THE TIME OF OUR LIVES

Also by Imogen Parker

MORE INNOCENT TIMES
THESE FOOLISH THINGS
THE MEN IN HER LIFE
WHAT BECAME OF US
PERFECT DAY
MY SECRET LOVER

THE TIME
OF OUR LIVES

IMOGEN PARKER

BANTAM PRESS

LONDON · TORONTO · SYDNEY · AUCKLAND · JOHANNESBURG

TRANSWORLD PUBLISHERS
61–63 Uxbridge Road, London W5 5SA
a division of The Random House Group Ltd

RANDOM HOUSE AUSTRALIA (PTY) LTD
20 Alfred Street, Milsons Point, Sydney,
New South Wales 2061, Australia

RANDOM HOUSE NEW ZEALAND LTD
18 Poland Road, Glenfield, Auckland 10, New Zealand

RANDOM HOUSE SOUTH AFRICA (PTY) LTD
Isle of Houghton, Corner of Boundary Road & Carse O'Gowrie,
Houghton 2198, South Africa

Published 2006 by Bantam Press
a division of Transworld Publishers

A catalogue record for this book is available from the British Library.
ISBN 978 0593 052945 (from Jan 07)
ISBN 0593 052943

Typeset in 11.5/14pt Janson by
Falcon Oast Graphic Art Ltd

Printed in Great Britain by
Mackays of Chatham plc, Chatham, Kent

1 3 5 7 9 10 8 6 4 2

Papers used by Transworld Publishers are natural, recyclable products made from
wood grown in sustainable forests. The manufacturing processes conform to
the environmental regulations of the country of origin.

6949

In memory of my beloved Gran,
who used to tell me stories.

. . . this little world,
This precious stone set in the silver sea,

William Shakespeare
Richard II

Historical Note

Dinosaur footprints discovered in the quarries indicate that a hundred million years ago, this region of Southern England was covered by tropical swampland, but an aerial view of Kingshaven demonstrates evidence of settlement by human beings since prehistoric times. On the South Cliffs, the ramparts of one of the largest Iron Age forts on the South Coast are still clearly visible.

The town was awarded its royal charter by Edward I, but trade began long before with the arrival of the Romans, and the first quarrying of the famous Kingshaven limestone, carved examples of which have been discovered as far away as Colchester and Hadrian's Wall. During the Napoleonic Wars, Kingshaven stone built many of the fortifications along the South Coast, as well as the gentlemen's clubs of London.

Before the advent of tourism, the town's other principal income derived from fishing. Boats plied the Atlantic in search of cod. Kingshaven supplied the preacher and the blacksmith for one of the first settlements in Newfoundland.

The picturesque but often treacherous stretch of coastline was the cause of many shipwrecks over the centuries, although locals strenuously deny reports of ships being lured on to the rocks for looting. There is evidence, however, that during the eighteenth and early nineteenth centuries smugglers secreted contraband in the storm drains running beneath the quay, and the lively harbour area supported some eighteen inns.

The Castle was donated by Elizabeth I to the Allsop family in recognition of its provision of a ship to join the fleet which sailed against the Armada. During the Civil War, a prolonged battle resulted in the destruction of the original castle, but following the Restoration, a new house was built on the site. The Allsop family remained pre-eminent in Kingshaven until the nineteenth century when a succession of wastrel and philanthropist descendants gambled or gave away most of the land adjoining the bay.

The inaccessibility from any major city and the geological instability of the land determined that, except for the occasional Darwinist in search of fossils, Kingshaven would not become a popular destination for holidaymakers until the opening of a branch line from Coombe Minster in 1875. The subsequent flurry of hotel building was halted temporarily by the landslip of 1890: seventeen recorded deaths endowing the town with a fame less propitious than had been anticipated.

The Palace Hotel, the imposing Victorian edifice on the North Cliffs, was originally constructed as a seaside villa by a successful London shopkeeper, Albert König, who believed that the healthful properties of the sea air would provide a remedy for his tuberculosis. Following his death, his enterprising widow, Beatrice, remodelled the house to its present form, naming it after one of the hotels she and her husband had visited for a cure in the Alps. The hotel and outbuildings were further extended by her son, who also financed the construction of a pier and the promenade to link the two ends of the town. These modern facilities, together with the increasing popularity of sea-bathing, ensured that Kingshaven became a fashionable and prosperous resort at the beginning of the twentieth century.

In 1936, Beatrice's great-grandson, Rex, then proprietor of the Palace, suddenly and scandalously emigrated to France, leaving the reputation of the hotel damaged and its management in the hands of his inexperienced younger brother, Basil. Shortly afterwards, the Palace closed for business, owing to its requisition by the RAF.

Thanks to their exemplary patriotism and generosity during

the war years, Basil, his wife Liliana and their two daughters, Elizabeth (known as Libby) and Pearl, succeeded in mending the reputation of the Palace as a family hotel after its civilian status was restored.

After Basil's untimely death in 1952, the hotel's management passed to Libby, her husband Eddie, and their young family.

(from *A Brief History of Kingshaven* © Michael Quinn 2000)

Chapter One

2 June 1953

A visitor's usual impression of Kingshaven, inscribed on the back of a Scenic Views postcard and read by Audrey Potter, the post-mistress, as she bagged up the mail, was of a picturesque seaside town, with well-tended gardens; a golden beach (which, if it appeared more sandy in the hand-tinted photograph than it felt to the naked foot, was left unremarked); a small harbour of colourful fishing boats; and wild cliffs where the fossilized skeletons of prehistoric creatures occasionally emerged from the eroding limestone. The town's attractions were virtually in-distinguishable from those of several other resorts dotted along the South Coast of England: a pier with a small theatre; a promenade with a clock tower; an imposing Victorian hotel; guesthouses painted in pale pastel shades with optimistic names like Sunny Side and Bella Vista; and a steep high street which, at the slightest glimmer of sunshine, bloomed with spinners of bright pink rock and bouncing nets of striped beach balls.

The second of June 1953 was not the clear and sunny day that had been prayed for by those more believing or patriotic than Michael Quinn. The sky was overcast and the air unwarmed by a visible sun. From the little bedroom window under the eaves of the Quinns' cottage the view was of drizzle and mist, the grey of the sea barely distinguishable from the grey of the sky.

In the kitchen downstairs, the announcer on the wireless was saying that despite assurances from forecasters that the date was the most likely in the calendar for picture-perfect conditions, the excited nation had awoken instead to a chilly, rainy gloom. In London, half a million people had spent a damp night camped out along the procession route. Everywhere else, rainy streets emptied as the rest of the population crowded into the living rooms of houses fortunate enough to have an H aerial on the roof.

Across the yard at the back of the cottage, Michael's wife Sylvia and their three-year-old daughter emerged from the outside lavatory and were inspecting the wild flowers that grew out of the cracks in the stone wall.

As if she had felt his gaze upon her, Sylvia turned to smile at him, her hand on her lower back, and then Iris looked up and shouted gleefully, 'It's raining!'

Michael opened the back door and scooped his daughter up in his arms. Beads of drizzle had attached themselves to her springy curls of red hair, making it both wet and dry against his newly shaven skin.

'Show your father your Coronation posy,' said Sylvia.

'Red, white and blue,' said Iris, opening her fist so close to his eyes that he had to adjust his focus to observe the damp remains of two daisies, a red campion and a speedwell.

'Shall I take this with me to the Palace?' Michael asked his wife playfully, bouncing Iris up and down.

Sylvia laughed.

Iris laughed too, the gloriously abandoned laugh of a child joining in without understanding the joke, which made Michael smile at his wife over the top of Iris's head with proud, parental pleasure, as if to say, 'Look at this little being we have created!'

'This one was kicking for England last night,' Sylvia said, placing her hand on her vast pregnant belly.

Michael held his palm over hers, and felt a fist, or maybe a foot – something hard and vigorous – drumming against the stretched flesh.

'I don't think you should be alone today,' he said.

'I won't be alone,' she said brightly. 'Half the town will be at Audrey's, including the midwife.'

2

'But I should be with you,' he said.

'No! You have to go. It isn't every day you're invited to the Palace!'

'It's only to stop the pupils damaging the furniture.'

'It's because you're their teacher. "Teachers are leading figures in the community,"' she told him, quoting the phrase the *Kingshaven Chronicle* had used to describe invitees to the Palace Hotel's Coronation Party.

Her earnestness made Michael smile.

'It is kind of them to think of the children,' she pressed on.

'*Noblesse oblige*,' he said.

'What does that mean?' Sylvia asked, sounding as young and innocent as Iris.

'Showing off,' Michael told her.

'No bless oh bleej,' Iris repeated.

'You are going to wear your best shirt, aren't you?' Sylvia suddenly asked him.

'What's wrong with this one?' He stretched out his arms. The sleeves were frayed at the cuffs.

'You can't wear that,' she told him.

His irreverence made her anxious, as if some harm might befall him if he failed to show proper deference towards the town's richest family. He had no intention of wearing his old shirt, but he couldn't resist teasing her.

'Why not?'

'It shows no respect!' Sylvia declared.

'They don't show much respect to us,' he said, looking at the mouldy whitewash of the walls. The property they were renting was owned by the hoteliers.

'They won't understand that, though,' she assured him with disarming accuracy. 'They'll just think you don't know any better.'

Two miles away, in the private wing of the Palace Hotel, Libby King was sitting at her dressing table enjoying a moment's reflection before dressing for the biggest day of her life.

The last time the hotel had thrown such a party was in 1937. That day, Libby remembered, the threatened rain had stayed away. Her mother, Liliana, had been in charge of arrangements. It crossed Libby's mind, as she gazed out of her bedroom window towards the South Cliffs, which were barely visible through the wet grey mist, that if she had asked her mother and her sister Pearl for help on this occasion, then perhaps the sun might now be shining.

Just as the 1937 Coronation Party had been organized with the dual purpose of celebrating the safe stewardship of the hotel's affairs through a turbulent period in its history, so today's marked another new beginning.

Libby and her husband Eddie had consented to take over the running of the hotel after the unexpected death of Libby's father, but only on condition that they would be allowed a free hand. Eddie, who might otherwise have continued his career in the Navy, had insisted on it. Her mother would still be there to offer advice if requested, and Pearl too, until she found a husband of her own, but the big decisions would be Libby and Eddie's alone – it would be demeaning for him otherwise. That, together with the continuing privations of rationing, restrictions which her mother had not had to contend with in 1937, was the reason that today's preparations were not perhaps as sumptuous as those Libby could remember when she was eleven years old.

Eddie was in charge of the budget, and Eddie had decided that circumstances demanded the purchase of not one but two television sets for the broadcast, despite the fact that the family already owned one for their private use. The children of the town would be allowed to watch in the ballroom, invited adults in the lounge. Two television sets were an investment which would last beyond the day, adding to the attractions the Palace had to offer to a new generation of guests.

Afterwards, food would be served to the children on trestle tables on the lawn. The adults would have a buffet in the dining room, which was a modern and convenient way of serving luncheon, although privately Libby feared for the new Axminster.

A timetable had been drawn up; orders given. Each member of the family and staff was fully briefed. After lunch, a photographer from the *Chronicle* would take a group photograph on the terrace and, later that evening, in recognition of the Palace's generosity, the Mayor, Mr Makepeace, had suggested that Libby herself should light the beacon on the South Cliffs.

Libby had bought a new full-skirted rayon dress with a white collar and buttons to the waist, and little white turned-back cuffs on the three-quarter length sleeves. Yellow would not have been her first choice, as it seemed to take colour from her complexion, but it was the only shade Farmer's Outfitters had in her size. Her appearance from behind the curtain in the changing room had conjured the word 'crisp' from Mrs Farmer. 'A New Look for a New Era,' she had added, and that was exactly the impression Libby intended to give.

Libby held the dress up in front of her and was looking at her reflection in the cheval mirror, enjoying the quality of the fabric (you'd never know it wasn't silk and yet it hung so well), when her five-year-old son Christopher wandered into her bedroom, still in his pyjamas.

'There is one thing I don't understand,' he announced, as if he were in the middle of a conversation. For a five-year-old, he had a peculiarly adult way of putting things.

'What's that, dear?' Libby asked, flustered by the realization that her son would have glimpsed the back of her slip as he walked in. She turned a full half-circle so that her front aspect was entirely covered by the dress. Where was Nanny?

'Why are all these children coming to our house to see the Queen?' said Christopher.

'Because most of them aren't lucky enough to have a television like we do,' Libby replied. 'And because your father is on the board of governors of the school.'

She was proud that Eddie's organizational skills had been harnessed by a number of the town's executive bodies since his return to the civilian arena. Even though there was no money in it, she couldn't help feeling it was good for him, and for the business.

'What is a board of governors?' asked Christopher.

'Very important people,' Libby replied, hoping that a succinct answer would hasten his departure.

'I wish I could go to school,' Christopher sighed, sitting up on their unmade bed.

Libby pivoted through another ninety degrees, one hand still on the coathanger, the other holding the dress to her waist. Where was Nanny? It really wasn't on. Today of all days.

'When you're old enough, you will,' she said tersely.

'To Daddy's school?' the child asked eagerly.

'To the school where Daddy went, yes.'

Libby sat down at her dressing table, now holding the hook of the coathanger under her chin to free her hands.

'With the children?' Christopher pressed on, oblivious to her eagerness for him to be gone.

'Not with the children who are coming today.' Libby popped a couple of kirby grips in her mouth and began to pull a brush through her wavy hair.

'Which children, then?' he said, sliding off the bed and standing beside her.

'Children like you, darling.'

She fastened her curls behind her ears with the grips and looked at his curious, wan little face reflected in the mirror next to hers.

'Children like *us*. Now please go and find Nanny and tell her to dress you. I have a number of important things to do.'

The natives of Kingshaven called the holidaymakers who came in the summer 'foreigners', and, although he was not a visitor, after almost ten months' living here, Michael Quinn still felt a stranger, especially this morning when he found himself completely alone.

Hanging baskets of red geraniums, bruised white petunias and luminous blue lobelia dripped from the lampposts along the promenade. Empty of people, the resort was more than ever a giant version of the model village in the Victoria Gardens and felt almost less real than when he had first searched for it in an *Atlas of Britain*, or when he had arrived with Sylvia and Iris after journeying the length of the country by train and bus, when the mother-of-pearl sunset had made them drop their cardboard suitcases and stare in wonder.

Sylvia had turned to him, her pale face glowing in the unnatural light, and said, 'I never knew there were palm trees in England.'

They had come to make a new life, and everything had been alien to them.

Kingshaven had seemed to him then the very embodiment of the comfortable Southern middle class, but, as Michael had become more familiar with the place, he had begun to realize that the strata of society here were as starkly delineated as the layers of rock in the unstable South Cliffs. This England was no less real than the England he had left behind. Here, the deprivation was easier to look at than the grinding grime of bombed-out slums in the industrial cities of the North, but behind the pretty façades and the artificial quaintness, people loved and lost and struggled and failed. Each of the houses, from grey stone to painted pink pebbledash, contained stories of passion and hatred, of disappointment and triumph, of human beings striving against the odds to achieve a kind of happiness.

They had rented one of the tiny quarriers' cottages in the Harbour End, now the poorest district, but originally the source of the town's wealth. These days, the quarried caves attracted only the more intrepid or foolhardy explorer and the quay was quiet except for yachts in the summer and a few local fishing boats whose longest journey had been to the beaches of Dunkirk.

After nearly a year in this place, Michael was still not sure whether he would ever feel at home, but he found pleasure in the smell of lobster pots, the sudden startling dialogue of seagulls, the ever-changing dome of sky.

It was a town of landladies and shopkeepers, Michael thought, as he reached the clock tower at the end of the promenade and began to walk up Hill Road. Damp flags flapped forlornly above his head and the shopfronts competed with patriotic displays. In the window of Green's Confectioner's there were trays of red, white and blue coconut ice. The blue, more indigo than royal, had seeped unevenly into the white, making it look as if the chunks had been dipped in ink. The Greens had lost both their sons in the war: one in the sands of Tobruk; one on the beaches of Normandy. When Michael sometimes stopped off there with Iris and watched the cheery way Mrs Green dispensed white bags of gobstoppers and licorice whirls into the grubby palms of little boys, he wondered whether her job reinforced the sadness of her

7

loss, or brought her the peculiar comfort of nostalgia. One lick of a newly derationed vanilla ice cream could take Michael back to summers before the war, playing in the street with his older brother Frank, and the delicious moment of anticipation when Frank would hold up his hand for silence, and they would hear the distant trundling of the ice-cream cart, and the staccato shout which Michael had always heard as 'I scream, I scream!'

The greengrocer, Mr Sweetman, who had fashioned a Union Jack from tomatoes, turnips and heads of purple sprouting broccoli in his window, had seen his older daughter spirited off to Iowa with her GI sweetheart. If Mr and Mrs Green had sold fruit and vegetables and Mr Sweetman humbugs and bon bons as their names suggested they should, might their tragedies have been avoided? Michael mused idly as he passed their adjacent windows. Had some trick of fate mixed them up? Were people born with an invisible map of their destiny imprinted on their souls, or did lives turn on tiny, random events?

Lines of red, white and blue rosettes divided the gleaming steel trays in the butcher's window. The dress shop, with the slogan 'Farmer's Famously First for Fashion' engraved on the window, had a framed photograph of the young Queen beside the headless models sporting a range of red, white and blue summer leisure wear.

In recent weeks, Michael had felt as if he was the only person in the country uninfected by the condition the papers were calling 'Coronation Fever'. If Sylvia's circumstances had been different, he knew she would have yearned to number among the crowds lining the streets of the capital, swapping sandwiches with her fellow subjects and cheering from the grandstands. When Michael expressed his view that the Coronation was nothing but an artificial charade, as he had on a couple of occasions when he stopped in for a half at the Ship, people looked at him as if he were dangerous.

When he had received the invitation to the Coronation Party he initially thought that it must be a mistake. His inclination had been to decline, until Sylvia had reminded him that Mr Eddie King was a school governor and might not look kindly on a refusal.

And a part of him was curious.

Michael had first seen the Palace Hotel on a black and white postcard his brother Frank had sent with one of his weekly letters. Servicemen weren't supposed to give away details of where they were posted, but Frank had never been much of a one for rules. He'd put an X on the roof to show approximately which room he was sleeping in.

You should see this place, Mike, he'd written on the back.

Was it fate or simply coincidence, Michael had wondered, almost ten years later, when the first education authority to reply to his request for teaching vacancies had informed him of a position in the very same town, that Frank's words had read more like a command than an exclamation?

Our billet's in the staff quarters in the attic, his brother had written in his scratchy, forward-sloping handwriting. *Can't stand up without bumping our heads. Keeps us in our place . . .*

Michael had often looked up at the hotel and tried to imagine his brother looking out of the high windows, but the building seemed almost to disdain the people who dared to gaze at it.

'Morning, sir.'

The word 'sir' still made Michael jump and look around for someone in authority.

'Good morning, Arthur,' he said, looking down at the small boy from his class, who had fallen into step beside him. He wondered how long he had been trailing him.

'You excited, sir? About seeing the Queen getting coronated on television, sir?' The child's face was pink as if it had been scrubbed and his too-small jacket was tugged and buttoned across his chest.

'It's sure to be a day we will remember,' Michael replied diplomatically.

'I can smell bacon!' said Pearl King, skipping into the Kings' private dining room.

'It's not for you,' said Libby, glaring at her sister.

Infuriatingly, Pearl was wearing the same dress as she was, but she had managed to squeeze herself into the cerise one with the little black collar and narrow black patent belt which had caught

Libby's eye in the first place. How maddening of Mrs Farmer not to have said! Libby would now look like that poor, drab Shelley Winters in the film they had seen at the Regal, *A Place in the Sun*, with Pearl taking the Elizabeth Taylor role beside her. People often remarked on the resemblance.

'It's Mr White's bacon,' their mother, Liliana King, explained. 'He brought it with him. And he's provided sausages.'

'I'll have a sausage then,' said Pearl mischievously.

Eddie lowered his newspaper. The headline said, 'Crowning Glory. British Expedition Conquers Everest.'

'They're for the buffet,' said Libby. 'So it's Family Hold Back, I'm afraid.'

'I can't see the point of owning a hotel if you're not allowed any benefits,' Pearl declared, shaking her napkin huffily across her lap as the waitress put down a plate with a fried egg in front of her. The edges were frizzled up like burnt cellophane. 'Six months ago, I'd have sold my soul for a fresh egg,' she added despondently.

'Apparently,' said Eddie, reading aloud from the paper, 'Edmund Hillary buried a Christian cross, and Sherpa Tensing left some food as an offering to their gods.'

'At least it will be properly refrigerated,' quipped Liliana.

'What is a Sherpa?' Pearl asked.

'Some Nepalese fellow,' Eddie replied. 'A native.'

'Sherpa Tensing is Mr Hillary's local guide,' added Liliana.

'He's a man?' Pearl said, astonished.

'Of course he's a man!' said Libby. 'What did you think?'

'I had in mind one of those dogs, you know, that pull sledges . . .'

As if recognizing a reference to themselves, Libby's spaniels, Duke and Duchess, started to bark. She smiled at them indulgently.

'A husky!' Eddie roared with laughter. 'You thought a Sherpa was a dog? Good God, is there no beginning to your knowledge?'

'Do I have to put up with this?' Pearl asked no one in particular.

'I think I'll see how Mrs Burns is getting on in the kitchen,' said Liliana.

*

Claudia Dearchild stood in the galleried entrance hall of the Palace staring at the elaborately decorated Victorian clock. Housed in a tall glass dome, it was an extraordinary porcelain confection of birds and flowers, reeking of excess and sentiment, which, in Claudia's opinion, had little artistic value; nor, she confirmed with a glance at her leather-strapped wristwatch, did it tell the correct time.

Claudia had been in the Palace only once before, when she and her father had received a dinner invitation from Commander Basil and Mrs King in 1947. Her father suspected that their interest was to do with the piece about him in the *Chronicle*: as a professor of Archaeology, he had been interviewed after a cache of Roman coins had been found by labourers digging the foundations for the new council houses.

The Kings had been full of apologies for failing to acknowledge their presence in the town earlier, citing the hotel's requisition during the war.

'Entertaining,' Claudia remembered Mrs King saying, leaning towards her father in her particular, over-familiar way, 'was one of the most unpleasant sacrifices we had to make.'

Claudia's father had muttered in his heavy accent that if that was all they had had to give up, they had been lucky.

It had not been a comfortable evening for any of them. Even though she could only have been about ten years old, Claudia already had a much firmer grasp of English etiquette than her father. Instinctively realizing that his politics would fail to find a sympathetic audience, she had spent the evening trying to put a gloss on the pronouncements he made, fortunately mostly incomprehensibly, in his broken English.

'Charming child,' she had overheard Basil King comment as they left.

'But the father's clearly a Communist,' Liliana had hissed.

There had been no further invitations to the Palace until one sunny day recently when Claudia was sketching on the South Cliffs. The Kings' younger daughter Pearl, whom Claudia recognized from her many pictures in the *Chronicle*, suddenly appeared in the long grass in the foreground, with a man whose hand she dropped the moment she spotted Claudia. The man hurried off, but Pearl had demanded to see Claudia's work in progress, and declared, 'That is my home!' in a tone which suggested that its pre-eminence was so absolute, a licence might be required to reproduce its image.

Capriciously, the next moment she was imploring Claudia to teach her to paint, vowing that she would buy the landscape as a Coronation gift for her sister, and engaging her in such lively conversation that only a true sceptic would have called it inter-rogation. Pearl had insisted she come to the Coronation Party, only suggesting afterwards, when it emerged that Claudia and her father lived in the almost derelict gatehouse at the edge of the Allsop estate, that Claudia might like to pop up to the hotel a little earlier to help out.

'We're all doing our bit,' she informed her, waving an airy farewell that reminded Claudia very much of the mother, who had often been pictured in the local paper during the war, sitting in a jeep with a group of young servicemen, smiling at the camera above a caption that read 'Keeping up Morale'.

A bellboy seemed to be inordinately preoccupied with polish-ing the board behind the reception desk where the keys hung. Claudia decided to wait in the arms of a large leather winged chair and make herself as invisible as possible.

A sharply dressed couple came down the main staircase, their arms entwined around each other's waists, and, imagining them-selves unobserved, kissed on the landing, their bodies pressed together, his grey chalk stripes grinding against her nubbly silk skirt, which was the colour of a freshly watered lawn. As they walked across the entrance hall towards the dining room, the man's broad hand spread over the left cheek of the woman's bottom and squeezed it hard, while her painted fingernails reached into her tortoiseshell handbag for a handkerchief to wipe the scarlet stain from his lips, and a compact mirror to check that her cupid's bow had not smudged.

A handsome man wearing chauffeur's uniform walked in through the front door and stood at the reception desk, as if he was waiting for someone.

'Are you going to watch it?' Claudia heard the bellboy say.

'Depends,' the chauffeur replied. 'Are you?'

'Chance would be a fine thing!'

And then Pearl King appeared through a door marked 'PRIVATE', creating a sudden tornado of the still air as she ran across the hotel lobby, her heels tapping on the inlaid marble floor, her wide, red mouth smiling. The chauffeur opened the glazed inner door of the porch and held it for her with an impassive expression on his face, but as she passed him, Pearl paused and brushed an invisible fleck of dust from his shoulder in such an intimate gesture that Claudia suddenly recognized him as the man who had been with Pearl on the South Cliffs.

A moment later the door marked 'PRIVATE' opened again, and an authoritative voice demanded, 'Can I help you?'

Libby King was wearing a full-skirted dress the colour of a daffodil and white shoes at least two sizes too big. Although she looked very much like Pearl, curiously she was neither chic nor attractive. Even their dresses seemed to be of the same design, the one almost like a photographic negative of the other.

Claudia stood up. 'My name is Claudia Dearchild. Your sister asked me to come and help—'

'Oh, for goodness' sake!' interrupted Libby. 'I do wish Pearl would tell me what she's up to!'

And then Mrs Liliana King appeared. 'I say.' She beckoned Claudia. 'You don't happen to know anything about mayonnaise?'

In the kitchen, the cook, Mrs Burns, picked up a piece of card with a floury hand, holding it as far as her arm would allow and screwing up her eyes to bring the words into focus, and began to read the menu for the luncheon buffet.

'Egg sandwiches for the children, bacon and egg pie for the adults, Mimosa salad . . .' She looked up. 'That's just a fancy name of Miss Pearl's for egg salad, except we have to *crumble* the egg yolks, if you please. Then there's the sausages.'

'Sausages?' squealed one of the maids.

'Courtesy of Mr White. That's why Mrs Liliana serves him herself. If a butcher from Spitalfields wants to think he's a friend of the family, well and good if you get sausages on your Coronation luncheon table. Mrs Liliana understands these things. Unlike some I could mention.'

The girl giggled.

'Coronation Chicken,' the cook continued, her mouth twisting out of shape. 'That' – she pointed at Claudia – 'is where you come in.'

Michael Quinn felt like the Pied Piper of Hamelin, leading a procession of primary-school children up the long gravel drive to the Palace Hotel. They were all wearing their Sunday-best clothes; their carefully combed hair was flattened by the rain, except Winston Allsop's springy black frizz which seemed to suspend the droplets of rain like dew on a cobweb. Some of the children were holding the paper Union flags they had coloured at school; the Carney boys had fabric flags attached to twigs, which looked a suspiciously similar size to the bunting the Shopkeepers' Guild had paid to have strung across the High Street. Millicent Bland had red, white and blue ribbons woven into her plaits. Una Adams, the undertaker's daughter, had brought her Coronation mug with her.

A black Bentley came down the drive towards them, the sound of the tyres on gravel like the drag of a wave on the pebble beach. Michael put his arms out like a scarecrow to protect the file of children as the stately car rolled past. A uniformed chauffeur was at the wheel; in the back, a beautiful face with luscious dark hair and full red lips seemed to float past at the level of his eyes, deliberately, it seemed to him, not looking at the line of urchins who peered into the car, intrigued.

You'll never guess what the owners of this place are called, Frank had written. *The Kings. The Kings in the Palace! How about that? And they live like it too. There are two daughters. One's a little princess all right. Some of the lads can see her playing tennis from their dormitory. When she knows we're looking, she bends over very prettily to pick up the ball!*

The lawn tennis courts to the left of the drive, Michael noticed, were marshy with rainwater.

'They weren't always called the Kings,' Percy Bland, the publican at the Ship, had once remarked with a dark chuckle.

Apparently, the family had changed their name during the First World War and it had been retained when Libby married a

14

distant cousin. The publican had been unable or unwilling to remember any details. The attitude in the town towards the Kings was a curious mixture of resentment and deference. The Palace was undeniably one of the reasons people came to Kingshaven, and it provided a substantial proportion of the town's employment.

The entrance hall was so exactly as Frank had described it, Michael shivered with déjà vu.

We're only allowed into the main part of the hotel for our meals. We're sat on wooden benches under ceilings embossed with fancy plasterwork and gold! The main staircase – you half expect to see Cinderella coming down – is strictly off limits to the men, because we'd wear out the carpet . . .

Michael gazed in awe at the elaborately carved banister, the ornate plasterwork of the high ceiling, the dark panelling.

. . . There's this huge fancy clock, so big they can't get it down to the cellars, a porcelain tree with birds and flowers stuck all over it. The lady of the house sucks in her breath whenever one of us walks past . . . Oh, the temptation to lose your footing and bring the bugger down! If we're bombed, God help me, at least I'll go to hell knowing that thing's shattered in a thousand pieces!

How could an object of such ugliness survive when so much had not?

A sudden stab of loss made Michael's eyes glaze with un-expected tears which he blinked back as a woman in a yellow dress tapped across to him. Two spaniels trailed behind her, jumping and yapping at the children.

'Welcome to the Palace,' said Libby King. 'If you'd like to take the children into the ballroom, the transmission is about to commence.'

'Come on, you lot.' Michael turned to his charges, who had fallen into an awed silence as if they had entered a church. The Carney boys, he could tell, were itching to test the slipperiness of the vast expanse of polished marble, as irresistible as a frozen pond, but they filed past him in an orderly manner until Mrs King suddenly cried, 'Wait!' and rushed across to the door marked 'PRIVATE'.

In the echoing silence, a couple of the smaller girls looked as if they might cry. A moment later, Mrs King returned with a great golden bracelet of cardboard crowns on each arm, which she handed to the children one by one.

'That's better!' she said, inspecting the line of solemn little crowned heads.

In the lounge, there was a pleasant fug of conversation, cigarette smoke and the slightly sharp scent of men's suits that have been rained on. The Reverend Church and his wife were there; Mr Makepeace; Mr Turlow, headmaster of the school; the Greens; Mr Maurice, the hairdresser; Mrs Farmer, of course. All the best people had turned out on this special day to show goodwill towards the hotel's new management, except for local landowner Sir John Allsop, but nobody had really expected him to come and, privately, Libby had been quite relieved to receive his refusal. She noticed that his adopted son, Winston, whom he had found in a basket under a hedge at the bottom of his land on VE night, and whose origins were unclear apart from the fact he was clearly the offspring product of one of the negro GIs, was with the school party.

Sir John's proper son, also called John, but who'd been known since he was a child as Jolly, was looking very smart in his Army uniform. Everyone knew that he was sweet on Pearl. He nodded politely while Eddie's uncle Cyril regaled him with one of his anecdotes from the Raj, but his eyes kept wandering over the old man's shoulder towards the door.

Where was Pearl?

Liliana was chatting with her friend Mrs Ruby Farmer and Ruby's daughter Jennifer, but her eyes were constantly roaming the room. On her face was a kind of unfocused pleasantness which sharpened into a scintillating smile whenever her eyes made contact with any of the guests who might be bored, irritated or simply lost for someone to talk to. In one smooth movement, Liliana would rise and swoop, guiding them to the safety of small talk with a new person. Her mother had a natural gift for such occasions, thought Libby. Everybody said so.

Libby tried to relax into the swing of things.

It was all going as well as could be expected, she told herself, apart from the slight embarrassment of one or two of the hotel's guests.

It was Libby's view that for a hotel to run harmoniously the guests should to a certain extent reflect the attributes and status of the proprietors. From the time of her great-great-grandmother onwards, the hotel had always attracted a clientele of solid, wealthy types. There had been a period of decadent notoriety when her uncle Rex was briefly in charge, but tradition had been re-established by her mother and father. Now it was up to Eddie and herself to attract a younger generation, still decent, of course, but she hoped just a little more stylish and modern.

When the woman had telephoned to reserve the best suite in the hotel for a Mr and Mrs Wilding, Libby had let herself hope, for a single self-deluding second, that the film star Wildings had come across a notice – perhaps Miss Elizabeth Taylor herself had been idling through *The Lady* whilst having her hair done – and decided to select the Palace as a discreet holiday location. But the loud specimen in the bright green costume and her companion were not Wildings at all. It never ceased to confound Libby that people could sign the register with one name and then hand over their ration books as if you wouldn't notice the discrepancy. Ironically, the man's real name appeared to be Smith, and the woman was a Miss Sally Lane, whose voice was growing more common with every sip of complimentary sherry.

The television flickered with pictures of cheering crowds as the Queen's Gold State Coach pulled by eight Windsor Greys left Buckingham Palace.

'I know where I'd rather be watching,' said Mr White, settling into the armchair that became his for the length of his stay in the hotel, a whisky and water in one hand, a small cigar in the other. 'You get a better view!'

There was a general murmur of agreement.

Mr White and his like were regular, clean clientele, Libby thought, as was the Squadron Leader, who'd been stationed at the hotel during the war and married a Land Army girl who'd unfortunately been killed in an accident involving a combine harvester. He came once a year to lay flowers. The Misses Flynn were perfectly respectable too, although they'd developed a habit of offering a picture or a small piece of antique furniture instead of cash for the bill. However, the New Elizabethan Age heralded a more youthful ambience.

'Believe it or not,' Uncle Cyril was saying to Jolly Allsop as he accepted another whisky from the drinks tray, 'elephants are rather partial to beer . . .'

Liliana was preparing to swoop to Jolly's rescue. Libby decided to check on the children's party downstairs.

The commentator on the television had to shout over the cheering of thirty thousand schoolchildren on the Victoria Embankment as the Queen passed by.

In the ballroom of the Palace Hotel, the thirty or so school-children were silently absorbed in the extraordinary pictures of the fairytale carriage rolling through the streets of London.

Outside on the terrace, with their hands and faces squashed low against the French windows, were Libby's own two children, Christopher and Angela.

'Where is Nanny?' Libby demanded, marching straight across and opening the French door.

'Don't know,' said Angela.

'It's not my fault,' Christopher said.

'You mustn't always do what Angela tells you. Angela is very naughty,' Libby told her son.

'I'm not naughty, I'm just a very strong character,' said the little girl.

Libby glared at Angela. Her bare arms were goosebumpy and her Start-rite sandals were dark with rainwater. What was Nanny thinking of?

'You'd better come in,' she said to the children. 'This is Mr Quinn.'

'How do you do?' said Christopher, holding out his small hand to shake.

Angela stared.

Michael Quinn squatted down to Angela's height. 'How old are you?'

'Six,' she announced.

'Oh, really, Angela, you're only four!' Libby corrected with an embarrassed laugh.

'I'm three,' said Angela.

'Nearly four,' said Libby hastily.

'My wife and I have a little girl just your age,' said Michael.

'What a coincidence!' said Libby. 'Perhaps she could come and play with you, Angela?'

'I don't want her to,' said Angela, her eyes fixed on the television.

The action had suddenly switched to the interior of the Abbey. The arcane ceremony was about to happen.

'Now we're here, we might as well stay,' said Angela, walking down to the front row of chairs and climbing on to an empty one.

Christopher hung back guiltily until Winston Allsop beckoned him over to the empty seat beside him.

Christopher stared at the older boy.

'Are you a monkey?' he asked.

Libby returned to the lounge, just as the bellboy was announcing that there was an urgent telephone call for Mr Smith. It couldn't have come at a worse moment; the Queen was being divested of her jewels and robes. There had been some public debate about whether the television cameras should look away from the Queen when she was being anointed, but in the hotel lounge, it almost felt as if the cameramen in the Abbey had themselves been distracted by the bellboy.

'Says it's important,' the bellboy added.

Libby was beginning to think that he was doing it on purpose. Perhaps her mother had been right to advise that it might be unwise to ban the staff from watching the ceremony.

'I think that may be for me.' Mr Wilding sidled guiltily round the back of the chairs towards the door.

On the television, the commentator was saying that the holy oil with which the Archbishop of Canterbury was anointing the Queen had been made to a formula originally devised by Charles I.

Wasn't he the King who was beheaded? A long-ago history lesson popped into Libby's mind. That didn't sound like a very good omen at all.

*

In the kitchen, the bellboy's report on what was happening in Westminster Abbey had been entirely superseded by the mystery of the telephone call to 'Mr Smith'.

'First he says, "What do you mean an accident?" Then he says, "Well, he shouldn't be riding a bloody motorbike, should he?"'

'Language,' said Mrs Burns.

'His words, Mrs B. Then he says he should have been in a car . . .'

'Who should?'

'I don't know who,' said the bellboy. 'All I know is your man's shouting his head off about how he's paid good money, how they'd better get someone down here straightaway, how he doesn't care if it's Coronation Day . . .'

'Not very respectful,' interjected the maid, whose name was Maudie.

'Then he says he's demanding a refund and damages, and slams down the phone, and then he stamps out the front door and smokes a cigarette out there.'

'And then what?' asked Maudie.

'Still out there.'

There was a moment of silent speculation.

'Where did you learn to do that, then?' the cook asked, peering into Claudia's bowl before putting her finger into it.

'I read it in a book,' Claudia told her.

'She read it in a book!' Mrs Burns licked her finger appreciatively. 'So that's mayonnaise, is it?'

'I imagine it would taste better with olive oil,' said Claudia.

'Olive oil?'

'That's the stuff mum puts in my ear when I've got earache,' said Maudie.

'In Italy, they cook with it,' Claudia told her, adding, 'France, too.'

Maudie, Mrs Burns and the bellboy all stared at her in disbelief.

'All I know about the French,' said Mrs Burns authoritatively, 'is that they charged the soldiers who was liberating them for water. Charged them! For a glass of water! Not the Eyeties,' she added, patting Claudia's arm with soft, fat, floury fingers, lest the girl think she tarred all foreigners with the same brush, 'the Italians was very welcoming.'

She had become so much more friendly since the mayonnaise that Claudia didn't think it was the time to remind her about Mussolini.

The moment he first saw Claudia would become a memory that made Michael feel as if he were smiling every time he recalled it.

The room was in cheerful disarray. After hours of fidgeting through solemn ritual in Westminster Abbey, the children were all cheering the bizarre spectacle of Salote, Queen of Tonga, braving the pelting rain in an open landau.

Little Angela King had climbed on to the blue velvet seat of her chair in an attempt to free some netted balloons, and her brother had followed her example and was jumping up and down. Then the balloons came down and through a bobbing sea of red, white and blue, Michael happened to look towards the door.

There was a girl standing in the gilded frame, her face inclined, her eyes dancing with eager amusement at the colourful chaos.

And suddenly, without knowing quite why, Michael found himself taking giant steps over the bobbing balloons towards her, as if she would vanish like a rainbow as suddenly as she had appeared.

'Are you a guest?' he asked.

Her forehead puckered as if she was trying to calculate the answer.

'I'm not exactly sure,' she said eventually. 'Are you?'

'I'm not sure either!'

They both let out a light laugh.

She had large clear brown eyes set far apart and long dark hair with a fringe cut straight across above arched eyebrows which made her look intelligent and quizzical. The red dress she was wearing was too big for her but the soft crêpe clung to her wisp of a body where it touched. With a backdrop of gilded curlicues and shining candelabras, she was so fragile and natural, she made him think of a single bright poppy in a field of ripe corn.

She smiled at him. 'We're to put trestle tables up in here and the kitchen staff will bring the children's picnic in.'

'You work here, then?'

'Only today,' she told him. 'My name is Claudia Dearchild.'

'Michael Quinn,' he said, so startled by the effect of her that he did not notice her outstretched hand until she started to withdraw it; he grabbed it with such haste that they both laughed again.

They were an instantly good team, ferrying the tables in, shaking the folds out of huge white tablecloths and smoothing them down like sheets. A convoy of platters was transported by the maids from the kitchen. A slight taint of hard-boiled eggs hung over the floor-polish scent of the ballroom.

Michael watched Claudia as she settled the children down on seats, tucking napkins into collars, and, occasionally, as if she had felt his eyes lingering on her, glancing up at him. He couldn't work out how old she was. Her dark beauty and her kindliness with the children made her seem like a woman, but her barely developed frame and the flustered innocence of her smile put her only just beyond childhood.

'You don't look as if you come from around here,' he said as they leaned side by side against the curve of the grand piano, each of them holding a large, heavy bottle of Corona (hers the stained-glass red of cherry flavour, his Belisha-beacon orange), watching the children tucking into their indoor picnic.

'I'm not,' she said. 'My father is Austrian. My mother was Italian. We were refugees,' she added quickly. 'Our real name is Liebeskind, but my father was advised to change it when I went to school,' she explained. 'Initially, he called me Claudia Lovechild, until it was pointed out to him that this was likely to be even more stigmatizing . . .'

Michael laughed.

'When did you arrive?'

'In Kingshaven? Nineteen forty-one,' she said. 'We came through Hungary.'

His face must have betrayed the rapid calculations going on in his brain.

'I was four years old,' she said, answering the question he hadn't asked.

Sixteen now, then.

'And your mother?' he asked.

'She did not survive the war.'

The words conjured in him terrible images of emaciated suffering.

'She was too ill to travel with us,' Claudia explained.

'Can you remember her?' he asked, not knowing what to say, but determined not to succumb to an embarrassed avoidance of the subject of death when his companion had so refreshingly flouted the conversational conventions of an English teatime.

Claudia considered his question for a moment.

'I'm not sure,' she said. 'I know that I remember my doll. She had a wonderful china face and long flaxen hair, and her eyes closed when I lay her down.' She gave a rueful laugh at the absurdity of the detail. 'I have pictures of my mother, of course, and when I see her handwriting, her name in the front of a book, she seems very close, somehow. Sometimes I think I can remember the sensation of her embrace, a faint smell of scorched cotton, the warmth of her chest wrapped up in an apron. Instead my father is all bones!'

He found he wanted to tell her that he had lost his mother too. He'd been ten. Both his mother and father had died in the first air raids on the docks. He thought of his mother whenever Sylvia made a cake, whipping his finger from the delicious raw mixture to his mouth to avoid the sting of a spatula on the back of his hand. And sometimes he could remember her voice singing one of her Irish songs, but he could never see an image and hear her at the same time, which puzzled him. But he said nothing. He did not want to sound crassly competitive.

The vicar's wife had a blob of whipped cream on her nose, and Libby didn't know whether it would be more embarrassing to alert her to it, or leave her to discover it herself in the Ladies. She took out her own handkerchief and blew her nose, hoping Mrs Church might follow her example.

'Hay fever?' Mrs Church asked in a concerned voice, taking another bite of her meringue.

The trouble was, Libby thought, replacing the handkerchief in her handbag, people were so unused to decent food they had forgotten how to eat it.

Mrs Burns had excelled herself. The Coronation Chicken was far more delicious than she could have believed from the ingredients list. Cook had even managed to find cocktail cherries to put on top of the Coconut Everests, which were a great success. The name had been Pearl's idea, not that it mattered what they were called.

Mrs Wilding – Miss Lane, or whoever she was – had one in each hand as she chatted to the Mayor. Was she holding them up to her chest deliberately, Libby wondered, to give the impression of . . . ?

Pearl had finally deigned to join the party and was giving Mr Smith the full beam of her charm. Her sister's face was almost as pink as her dress. Libby wondered spitefully whether the high colour and downright flirtatious behaviour had anything to do with the fact that Jolly Allsop was talking very animatedly to Jennifer Farmer and had yet to acknowledge Pearl's disgracefully late arrival.

'Your wife's really got her snout into those meringues,' Mrs Wilding informed the Reverend.

Was he just being polite, or was it such a special day that nobody minded this kind of crude behaviour? Libby wished she was a better judge of this sort of thing.

She took a deep breath. 'Have you met my husband Eddie?' she asked.

'I certainly have,' said Mrs Wilding. 'We had a right old giggle in the bar last night.'

Eddie had got into a bit of a habit of drinking with the guests. It was something her father would never have dreamed of doing. Libby didn't know quite how to broach it with her husband.

At school, Claudia and her friends had talked about love at first sight. Edith Payne thought she had experienced it the first time she saw *Wuthering Heights* starring Laurence Olivier. Now Claudia realized that those giddy feelings were nothing but adolescent silliness. When you fell in love, it wasn't butterflies in your tummy, it was a wonderful symphony of unexpected melodies playing all over you. Standing beside Michael, leaning against the piano, she was afraid that the sensation that made her feel as if her whole body was trembling would reverberate through the instrument into his body, and he would be able to tell. She stood up straight, taking her weight from the piano.

'Do you play?' he asked.

'No,' she replied.

'Would you like to learn?'

'Very much,' she replied.

'Now?'

'Now?'

He had a serious way of asking questions, but a smile danced around his pale blue eyes, gently mocking her, as if he had known her a very long time.

'I don't think it is possible,' she said.

'Of course it's possible. In five minutes, I can guarantee you'll be playing a very famous piece of music!'

He opened the piano lid and pulled the stool out from beneath the keyboard. Then he bowed and indicated that she should sit down. Standing close behind her, he took her left little finger and placed it on a low white note, her thumb on an ivory key further up the keyboard. Then he took her right hand, and made a chord from her thumb and third finger.

'That's good,' he said, as she struck the keys as instructed. 'Now all you need is a tune.'

Then he was sitting next to her on the piano stool, his thigh almost touching hers, and Claudia's rhythm fell apart.

She could feel her face going red.

'Again!' he said, putting her fingers back on the keys.

She laughed. 'I can't!'

'You can!' He pushed a hand back through his light brown hair and counted them in again.

This time she managed to keep up the oom-pah-pahs as Michael played increasingly complicated 'Chopsticks' accompaniments in the high register, and ended with a tinkling flourish worthy of Chico Marx.

They both sank across the piano laughing, their faces so close that she could feel his breath on her eyelids.

'You're a good teacher,' she said.

'My mother taught me to play,' he said very quietly. 'I found two of our piano keys in the wreck of our house.'

His eyes were such a pale blue they looked as if pain lay just beyond. His lower lip was full, sensuous, almost bruised-looking.

The children gathered around the piano.

'Can we play musical chairs?' the little King girl demanded.

Michael looked at the empty rows of chairs in front of the television, which no one was watching any more. 'I don't see why not,' he said.

He began to play:

> Half a pound of tuppenny rice,
> Half a pound of treacle,
> Mix it up and make it nice,
> Pop!

When he stopped, all but one of the children had sat down. Claudia took away a chair, and on they played, until there were just two chairs left and three children – the King children and the little boy called Arthur.

Claudia could tell that Michael tried to give the boy from the town the best chance, but Angela King barged him off the chair, and in the last round did the same to her older brother.

'When this hotel is mine,' Christopher King informed her in a pompous little voice, 'you won't be able to do that any more.'

Claudia found herself looking over the top of the children's heads at Michael, and he was smiling at her, a truly adult, complicit smile, which made her blush again.

There was a spontaneous round of applause in the lounge when the Queen appeared on the balcony of Buckingham Palace.

Everyone clinked glasses with his or her neighbour.

Mrs Wilding shouted, 'Hip Hip!'

To Libby's astonishment, the rest of the party chorused back, 'Hooray!'

The atmosphere was so convivial, Libby wouldn't have been surprised if they'd all broken into a chorus of 'Rule Britannia'.

It was a propitious moment for the photographer from the *Chronicle* to arrive. He was a nice-enough young man, although he seemed a little overwhelmed by all his equipment, and she hoped he was up to the task. But Mr Otterway, the editor of the *Chronicle*, was a guest, she reassured herself, and wouldn't have employed an incompetent.

'Excuse me!' she called loudly to make herself heard above the racket of piano coming from the ballroom. 'If you could all step out on to the terrace,' Libby instructed. 'It'll only take a minute, and nobody should get too wet.'

When it had been developed and printed, the photograph would show the entire King family, the spaniels Duke and Duchess, and all but two of the guests who had been invited to the Palace on Coronation Day 1953.

The photographer managed to capture most of the faces smiling at the camera, but there were two slightly blurred: the teacher and the foreign girl in the dreadful dress who were standing at the opposite ends of the group, like Spode dogs on a mantelpiece, as if they had turned to look at each other the moment the shutter opened.

What the picture did not record was the excruciating sound drifting down from the open windows of the Windsor Suite as the Wildings engaged in a particularly vigorous act of copulation, which had been all too audible during the moment of silence after the photographer called, 'Ready!'

'On the whole, I think it was a success,' Libby said to Eddie that night as he hopped around the room trying to dislodge his foot from a trouser leg.

She had been waiting for him to come upstairs for over an hour, going through the events of the day with satisfaction.

The arrival of the photographer had broken up the party a little prematurely, but all the adult guests had been effusive in their thanks. One of the children had been sick on the sprung floor of the ballroom, but it was only to be expected after all the rich food.

Even though it had been rained on all day, the beacon on the South Cliffs had lit immediately she touched it with her flaming torch. The whole town had cheered and Libby had known for a single, blissful second how it must feel to be Queen Elizabeth herself.

It was a shame about the yellow dress, but very lucky that there had been fire buckets strategically placed. And if the charred bit of the skirt couldn't be repaired, Mrs Farmer knew a girl who might be able to alter the bodice to make a blouse.

Nobody could work out how Nanny came to have been locked in the linen cupboard. Nanny's claim that Angela had been responsible met with the derision it demanded. The key was far too high for a child to reach, and Christopher insisted that neither of them knew anything about it. If Nanny hadn't immediately tendered her resignation, the disloyalty alone would have been grounds for dismissal. It was fortunate, in one sense, that the Wildings had repaired to their room at that particular point in the afternoon and heard the banging. Left any longer, Nanny might well have suffocated.

'You haven't been associating with Mr and Mrs Wilding, or Smith, or whatever they're called, in the bar this evening, have you?' Libby asked as her husband plonked heavily down on the bed in his shirtsleeves.

'It's a rum do,' he said, puffing brandy fumes at her. 'Fellow's got a lover—'

'Well, I had actually guessed that,' said Libby with a sniff.

'No . . . not the one who's here. She's quite a catch, apparently. Very much NOT the sort of woman who would like to find herself cited as a co-respondent in a divorce court. So, Mr Wilding—'

'Mr Smith.'

'The same, decided to hire himself a floozy, and a private detective, and to pretend to engage in a very public adultery . . .'

'It didn't sound like pretending,' Libby remarked curtly.

'Thought he'd get his money's worth!' Eddie chuckled. 'It was a bit of a wasted visit, you see. The detective had a nasty accident on the way. Therefore no witness to the liaison.'

The deviousness of people. And on Coronation Day!

Eddie's hand reached for her inner thigh and began to stroke in soft little circles. Surprisingly gentle.

'I really don't think . . .' Libby began.

His finger popped inside her.

'Eddie, I really don't . . . not on Coronation Day . . .'

Her husband kissed her. His mouth tasted of brandy and tobacco. Despite her respectful intentions, she found herself responding.

They were definitely going to have to do something about the sound-proofing.

Sylvia Quinn's baby had arrived very suddenly and was blue. Dr Payne had been watching the Coronation with his family on his television when he had been summoned by the midwife who had been watching with most of the rest of the town in Audrey Potter's parlour. The doctor had driven mother and baby to the hospital in Lowhampton where they were both recovering well, he told Michael, with a reprimanding look for leaving Sylvia in her advanced condition.

Miss Potter offered to have Iris for the night, but Michael carried her home asleep on his shoulder, and lowered her gently into her bed. The child sighed and snuffled, then stretched her hands up above her head, her skin so pale and still that he touched her chest just to make sure she was still breathing. The red curls spread out on the pillow were just like Frank's. They'd called him Carrots at school, but if you looked closely you could see at least ten shades of gold.

Michael adjusted the blanket, almost hoping he would rouse Iris so that she could keep him company with her stream of idiosyncratic chatter. But Iris slept on, and eventually her even breathing began to work its soporific magic on him, but every time his eye-lids closed he started awake again.

Claudia Liebeskind. Claudia Dearchild.

That beautiful face amidst swirling balloons; those delicate little hands, so trusting as he placed them on the piano keys; that look of puzzled disbelief when the bellboy had shouted to the assembled guests on the terrace that a Mr Michael Quinn was wanted urgently on the telephone, because his wife was having a baby.

Chapter Two

March 1954

It had been generally assumed when Mr Jolly Allsop announced his engagement to Miss Jennifer Farmer that his father, Sir John Allsop, would make way for his son at the Castle.

The question of where her daughter would live after the nuptials was very much on Mrs Ruby Farmer's mind when she took tea with her oldest friend, Mrs Liliana King, in Liliana's private apartment at the Palace Hotel.

'He refuses to budge! Or even share!'

'Sir John is impossibly eccentric!' said Liliana sympathetically, picking up the heavy silver teapot and pouring the steaming amber liquid into Ruby's cup.

'Apparently, he calls Jennifer "the shop girl",' Ruby confided.

'The nerve!'

'I've half a mind to tell him that I wouldn't have my daughter sharing his house with him and his piccaninny,' Ruby went on.

'You could still refuse permission, of course,' said Liliana, buttering a scone and passing it on a small plate to Ruby. 'Jennifer is only eighteen, after all.'

'It's too late for that,' Ruby said.

'Has it gone beyond the point of postponement?' Liliana enquired.

Ruby was halfway through a mouthful of scone, but didn't want a prolonged pause to be taken as a positive response, so shook her head vigorously. The scone took an age to go down. The sip of tea she took to help it on its way turned to burning glue on the roof of her mouth.

'Certainly not!' she finally managed. 'But the invitations have gone out. And,' she added, suddenly remembering the point of it, 'they are in love!'

'Has Jennifer decided on a dress?' Liliana asked, selecting a finger sandwich from the lowest tier of pretty floral plates on the tea stand.

'White.' Ruby Farmer allowed a slightly sanctimonious smile to play around her lips. 'We considered an oyster satin with pearls, but there's always a slight feeling, isn't there, with oyster, or even cream?'

Liliana said nothing.

'Which is a shame for the girls whom white doesn't suit, but there we are. Luckily Jenny is one of the few. Silk chiffon with a boned bodice.' Ruby stood up to demonstrate the shape on her own trim figure. 'A removable bolero. White lace, scalloped edges, tight long sleeves,' she went on, stretching her right arm in front of her and running her left hand lightly from shoulder to wrist. 'I'm having it taken in a little. The girl who did Libby's invisible mending. Jenny is so . . .' She searched for the right word.

'Lanky?' Liliana interjected.

'Slender,' Ruby substituted. 'No embroidery; no beads. The quality of the fabric speaks for itself . . .' She smoothed imaginary yards over her narrow hips and allowed her hands to float out by her sides to demonstrate the fullness of the skirt.

'Classical,' Liliana decided as Ruby twirled, modelling the invisible frock.

'*Very* classical,' Ruby echoed.

'Sounds perfect,' Liliana said.

Everything about Jennifer's upcoming nuptials did sound perfect. She had been swept off her feet by the most eligible man in the county (right under the nose of Pearl King too, although mention was never made of that at the Palace, of course); there was the prospect of a title and acres of land to come; an Easter wedding: a very *à la mode* wedding gown – it was all, as

Audrey Potter had tellingly remarked, almost too good to be true.

'Yes,' Ruby agreed with a slight hesitation. 'Except for the problem of having nowhere to live,' she added, returning to her theme.

'They say the new council houses have better facilities than most of us can afford,' Liliana observed.

Ruby did not want to dignify the suggestion, if it was intended as a suggestion, with a rebuttal. She had heard all about the new Scandinavian-style council houses which were going up in the fields above Church Lane. They were to have upstairs bathrooms and kitchens with built-in cupboards, but she would die before she saw Jennifer live in one. If her own years of hard work meant anything, it was certainly not to see her daughter living amongst those the State provided for. In any case, she doubted very much that Jolly Allsop would qualify as deserving. Neither immediately wealthy, nor deserving! That was the problem.

'They can hardly share with me,' Ruby pressed on.

Mrs Farmer resided with her daughter in the apartment above Farmer's Outfitters. It was spacious and light, with a balcony above the roof of the little arcade, but it was clearly not a suitable place for a well-to-do young couple to begin their married life.

Jennifer's bedroom walls were lined with rows of dolls all immaculately kitted out in national costumes of the world, which Ruby had sewed from off-cuts during the blackouts. They would stare at the honeymoon couple in that slightly sinister way that dolls did. It would be most off-putting.

'They need a place of their own,' Ruby continued, slightly desperately.

'If only I could help,' said Liliana, leaning forward and putting a hand on her friend's arm. 'But it's all out of my hands now, as you know.'

Disappointment coursed through Ruby's veins. She'd been sure that Liliana would come up with something in exchange for all her generosity over the years. A suite of rooms perhaps, if only on a temporary basis. It wasn't as if it would make much difference to the Kings. And she'd made Pearl's clothing coupons stretch much further than they would have done elsewhere. She began to wonder whether Liliana wasn't secretly a little envious.

Even though Pearl had always made fun of him, the fact remained that Jennifer had stolen Jolly's heart. If the Allsops weren't quite the top drawer, at least they were the middle drawer of a genuine antique chest of drawers (if that is where the expression originated), unlike some of the men rumoured to be Pearl King's suitors, whose origins were very much more the utility furniture end of things.

The Summer House, which stood at the far reach of the Palace land, had been built by Pearl's Victorian great-great-grandfather for the amusement and education of nine children (and later modified by the oldest son, as he waited to take over the hotel, for the accommodation of his mistress). Designed to three-quarter-scale, it gave the appearance of a Swiss chalet with a carved gable, and flower balconies at the first-floor windows, but the wooden frontage and large stones on the roof were cosmetic attachments concealing the solid brickwork of Victorian builders.

During the war, the Summer House had been requisitioned as part of the RAF's occupation of the Palace and remodelled again as living quarters for the senior officers at the expense of the War Office. The track from Hill Road had been created for access. It was said that Mr Churchill himself had slept here when the Summer House had been the secret location for one of his meetings with General Eisenhower and Field Marshal Montgomery during the early stages of planning the D-Day landings.

Inside it was cold, and there was a smell of old dust, like an attic. There were a few items of normal-sized furniture: a wide mahogany desk with a leather top and three wing-back armchairs in front of the fireplace where Pearl could envisage the great leaders plotting like giants. The gravity of Mr Churchill's presence (was it her imagination, or was there still a vanilla hint of cigar?) still lingered.

What must Mr Churchill have made of this Tyrolean idyll in the depths of the English countryside? Pearl wondered as she gazed at the barn-like eaves, with Mr Rogers, the chauffeur, asleep beside her, his head in her armpit, slow even breaths blowing across her right breast.

For a moment she allowed herself the daydream of waking up

every morning beside this man whose body fitted so exactly with hers, the two of them living permanently in the forest. She pictured herself in a white apron, doing something wifely like rolling pastry, Rogers polishing boots in the hearth behind her, unable to resist picking up her skirt and taking her on the long oak kitchen table, both of them rolling blissfully, unashamedly, in clouds of flour.

Her reverie was brought sharply to an end by pins and needles prickling her foot. Mr Rogers's left leg was flung across hers and was beginning to cut off the blood supply. The warm, listless pleasure of an afternoon nap after love-making had suddenly turned to intense discomfort. Her exposed skin shivered with a rash of goosebumps.

'Rocky,' she hissed her pet name for him. She thought it suited his Hollywood good looks. 'Rocky!'

He did not stir.

'Mr Rogers!'

Still his breath ebbed and flowed against her chest. His trusting unconsciousness, so tender it had made her want to cry after the urgency of their love-making, was fast becoming a source of irritation.

Unable to move her limbs, Pearl took a mouthful of his curly hair between her teeth and tugged as hard as she was able.

'What the bloody hell did you do that for?' Mr Rogers sat up, rubbing his scalp.

Men were terrible sissies about hair-pulling, Pearl thought. Women endured the pain without nearly as much fuss.

Mrs Liliana King's choice of a suite without a sea view had not been the entirely selfless act that people had given her credit for. Although the west-facing aspect of rooms which overlooked the bay brought an attractive opalesque quality to the light at sundown, having grown up by the seaside, Liliana hardly noticed the ever-changing vista of ocean which made visitors gasp after the long journey down. For her, a hotel was and had always been, from her very first memories, what went on inside, and from her window overlooking the front door, she could see everyone who came and went.

Hotels, she had sometimes thought, had a similar effect to those wavy mirrors at funfairs, exaggerating all the guests' worst features. Would-be wits spoke a little louder in hotel lobbies; people with something to hide became a touch too confident in their anonymity; strained marriages were stretched beyond breaking point in the effort to appear happy in public.

As a child, she had crouched at the upstairs window of her family's more modest establishment, and watched the guests arriving, allocating names to each – the Dashing Cavalier, the Suffragette, Beauty and the Beast – and stories which brought them to the point of their arrival in her world. Sometimes the lives she guessed at were revealed as uncannily accurate; more often the intrigues would exceed the limits of a child's imagination. The candid sunlight of the seaside drew out secrets kept all year in the dark halls of suburban villas. Even the dullest-looking guests would return for their evening meal with the sun's flush on their cheeks and a certain unburdened quality to their step.

Liliana learned when she was quite young to read and write, but she gained her real education through observing the many lives that glanced against hers. The labels on the luggage they brought, the stains they left behind, the constant drift of perfume and murmured conversation taught her the complicated, duplicitous nature of human beings: a useful lesson for a solitary child with no brothers or sisters to talk to.

This afternoon a little Morris drew up and a slight man in a single-breasted three-piece navy suit and a black trilby emerged from the car, brushed first his left and then his right shoulder, and paused for a moment, looking up at the frontage. His gaze seemed to linger on certain details: the ragged flashing the builders had yet to finish around the roof repairs; the single dripping overflow pipe. Not a guest, Liliana decided. Although the suit was undoubtedly the latest style, it was a little too flashy for a gentleman on a visit to the country, and, in any case, the hotel had yet to open for the season.

The almost indecently long time he was spending looking at the minor blemishes on the façade led her to think, momentarily, inspector; but something about the cut of the suit said not. A little too smart for a salesman. Natty was the word that kept popping into her mind. It was a very natty suit. This must be Mr Pocock, Liliana surmised, the under-manager Libby had decided to employ. Everything about his demeanour, the precise steps he took to the front door, his failure to turn and gawp as the hotel Bentley drew up and Pearl, in her tennis dress, hurtled past him up the steps, made Liliana instantly award him the private soubriquet the Confirmed Bachelor. On the whole, Liliana decided, she was in favour of Mr Pocock and his natty suit. In her experience, things went with more of a swing when there was a confirmed bachelor around.

'It's a bit rainy for Pearl to be playing tennis, isn't it?' said Ruby Farmer, who was leaning as far as she could across the tea table in order to get a better view of what it was that had caught Liliana's attention.

'I think the weather's got worse since they started forecasting it on television,' said Liliana neutrally.

'Didn't seem to have her racquet with her, either,' Ruby observed.

'I say,' said Liliana, pointing at the teapot and checking the time on her wristwatch. 'How about something a little stronger?'

When Liliana made the suggestion at dinner that Jolly and Jennifer should move into the Summer House until the Castle became available for them, Eddie, who was already feeling a little put out by Mr Pocock's arrival, objected. 'I thought I was supposed to be in charge!'

'You'd get an estate manager for virtually nothing,' said Liliana. 'Jolly needs something to do now he's finished his National Service.'

'Estate manager!' Eddie scoffed.

'Groundsman, then,' Libby suggested to her husband.

She could see him turning it over in his mind. Whilst he didn't like his authority to be undermined, there would be more time for working on his yacht, the *Brittany Anna*. The fact was that Eddie was far happier with the deck of a ship beneath his feet than an Axminster carpet. He was inclined to be either over-friendly or irascible with the guests. On the whole, things ran more smoothly when contact was limited to the bar before dinner. She could see that he was about to concede the point when Pearl suddenly banged both her hands down on the table and said, 'No!'

Her voice was so unexpectedly loud that the waitress dropped the buttered new potato she was serving on to the carpet where it rolled uncomfortably close to Pearl's new kid shoe.

'Oh, do go away!' said Pearl to the waitress as the girl knelt on the floor trying to retrieve the potato. Still crouching, she hurried out of the room.

Everyone looked expectantly at Pearl. With three pairs of eyes on her, Pearl shifted a little uncomfortably on her dining chair. 'I might be planning to use the Summer House myself,' she said, avoiding direct eye contact with any of them.

'What on earth for?' Libby asked.

'If it's good enough for Jolly and Jenny, why should it not be good enough for me?' Pearl argued. 'When *I'm* married,' she added through gritted teeth.

'By the time *you're* married Jolly and Jennifer will have inherited the Castle!' Eddie joked.

'Do I have to put up with that?' Pearl appealed to Libby, who issued Eddie with a duly critical look.

The waitress, who had returned with a silver bowl of peas, held them high above her shoulder as if to keep them out of range of attack.

'Do you have anyone in mind?' Libby asked, trying to mollify the atmosphere.

Pearl squirmed slightly on her dining chair. 'Possibly.'

'Oh, Pearl, you're such a one! Who?'

The crash of silver on china as the waitress misjudged the distance to Liliana's plate alerted the diners to the fact that she was listening in. Silence fell round the table until the door of the Kings' private dining room had clicked shut behind her.

'As your mother, I think I'm entitled to ask whether the gentleman in question has the means to keep you?' said Liliana.

'I am over twenty-one. I am allowed to do as I please,' said Pearl airily.

'Well, yes, I suppose you are, legally,' said Liliana, cutting the meat from the bone of her lamb chop.

Eddie picked up his knife and fork again, as if he simply wasn't capable of listening and eating at the same time.

'I inherit what Daddy left me next year,' said Pearl, confidently brisk.

'Only at my discretion,' said Liliana, fixing her with one of her significant looks.

Pearl stared back at her. 'Perhaps I should marry Jolly Allsop after all, then,' she said, defiantly.

'You wouldn't ... Oh, Pearl, you couldn't ...' said Libby, thinking of poor Jennifer, and the scandal.

'Of course I wouldn't,' Pearl snapped. 'Kissing him is like kissing a slug.'

Liliana sighed.

'I do wonder what Jenny sees in him,' Libby mused.

'What Ruby Farmer's daughter sees in the heir to the Castle and two thousand acres? I simply couldn't say,' said Pearl.

Several peas spluttered from Eddie's mouth on to the white damask tablecloth. Pearl stared at the tiny coronas of gravy spreading out around each pea.

'Please don't give them the Summer House,' she pleaded with Libby.

'I'm afraid it's already settled,' said Liliana, firmly.

'Well, I think you're all completely beastly,' said Pearl and rushed from the room.

'It makes me think of the darling little weather house I had as a child,' said Jennifer Farmer. She was looking out of the first-floor window of the apartment above the shop. Even though it was only mid-afternoon, the rain, which had persisted for several days, made it feel dark already. 'Do you suppose I shall be the smiling lady who comes out when the sun is shining, and Jolly will be the grumpy man who only shows his face when there's bad weather?'

'I hope you will both be smiling,' said Sylvia, immediately realizing that the appropriate response would probably have just been a light laugh. Jennifer was passing the time of day, not really trying to engage her in a conversation.

'It hasn't stopped raining for weeks,' said Jennifer.

'Let's hope it rains itself out in time for your day,' said Sylvia.

Jennifer flashed her a brief smile, and continued to stare out of the window, sighing occasionally as Sylvia silently stitched the seam that joined the bodice to the skirt of the wedding dress. Half the Farmers' drawing room seemed to be billowing in the dreamy white fabric. It was like sewing in a cloud.

'Mummy?' said Iris, who was perched on a small upholstered footstool at the far end of the long room, turning the onion-skin pages of a volume of the *Encyclopaedia Britannica* which she had asked permission to take from the special bookcase. 'Mummy?' she said, again, looking up.

'Yes, dear?'

'Sarah Bird would like to go home now.'

'As soon as I've finished,' said Sylvia.

The child turned another page solemnly. Iris could sit for hours with a book in her hands.

'She's terribly well behaved, isn't she?' Jennifer remarked, staring at Iris as if she were a curious exhibit. 'I wish I could have your little girl as my bridesmaid instead of horrid Angela King.'

Jennifer pulled the net curtain back again. The rain was bouncing off the roof of the arcade.

'Jolly wants to have lots of children straightaway . . .' she said with a sigh.

Sylvia concentrated hard on the tiny stitches, not wanting to jump in again.

'. . . but I'm rather hoping that we won't be immediately blessed. Does that sound awful? I'd like it to be us, just the two of us, for a while at least . . .'

Sylvia carefully snipped the thread, and brushed the seam lightly with the back of her hand. She was thinking what a lovely expression 'immediately blessed' was. Much prettier than the phrases that had been used about her first pregnancy.

She would have liked it to be just the two of them too, for a while, in their own home. But it would never have been like that. Michael had proposed without hesitation when she told him she was pregnant, reassuring her that it was only a matter of timing, but she knew that wasn't the truth. His willingness to lie had made her love him all the more.

'Mummy, Sarah Bird needs to go,' Iris whined.

'Who's Sarah Bird?' Jennifer asked.

'Just an imaginary friend,' Sylvia explained. 'It's quite normal in children her age. I'll be finished in a minute,' she said to her daughter, annoyed with her for breaking into the quiet exchange of confidences that might have paved the way for friendship with Jennifer Farmer, who reminded her of the confident, richer girls at school that her mother had always wanted her to be friends with.

'Are you any good with curtains?' Jennifer asked.

'I'll be making ours for our new home,' Sylvia replied.

'You're moving too?' Jennifer asked, although Sylvia had mentioned it on several occasions.

'One of the brand-new houses on the estate,' Sylvia explained again. 'They'll be finished in a month or so.'

'I don't suppose you'd be a darling and consider doing mine in the meantime?' Jennifer asked.

'I'd be pleased to,' Sylvia agreed.

Jennifer beamed at her.

Sylvia looked shyly down at her sewing.

'Did you hear about Pearl King?' Jennifer asked.

Sylvia, who had heard the gossip via Audrey Potter, whose best friend cooked at the Palace Hotel, shook her head innocently.

'She's fallen in love with the chauffeur but Liliana King won't let them marry. So sad for Pearl, don't you think?'

Sylvia nodded.

'He *is* good looking,' Jennifer went on airily, 'and, between you and me, Pearl is no angel . . .' She lowered her voice to relay a confidence. 'Do you know she used to set the fire alarm off on purpose just so she could be carried down a ladder by a fireman . . .'

'Isn't that against the law?' Sylvia asked.

'Oh, the Kings are above the law!' Jennifer giggled. 'Didn't you know?'

'Mummy!' said Iris.

'In a moment!' Sylvia snapped.

She suddenly noticed the time on the clock. It was gone four o'clock. Gathering up the yards of skirt, she draped the dress over the back of the sofa, running her hand along it one last time.

'You're going to look perfect,' she whispered, not quite daring to look directly at Jennifer.

'I'll be in touch then, shall I?' said Jennifer. 'About the curtains?'

'Yes, of course.'

Sylvia grabbed Iris's hand and yanked her towards the stairs.

Halfway down, Jennifer called out again, 'Mrs Quinn?'

'Yes?' Sylvia turned.

'Do we owe you anything?'

'I was pleased to be able to help,' Sylvia replied, flustered.

'Sweet of you!' said Jennifer. 'You must choose something next time you're in the shop.'

Anthony, who would normally have woken up and alerted her to the time, was still sleeping soundly in his pram at the foot of the stairs, probably lulled, as she had been, by the gloom of the day. Sylvia pushed the pram along the promenade, tugging an uncharacteristically crotchety Iris behind her, trying to keep an umbrella over them both.

'Can we go a bit slower, because the Birds are out of breath?' said Iris.

'There aren't any Birds,' said Sylvia crossly.

Sometimes she was prepared to go along with Iris's family of imaginary friends, sometimes she didn't have the time for it. She wasn't quite sure whether they were actually birds who floated around like the twittering cartoon ones in *Snow White*, or whether they were a family who had the surname Bird, and she didn't think she ought to encourage Iris by asking.

'Come along, Baby Bird,' Iris said, holding out her hand to help a creature only she could see, and walking at her own slow speed. Sylvia pressed on in the hope that Iris would quicken her pace without the shelter of the umbrella, but by the time they reached home, Iris was at least fifty yards behind, still holding out her hand and talking to her invisible companion.

'I'm all wet!' said Iris, when she eventually reached the doorstep.

'Come on then!' Sylvia said, smiling at her. Iris could be infuriating, but you had to admire her consistency. She bent forward and hugged her curiously determined little girl, holding her cold little wet face against her own. Iris's arms went round her neck in a tight forgiving hug.

'Come on then,' Sylvia said again, straightening up and putting her hand under the child's bottom to carry her inside. 'Iris, what have you done?' She drew her face away to look into her daughter's.

'Sarah Bird was very naughty and splashed a puddle right up into my knickers,' Iris explained.

Sylvia was filled with remorse as it dawned on her that Iris had been trying to tell her all along that she wanted to go to the lavatory. For one awful moment she wondered whether Iris had done her wee on Mrs Farmer's upholstered stool.

The slices of mutton were cold and dry. Unappetizing fat coated the roof of Sylvia's mouth. She had been intending to make a shepherd's pie from the remains of Sunday's shoulder roast, but there had barely been time to peel the potatoes and set them to boil before her husband arrived back after school.

'What did you do today?' Michael asked his daughter.

'I read a book that crackled with Sarah Bird. Mummy did sewing. Anthony just did sleeping,' Iris replied.

Iris had insisted on tackling her food with a proper knife and fork because she was eating with Daddy, and she pushed Sylvia's hand away when her mother attempted to cut her meat up for her. After struggling manfully, she finally decided to put it into her mouth whole.

'Is Mummy sewing a nice dress for you?' Michael asked.

'Not for me!' Iris said, as if it were a very stupid question. Little gobbets of meat flew out of her mouth.

'Don't speak with your mouth full!' Sylvia reprimanded.

Chastened, Iris chewed and chewed.

'Is it for Sarah Bird?' Michael asked.

'Sarah Bird doesn't wear dresses!'

'How was your day?' Sylvia asked.

'We made Viking boats out of matchboxes,' said Michael. 'Would you like to make a Viking boat one day?' he asked Iris.

'No thanks,' said Iris, opening her mouth wide to demonstrate to Sylvia that it was empty, before trying her luck with a boiled potato. 'But the Birds might,' she added. 'You just never know with the Birds.'

Sylvia found it slightly uncomfortable recognizing grown-up phrases issuing from her daughter's mouth, but Michael was always amused by it. He didn't have to deal with the looks people gave Iris when she came out with precocious utterances in public.

'Mummy is sewing a big white dress,' Iris informed her father.

Sylvia put down her knife and fork. 'Mrs Farmer asked me if I would mind altering her daughter's wedding gown,' she admitted.

'Which one's Mrs Farmer?' he enquired distractedly.

'Farmer's Outfitters,' Sylvia reminded him.

'The merry widow with the ghastly hats?'

Sometimes Sylvia thought Michael never noticed anything that went on around him, but then he would come out with comments so perceptive she had to bite her tongue to stop herself laughing out loud.

'Sorry it wasn't very nice,' Sylvia said, clearing away his plate.

Iris pushed her plate away too.

'Finish your tea,' Sylvia instructed her.

'But it's not very nice,' Iris said.

'There are plenty of people in the world who'd be grateful for that food,' said Sylvia.

'Give it to those people, then,' Iris countered.

'You can't fault her logic,' Michael said.

'It's not her logic I'm worried about, it's her manners,' said Sylvia crisply, hating the phrase as it came trotting out. It sounded just like her mother. Michael never said anything, but she knew she was not how he wanted her to be with the children. She scooped Iris up. 'Bed for you, young lady!'

'One day, Mummy,' Iris said, as Sylvia kissed her goodnight, 'I'm going to fly away.'

'People can't fly.'

'The Birds can.'

'Never mind about that now,' said Sylvia, turning off the light. 'You go to sleep.'

Michael was reading in the dark little front room when she came downstairs.

'I think those blooming Birds keep her awake,' said Sylvia, perplexed by the way she could slip into lending the Birds the dignity of reality herself. She sank into the other armchair. The stuffing in the seat cushion was so old that the feathers inside had collapsed into hard little quills which prickled against the backs of her legs. However often she hung the cushions on the washing line on fine days, and whacked them with a carpet sweeper, they still smelled of dust. She couldn't wait to leave the ingrained grime of the little rented cottage. In the new house, the living room was open plan. It would be light and clean and everything would be much nicer.

The room was silent apart from the patter of rain on glass.

'April showers,' she said, racking her brain to find something interesting to say to keep Michael from going upstairs as soon as he was sure that Iris was asleep.

She wished they could sometimes spend a normal evening together, like normal couples did, talking or listening to the wireless, or just sitting. But he always wanted to do his writing.

'In the new house, it won't be so damp,' she ventured.

'No?' Michael turned a page.

'Would you like to look at curtain material on Saturday morning?' she asked. 'Mrs Farmer's got some new stuff. Very modern. I don't know whether you'd like it.'

'You decide.'

'I'm hoping to get a discount,' she announced. 'This sewing I'm doing . . .'

'Isn't she going to pay you?' he asked, looking over the top of his book.

'Mrs Farmer gave me a scarf when I did some invisible mending.'

'A scarf!'

'It's real silk,' she defended herself.

'In the new house . . .' Michael suddenly volunteered.

'Yes?' Sylvia sat forward eagerly. It was a phrase she had found herself using at the beginning of lots of sentences, but she didn't think she'd heard him say it before.

'I thought I'd have the little box bedroom as a study,' Michael told her.

'A study?' Sylvia repeated.

'So that I don't disturb Iris.'

Sylvia hesitated.

'What about Anthony? He'll need his own room soon,' she replied. 'We don't want him sleeping in ours for ever, do we?'

For a second, a flash of unmistakable lust gleamed in her husband's eyes at the implicit invitation. It made Sylvia feel guilty for not pleasing him more often.

In the new house, she decided, everything would be different. Everything would be much better.

The sun came out on Jennifer Farmer's wedding day.

Jennifer lay on her single bed in her new white bra and suspender belt, white stockings already fastened, smoking a cigarette and staring at the ice-white dress which was hanging from a padded hanger in the doorframe.

'Buck up. You'll be late if you don't get a move on,' Ruby Farmer said, poking her head round the dress.

She was ready, wearing a striking black and white checked dress and jacket with an elaborate corsage of roses the same fondant pink as those Jennifer had chosen for the bouquet. A stiff little pink handbag hung from her arm.

'Isn't the bride supposed to be late?' Jennifer said loftily.

'Not too late,' said Ruby, looking at her watch for the hundredth time, and retreating to the kitchen before her daughter became annoyed with her.

It was a lovely day, she told herself. The happiest day of Jenny's life, although Jenny herself did not seem to be very happy. It was down to nerves, she thought, taking a little nip of brandy to calm her own.

Then suddenly Jennifer was standing in the door, her chestnut hair loose around her shoulders, and she looked so beautiful that tears sprang to Ruby's eyes. She rushed forward to hug her daughter, careful to keep her mouth away from the dress and veil in case of lipstick stains. When she released her, she could see that there were tears in Jenny's eyes too.

'Come on, I'll do your hair for you,' said Ruby.

'I don't want to get married!' Jennifer said.

'We'll still see each other all the time,' said Ruby, touched by her daughter's sudden display of affection.

'I'm not sure I love him.'

'Of course you do. It's just nerves. Every bride gets nerves.'

'I don't think so,' said Jennifer, lighting another cigarette.

Ruby wished she wouldn't. Not with all that floaty fabric around.

She sat Jennifer down and tried to pin her hair up, but she was all fingers and thumbs. She poured another little glass of brandy, just to steady herself.

It wasn't that she hadn't wondered herself what it was that Jennifer saw in Jolly. She'd put the attraction down to the Army. Like so many men, Jolly had cut a much more substantial figure in uniform – the cap gave him several inches in height, the jacket added breadth to his slight shoulders. Even though Ruby had spent a lifetime studying ladies' fashions and knew how much the correct height of heel and a good hat could add to a woman's powers of attraction, she had never paid the same attention to the study of men's attire, until she had been forced to think about what it was that her tall, beautiful daughter might see in the feeble young man. The separation National Service demanded was another factor which fostered romance among so many young couples. There was never a truer saying than Absence Makes the Heart Grow Fonder, Mrs Farmer had often thought when dusting the photograph of her own late husband, who had been so very much easier to love and honour since his death had parted them.

'Do you think I'm doing the right thing?' Jennifer looked pleadingly up at her.

'It's too late for all this now,' Ruby snapped at her daughter. 'You should have thought about it before.'

It was the kind of sparkling spring morning Sylvia had never known before coming to live in Kingshaven. The sunshine bouncing off the choppy silver sea seemed to double the brightness, and the chilly breeze made her feel as if she were breathing in great lungfuls of sunshine.

She had dressed Iris in the smart tartan coat with a black velvet collar Mrs Farmer had pressed on her in exchange for her work on the wedding dress, and tied the silk scarf patterned with sketches of Parisian scenes around her own neck.

'Where are we going?' Iris asked.

'For a walk.'

'Why isn't Daddy coming?'

Sylvia sighed. 'He's doing his writing.'

'Why?'

Why did Michael have to write? Sylvia wondered. Sometimes it felt to her as if he was dissatisfied with his life and had to make things up for interest.

He had written stories ever since she'd known him. He'd even won a competition back home just after they were married, and been awarded a certificate and a guinea. A photograph of him had appeared in the regional newspaper, but it was only when one of her mother's friends had seen it that Michael had owned up to sending the story in. He had claimed that he didn't want a fuss, but Sylvia had suspected that he hadn't really wanted anyone he knew to read it.

He was definitely very good at describing things, but some of the things he chose to describe, were, as her mother had pointed out, better left unsaid.

'It made me feel quite sick,' had been Doreen's exact words at Sunday lunch in the cold dining room at home.

Sylvia had frozen, imagining in the ensuing silence that Michael was about to do something wild like smashing the gravy boat into the glass-fronted cabinet that contained her mother's collection of china figurines. The mantelpiece clock marked each long second of dread anticipation until Michael suddenly started laughing very loudly and for a long time, as if her mother's verdict had given him enormous pleasure. Her mother had stared at him as if he were mad.

He'd never been like other people. Even as a boy when he'd come to spend summers with his aunts, their next-door neighbours in the Yorkshire market town of Etherington, he never did boys' things like climbing fences and catapulting stones at the greenhouses on the allotments. He never showed any interest in pulling the Shirley Temple ringlets her mother tied up in rags each night. Michael had preferred to sit hidden in the branches of the old apple tree at the bottom of his aunts' garden, reading books.

Like any enigma, Sylvia had found him a little frightening at first and had to dare herself to look up at him from the safety of her garden. Sometimes he would wave at her. Once he smiled. That was the moment she had fallen in love with him. She was six years old; he was nine.

When he came to live permanently next door they explored the area together, playing games based on the books he had read. The rough ground beyond the end of the gardens became the sands of Arabia, the cricket pavilion a fortified castle, the recreation ground, with its shallow paddling pool, served as the Lake District for a re-enactment of *Swallows and Amazons*. Sometimes Michael would get cross with her when she got details wrong. She preferred to be his audience as he recounted stories, or acted out swashbuckling scenes, or terrified her with sudden howlings from *The Hound of the Baskervilles*.

At the time, she had thought it a bit odd that her parents had let her play out, especially with a boy whose relations they didn't much approve of, but she'd realized later that they, like many other parents, had been so frightened of invasion that they hadn't had the heart to stop her enjoying her life while she still had it.

Sylvia had never wanted the war to end.

'Why are we stopping here?' Iris wanted to know as Sylvia lifted her on to the wall at the back of the churchyard to get a better view of the wedding guests arriving.

'I just want to look,' Sylvia replied.

'Why?'

'That's enough questions.'

'I say!'

To Sylvia's horror, Jennifer Farmer, yards of skirt over her right arm and a cigarette in her left, was walking towards her.

'I say,' she called again. 'You don't happen to have a match, do you?'

'No, I'm sorry!' Sylvia was covered with embarrassment to be caught peeking. She patted coat pockets she knew to be empty in an effort to appear co-operative.

'Mr Rogers picked me up first,' Jennifer explained. 'So much skirt we couldn't fit the bridesmaids in at the same time.'

For some reason, Sylvia felt a little guilty, as if it were the fault of her sewing that Jennifer was early for the wedding.

'I feel as if I'm being offered up for sacrifice,' Jennifer said, waving the unlit cigarette around.

Sylvia wasn't sure what she meant. 'Well, you look very nice,' she said.

Jennifer looked over the wall towards the front of the church where the congregation was arriving in groups of two and three and suddenly grabbed Sylvia's arm. 'Did you have doubts on your wedding day?' she asked, sounding uncharacteristically nervous.

Sylvia thought of Etherington Town Hall, the institutional smell, the horrible unadorned wooden staircase which creaked as they walked up it. There were two doors on the landing, one with a big sign saying 'Marriages and Births', the other 'Deaths': the future laid out before them with sudden terrible starkness. Then Michael had squeezed her arm, and said, 'Come on then!' and she'd known she could face anything with him beside her.

'Everyone does,' she told Jennifer because she thought that was probably the most steadying thing to say.

'I'm just not—' Jennifer began.

'There's the merry widow in the ghastly hat!' Iris suddenly announced, pointing across at Mrs Farmer who had come out of the church and was anxiously looking at her watch.

Sunlight streamed through the clear glass window above the altar, making the church unnaturally light. Libby wondered how much it would cost to replace the window with stained glass. The previous window had shattered into smithereens when the only bomb which had fallen on Kingshaven during the war missed St Mary's by yards, blowing a crater in the churchyard instead. Several of the old graves had been disturbed, but fortunately no new ones created.

The Allsops' window had withstood the blast.

There was no good reason why the Kings should not have a window too, Libby thought. It would be a fitting memorial to her late father.

As the congregation rose, Libby turned towards the rear of the church and saw Jennifer, on the arm of Dr Payne, framed in the door of the church. Then Mrs Farmer gave her daughter a little push, and Jennifer set off down the aisle. Libby remembered at her own wedding how her father's arm had trembled as he'd offered it to her, and she'd suddenly realized that he was much more nervous than she was. She'd grasped his arm tightly, holding him up, never in any doubt that she was doing the right thing.

Eddie had been standing in almost exactly the same place on that day as he was now, looking wonderfully handsome in his uniform. It was a shame, Libby thought as the bride passed beside her, that Eddie couldn't give Jennifer away today, but Jolly had asked him to be best man before Ruby Farmer had suggested it.

A few steps behind Jennifer, Pearl brushed past the family pew in her candyfloss pink dress with its fashionable stole collar and stiff underskirt, her face a solemn picture of piety. Next to her Angela was taking giant steps, taking the instruction to follow Pearl to the letter. Libby smiled approvingly at her daughter. Angela scowled back at her.

The two ill-matched bridesmaids slowly processed behind the bride and groom towards the altar. Unfortunately, no one had had the foresight to teach Angela how to kneel in a skirt with a hoop. She had not worn the dress at the practice for fear that she would dirty it. Energetically resisting Pearl's attempts to help her, the little girl eventually decided to kneel on the front of the skirt, making the hoop spring up vertically behind her, and affording the congregation a clear view of her white knickers.

A trace of a snigger reverberated through the church. Several women made a point of turning round to smile sympathetically. The loud opening chords of 'Oh Jesus, I Have Promised' blasted out from the organ.

'My lord, ladies and gentlemen,' Eddie began. 'And any other riff-raff gathered here today . . . !'

A murmur of slightly nervous amusement rumbled round the horseshoe-shaped wedding breakfast table. He felt Libby tense in the seat beside him.

'Promise you won't be too naval?' she had asked anxiously whenever the subject of his speech had arisen.

'I'm told it is the duty of the best man to gather as many embarrassing facts about the groom as possible . . .' Eddie paused for effect, and looked around the table. Liliana King's cornflower-blue eyes had him fixed in a gimlet stare. Next to her, Jolly Allsop was smiling inanely into the middle distance; his bride was toying sulkily with her pudding. The bride's mother didn't seem to have noticed that everyone else round the table had fallen silent and was still attempting to make conversation with Sir John Allsop who, much to everyone's surprise, had attended the ceremony.

'. . . the thing about land,' Mrs Farmer was saying. Her voice had grown progressively louder and more slurred with her continual failure to elicit a response, 'is the responsibility that goes with it. For example, my father's dahlias really took over his life. Even a couple of hanging baskets, which you wouldn't think could be a chore—'

A sharp nudge from her daughter brought her up mid-sentence.

'. . . unfortunately, I could find nothing of salacious interest in the life of Jolly Allsop!' Eddie resumed.

Which wasn't entirely true, but the incident dated from school days and he judged that it would be considered below the belt, in more ways than one.

'In fact, the most astonishing thing about Jolly Allsop is how on earth he managed to win the heart of the very beautiful girl he has married today,' Eddie went on.

His effort was rewarded with the first smile of the day from the bride.

'So young, so radiant . . .' Eddie continued.

There was something about a wedding dress, Eddie thought. The more buttoned up, the better. He wondered if Jennifer's body was freckly, or whether her skin was as creamy smooth as the nape of her neck, a particularly beautiful specimen, he had noticed, as he walked behind her out of the church.

'Any man who saw Jennifer today would envy Jolly tonight,' he continued.

Was the hair down below the same soft silky texture?

Eddie detected a cold wind on his starboard side. 'And I'm sure that if her father were here today, he'd be very proud,' Eddie concluded.

There was a murmur of 'Hear! Hear!' and a cry of 'Oops! Sorry!' from Mrs Farmer as she failed to notice Mr Pocock attempting to charge her glass for the toast, and knocked the bottle up just as it passed her elbow.

A napkin was placed over the spillage. Eddie waited for the under-manager to complete his round.

'So, may I ask you all to join me in toasting the beautiful bride and the lucky groom?' he said.

Chairs were pushed back. Everyone in the room, including the dogs, stood up.

'The bride and groom!'

Everyone sipped their champagne. There was a short enthusiastic outbreak of applause from Ruby Farmer, who stopped when nobody else joined in.

Then Jolly Allsop rose to his feet. 'I'd like to thank the bridesmaids,' he said.

Eddie watched his Pearl preening in her bubble-gum pink, knowing that his sister-in-law would like nothing more than to steal the show.

'I don't think that my wife and I ... I'd better get used to saying it ...'

Eddie put his fingers in his mouth and whistled loudly, which made Jolly jump and lose his thread. Jennifer Farmer looked up and blushed prettily.

'Well, that is, we didn't expect Angela to be so well-behaved, did we?'

Jolly was clearly struggling to recall the rest of the speech.

'I think we could all agree that the bridesmaids were very much in the pink!' he finally remembered his closing joke.

A small polite titter rippled round the table.

'So I'd like to propose a toast to the bridesmaids.'

Chairs went back again. Everyone stood up, Pearl rising rather reluctantly after a prompting stare from Liliana.

'The bridesmaids!'

Everyone sat down again.

That was that, then. A wave of anti-climax lapped around the room.

Ruby Farmer got to her feet, stood for a moment looking

as if she were about to say something, then sat down again.

Two waitresses carried in a heavy three-tiered cake, which swayed alarmingly and came to rest at a perilous angle, like the leaning tower of Pisa.

There was a collective intake of breath as the cake wobbled.

Jolly and Jennifer saw immediately that urgent action was required, but as they sprang to their feet, grabbing the ceremonial sword from Eddie's hand, Mrs Farmer rose again and said, 'Ladies and gentlemen, and Sir John, of course, it's my daughter's big day and I just want to say . . .'

There was a small thump as one of the pillars supporting the first tier collapsed, then all eyes were on the second layer of cake as it began its unstoppable slide, sending all four pillars and the top cake crashing down on to the table in a clatter of silverware and crystal.

The tiny statuette of a bride and groom, which had been standing on the top tier, flew across the room, hit a wall, fell to the ground and was immediately retrieved and presented to Libby by her spaniel, Duke.

In the ensuing silence, Mrs Farmer's eyes closed and her body gradually sank until it disappeared entirely beneath the floor-length white tablecloth, except for her pink straw hat, with its contrasting frill of black organdie, whose wide brim caught on the table. There it rested, as a uniform cap might sit on the coffin of a dead officer, Eddie thought, symbolizing much about the person who lay beneath.

'Guess who this is?' Jolly rolled his eyes and flopped back on the large double bed of the Windsor Suite.

'I think she was a little overcome by the occasion . . .' Jennifer said, trying to unpin the flowers from her hair and suddenly missing the help of her mother's nimble fingers so much she wanted to cry.

It had not really occurred to her that her mother would no longer be there to do things for her. Perhaps her mother had thought about such things. Perhaps that was the reason she had drunk so much.

At the time, Jennifer had wished her mother had simply died, because it would be the only respectable explanation for her behaviour. She could have forgiven her mother the wedding dress, which Jolly said made her look like a meringue (Jennifer wasn't sure if he intended this as a compliment or a criticism), and even her mother's own outfit, which Jolly said made her look like a licorice allsort (definitely criticism), but Mrs Farmer's increasingly embarrassing efforts to engage Sir John in conversation, and then the attempt at a speech, would always be stains on the memory of her wedding.

Even so, Jennifer thought it cruel of Jolly to harp on about it the first moment they were alone together as man and wife, especially when his own father was so mad. He'd brought them a wedding gift wrapped in ancient yellowing newspaper, which had turned to dust when they'd opened it and found a horrid dirty little vase with a crack in it.

'Come here!' said Jolly.

She glanced in the wall mirror at her husband, who was still in his grey and black striped trousers and his shirtsleeves. He had loosened the wing collar and cast aside his white silk cravat.

'Wait a moment.' Jennifer finally managed to disentangle the flowers and her thick hair swung like a curtain around her shoulders.

'I can't wait,' Jolly growled.

As she made to walk past him to the en suite bathroom, he caught her hand and pulled her down on top of him.

'Jolly!'

'I want you now,' he said, kissing her.

'But the dress!'

'I want to take you in the dress. I want to bloody that virgin white.'

'It's a little late for that, isn't it?' she giggled, kissing him back, and rolling him over on top of her.

They had been carried away a couple of weeks earlier, the afternoon they went to the Summer House to measure up.

After years of trying to imagine what sexual intercourse might be like, and privately studying the pages of a book called *What a Husband Should Know* which she had found in the drawer of her late father's bedside table, Jennifer had found the experience unexpectedly disappointing. Although she hadn't actually seen one before, she had imagined that the male member would *feel* bigger. She had braced herself for pain and when it had not happened, she had felt strangely let down. The blood on the skirt of the dress she had been wearing (fortunately, a Horrock's print with a horizontal striped pattern of red and pink roses, so the traces didn't show on casual inspection) confirmed that the deed had been done, but the worry that she had not felt what she was supposed to feel, that perhaps there was something wrong with her, had niggled.

Now Jolly was burrowing underneath the yards of skirt, trying to find the entrance to her body through the layers of chiffon and lingerie, and when his head appeared from under the skirt admitting defeat, she laughed.

'What's so funny?' he demanded.

At this unaccustomed angle his face looked strange, his nose redder and more bulbous, his eyes smaller and steelier. There was a sheen of sweat on his forehead.

'Nothing,' she said, suddenly swamped with dread.

He grabbed her skirt ferociously, and threw it up over her body, covering her head, then he tugged her legs until her bottom was aligned with the edge of the bed. The sound of the lace ripping as he tore her knickers off made her breathing quicken, and then he was pumping on top of her. When he stopped abruptly and pulled her dress back down, his face all hangdog, she had no idea what to say to him.

Ruby Farmer was the last guest to leave, having spent an inordinately long time in Liliana's personal bathroom freshening up. When Liliana went to kiss her friend farewell, the sour stink of bile still hovered, eliciting simultaneous feelings of revulsion and tenderness.

'On the whole,' said Ruby, with a brave attempt at insouciance, 'on the whole, a great success, don't you think?'

'I should say so,' replied Liliana.

'Do you remember how I used to faint at school?' Ruby continued. 'At the least provocation, bang, down I went!'

Liliana, who could only remember Ruby in robust good health, smiled and nodded, understanding that the explanation Ruby was preparing for her indignity needed the addition of a little history to give it credibility.

'Still, I must only have been out for a second or two,' said Ruby, her voice going up queryingly at the end of the statement.

'Quite,' said Liliana.

Emboldened, Ruby went on. 'The sherry trifle was too rich. We're just not used to it, are we?'

'Perhaps a second helping was not advisable,' said Liliana.

Ruby's face greened alarmingly. 'Did they manage to get the glass out of the cake?' she asked.

'The top tier was intact,' Liliana informed her. 'There was enough for a small cube for everyone.'

'And Jennifer looked happy when they went upstairs?'

'Very happy.'

'Did Pearl catch the bouquet?'

'She did,' said Liliana without expression.

'I only hope you will be as lucky as I in your son-in-law.'

'The car is waiting,' said Liliana crisply.

As it was quite dark, Mr Pocock escorted Mrs Farmer down the steps and held the door of the Bentley for her as she unsteadily lowered herself in.

Liliana waved feebly as the car purred down the drive towards the gates and stared for a moment into the darkness as it turned out on to Hill Road.

'I say,' she said as Mr Pocock came back up the steps. 'With all these cars around' – she waved at Eddie's Vauxhall, and the under-manager's own Morris – 'I wonder whether we really need a chauffeur any more?'

'In the new house, you'll be able to leave a bit later,' Sylvia said as Michael was about to go to work the first day back after the Easter holidays.

'What do you mean?' he asked.

'It won't be such a long a walk, will it?'

A twitch of a frown appeared on his face in the mirror as he combed his hair back from his forehead.

Michael kissed his wife's cheek and the top of the baby's head, then he bent over so that Iris could clasp her hands around his neck and clamber up his body to embrace him with her legs wrapped round his waist, leaving a smacking wet kiss on his cheek.

A good wife, two healthy children, a little pyramid of domestic bliss. He waved at them when he reached the end of the street, then went on his way.

He had not envisaged what it would be like living in the new house, nor even considered that his route to work would no longer take him along the promenade.

He would no longer pass the bus stop.

Today, Claudia was wearing a panama hat with a navy hatband and her yellow and white checked school dress. When she looked at him from under the brim, he realized that he had simply stopped in front of her and forgotten to smile or say hello.

Claudia's tiresome friend Edith Payne was walking towards them.

'We're moving house,' he said quickly.

'I know,' Claudia replied.

'You know?'

'Everyone knows everything in Kingshaven!'

'I won't be seeing you in the mornings, then,' he said, glancing nervously to his left as Edith approached.

'I often work in the library after school,' Claudia said, and turned to her approaching friend. 'I was just telling Mr Quinn about the mountains of homework.'

'Reams,' said Edith, giggling.

'Hope your bus comes along soon.' Michael nodded at both of them and walked quickly on.

He had not encountered Claudia after their meeting at the Palace until one bitter winter morning, as he walked to school in semi-darkness, she was standing at the bus stop in her school uniform. All the things he had rehearsed to say to her if their paths should ever cross again went out of his mind as he walked straight past. From a safe distance, he saw her looking at her watch in a way that suggested that the bus was late, and deduced with a jolt of satisfaction this was the reason why he had not passed her before. After that, he left his house a little earlier each day until he encountered her again.

She was the first to say 'good morning', enunciating it with a certain amusement. And then their conversation had begun. He found he could talk to her about all sorts of subjects he was able to speak of with no one else in Kingshaven, like books and politics and the horror of the hydrogen bomb. For a few minutes at the start of each day, her bright mind turned his monochrome world technicolor.

There was nothing clandestine about where they met, nothing personal or improper in what was said, and yet . . . and yet there was something, some invisible thread of understanding between them, which made him perpetually apprehensive that they would be found out.

Chapter Three

July 1955

For as long as anyone could remember, a travelling fair had arrived in Kingshaven during the third week of July, pitching up just beyond the railway station in a large field at the edge of Sir John Allsop's estate. The shops on Hill Street trembled as lorries trundled through with rides on top folded up like giant Meccano. Excitement rippled through the town as the turbines began to hum and snatches of popular tunes were carried down to the beach on the off-shore breeze.

When Libby and Pearl were children, the fair had always been their father's treat – to clamber aboard the painted horses of a merry-go-round would have been considered undignified for a lady of their mother's standing – and because outings with him were rare, it had added to the excitement. After the war, with her father's health failing, Jolly Allsop had usually escorted Pearl, but now that he was happily ensconced with Jennifer and their new baby, Joanna, Pearl had asked Libby to go with her, although Libby suspected that the invitation had more to do with Pearl wanting a lift in her new car than with a particular desire for her company.

There was still something childishly thrilling about walking across the darkened field towards brilliant snakes of light which chased over the outlines of the rides; something strangely nostalgic about the smell of frying onions; something scary about the faces of the fair people, their black hair and white skin accentuated by the artificial light, the menace exacerbated by the sudden, unexpected hiss and sigh of the machinery. Libby slightly missed having a strong, masculine hand to hold on to.

The idea, she remembered, as she fished for a yellow duck with a hook on a long stick, was to start with the least challenging attractions and gradually dare yourself up to faster, more thrilling experiences, but she'd forgotten how addictive the desire for cheap, sparkling prizes could be, like the gilt trinkets which were piled tantalizingly high within a glass case, but which the mechanical claw inside stubbornly refused to grasp.

'Come on!' said Pearl, linking her arm. 'Let's go on the dodgems!'

'I don't know if I'm dressed for it . . .' Libby looked despairingly at her full summer skirt, wishing that she had worn more practical pedal pushers as Pearl had.

'Oh, don't be so square!' said Pearl, tugging her arm. 'My turn to drive.'

Everyone became a child at the fair, Libby thought as Pearl accelerated towards Dr Payne and one of his daughters, who seemed not to mind in the slightest their car being punched into the barrier.

'Stop saying sorry!' Pearl shouted at her.

'Sorry!' Libby shouted back, getting into the spirit of it as another car thumped into them from behind, rendering them motionless until one of the fairground men jumped on to the back and leaned over Pearl, spinning the steering wheel expertly to start them up again.

Libby looked up at their rescuer and was startled to recognize their former chauffeur. 'Mr Rogers! What are you doing here?'

'Working,' he said.

'Oh . . . good!' Libby said, slightly embarrassed.

She had felt a little guilty about making the chauffeur redundant last season. He'd been such a favourite of her father's, and although the upgrading of the hotel, and plans for a heated outdoor swimming pool, did mean a tightening of belts all round, it had seemed rather ungrateful, after all his years of loyal service, to ask him to be the first to go. Still, as her mother had pointed out, this was exactly the reason she had employed Mr Pocock to make an objective assessment of the costs.

'Please will you come on the Ferris wheel with me?' Pearl pleaded childishly with Mr Rogers. 'Libby won't go because she's worried about people seeing her knickers!'

Mr Rogers smiled. He had always indulged Pearl's whims, taking a lead from their father. If someone had been a bit firmer with her sister from the beginning, Libby thought, perhaps she might not have grown up so wilful.

'I'm working,' he told her gently. 'Come back tomorrow afternoon. You'll have the fair to yourself and I'll give you the ride of your life.'

He winked at Pearl and then he was gone, leaping on to the back of another car as it sped around the rink.

Libby bought toffee apples to take home for Christopher and Angela and won a goldfish on the rifle range, while Pearl went on the waltzer alone and stumbled off drunk with dizziness.

'Had enough?' Libby asked, trying to hold the bowl still so that water didn't slop over the top. '*Never win a goldfish early on,*' she could remember her father advising.

'I suppose,' said Pearl, looking longingly at the big wheel. The coloured lights lit up her face. 'Since I'm coming again tomorrow.'

They began to walk back across the field. Away from the lights, it was suddenly very dark, and people arriving at the fair loomed unexpectedly close in the shadows, making Libby remember the stern warnings never to go near the fair alone when she went on bike rides before the war. The fair people were hardly more than gypsies, her mother had told her, and gypsies stole children.

It was an odd place for Rogers to have ended up.

'You're not really going to come back, are you?' Libby asked, a shiver running down her spine.

Pearl was fumbling in her impractical little handbag for a cigarette. 'You can't stop us, you know,' she said.

'Stop you?' Libby echoed.

'Can't you see we're still in love, despite your best efforts?'

'In love?'

'Rocky and I?'

In the darkness Libby could not see her sister's face to know whether she was teasing.

'Mr Rogers, for heaven's sake!' said Pearl, exasperated.

'In love?' said Libby incredulously.

She opened the passenger door of the car and tried to hand her sister the goldfish bowl.

'Oh, wait a minute, would you!' Pearl insisted on lighting her cigarette first.

They sat in silence as Libby put the key in the ignition. She was still not a confident driver and needed to concentrate. The car started straightaway, but Libby lifted her foot too quickly from the clutch and stalled it and it took several attempts to get it started again. She could feel a sheen of sweat on her forehead.

'I told you ages ago!' Pearl resumed where she had left off when Libby eventually manoeuvred the car out on to the road. She blew out a long stream of smoke.

Libby racked her memory for any such conversation. Surely Pearl couldn't mean that time years ago, when they'd confided their crushes to one another? Her own heart-throb had been the actor Kenneth More, she remembered fondly. Pearl had admitted a pash for the new chauffeur. The attraction was so magnetic, the slightest touch would render them impossible to prise apart, she had declared, or some such nonsense. Pearl was always so melodramatic. Mr Rogers was a man, more than ten years her senior, and Pearl had still been a child.

Libby glanced across at her. Was this all an elaborate practical joke?

'You're surely not serious?'

'You can't stop us! You thought if you sent him away, we would drift apart, but we haven't. We write every week. Can't you see?'

'But . . . Mummy will stop your allowance.'

'Not if you would support us.' Pearl's voice took on a wheedling tone. 'She listens to you and you're fond of Mr Rogers, aren't you?'

'Well, yes, in a way . . .'

'I supported you when you wanted to marry Eddie . . .' Pearl pressed on.

'But it's not the same thing at all!'

'Eddie had no money,' Pearl said.

'It's not just a question of money,' said Libby.

The engine made a dreadful sound as the car reached the fork at the clock tower and Libby changed gear without fully depressing the clutch pedal.

'What is it a question of, then?' Pearl demanded to know.

'We know nothing about his family,' Libby said.

'Unlike Eddie, of course, whose family we know everything about because it's our family too, and whose mother's in a madhouse,' Pearl countered.

'It's a sanatorium,' Libby corrected her. 'Anyway, Mr Rogers is married!'

'His wife left him. They're divorced now.'

That hardly made it any less of a scandal.

An awful thought occurred to Libby. Was it her duty, as the older, married sister, to warn Pearl?

'Married men . . .' she began. 'That is to say, men who have been married, might have certain expectations . . .'

'Oh, for goodness' sake!' said Pearl. 'I wasn't a Girl Guide for nothing. Be prepared, and all that!' she added with a cool laugh.

Libby stared at her with grudging admiration.

'As a matter of fact, you didn't support me,' she suddenly remembered. 'You were always saying horrid things about Eddie.'

'Don't I deserve a little happiness?' Pearl suddenly wailed. 'Why do you have everything, and I'm not allowed to have the only thing I want?'

Pearl was terribly adept at self-pity, but over the years Libby had become immune to it. 'That's one way of looking at it,' she replied, grinding up Hill Street in second gear. 'Or you could say I do all the work, and you do nothing at all,' she finished, as the interior of the car filled with hostility that seemed to press at the doors and windows, searching for an outlet.

It was the last day of the last term of the last year Claudia would spend at Lowhampton Grammar School for Girls. After the final assembly, leavers were free to go, although most of the other girls seemed reluctant to prise themselves away, and sat in the sunshine on the top hockey field swapping reminiscences about their time at the school, writing addresses in the slim alphabetized note-books their grandmothers had given them for Christmas, and promising to keep in touch. Claudia had always felt an outsider in the rituals of English schoolgirls, and today, as she walked down the tarmac drive towards the school gate, she fancied there was still a whispering about her oddness, her suspicious Jewish cleverness, her interest in politics.

Intelligence was not prized in the way that sporting prowess was. The headmistress's view, which she had expounded from the pulpit of All Saints' Church in Lowhampton at the Leavers' Assembly that morning, was that a girl's education should be a preparation for her responsibilities, and the congregation of civic dignitaries and well-to-do parents understood this to mean as the wives and mothers of the county's future men of substance. Occasionally, the school produced what the headmistress dis-missively referred to as a bluestocking, but, on the whole, excessive concentration on academic study was deemed slightly peculiar.

Claudia took a final look back at the frontage of the school. The rows of dark arched windows had always seemed to her like hollow skulls' eyes.

On the coast road back to Kingshaven, she stared out of the window of the bus. She was in what psychologists would call a liminal place, she thought, where one world meets another. As she climbed down the steps at the seafront, it occurred to her that although she was dressed in school uniform, she was now no longer a schoolgirl, and she thought she should do something outrageous to mark the occasion.

A warm blast of menthol and disinfectant greeted her in the chemist's. She could sense the pharmacist's bespectacled eyes tracking her as she dared to pick up and sniff a Bronnley soap in the shape of a lemon, and to test a smear of Coral Ice lipstick at the base of her thumb. Why was it that women always tested cosmetics in that particular place, Claudia wondered, which bore no relation to the colour of lips or face? For a moment, she wished that her friend Edith Payne was there to advise her on the colour. Edith read the copies of *Woman* in her father's waiting room, and knew about such things. Coral Ice. To the astonishment of Mr Poots, Claudia purchased the lipstick at the till, then used the little mirror above the carousel of sunglasses to apply a coat to her mouth.

The warm appetizing smell of fresh bread puffed out of the baker's shop. Claudia bought herself a pink iced bun. The sweetness of the icing mingled with the greasy perfumed taste of the lipstick. The half-eaten bun had a ring of orange on it. She touched the sides of her mouth for crumbs.

Was it sheer madness to spend the whole afternoon in town for the very slight possibility of seeing Michael? After school on Thursday was their usual time, but it was the last day of the school year. It was very unlikely that he would want to make an unnecessary journey to the library.

And yet . . .

And yet if there was only the slightest chance, Michael was the person she wanted to share her freedom with.

As she walked past the coffee bar, the sinfully delicious aroma of ground coffee curled temptingly around Claudia's nostrils. The newly opened Coffee Bean had been the cause of some consternation amongst the inhabitants of Kingshaven and had gained the reputation of attracting the wrong type to the town. Teddy Boys loitered at its tables. There was a jukebox! No decent person would be seen there. The school had explicitly banned its Kingshaven girls from entering.

Claudia hesitated outside the glass door. There was no particular reason to go home. She had a library book to finish in her satchel. *The End of the Affair* was not a title the headmistress of Lowhampton Girls' Grammar School would approve of, but Claudia found it compelling. The dark chaos of London in the aftermath of bombing, where bargains were struck with God and miracles might happen, was a long way from her own experience of the war, and yet she identified with the character, Sarah, and hoped, right until the end, that she would go back to her lover, Bendrix, despite his flaws.

With revolutionary audacity, Claudia pushed open the door.

In daylight, the fairground looked shabby. A couple of unkempt Alsatians tied to posts by frayed bits of rope jumped and barked at Pearl as she made awkward progress across the bumpy field in her unsuitable shoes. It had probably been a mistake to wear stilettos, but she could hardly put sensible shoes with her new red circular skirt with a large black poodle appliquéd on the front.

Pearl knocked at the door of a caravan.

Mr Rogers had a cap on and a slightly grubby Aertex vest which hung around his chest. 'I didn't expect you so soon,' he said as she stared in dismay, which rather begged the question of whom he was expecting to see when he opened the door half dressed.

He took off his cap. His dark wavy hair was greasily flattened against his head and for a moment he didn't look handsome at all.

'Come here,' he said, gently pulling her inside by the tails of the tight-fitting black cotton blouse she had knotted at her waist. Her back arched as she resisted, and then succumbed to his kiss. He kicked the door of the caravan shut behind her. She closed her eyes tight, inhaling the petrol smell of him, giving her body up to his strength.

When he drew away and looked at her in that heart-stopping way he had, as if he couldn't believe his luck, she said, 'Take that off, then!'

In one swift movement he removed the vest and threw it on the floor.

'God, I've missed you,' he said, drawing her towards him again, kissing her mouth, her neck, her cleavage, then falling to his knees in front of her, ducking his head under her skirt, running the rough tip of his tongue around the exposed flesh at the top of her stockings.

'Rocky!'

The appliquéd poodle began to bob up and down.

The roof of the caravan, Pearl couldn't help noticing as they lay down on the narrow bed together, was growing black spots of mould. It wasn't the bright space she had imagined when he'd written that he was living in a caravan. She'd had an image of a wooden dresser with painted enamel crockery, a vase of wild flowers, a friendly carthorse with a nosebag outside. Her dream had been halfway between the Summer House and a painted canal boat, she realized, not this flimsy hardboard box with a mean bit of frayed curtain at the window.

She climbed on top of him, exchanging the view of the ceiling for the view of his face, and gave herself up to sensation as he inched his enormous penis inside her and murmured, 'That's good, that's good, oh, that feels like coming home.'

Afterwards, he put on a clean shirt and got one of the fairground men to give them a go on the Ferris wheel as he'd promised.

Round and round, up and down, so exciting, so dangerous: Pearl was on the point of climaxing again when they stopped just past the top, hanging in the air with the whole of Kingshaven spread out below them. There was a sparkling light coming off the ocean; the terraced lawns of the Palace Hotel were like a staircase of bright green carpet going down to the sea; the windows glittered like diamonds.

'Whoops, we're stuck,' said Mr Rogers, leaning over the side of the carriage, giving the thumbs up to the operator.

'I don't care,' Pearl said, kicking her legs. 'I could stay here for ever.'

As she turned to kiss him, he took both her hands in his and looked at her very seriously. 'Marry me?' he said.

Her first impulse was to giggle. For all her dreams of this moment, she had never really expected him to ask.

'Aren't you supposed to go down on one knee?' she protested coquettishly. Then: 'No!' she shrieked as he started to do so and the seat swayed alarmingly. For a moment her face looked straight at the ground, and then it righted again.

'So, where's my ring?' she asked, playfully.

From the pocket of his trousers he took out a ring which looked as if it had come from the glass case with the mechanical claw in it. It was bright gold with a huge blue stone.

'I'll buy you a real one as soon as I can afford it,' he said.

Pearl knew this was the most romantic moment of her life, and yet she couldn't seem to make herself feel how she knew she was supposed to. Instead, she couldn't help wondering whether he had bought his first wife a proper ring, or whether he had said the same thing when he proposed to her.

'We leave Sunday morning at sun-up,' said Rocky.

'You mean elope?'

'Why not?'

'Oh, Rocky, darling!'

The words sounded like an actress speaking a line from a film. There was exactly the right tremble of emotion in her voice.

Below her, the tops of the caravans had little sooty chimneys like bits of drainpipe, with smoke puffing out.

'I won't have any money, you know,' she told him.

'I'm not interested in your money,' he said in his tough-guy voice, like Humphrey Bogart.

'But how would we manage?' she asked. Surely he didn't expect her to live in that caravan?

'I've got some ideas.'

'What sort of ideas?' she queried excitedly, linking her arm through his.

'Second-hand cars,' he said. 'There's money in it if you know what you're doing.'

'Who on earth would want a second-hand car?' Pearl asked.

He looked a little wounded.

And then the seat jerked and they started moving again.

'All right, Bert?' the operator at the bottom said with a knowing smile, giving Pearl an appreciative up and down as they got out.

'Thanks, mate!'

'Bert?' Pearl repeated.

'Short for Herbert,' said Mr Rogers.

He put his arm around her waist and pulled her gently to his side. Their first public togetherness, Pearl thought, resting her head on his shoulder. Her body fitted his. It was as simple as that.

'What shall we do now, then?' she whispered invitingly.

'I've got maintenance to do. Work, ' he explained, tilting her disappointed face to his and dropping a brief, dry kiss on her lips. 'One of us has to!'

'I can't see what all the fuss is about if they love each other,' said Verity Dyer, the junior in Mr Maurice's Hair Salon, talking into the mirror at Audrey Potter as she fixed tight little curlers into her hair.

'It's not as if she's ever going to be running the Palace!' replied the postmistress.

'I'd have thought they'd be grateful anyone *wanted* to marry her,' said Verity Dyer.

'Come along now, ladies, Miss King is a very attractive woman,' said Mr Maurice. 'With assets!'

'Large assets,' said Verity with a lewd chuckle, and was clearly about to add some further observation when Mr Maurice looked up and noticed Libby standing in the doorframe.

Usually the ping of the bell would have alerted them to a new arrival, Libby thought, but it was such a pleasant day they'd left the door open. The rotten odour of perming lotion wafted on to the pavement, polluting the fresh sea air.

Mr Maurice coughed loudly and, looking rather pinker than usual, came across to greet her.

'Can you fit me in?' Libby enquired. 'My daughter's toffee apple somehow got caught in my hair, and I think you're going to have to cut it out.'

After a cursory inspection, Mr Maurice ordered a sulky girl to wash her hair in the basin in the shadows at the back of the salon.

Was she the only person in Kingshaven, Libby wondered as the girl hosed her hair with lukewarm water, who had not been aware of Pearl's liaison? If Miss Potter knew about Pearl's scandalous behaviour, then everyone must. Audrey Potter distributed salacious titbits with the same efficiency she distributed the first post.

The girl lathered her head vigorously.

Was she being too hard on Pearl? Libby wondered. Her sister was nearly twenty-five, after all, and clearly experienced enough to make up her own mind. Why shouldn't she marry Mr Rogers if she wanted to? He had always been such a friend to her father – at times almost like a son. Perhaps Daddy would even have approved? Perhaps he had actually known? Surely it couldn't have been going on then?

It didn't make any difference anyway, Libby thought, because she couldn't see her mother changing her mind. Liliana had fought so hard to repair the reputation of the hotel after Uncle Rex. It had made her very unbending about standards.

The conversation at the front of the salon had turned to a new television programme called *Dixon of Dock Green*.

'It's so true to life,' said Verity Dyer.

In Libby's view, the idea that an ordinary policeman would light upon and solve a serious crime each week was distinctly untrue to life, and she was quite sure that television viewers would tire of it as rapidly as she had, but she regretted offering her opinion, when she realized she had killed the conversation dead.

The girl dragged a comb through her hair with such ferocity that Libby looked up sharply, only to recognize, in the round mirror, the face of the chambermaid she'd dismissed the previous summer, unswayed by Eddie's explanation that the two of them had been searching for a dropped cufflink. The girl had no business being in the private wing in the first place, and she had a distinctly defiant look about her which Libby cared for no more now than she had then. The trouble with employing locals was that when there were problems, they came back to haunt you.

'I say, be careful!' Libby said, loud enough to appeal to Mr Maurice.

Mr Maurice waved the girl away and began to apply his expert scissors.

'How is Mother?' he asked.

There was a slightly unctuous quality about him which always made Libby feel at a disadvantage.

'My mother is very well, thank you,' she replied, regretting the need to introduce the personal pronoun because it sounded as if she was correcting him. She wished she had Liliana's gift of keeping the small talk bubbling along.

It was one of the many aspects of going to the hairdresser Libby dreaded. She was never quite sure whether you were supposed to tell the hairdresser what you wanted, or let him decide, and she normally struck exactly the wrong balance so that both she and Mr Maurice came away from the encounter feeling somewhat dissatisfied.

Another worry which niggled from the moment she stepped through the salon door was whether or not to tip him. As the proprietor of a business herself, and considerably younger than he was, she thought that to tip might be seen as patronizing, and yet she had spied other women discreetly palming him money, and he had not appeared offended. The only occasion she had attempted the same gesture, she had accidentally dropped the change on the floor, and he had bent down to pick it up for her, which had not clarified matters.

'Your mother has a strong head of hair,' Mr Maurice said, pulling a section of Libby's hair up from the crown of her head. 'Miss Pearl takes after her.'

Miss Potter glanced up from under her dryer.

'You're more like your father,' said Mr Maurice.

Libby smiled in the mirror. Her father had been a well-respected figure in the parish. Any comparison with him was welcome, although, as far as hair was concerned, she remembered, he had been noticeably thin.

'Can we go to the fair, sir?' Iris asked Michael.

His daughter had joined the Infants' class in the spring term and taken quite literally Michael's instruction to treat him no differently to the other teachers.

He enjoyed their walks to and from school, just the two of them, and the glimpses he caught of her serious little face during the day.

'Maybe tomorrow,' he said. 'It's the holidays, remember.'

'But it's Penny Night tonight!' said Iris. 'It means you don't spend so much money. Everyone goes on Penny Night. Brendan Carney said so.'

'But you're tired after school,' Michael said.

'I'm not tired.'

'What did you do today?' Michael tried to change the subject.

'Nothing,' said Iris.

At only five years old, she was already quite good at punishing him when she didn't get what she wanted. He tried to humour her. 'Did the Birds do anything interesting?'

'The Birds don't go to school!' Iris told him scornfully.

He hoped that her imaginary friends had become less important because she had found little friends, but he often spotted her in the playground, a solitary figure playing hopscotch, and it made him ache with loneliness for her. He had to stop himself using his authority to demand that other children go and play with her.

They walked the rest of the way back to the new house on Cherry Avenue in silence. Sylvia had a hat on when they arrived, and Anthony was sitting in his pushchair.

'It's such a lovely afternoon, why don't we all go to the fair?' his wife suggested brightly.

'Won't that make the children late to bed?' Michael said.

Sylvia's face fell.

'The holidays start tomorrow,' he offered as compensation. 'There'll be plenty of time to do nice things.'

'I suppose,' said Sylvia.

'I have to get my library book back,' he said.

'I don't suppose the world would end if you were one day late,' Sylvia muttered.

The sarcasm chafed, providing him with an internal excuse to resent her, but he knew that if she had said something as neutral as 'Please don't go tonight', it wouldn't have made any difference.

Did she know that he met Claudia in the library? Michael wondered. Had one of the other young mothers she sometimes invited round for morning coffee seen them passing notes to one another and decided to tell? He had never lied about his whereabouts on Thursday evenings, but he had not told Sylvia the whole truth either. After what he had done in Etherington, he couldn't blame her for being suspicious of him, but he wondered whether hers was the reaction any wife would have to her husband spending an evening away from home. His father had always gone to the working men's club. That's what men did where he came from, but here, on the rural edges of Wessex, expectations of marriage seemed to come straight from Gabriel Oak's proposal in *Far From the Madding Crowd*: 'Whenever you look up, there I shall be – and whenever I look up, there will be you.'

Michael instinctively shrank from the claustrophobia of Hardy's portrait. But as he walked away from his wife and daughter, feeling their disappointment trailing him down the avenue, he wondered why he always chose to make his life complicated.

*

'Hey! Roger Bannister, where're you going?' Michael's colleague Ivor Brown called after him as he hurried down Hill Street.

Ivor, a recently qualified teacher, was a local lad whose mother ran the Riviera, one of the terrace of Edwardian guesthouses with wrought-iron balconies off Hill Street. Ivor had been employed the previous September as the fourth teacher at the school because of the post-war rise in children on the school roll. From the moment he had announced himself as 'Ivor Brown, don't bother, I've heard all the jokes' Michael had sensed he had found an ally, but although Ivor was great fun and a brilliant mimic whose accent changed depending on whom he was talking to – with the headmaster he became a toff, with the dinner ladies a gossip – Michael had slowly realized that it was a kind of magic trick: to appear to be open to the point of indiscretion, but to reveal nothing at all.

Initially they had made the usual routine enquiries about each other's National Service. (Ivor had been invalided out after six months in Egypt. Michael had been in Burma. Neither looked for further elaboration. Their generation of men had lost their child-hood to war and their youth to the messy decline of Empire. Some carried visible scars; mostly they carried their wounds inside.) They swapped pleasantries about the weather, recounted favourite bits of the Goons (one on occasion bursting into a spontaneous chorus of the 'Ying Tong Song', much to the dis-approval of the Infants' teacher, Mrs Evans). But, after almost a year as his colleague, Michael knew little about him. He wasn't good at drawing friendship out of people as Sylvia was.

'Where are you off to, then?' Michael asked as they walked along together.

'*The Deep Blue Sea*,' said Ivor.

'Going for a swim?'

Ivor laughed. 'It's the new Rattigan at the Pier Theatre. They usually drag me in as prompt.'

'What's it like?' Michael asked.

'The play? Well constructed, but rather gloomy, I'm afraid. Not exactly the thing for the summer holidays. Not nearly as entertaining as last year's show.'

'What was that?'

'*Toreadors on Ice*. Sadly, the ice only worked for one evening. After that it was *Toreadors Slopping About* and the manager flapping about the electricity shorting.'

Michael laughed. 'How come you work there?'

'I've got theatre in my blood, darling!' said Ivor archly. 'Mama was in the theatre herself. And I imagine my father was too.' He arched an eyebrow for effect. 'Wanted me to follow in her dance steps, but I've two left feet, so I became a teacher. Those who can't and all that. All the stars stay at the Riviera, you know.'

'I didn't,' said Michael.

They'd reached the fork for the seafront.

'Are you going to the fair?' Ivor asked.

'Not tonight,' said Michael.

'Well, where are you off to in such a hurry?' Ivor asked.

'Library,' Michael said.

'You'll have to do better than that,' said Ivor, winking as they parted. 'Nobody in their right mind *runs* to the library.'

Through the slightly steamed-up window of the Coffee Bean, Claudia was suddenly aware of somebody waving at her.

Pearl King.

Pearl pushed open the glass door and the tap of stiletto heels echoed on the tiled floor.

'It's Claudia, isn't it? I knew I knew the face,' she said, rather loudly. 'What are you reading?' She closed Claudia's book so that she could see the cover. '*The End of the Affair*! Oh dear!' she sighed dramatically and, without waiting to be invited, sat down in the booth opposite Claudia. 'Any good?' she demanded as Claudia returned to her reading.

'Unputdownable,' said Claudia.

'Have another coffee,' Pearl said.

'Er . . .'

'My treat!' said Pearl. 'I've got ages to kill before my sister finishes at the hairdresser. I can't walk another step in these shoes!'

Pearl King had a kind of aura, Claudia thought, an expectation that people would know who she was and behave accordingly, but the girl behind the counter barely looked up as she ordered. A group of youths lolling on high stools near the jukebox stared and nudged each other as she strutted past them in her fashion-plate clothes and with her scarlet lips, carrying two glass cups of frothy coffee back to the booth.

'Shouldn't you be in school?' Pearl asked, as if she had only now noticed Claudia's uniform gingham dress.

'Today was my last day,' Claudia said.

'And what will you do?' Pearl asked, the forefinger of her left hand pushing a grain of demerara sugar around the yellow and black pattern of blobs and lines on the Formica surface of the table.

'I have a place at Cambridge University,' Claudia said.

Pearl began to spoon amber granules from the chrome sugar bowl into the milky coffee. 'I wonder if I should have gone to university,' Pearl said. 'What do you think?'

'I couldn't say,' Claudia replied diplomatically.

The serving girl at the counter went over to the jukebox and put in a coin. The robotic arm selected a vinyl disc and placed it on the turntable. The voice of Doris Day filled the room. The girl glanced at one of the youths shyly. The youth tapped his feet in time to the bossa nova rhythm, then stopped, a little embarrassed.

' "Secret Love",' said Pearl. 'How appropriate! Have you noticed anything?' She dangled her left hand in front of Claudia's nose.

'It's very pretty,' said Claudia, looking at the size of the stone. Surely it wasn't real?

'It's just a token, of course,' said Pearl.

'I like it,' Claudia said.

'A symbol of my secret love . . .' Pearl's voice lowered to a whisper as the song stopped abruptly, the disc went back with a mechanical whirr, and silence returned to the Coffee Bean.

The youths got up to leave. They stood in a line in front of Pearl as if about to say something saucy, the row of spotty faces and oily quiffs slightly threatening en masse.

'Can I help you?' Pearl asked.

The collective nerve failed and, one by one, the youths slunk out of the coffee bar.

'Do you think I should?' Pearl asked when they were alone again.

'What?' Claudia asked.

'Elope!'

'I'm really not qualified . . .' Claudia said. For a moment she felt slightly sorry for Pearl if she had no one better to advise her.

Pearl took out a packet of cigarettes, put one in her mouth and lit up. 'It's a terribly complicated business,' she said, blowing a sigh of smoke at Claudia.

Claudia smiled sympathetically at her.

'Have you ever been in love?' Pearl suddenly asked.

Claudia had been dreading the moment when Pearl would suddenly demand confidences in exchange for hers.

She said nothing.

'You won't tell anyone, will you?' Pearl asked.

Claudia shook her head. She didn't feel it was her place to reveal that everyone in Kingshaven knew of Pearl's relationship already. The town was almost equally divided between those who considered it disgraceful, and those who thought it desperately romantic.

And then Michael walked past outside.

'I really must be getting to the library,' Claudia said to Pearl.

How maddening to have waited so long, and then to run the risk of missing him!

Inside, the library was cool and dim after the glare of the sunshine. Michael's eyes took a moment to adjust. In the bright shafts of light coming through the high windows, dust motes danced. The clock on the wall seemed to be ticking time away particularly slowly. Miss Phelps, the librarian, looked down as he ventured a smile at her. She was such a timid woman, she could never bring herself to make eye contact even as she stamped the borrowers' books. There was nobody else there. Michael's chest deflated with disappointment.

It was Claudia's last day of school, he told himself. She was probably celebrating with her friends, setting fire to her panama hat, or whatever they did at Lowhampton Girls'. It was mad of him to have expected her.

He would take his family to the fair, he decided instantly, and drive away this absurdly adolescent pining with a ride on the waltzer which spun so fast it felt your head was coming off your body and made you forget who you were.

And then the heavy Victorian door was pushed open and Claudia was standing there with another woman behind her, a glossy hourglass of a woman, who stared at him for a moment, then said goodbye to Claudia in a loud voice and went out into the street again.

There was something different about Claudia, he thought, not immediately able to work out what it was, as she returned her book at the desk. She went to the shelves, flicked through a couple of novels before selecting, and brought the book back to the desk opposite his.

Michael wrote on a piece of paper, *How was your last day?* and passed it across to her.

A great relief! And yours?

Why are you wearing lipstick? he wrote.

Her little hand went to her lips.

You're much prettier without it, he wrote.

Her smile made him feel as if the blood in his veins had suddenly become warm and he could feel it shooting through every inch of his body.

I don't know what I'm going to do without you, he wrote.

He saw her deliberate, write something, rub it out, and then pass the paper back to him.

Can we still write to each other? he read.

May I walk you home? he wrote.

She looked up nervously and nodded.

It was the quiet time just after the shops had closed when the retired couples and mothers with young children, who came on holiday before the beginning of the school vacation, had already left the beach and returned to their guesthouses for tea, but there was still a frisson of danger walking beside her even though they kept as far apart as the pavement would allow.

It was still hot. Michael took off his jacket and slung it over his shoulder.

'Are you excited?' he asked. 'About Cambridge?'

'I probably won't like it there at all,' she said, brushing her fringe from her eyes. 'All those silly boys with their teddy bears!'

They had read *Brideshead Revisited* at the same time. He had loathed its nostalgic portrait of privilege, but felt that Waugh wrote as well as anyone about faith. He couldn't understand why he was so drawn to the Catholic novelists, Waugh and Greene and Spark, he had written to her in the notes they passed back and forth across the desk in the library. Perhaps they represented the last vestiges of his lapsed faith, which he had expunged from his life after the loss of his parents? And she had written back: *It can be lonely without faith, can't it?*

Which had articulated something he had not been conscious of feeling.

Their friendship was rooted in the books they shared. For Michael, reading had previously been a private pleasure, but his discussions with her lent another dimension of intimacy. In talking about characters and themes, they discovered things about each other far more revealing than anything an ordinary conversation between an eighteen-year-old schoolgirl and a twenty-five-year-old married man might uncover. Sometimes he thought they were speaking in a secret code which allowed them to discuss motivations and desires under the cover of a quasi-objectivity.

As they walked past the railway station, the five-thirty direct to London tooted and pulled out of the station. They watched it gathering speed, and waved the sooty smoke from the air in front of their faces.

The generators for the fair in the field were already chugging.

'Have you been?' he asked.

'No,' she said. 'I would like to, but Papa will not let me go on my own.'

He wanted to offer to take her. The fair didn't really get going until after dark and few people would see them. But he knew that to be thrown against each other in the spinning carriage of a fairground ride would be unacceptably intimate, and he didn't know whether he would be able to control himself.

'I had a place at university, you know,' Michael said as they turned up the steep little high-sided lane off the main road, which wound up from the valley floor towards the Castle.

'What were you going to study?' she asked.

'History.'

'Yes, of course. Why didn't you go?'

'I got married. Iris came along soon after,' he said, kicking a loose stone into the hedgerow.

'Do you regret it?' she asked.

'I wouldn't wish Iris away,' he snapped, wondering why he was spoiling these precious moments which might be their last together.

'I meant missing university?' she said patiently.

'What do you think?' he asked.

As she looked up at him with her wide, sympathetic brown eyes, the urge to kiss her was so strong he had to look away.

The mansion known locally as the Castle had been built on the site of a real castle which had been destroyed in the Civil War. Some of the original blocks of stone had been used in the construction, but otherwise the house bore no resemblance to a castle apart from the ornamental battlements which had been added in the late eighteenth century to disguise the new guttering for the roof. Standing a little way up the valley at a point where the river would still have been navigable in times gone by, the original castle would have boasted a view of the bay without being immediately obvious to any hostile invaders. The present house was entirely concealed by an avenue of mature beech trees. Nowadays, the gatehouse, a late-Victorian addition to the estate, gave the only clue that a grand residence lay beyond. It was built of red brick in a faux-Gothic style with mullioned windows and a tall chimney and looked out of place in the landscape of grass and stone.

'Do you ever see Sir John?' Michael asked.

'Sometimes he comes down to chat to Papa.'

'I don't even know what he looks like!' he said.

'He's actually very kind,' Claudia told him.

'I expect I'll meet him next year because Winston will be in my class.'

She nodded. The conversation had come to a natural end.

They stood awkwardly at the wrought-iron gate. What a peculiar place it was for a little girl to have grown up, Michael thought.

'Well, goodbye then,' he said.

'Goodbye!'

Turning to go, he felt her hand on his shirtsleeve.

'Perhaps you'd like to come in and meet Papa?' she asked with a nervous smile.

Claudia's father was small and fine-boned as she was, but although his body appeared frail, his eyes were bright.

'Papa, this is my friend, Michael Quinn,' Claudia introduced him.

The old man walked around his desk, picked up a sheet of paper, read a little, then put it down again. Michael wondered whether he had heard.

'You must be very proud of your daughter,' Michael ventured. 'Going to Cambridge!'

'I didn't doubt it for a moment,' the professor informed him briskly.

He constantly fidgeted as he spoke, as if the subject of the ongoing conversation was not enough fully to occupy his mind. He reminded Michael of a bird who kept pecking, then flying off for no obvious reason, before returning to peck again in a slightly different place.

Every available surface of the room was covered in papers; every inch of wall was lined with books.

'You've quite a library here,' Michael said.

The professor peered at him from under his eyebrows, as if he expected him to say something else.

'A lot of books!' Michael said, a little louder.

'Certainly,' the professor replied dismissively. Although he had been in the country fifteen years, his accent was still strong.

'I'll make some tea, I think,' said Claudia.

'English tea,' said the professor to Michael. 'One of your more agreeable customs. Did you bake a cake, Claudia?'

Michael noticed that he pronounced her name differently. Cloudia. It sounded foreign, exotic.

'No, Papa!'

'What about the fruit pie in the box?' suggested the professor. 'Did you ever hear of such a thing, Mr Quinn?'

Michael was taken aback that the old man had remembered his name.

'A fruit pie in a box?' he repeated, wondering what was so remarkable about this.

'Bring it in, Claudia,' her father told her.

She returned from the kitchen with a tray bearing three cups, a chipped teapot and a Lyons' individual apple pie.

The professor handed a cup to Michael. The tea was pale and smelled of wood smoke.

'A bit hot,' Michael said, returning his cup to its saucer.

'Apple pie in a box.' The professor was chuckling as he opened it. 'So very English!'

'My father likes to experiment with foods he doesn't know,' Claudia tried to explain.

Michael smiled to let her know that he wasn't in the least offended. She blushed and looked away.

'In Austria, we have very delicious pastries. This thing' – the professor looked at the pale sugared disc into which he had just bitten – 'does not deserve the name of apple torte.'

He broke off a small piece and handed it to Michael.

Michael took a bite of the soggy sweet pie. 'Perhaps if you think of it as something different?' he suggested.

'Explain,' the professor demanded.

He hadn't intended to start an argument, or even to defend the pie, which was nondescript, but not altogether disagreeable if you were as hungry as he was.

'I just meant that if you put your pastries from your mind and think of it as something that has nothing to do with apples or pie,' Michael said, 'then it becomes acceptable, as a filling food.'

'Your point is that the pie *qua* pie is not successful, but *qua* sustenance it is?'

'Possibly,' said Michael, wishing he had not said anything.

The professor closed his eyes and took another small taste, rolling the morsel round his mouth as if savouring a vintage wine.

'An ingenious proposition,' he said. 'But I'm afraid, in my

opinion, it makes it no less inedible.' He smiled warmly at Michael, as if by his willingness to debate the identity of the pie his guest had passed some kind of test. 'Come and see me again,' he said.

'Well, I'd better be on my way,' said Michael, confused by the professor's words, feeling he was being welcomed and dismissed at the same time.

'I'm sorry about Papa,' Claudia whispered at the door.

'Why?' he asked.

She was so covered in embarrassment that, without really thinking about it, he put his forefinger under her chin so that she would look at him. A spark of static electricity shot between them.

'Sorry!' he said, snatching his hand away.

She touched the skin where the shock had pricked it.

'Will you really write to me when you're at Cambridge?' he asked.

'I will,' she replied solemnly.

He turned at the bend in the road home. Claudia was waving at him enthusiastically with her right hand, her left still touching her face.

Pearl could pinpoint the exact moment she fell in love with Mr Rogers.

It had been a hot summer afternoon. He was in his shirtsleeves, polishing the Bentley. She did not know whether it was her reflection in the shiny black bonnet, or whether he had simply sensed her presence, but when he turned round, his smile was so knowing, so conspiratorial, it had sliced right to the heart of her.

In that window of euphoria just after the war, new social rules were being written. A Labour government had been elected with a sweeping mandate and suddenly the boundaries between master and servant had seemed completely out of date. The only obstacles to their passion were her age and his wife, but by the time Pearl was old enough and Mr Rogers's wife had left him, the hierarchies of class and money had reasserted themselves.

Ironically, it was her father's untimely death, quite suddenly in his sleep, which finally brought them together. At the funeral, her eyes, glassy with tears as she stared across her father's grave, had met Mr Rogers's staring back.

Spadesful of earth hitting the solid oak of the coffin thumped in time with the heartbeat in her head.

That afternoon, nobody seemed inclined to notice or care whether she cycled or was driven to her weekly tennis game. The Ladies' club put her non-appearance down to bereavement.

'You're the woman of my dreams,' Rocky had told her, his chest smacking down on to hers. She adored his looks, his body, and the way he said things with a total absence of irony. Like a film star.

Pearl could not pinpoint with the same certainty the moment she had fallen out of love.

The image that kept returning was the vest, but surely a vest alone could not unravel the complex knot of passion that tied them together?

Or was it the name? Herbert. She simply couldn't imagine herself ever saying the words 'I take thee, Herbert' out loud. She wondered if she'd known that at the beginning whether she'd ever have fallen in love with him at all.

Or was it the ring? The hideous glass stone?

'I'm not interested in your money.'

Had that been the moment? Poverty was terribly romantic until it was staring at you down the barrel of a gun.

Or was it really nothing to do with Mr Rogers at all? Had her fate changed irrevocably the moment she walked into the library behind Claudia?

The man had something of the good looks of Richard Burton: that dimpled chin, those pale penetrating eyes. But his glower had peeled away when he caught sight of them, and his face had lit up with delighted surprise, as if he had given up believing, then witnessed a miracle. And Pearl had thought for one blissful second that the transformation was due to her, then realized just as rapidly that it was not. But she had known she would ditch Mr Rogers in an instant to have this man look at her like that.

It made her see Claudia quite differently – little minx for not telling – one moment a flat-chested little schoolgirl; the next a beguiling waif with a distinctly Audrey Hepburn insouciance about her.

All the curlered heads turned as Pearl walked into Mr Maurice's Hair Salon.

'You might as well know I've decided not to get married after all,' she announced in a loud voice so that Libby could hear under the bell of the dryer.

Sometimes Pearl wondered how long Rocky (as she would always think of him) waited shivering in the chilly grey dawn before starting up the engine of the lorry and driving his caravan away from Kingshaven.

Occasionally, she would take the ring from a twist of tissue paper at the bottom of her lingerie drawer, and look into the stone as if it were a crystal ball which could tell her what her life would have been like.

She tried always to remember him naked, but was surprised how often the vest would jump into the image of his strong sculptured chest, his curly hair and the rough workman's hands that had given her such exquisite pleasure.

Chapter Four

November 1956

Before Michael Quinn arrived at Kingshaven Primary School, history lessons had consisted solely of learning the dates of the kings and queens since 1066. It had occurred to him early on that the story of Kingshaven neatly reflected the history of England, and he had embarked on a project of researching and designing with the children a collage depicting their town through the ages.

'A very modern approach,' the headmaster, Mr Turlow, had remarked.

The area had been underwater during the Jurassic period, and the first section of the frieze showed ichthyosaurs made of egg boxes swimming amongst nautilus shellfish made of corrugated cardboard, in a rippling sea which glinted with bits of milk-bottle top.

It was Ivor Brown who had the bright idea of inviting the *Chronicle* to photograph the work, and after that it had been displayed in St Mary's Church during the previous summer's Flower Festival.

At the beginning of this academic year, Michael had introduced early human settlers and invaders to the school curriculum, and he had suggested that the study should include a field trip.

The children were walking in a crocodile along the promenade towards the Harbour End chattering, excited to be out of the classroom. Michael observed that none of them so much as glanced at the sea, which was flat today, gleaming like wet slate. It made him wonder whether Turner or any of the other great seascape artists had grown up beside the ocean, or whether the magical palette of sunlight playing on water captivated only those who were not accustomed to it.

'What's a field trip, sir?' asked Winston Allsop.

'It's a trip to a field, stupid,' said Simon Ironside.

'Not exactly,' Michael corrected. 'A field trip' – he turned to Winston, who was walking beside him because none of the other children ever chose him to be their partner – 'is where we look at the geography and the history of a place on the ground. You've probably played up on the South Cliffs dozens of times,' he went on, 'but did you know that those little hills that you run up and down are evidence of people who lived here before us?'

'Do you mean the Iron Age fort, sir?' Winston said.

The other boys stared at him.

'Yes, Winston, I do.'

'My father owns the land, sir,' Winston explained.

'I see,' said Michael.

Perhaps he should have asked permission from Sir John Allsop before taking the children up there. He had always assumed that it was common land. It had not crossed his mind that the sheep who grazed so placidly on the defensive dykes actually belonged to someone.

In the fields beyond the last row of quarry cottages where he, Sylvia and Iris had lived when they first arrived, Michael noticed two men with plumb lines and tapes measuring up. Their trench coats and unsuitable town shoes marked them out as strangers.

'I wonder what they're doing,' he asked Winston.

'They might be from the camp,' said Winston.

'The camp?' Michael enquired. There was an Army firing range on the other side of the ridge, but the nearest barracks were in an inland town some miles away.

'Something to do with holidays for poor people,' said Winston.

'You mean a holiday camp?' Michael clarified.

'I think so, sir. My father doesn't see why children in cities shouldn't have the benefit of sea air.'

Michael had never met Sir John Allsop, the reclusive aristocrat whose idiosyncratic philanthropy was considered little less than lunacy by most of the town, but he thought that building on a landscape of such historic interest, even for such a worthy motive, seemed out of character.

As they walked towards the South Cliffs, the sharp yeasty smell of ploughed earth and rotting apples filled the air. It was the time of year when Michael felt as if he should gather every moment of golden sunshine and store it in his heart to see him through the cold, dark days ahead.

Not far from the triangulation point, the skeleton of the town's annual bonfire was already visible. In the coming days it would grow into a pyramid which could be seen for miles even before it was lit on Guy Fawkes' Night.

Michael stood on a hillock and spread his arms out as the children gathered in a semi-circle around him.

'Why do you think that people chose to live up here?' he asked.

They shuffled awkwardly and looked at each other as if uncertain whether to put their hands up outside the classroom.

'Because of the lovely view?' Alice Payne, the doctor's youngest daughter, finally piped up.

Some of the children tittered.

'Alice is right in a way,' said Michael. 'It wasn't exactly that they liked to look at the view, though perhaps they did. Perhaps the chief of the tribe got out his deckchair on sunny days and knotted his handkerchief to make a sunhat . . .'

The children giggled as he enacted a little mime of a typical holidaymaker.

'Please, sir, I'm not sure deckchairs were invented in those days,' Winston interrupted, his voice full of concern.

'Did they send postcards, sir?' asked Simon Ironside, laughing.

'As a matter of fact, the Romans did send a kind of postcard,' Michael informed him. 'Archaeologists have found little wooden tablets with messages carved on them . . .'

Michael shot a look at Sam Coral, who found it difficult to concentrate and was attempting kicky-uppies with a lump of turf.

'Why do you think they lived up here, Sam?'

'Dunno, sir.'

'Sir, it was so they could see if anyone was trying to attack them.'

'Well done, Winston,' said Michael. 'And another reason why they built their fort up here' – he climbed up one of the ramparts – 'was because the enemy would be quite worn out by the time they got here.' He flopped down on the grass, dramatically exhausted.

Several of the children copied him. Michael stood up quickly. Taking the children out of the school building was revolutionary enough. There would be hell to pay if they came back covered in sheep droppings.

'They lived with their animals in little round huts until one day, out on the horizon . . .' He shielded his eyes with his hand, looking out to sea. The children's eyes followed. '. . . they saw boats, and as the boats grew nearer, they could see the glint of metal armour. As the boats approached the beach they could hear the sound of a drum beating out the rhythm for the men who were rowing, and then they landed and the men started jumping off the boats and running up the beaches. Does anyone know who these men were?'

'Please, sir?'

Michael looked round trying to give someone else a chance.

'Go on then, Winston.'

'Romans, sir?'

'Correct! So what do you think the tribe thought when they saw the Romans running up to attack them?'

The children were all staring down at the beach where he was pointing.

'Help!' Michael shouted suddenly.

Some of the children jumped.

'The Romans were very good and clever fighters,' Michael went on. 'The people up here didn't stand a chance. Now, try to imagine what it must have been like because that's going to be the next section of our collage.'

Since Christopher had gone off to prep school, the act of opening the post, which Libby had previously enjoyed, had taken on the quality of a game of Russian roulette. A quick flip through the envelopes would determine whether the day was going to get off to a good start. If there was one addressed in her son's distinctive backward-sloping handwriting, she would tuck it to the bottom of the pile, hoping that the other envelopes would contain some urgent news that would require her immediate attention and put off the moment of reading another of his barely decipherable catalogues of misery. The strict regime of the school seemed to have had little effect on Christopher's spelling.

Eddie had dismissed the outpourings as new-boy nerves, best ignored unless she wanted Christopher to become a sissy. But now that her husband was away sailing with Gerald Rackett and some other old Navy chums on the yacht he had spent such an inordinate amount of time refitting, there was no one to reassure her that the cruelty inflicted on her son was quite normal, and wouldn't do any permanent damage. This morning's envelope appeared to be smudged with tears.

Among Liliana's morning post was a card with a photograph of the Empire State Building on the front and on the back the message: *On top of the world! Rex and Regina.*

Regina! Is that what his lover was known as these days!

Liliana carefully ripped the card into four pieces and deposited it in the ashtray on the breakfast table.

'Do you think fireworks are U or non-U?' Pearl was gazing out of the window towards the South Cliffs.

'I suppose it depends who is lighting them,' Liliana replied.

'I think they're U,' said Angela, who assumed from Pearl's frequent usage that U meant good and non-U bad (which, in a way, it did). Angela was keen to go to the town firework display later in the week and she clearly thought that Pearl, who frequently went down into the town, was her best hope of achieving this.

'There's a reservation for a Mr Butlin,' Libby exclaimed, brandishing a letter on headed notepaper.

'Billy Butlin?' asked Pearl.

'How many Butlins can there be? Pass the marmalade, will you, Mummy?'

'What's he coming here for?' Pearl asked. 'Doesn't he have his own hotels?'

Libby and her mother exchanged looks.

'I say, you don't think he's after the Palace?' Pearl continued. 'Isn't he rather non-U, even if he is terribly rich?'

'I imagine even Billy Butlin needs to get away sometimes, in the low season,' Liliana said. 'Peace and tranquillity, a bracing clifftop walk, the impeccable attention to detail of a truly English holiday. We'll show him how it's done properly.'

Libby made a mental note to reword the hotel's brochure, which suddenly sounded rather old-fashioned.

'I for one rather hanker after a Butlin's holiday,' said Pearl. 'Non-stop dancing and roller-skating! It must be tremendous fun. Perhaps he'll offer me a job? I've always looked good in red.'

'Oh, really, Pearl,' said Libby.

'Well, there's nothing for me to do here,' Pearl sulked.

'Darling, we couldn't manage without you,' said Liliana.

'You give us a certain *je ne sais quoi*,' Libby said.

'Do I really?' said Pearl, instantly cheered.

'Mr Pocock was saying so only the other day.'

'Was he?' said Pearl. 'How adorable of him!'

It occurred to Libby that if she had been paid the same compliment, she might have wondered why it was that her usefulness was being discussed in the first place. In a way, she felt fortunate to have been born the plain sister. Plain people had to have an occupation, and she had found that a great deal of satisfaction could be derived from reading ledger sheets, balancing the books and organizing staff rotas. It had all taken effort to master, with Mr Pocock's assistance, but it had made her proud of herself.

Pearl had never shown any inclination to do anything. Occasionally, she entertained bursts of enthusiasm for taking up a worthwhile profession such as nursing, but her interest soon waned as the reality of emptying bedpans or wearing ugly shoes occurred to her. The fact was that the allowances which had been made for Pearl being the baby of the family, together with the self-absorption of great beauty, had rendered her sister incapable of independence.

In the time of Uncle Rex's proprietorship, when the hotel had been renowned as a getaway for the more rakish elements of London society, Pearl would have fitted in splendidly, but the

New Elizabethan Era they had all greeted so optimistically had turned out to be more frugal than anyone could have imagined. There simply wasn't a role for her glamorous sister to play in the new family-orientated ambience of the Palace.

Their mother still held out the hope that an appropriate man would present himself, someone from outside the county, perhaps, with no knowledge of Pearl's reputation, or even a guest (the usual rule to keep a professional distance might have to be stretched). Yet as she grew older the possibility grew more remote, and it was tacitly understood that she was better off where they could keep an eye on her, rather than being encouraged to break free and land herself in all sorts of trouble.

The problem with visiting the new family-planning clinic in the port of Lowhampton was that everyone knew what you were there for, and if that made it less embarrassing to talk to the doctor – Sylvia had tried and failed three separate times to get the message through to Dr Payne that she wanted to be fitted with a Dutch cap. 'A pretty woman like you,' he'd said on the last occasion, 'should have lots of children!' – it made it correspondingly more embarrassing to encounter someone you knew.

When Sylvia spotted Jennifer Allsop on the other side of the room, she was faced with an instant decision. Should she pretend not to have seen her, which might be impossible to sustain, since the number of women in the room indicated that the waiting time might be as much as an hour, or should she boldly make herself known?

At that moment, Jennifer looked up from her magazine, greeted Sylvia with a surprised smile and patted the vacant seat next to her.

'Is it your first time?' Jennifer whispered.

'No,' Sylvia admitted.

'What a bit of luck to run into you! You can tell me the ropes.'

Just then, to Sylvia's relief, the nurse called Jennifer in for her appointment.

'I'll wait for you afterwards,' Jennifer hissed. 'We'll have lunch!'

And there was no time for Sylvia to explain that she couldn't because she had left Anthony with Audrey Potter for the morning since she didn't think this was a suitable place to bring a three-year-old child.

'I'm sure Audrey won't mind,' Jennifer said, when Sylvia emerged from her appointment. 'I should think we deserve a bit of cheering up after that ordeal!'

Sylvia smiled shyly. Audrey probably wouldn't mind. And why shouldn't she have a bit of fun?

'That,' said Jennifer, as they walked briskly towards the city centre, 'was almost worse than having another baby, which is something I don't intend to do again if at all possible. Not that Joanna isn't the sweetest little thing!'

In the restaurant on the top floor of Gillie's department store, which had a panoramic view of the docks, a waitress handed Sylvia the menu.

'I'm going to have the fish pie,' Jennifer announced. 'How about you?'

'I think I'll just have a sandwich.' Sylvia selected the cheapest item, unsure whether Jennifer's invitation extended to picking up the bill.

'Well, they've got all sorts,' said Jennifer peering at the menu. 'How about prawn?'

'Oh no, not prawns,' said Sylvia. 'Shellfish doesn't agree with me at all. Makes me swell up. Can't breathe,' she explained.

'What a nuisance,' Jennifer snapped the menu shut and handed it to the waitress. 'Just a ham sandwich, then, and the fish pie,' she said.

They sat in silence as they waited for their food. Jennifer took out a packet of cigarettes and offered one to Sylvia, who shook her head.

The useful thing about smoking was that it gave you something to do, but it made her feel sick every time she tried it. Sylvia glanced around the room. It was just gone noon and they were the only customers in the restaurant. She slipped the jacket off her shoulders, put her handbag on the floor, looked up at the chandelier and noted that two of the droplets were missing from the outer circle of sparkling crystal.

'Is that one of your own creations?' Jennifer pointed at Sylvia's olive-green A-line dress.

'Yes,' said Sylvia, feeling herself colour a little.

'You're terribly clever. Pearl King never stops talking about you. Mummy says you'll be putting her out of business!'

'Oh, no! Your mother's been so kind to me!' Sylvia stammered, and then, seeing Jennifer's mystified look, realized that her companion had only been joking. This sort of exaggeration was a way the better class of Southerner had of paying compliments and keeping you in your place at the same time. It wasn't the first time she'd been caught out.

Sylvia gazed around the high-ceilinged room with its padded pink chairs and eau-de-Nil carpet.

'I suppose you get used to it?' Jennifer asked, blowing out a cloud of smoke and pointing at Sylvia's lap.

'Excuse me?'

'They told me to squeeze the sides together and it jumped right out of my hand!'

Sylvia realized with shock that Jennifer was talking about the diaphragm she had just had fitted. She looked around nervously to check that there was no one within earshot. 'I suppose you do,' she said.

'What we girls have to put up with!' said Jennifer.

Sylvia looked up at the chandelier, and then back at Jennifer, and suddenly both of them burst out laughing.

'The trick is,' Sylvia whispered, leaning forward confidentially, 'not to use too much of the cream that goes with it, otherwise it can slither about a bit.'

Jennifer pulled another funny face.

'But it does work?' she asked anxiously. 'You know . . . ?'

'So far,' said Sylvia, relishing being the woman of greater experience. 'Best get yourself ready before, though, because it can be a bit of a, well' – her voice dropped to a whisper – 'passion killer.'

Jennifer grimaced with distaste and Sylvia thought perhaps she'd gone too far, giving the impression that she and Michael did it far more than was the case. Most evenings, Michael stayed up scribbling in his illegible handwriting in exercise books on the dining table. If Sylvia ever asked him what it was that he was writing he shielded his work with his arm, like the clever child at school who didn't want to be copied.

Instead of sitting like a lemon waiting for him to finish, Sylvia now spent her evenings sewing. She was making dresses for several ladies, and secretly putting half the money aside to surprise Michael with a typewriter on his next birthday.

Usually he came to bed long after she did, and if she wasn't pretending to be asleep, the gap of cold sheet was a chasm between them. As they lay there, she would feel as if there were thousands of impatient words jostling noiselessly in the chilly air of the bedroom. Sometimes she thought these were the words he wrote down, which was partly why she never asked to read them.

Sometimes she found herself wishing he were the sort of husband who just gave you no choice in the matter, but he said that there was no pleasure in it for him unless it gave her pleasure too, and that only seemed to make it all twice as difficult.

The waitress arrived with their lunch.

Sylvia took a tiny self-conscious bite of her sandwich. It was nice to eat something prepared for her. She had not eaten out once since they moved to the South Coast. Back home, she and her mother often treated themselves to tea in the restaurant in Stapely and Penney, and watched the mannequins strolling around in the latest fashions, carrying discs with numbers on, so you could look in the programme and see how much the outfits you liked were going to cost.

'This is a bit like our department store back home,' Sylvia said, dabbing the corners of her mouth with a pink linen napkin.

'Your department store?'

'My mother and I—'

'I had no idea,' said Jennifer loftily.

Surely she hadn't conveyed the impression that her family owned a department store? Sylvia felt slightly panicky, and told herself not to volunteer any more information. It wasn't as if she had told a lie, and sometimes if you tried to explain you made yourself look more stupid.

'Does your husband know?' Jennifer asked.

'Pardon?'

Jennifer pointed at her lap again. 'About it.'

'It was his idea,' Sylvia confessed, with another anxious glance around.

Michael had thought that getting a Dutch cap would make her more eager to do it, if she knew she wasn't going to get pregnant every time, but Jennifer didn't need to know about that.

'You're in luck,' said Jennifer, lighting another cigarette. 'Jolly wants another baby straightaway. A boy. Ridiculous, don't you think? I mean Winston's so clearly *not* Sir John's offspring. He'd never be allowed to inherit after Jolly, would he?'

'I've really no idea.' Sylvia racked her brain for a more neutral subject to talk about. 'I hear there's to be a holiday camp,' she said.

'I'm sorry?' Jennifer said, pushing her barely touched plate away.

'Michael saw the men measuring up yesterday,' Sylvia said. 'At the Harbour End.'

Jennifer stared at her as if she had somehow overstepped the mark. 'Anyway,' she said, returning to her theme, 'what the eye doesn't see . . .'

'Pardon?'

'Jolly won't know, will he?'

'But won't he, well—' Sylvia stopped abruptly, deciding not to finish the sentence.

'What?' Jennifer insisted.

'Won't your husband . . . erm . . . feel . . . the . . . you know?' Sylvia's voice trailed away.

'I thought that was the whole point!' said Jennifer crossly, throwing her napkin down on the table. 'They told me that once it's warm, you can't tell the difference!'

Sylvia felt flustered by the outburst and wished she hadn't said anything.

'Can your husband feel it?' Jennifer demanded to know.

'I really couldn't say,' Sylvia stammered. It wasn't the sort of thing you asked, was it?

The silence felt charged with Jennifer's irritation.

'He's awfully handsome, your husband, isn't he?' she said suddenly.

Sylvia blushed. She didn't feel it was quite decent to be talking about you-know-what one minute and Michael's looks the next.

'I'm not the only one who thinks so, you know,' Jennifer added, squashing out her half-smoked cigarette.

There was something about Jennifer's tone that made Sylvia slightly uncomfortable, as if she might be hinting . . . She told herself not to be so silly. The new start she and Michael had made to their marriage wasn't perhaps quite what either of them had hoped, but there was no reason to suspect him. There wasn't the opportunity for it in a small place like Kingshaven.

Claudia's father handed Michael a chipped and stained cup of the special tea one of his relations sent him by post from London. He sometimes remembered to add a splash of milk for Michael, but the flavours did not marry well and, since the professor did not use a strainer, the spiky leaves lurked mischievously below the surface, making every mouthful of the pale smoke-scented brew an ordeal almost as challenging as his attempts to engage the professor's interest.

'I think Mr Eden has made a big mistake,' Michael ventured.

'Paaah!' the professor now snorted dismissively. 'Suez is but the last little adventure of a dying imperial power. A lot of fuss over a damp squid.' He stood up, walked around his desk, picked up a paper, read a little, put it down again, cocked his head at Michael.

Was this the sort of battering students received in university tutorials, Michael wondered. 'A damp squib,' he corrected the professor's idiom.

'Thank you,' said Claudia's father. 'You are looking in the wrong place,' he added more gently. 'Look East.'

'Hungary?'

'But of course. This is the interesting question for the world. What will the Russians do now?'

Michael was never sure whether he was supposed to suggest answers to such questions, or simply nod thoughtfully.

After a suitable pause, he asked, 'I was wondering whether you might consider coming to talk to my class about the Romans?'

'In fact, I don't think this is what you came for,' said the professor.

Michael focused his gaze on the bookcase behind the professor's head.

'I think what you have come for is this,' the professor said, holding out a pale blue Basildon Bond envelope with Michael's name written on it in Claudia's handwriting.

As he went to take it, the professor suddenly withdrew his outstretched hand as if he had changed his mind. Michael forced himself to swallow the surge of anger that swelled in him. These games were the price he had to pay for using Claudia's father as a post office.

The professor took off his glasses again, looked down and sighed. 'My daughter is very young, and I think quite attractive,' he began, his voice quivering and then growing stronger. 'And Cambridge is a chance for her, do you understand?'

'I don't see what—' Michael began.

'Mr Quinn. I ask you please to try to be a good man, a very unselfish man—'

'We write to each other about books,' Michael interrupted.

'I'm sure you do,' the old man said. 'And literature is a most potent aphrodisiac.'

'I am a married man,' Michael retorted indignantly.

'But I do not think you discuss books with your wife,' said the professor evenly.

Michael felt colour rising above the clean white collar Sylvia starched and ironed for him each day.

The old man was staring back at him now, his eyes watery-bright but determined.

'I understand what you are saying,' Michael said finally.

'And you agree?'

Michael nodded.

'Good,' said the professor, picking up another paper from his desk and putting it down again. Then, without looking at Michael, he handed the letter over.

The tutorial was at an end.

'May I still visit you?' Michael blurted, suddenly realizing that he would miss the professor's company. He was a cantankerous old so-and-so, but Michael always came away feeling that his brain had been sharpened. 'When your daughter is not here?'

The old man took off his glasses and stared at him, as if surprised. 'If you would like to,' he said, after a moment of consideration. 'There are few people I can talk to in these parts. John

Allsop is a good man, but not, I think, a comrade.' His face broke into a rare smile that made him seem a little vulnerable. He held out his bony veined hand for Michael to shake.

Dear Michael,
    I think, if it's possible, that it's even colder here this year than last. I've found a new use for my college scarf – to wear it last year was a badge of honour, but now nobody does for fear of being marked out as a Fresher. How sophisticated we've all become! – it serves as an invaluable draught excluder wedged along the bottom of my window frame. I'm sitting here as if in a scene from *La Bohème*, wearing two pairs of socks, a blanket and fingerless gloves, but still my *manina* is *gelida* . . .

Michael sat in the corner of the Ship, his half-pint of beer untouched on the upturned barrel which served as a table. Around him, fishermen conversed in accents so broad they might have been talking a foreign language for all he understood.
    He thought *La Bohème* was an opera. He would ask Ivor.

The price you pay for having large windows is the cold, but I wouldn't have it any other way at this time of year. The colours of the garden range from the palest gold to the brightest scarlet, all framed with the black-green of conifers. The Backs are at their best now. When the sun is shining and a slight breeze blows flurries of leaves down in a shimmer of golds, it is almost like watching a great exotic bird of paradise shed a little of its plumage – a truly enchanted place.
    I should of course be writing my essay now, but have been meaning to write to you since the beginning of term, and at this point of increasing panic before my tutorial, any distraction takes on a quality of pressing importance . . .

Michael read through the first page of the letter again, wounded by the idea that writing to him was simply a distraction for her.

This term, you will be glad to hear, I have joined the Labour Club, and have auditioned for a play, not, I have to confess, because I entertain theatrical ambitions, but because acting is something women are allowed to do within certain limits. The powers that be have reluctantly accepted that a few women may have the intelligence to participate in study, but we are still not deemed suitable to debate in the Union or join the Footlights, where there's apparently much hilarity. A friend tried to sneak me in the other evening claiming I was a student of existentialism from the Sorbonne in Paris. With my hair hidden under a beret, a jacket and slacks, I looked quite like a boy, but his shoes gave me away, flapping off my feet, and my French was not as fluent as that of some of the students of Modern Languages! I was unceremoniously put out on the pavement and then, irony of ironies, stopped by the porter on my way back into college, who was distinctly unamused by a man trying to enter the college late at night!

The lessons I am learning here are so very different from those I anticipated. Mr Leavis's lectures are simplicity itself compared to the complicated rituals of formal English manners – which fork to use, which way to pass the port if you are invited to dine at High Table. One of the only benefits of being a woman in an overwhelmingly male environment is that one is such a rare creature, one's gaucheness is overlooked!

I thought of you so much when a group of us went up to the Royal Court in London to see John Osborne's *Look Back In Anger* the other evening. It's tremendously powerful and raw, and everyone is talking about it. Sadly, I don't think it would find a sympathetic audience at the Pier Theatre, Kingshaven. But there were elements which reminded me of some of your stories.

I wonder if you have ever thought of turning your stories into a novel? The ones you have sent me are all in the first person and, even if the narrator is not always the same character, you write about a distinctive physical and emotional landscape. Please take this suggestion as praise not criticism, for I mean only the former. Short stories, while satisfying in their way, are never, in my view, going to find a big enough readership for you. I have a friend whose father is a publisher and he says that everyone is looking for a novel from the next Angry Young Man. I keep thinking that it will be you!

I long to read more of your work, as I long to read any words
you write. What happiness when I visit my pigeonhole and
discover an envelope from you! The presence of your words
makes it seem for a glorious few minutes in a secluded place in
the college library that you are there across the desk from me!

What distinguishes the writer is the voice, which you have,
and I do not. Reading back over this, I find nothing in it that
sounds the way I feel. I have donned a disguise for Cambridge!
My life here is something separate, that bears no relation to
what I am or what I will become when it is time to leave.
The sensation is a little like finding myself in the middle of a
strange, wonderful dream. I give my subconscious permission
to stay until I wake up.

It is late now, and there are blank sheets of paper to be
covered in writing, not for you, but for my terrifying tutor,
who listens in deafening silence as I offer thoughts which seem
suddenly unbearably naïve.'

I hope that you are not so critical!

Wishing you were here to exchange notes with me about it all.

With fondest regards,

Claudia

Michael held the letter in both hands, tormented with the
tantalizing glimpses she gave of her life at Cambridge. Who was
this friend whose father was a publisher? Was he someone she
had run into at one of the many parties she seemed to go to? Had
he been the one who tried to smuggle her into the Footlights,
whatever that was? He imagined her dancing and laughing in a
crowded smoky room unaware of the men watching her, wanting
her. Flirting over the top of a Martini glass, laughing at the wit of
all the bright young men who desired her.

He imagined a tall man with rakish long hair swept back
from his face, baggy tweed trousers and a gown, cycling beside
Claudia ('from the back we students look like giant bats on
wheels!' she had written in a previous letter), both of them
laughing. Had she told this friend whose father was a publisher
that there was a man she knew back home who wanted to be
a writer? He saw them climbing off their bikes, gathering up

their books, making their way into some columned lecture hall.

'I've advised him to write a novel.'

'Your very own angry young man! How super! Do come to my room for tea and crumpets!'

Was this son of a publisher one of the group who had gone up to London to see the Osborne play? Had they stayed in London together, or were there trains back to Cambridge late at night?

Michael could see them crowded into a compartment, loud and confident, making pronouncements in their upper-class accents about the brilliance of Osborne's depiction of the working class. He hated their flippancy, their laughter, their self-importance.

Claudia!

He tried to picture her alone, serious, framed in her window on the ground floor, with its fifty-six panes of glass, sucking her pen as she composed her letter to him.

He imagined her delicate hands in fingerless gloves scribbling and crossing out the words.

The ways they had found to avoid an open declaration of love were almost exhausted. For one awful moment, it crossed Michael's mind that Claudia's father had steamed open the letter and that this was the reason for his stern warning this afternoon. But he doubted the professor would intrude into his daughter's privacy. The truth was that Claudia's father did not need to read their correspondence because her feelings and his were transparently obvious. And if the exchange of billets doux were allowed to continue, reputations would suffer.

His reply took as long to compose as a letter of several pages.

It was the oddest love affair, for there had been no impropriety, no declaration, not even a kiss, and yet his longing for her was so physical he could feel it not just in his groin but in his chest, his head, even the muscles of his face when he thought about her.

The letter dropped irrevocably from his hand into the mouth of the post box. He felt a profound emptiness and a kind of despair for the loss of something that had never been.

In person, Mr Butlin was both shorter and smarter than Libby had imagined. With his background in travelling circuses, she had been expecting if not exactly the baggy checked trousers and red nose of a clown, then certainly a flashier suit and a coarser complexion. It was extraordinary what money could buy. A man's fingernails were often a useful indicator of his bank balance, and Mr Butlin clearly enjoyed a regular manicure. He was an amiable man, polite enough, but Libby felt at a disadvantage with Eddie away aboard the *Brittany Anna*.

The last she'd heard was a telegram from Gibraltar: *All well. Sporting whiskers. Eddie.*

She imagined that five must be the limit of words, but she felt Eddie could have used his allocation to impart something more useful than the information that he had grown a beard.

She missed him in all sorts of ways, but especially at drinks before dinner. From years of mute observation of men in the bar, Libby had learned that there was a kind of instant hierarchy created by the way in which conversation was struck up. The man who was first to put forward a proposition (even something as banal as 'Nice weather for ducks!') was usually in charge as the others chuckled and agreed. There were certain subjects which lent themselves perfectly to this leading-the-consensus approach: the weather, of course, with cricket not far behind, and recently, as more and more of the guests arrived by road, the performance of different makes of motor car had become a rich source of the uncontroversial debate which men employed as a way of sizing each other up. It was a form of communication which simply didn't work if a woman got involved. Even though she was the proprietor of the hotel, Mr Butlin seemed to have the upper hand straightaway, and his direct questions in the area of business made her uneasy about the motives for his visit.

'Nice bit of land you've got here,' he said after taking a turn in the gardens. 'Must be enough for nine holes out the back.'

'There are a number of well-established courses in the area,' Libby informed him.

Her dream was eventually to have horses on the fields at the back of the hotel. Eventually, even a stables. At the moment, she kept her stallion liveried.

'These days people want their facilities on site,' he said.

'We're getting a swimming pool next year,' she said.

'With your capacity, I doubt you'd see enough return for your investment,' Mr Butlin told her, lending a certain weight to Mr Pocock's ideas about expansion.

'My children will enjoy it,' she told him in as grand a voice as she could muster.

'Think of the maintenance,' said Mr Butlin with an avuncular grin. 'Could be a popular little place, this,' he said, lighting a cigar. 'You've got the best spot here.'

'Indeed.'

'Pity there's talk of closing the branch line.'

She wondered to whom he'd been speaking. 'Most of our guests travel by motor car,' she assured him. 'With the exception of Lord and Lady Docker who moor the *Shemara* in the harbour.'

Libby congratulated herself on the way she had made one overnight visit by the Dockers sound as if they were regular guests.

'I've heard Bernard's in a bit of hot water,' said Mr Butlin.

'Bernard?'

'Lord Docker,' Mr Butlin said with an almost indiscernible chuckle. 'Her ladyship might not be travelling by gold-plated Daimler in the future.'

'What a pity,' said Libby, who treasured the memory of the glamorous couple's fleeting visit. When the Dockers discovered that the Palace did not have a stock of pink champagne (the one occasion Libby did have to have words with Mr Pocock), they had invited the entire King family on to their yacht for drinks. The boat had almost as many staff as the hotel itself.

It was Jolly Allsop who inadvertently solved the riddle of Mr Butlin's visit.

'Apparently, there's going to be a holiday camp on the South Cliffs,' he said, apropos of nothing as they ran through next year's colour scheme for bulbs.

It was such a relief to discover that Mr Butlin was not engaged in an unfathomable scheme to make the Palace his, Libby did not fully appreciate the sheer awfulness of the alternative reason for his visit until she mentioned it to her mother later on. Liliana put her Dubonnet down so angrily on the marble mantelpiece that the stem of the glass snapped, leaving her holding only the intact bowl in her hand.

'Quite impossible!' Liliana declared. 'It will ruin the view and bring the tone of the place right down.'

'It's Jolly I feel sorry for,' said Libby. 'Apparently everyone knew except him. Jenny heard about it when she was shopping in Lowhampton, of all places! At this rate, there'll be nothing for him to inherit.'

'Never mind about Jolly Allsop,' Liliana scolded her. 'Think of what it will do to the value of the Palace! Sir John has finally taken leave of his senses. It's one thing to take pity on foundlings and refugees, but to invite the nation's hoi polloi to spend their summers . . . !'

The corridor that ran from Claudia's hall of residence to the college lodge was said to be the longest in the world. How on earth did people light upon such information? Claudia had developed an absurd ritual: if she reached the pigeonholes in fewer than five hundred paces, then there would be the possibility of a letter; if it took more, there would not. If another student fell into step with her for a chat and she lost count, there was no chance at all. Running was forbidden, and all the way she told herself, over and over, that there would not be a letter, hoping that if she could stop wanting it so much, her restraint might be rewarded. It was ridiculously superstitious behaviour for someone who proclaimed herself an atheist, as silly as a child not stepping on the lines between paving stones, but it happened twice a day, sometimes three or four times when she suspected that the post was late. Sometimes Claudia even found herself going to check again late at night after working in the library, in case someone with a surname beginning with D might have mistakenly picked up her letter along with their own, only returning it when they went to supper.

Four hundred and ninety-eight. Claudia did a big leap for the last pace. Four hundred and ninety-nine!

There were three folded notes with her name scribbled on, and – miracles! – a white envelope addressed to her in untidy writing which always surprised her because of some idea she had that a person as attractive as Michael would naturally have beautiful handwriting too.

With a swift glance around to check that she was alone, Claudia clasped the envelope to her chest, as if trying to extract the essence of him from it. She could feel that there was only one sheet of paper inside the envelope, which was disappointing, but she couldn't really expect a long letter, she told herself, since it was only a few days since she had sent hers to him. Once she had had to wait five agonizing weeks, but at the end of it (four hundred and sixty-three paces down the corridor, which she'd never managed to achieve again for fear of being observed taking giant strides as if playing grandmother's footsteps), there had been a manila envelope stuffed with school exercise books containing stories in raw, ferociously honest prose which she sat up all night reading, with increasing excitement, like a scientist on the brink of discovering a new element.

Now, she turned the flimsy envelope over in her hands wondering whether to open it straightaway, or save it for a moment when she was alone in her room

'How many have you got?'

Claudia's American friend, Josie, whom she admired for her articulacy and confidence, but was also slightly in awe of, was suddenly beside her, rifling through her own pigeonhole for notes.

Claudia hastily tucked Michael's letter into the bottom of the pile and scanned the notes she had received.

In recent weeks, a fashion had developed among students visiting other colleges of scribbling messages in verse if their intended hosts were out – *Drowning in* Journal of Aristotelian Studies, *Desk 37P. Will someone, taking pity, rescue me?* – which, in turn, spawned lengthy sonnets whose studied wit gave the lie to their spontaneity.

'Everything here becomes a competition,' Claudia observed, reading the latest offerings from her current admirers.

'You've got three!' Josie exclaimed, looking over her shoulder. 'Only one for me.'

'Who from?'

'Ted.'

'I'd rather have your one than my three,' Claudia said. 'Ted's a real poet.'

'Do you think he leaves poems in other women's pigeonholes?' Josie asked, sounding uncharacteristically vulnerable for once.

'I'm sure he doesn't,' Claudia reassured her.

Josie looked doubtful.

'Tim's is very good,' said Josie, reading Claudia's poems over her shoulder.

'Hmm,' said Claudia.

'What is the matter with you?' asked Josie with a directness none of the English girls would have dared to employ. 'Tim's completely gorgeous. If he weren't so besotted with you, I'd snap him up myself!

'Poor Ted!'

'I don't think Ted will ever make anyone happy,' said Josie, suddenly wistful. 'Far better to be in love with someone like Tim.'

'Except I'm not,' said Claudia. 'There's nothing very rational about love, is there?'

'Oh, this place is crazy!' Josie said, strong and forthright again. 'We're here because of our brains, but we mope about men with all the sophistication of a woman's magazine! Are you coming to the Suez protest?'

'Of course!'

As an immigrant marooned in the rural shires of England, Claudia had found that it was best to keep her political opinions to herself, but at Cambridge she had been liberated to find people her own age who felt the same as she did about the issues of the day – and were prepared to demonstrate in support of their views. She knew that Michael would most certainly approve of her going on the protest. He was a supporter of Nye Bevan and was sure to have applauded his marvellous mockery of the Prime Minister on the wireless. She was going for both of them, Claudia thought, and she would tell him all about it in her next letter.

'Come on, then!' said Josie, impatiently.

'I'll catch up with you,' Claudia told her, suddenly unable to resist reading Michael's letter straightaway.

Claudia slid her finger under the envelope flap and took out the sheet of paper. A little dip of disappointment when she saw that there was only writing on one side.

Dear Claudia,
    I cannot continue our correspondence. I'm sorry.
    In my mind, you will always be sitting across the desk from me.
    With best wishes for your future,
    Michael

It was customary on Guy Fawkes' Night for the inhabitants of Kingshaven to shame wrongdoers by putting their likeness to the flames. In days gone by, images of local embezzlers, fraudsters and adulterers had been publically torched, along with an occasional greedy smuggler who had made the mistake of trying to cheat the town's folk as well as the government. The accounts reminded Michael of the skimmity ride in *The Mayor of Casterbridge*, and when he looked into it further, he had found documents in the county library which referred to a practice known as skimmington riding only half a century before, in villages not so very far away.

In more recent times, the targets singled out for public humiliation had been more universally recognizable: Hitler; Mussolini; the Emperor of Japan. Tonight, a crude version of General Nasser's features was sitting on top of the pyre.

The bonfire was so huge that the warmth of it could be felt from a hundred yards. The kindling spat and crackled. The greediness of the blaze and the collective cheer that went up as the guy caught and folded into the flames made the gathering feel almost orgiastic.

Michael recognized the features of children in his class illuminated momentarily by yellow tongues of light, but not one of them bounced up to greet him as they did each morning in the playground. Instead, they looked at him with suspicion, as if he were spying on their rituals; and with reason, he thought, for he had little sympathy with the insularity of the place, and his involvement was only as an observer.

'Is the fire alive, sir?' Iris asked, warily backing away from the blaze.

'No,' he said. 'But you can see why people used to think it was.'

Her hand gripped his tighter. 'When are we going home?' she said.

'You don't want to miss the fireworks, do you?'

Iris had been looking forward to the fifth of November for weeks, demanding first thing each morning how many days to go, but he sensed it was intimidating to be surrounded in the dark by bodies whose faces she couldn't see.

'Would it help if I picked you up?'

Without further invitation, Iris sprung up into his arms as she had done when she was a toddler.

She was a little heavier now, but not much, as if her weight had simply been stretched. Her legs dangled down, heels knocking against the back of his knees. It wasn't often that he held his daughter now that she was growing up and each second of her clinging grip felt intensely precious.

A feeling of kinship with Iris had rocked him from the first moment he saw her. Iris was so much a Quinn. Her flashes of temper and charm came directly from his mother who, he now understood, had been a very intelligent woman without the education to fulfil that intelligence. As a child he'd always lived in fear of her unpredictability. The simple recognition that Iris and he were made of the same stuff was something Michael had never felt with his son. He could see that Anthony was a good-looking child, with an even, placid temperament, but his admiration for him had never extended beyond a kind of curiosity and a wish to protect him when people remarked that the boy was so pretty, he could be used in an advertisement for Heinz baby food.

With Iris, especially when he held her and could feel the expansion and contraction of breath inside her bony ribcage, he felt as if they were bound together by an invisible force as funda-mental as gravity, as if her presence was what anchored him to the world, as if she was in some way the answer to the question of his existence.

As the rockets whooshed silently up into the sky, bursting into great constellations of brilliance above, Iris's limpet body gradually relaxed and her face broke into a marvellous smile. Her features were becoming more angular, and in the strange orange light of the fire, she looked so very much like his brother Frank, it made Michael wonder whether Frank had ever stood on this spot where they were standing right now.

Perhaps there had been a bonfire on VE night?

What had Frank made of these small-town people who whooped and hollered at the demise of a hated foreigner?

Michael gripped Iris tightly, not wanting her to see the tears that had involuntarily welled in his eyes.

The last fountain of orange and purple stars vanished, leaving trails of smoke in the clear dark sky.

A loud, confident voice made Michael suddenly aware again of where he was. 'It's Mr Quinn, isn't it?'

There was a woman standing right in front of him. The elemental glow of the fire gave her the appearance of a gypsy with loose dark curls and full red mouth.

'I'm Pearl King. Your wife has run up a couple of dresses for me. I really don't know what I'd do without her,' she said, offering her right hand.

Michael had no idea how he was supposed to respond to this information, so he said nothing, but let Iris slip down, and then extended his own hand to shake, but Pearl King had already dropped hers, and there was a moment of embarrassment as Michael quickly ran his hand back through his hair, as if that was why he had stuck it out in the first place.

'My niece, Angela.'

'Hello!'

Michael remembered the little girl from the Coronation Party. She had lost her childhood prettiness with her milk teeth. Uneven halfgrown incisors stuck out above her lip even though she was not smiling.

'We were just leaving,' he said. 'It's past Iris's bedtime.'

'Angela's too,' said Pearl, falling into step beside him.

'No, it's not!' retorted Angela as her aunt tugged her arm viciously.

The four of them tramped across the rutty field in silence.

'How is Claudia getting on in Cambridge?' Pearl asked.

'I don't know,' Michael answered carefully.

The question seemed almost to contain the subtle weight of blackmail.

'But I thought you two were such friends!' Pearl declared.

Afterwards, he thought how strange it was that the moment he had wished for the ground to open up and swallow him, it had almost literally done just that.

The eyewitness accounts printed the next day in the *Chronicle* related that there had been no warning, but Michael was sure that there had been an explosion so loud they had looked up for another great chrysanthemum blossom of stars, but found the sky empty.

As his mind struggled with the illogicality of not seeing what he expected to see, Michael had the peculiar sensation that he was moving, even though he knew he was standing still, rather as if he were sitting on a stationary train with another train pulling away from the platform alongside.

Then the children, more in tune with the natural rhythms of the earth, like animals before an earthquake, began to shriek wildly.

Only then did Michael's mind let him believe that the ground was moving.

The sensation was like being on a slow raft moving down the hillside, peculiar but not in itself frightening, but then all the facts he had read about the nineteenth-century landslip came hurtling into collision with his imagination, and he was finally conscious of the peril.

The noise of thousands of tons of earth sliding towards them was so deafening, he felt he couldn't think. He heard himself shouting, 'Run!' and picked Iris up again. She was stiff with fear and felt heavy now.

'Come on!'

'I can't run!' Pearl King cried, frozen with panic.

'Don't be so stupid!' he shouted at her, grabbing her hand and pulling her, leaping and bouncing up the uneven turf to the edge of the chalk cliffs, where he stood, praying to a God he did not believe in for the land to stay solid under his feet. And then he realized he was still holding Pearl's hand, and dropped it abruptly as they stood and watched the awe-inspiring sight of the hillside pouring inexorably down towards the Harbour End, rolling into the row of cottages where his family had lived when they first moved. He suddenly knew, with horrible certainty, that if his instincts had told him to go left instead of right, they would all have been buried alive. The nearness of a different fate made him feel humble, as he stood holding Iris very tightly in his arms, hiding his fear in her hair.

Miraculously, unlike the previous landslip of 1890, there was no loss of life apart from three of Sir John Allsop's sheep.

Rescue parties of the Civil Defence Corps had been despatched from all over the county, and together with the lifeboat crew, who had been amongst the revellers around the bonfire, they worked from opposite ends to secure a safe path above the line of the landslip, enabling the people of Kingshaven to return to their homes.

The Food Flying Squads hadn't been required, and it was generally agreed that it had been a much more worthwhile exercise in civil defence than any of the recent pretend scenarios supposing the explosion of a hydrogen bomb over the nearby port of Lowhampton.

Those who were left without a roof over their heads had been allowed to spend the night in the vacant bedrooms of the Palace Hotel, whose comfort and luxury was indelibly printed on their memories, and became an important feature of the subsequent telling of the story of that momentous evening.

At breakfast the next morning, Liliana King remarked, 'I did warn Mr Butlin that the land on the South Side was unstable.'

Libby was relieved to see that her mother had regained her composure after losing it so uncharacteristically the previous evening when she had told Liliana that Pearl and Angela had gone to watch the town fireworks.

Chapter Five

August 1957

The newsagents had sold out of copies of the *Radio Times*. Everyone wanted a souvenir of the day Kingshaven found fame on the radio. The West Home Service was going to broadcast 'The Good Old Summertime: A Holiday Visit to Kingshaven' from seven-thirty to eight-thirty. Cliff Michelmore himself had arrived at the Palace Hotel the previous evening, and was recording behind-the-scenes interviews at the resort's attractions. The news from the Palace was that he had eaten a substantial breakfast, requesting coffee rather than tea, and was wearing light trousers and a striped blazer. It was a funny thing putting a face to a voice, the night porter told the queue in the Post Office. If he'd been asked to describe Mr Michelmore before having the pleasure of meeting him, he would have made him a less substantial figure.

'Which just goes to show,' said Audrey Potter, who had taken off her apron in case any of the BBC reporters who were said to be roaming the town, stepped into the Post Office.

'If the weather stays like this, we're going to run out of hats.' Sylvia wished she could find something interesting to say for the woman with the clipboard to record for the programme, and then Mrs Farmer, who was in hospital for an operation, would hear it on the wireless beside her bed in the ward. Sylvia was standing beside the till of Farmer's Outfitters, in charge of the shop.

There were only two panamas, one a deceptively small size whose binding inside was now wet with the sweat of several bald men who had tried it on, and three ladies' straw hats, one of them navy blue with a wide brim which was far too smart for the beach. There were still a few gingham Bo-Peep bonnets, the sort she always tried to get Iris to wear, but they were green, never a popular choice with children.

'With the Bank Holiday coming up, we could do with a few extra bathing costumes, but you don't want to be left with this year's look next season,' Sylvia said. 'People in Kingshaven like to be up to date. That's why they come to Farmer's.'

The researcher, who was dressed in a black boat-neck tunic and narrow-legged black trousers, raised a supercilious eyebrow, thanked her, and left. The shop seemed emptier than it usually did for a moment. Sylvia noticed that a wisp of one of the chiffon scarves in the glass-fronted drawer below the counter was out of place. She pulled the drawer out and began to tidy it.

'Who was that?' asked Jennifer, sauntering in late, as usual.

'A researcher from the BBC,' said Sylvia.

'It's so stifling in here, I can hardly breathe,' Jennifer said distractedly.

Sylvia experienced a kind of mild panic whenever Jennifer expressed any negative views, as if her discomfort or boredom must somehow be her fault. 'Perhaps we could prop the door open with a chair?' she suggested.

'It's even hotter outside,' said Jennifer, fanning herself with a lingerie catalogue. 'I don't even know why we open in this weather. There are so few customers, it's hardly worth bothering.'

'Why don't you go and have a nice cool drink upstairs,' Sylvia suggested. 'I'll be fine down here on my own.'

'You are such a brick,' said Jennifer.

Some people just didn't know when they were lucky, Sylvia thought as Jennifer's shoes tapped up the staircase to her mother's flat. Ruby Farmer lavished money and attention on her daughter and yet she couldn't even be trusted to look after the shop properly when she was in hospital. Hardly any customers? The town was swarming!

Not that it was any skin off her nose, Sylvia thought. When Mrs Farmer had asked her to help out, it meant more than just the extra money, it was a sign that they were accepted as locals, after just five years in the town, which was something of a record from what Sylvia could gather. The people of Kingshaven did not readily welcome new residents into their midst. And it was all down to her, too, Sylvia thought, because, if truth be told, Michael, for all his pronouncements about equality, was not very good at mixing with people.

Sylvia pushed the glass drawer with its rainbow arrangement of nylon gauze roses closed. There was nothing she liked better than to be in the shop alone, to run her hand over the cool, almost liquid surface of a pristine satin slip, to pinch the creamy leather interior of a quality handbag, or hear the satisfied chime of the cash register closing a sale. Alone, she could imagine it was her own shop. When the end of the day came and she pulled down the blind on the door and turned over the sign in the window, she often stayed a while, plucking the stiff gathers of new cotton dresses back into shape, or folding piles of cardigans into perfect square towers.

'And still they come . . .' Pearl read from the *Chronicle*, her mouth twisting into an expression of distaste. 'In their thousands apparently, mostly from the North. They've put on special trains.'

Michael looked up.

'Poor things,' she added sympathetically, remembering his origins, 'they'll hardly see a grain of sand with the beach so packed.'

Michael went back to his book, an American novel entitled *Lolita*, which the professor had been sent by friends in New York where it was the subject of great controversy. It was not an easy read. The writing was so crazily, poetically original, it made Michael think it was mad for anyone else to bother. It was the sort of book you had to be careful not to leave lying around in case someone too young like Iris, or too conservative, like his mother-in-law, Doreen, who was staying with them for the summer holidays, picked it up and started to ask questions about the unusual vocabulary.

Michael wondered whether Claudia had read the novel yet. There was evidence of her return for the vacation in the gatehouse recently: the mahogany bookcase shone like a conker; the professor's papers were stacked tidily on his desk. On Michael's last visit, the tantalizing aroma of newly baked scones had filled the house. He had been disturbed by the fierceness of the wanting that still clutched at him whenever he thought about her.

Michael and Iris had spent much of the holidays going for walks. At seven, Iris was old enough now to keep up with his pace, and to learn historical and archaeological facts about the area. They gave each adventure a different name: the Treasure Trail, which culminated at the wishing well in the Victoria Gardens where Iris attempted to count all the shiny sunken farthings and halfpennies holidaymakers had invested with their secrets; the Fossil Hunt in which they chipped open the round flat stones where ammonites hid with the hickory-handled hammer he had purchased in Mr Barratt's hardware shop; the Wild-flower Walk where they collected buttercups and dandelion clocks whose petals and gossamer blew away, leaving just a bunch of stalks to present to Granny when they arrived home. Together they had explored every street and lane, but they had not caught one glimpse of Claudia.

The person they bumped into with improbable frequency was Pearl King. It occurred to Michael that she must be the little princess Frank had mentioned, whose tennis knickers had been the subject of the squaddies' wet dreams, a dozen years ago. Lolita then, now an undeniably attractive woman.

In conversation, she positioned herself just an inch too close and she wore perfume that was a little too heavy for the pale summer days. Her eyes, a startling, almost violet blue, froze into an icy stare if something displeased her, or melted in a puppyish plea to be liked. Michael suspected she was the type who got aroused by a plain-speaking working-class man. He found himself colluding in the flirtation, becoming more reticent and monosyllabic, amused to see how this made her all the more breathless and eager.

But it was difficult to maintain the upper hand when she offered enticements to Iris.

When Michael declined the invitation for his daughter to learn to swim in the hotel's new pool, Iris demanded to know why.

'I'm bored with just you all the time,' she told him with a casual cruelty that rendered him temporarily incapable of thinking of a plausible excuse.

So they had come, Iris carrying a new costume, which Doreen had spent all night knitting from a pattern in *Woman's Weekly*, in a straw beach bag with plastic handles; he in his best suit because Sylvia had insisted.

He had watched Sylvia weighing up whether to chaperone Iris herself, and listened to the convoluted debate with her mother in which the immediate attraction of one privileged visit was weighed against Sylvia's long-term plan to better herself by becoming someone Mrs Ruby Farmer (herself a close associate of the Kings) could rely on.

Sitting stiffly on a sun-lounger in his suit, Michael very much wished Sylvia had come instead of him. It was more difficult to despise the wealth and privilege of the Kings while accepting their hospitality. He was the comical figure now. Under his jacket, he could feel the sweat soaking into his shirt. He didn't know whether it would be the done thing to take his polished brown shoes off, or leave them on.

'Shall I see if you could borrow some of Eddie's trunks?' Pearl asked. Her halter-neck swimming dress had a loud pattern of blue and yellow roses and a tiny skirt around her hips.

'Don't bother,' Michael said. 'I'll just read.'

Pearl flung herself down on the next lounger, droplets of water cascading from her bronzed legs and snaking between her cleavage; then she put on white plastic sunglasses with lenses so dark he could not see where she was looking.

In the ballroom, Mr Ray Moore and his Orchestra were rehearsing tunes for the ballroom dancing which was going to be broadcast live from the hotel that evening. After several attempts at the first few bars of 'Spanish Eyes', angry shouting was clearly audible through the French windows open on to the terrace.

'Sidney, the usual drummer, came off his bike last night,' Pearl announced. 'Broken collar bone.'

There was a ripple of sympathetic applause from the guests

who were lounging round the pool when the right tempo was eventually achieved.

'Will you be listening to the broadcast this evening?' Pearl asked Michael.

'A friend of mine's playing at the end of the pier. A skiffle band,' said Michael. 'How about you?' he asked, politely.

'Oh, I'm afraid I'll have to stay for the dancing,' Pearl said, as if he had invited her to go with him. She pulled a face.

'Daddy, watch!' Iris shrieked, diving into the pool.

He stared at the spot where her body had pierced the water for several anxious seconds. The reflection of the sun made the surface opaque. Suddenly she burst up at the other end of the pool, laughing at the worried expression on his face.

Pearl applauded her achievement.

'Such a perfect afternoon,' she said. 'I know, let's have tea out here.'

She slipped her bare feet into canvas mules with high cork heels and sashayed up the flight of steps between rows of terra-cotta pots spilling over with pink geraniums. At the top, the sunglasses looked back over her shoulder, as if she knew that Michael's eyes were following her. He fixed his focus so as to appear to be looking beyond her at the upper floors of the hotel.

From one of the balconies on the top floor, someone was leaning over, looking at him, but just as he became aware of the figure, it disappeared, and he couldn't decide whether he had been fooled by sunlight. He looked away, and then up again, as if to catch whoever it was unawares, but there was still no one.

At the Pier Theatre, pump failure had caused the Dancing Fountains of the Aquafantasia to leap no higher than punctures in a garden hosepipe. Archie Mills, the resident stage manager, who had always had his doubts about the advisability of mixing water and electricity, stood at the back of the stalls with his arms folded.

The Director of the Summer Season flustered about the stage ordering his assistants to turn things off. The crew held their breath each time his arm made the decisive signal to switch on again, and when nothing dramatic happened, a shudder of suppressed laughter spread through the auditorium. It was very warm inside. People fanned themselves with the commemorative programme. A half-hearted slow handclap was quickly shushed, but the general restlessness of the audience was sliding irrevocably towards an almost audible impatience.

The recording of the spectacle was already behind schedule.

'How about if the orchestra were to play,' Ivor Brown suggested half seriously to the producer, 'and we got the crew to throw fire buckets on cue?'

'It's more difficult to fool our listeners than you might imagine,' the producer explained. 'And very much against the spirit of the BBC.'

'You're forgetting our audience here,' Archie Mills reprimanded Ivor.

'Oh, they'd go along with anything to be on radio,' said Ivor breezily.

'Should have stuck with *Gay Time*,' said Archie Mills. 'You knew where you were with that.'

'*Gay Time*?' the producer echoed.

'The Summer Show that's in rep with the waterworks,' said Mr Mills.

There was a whispered debate among the BBC people.

The female researcher looked at her clipboard. 'We've got the military band at the railway playing "See the Conquering Hero", tennis, the Gardens with the head gardener's planting tips and the man with his sand sculptures.'

'We need more sound,' said the man with the mike.

'How about a skiffle band?' Ivor suggested.

'That's more like it.' The producer clapped his hands. 'The contemporary mood.'

'We could offer you the *Gay Time* overture medley,' offered the Director of the Summer Season.

'Followed by the skiffle band. We'll wrap up with the ballroom dancing,' said the producer with a wide smile. 'An eclectic symphony of musical tastes.'

'I'm off now,' Sylvia called up the stairs to the apartment as she let herself out of the back door of the shop.

There was no reply.

'Bye!' she called again.

Sylvia tiptoed up the stairs. The door of the flat was open.

There was no one in the kitchen, but on the table there was a dark green bottle, its screw cap beside it on the checked cotton tablecloth, and only a measure or two of gin left.

Tentatively, Sylvia pushed at the door of Mrs Farmer's bedroom. The shiny satin counterpane and matching pillow slips were undented.

In Jennifer's childhood bedroom, the candlewick counterpane was straight and tidy. Dozens of dolls' eyes stared at Sylvia. Even though she was doing nothing wrong, she felt as if she was snooping.

In the long drawing room directly above the shop, heavy pink velvet curtains were drawn against the sun, but a slight draught from the open casement door made a slice of light on the dark carpet.

On the balcony, Jennifer was standing beside the parapet looking down at the street. Most of the shops were closed now, but there was still a small queue of children dragging coloured spades outside the window of Green's, waiting for an ice-cream cornet.

Jennifer took a swig from the glass she was holding and held the liquid in her mouth before swallowing it with a shudder.

'I've locked up,' Sylvia said quite loudly.

Jennifer turned sharply, as if woken from a dream. 'What are you doing up here?' she asked in a tone that made it sound as if Sylvia's place was downstairs.

'You didn't reply when I called up,' Sylvia faltered.

Jennifer stared at her, as if she didn't understand what she was saying.

'Are you all right?' Sylvia asked.

Jennifer's shoulders suddenly started heaving like a child's. Embarrassed, Sylvia ushered her back into the dark drawing room where no one would be able to see. 'Whatever's the matter?' she asked.

Sylvia stroked wisps of Jennifer's chestnut hair back from her wet cheeks and forehead. The pungent smell of gin was all around her like the petrol vapour that hung around the pumps outside the garage.

'Come on, blow your nose, dry your eyes and tell me all about it.'

The appropriate formulae of comfort sprang to her lips like nursery rhymes learned at an early age, the words of which stayed with you and could be recalled instantly, even though there were other far more important things you forgot.

Jennifer stopped crying abruptly and blew her nose on the clean white handkerchief Sylvia offered her from the pocket of her skirt. 'I'm pregnant again,' she whispered between sniffs.

Instantly, Sylvia felt guilty. Hadn't she been there when Jennifer was fitted with her diaphragm? Hadn't she told her to be sparing with the spermicidal cream?

'Jolly found the thing and threw it away,' Jennifer explained, to Sylvia's relief. 'I left the box in the bathroom by mistake. It looks so much like a powder compact. Terrible row . . .' She blew her nose again.

'Does he know?' Sylvia pointed to Jennifer's flat stomach.

Jennifer shook her head.

'But he'll be pleased, won't he?' said Sylvia.

'He will. It's just that I don't think I can bear . . .' Jennifer stammered. 'You don't know any way of . . . I thought gin was supposed to . . . ?'

'It's not as bad as all that, is it?' Sylvia asked.

Jennifer looked at her, the confessional shine of alcohol in her eyes. 'If you must know, I hate everything about my life,' she blurted. 'I hate that horrid little house, and I hate the bloody Kings, I hate my husband . . .'

It was the gin talking, Sylvia told herself. She was sure Jennifer didn't really hate her husband or the Kings. How could anyone hate the Kings? The Kings were what made the place special. They gave the place a bit of glamour. *Noblesse oblige*, or whatever it was that Michael always said.

Jennifer was really very spoilt. She'd married Jolly Allsop and one day she'd have the Castle and all that land. She couldn't just get out of her side of the bargain now. It was important for people like Jolly Allsop to have heirs.

'There has to be a bit of give and take in any marriage,' Sylvia said sagely.

'But it's all take with Jolly. You've no idea, none of you, what I have to put up with. Nobody does!' Jennifer started sobbing again.

Sylvia knew there were some things you couldn't speak about, even woman to woman, such as what went on behind closed doors.

The bar at the Yacht Club, which had originally been the harbour master's office, stuck out over the water and gave the impression of being on a liner at berth.

At a table by the window, Eddie King was discussing his friend Gerald Rackett's proposals for a new development at the Harbour End.

The problem, as far as Eddie could see, was that all the cottages would need to be knocked down. Some of them had sitting tenants whose families had lived there since time immemorial, before the Kings had ever purchased the land.

'Everyone has their price,' said Ratty.

His nickname had been coined by Libby because of his fondness for messing around in boats. At least, Eddie thought that was it, and not the fact that Ratty's wife had divorced him on several counts of adultery on their return from their voyage on the *Brittany Anna*.

Eddie watched a little boat laden with tourists chugging out of the harbour on a mackerel-fishing trip. Even on a calm day like this most of them would be sick as dogs when they returned. But at least on a boat you got a bit of a breeze. It was a sweltering afternoon.

'All you need to do is to come up with the readies,' said Ratty.

'Steady on!' said Eddie.

'Oh, come on, you must be raking it in up there this summer!' Ratty said, inclining his head in the direction of the Palace Hotel.

'It's a question of liquidity,' Eddie said, loosening his tie.

'Liquidity! A capital idea!' said Ratty, waving at the peroxide blonde with the hourglass figure who'd been a most welcome recent addition to the bar staff at the Yacht Club.

'Another couple of brandies?' she asked.

'You bet!' said Ratty. 'And whatever you're having, my darling.

On Mr King's account! So.' He turned back to Eddie. 'How's your liquidity now?'

Ratty must know that the decision wasn't really in his hands, Eddie thought. To all intents and purposes in recent years he had lived like a lord, but Liliana King owned the freehold of the Palace and its land, and although he was nominally a director of the limited company that ran his father-in-law's estate, there were no shares in his name. Any money he drew was carefully scrutinized by his wife, who'd become quite sharp at spotting accounting oversights.

'It's a matter of cash flow,' muttered Eddie, hoping Ratty would leave it there.

'You're not telling me you're broke!' Ratty exclaimed.

'Put a bung in it,' said Eddie, looking round the empty room.

'Nobody here!' said Ratty. 'Apart from the delightful Miss Monroe.' He pinched the barmaid's bottom as she placed the brandies down in front of them.

'Ooh, Mr Rackett!' she said, in the husky little-girl voice of the movie star she slightly resembled.

'She'd give me the seven-year itch any day,' said Ratty, watching the bottom shimmying back to the bar. 'Of course,' he added leaning across the table when the waitress was out of earshot, 'You don't always have to *pay* to get people to leave their homes. Sometimes they go of their own accord, so to speak.' He tapped the side of his nose, which was shiny with sweat and almost as deep a pink as the bottle of claret they'd just consumed.

'What are you getting at?' Eddie asked. His mind was a bit of a blur. Ratty appeared to be speaking in riddles. He couldn't remember whether Yacht Club rules prevented him from removing his jacket.

'Sometimes people move if they get a bad feeling about a place,' Ratty said in a very low voice. 'Like after the landslip . . . that cleared a few out, and not just the ones who were left without a home. Fire's another possibility, of course. Chip fat from the chippie catches one minute, the next thing you know, conflagration's spread over the Harbour End. Happened before, after all. The entire Harbour End was wiped out.'

'That was in the seventeenth century and most of the houses

were made of wood. Isn't it a bit unlikely? Lightning striking twice and all that . . . ?' said Eddie.

'Lightning. Ingenious! I hadn't even thought of that!'

Eddie was puzzled. 'You're not suggesting . . . ?' he said, slightly concerned.

'Far be it from me . . .' Ratty smiled, and then suddenly jumped out of his seat. 'What the hell's that?'

A microphone on a stick appeared just outside the window, and seemed to hover.

Eddie pushed back his chair and leaned out of the window.

In a rowing boat below, a man and a woman were standing holding the stick and trying to keep their balance at the same time.

'What the hell do you think you're doing?' Eddie shouted down.

'BBC!' the man shouted up.

'BBC?'

'We're recording the sounds of the harbour!'

'That lovely sort of chink chink chink!' the woman added.

'Well, record it somewhere else, damn you!' Eddie swiped at the microphone.

Attempting to whip the gun mike out of Eddie's range, the man in the boat began to sway.

There was a loud splash below.

'Should we chuck them a ring?' Ratty asked.

'Bugger that!' said Eddie. 'Ghastly people, the lot of them.'

There had been major changes in the staffing since the first occasion Claudia had helped out. Mrs Burns and her girls who had reigned in the kitchen had been replaced by an entirely male staff of chefs, sous-chefs and kitchen boys, all of whom came from the London area and lived in the old coach house which had been extended and converted into staff quarters. They were viewed with suspicion by the female staff who now ran the housekeeping and waitressing side of things, and came up each day like a group of Land Girls from the town. But both camps were united in their contempt for the other type of employee: the student. They continually sought to make a fool of Claudia by misleading her in the simplest of tasks, and she had lost count of the number of times she had heard a sentence that began, 'Students! Thought they were supposed to be clever . . .'

Mr Pocock, who ran the place like a benign general, had warned Claudia when he interviewed her for casual work in the long vacation, but even though she had precisely one day's experience in hotel work and he a lifetime, she had not really believed that people could behave so unreasonably.

After the first few days, Claudia had stopped even trying to make friends with her colleagues, and given herself up to a mind-less routine of making beds and cleaning baths which she found curiously restful after the intoxicating whirlwind of lectures and parties at Cambridge.

In this part of the world, where the pace of life was slow and attitudes unchanged since the previous century, Claudia some-times wondered whether she had made Cambridge up. Had she really stayed up all night arguing about the witch-hunt of Communists in America? Had she really played Puck on Midsummer Night in the magical shadows of medieval cloisters? Did flamboyant boys in brightly coloured waistcoats really smoke French cigarettes and declaim verse from high windows? Had she really gone to a May Ball wearing a borrowed dress, danced all night, and watched the sun rise from a punt gliding along the Backs in the misty morning? The passionate political arguments, the poetry readings, the hours of studying for exams that made her head so hot she had to wrap it in a damp towel were completely irrelevant here.

The smell of the evening meal wafted up from the kitchen. Lamb, she thought, wondering how anyone would be able to eat a roast in this heat, and then she remembered she had still to clear the lounge.

Several of the tables were covered with the debris of tea, the corners of sandwiches dry and curling, little pots of clotted cream melting to yellow oil in the heat. The Steinway piano on which Michael had taught her 'Chopsticks' had been moved in from the ballroom, she noticed, to make room for Ray Moore and his Orchestra, who were now rehearsing a lively version of 'In the Mood'.

The Palace was the last place Claudia had expected to see Michael. But it had been him, she was sure of it, lounging by the pool, chatting to Pearl King, of all people. Claudia was disconcerted by the feelings she still had for him. She had exhausted every imaginative resource she possessed to extract meaning from his brief goodbye letter, like an alchemist trying to extract gold from stone, and she had never grown accustomed to the thump of disappointment when there was no further envelope from him in her pigeonhole. These days, she did not even count the number of steps from her room to the lodge. She missed his descriptions of the sea and the seasons, the little bits of history of the area that fascinated him, the funny things the schoolchildren said, all details that made Kingshaven seem like a far more interesting place than it really was. She missed having a secret from the confident girls around her in college, most of whom had come up with the intention of falling in love and found her lack of interest in the opposite sex perplexing. She was still in love with Michael Quinn, faithful in body and soul.

The last place she wanted to bump into him was here, dressed as she was in a little white net hat and pinny.

When Libby went to find her mother for the dress rehearsal, Liliana was in her day room, wearing a gold brocade blouse over a floor-length black satin skirt.

'How do I look?' she asked.

'You always look lovely, Mummy,' said Libby automatically.

'What's wrong with it?' Liliana asked, because Libby wasn't very good at dissembling.

'It's just . . .' Libby searched for a diplomatic response. What with the heat and the BBC people, everyone seemed to be walking on hot coals this afternoon.

The gold wasn't very flattering in the harshness of daylight, and the off-the-shoulder neckline accentuated a crêpiness of skin around her mother's neck area, which she hadn't noticed before.

'Isn't it rather early in the day for evening dress?' she suggested.

'I thought it was a dress rehearsal.'

'Don't worry. It's not as if the world's going to see you,' said Libby, which seemed to make matters worse.

Liliana sucked in her breath and stared out of the window at the front entrance to the hotel.

'Who is that child?' she demanded, pointing suddenly.

Libby followed her mother's outstretched finger.

The little redhead who'd been playing with Angela this afternoon and her father were just leaving. The child jumped down the front steps beside her father, snatching her hand away as he tried to hold it. The chlorinated water had turned her curly hair into an unruly mop, which swung round every few seconds as she turned to wave at Pearl, who stood watching after them as they walked down the drive.

'I believe her name is Iris. Her father teaches at the school.'

'The school?' Liliana repeated.

'According to Jennifer, her mother's family owns a department store in the North of England.'

'The North of England? Whereabouts?'

'I've really no idea,' said Libby, wondering why her mother was so interested.

'A teacher, you say.' Liliana's eyes followed father and daughter down the gravel drive.

'Mr Turlow says he has rather modern ideas about discipline, but the pupils worship him.'

'Not just the pupils,' said Liliana curtly, watching as Pearl waved, heaved her shoulders in a great sigh, and reluctantly walked back into the hotel. 'Is it really appropriate for Pearl to be entertaining a married man on the premises?' she asked.

'Perhaps the child can come on her own next time,' Libby said.

'Redheads are often temperamental, you know.'

'In fairness, her manners are a great deal better than Angela's,' said Libby.

'What is the point of encouraging Angela to mix with town people when she'll be going off to school in a month or so?' asked Liliana.

It was simply too hot for all these questions. Usually Libby was grateful for her mother's guidance, but sometimes she overstepped the mark. On this particular afternoon she really couldn't be doing with Liliana nagging her, and Eddie staggering in from the Yacht Club stinking of brandy.

'We have to move with the times,' Libby said pointedly. 'Shoes on, Mummy. We're relying on you to start the dancing!'

'I don't know if I'm in the mood for dancing.' Liliana sat down at her desk as if she suddenly had urgent business to attend to.

'Don't be silly. Eddie will lead off with you. You're the best dancer and it really is all hands on deck for the BBC.'

She saw the glimmer of softening in her mother's face.

'I expect the Squadron Leader will want a turn,' Libby pressed on.

'If his new wife will allow it,' said Liliana sulkily.

In recent years, Libby had begun to think that the Squadron Leader's purpose in visiting Kingshaven had more to do with Liliana than the poor soul in the churchyard. Anyone watching him and Liliana playing a round of croquet could see there was an attraction between them. Liliana had always acted younger than her years. Nobody would have put her in her late fifties, Libby thought, especially when she wore something a little more forgiving in the neck area. But, to the surprise of everyone, this year the Squadron Leader had arrived with a little oriental woman who smiled a lot and said nothing at all.

'I can't imagine she's much of a dancer,' Libby said.

'Not a ballroom dancer, at any rate,' said Liliana tartly.

'She's so tiny, she'd have to stand on his feet like Angela does when Eddie's trying to teach her,' Libby added.

The image seemed to cheer Liliana up. 'She hangs on his arm like an umbrella,' she remarked.

'Oh, Mummy, that's unfair.' Libby paused, timing a rare moment of acerbic wit to perfection. 'She's much more like a paper parasol.'

Liliana rewarded her with a smile. Friendship was restored.

Which was just as well, Libby thought, wiping the perspiration from her forehead as she hurried back downstairs, because she was absolutely determined that nothing was going to spoil the day that the Palace appeared on the radio.

Sylvia was feeling as excited as a little girl dressing up for a party. It was ages since they'd been out, just the two of them, for the evening. It was one advantage, she'd have to point out to Michael, of having her mother staying to look after the children. The town was buzzing tonight, and although a part of her wanted to listen to the broadcast on the radio, it was much more special to be in it, if only as part of the crowd.

Sylvia stood on tiptoe so that she could see all of herself in the mirror over the basin in the bathroom. She had run up a sleeveless summer dress from the end of a roll of printed fabric Mrs Farmer had let her have for nothing. It was green and white check with an embroidered pattern of white daisies. It had turned out so well, she'd thought about offering it to one of the ladies she sewed for, but the colour suited her, and sometimes when a pattern fitted perfectly first time, you didn't want to start altering it.

'Mummy, where have you put my shoes?' she called downstairs.

Doreen, who did not yet have a vacuum cleaner of her own at home, insisted on using Sylvia's every day, but she tended to pile items which had been left on the floor on to other surfaces with a logic Sylvia did not yet understand.

'On top of the wardrobe in your room,' her mother called back up the stairs.

There were two boxes, one containing a number of toys the children had lost, the other assorted pairs of shoes among which Sylvia found the pair of pale tan slingbacks she was looking for. At the bottom of the box, there was a neat stack of paper.

Twenty pages, the product of Michael's painfully slow night-time typing. The top sheet read: *Chapter 1. The Beginning of the Affair.*

It had been easy not to read his exercise books. His hand-writing was so bad, it had crossed Sylvia's mind that he made it like that deliberately to prevent her.

Typed neatly, black on white, each word stabbed a fresh wound.

She had to keep reminding herself that his affair was not happening again, he was simply describing it, but there was a horrible kind of fascination as she read the answers to questions which had tormented her. Like how he'd actually started it in the first place – the Labour Club; she might have known.

The town wasn't called Etherington in the novel, and the man wasn't called Michael and the woman wasn't called Rachel, but

Sylvia somehow knew that he couldn't have invented the emotions. This must have been how he felt.

When the typing suddenly stopped at the bottom of a page and there was no more for her to read, she was filled with curious disappointment, but the desolation was as bleak as the day she had confronted him with her suspicions. He'd denied having an affair at first and she'd been so prepared to believe him that she'd felt foolish and suspicious. But then he'd heaved the most enormous sigh, and told her it was true, and she'd wanted to say, No, it's all right, I believed you, and I'm sorry I brought it up. Let's just go back to how it was a minute ago.

When he left the house, Sylvia thought he'd gone to the woman, and she'd never see him again. She'd made the mistake of telling her mother. But then he'd come back the next day and asked to try again. Not likely, her mother had said at the door, but he'd pushed past her and grabbed Sylvia, and they'd gone for a long walk by the canal together. Her memory of it was all watery. It was raining, and she'd left the house without her raincoat, and then he'd cried. She and Iris were his only family, he'd said. And she'd felt so sorry for him, and found she loved him just as much as before she knew, except that she felt even more unworthy of him, somehow.

They never talked about it any more and she'd thought that they'd both done their best to put it behind them. There were whole days now when she didn't think about it even once! But it had clearly never left his mind.

As they stopped to cross Hill Road, Michael dropped his hand to his side, but Iris did not take it as she usually did.

'Why did you say we weren't hungry?' Iris asked. 'I'm half starved!'

'We'll be home soon enough,' he told her.

'Why do you say I shouldn't tell lies, when you're always telling them?'

He was very hot and his mind was still blurry from the squawks and screeches of children playing around the swimming pool.

'Next time, I shall have tea, with jam and cake and clotted cream and everything,' Iris went on defiantly.

'*If* you go again.'

'Auntie Pearl says I can go whenever I want,' said Iris.

'You're not to call her that,' Michael said firmly.

'That's what Angela calls her,' protested Iris.

'I don't give a damn what Angela calls her.'

Iris was so shocked by the harshness of his voice, she was quiet for a few hundred yards.

'Why do I have to sleep in the same room as Granny?' she said as they turned into the long road of houses just like theirs, each with a garden path, a neatly clipped front lawn, and an ornamental cherry sapling on the green verge between pavement and road, which bent like a reed when there was any wind.

'There isn't a bedroom for her,' Michael replied.

'Why can't she sleep in Anthony's room?'

'Because your room is bigger.'

'I'd rather have a smaller room and no Granny sleeping there,' said Iris grumpily.

This brought a smile to his face.

'She snores,' said Iris, encouraged. She did a loud impression which sounded much more pig-like and exaggerated than the grunts he had heard emanating from the back room, but he didn't bother to correct her.

'She'll be gone soon enough,' he said.

'Why does she have to be here, anyway?'

'Because she's helping Mummy in the house while Mummy's at the shop.'

'Why can't you help Mummy in the house?' Iris demanded.

It simply hadn't occurred to him to offer this alternative solution when Sylvia had presented him with her proposal that her mother, who had been longing to visit her grandchildren, might come to help out over the summer.

'It wouldn't kill you to lend a hand, you know,' said Iris.

Michael forgave her because he knew the words were not hers, and braced himself as they walked up the front path.

The first thing he noticed when his wife opened the door was that she was wearing a lime-green dress he hadn't seen before; the second was that she had been crying.

'Mummy, we had such a super time!' Iris said.

In one afternoon, she had learned a new vocabulary.

'Go and play in the garden,' Sylvia told her.

'I should think you'd be ashamed of leaving that filth lying around,' Doreen declared as Iris stamped off.

At first, he assumed that his mother-in-law was talking about the novel *Lolita*. It was only when she flapped typed pages in front of his face that he realized she was talking about his work.

'That wasn't lying around,' he protested. 'It was in a box on top of the wardrobe in our room.'

He saw Sylvia look at her mother. She was holding Anthony's hand. The child was looking from his father to his grandmother like a spectator at a tennis match.

'I needed the box for the shoes,' Doreen explained.

'And you thought you'd have a good look through my private papers while you were about it?' Michael said.

'There was nothing to say they were private,' said Doreen. 'I'm glad I did,' she went on the attack again. 'As if it's not bad enough to do the things you did, without telling the world all about it.'

'You don't know what you're talking about,' said Michael, turning his back on her.

'I know enough,' she said.

'No you don't.' He spun round. 'You wouldn't recognize literature if it walked up and introduced itself.'

'Literature, is it? Filthy lies is what I call it.'

'One minute it's real, the next it's lies. Make up your mind.'

'Don't you talk to me like that.'

'I'll talk to you how I want in my own house,' he said.

'Michael,' Sylvia pleaded.

'I'm not the one who carried on with a married woman—' said Doreen.

'Mummy!' said Sylvia, nodding at Anthony.

'Syl?'

'It was just a shock, seeing it all in black and white . . .' Sylvia faltered. 'When I saved and saved to buy you that typewriter.'

'It's fiction,' he appealed to her. 'It's a work of imagination.'

'But why do you have to imagine things like that?' asked Sylvia.

'If it's fiction, why don't you want anyone to read it?' Doreen intervened triumphantly.

'Mummy, please,' said Sylvia.

'Because it's not finished!' Michael shouted.

'If you made it all up,' – Doreen put down her trump card – 'why does the mother-in-law have a collection of porcelain figurines?'

Sylvia cupped her hand over Anthony's eyes, as if she half expected her husband to hit her mother. There was a moment of hot, tense silence. Then, suddenly, Michael threw back his head and laughed.

'You're quite right, Doreen. Nobody could invent anyone quite as awful as you,' he said.

His mother-in-law glared at him and then dissolved into histrionic tears.

'Don't talk to my mother like that,' said Sylvia, going to comfort her.

'Syl . . .' Michael couldn't bear to see her falling for it.

The two women stood staring at him with big teary eyes, excluding him from his own living room, and then Anthony started crying too.

'Just get out,' said Doreen.

The only compensation for the awfulness of being unrequited in love was that it made you slim, Pearl thought as she walked along the pier. The white cotton cocktail dress with its tiny black velvet straps and stiffened fitted bodice simply would not have been possible the previous summer. White was not a colour she ever thought of, but Sylvia assured her that men generally preferred women in the paler shades, an opinion which seemed to be borne out this evening when Pearl had appeared in the ballroom. Eddie had sidled up to her and asked her why she was dressed for bed, his lowered voice and the appreciative leer making it plain that this was intended as a compliment.

Stiletto heels, in spite of all the danger stories about broken ankles and hammer toes which Libby read out loud from the newspaper at breakfast time, gave Pearl that little extra height that made men stare at her and women frown as she sauntered past.

Pearl paused to lean against the railing. Although the sun was going down, the beach was still swarming with people. There were large groups of youngsters, factory workers from the North, she imagined, larking around. Occasionally a boy would break away and gallop over the sand howling like Tarzan, then his friends would follow, dragging reluctant girlfriends by the hand, or picking them up and carrying them like squealing, kicking sacks of coal into the gentle waves.

On the promenade, a crowd had gathered around a West Indian man who was lying almost horizontal in a deckchair, a pork-pie hat tilted over his forehead, strumming calypso on a guitar. A couple of his compatriots, a tall man in a suit much too big for him and a woman in a tight shiny red dress which accentuated her firm, rounded contours, were dancing sinuously together. Such explicit display would never normally have been tolerated in Kingshaven, and yet the faces of the spectators were smiling, as the balmy evening air and the lilting nostalgia of the tune cast their spell.

Pearl wandered on, swinging her handbag, closing her eyes to let a whisper of salt breeze refresh her face.

Was life always slow and evenings always sweet in faraway lands where the sun always shone? Could happiness be as simple as a curve of tropical beach and nothing to do but lie down? If this *were* the answer to life, why were all these coloured people leaving their tropical homes to take jobs as bus conductors in rainy old London?

The spike of Pearl's heel caught in the gap between the wooden boards, and without being able to do anything about it, the forward momentum cast her down on to hands and knees with a sudden humiliating bump.

Lucky that she wasn't wearing nylons, Pearl thought as she brushed her palms. There was no visible damage to her knee.

'Are you all right?'

A man she half recognized was offering his hand to help her up. His teeth, she noticed when he smiled, were slightly too big for his mouth, but he was handsome, in a smart, conventional sort of way, and she was slightly disappointed to find when he pulled her to her feet that he was not very much taller than she was. She shook out the tiers of her skirt.

'Tom Snow,' he said. 'I've been watching you daydreaming.'

A good voice, well-spoken.

'Oh, I wasn't aware . . .' she said.

'I wouldn't be very good at my job if you were,' he said.

Belatedly noticing the camera that hung around his neck, she placed him as the photographer from the *Chronicle* who'd been to a couple of the hotel's functions. She had seen him round town during the summer, taking pictures of the holidaymakers who'd pay for him to send prints. She'd always wondered how he knew which name and address went with which snap. Did he make little notes – *Fat man with cap and wife with varicose veins* – to remind him?

'Pearl King,' she said, taking his proffered hand.

He smiled. 'I know.'

She took her hand back. It went automatically to her hair. Ought she to feel offended or excited by the idea of being secretly photographed?

'Don't worry. Too dark now.' He laughed. 'Perhaps another time?'

'Perhaps,' Pearl replied cautiously.

'I'd love to have you in my portfolio.'

The way he said it sounded a bit risqué.

'I'll see you around, then,' he said.

'But I won't see you,' she countered, beginning to enjoy the game.

'Unless I reveal myself to you,' he replied, almost suggestively.

She was about to reply in the same bantering manner when, through a gap in the wrought-iron shelter that ran down the centre of the boardwalk, she caught sight of Michael walking towards the skiffle band playing at the end of the pier. He had a dark expression on his face. And he was alone.

'See you later, alligator!' she bid the photographer a hasty farewell.

'In a while, crocodile,' he called after her as she set off, taking little tiptoeing steps so as not to get caught by the boards again.

'Here's one of the numbers we recorded earlier,' Ivor announced, 'for the BBC.'

A cheer went up from the little crowd gathered at the semi-circular bit at the end of the pier beyond the theatre, which had been destroyed during the war in case of an invasion and recently rebuilt with a large donation from the Yacht Club committee.

The bass player, whose instrument was made of a tea chest, a broomhandle, and a parachute cord, plucked the rhythm. Peter Ironside, the station master's older son, was playing clarinet, still dressed in the maroon trousers of his military band uniform with a gold stripe up the side of the leg. The jacket and cap were piled on to a deckchair; his white shirtsleeves were rolled up.

'Shake, rattle and roll,' sang Ivor. His guitar was slung on a strap, his quiff slicked back with Brylcreem. He smiled at another lad scraping the rhythm on a washboard.

Two of the girls in the crowd began to dance a jitterbug with one another.

Michael took off his jacket and slung it over his shoulder, loosened his collar, removed his tie and shoved it into his trouser pocket. Sylvia would have a fit.

'Shake, rattle and roll,' said Ivor, in a deep voice at the end of the song, his right hand trailing through the final chord on his guitar.

As the band struck up another tune, Michael felt a light, tentative touch on his sleeve from behind.

'Hello, again,' whispered Pearl King.

'I thought there was dancing at the hotel?' Michael said abruptly.

'There's a bit of a storm brewing,' Pearl whispered confidentially. 'Apparently the BBC have got so much recorded, they're thinking of doing without the ballroom dancing. You can imagine the negotiations. My sister was expecting a full fifteen minutes. So, I find myself all dressed up and nowhere to go.' She ran her hands down the sides of her dress as if expecting a compliment.

She looked, he thought, like a courtesan who hadn't bothered to put on a frock over her petticoat. But he didn't think he would tell her that. He raked his hair back from his face.

'Where's Sylvia?' Pearl enquired.

'Sylvia and her mother are listening to the broadcast at home,' he said.

'I expect most people will be,' said Pearl as the crowd began to disperse around them. 'But it's a shame to be indoors on a night like this.'

She waved a hand just at the moment the string of fairy lights above their heads came on, and it almost seemed as if her gesture had illuminated the length of the pier with multicoloured bulbs.

'How did you manage that?' Michael asked.

'It's a talent I have,' she replied, laughing.

He looked at her, right at her, as he never had before, and grinned.

They began to walk back down the pier side by side, neither of them in any hurry.

'Do you have a beach hut?' she asked casually as they turned along the promenade in the direction of the clock tower. Most of the crowds had gone back to their boarding houses and caravans, or to the station, sore with sunburn as they struggled with windbreaks and picnic baskets to catch the last train back to Lowhampton.

'No,' he said. And then, remembering his manners, 'Do you?'

'The hotel owns all of those over there.' She pointed at the block of white huts at the far end of the promenade, below the North Cliffs.

Inside, it was warm and steamy, like a garden shed, and his forehead broke sweat instantly. Pearl fumbled for matches and lit a candle in the glass lantern which hung from a hook in the eaves.

'Deceptively spacious,' she said, as if she was showing a property to a potential tenant. She pointed out the row of cup hooks, the folded canvas chairs, a calor-gas bottle with a cooking ring attached.

From the moment he had chosen to walk with her along the dark stretch of the promenade where the illuminations ended, instead of going home, he had known what would happen. The hot musky scent of her was beginning to permeate the hut, overlaying the distinctive seaside bouquet of wood preserver, sun oil and damp towels.

In the ballroom of the Palace Hotel a hundred yards above them, Cliff Michelmore's voice was saying, 'And so, from Kingshaven, we bid you goodnight. Take it away, maestro.'

The mellow sound of Ray Moore and his Orchestra drifted through the open French windows, over the terrace, past the pool and down the private steps to the row of white beach huts beside the phosphorescent sea.

In the flicker of candlelight, in her little white dress with its tiered frills, Pearl's face was endearingly uncertain as they stood looking at each other.

'Would you like to dance?' Michael found himself asking.

She stepped closer to him, taking his right hand, letting his left hand touch her waist in a chaste and formal clasp. They danced round and round on the spot, smiling at each other, their bodies drawing closer with each turn.

And then the tune that they had heard a hundred versions of that day as if rehearsing for this moment: 'Spanish Eyes'.

'I . . .' Pearl King started to say something, but he pressed the tip of his finger to her lips.

And then he dropped his mouth to hers and kissed her. As he closed his eyes he saw Sylvia and her mother staring reproachfully at him, so he allowed them to open, to look at the simple, gorgeous sight of a woman who wanted him.

He had been so long without the soft, melting curves, the taste of lips that kissed him back, the energetic abandoning of clothes, the willingness to give and receive pleasure. The reckless joy of it bubbled up inside him like champagne, but he held himself back by logging each glorious sensation in his consciousness, so that he would remember when he came to write it down.

Chapter Six

April 1958

On a sunny day, when visitors were flocking into Kingshaven, no one would particularly notice a person heading towards the station, but it was raining, and Michael was aware that his progress was being watched by small observers trapped inside. Curious voices, fed up after just one morning of the school holidays, were bound to be asking, 'Where's Sir going? Why d'you think he's got a rucksack?'

And for a few moments speculation would alleviate the boredom of racing rivulets of rain down the windows.

A bright poster on the front wall of the station read, 'Kingshaven! A Sunny Welcome Awaits!'

Water cascaded from the scalloped canopy. Michael's hair was plastered to his forehead and cold drips of rain ran down behind his collar as he stood at the ticket office.

'Return to London, please.'

'Must be something important to brave this weather,' Stanley Ironside commented cheerily.

Warm fumes from the paraffin heater drifted out of the hatch.

'First, second or third?' Stanley asked.

'Third.'

A tight bud of guilt bloomed as Michael handed over a pound note and coins. Even in third, the fare was more than they could afford when there were shoes to buy for the children. Iris's feet seemed to grow a size each term, and none of them could be passed on to Anthony because his feet were wider and Sylvia said he'd end up with hammer toes if they tried to force them, a prognosis Michael privately questioned, given that he hadn't owned a pair of new shoes until he earned his own money. He'd had to wear Frank's cast-offs whether they squeezed his toes or not. Even after Frank died, Michael thought ruefully, his shoes had been passed on. A pair of handmade shiny black lace-ups, with leather soles, which had never been worn outside, had come back along with Frank's demob suit, shirt, two collars, two pairs of socks, and hat.

Occasionally Michael would take them out of their stiff cardboard box, which bore the name of a Bond Street shop, slide his hands into the cavity where Frank's feet had tried them on, and wonder what on earth must have been going through his brother's head as he handed over a small fortune for this last purchase. Sometimes the thought made Michael smile, recalling how careful Frank had always been about his appearance. With a tea towel tucked into the collar of his starched white shirt to prevent spatters, Frank had polished and buffed his shoes with an array of brushes lined up on the back doorstep, and checked the smoothness of his shave and the flatness of his hair in the mantel mirror before he went out dancing. Sometimes simply touching the velvety nap of the beige leather lining, just a sock away from his brother's skin, made Michael choke with grief.

'London Waterloo!' The station master smiled at Michael expectantly, as if an explanation was required before he would hand over the ticket.

Mr Ironside was only trying to be friendly, Michael realized, and he had aroused his suspicion far more by his silence than if he had obliged with a brief exchange of pleasantries.

'He caught the seven-fifteen,' Michael could imagine Stanley saying later that day, like a witness for the prosecution at the bar of the Railway Arms. 'I'd say his demeanour was somewhat shifty.'

Half a mile down the track, as they began to pick up speed through the rain-drenched valley, Michael was liberated by a feeling of exhilaration he remembered from summers before the war, when his parents had packed him off to Etherington, a luggage label with his name and destination round his neck. Freedom beckoned, and the prospect of throwing off the history which defined him. In his family, Michael had always been characterized as the quiet one, the moody one, the altogether-less-easy one than his golden brother Frank. But at his Auntie Jean's house, he could become the clever one, the polite one, and, when the war came, even the charming one, who looked mature enough to escort Jean and her younger sister Rita to the dance hall, and, just as importantly, knew when to slip off home on his own.

This was why people went on holiday, Michael thought as the train whistled across the viaduct, not just to go somewhere different, but to be someone else.

He stood up and attempted to manoeuvre his rucksack on to the overhead luggage rack, but it was packed with awkward, rigid shapes. In a square biscuit tin with a scuffed reproduction of Constable's 'Hay Wain' on the lid, Michael discovered a dozen sausage rolls. A round tin, which had originally contained Quality Street, was filled with squares of gingerbread. Sylvia had cut a whole loaf of sandwiches. Those with cheese and pickled onion were wrapped in a separate sheet of greaseproof paper from those with blackcurrant jam. There was a large Thermos flask of tea.

Michael felt a bit guilty about Sylvia providing so well for him when she disapproved of what he was doing. He unscrewed the cup from the top of the Thermos. The tea was too hot to drink straightaway. He held the cup in both hands, sniffing the steam, staring out of the window as the train thundered through swathes of green countryside, past signal boxes and villages whose names sped by too quickly for him to read.

'People here won't understand,' Sylvia had said when he'd told her he intended to go on the Campaign for Nuclear Disarmament march.

'I'll not tell anyone, if that's what's bothering you,' he had offered, joking, though it grieved him that she was more concerned about what the neighbours might make of his subversive views than that the world might be blown to smithereens.

'I don't know how to tell you this,' Josie said to Claudia at breakfast in college.

'You're not coming?' Claudia guessed.

'Not my decision,' Josie confessed. 'I made the mistake of mentioning it to my father. He won't have me protesting against the US of A. Not in someone else's country.'

Claudia couldn't believe what she was hearing. 'It's not against America. It's against the proliferation of nuclear weapons!' She stirred her bowl of porridge to make it cool down quicker.

'I didn't think you'd let me get away with it,' said Josie.

'What about not bowing down in the face of patriarchal institutions?' Claudia continued, quoting a phrase Josie often used.

'I figure the patriarchal institutions will suffer more by financing my post-graduate studies . . .' Josie faltered. 'No, I can see that doesn't do it either. Look, I'm sorry.'

'There are plenty of other people,' said Claudia, surprised by a sudden welling of anger.

This was surely the battle of their generation, just as fighting fascism had been the battle of their parents' generation. Unless right-minded people joined together to throw out this new man-made evil, then it would destroy the entire human race. Nevertheless, the prospect of three nights on the road without Josie's lively company was a good deal less appealing than it would have been with her there.

'Don't go, then,' Tim said when she bumped into him outside his college lodge. He was dressed in full rowing kit, just about to leave for the river. The rest of the college boat whistled as he stopped to talk to her. He waved them on.

'Of course I'm going,' Claudia said hotly. 'I'm secretary to the university CND Group. I was the one who booked the coach. I can hardly not go.'

'I say,' Tim suggested suddenly, 'can I come instead of Josie? It'll be fun!'

It's not supposed to be fun, Claudia almost said, but stopped herself. There was no reason why protesting shouldn't be fun as well as having serious intent, was there? It just didn't seem an appropriate word to use.

'I'm told it's the battle of our generation,' Tim added with a wink.

He treated politics with a blasé indifference typical of most of the male students who had been to public school. Claudia wondered what his father, originally a refugee from Poland, made of this. Did he despair of his son's expensive education, or was he secretly relieved at his assimilation into English society?

'Where is bloody Aldermaston anyway?' Tim asked.

She was about to explain the route of the march, when she saw that he was teasing her.

'Give me a few minutes to change,' said Tim.

'I think it may take much longer than that,' Claudia said under her breath as he disappeared through the little door which was cut into the huge oak door of his college.

As the train approached London, Michael saw that the urban landscape was still pocked with scars the bombs had inflicted and nature had sought to heal with waving pink rosebay willowherb. There were people waiting for stopping trains on suburban platforms: individuals with newspapers who stood at a certain distance from one another, unaware of their fellow passengers. In a city, you could be anonymous in the crowds. It was a kind of solitude Michael missed.

Once inside the cavernous station, he sniffed the air. The sharp wet smell of soot and sour disinfectant was refreshing after the stale-carpet air of the compartment.

It was his first time in London.

The Thames was much wider than he had expected. The gleaming span of the Waterloo Bridge must be almost a mile across, and the view each side was astonishing. The landmarks were so startlingly familiar they almost looked artificial, like stage sets. Big Ben, the Houses of Parliament and, in the distance, to his right, the dome of St Paul's Cathedral. On the south bank, the modern lines of the Festival Hall, and the acres of wasteground where the Festival of Britain had been. The water was high and bulging; the great river was throbbing with boats and barges.

Trafalgar Square was exactly as it appeared on newsreels except that it was in colour: the classical columns of the National Gallery were grey, but the double-decker buses skirting the perimeter were red. It was swarming with people like him, people with shabby overcoats, rucksacks and banners, all buzzing with the excitement of common purpose, creating such a noise he couldn't hear what the man addressing the crowd from a podium was saying.

'Who's that?' he asked a man with glasses standing next to him.

'Bertrand Russell,' the man told him in a posh, supercilious accent which made Michael suddenly as nervous as a new boy on his first day in the school playground. Would anyone talk to him? Would he have to march alone?

And then behind him, a voice he had not heard for a very long time said, 'Hello, stranger!'

Six years was a long time in a woman of Rachel's age. The voice, husky with years of cigarette smoke, was the same, and it was the same smile, but the little wispy bits of hair that had escaped the chignon she always wore were grey and brittle, not the rich silky brown it had been when Michael last saw her.

He didn't think he disguised his shock at her appearance very well.

'I thought we'd see you here,' she said.

'It hadn't occurred to me . . .' he said.

'The Labour Club goes on without you, you know,' she teased, pointing at a group of men and one young woman in a duffel coat standing just a few yards away under a banner with Etherington painted on it. A couple of the men waved at him. They were organizing themselves into lines of six.

'On your own?' she asked.

Michael nodded.

'Why don't you walk with us?' Rachel offered. 'Back to the fold!' She smiled with a directness that made him look away.

'Who's the girl?' Michael asked.

'My daughter. You remember Clare?'

'She's grown up,' said Michael stupidly. She must have been about nine when he last saw her. Only a year or two older than Iris now. She'd grown up quite attractive, with long chestnut hair like her mother's used to be, which she kept flipping back off her coat.

'Hands off,' said Rachel. 'She's sixteen.'

143

'I wouldn't dream . . .'

'Wouldn't you?' Rachel asked.

The same direct look.

'George not with you?' Michael asked, casually.

'George's at home with our son, who's a bit young yet for marching.' Rachel looked away as an announcement over a loudspeaker stated that the march was moving off.

'I've a son too,' said Michael, falling into step beside her. 'Anthony.'

'We called ours Clem,' said Rachel.

'Good name,' he said. Typical of Rachel to wear her politics on her sleeve.

Someone a few rows behind them began to beat time on a drum.

A cry of 'Yankee bases out!' went up.

The drumbeat took up the rhythm. Quaver, quaver, crochet.

'Yankee bases out!' Michael shouted in unison with Rachel.

'Yankee bases out, out, out!'

A few rows behind them, a brass band started to play 'When the Saints Come Marching In'.

Michael couldn't seem to stop his face from smiling.

'I've missed this,' he said, extending his hand towards Rachel's.

'It's political, not personal,' she said, ignoring his hand and opening a large black umbrella on which she'd painted a white CND sign. 'But you can come under, if you like.'

'No, I'm all right,' he said, pulling up his collar and walking stoically in the drizzle.

'Oh, don't be so daft,' Rachel said, taking his arm and pulling him in with her.

The first time he'd seen her at the Labour Club, she was like no woman he'd met before. Strong, funny, unwilling to hide her intelligence. They'd hit it off straightaway – a similar sardonic sense of humour, an undercurrent of attraction despite a good fifteen years difference in age. He hadn't known whose wife she was.

He and Sylvia were only just married at the time, living with her parents, occasionally having sex silently on the living-room floor as the white dot in the centre of the television faded to grey, because their bedroom was next door to Sylvia's parents', and Sylvia tensed every time the house creaked in case her mother was listening.

Ironically, the person Michael had probably loved most at the time was George, the headmaster of the school where he was doing his probationary year. George was the teacher he'd never had, and the father, and the friend – a fine, decent, good man. George's passion for education extended beyond the children he taught. He lent Michael books, invited him back to his house to listen to opera, and introduced him to his wife.

Sitting next to Rachel on a broken-down sofa, with *Così fan tutte* on the gramophone, sipping gin from an unwashed tumbler which still bore the imprint of her lipstick – their house was the very opposite of Sylvia's parents': newspapers all over the floor, brimming ashtrays, opened packets of biscuits left to go soggy in the air – the attraction had swelled from an inconsequential flirtation to a desire so urgent, Michael had to put all his concentration into thinking down his erection before he could find words to express his appreciation of the Mozart at the end of the aria.

'Beautiful,' he'd managed.

'And tremendously sexy, don't you think?' George had said.

George and Rachel used words that were banned in any home he'd lived in.

When he'd thought about his betrayal, afterwards, Michael wondered whether it was sheer admiration and the desire to emulate everything about George which had extended to bedding his wife.

'How's your new life turned out, then?' Rachel asked beneath the little dome of privacy the umbrella gave them.

'I can hear seagulls when I wake up in the morning. The sea is never the same colour twice . . .'

She waited for him to go on.

'Full of bloody Tories, though,' he said.

Which made her laugh.

'I thought you looked desperate,' she said.

He raised his eyebrows, alarmed.

'For a bit of socialism,' she said. 'Sylvia's not interested, then?'

'She's looking after the children,' he said defensively, echoing the way she'd described her husband. 'Sylvia's not interested in politics,' he added.

'That's what Tories always say,' said Rachel.

He remembered George warning him the evening of the Mozart: 'You have to watch my wife. She can change from pussy cat to tiger in an instant . . .' and Rachel smiling, as if he'd paid her a particularly wonderful compliment.

Had George seen what was happening? Had he known all along?

'And the school?' Rachel was asking.

'It's a small place. Somewhere I can make a difference.'

'Congratulations,' she said, mocking his self-importance.

He shoved her arm, playfully. She shoved him back. And for a moment, her happy face looked ageless.

Her daughter, two down on the other side of Rachel, noticed and looked away.

In the beam of the girl's disapproval, Michael wondered whether Sylvia had guessed at the likelihood of Rachel's presence on the march, and whether this had been the real reason for her opposition. Women were better at such conjecture.

Pearl dragged the back of her hand all the way up the keys of the Steinway to the top, bell-like notes, paused a moment, then ran it all the way back down to the lowest, portentous A.

'Are we in tune today?' asked Mr Pocock, coming into the lounge. He walked with small steps, his eyes alert for any imperfection. Mr Pocock could spot a flake of peeling paint or a ghostly loop of cobweb at a hundred paces.

'I couldn't say,' said Pearl.

'Pity we're not played more often,' he remarked.

Mr Pocock talked about most things in the first person plural. It was a way of speaking Pearl had found herself slipping into on occasion.

'A great shame,' she agreed.

'Have you ever considered taking lessons yourself?' the deputy manager asked her as he walked soundlessly across the lounge with its armchairs from the 1930s, which were next in line to be replaced with a much more up-to-date look.

'I don't seem to be very good at learning lessons,' Pearl told him with a sigh.

Even the rats in those experiments which they were always showing on television showed more intelligence, she thought. Rats soon seemed to get the idea that if they went down one particular route they got an electric shock, and so avoided it, whereas she didn't seem to be able to stop doing the wrong thing however much pain it caused her.

Pearl wondered if Mr Pocock knew. Probably. He knew every-thing that went on in the hotel, but Mr Pocock's second name was Discretion. ('How appropriate!' Libby had exclaimed the first time he'd made the remark, when Mr Rackett was arrested, as if she didn't realize it was just a way of saying things.)

At least rats were given choices in the mazes they ran around, Pearl thought, whereas she didn't appear to have a choice. She could tell herself a million times that it must stop, but as soon as she saw Michael the compulsion was as unavoidable as the com-pulsion to smoke a cigarette when she hadn't had one for a few hours.

Cigarettes were an addiction. They had done some experi-ments with rats in America to prove it.

Was it possible to become addicted to a man, Pearl wondered, and what sort of experiment might the scientists dream up to prove that?

There were still three whole days to go before there was even the chance of seeing him and he wouldn't tell her why he was going away.

Was it a funeral? Pearl had asked him.

'No.'

Visiting an infirm relative?

'I have no relatives,' he had told her.

A ball?

That, at least, had made him smile. 'No, I'm not going to a ball.'

Another woman, then?

'You'd hardly be in a position to object,' he teased.

'Or care,' she retaliated, because she knew that the only hope she had of keeping him was to affect as little interest in him as he did in her, even though they both knew that they were dying for each other.

No, it wasn't another woman, he said, but he still wouldn't tell her. He doubted she'd understand.

When she'd tried to slap him in frustration, he'd caught her wrist and grasped it so tightly that his grip had scorched a mark on the delicate skin above her pulse. It was as if he had given her a bracelet to remember their passion, Pearl thought, touching the tender weal gently.

Pearl stabbed randomly at two of the white piano keys, sounding a disharmonious chord. Sometimes Pearl wished Sylvia would just die. Then Michael would need her. She would be kind to his children. She could teach them how to play tennis. They could swim in the hotel pool. And everyone would say what a marvellous stepmother she was.

Ridiculous!

In her clean little box of a house, a few hundred yards away, Sylvia Quinn, with her perfect complexion and her shining fair hair, was in radiantly good health, like a wife in a television commercial. She wasn't about to die, unless she met with a terrible accident. And, oddly enough, Pearl quite liked Sylvia. She suspected that there was a sharper brain behind the pearly smile than the flow of clichés would indicate. Sylvia was terribly clever at copying the latest fashions and could turn perfectly ordinary fabric into haute couture. Pearl had noticed she was rather adept at copying people too. Sylvia had almost completely lost the short Northern vowels which Michael still retained, and, once learned, she never forgot the little lapses of etiquette that gave her away, like adding milk to tea, instead of tea to milk.

In other circumstances, they might have been friends.

'Ow!' Iris protested as the sharp point of a pin nicked her neck.

'Don't be such a baby,' said Sylvia.

'What is it supposed to be?' Iris asked, standing on a chair to see her reflection in the oval mirror over the sideboard.

'It's a surprise,' said Sylvia with an infuriating little smile.

Sometimes her mother behaved just like one of the big girls at school with their stupid secrets which never turned out to be very interesting anyway. The worst thing was when one of her ladies came round for a fitting: the way they giggled together and whispered and stared at you if you walked into the room, and made you feel horrible.

'Why doesn't Anthony have to wear a stupid bonnet?' Iris asked.

'Boys don't wear bonnets.'

'Angela's seen a *man* wearing a dress, so there!'

'You don't want to believe everything Angela says.'

Her mother couldn't seem to make up her mind whether Angela ought to be her best friend or not. Some days it was 'Angela this, Angela that'; others, it was 'Angela King knows a bit too much for her own good, if you ask me.'

Not that anyone ever did ask her.

'Perhaps I should make something for Anthony,' her mother was saying. 'There's enough of this fabric.'

'Christopher King is dressing up as well as Angela,' Iris told her.

'What as?'

Iris was about to reveal, but she saw the eagerness on her mother's face.

'It's a surprise,' she said, getting her own back.

'You little . . . Take it off then.'

Iris gingerly took the hat off her head.

'Get a move on!' Her mother snatched it from her.

'You did that deliberately,' said Iris, looking at the little line of blood bubbles oozing from a scratch on her cheek from the pins. 'I'm going to tell Daddy.'

'Daddy's not here, is he?' said her mother.

Iris didn't dare ask when he was coming back, because she was half beginning to suspect that the answer would be that he wasn't coming back, ever.

'Go to bed, now,' her mother said with the look that meant a slap on the back of the legs if she didn't get up the stairs quickly.

Iris chewed the end of her pencil considering what to write in her diary.

'Daddy still gone. Mummy horrible as usual. Today she

stabbed me with pins. One day I will run away for ever. Mince and carrots for tea.'

She shoved the diary back under her mattress, where she kept it except on Mondays, when her mother took the sheets off to wash.

The library book Iris was reading was about a family of children who had been orphaned. They found a barn to live in, and cooked delicious food in a hay oven, whatever that was. Iris was dying to try it herself when the summer came. She was sure she could find a barn on one of her walks with Daddy.

If he came back.

If he didn't come back, Iris thought, she would be virtually an orphan herself. She turned over and buried her face in her pillow.

Secretly, she often imagined what it would be like to be an orphan, devising various deaths for her parents. Her mother usually drowned. Her father sometimes died fighting a dinosaur which had crawled out of the rock pools beneath the South Cliffs and threatened the town with its thundering footsteps and fiery breath. Other times he caught consumption, which was an illness writers often had, and after he was dead, the stories he wrote became famous and everyone hailed him as a genius, like Vincent Van Gogh, the artist in the film showing at the Regal called *Lust for Life* which only grown-ups were allowed to see.

Her brother usually died alongside her mother, but sometimes Iris let him survive. It would be quite useful to have him around because people tended to like Anthony. With his blond hair and his good manners, he was the sort of child who might attract a rich and kindly benefactor, like Pip in *Great Expectations*, which Daddy was reading her.

Iris closed her eyes and listened to the regular bumpity trundle of her mother's sewing machine, trying to ignore the nagging worry that by thinking about being orphaned she might have made it happen.

Where was Daddy?

Was he thinking about her too?

*

Rachel's eyes were closed, but Michael couldn't tell whether she was sleeping. The embers in the grate were cold and grey now, and the pale light of dawn filtering in through the leaded windows seemed to chill the room.

An apple-cheeked vicar's wife with a voice like Joyce Grenfell had welcomed several dozen marchers into the Elizabethan rectory for their second night on the march, and served them cocoa and fruitcake still warm and gooey from the oven, before settling them down for the night on the uneven floors of the downstairs rooms, with a cheery shout of, 'Lights out!'

In the darkness, Rachel had remarked, 'My, but doesn't adversity make strange bedfellows. A group of atheists like us kipping down in a vicarage.'

'Praise God for the Women's Institute and their cakes,' someone else had called out in the darkness.

And then they'd been shushed, and even though they'd been shouting their lungs out about banning the bomb for two days, none of them had quite had the courage to defy the vicar's wife and whisper after bedtime.

Michael had not slept much. One of the party had such a loud and irregular snore that every time Michael's consciousness began to drift, a massive snort from the other side of the room would blast him back to the discomfort of the unforgiving stone floor. In the darkness, he couldn't make out who it was, but he suspected the bus drivers' shop steward, a large man with a pitted, publican's nose. Curiously, he was filled with a strange kind of affection for the fat man. Even though he didn't know most of these people, their shared belief in the cause made them feel like family.

Rachel opened her eyes and sat up, shivering. She looked blearily at him, then she said, 'Let's go outside.'

It was still winter in the walled garden of the vicarage. In Kingshaven, the daffodils' succulent yellow lit every verge and hedgerow; here the golden trumpets were still wrapped up in their brown paper buds. The lawn was grey and matt with dew. Their boots made flat wet prints across it.

Rachel pinched a rosemary bush and held her fingers up for him to sniff the aromatic scent. 'You never said goodbye,' she said.

Whenever Michael had tried to write about her, there were things he found impossible to describe, like the fleeting vulnerability that shadowed her forthright challenges.

A weak sun began to filter through the damp mist. They were alone in the garden and there was going to be no avoiding the conversation that had been unspoken since he spun round at the sound of her voice in Trafalgar Square.

'I didn't dare,' he said.

'Was I so frightening?'

'I thought you might persuade me not to go.'

'You've a big idea of yourself,' she said. 'I'd not leave George.'

'So why sleep with me, then?'

'I don't remember a lot of sleeping,' she said with a laugh.

He had never managed to capture the way she laughed in words, the feeling of well-being it created inside him.

They used to make love on the way home from the Labour Club, in a rain shelter at the top of the park with the scrawled initials of other sweethearts all around them. His mind had been gripped as passionately as his body. She knew how he worked. If he'd let her down, he'd tried to absolve himself by telling himself that she'd known all along that he would.

'Are you happy?' he asked her.

'George is a good man. A good father. They're boys together, him and Clem, playing football, fishing. It's given him a new lease of life. Like you and Sylvia,' she said encouragingly.

He nodded earnestly, but couldn't look her in the eye.

'Oh, Michael!' she said, as if she could see inside him. 'Not the headmaster's wife again?'

'No!' He laughed hollowly as an unwelcome image of stout, tweedy Mrs Turlow flew across his mind.

'This one's very beautiful, isn't she?' Rachel said quietly.

'How do you know that?' he asked, bewildered.

'I saw you look at me in London, and wonder how you could have . . .'

Stripped bare by her uncompromising candour, he tried to excuse himself. 'It's different from how it was with you. It's just . . . It doesn't mean anything . . .'

A short acerbic laugh. 'Who to?' Rachel asked. 'It might mean something to her, you know. And it might to Sylvia, if she knew about it.'

He had toyed with the idea that Sylvia must know, at some sub-conscious level.

It was Sylvia who had volunteered Michael's services as a piano player at the Palace, almost as if she was trying to engineer a rendezvous for him and Pearl during the winter months. Sometimes he thought his wife's admiration for the Kings was so devotional she was prepared to offer him up for their amusement. But now, as he thought about her sitting at the table with their children eating tea when he returned each Sunday afternoon, her anxious smile, and the way she fussed around bringing him a fresh brew and cake, he was ashamed of himself for imagining her complicity.

High above them in the church tower a bell began to summon early worshippers with a sad, low toll.

'Saved by the bell,' said Rachel, lighting her first cigarette of the day. 'Come on, they'll have us singing hymns if we don't get a move on.'

Sylvia always woke up in the exact position she went to sleep, on her left side, at the very edge of the bed and usually uncovered because Michael had managed to twist the bedclothes up like a great heavy pile of dirty washing. Sometimes she wondered how he got any rest, thrashing around as he did. It was only in the early hours of the morning that he seemed to settle, and then it was a battle to raise him for work. The cup of tea she took up to him would grow cold on the bedside table, and when she gently told him the time, he would snap at her, 'I know!'

Eventually, she would send up Iris with a five-minute warning, and then she and the children would sit at the kitchen table look-ing at the ceiling as he thumped about, cursing, before clattering down the stairs with little flecks of shaving soap still clinging to the rims of his ears.

She missed his presence – she'd kept her bra and knickers on under her nightdress in case of emergency during the night – but it was a nice feeling, lying tucked up in bed like a child. Sylvia inched her way across to the middle of the bed, where the mattress springs were still firm. Tentatively, she spread first her arms and then her legs into the cool corners of the envelope of sheets.

An almost inaudible knock at the door made her spring back, as if she'd been caught trespassing. 'Come in?'

There was shuffling outside the door. The handle was lowered and then returned to the horizontal position. Eventually, the door opened revealing Iris bending down to pick up a cup she'd placed on the floor.

'What's this then?' asked Sylvia, sitting up.

'Happy Easter! I've made you a cup of tea,' said Iris.

'You boiled a kettle?'

'No.' Iris looked a bit sheepish.

'How many times have I told you not to turn on the Ascot without me there?' Sylvia demanded.

Iris was crestfallen. 'It was a surprise!'

'Well, it's certainly that,' said Sylvia. 'It's dangerous carrying hot tea upstairs,' she said, more gently.

'I am eight years old,' said Iris.

Sylvia took a sip. Iris had wasted a week's worth of tea leaves, and she hadn't used a strainer.

'It was a very kind thought, Iris,' she said, trying to smile. 'I'll teach you how to do it properly later.'

Anthony appeared in the door in his brushed-cotton pyjamas. He ran in and presented her with a biscuit.

'A lovely Rich Tea!' said Sylvia, pulling her son up on to the bed. 'Well, this is a treat!' she went on, extending a hand towards Iris, but her daughter stood just out of reach.

'Is Daddy coming back today?' Iris blurted out.

'No, he's not.'

Sylvia saw her daughter's face fall, and wondered whether Iris'd be quite so disappointed if she'd been the one who'd gone away for the weekend. She was surprised that Iris hadn't demanded to know where her father was, but she'd tried to close each line of enquiry as it arose. Luckily the child hadn't pressed further because she wasn't sure what she should tell her. Iris was good at chivvying out lies. And if she told her the truth, the whole town would know. Going on protest marches just wasn't the sort of thing people in Kingshaven did.

'What are we doing today?' Iris asked.

'What would you like to do?'

'Make a hay oven and cook a chicken in it.'

'A chicken? We can't afford a chicken for just us three!'

'You don't afford it, you catch it and wring its neck.'

'Why don't we go to church?' Sylvia asked brightly.

'I don't want to go to church,' said Iris.

'Most people go every week.'

'But we only go with school, and Daddy says that's different.'

'It's Easter Sunday,' said Sylvia firmly.

When she felt guilty about taking them sometimes behind Michael's back, she told herself that if he really didn't believe in God, as he was always saying, then it shouldn't matter if they went to church or not. A God that didn't exist was hardly going to punish them for being two-faced about it. Her view of things was that unless you were sure, and she didn't see how you could be, then wasn't it just as well to be on the safe side?

The Church of England wasn't as strict and serious as all the Roman Catholic ritual and incense he was brought up with. It was much more of a social thing, and she couldn't see what was wrong with that.

> *'All things bright and beautiful,*
> *All creatures great and small,*
> *All things wise and wonderful,*
> *The Lord God made them all.*
>
> *'Each little flower that opens,*
> *Each little bird that sings . . .'*

Anthony had a lovely, clear high voice, Sylvia thought. She wondered if she dared suggest to the vicar that he join the church choir.

> *'The rich man in his castle . . .'*

'That must be Sir John!' whispered Iris.

'The poor man at his gate . . .'

'And that's the professor Daddy sometimes goes to see . . .'

'God made them high and lowly,
And ordered their estate . . .'

'What is their estate?' Iris wanted to know as the congregation spilled out of the church.

'I think it means we're rich or we're poor because God wants us to be,' Sylvia said, thinking that couldn't be right. What about the people who got on through hard work? They were often churchgoers.

'Is it a bit like capitalism?' Iris asked.

Sylvia wished Michael wouldn't put all these things in her head. 'I don't think so,' she said.

'Is God Russian?' Iris asked.

Whatever next? 'Of course he's not!' Sylvia hissed.

'Who invented Sputnik, then?' Iris whispered.

'Space rockets weren't around when God was inventing things,' Sylvia assured her, counting four women coming out of the church who were wearing dresses that she had made for them.

The headmaster approached. 'Mrs Quinn. Iris. Anthony.'

Anthony stepped forward and said, 'Good morning, sir!'

'I hear you'll be coming to my school in September,' said Mr Turlow, looking down at the little fellow.

'I'm looking forward to it, sir.'

Sylvia was very proud. With only one rehearsal, Anthony could speak his lines on cue. Part of her knew that, come September, she would miss his company doing the shopping and eating dinner and listening to *Listen with Mother*, but part of her couldn't wait to see him go out into the world. Anthony was going to be someone. She was sure of it.

The headmaster looked at Iris. Her hair was whipped up like candy floss by the blustery wind. It wasn't fair really, Sylvia thought, that their boy had inherited her blond hair, whereas Iris was so much of a Quinn. When people commented on Iris's appearance, they usually said that she had a face she would grow into. It was the look she gave that unsettled. As if she knew all your weaknesses.

'Stanley Ironside tells me your husband's gone to London?' Mr Turlow said.

Sylvia nodded. Least said, soonest mended.

'When did you see Stanley Ironside?' enquired the head-master's wife.

Everyone knew that Mr Turlow often enjoyed a pint or two in the Railway Arms at lunchtime, except Mrs Turlow, whose firm teetotal views were regularly expressed in her letters to the local paper.

Without answering, the headmaster turned to greet Pearl. 'Miss King, looking as pretty as a picture!'

'What an unusual coat!' said his wife.

Pearl was wearing a pink seven-eighths-length coat with three outsized black buttons, and a matching straight skirt underneath.

'It's the very latest thing,' said Pearl. 'Sylvia copied it from a picture in a magazine.'

Mrs Farmer gave Sylvia a thin smile. 'You'll be putting me out of business!'

'Perhaps you ought to sell Sylvia's creations in your shop?' Pearl suggested.

Mrs Farmer's mouth opened to say something, but Libby King butted in, 'How's Jennifer getting on with the new baby?'

'Oh, she's beautiful,' said Mrs Farmer. 'They're calling her Jacqueline.'

'Mummy, have you met Sylvia?' Pearl asked.

The older Mrs King stepped forward.

In her youth, Sylvia had heard that she had been a great beauty, and she was still a very handsome woman who knew how to make the most of herself. A pale lavender jacket enhanced clear blue eyes. Pearls beamed a flattering light up on to her face.

'I understand you indulge my daughter's greatest passion,' Mrs King said with a searching look that made Sylvia slightly un-comfortable. She didn't know whether to agree or not. 'Fashion,' Mrs King said, breaking into a beatific smile.

Opinions in the town about Mrs King were sharply divided. There were those who thought that she still ran the Palace and most of the council, and were grateful for her fortitude and the upkeep of tradition. They remembered the blankets she had handed out during the war, and her hospitality after the landslip, and saw her as a figurehead of all that was good and decent in Kingshaven. There was a growing minority of others who thought the town would decline if it failed to move with the times. They sought permission for ice-cream parlours, a bowling alley on the pier, an amusement arcade, all of which Mrs King and her generation had so far been successful in opposing.

Sylvia could see the arguments on both sides, but she hadn't reckoned on the sheer presence of the woman, even though she couldn't be much more than five feet tall, and the penetrating gaze of those famous cornflower-blue eyes. She now understood why Pearl had once remarked sulkily, 'My mother sees everything.'

'You're from the North, I understand?' Mrs King made it sound like an affliction. 'May I ask which part?'

'Etherington,' Sylvia answered.

'I see.'

'It's much nicer here,' Sylvia said quickly.

'Quite.' Mrs King smiled at her again.

'We will be seeing you at the Bonnets?' said Libby King, following in her mother's footsteps as the King family entourage moved towards the cars they'd arrived in.

'Oh, yes! Thank you!' Sylvia said.

The Easter Bonnet Parade was an annual event at the Palace Hotel. The young ladies of Kingshaven were invited to create an Easter bonnet to be judged by a panel of the town's most eminent personages. The prize for the most attractive bonnet was a pound of Milk Tray, but the position was coveted more for the picture in the paper which gave a headstart in the annual race to be crowned Miss Kingshaven and ride on the first float in the carnival. This year, Sylvia had made several hats for the older girls, and thought that Iris had a good chance of winning the junior category.

As the third evening began to draw in, Claudia's mood sank at the prospect of a third night sleeping in clothes that would not dry, on a church hall's dusty floorboards. When a sharp wet soreness at the back of her heel indicated that the blister there had finally burst, she had an overwhelming desire to cry.

Tim noticed her limping almost immediately and sat her down on the wall of a suburban garden somewhere on the outskirts of Reading.

'We have to keep up with our lot,' Claudia urged, trying to swallow her tears.

'Save us a place in the billet,' Tim called after the small group of marchers left from the Cambridge contingent. Then: 'Come on, take your shoe off,' he instructed.

They made a good team, Claudia thought, staring at Tim's thick sweep of black hair as he bent to inspect her foot. When his feet were sore the first night, she had bathed them in a bowl and found a retired nurse from Bury St Edmunds with a supply of surgical spirit and sticking plaster.

They'd kept each other's spirits up throughout three gloomy days with games and forfeits such as reciting a Shakespearean monologue, composing nonsense verse, and eventually embarking on an epic poem about the march in iambic pentameters, but she knew that if any verse was likely to last beyond the march, it was his clerihew:

> Bertrand Russell
> Said I'm taking the bus – Hell!
> Nobody told me I'd have to put
> Up with three days of Michael Foot

Claudia was aware that she was the envy of all the other female students in their group, and some of the men. Tim was handsome, accomplished and great fun, a cricket blue, a tennis blue, a fine actor, universally admired, and madly devoted to her.

Claudia had never quite understood the persistence of his affection. In the first year, she had wondered whether she was the butt of a joke she didn't quite understand, but, as time passed, her failure to succumb to his undoubted attraction had created an oddly intimate bond between them based on the clear knowledge of this boundary.

As their destination grew closer, the enthusiasm of the

marchers seemed to dim instead of swell. Claudia could understand why people with small children would find it impossible to continue in such inclement conditions, but she would not forgive her fellow students for giving up. To arrive at the Atomic Weapons Establishment with fewer supporters than had left London was shame Claudia could not countenance.

'The trouble is, they've got the tactics all wrong,' Tim explained. 'The march should finish in London.'

'Why?' she asked.

'London's where the press is. Ask yourself how many journalists are going to drag themselves out to Aldermaston on a wet Easter Monday. More importantly,' he added with a wink, 'people too lazy to march could join in at the end, and look as if they'd walked the whole way! Imagine a crowd all the way down Whitehall. That's the photograph you want!'

To her surprise, Tim had never once suggested going home. On several occasions he had expressed a desire to check into a hotel for the night, offering to pay for separate rooms and a slap-up dinner, declaring that he didn't see why they had to suffer in the name of nuclear disarmament.

Now, as she watched him improvising a bandage for her heel from his last clean handkerchief, she thought that if he were to suggest staying at a hotel this evening, she might find it harder to resist.

'Come on,' he said, pulling her to her feet. 'I've heard tonight's church hall has been awarded three stars by the AA, and the local fish and chip shop is renowned for the crispness of its batter!'

The Etherington contingent was among the first to arrive, and immediately bagged the little stage to sleep on. They operated as a unit now, as if they'd been together all their lives. The older men would set up camp while the women searched out and reported back on the amenities. Michael reconnoitred the perimeters.

He discovered an upright piano covered with an old curtain. It was just about in tune. A couple of the lads helped him push it out to the front. Rachel brought him a chair. He played as the hall filled with marchers and requests were shouted up at him;

'Lambeth Walk', 'Me and My Gal', 'Roll Out the Barrel'. The music brought smiles to the faces of the weary walkers who seemed to gain new energy as they stepped over the threshold. Pint glasses of the local bitter lined up along the top of the piano as a chain of hands ferried refreshment for the piano player from the next-door pub.

In one of his breaks, someone called out, ' "The Red Flag"!'

It was an age since he had played it. He took another sip of beer, thought for a moment about the chords, then thumped out the refrain. As the packed hall rose to its feet, some picking up their banners, others holding fists in salute, Michael felt as if he were being lifted up on the unity of the song and transported to a place he had not been before. It was suddenly obvious to him why people were prepared to die for a cause, because it was only by being part of something you believed in that you truly discovered what it was to be alive. His fingers found the harmonies, and his vision blurred with emotion as he looked across the ranks of singing faces, and saw, there at the door, stamping the mud off her feet, her right fist raised and singing in a clear soprano he could pick out above the mass of voices – Claudia.

He looked back down at the piano, trying to focus on the black and white pattern of keys, and when he looked up again, she had disappeared.

He hurried the last flourish of chords and stood up. 'I need some air,' he said.

Michael picked his way over the lines of unrolled sleeping bags, skirting groups of comrades who were beginning to settle down for the night. A man strummed an acoustic guitar, and began the refrain:

> *'I'll sing you one – O!*
> *Green grow the Rushes – O!*
> *What is your one – O!*
> *One is one and all alone and ever more shall be so.'*

Michael found her under the lych gate of the church.

'What a coincidence!' he said.

'I expected to see everyone I knew on this march,' she said in a judgemental tone which made him very relieved that he had made the decision to come.

She was wearing a duffel coat. The hood was up and, with her eyes lowered, he thought she had the slight air of a nun. She looked older, more sophisticated. The fringe was gone.

'Have you been walking since Friday?' he asked.

'Of course!'

'How . . . ?' they said simultaneously.

'You . . .' he said, giving way for her to speak.

'No, you . . .'

They both paused, an absurd silent game of chivalry, and then they both opened their mouths to speak again.

'Quite a crowd!' he said, pointing at the hall, kicking himself for his banality.

'Yes!' she said. Then her face fell suddenly. 'Not as many as started, though.'

'Who are you walking with?' he asked her.

'Just some friends from Cambridge,' she said.

He wondered immediately what had made her qualify their status with 'just'.

'And you?' she asked.

'Just some people I used to know,' he replied, equally cagey. 'I sometimes see your father. He wanted to come on the march, but thought he was too old for sleeping on floors.'

'Yes, I know. He enjoys your company very much.'

'I enjoy his,' said Michael, finding it a little unnerving that Claudia and her father would still mention him, when he was not allowed to mention her. 'Are you enjoying Cambridge?' he asked.

'Very much,' she said.

'At least we're all enjoying ourselves, then,' he said.

'We've never had it so good,' Claudia quipped.

God, how he had missed her!

'Are you writing?' she asked.

'I'm trying to turn some of my stories into a novel,' he told her with a rueful grin.

She did a little jump of joy, so charming in its girlishness, it made him think she wasn't so sophisticated after all.

'I can't wait to read it,' she said.

Another cycle of 'Green Grow the Rushes, O!' wafted over from the hall.

'Have you ever had any idea what this song means?' Claudia suddenly said. 'Who are these lily-white boys, after all?'

Michael laughed. She asked questions just like her father did, forcing you to consider things you had always taken for granted. Whenever he let himself think about her, he could recall the intelligent face, the slender body, the almost puritanical seriousness, but it was this charming unpredictability he could not replicate in his mind.

'You're nearly finished at Cambridge, are you?' he asked casually, as if he'd lost count of the time she'd been away.

'In three months it will be over,' she said.

'What will you do then?' he asked.

He knew before she said anything that she would not be coming home.

'I'm still weighing up,' she said, as if she had given the matter a great deal of consideration. 'Possibly the BBC.'

'The BBC?'

'I had an interview with the radio drama department. Maybe one day I'll commission a play from you?' she said.

It was as if she spoke a different language now. She had joined the elite class who created the culture, and left behind those who merely consumed it. He remembered how he used to be the one who would tell her about things he'd heard on the Third Programme. The BBC had been an oracle, not somewhere you might think of getting a job.

'Claudia?' A toff's voice in the darkness.

Michael could see the shadow of a tall man against the rosy light emanating from the windows of the hall.

'Over here!' she replied.

The figure followed the direction of her voice.

'Are you OK?' he said, ducking under the eaves of the covered gate.

'Tim, this is my friend Michael,' she said. 'The writer I've mentioned.'

'Of course,' said Tim, indifferently. 'How do you do?' He

turned to Claudia. 'I managed to book us a lovely room. It's quiet and private, and there's hot and cold running water . . .'

The intimacy between them was a blade through Michael's chest.

'I hope you managed to find a well-appointed spot?' Tim asked him.

Claudia raised an eyebrow. It was clearly some sort of running joke they had.

'Up on the stage,' Michael said flatly.

'A first-floor room with a view! Lucky you!'

In the porch of the hall, Michael recognized the glowing arc of Rachel's cigarette before her face became visible. She was curious about his hasty departure and his return with younger friends. He thought that he detected a glance between the women as they approached her, a mutual suspicion, or perhaps an understanding, a conversation where no words were spoken.

A boy wearing a large yellow chicken head was standing at the top of the steps that led up to the Palace entrance.

'Hello, Christopher,' Iris said in a bored voice as they passed.

Angela King was wearing a white party dress and, on her head, a bonnet of white velvet with two long stiffened ears lined with pink satin.

'You look nice,' Sylvia said untruthfully.

Angela King had reached that puppy-fat stage between sweetness and womanhood earlier than normal, and the smocking across her chest was stretched to breaking point. The rabbit hat drew cruel attention to her large front incisors. What had Mrs Farmer been thinking of?

'You have to go through there,' Angela ordered.

Sylvia paused to gawp at the magnificent reception hall. It was her very first time inside the building. She had fished for an invitation from Pearl, suggesting that it would be no trouble to come up to the Palace for her fittings, but Pearl had never taken the hint. Neither Michael nor Iris's descriptions had given any idea of the sheer scale and luxury of it. The beautiful china clock reminded Sylvia of one of her mother's precious china ornaments magnified a thousand times.

A sudden flash behind her made her jump.

A photographer was leaning over the grand staircase, resting his camera on the top of the carved wooden banister.

'Sorry,' he said. 'But you looked like Alice in Wonderland!'

Sylvia was wearing a lightweight two-piece. The jacket had three-quarter sleeves and a standaway collar. It was blue, but otherwise she couldn't see the resemblance. Didn't Alice in Wonderland wear an apron?

'I meant your expression,' the photographer explained, observing the disquiet on her face. 'And I'm sure I saw a white rabbit earlier.'

Sylvia smiled.

'Your daughter's a picture!'

Sylvia couldn't help her smile widening. Modesty apart, Iris really did look a treat. She wouldn't normally have thought of putting yellow next to her daughter's red hair, but there was a particular variety of narcissus which had a deep orange edge to its trumpet, and when Iris's untameable curls had peeped out of the daffodil bonnet when she'd first tried it on, Sylvia had decided to leave it just so, rather than shoving the hair back in to hide it. She'd made Iris a dress of green lining material cut on the bias to look like a stalk, and she was carrying a bunch of daffodils to present to Mrs King.

'Iris, hold the flowers nicely,' Sylvia hissed at her as the photographer snapped. 'Stand up straight and smile.'

Iris posed for the camera, her expressions ranging from outright hostility to goofiness.

'You're from the *Chronicle*, aren't you?' Sylvia asked, trying to keep up a good impression in spite of Iris's behaviour.

'Hurry up, hurry up!' shouted Angela King. 'Or you'll be late!'

When the marchers finally caught sight of their destination, their tired, blistered feet itched to run the last few hundred yards towards the battalion of policemen deployed to protect the base, but they kept their discipline. They had come in peace but they couldn't resist teasing the po-faced policemen, trying to get them to join in the celebrations.

Michael found himself hugging each member of the

Etherington Labour Club, even Rachel's daughter, Clare, who initially hung back, then returned his embrace, embarrassed.

It was almost like VE night again, when the streets had been full of strangers hugging one another, common happiness outweighing all differences. For a few uplifting moments outside the bleak and forbidding railings of the AWE, it didn't matter if they had achieved anything, because their endeavour felt like a great victory.

There were speeches, a chorus of 'Auld Lang Syne', and then the ambition uniting them was fulfilled, the Bank Holiday almost over, and it was time to go home.

Rachel was the quickest to sense it, and the most practical. First to leave would be first on the train. There were bound to be queues.

Michael stood facing her, holding both her hands, a million words in a look. He was filled with a need to tell her that talking to her had made him think about his life, put things in perspective, that he would be good from now on, treat people better. He wanted to tell her that he was sorry for hurting her, that he admired her and missed her, and wished they could stay in touch, but he thought she probably understood all of it anyway.

And then she was gone.

He tracked her as she pushed back through the crowd, arm in arm with her daughter, until he was no longer able to distinguish her brown raincoat from any of the others. Suddenly he wondered why he hadn't gone with her to say goodbye at the station, and started pushing back through the crowd himself, following her route, certain that she would have worked out the right direction. But the Etherington contingent had departed by the time he reached the station.

'Pray silence,' said Libby, 'for the Easter Bonnets of nineteen fifty-eight!'

A line of young women dutifully marched in and stood before the judges' table.

Eddie looked at them smiling at him and decided to select winners on what he imagined they would look like in bathing costumes. Percy Bland, the proprietor of the Ship, had hinted at certain fringe benefits accruing from being on the judging panel for Miss Kingshaven, but Eddie doubted that any of this lot would be prepared to oblige in exchange for a pound of Milk Tray.

His first choice was a brunette with green eyes like a cat, and his second the delicious blonde who served in the bar of the Yacht Club.

'I'm afraid I can't agree,' said Liliana, as they conferred. 'For workmanship and sheer ingenuity, I would have to choose number three.'

Number three's bonnet was in the shape of a bird's nest with three speckled blue eggs nestling in it.

'Ingenious, certainly, but is it practical?' argued Mr Makepeace. 'I think I'm going to plump for number seven.'

A simple headdress of silk tulips.

'Isn't that Ronnie Cadd's daughter?' Eddie asked.

Mr Makepeace coloured slightly.

Good Lord! It was one thing for the Chair of the Planning Committee to take sweeteners when it came to smoothing the way for planning permission, but it beggared belief when an elected councillor would accept a bribe for swinging a bonnet competition!

'I think I'll have to agree,' Eddie said, feeling a waft of approbation from Liliana next to him. 'Two to one, I'm afraid, Liliana.'

'It's a particularly lovely display this year. Each bonnet a work of art in its own right, but I'm afraid there has to be a winner. And the winner is ... Susan Cadd!' Libby announced, somewhat surprised as Eddie passed her the judges' decision.

'And the winner of the Junior Bonnets ... Iris Quinn! Both bonnets, incidentally, made by Sylvia Quinn.'

Ruby Farmer was first to congratulate Iris's pretty little mother through clenched teeth. It was customary for at least one of the winning girls to be dressed by Mrs Farmer.

Eddie sensed that there was a slight feeling about the delectable Mrs Quinn. The crones did not easily forgive her sewing things which women actually looked nice in.

Susan Cadd and Iris Quinn posed by the marble fireplace while the photographer from the *Chronicle* took their picture.

'You can share those with me,' said Angela, snatching the New Berry Fruits from Iris's hand.

Angela tore out of the room with the prize; Iris hitched up her dress, in a most unladylike manner, and gave chase, followed by the sulky chicken.

'We can't all be winners, can we?' said Libby with an approximation of a light laugh as a cloud of anti-climax descended on the room, and the disappointed contestants and their families began to make their excuses and leave.

The Easter Bonnet Parade at the hotel had been one of the traditions invented by Liliana to give the Palace a more wholesome image after the departure of Libby's Uncle Rex, but it had become an absurd spectacle of corruption and wounded pride, Eddie thought.

'Nobody really bothers with Easter Bonnets these days,' Eddie said to his wife. 'I think we should make this the last year.'

'Ban the Bonnets!' said Pearl. 'Good. I've always hated it.'

'Only because you were never allowed to win,' Libby remarked.

The photographer seemed to appear from under the bar as Eddie pushed the optic on the brandy up with his right hand, and held the teacup under with his left.

'You look like a man who appreciates photography,' he said.

'Do I?' Eddie chuckled. 'Will you join me . . . er?'

'Tom Snow. I wouldn't say no to a g and t.'

'That's the spirit!' said Eddie, helping himself to a double brandy in a glass, now that he had company.

The photographer had been to several hotel functions in recent years. He was an engaging enough fellow.

'I thought you might like to view my portfolio,' the photographer said, opening a large folder on the bar.

'Portfolio, eh?' said Eddie.

From the photographer's slightly furtive demeanour, Eddie was anticipating rather more risqué photographs than at first appeared. There were shots of the beach, boats in the harbour, all perfectly pleasant and unexceptional. It was only when he saw the distant shot of Ratty on the deck of the *Brittany Anna*, himself and Ronnie Cadd going into Offard's Estate

Agent's, the silhouette of a couple in the alleyway by the Yacht Club, the familiar exterior of a boarding house in the port area of Lowhampton, that he began to realize there was something more on the agenda.

'You're very observant,' Eddie said.

'Thank you,' said the photographer.

Eddie didn't know how the conversation was meant to go next. It was an opportune moment for the door to open.

'Ooops! Sorry!' said the delightful Mrs Quinn, holding her handsome little boy by the hand. 'We're looking for Iris.'

'I think I know exactly where she'll be,' said Eddie, coming out from behind the bar and taking Mrs Quinn's arm. 'You will excuse me, Mr . . . ?'

'Snow, Tom Snow,' said the photographer.

The curtains were drawn in the private sitting room and the children were sitting in a line in front of the free-standing television cabinet; Christopher had the head of the chicken on the floor between him and Angela. Next to her, and glued to the screen, was the little daffodil girl.

'Iris!' Mrs Quinn hissed at her daughter.

The girl looked up, frowned and looked back at the screen, impatient with the disturbance.

'Let's be off now, Iris,' said Mrs Quinn.

'Ssssh. The news,' said Christopher, pointing at the screen.

'Members of the Campaign for Nuclear Disarmament arrived at the Atomic Weapons Establishment in Aldermaston today . . .' the newscaster began, over images of scruffy-looking types walking along beside some iron railings.

Eddie ventured a companionable squeeze of the delectable Mrs Quinn's arm. He felt her stiffen. Nothing doing. But worth a try. Always worth a try.

'Police estimate that four thousand protestors marched . . .'

'They look more like beatniks and Communists to me!' Eddie muttered at the television.

Mrs Quinn was staring at the screen as if she'd never seen one before.

The report cut back to the newscaster who began to read the next item.

And then Iris suddenly piped up in the darkness, 'So that's where Daddy's got to!'

Michael stared out of the compartment window as England drifted past, and station by station the train emptied of marchers, until there was no one with the tell-tale black and white badge or the grime of four days' walking left except himself.

Outside, the light gradually faded until it was so dark he could see only his reflection looking back at him.

He kept thinking about Claudia, shining with purity like an angel in a duffel coat. Claudia who had introduced him as a writer although he hadn't written a word for months. How disgusted she would be if she knew what he was really like!

The weekend had after all been about the personal and not the political, he thought as he climbed down from the train at Kingshaven station.

The rain had stopped. His rucksack was much lighter than when he had set out. A thin crescent moon rose above the bay.

The sound of his boots on the pavement echoed through the sleeping town as he made silent resolutions to the rhythm of his paces.

He must return to his writing each day; he must be a better father; he must stop seeing Pearl King; he must try harder to be a good man.

As he walked down the street to his house, cherry blossom petals swirled around him and drifts of pink snow filled the gutters.

A light was on at home.

He opened the door as quietly as he could so as not to wake his sleeping family.

Sylvia had waited up for him, but she was asleep in the chair.

He knelt in front of her, kissed her forehead and smoothed her white-gold hair from her eyes.

She woke up with a frightened start, her features firming into a frown as she recognized his.

'How could you?' she asked in a cold voice. 'How could you do that to me?'

'What?' he asked nervously.

'With her,' she said, her voice rising as the anger spilled out.

'Who?' he faltered.

'Don't lie. I saw you on the television. Arm in arm. With *her*.'

Chapter Seven

December 1959

Once a year, when the Palace Hotel closed after Christmas, the King family threw a party for the staff who remained and anyone else who had helped in the successful running of the business. For one night, New Year's Eve, the King family served those who served them, and, by all accounts, Mr Eddie King poured the drinks very liberally, and Mrs Liliana King's famous steak and ale pie was as sustaining as it was delicious. There was Scottish dancing before dinner, and party games after.

Sylvia wasn't sure which of the engraved invitations on the shelf above the electric bar fire she liked most. She doubled up the Christmas cards to make enough room to display them side by side. The one on the right requested the pleasure of the company of 'Mr and Mrs Michael Quinn', the names neatly written in the top left-hand corner in royal-blue ink, and the other had 'Michael and Sylvia' scrawled in black by a different hand. The more formal style of address pleased her because it signified that they had now been recognized as the sort of people no respectable occasion in Kingshaven could be without. However, the informality of Pearl's handwriting showed that they were considered friends.

Sylvia carefully pressed the seam of the tartan edging she had stitched to the dark green silk dress she'd been married in. The dress had cost a fortune at the time, and she'd only worn it once.

It was one of the few dresses she had left with a full enough skirt for country dancing. Skirts had become narrower and narrower, which was peculiar if you thought about it, because fabric was in much more plentiful supply than it had been when the New Look was invented. If the fashion continued, she'd joked to Pearl King recently, they'd be straight up and down in a couple of years, which wouldn't suit anyone with a nice curvy figure.

Her mother had come with her to buy the dress. 'Married in green, wish you'd never been!' Sylvia remembered her saying, when she'd picked it out in Stapely and Penney of Etherington.

She'd had an ominous rhyme for every colour except white.

That was almost ten years ago now.

Mr and Mrs Michael Quinn hadn't done so badly, Sylvia thought.

They'd had their ups and downs like any other couple. It had been very hurtful to see Michael on the television arm in arm with that Rachel again. He said that they hadn't done anything, and with all those other marchers, Sylvia couldn't see where they'd have found the privacy, but she hadn't let on that she believed him. Sometimes it wasn't wise to forgive too readily. He hadn't even asked whether he could go on the march this year.

To an outsider, they were the perfect example of a modern marriage: two healthy children, one of each; a nice new house with an array of modern conveniences. In the last year, they'd become proud owners of their own television and an electric iron.

Sylvia manoeuvred the point of the iron carefully around the covered buttons at the shoulder of the dress, remembering suddenly exactly how it had felt when Michael unfastened those buttons on their wedding night, standing behind her, looking at her reflection in the mirror as she brushed her hair. The touch of his lips on her shoulder blade; the tingling down her spine. And her worrying that, with the light on, people would see them through the pink net curtains.

'Let them look. They'll not see anything as gorgeous on the Golden Mile,' he'd said.

That terrible guesthouse: pink bedspread, pink lampshade and red flock wallpaper, which made it look like a Shanghai brothel, he'd said. Her parents had offered to pay for a week in a nice hotel in the Lake District, but he was too proud for that, so it had been three nights in Blackpool, but what a time they'd had, and how they'd loved! And laughed – at the squeaking bedsprings; and the stains on the carpet; and the two brothers who'd owned the guesthouse, one of whom wore a frilly apron to serve the breakfast and kept putting his hand on Michael's arm.

'It's a queer place to begin your married life, this,' Michael had said, making her giggle and spray her tea all over the pink tablecloth.

Mr and Mrs Michael Quinn.

You couldn't expect those giddy feelings to go on, could you? Not when you had children and responsibilities. Theirs was a lot better than some marriages, like the Allsops, which had a bit too much on the physical side, if you believed what Jennifer said (which Sylvia didn't entirely).

They'd been young then, Sylvia thought, shaking the dress out and putting it on a hanger, and things changed. (Although not her waistline. She'd been delighted to find that the dress was looser than it had been when she'd first tried it on in Stapely and Penney.)

Mr and Mrs Michael Quinn.

The way her mother had talked about their prospects that day, you'd never have thought that, ten years later, they'd be the sort of couple to get invited to an At Home with the Kings.

'Why does Friday always smell of fish?' asked Christopher at the lunch table in the private dining room of the Palace Hotel.

'Because we eat fish on Friday, idiot!' said Angela.

'Angela . . .' Libby warned.

'We do eat fish on Friday,' said Eddie, who was always inclined to defend his daughter even when she was being rude.

'But why?' Christopher persisted.

'Why what?' Eddie asked impatiently.

Libby filleted the lemon sole on her plate and popped a morsel into her mouth. It was rather watery, and the mornay sauce had separated a little, but it wasn't quite bad enough to send for Chef. She wished he'd be a little more careful about draining food properly, but he was extremely temperamental, so she usually took a list of complaints to any confrontation to get it over with in one go.

'What I mean is, why do we have to eat fish?' Christopher persisted. 'Did Jesus tell us to?'

Libby had the uncomfortable feeling she didn't actually know the answer to this. Was it something to do with the communion? Something about not wanting to consume blood on the day he died? In which case, would veal do just as well? She put down her knife and fork, struggling to come up with a satisfactory answer. Or was it simply because Christ had been a fisherman?

It was absolutely typical of Christopher to question a practice that everyone else just took for granted. He had a knack of upsetting the balance of things.

'You're eating it because I tell you to!' Eddie ordered, pointing at his son's plate with his knife.

Eddie could be heavy-handed at times, but Libby was grateful for his intervention. Whereas she had a tendency to read her son's questions as a sign of a peculiar intelligence, her husband viewed them as simple insolence. She suspected that the truth lay somewhere in between, but it was generally better to stamp on the boy's curiosity at an early stage, otherwise things could get terribly convoluted.

'Why does fish stink the whole hotel out?' Christopher asked.

'Don't speak with your mouth full,' said Libby.

Christopher swallowed his food with exaggerated difficulty. 'I mean, why does the fish smell last longer than the smell of meat?' he pleaded.

'Are you allowed to talk at mealtimes at school?' asked Eddie.

Christopher shook his head.

'Well, then,' said Eddie, pointing again at his son's plate.

Libby watched her children making faces at each other as they continued the meal in silence. It wasn't often that she saw them together now that they were both at boarding school. They had reached a particularly unattractive stage. Their teeth were too big for their faces; their bodies had lost their childish roundedness. She couldn't remember the last time either of them had wanted to clamber on her knee when they'd hurt themselves, or put their arms around her neck to kiss her goodnight. She had never encouraged public displays of affection, but there was something uniquely comforting in the innocence of a child's embrace, and it suddenly occurred to her that that time had gone for ever. Unless they decided to have another child. The thought popped into her head from nowhere. In your mid-thirties, you only had two choices: to become middle-aged, or to be young again.

What an appropriate way to start the new decade!

The tradition at the Kingshaven Primary School Christmas Party was that, after Pass the Parcel, Mr Turlow would read 'How the Camel got his Hump' from the *Just So Stories* by Rudyard Kipling, employing all the vocal skills he had honed over many years' membership of the Kingshaven Amateur Dramatic Society. This year, as the headmaster settled himself in his usual seat and started on the first line, Jim Carney, the youngest of the eleven Carney children, whose father ran the stables, and who was usually addressed as the Naughtiest Boy this School has Ever had the Misfortune of Teaching, shouted out: 'Oh, not this auld one again! Can't we be having one of Sir's stories instead?'

Mr Turlow dragged Jim by the ear to his room and Mrs Evans decided that the plates of sandwiches and biscuits sent in by the children's mothers would be devoured ahead of schedule, to distract the children from the howling as Jim was caned.

Michael had to summon up all his self-discipline to stop himself from walking out of the school. He had never agreed with corporal punishment, knowing from his own experience that it only made naughty children better at hiding their misdemeanours. But he sometimes wondered whether his refusal to perform it was self-defeating, since Mr Turlow seemed to relish meting out particularly sadistic beatings to the children in Michael's class.

By the time the vicar arrived to say Grace, most of the food had been eaten.

'Just in time to hear one of Mr Quinn's stories,' said Ivor, diplomatically steering the Reverend Church to an empty chair as Michael began.

'I'm not at all sure that my story today is one that you will wish to hear . . .'

A hush fell over the children almost immediately. Years of bedtime practice with Iris, who was a most demanding audience, had taught Michael that a child's attention was best grabbed by engineering the protest, 'Yes it is!'

'My story is not, by any stretch of the imagination, a merry Christmas story at all. In fact,' Michael went on, 'one might almost call it a tragedy. It concerns a little girl I may have told you about before called Rose.'

He looked around the school hall strung with the paperchains and paper lanterns the children had spent the previous week making. Several of the children were nodding their heads.

'If you are thinking that Rose, as her name would suggest, was a pretty girl whose favourite colour was pink, then I'm sorry to say that you are much mistaken. Rose was a gangly girl whose elbows stuck out. Her hair was black as a beetle and her eyes were as green as lime jelly. Everyone remarked how odd it was that Rose was so odd-looking and thin, when her parents were pink-cheeked, fat bakers called Mr and Mrs Bun, but Rose didn't think it was odd at all, because Rose knew that she was really a witch.'

Michael was gratified to hear a sharp intake of breath not only from the younger children, but also from the vicar.

'Now, you may or may not know that witches come in two varieties. Some are bent on sorcery and all manner of bad deeds like the ones you've probably encountered in other stories like *Hansel and Gretel*. But there's another sort of witch, who's really just like you and me, except that she has a little bit of magic inside her. Rose was this sort of witch. She went to school, just like you do, and she learned her times tables, but she wasn't any better or worse at them than you are. It wasn't that sort of magic . . .'

Michael looked up and smiled at Jim as he returned to the room, digging his knuckles into his eye sockets to grind away any trace of tears. The boy shot him back a defiant look which seemed to say: 'It's you that's weak for pitying me.'

'I'm sorry to say that Rose was not a very popular child. Her black hair and green eyes made a lot of people a little bit frightened of her, and her face was not naturally smiley, which made some people think that she was up to no good, which sometimes she wasn't . . .'

He could see Iris looking round at the faces closest to where she was sitting. Rose was an only thinly disguised version of his daughter, which he'd made up in an attempt to make her feel better when some of the more stupid children had started teasing her for her precocious intelligence. None of the other children seemed yet to have made the connection.

'Now, Mrs Bun was usually very indulgent of Rose and let her do almost anything she wanted to do, like walk around the house in her best shoes (only upstairs because they were far too big for Rose and the heels might be dangerous on the staircase) and even try her lipstick (which Mrs Bun only ever wore on special occasions), but there was one item that she was not allowed to fiddle with (which was, of course, the one Rose most wanted to), and this was her lucky charm bracelet.

'Now, Christmas is always a busy time for bakers, and it was an especially busy time for Mr and Mrs Bun. Aside from all the extra bread, Mrs Bun also had to make the town's Christmas puddings. The one thing the whole town could agree on was that Mrs Bun's puddings were the best. Nobody knew how she did it, and when people asked Mrs Bun what she put in the mixture, she would smile and say, "Just the usual things, and a bit of magic!"

'When the time came for Mrs Bun to make her puddings, she would always take twelve of the charms off her bracelet and stir one into each of twelve puddings, and she would tell the people who bought the puddings that whoever found a charm must bring it back to Mrs Bun, so that the magic would go on . . .'

'Rather a moralistic story for you,' said Ivor in the Ship afterwards. 'But I'm sure the vicar appreciated your "cast your bread upon the waters" message.'

'I meant it more as a parable of the redistribution of wealth,' Michael replied.

'Ever thought of putting them down on paper, your stories for children?' Ivor enquired brightly.

'No,' said Michael, guessing what was coming next.

'Heard from that publisher yet?'

'No.'

Ivor had become a friend, someone he often went for a drink

with, but Michael wished he had never told him that he had sent his novel to some publishers. He realized now that he'd been assuming the book would be accepted. The difficulty, he had innocently imagined, was finishing the novel and having the courage to send it off. He had never envisaged the acute shame of opening the door to the postman and having to take the parcel back, or the terrible powerlessness of reading a letter of rejection.

The novel had gone now to the publishers of Alan Sillitoe, and to the company which had published John Braine's *Room at the Top*, whose work Michael privately felt his work bore comparison to. Both firms had rejected him with bland words which his imagination twisted in disproportionate ways depending on his mood, sometimes offering a glimmer of future success, more often bringing an angry despair.

When he handed the parcel over to Audrey Potter for a third time, addressed to a third publisher, he had promised himself, in silent secular prayer, that if they were to decline, that would be an end to it. Tantalizingly, their rejection letter had suggested he try Portico Books, a well-known publisher of left-wing pamphlets, which was starting a fiction list. So he had given himself one more last chance, but now he wished he had not, because it had been over two months now.

'Maybe you'd have more luck with your children's stories,' Ivor suggested sympathetically. 'You sail a bit close to the wind sometimes. But that's the way with you, isn't it?'

'What do you mean?' Michael said.

'How you behave's your own business,' said Ivor. 'But it doesn't go unnoticed. There, I've said it now. Don't say you weren't warned.'

Michael suddenly understood that Ivor was not offering up a critical judgement of his work. 'Warned?' he repeated.

'Believe me, I'm in no position to comment on other people's morals . . .' Ivor went on.

'I don't know what you're on about,' Michael said. He wasn't going to be caught out by Ivor's teasing.

'Oh, I think you do.' Ivor put his empty glass down on the table and picked up his coat. 'Happy Christmas, anyway.'

'Come on, let's have it,' Michael said.

'People are talking about you and Pearl King,' Ivor whispered.

It was as if Michael had been waiting for a punch and, when it landed, it didn't exactly hurt, but winded him with the sudden reality of the horror he had brought upon himself.

Seconds of incriminating silence ticked away.

'What's the matter with you?' Ivor asked him. 'Sylvia's a lovely girl, and your kiddies—'

'You've always fancied Sylvia,' Michael lashed out.

'You've got a bloody nerve.' Ivor got up to leave.

'Ivor!' Michael put his hand on his friend's coat. 'You won't tell anyone?'

'Oh, for God's sake!' Ivor said. 'I'm the least of your problems.'

Michael stood on the promenade staring at the moon's path over the cold steel mirror of the sea. Sylvia had been so determined he was having an affair, with her pursed lips and the way she stiffened when he touched her, that he had told himself he might as well be. Ironic that she'd been so fixated on Rachel, she hadn't seen what other people obviously had. His brain had come up with myriad ways of lessening the guilt, but the truth was banal. He had behaved badly because he thought he could get away with it. It broke the routine of his existence. It had felt like strength, not weakness: his private two-fingered salute at Kingshaven's establishment. But now it had to stop.

A cruel wind swept down Oxford Street, ripping right through Claudia's clothes to her skin. She'd been into each department store looking for a suitable party dress and had tried several on, but hadn't been able to decide. With her flat chest, cocktail dresses tended to make her look like a child trying on her mother's clothing, and she knew that Tim would not approve of the plain sack dress which was the only item she'd felt had the right kind of sophistication.

'Why do you always wear black?' he had said to her the last time they went to the theatre together. 'It makes you look as if you're permanently in mourning.'

Part of her resisted a purchase because of the hole it would leave in her budget. It seemed such a silly amount of money to spend on something she would wear only once or twice. And so she whirled out of yet another revolving door empty-handed into the biting night air.

'Claudia! It *is* you. I was sure it was! I've been calling after you all the way through Perfumery!'

'Edith!'

Claudia wondered if she would have recognized her old friend if she'd passed her in the street. She had lost all her puppy fat and looked quite the girl about town in her scarlet lipstick, floury dusting of pale face powder on flushed pink cheeks.

'What are you doing here?' Claudia asked.

'Same as you, I should think. Christmas shopping.' Edith raised both hands, which were clasping several carrier bags each.

Claudia's Christmas shopping had been easy enough. A book on Dadaism from Zwemmers in Charing Cross Road for her father. Wisden's *Almanack* for Tim.

'Did you come to London especially?' she asked Edith.

'You must be joking. I live here now. I'm personal assistant to the chairman of an oil company. I can't tell you how ghastly two years at Pitman's was, but with decent shorthand and typing the world really is your oyster. How about you?'

'I'm at the BBC,' said Claudia.

'Secretary?'

'General factotum,' said Claudia.

'That sounds rather grand,' said Edith.

Claudia smiled. She hadn't wanted to give her real title, Studio Manager, because she thought it gave a totally misleading impression of what was essentially a menial job producing sound effects, but she had unwittingly elevated herself in the eyes of the impressionable Edith.

'Look, why don't you come and have a coffee at my "pied à terre",' Edith suggested. 'I call it that because it sounds so much better in French. We've so much catching up to do.'

Edith had always been a rather silly girl, but very good-natured. Claudia followed her friend's good-quality black-and-white-checked coat as she pushed determinedly through the crowds. 'I'm glad we ran into each other,' she said as they turned off the busy shopping street into a suddenly quiet side street. 'I could do with your sartorial advice.'

'Oooh, sounds interesting,' said Edith, clearly imagining something much more intriguing than Claudia had in mind.

At the flat, Claudia explained the dilemma of the party dress.

Edith thought for a moment while she ran the tap in a kitchen that was so small only one person could fit in it.

'Tinsel,' she said finally. 'Wind a strand of it round the neck of the black dress and you've got the effect of a sparkling fur collar. No need even for a necklace.'

'That's inspired!' said Claudia.

'A girl at the office did a similar thing,' said Edith, and Claudia warmed to her even more for her honesty in not claiming the idea for herself. She couldn't imagine such a thing happening at the BBC where the culture was so competitive everyone claimed any good idea as their own.

As Claudia settled into the only armchair with her cup of tea, she thought how much she missed the comfortable ease of female friendship. Sometimes it was relaxing just to pass the time of day and not feel you had to have an opinion about everything.

Edith's flat was in the basement of a big red-brick mansion block, with a window which looked out on to a wall along the top of which the shoes and ankles of passers-by could be seen. It was tiny, but it was luxury to Claudia, who was still in a bedsit in Camden, sharing a bathroom with six other people.

'How many proposals have you had?' Edith asked her.

'Of marriage? None at all,' Claudia said, feeling a little disingenuous because she suspected that Tim had planned to ask her on several occasions, but she had always managed somehow to steer the conversation in another direction. Sometimes the effort to keep talking about any neutral subject felt like bicycling madly in order to stand still.

'I've had three,' said Edith.

'Congratulations!'

'I've turned them all down. Two from medical students – so we know what they were after . . .'

'And the third?' Claudia asked.

Edith blushed. 'He's in the geology department at the company. I turned him down because it doesn't do to let them know you're keen, does it?' she said. 'Course, now I'm desperate because he hasn't asked again!'

'Perhaps he will at Christmas?'

'Do you really think so?' Edith brightened considerably. 'Do you think I should give him my telephone number in Kingshaven just in case?'

'That might appear a little keen,' Claudia said.

'Hmm,' Edith pondered. 'Are you going back?'

'No, I've volunteered to be skeleton staff at the Beeb.'

'You don't observe Christmas, anyway, do you?' said Edith.

In cosmopolitan London, Claudia had quite forgotten the significance still attached to being Jewish in a place like Kingshaven. There was still prejudice against immigrants, of course, especially the more recent immigrants from the West Indies, which had grown ugly in Notting Hill the summer of the previous year, but Jews were so integrated into the society she moved in, she didn't even know whether her friends and colleagues were Jewish or not.

'I don't observe Christmas because I am an atheist,' Claudia explained.

'What a shame!' said Edith. 'I love all the pretty lights and carols, and presents of course. And I do miss my mother's cooking! I say, you don't have a shilling for the meter?'

Claudia looked into her purse and found one.

The room took on an intimate glow as Edith lit the gas fire.

'What's the news from Kingshaven, then?' Claudia asked. Her father wrote to her regularly, but he didn't know the gossip.

'Sir John's as alive and as batty as ever,' said Edith, warming her hands. 'Jennifer Allsop is pregnant again. That's her third. Of course, everyone's hoping it will be a boy for her sake, poor thing. How on earth they're going to fit more into that little house, I do not know. Why do you think it is Sir John won't give over the Castle to Jolly?'

'They haven't really spoken to each other since Sir John decided to take Winston in, I believe,' said Claudia.

'Oh, I see. Poor Jolly. You couldn't really blame him for objecting, could you?'

Claudia decided it would be diplomatic not to say anything more on this subject.

'You heard about Mr Rackett, presumably?' Edith went on.
Claudia shook her head.

'It was in the national papers! He was terrorizing the sitting
tenants in the cottages down the Harbour End, so that he could
raze them all to the ground and develop a marina, if you please!'

'A marina?'

'The money's in sailing these days,' said Edith with authority.

Claudia noticed that Edith issued diagnoses in exactly the same
tone as her father Dr Payne. It was as if she thought that in order
to sound grown-up, you had to say the things that middle-aged
men said, and with the same assurance.

'Yachting used to be a rich man's privilege, but with all these
dinghy kits around, just about everyone has one,' she continued.
'Mr Rackett would have happily turned our centuries-old harbour
into a floating caravan park, if he hadn't been found guilty of
arson and ended up a guest of Her Majesty!'

'Goodness me! In a little place like Kingshaven,' said Claudia.

'Mummy says that more goes on in Kingshaven than does in
Peyton Place! Beneath the picturesque façade beats a scandalous
heart.'

Claudia laughed at the melodramatic mixed metaphor,
wondering whether Edith had intended it to be so funny.

'It's top down, of course,' Edith pronounced in her grown-up-
speak. 'If certain people set a better example, things might be
different.'

'Such as?'

'Oh, honestly, Claudia! The Kings of course, especially Pearl
King.'

'Oh, but that was ages ago,' said Claudia, dismissively.

She'd never been able to see what all the fuss was about. Pearl's
lover had been divorced, after all, it wasn't as if their affair had
hurt anyone.

'But it's still going on,' said Edith.

'I thought he moved away.'

'Hardly! My youngest brother's in his class!'

'What?' Claudia asked, her head beginning to swim in the
fumy heat of the gas fire.

'Mr Quinn,' said Edith.

'Mr Quinn?'

'You must remember him. The one who sometimes said a few words at the bus stop. He is terribly handsome, of course . . .'

'But that's impossible!' said Claudia.

'I thought everyone knew,' said Edith.

But he hates the Kings! Claudia was about to protest. He hates everything they stand for! And then she remembered shaking out a pillow on the balcony and seeing him sitting with Pearl beside the swimming pool.

It couldn't be true, she told herself. He would never do such a despicable thing to his wife. Then she remembered the march. The woman who'd come out to see where he was, and the invisible, inaudible pull of sexuality between them. Perhaps he *was* the sort of man who had other women.

No.

People didn't understand him. Because he was different from them, because he was so handsome, and unknowable, they jumped to conclusions.

It was just people jumping to conclusions.

But if he was a womanizer . . . However hard she tried to dismiss it, Claudia's mind kept returning to the thought the whole bus journey home. If he was a womanizer, why had he not attempted to proposition her?

When the photograph of Anthony sitting next to Father Christmas appeared on the front page of the *Chronicle*, Sylvia bought two copies, and cut one out to enclose it in the card she was sending to her mother and father.

'*Everyone here well*,' she wrote, and, as an afterthought, she took one of the invitations down from the mantelpiece (the one addressed to Mr and Mrs Michael Quinn) and enclosed that too.

'Who's that one to?' asked Anthony, who was sitting next to her, licking the envelopes.

'To Granny and Grandpa,' said Sylvia.

'Is Granny coming to see us?' he asked.

'Not this year,' said Sylvia.

'Why? I like Granny!'

'Daddy doesn't,' said Iris, who was carefully cutting snips in concertinaed sheets of sugar paper to make lanterns.

'Iris!'

'He can't stand her!' Iris persisted. 'And he won't have her in his house again.'

'One more word from you, young lady, and I'll have to have words with Father Christmas!' said Sylvia.

'Father Christmas doesn't exist anyway,' said Iris.

'Don't be silly,' said Sylvia.

'Daddy said he doesn't, so there.'

Sylvia was furious. It was bad enough Michael filling her head with irreverence about God, but Father Christmas!

'It makes it more exciting for them,' she'd tried to explain, thinking how killjoy his socialist principles always were. 'The one who tells the other children Father Christmas doesn't exist is never very popular,' she'd added, knowing that he wouldn't want to make things worse at school for Iris.

Anthony was looking from his sister to his mother, as if they were both insane. 'Father Christmas does exist, Iris,' he said patiently. 'He's in the photo.'

'Of course he does,' said Sylvia with a wink, hoping to appeal to Iris's desire to be one of the grown-ups. 'There's Father Christmas sitting right next to Anthony.'

Iris said nothing this time.

'What I don't understand,' said Anthony, 'is why Father Christmas came to our school party. It wasn't Christmas Eve, and he didn't come down the chimney. In fact, I think he came in a car!'

'Well, it wasn't his official visit,' said Sylvia quickly.

She looked at the photo. Father Christmas's beard was slightly askew, revealing the distinctly rakish smile of the chairman of the school governors, Mr Eddie King. It was good of him to dress up each year and bring a sackful of penny chocolate bars for the children. The Kings were full of such acts of generosity, bestowing largesse, as Michael put it in the French way.

'Where's our chimney?' said Anthony suddenly.

'Modern houses don't really have chimneys,' said Sylvia, anticipating what was coming next.

'Well, how is Father Christmas going to get in?'

'We'll leave the door on the latch for him.'

'What about his sleigh? It's not snowing yet.'

'I'm sure it will later,' said Sylvia, beginning to wonder whether Michael's denial of Father Christmas's existence wasn't easier after all. 'That's lovely,' she went on as Iris held up the lantern she'd just glued.

'I'm going to make about a hundred and Daddy can string them up all round the room,' Iris told her.

'Where is Daddy?' asked Anthony, as if he'd only just noticed he wasn't there.

'Daddy's at the Palace Hotel playing the piano for the Kings' Christmas carols,' said Sylvia.

'We three Kings of Orient are!' Anthony started singing.

'Oh, that's funny, Anthony,' said Sylvia, clapping her hands. 'We three Kings! I wonder if that's one of their favourites?'

'But will he be home before Father Christmas gets here?' Anthony wanted to know.

'Daddy sometimes sleeps at the Palace,' Iris chipped in.

'No, he doesn't,' said Sylvia. 'He sometimes gets back after you've already gone to bed.'

'But sometimes he sleeps there,' Iris insisted.

'Don't be silly,' Sylvia scolded.

'He does too. Angela told me and she's seen him, so there!'

The King family were all present and they were all looking at him.

In full plumage, Michael thought, recalling the first page of *The Forsyte Saga*. He'd read all nine volumes at his Auntie Jean's house, at that age when the words were absorbed quickly and had formed, he now realized, most of his views about English upper-class society. Or, more accurately, the upper echelons of the English middle class. The families who were responsible, in their ruthless pursuit of wealth, for all the country's division.

Here they were, arrayed before him, as formidable a unit of society as they had been in Galsworthy's era. Christmas Eve, and its opportunity for a very public display of piety, had brought the Kings out in force.

En masse, their faces displayed the same genetic heritage. Unlike most families where the DNA was diluted down the generations, theirs had been concentrated by the union of cousins Libby and Eddie King, ensuring that their more unfortunate features were exaggerated in their children. Standing between their parents, Christopher and Angela brought to mind those portraits of Tudor children, their faces adult in miniature, disquieting and a little sad. On the peripheries, the more down-at-heel relations hovered. Eddie's Uncle Cyril cracked jokes between songs, which only young Christopher laughed at. A number of other cousins were designated harmonies by Liliana King, which their feeble baritones and faltering sopranos attempted, and failed, to follow.

It was the older Mrs King's looks, he observed, which had made one of her daughters a beauty, although, seeing them side by side, Pearl's features seemed coarsened by the input of King blood. Mrs Liliana King, when she chose to employ her scintillating smile, must have been stunning in her day.

Each family member had a turn to choose the carol and now the choice had fallen to Uncle Cyril.

Michael sat with his hands poised above the piano.

'I'm blowed if I can think of another!' said Uncle Cyril. 'We've had all the usual ones, haven't we?' he said, looking optimistically towards the door of the lounge from where the spicy smell of mulled wine wafted.

'How about "Silent Night"?' Pearl suggested. 'It's short, at least.'

They had sung all seven verses of 'In the Bleak Midwinter', at the end of which she had stated, 'Well, if it wasn't bleak before, it certainly is after that!'

It was strange seeing her with them all, behaving like a naughty schoolgirl showing off because she had a friend round for tea. Everyone pretended to ignore her, but sometimes her asides hit the spot quite wittily and forced involuntary smiles on to the disapproving faces.

' "Silent Night" is Mummy's choice,' Libby hissed at her sister. 'It's the last one we do.'

'Why does it always have to be the same?' Pearl asked. 'Let's be devils and do something new!'

Everyone in the room was focusing on her, waiting for her next caprice. She stirred in Michael the desire either to kiss or to slap, but very occasionally there was a surge of tenderness. In her own way, she was an outsider too, a free spirit trying to break from the clutches of expectation. He smothered any such thoughts, knowing that if he began to pity her, he would never be able to tell her it was over.

'How about that Christmas tree one you like?' the boy Christopher said to his great-uncle, trying to help him out.

' "Tannenbaum"! A first rate idea!' said Uncle Cyril, joshing the boy affectionately around the head. 'You know, it goes "O Tannenbaum, O Tannenbaum . . ." ' He started singing.

Liliana King glared at him disapprovingly.

'O Christmas tree, O Christmas tree,' Eddie translated. 'Come along, maestro!'

'I'm not sure I know that one,' Michael said, struggling to discern a melody.

'But I'm sure you must!' said Eddie loudly. 'It's the same tune as "The Red Flag"!'

Over the course of the year, all the original Victorian features, along with all the art deco furnishings and furbishments from the previous major updating in the thirties, had either been stripped out of the hotel, or, like the panelled doors and stucco ceilings, concealed behind plywood boards.

On Sunday afternoons, when Michael arrived to play during afternoon tea, the entrance hall had something of the atmosphere of a railway station about it, with people coming and going, suitcases stacked up, and enough happening for his own arrivals and departures to blend in with the general movement.

This evening, with most of the guests still in the lounge drinking mulled wine and nibbling cinnamon biscuits, it felt very different. There was new carpet on the floor and his shoes no longer made a guilty echoing tap across the marble.

The Windsor Suite had a notice on the door saying 'Closed for redecoration', but the key Pearl had slipped into his pocket slid in easily enough, and when he found the switch and flooded the room with light, it was clear that the decorators had yet to make a start.

Pearl usually gave him the key to one of the smaller rooms at the back of the hotel, the one with the brown ring on the ceiling where a radiator above had leaked, or the one with the view over the yard, where, on Mr Pocock's Sunday off, the kitchen boys played football, towelling the sweat from their faces with tea cloths they kept draped over their shoulders. Once, when a reunion of RAF officers had filled the hotel to capacity, Pearl had beckoned him into a linen cupboard and knelt in front of him. He'd not been able to smell ironing since without shuddering at the memory of it.

The opulence of the Windsor Suite was incredible. A whole family could live in a place like this, Michael thought, trailing his hand along the carved gilded frame of an armchair, then sitting down at the walnut veneer desk, taking a sheet of the thick white notepaper, with the hotel crest embossed at the top, and miming his signature over it.

The brocade curtains were drawn. Outside it was black as pitch, and he quickly let the curtain drop, in case anyone should look up from the town and catch him at the window, silhouetted in the bright white light of the teardrop chandelier.

Double doors led through to the bedroom. A further door opened into the biggest bathroom he had ever seen, with two basins side by side in a long pale green marble counter, and a bath big enough to swim in.

The bed was vast. It took two and a half complete rolls of Michael's body to get from one side to the other.

He lay on top of the quilted counterpane of jade-green silk and stared up at the ornate light fitting suspended from an elaborate ceiling rose, a great upside-down palm of green and golden glass leaves which diffused a mellow light around the room.

Suddenly, he narrowed his eyes to focus. The shining fronds were not leaves as they first appeared, but peacock feathers.

Dear Mike,

Still no call to arms, so we're stuck here, twiddling our thumbs (and some other parts of our anatomy!) and I've been sampling the amenities! The posh rooms have names painted on the door.

The other day, I partook of a cigarette on the balcony of the Windsor Suite and waved at my invisible subjects! You've never seen anything like it, mate. There's a chandelier of peacock feathers, like something out of Tsarist Russia. Long live the revolution, I say, although, 'til that day comes, it's nice to have a bit (of luxury, that is!). The beds are so soft it's like you're sinking into a cloud.

Write with news.

Your brother,

Frank

Michael jumped up from the bed and walked to the door, staring at the chandelier all the time. Then he went and lay back down. It was only when you were lying directly underneath it that you could see that the leaves were peacock feathers.

Frank must have been lying in this very spot!

He imagined his brother sneaking up the staircase, finding the door to the Windsor Suite open, slipping in and strolling round, checking the furniture for dust as if he owned the place. Flopping down on the bed, staring at the light . . . There was something that didn't quite work in the little reel of images running through his mind. The Windsor Suite would not have been left unlocked. It wasn't now. It certainly wouldn't have been when there were servicemen milling around the building. Like him, Frank must have had a key, or he must have been with someone who had a key.

A chambermaid!

Now it made sense. It was perfectly easy to imagine his brother ensnaring a chambermaid, having his way, and smoking a cigarette afterwards.

Two brothers lying in the same sinful spot, fifteen years apart. If Frank were alive, he would have laughed at that. Pearl had unwittingly chosen a memorable place for their last encounter! Miss Tennis Knickers herself, Michael could almost hear Frank saying.

The click of the outside door to the suite startled him.

He slipped underneath the counterpane to hide and surprise her just as the door to the bedroom opened . . .

'It's a lovely room, isn't it?' said Liliana King.

*

Unlike some of her daughter's other suitors, Liliana could see the attraction of this one. He exuded a kind of suppressed anger that women often found irresistible. The desire to make a solemn man smile, an unhappy man happy, was very potent. But would her daughter find him quite so attractive if she could see him now, Liliana wondered, looking frightened instead of dangerous, a little panicking face peeping out from the coverlet?

Liliana wondered if he still had his clothes on.

'Perhaps it's too fancy for your taste?' Liliana went on, with a wave at the Murano glass chandelier. 'My husband's older brother, Rex, lived in this suite, you know.'

She walked around the room, pointing out objects of special interest.

'He didn't see why the guests should have better than he did! He didn't really understand the duties of a hotelier, you see. I often think that Pearl is rather like him.'

She stopped and shot a glance at Michael.

'What happened to him, then?' He sat up, revealing himself still fully clothed.

Liliana felt a slight sting of disappointment. She would have preferred the humiliation to be complete. He was clever too. Clearly knew something of the scandal and had grabbed the opportunity to put her on the back foot.

'He went to live abroad,' she said in a clipped voice. 'In exile, one might say. The King family doesn't tolerate scandal, you know.'

The young man raised his eyebrows insolently.

'My son-in-law informs me that you're a Communist.' Liliana decided to get to the point.

'Well, he's wrong about that. I handed in my card in nineteen fifty-six.'

'Nineteen fifty-six?'

'When the Russians invaded Hungary.'

'I see.'

Typical of Eddie to get the details wrong, thought Liliana. Rather admirable of the pianist not to dissemble. Sometimes that kind of Northern bluntness could be very refreshing. Exciting, almost. If she'd been her daughter's age, she thought she would have been tempted herself. He was much less cowed than she had expected him to be by this stage of the encounter.

'My daughter will be thirty next year,' she said, perching on the end of the bed, as if he were a sick child she'd come to comfort. Not at all the tactics she'd planned.

His silence was one of his strengths. It made you think that there were unknowable thoughts going on behind those pale blue eyes. It was terribly difficult to read him. Did he have any feelings for Pearl, she wondered, or was he just playing with her?

'Thirty is quite a crucial age for a woman who has not married because it marks the end of not-lucky-yet and the beginning of never-will. And I'm sure you would agree that Pearl is not designed for spinsterhood?'

No expression except a kind of sullen attention.

'In other words, my daughter needs to find a husband quickly. Now, it's clear to me that you are not a suitable candidate for a number of reasons . . .'

His eyebrows lifted again.

'Apart from your politics,' she said, with a little laugh to acknowledge the inaccuracy of her intelligence, 'there's the rather more pertinent question of your wife and children.'

This elicited a wince and a defiant toss of the thick tawny hair.

'And your job, of course,' she pressed home the advantage. 'I think it's very unlikely that Kingshaven Primary School would want to employ a man who has been cited for adultery in divorce proceedings . . .'

'That'll not happen,' he said.

'You're confident of that?'

He nodded.

'In my experience, it doesn't do to be too confident,' said Liliana. 'I imagine it would be most distressing for your children to lose their father and their teacher at the same time. I don't know how anyone would live that down, do you?'

'What's your point?' he suddenly asked.

'I should have thought I'd made my point abundantly clear.'

It unsettled her, this way he had of looking at you as if he could see you naked, as if every sag and blemish of her fifty-nine-year-old skin were visible.

Ten years ago, he would not have looked like that, she thought. At forty-nine she had still passed for mid-thirties. The Change had come to her late and it had made her suddenly old. Sixty this coming year! Now she wished she had started knocking years off long before she got here, but it was difficult when everyone knew that you were the century's child.

'I advise you to end your association with my daughter immediately or the consequences for you will be catastrophic,' she said, unable to keep the shake of anger from her voice.

There was quite a long silence.

'It's not as easy as that,' he said.

Liliana sucked in her breath. Surely Pearl hadn't been quite so reckless?

'She's always threatening to tell my wife,' he explained.

Liliana laughed with relief.

'Pearl won't tell anyone,' she explained, 'because she knows that another scandal would put her on the shelf for ever.'

'But she doesn't want to get married,' he said.

'You're more of a fool than I thought,' said Liliana. 'Every woman wants to get married.'

He leaned forward aggressively. 'I was going to end it today anyway.'

Liliana was suddenly bored with his disrespect. 'Oh, do get out!' she said.

In the end he was a coward, Liliana thought, staring at the door as it clicked shut behind him. She hadn't particularly wanted him to insist on telling Pearl face to face, because that would only create another melodrama, but she didn't particularly relish the prospect of telling Pearl herself. They were all the same, these socialists, always passing the buck.

Eddie couldn't help noticing that it was the second night in a row that his wife was already in bed when he came up, and that she was wearing her satin nightdress, which was about as clear a signal for Go! as a green traffic light in the narrow bit at the bottom of Hill Street that the council had recently decreed one way.

The previous evening, his response had been an exaggerated yawn, lights out and his back towards her, but her sigh of thwarted reproach had remained in the air long after he had pretended to be asleep.

Tonight he sensed that he wouldn't be allowed to get away with giving her the red traffic light again.

'Doesn't time fly?' Libby asked.

'Yes,' he agreed. He usually took the route of least resistance when his wife was in one of these moods.

'And?' Libby wasn't going to let him get away with that.

He shrugged, defeated.

'Before you know it, your children have grown up,' Libby said.

The mare was broody. Now he understood.

'Absolutely!'

'You hardly notice it, especially if you're busy ... And suddenly, they're all teeth and their feet smell.'

'Couldn't agree more,' he said.

In his view, the benefits of fatherhood were grossly exaggerated. The mild amusement caused by the things your offspring said and did was vastly outweighed by the restrictions they put on your life. Children were a convenient excuse for your wife to order you not to swear, not to drink as many brandy sodas as you wanted, not to do anything you used to enjoy doing.

His wife was wriggling down next to him, her satin rucking up against his cotton nightclothes.

'Aren't you going to take this off?' she whispered, pinching the sleeve of his pyjama jacket.

What had happened to it being indecent to go to bed naked?

Now she was unbuttoning his pyjama jacket with fingers almost as nimble as a professional. Libby could be quite a minx when she chose to be. It was one of the things that had drawn him to her in the first place. The plain ones were often more eager to please.

But there was no familiar stirring in his groin.

They'd produced a boy and a girl. Nothing special, either of them, but with the requisite number of fingers and toes. Since then, children hadn't come into it. And nor had the act of procreation much, in recent years. There'd been a prolonged period of icy rebuff after Libby walked in on him with the chambermaid, but she'd melted gradually to allow sporadic romps on his birthday, or the rare occasions he'd poured a particularly strong gin and tonic, but neither of them had ever been so carried away that they hadn't taken sensible precautions.

He'd always assumed it was something they were of a mind about. Now that both children were at boarding school, the hotel was a much more agreeable place than when they were loitering around in the holidays.

'What is the matter?' Libby wanted to know, looking up from the task in hand.

The part of his anatomy which usually sprang into action at the slightest provocation appeared to have gone into a limp state of shock.

'I've got a lot on my mind,' he said.

Libby regarded him sceptically. He hoped she wasn't going to ask him what, because he would either have to lie, or say 'Nothing', which would get him into more trouble.

'You used to say it took a lot off your mind,' she said with her approximation of a coquettish smile. Her right hand slid down again to greet Little Eddie but he seemed even less inclined to stand up and say hello.

'Out of practice?' he suggested with a laugh which didn't go down at all well. 'Machinery gets a bit rusty when it hasn't been oiled for a while.'

'More like too well oiled,' Libby said disapprovingly.

He hoped that was a reference to the brandies he'd consumed after the carols rather than anything else she'd discovered.

'I'm not sure I feel as you do about the idea of more children,' he ventured, trying to voice the rational explanation for his present deficiency.

'Well, what is the point, then?' Libby snapped.

Without waiting for an answer, she rolled over and switched off her bedside light, leaving the taste of her anger in the sudden darkness.

The point of what, Eddie wondered, as his eyes adjusted.

The point of life?

The point of marriage?

Surely she didn't mean the point of him?

*

Anthony's present was so big it had to be wrapped in newspaper. Iris watched as he pulled off the yards of red ribbon their mother had tied around it and revealed a brand-new scooter. Its turquoise paint was so shiny it still looked wet, and it had bright yellow wheels with white rubber tyres.

'Yippee!' said Anthony, pushing off round the room. 'Thank you, Father Christmas!'

'Not indoors,' their mother warned.

'Can I go outside?'

'After Iris has opened her present.'

'Where is it?' asked Iris.

Perhaps her present was so big, even newspaper wouldn't do. Perhaps it was hidden upstairs in her parents' bedroom, like the dolls' house had been two years ago: a perfect replica of their own home made of plywood, with little curtains sewn from material left over from their curtains, and a television set made of a match-box, long before they got a real one. Perhaps it was a bike! Iris told herself she would be happy to settle for a scooter herself, or even a pair of roller skates.

'In your stocking, of course,' said her mother.

Iris was sure she had taken everything out of her stocking. There was the usual tangerine, an apple, a little yellow net of golden chocolate coins. She plunged her hand in to feel around again. Whatever it was must be very small.

Perhaps it was money. Angela King had boasted that she sometimes received money from her relations. Lots, she said, when Iris had asked how much. What would a bike cost, Iris wondered, as her hand closed around a small flattish square parcel right in the toe.

The wrapping paper had sprigs of holly on it and her mother had tied it very prettily with a little rosette of red silk. Iris made sure she took the ribbon off intact and unfolded the paper carefully without tearing it.

Inside was a maroon leather box. Iris glanced up at her father to make sure that he was looking at the moment of opening. His anxious smile was the first indication that something was wrong.

'What is it?' Iris asked, lifting the little silver chain off its red velvet bed. It had the smallest padlock she had ever seen at one end.

'What do you mean, what is it?' her mother asked. 'It's a charm bracelet, of course.'

'But it hasn't got any charms on it.'

'The whole point of a charm bracelet,' said her mother, whose mouth had gone all thin, like it always did when Iris did something that drove her mad, 'is that people buy you charms to go on it.'

'In Daddy's story, the charm bracelet had lots of charms!'

'What story?' Her mother stared at her father.

'The story about Rose Bun and the charm bracelet!' said Iris.

'People will buy you charms on special occasions,' Sylvia explained.

'Who will?'

'Granny, for instance. She never knows what to buy you.'

'Tell her I want a bike.'

'For heaven's sake!' Her mother was unable to contain her temper. 'I've never known such an ungrateful girl.'

She sounded as if she hated her. It was all Iris could do not to cry. It was unlucky to cry on Christmas Day.

'Even a scooter would do,' pleaded Iris.

They didn't even have to be new, she wanted to add, as long as she could zip along the promenade like the other children in her class did.

She saw her mother shoot a look at her father, who shrugged his shoulders. There was one of those horrible silences that felt so full of anger Iris longed for it to end, but dreaded it too, in case the anger burst out all over the place.

'I want to try my scooter outside!' Anthony shouted.

'Oh, run along, then, both of you,' said her mother impatiently.

'Give me first go,' Iris ordered.

Without looking back, she scooted all the way to the end of their street. It was a super feeling, flying along at speed, the cold air blowing her mother's words out of her hair. She slowed at the junction with Hill Road, putting her foot on the back wheel to bring it to a halt. Looking down towards the sea, she was tempted to zoom straight off down the hill, but Anthony, who was running after her, was bound to rush back and tell.

'You've broken my scooter,' he wailed.

'Course I haven't!'

'You have, look, you've made it all dirty!'

He pointed at the charcoal skid marks on the brand-new tyres.

'Here, have your stupid scooter then.' Iris thrust the handle-bars at him so roughly he fell over with the scooter on top of him.

She could hear her parents arguing from the road.

'It's not my fault she didn't like it. You were the one who insisted,' her father was saying.

'You're the one who tells her daft stories, raising her expectations.'

'I thought it might make her like it more. How was I to know it came without charms?'

'How could we afford charms as well?'

'I told you she wanted a bike.'

'When I was her age, I loved my charm bracelet!'

'But she's not you,' he said, more gently. 'You can't force her to like the things you liked. Iris has an independent mind.'

'And whose fault is that?'

'I don't consider it a fault. That's the fundamental difference between us!' her father said.

And then her mother started crying, as she often did when he used long words.

From the bridleway on the top of the ridge, Libby could see the whole of Kingshaven spread out before her. The view of the town from high up, all of a piece, gave her a nice, settled feeling that everything was manageable. The frost made all the buildings, from the slums around the harbour to the stepped Edwardian terraces of the New End, look as if they were coated with icing sugar, like a Christmas honey biscuit.

'Come to survey your kingdom, Lady Elizabeth?' Mr Donal Carney, who managed the Kingshaven stables, always asked as he handed over the reins of her black stallion. He was the only person in the world who called her by her full name. Libby had never liked the diminutive coined by Pearl when she was learning to speak, and used by the family ever since, but she wasn't sure whether Mr Carney's awarding her a title on top was simply a mistake or whether his mischievous Irish eyes were teasing her. The cheek of it was softened somehow by his accent, and she never bothered to correct him. Sometimes he would ride alongside her. Their conversation was limited, but there was an easiness between them based on their shared love of horses.

From this distance, in the cold, clarifying air, it was easier to get a perspective on things. Up here, she always felt privileged rather than burdened by her responsibilities. If she narrowed her eyes and allowed herself to imagine that the deep blue of the sea was a lake, the Palace Hotel, with its pine trees behind and virgin white terraces in front, brought to mind the January photograph of St Moritz in the Views of Switzerland calendar Eddie's mother had sent her for Christmas.

'It sounds awful, I know,' Libby said to Mr Carney as they trotted beside each other along the bridleway, 'but I do love to get out for a ride on Christmas Day! There's such pressure to enjoy yourself at Christmas. Not that it isn't a special time, in its way . . .'

'Far too many of us in our house,' said Mr Carney, who was the father of so many children Libby had lost count.

'Absolutely,' she said.

'All the little ones arguing over their presents!'

'Quite! We bought Angela a brand-new bicycle, a Raleigh in fact, with a pump and a bell, and do you know what she said?' Libby didn't wait for an answer. 'She said bikes were boring and she wanted a pony! Can you imagine?'

The horses snorted clouds of warm breath as they walked the steep incline. A few blood-red berries spotted the spiky skeletons of hedge, and the peaks of the ploughed furrows were dusted with frost.

'You'll be having her company on your rides then, Lady Elizabeth,' Mr Carney commented.

Libby sighed. 'Between you and me, I think I prefer riding alone.'

'In that case, I'll be leaving you here,' he offered immediately.

'Oh, no, you don't count!' Which didn't sound quite right. 'I never tire of your company,' she said, making direct eye contact with him to emphasize her sincerity.

In fact, Libby thought, she'd rather come to rely on it. He was so easy to be with. She was never certain whether he was friendly out of genuine affection or because she was paying him, but there were plenty of people she paid who weren't, and he possessed the most expressive dancing blue eyes she had ever seen. They had the most curious effect on her, sending a pulse right up through the horse's body into hers. Recently she had begun to have the same sensation at the mere thought of a ride, a pleasurable, warm rush, which felt so rude she hoped people couldn't see what she was thinking.

They paused at the top of the ridge.

Kingshaven was perfectly still. No traffic moving.

All those little boxes, Libby thought, were full of families getting on each other's nerves, and yet it all looked so peaceful as dusk began to fall and, one by one, the lights came on inside and lit up the windows like lanterns.

'Peace on earth,' Mr Carney said softly, almost as if he were reading her thoughts.

Her hands must have loosened on the reins for a moment, because the stallion suddenly decided to bolt. A less accomplished rider might well have been thrown off. The uncontrolled gallop back to the stables was terrifying and somehow at the same time so wonderfully pleasurable that she felt almost disappointed when they finally came panting to a halt.

'You are coming to the party?' Libby asked, handing over the reins, for some reason unable now to look Mr Carney in the eye.

'I most certainly am, Lady Elizabeth,' he said.

'I'm not sure what that horse does to you,' Mr Pocock always said when she arrived back. 'But you're always full of the joys of spring when you return from your ride.'

Since Christmas Day, everyone had been in a bad mood, Iris thought.

Her mother's spirits only seemed to lift when she was trying on the big dress with the tartan border.

'What do you think, Iris?' she would ask, twirling in front of her.

And, even though Iris hated the colour green, she kept quiet because she knew her mother wasn't really asking for an opinion. Her mother would rustle about in the dress keeping one eye on the mirror, trying to see how it looked at the back, and then she would brush her hair in different ways. One day, she sewed a scattering of little tartan bows all over the skirt. The next, she unpicked her work.

'You don't want to gild the lily,' she said when Iris asked her why.

The day before New Year's Eve, Sylvia was in the dress, trying to decide whether her hair was best loose or tied with a broad tartan bow, when her father looked up from his newspaper and dropped his bombshell.

'We're not going.'

'What do you mean?' her mother asked.

'Which word didn't you understand?' he replied in the cold voice he used in class when one of the boys was being silly.

'What do you mean?' Sylvia repeated.

'I'm not prepared to kowtow to the Kings.'

'But you play the piano for them.'

'Not any more.'

'What? Have you done something to upset them?' her mother wanted to know.

'Oh, for God's sake!'

'But we've accepted the invitation . . .'

He walked out.

'You can always go to the Palace by yourself,' Iris said.

Her mother's disappointment was so heavy it seemed to weigh the air down. 'I can't,' she replied.

'Daddy does!'

Sylvia sighed. 'It's not the same for women,' she said.

Iris didn't say anything, because she knew what she had in mind would only make her mother cross again, but the very next day the chance presented itself when they encountered Angela's mother coming out of the hairdresser. Iris waited while her mother and Mrs King said the usual things about the weather, then Mrs King opened her car door and got in, and Iris knew it was the moment.

'Can a lady go to your party without a man?' she asked, crossing both sets of fingers hard in the pockets of her winter coat.

From her car seat, Mrs King looked up, surprised at being spoken to by a child, but then smiled. Iris didn't think she'd ever seen her smile before. It made her look pretty.

'It wouldn't be much good if they couldn't,' Mrs King said. 'Mrs Farmer, and my mother, and, for that matter, Pearl. Jolly Allsop, not that he's a lady of course, but I very much doubt Jennifer's in a state to . . . All sorts of people. It's the beauty of Scottish reeling. You're always changing partners!' Mrs King gave a little wave and drove away in a cloud of exhaust fumes.

'There you are, you see, Mummy,' Iris said to her mother, thinking that she was probably a good witch just like Rose Bun. 'You shall go to the ball!'

The large semi-detached villas of Belsize Park were a curious mixture of houses that had been converted into bedsits with twenty bells beside the door and a whole continent of lives colliding on the staircase, and an occasional single dwelling recently converted back to its original high-ceilinged elegance. The early Victorian façade of Tim's parents' house gleamed with new paint the fresh, dense colour of vanilla ice cream. There was no reply when Claudia knocked on the brass knocker but the shiny black front door opened when she pushed it. The hall was tiled; one of the walls was covered in framed drawings, the other shelved with books. There was a wide staircase with wooden banisters draped with guests' overcoats.

Claudia walked towards the general drift of jazz, which became a loud blast as she opened the door at the end of the hall and found herself standing on a balustraded gallery, overlooking a space like no room she had ever seen. The basement had been opened up, so it was the height of two rooms, and the rear aspect on to the garden was entirely made of glass. The building work was recent and unfinished. The word 'Top' daubed in thick white paint had yet to be cleaned from several of the giant panes of glass. One of the side walls was only half plastered. The brackish whiff of freshly broken brick mingled with the spicy fug of foreign cigarettes.

Steps led down to a mezzanine kitchen, where a saxophonist, a drummer and a double bass player were playing beneath a hanging frame of saucepans and kitchen utensils.

Below there was a sea of people, talking in loud groups, or sprawled over shabby armchairs. The women were dressed in muted colours, with coloured stockings, wine, olive and black, the men in corduroy trousers and shirts without ties. Filled with sudden panic, Claudia wanted to do an about turn and disappear before anyone noticed the ridiculous tinsel, which made her feel about as sophisticated as a child dressing up as a Christmas fairy.

Then, suddenly, Tim's face emerged from the crowd, shouting, 'Claudia!' and he bounded up the stairs. His delight at seeing her was so public and unabashed she couldn't help smiling as everyone else in the room turned to look at her, and the saxophonist played a riff that sounded curiously like an echo of her name.

Tim's mother was willowy, upper class and a little distant.

'Pippa,' she said, holding out a languid hand.

They were first-name sort of people.

His father, Roman, was short, serious and very charming.

When Claudia expressed polite interest in his collection of drawings, he took her to see them, pointing out those with a particular story, explaining how he came by them, as if he had all the time in the world and she was the only person he wanted to talk to.

When a film director lurched at her and suggested she take a screen test for him, Roman fended him off. 'She's far too clever to be an actress, Ken.'

The vast space was full of writers, artists, film-makers: the sort of people she had dreamed of meeting when she was growing up. She had always expected that there would come a moment at Cambridge that she would recognize as a kind of watershed between youth and adulthood, but somehow she had still always felt like a provincial schoolgirl there. Tonight, as the jazz washed over her, the wine and conversation flowed and the hours slipped away before the beginning of the new decade, she was buoyed by optimism for the future.

When someone turned on the radio so that the party could listen to the chimes of Big Ben, Claudia remembered momentarily how she had felt on the eve of 1950, the first time her father had allowed her to stay up to see the New Year in. They'd listened to the wireless and he'd let her taste his tiny glass of schnapps. It had burnt her tongue. She'd closed her eyes and wished the coming decade would be better for them, crossing her fingers hard, like the little girl she then was, her hair still in plaits.

Now, as she gazed around this gathering, catching Tim's adoring eyes watching her, she wondered fleetingly where she would be in another ten years, at the beginning of the seventies. But that seemed unimaginably far away. Here and now was the beginning of her real life. This place, this milieu, this new decade was where she belonged.

The ballroom of the Palace Hotel was decked out with garlands of holly, and balls of mistletoe were suspended from the ceiling on tartan ribbons. A fiddler and a drummer, both dressed in kilts, played in one corner. The room seemed to be swirling with skirts as the caller called the Gay Gordons.

Mr Pocock announced each guest as they arrived.

'Mrs Michael Quinn!'

'Sylvia, darling!' Pearl rushed towards her. 'What have you done with that husband of yours?'

'I'm afraid he's indisposed,' said Sylvia.

'Indisposed?' Pearl repeated. 'Do you mean he's not coming?'

'Mrs Quinn.' Liliana swooped in. 'You know Jolly, of course?'

'Yes. By sight, I mean,' said Sylvia.

'I don't believe I've had the pleasure,' said Jolly Allsop, offering his hand.

'Oh, don't be silly, Jolly,' Pearl snapped.

'But we've never been introduced,' Sylvia defended him.

'I certainly would have remembered if we had,' said Jolly, gallantly, which settled her nerves a little.

*

'Mr Tom Snow!'

Eddie looked up sharply from his task of ladling punch into bowls. 'Who the hell invited him?'

'He's the photographer,' Libby told him.

'I know he's the photographer, for God's sake!' Eddie said. 'But why does he turn up at every occasion? Can't they send someone else occasionally?'

'Are you blind?' Libby asked.

'What do you mean?'

'Can't you see he's got a crush on Pearl?'

Eddie's eyes followed the photographer as he made his way round the room, smiling with his big teeth, like the cat that got the cream.

'That's why he's always here?' he said.

'Of course,' said his wife, smiling as if she were floating on a cloud of bonhomie.

Was it the advocaat? Eddie wondered. She'd not been herself since Christmas. When he'd pointed out that she seemed happier than usual, she'd come up with some tripe about the season of goodwill to all men.

Well, there'd be no further seasonal cheer for the photographer, Eddie thought. Snow needn't think there'd be any more surreptitious tenners turning up in his pocket. If he wanted Pearl, he was welcome to her, but Eddie wasn't going to pay to have her taken away.

'Miss Norma Barker!' announced Mr Pocock.

That was more like it. The barmaid from the Yacht Club looked absolutely stunning in a white halter-necked dress with a full skirt of pleated chiffon which the draught from the main door played with around her legs.

'Who is Norma Barker?' asked Libby. 'And what has she done for the hotel's fortunes this year?' she added acidly.

'We couldn't do without her at the Yacht Club,' said Eddie.

'Mr Donal Carney!' Mr Pocock announced.

'Who the hell is Mr Donal Carney?' said Eddie.

'He manages the stables,' Libby informed him crisply.

'Sounds Irish to me,' said Eddie.

'Second generation, I believe,' said Libby.

'Any other riff raff I should know about?' said Eddie.

*

'How is Jennifer?' Sylvia asked Jolly Allsop, trying to keep a conversation going so he wouldn't have the opportunity to leave her stranded.

'A bit like a beached whale at the moment,' he said.

'The baby must be due any time now?'

'Can't be much longer.'

'Poor Jennifer,' said Sylvia. 'She's been so poorly this time.'

'We're rather hoping that's a good sign,' said Jolly.

'I was very sick when I had my boy,' Sylvia told him.

'Oh, good!' Jolly smiled at her happily. 'I say, do you think we should join in the dancing?'

'If looks could kill . . .' said Tom Snow.

'Oh, it's you,' said Pearl King, taking her eyes off the dancing for a moment. 'What do you want?'

'I want to dance with the prettiest girl in the room.'

'Everyone's queuing up for Mrs Quinn. Look at Eddie. Practically drooling in anticipation . . .'

'I'm not interested in Mrs Quinn,' said the photographer.

'Why ever not?' Pearl turned round to ask him.

'I sometimes find blondes a little . . . icy,' he said.

'Do you know, I've often wondered myself if Sylvia isn't a little . . . glacial,' said Pearl, cheering up a little.

'Brunettes have so much more . . . warmth,' he said, holding out his hand.

'Sssh!' said Angela to Christopher. The door to the broom cupboard creaked as he closed it behind him.

'After he's played the piano, Mr Quinn pretends to leave, but in fact he comes up here and waits for Pearl.'

'I can't see,' said Christopher, trying to get a turn at the little spyhole a couple of feet off the floor where his sister was kneeling.

'You can't see anything until they turn the light on, stupid,' said Angela.

'I don't think Mr Quinn's here, anyway,' said Christopher.

'Well, sometimes she does it even if he's not here,' said Angela. 'With a pillow!'

Christopher shifted his position slightly, bringing a broom-handle down with a clatter.

'Sssh!' said Angela. 'Listen, can you hear anything?'

'No!'

'That means they're eating. I expect she'll be up soon.'

'I'm hungry,' said Christopher.

'We can't go now, or she might catch us,' Angela told him, pressing her face back to the spyhole.

'Do *you* have any idea why Mr Quinn isn't here?' Pearl asked her mother, who was in the kitchen serving out the pie with a big white apron tied over her dress.

Her mother concentrated on the task of carefully cutting the second huge tray into squares. Clouds of deliciously meaty steam rose as the golden crust was pierced.

'Mummy?' Pearl asked, immediately suspicious.

'Can't you see I'm busy?'

Her mother levered out a portion with a fish slice, and handed the plate to Pearl, who kept her hands by her side, refusing to take it.

'I won't play waitress unless you tell me!'

'Oh, do grow up, Pearl!' her mother retaliated, wielding the fish slice at her.

Little globules of gravy flew off in all directions; one burning drop landed right in Pearl's cleavage.

'I told you to wear an apron,' her mother said as Pearl blotted it off, leaving an inflamed red spot on the firm white skin.

'It was you, wasn't it? What have you done with him?' Pearl demanded.

'I merely told him what any concerned parent would,' Liliana replied, trying to be conciliatory.

'I don't suppose you were concerned about ruining my life?'

'Pearl, you're too old for this kind of tantrum!'

'Tantrum! You play with other people's lives and you don't care what happens, do you? Do you?' she screamed so loudly across the pie that Liliana took a step back.

'People will hear you,' Liliana said quietly.

'And that's what matters. That's all that really matters. What other people think. Well, damn you all!' Pearl's voice was rising to a climax. 'And damn your bloody pie!'

She pulled an empty saucepan off the huge cooker and slammed it down right in the middle of the pie. Then she ran out of the kitchen through the staff door.

The dining room had fallen silent as the shouting in the kitchen grew louder.

'Delicious pie!' said Jolly Allsop loudly, and, as if his words had given permission, the room began to murmur with reinvigorated chatter again.

'I say,' said Jolly, looking across the table. 'I say, are you feeling all right?'

Sylvia could tell from only one taste of the gravy. Her tongue started to tingle almost immediately, and she was gripped by a horrible prescience of doom.

'There's something in the pie,' she whispered hoarsely. 'Doesn't agree with me.'

'I say, you've gone very red. Do you need some air?' Jolly asked.

'Yes, some air. Some water.' Sylvia clutched at her throat.

'I say,' said Jolly again, 'is Dr Payne around? Mrs Quinn doesn't appear to be very well.'

'Here she comes now,' said Angela.

Christopher was curled up on the floor asleep, a mop head as his pillow. His sister nudged him viciously. But the tap of Pearl's footsteps did not stop outside the room, but carried on up towards the tower.

'What?' said Christopher, rubbing his eyes.

'Come on!' said Angela.

'Where?'

'Up the tower.'

'I don't want to go up there,' he said. 'It's haunted.'

'Oh, don't be such a sissy!' said Angela.

'Anyone for Murder in the Dark?' Libby tried to distract the crowd from the commotion on the balcony, where Mrs Quinn appeared to be having some kind of fit. Dr Payne would soon have things under control and there was no point in spoiling it for everyone.

'How about Sardines?' Eddie suggested.

Wasn't that the one where if you found someone you squeezed in with them? Libby was about to suggest Hide and Seek instead when she caught the sparkling eyes of Mr Carney.

'Sardines, everyone!' she called.

'Oysters,' said Liliana. 'I hope I can rely on your oath of confidentiality, Dr Payne. They're my secret ingredient. I find they just give the pie that certain *je ne sais quoi!*'

'I'm afraid therein lies the problem,' said Dr Payne. 'Shellfish most certainly do not agree with Mrs Quinn. There was a similar incident at the Flower Festival in the summer when she mistook a lobster mousse for a strawberry fool. Fortunately, this time, she has only ingested a little of the gravy.'

'They're perfectly fresh, I can assure you,' said Liliana.

What a nuisance the Quinn woman was turning out to be. Arriving alone, then collapsing in the middle of supper. The implication that her pie was somehow to blame! Quinn was most definitely a name to be crossed out of the Palace's address book.

A sudden overbearing feeling of *déjà vu* gripped Liliana for an instant. And then released her.

'Found you!' Tom Snow's head pushed up the trap door which led into the attic.

'Leave me alone!' shouted Pearl from beside the window.

'Sssh!' he said. 'You'll give us away.'

'What?' she asked.

'Sardines,' he said.

'I'm not playing!'

'What are you doing up here, then?'

'Actually, I'm about to throw myself out of the window!'

Eddie pushed the optic on the brandy bottle up, holding his punch cup underneath. While the guests were seeking out the far reaches of the hotel, the best place to hide was often one of the public areas. Nobody ever dreamed of looking there.

'Mine could do with a bit of stiffening up as well,' said Norma from her hiding place under the bar, squashed against the cider barrel.

Extraordinary the effect her voice could have on Little Eddie!

'It's true, then,' she went on, from her privileged vantage point, 'what men wear under kilts.'

Tom stood beside Pearl, looking down at the drop.

'Splat!' he said. 'What a waste of someone so special.'

'Do you think I'm special?' Pearl asked with a little sniff.

'I think you're very special, very gorgeous,' he said, putting a finger under her chin. 'And very clever.'

'Clever? Really? Nobody thinks I'm clever.' Pearl sniffed again.

'And witty!'

'Really?'

'I've been pining for you for years,' he said sadly. 'And now? Splat!'

'How many years?' Pearl couldn't help asking.

'The first time I saw you was Coronation Day. You were wearing red then too.'

'I think it was pink actually. Very dark pink.'

'I've been in love with you ever since,' he said.

She couldn't tell whether he was joking. She thought he was, a bit, but also that he half meant it.

'And now I'll have to content myself with a mere photo album,' he said, looking out again.

'A photo album?'

'Full of pictures of you. Can't help myself, I'm afraid. I follow you around like a devoted disciple.'

'Could I see?' she asked.

'Of course. Why don't you come back to my studio?'

'Now?'

'Why not?'

'I don't think Mummy . . .'

'One minute you're going to kill yourself, the next you're worried what Mummy will think?' he teased. 'How old are you?'

'Twenty-nine,' Pearl admitted.

'You're a big girl now. You're allowed to go to your friend's house.'

'Are you my friend?' she asked, a little nervously.

'I'd like to be,' Tom said, taking her hand and drawing her away from the ledge.

'Everyone's playing Sardines,' Jolly Allsop said to Sylvia as they came back into the empty bar. 'Are you well enough to join in?'

'I think I'd be better off going home,' she said.

The coolness of the air outside had helped the itchiness to subside on Sylvia's face and neck, but she was sure she was all blotchy, and she didn't want the whole of Kingshaven to see her like that when they returned to the ballroom for the next game.

'Will you allow me to accompany you?' he said.

'No, I'll be fine on my own,' she said.

'But I absolutely insist,' said Jolly Allsop, ushering her out of the room.

Beneath the bar, Eddie and the blonde simultaneously exhaled.

Libby was crouched behind the door of the Windsor Suite as it was slowly pushed open.

'Lady Elizabeth?'

'Quick. Close the door.'

Mr Carney found her in the darkness, as quickly as hounds would sniff out a fox in a barn. And suddenly – she wasn't quite sure how it happened: did she lean towards him, or he to her? – they were kissing. His lips were soft and exploratory, more like a horse's muzzle than a hard, demanding man's mouth. And then he was coaxing her mouth open, his tongue flickering in.

'You've got a Mini!' squealed Pearl when she saw Tom Snow's car. 'How on earth could you afford that?'

'Private income,' said Tom with a wink.

'Really?'

'All will be revealed,' he said.

'How perfectly intriguing!' said Pearl, lowering herself into the passenger seat and squashing her skirt inside.

'Who was that?' Jolly Allsop asked Sylvia as a new Mini car accelerated down the drive, spraying them with gravel.

Sylvia had only seen one on television before. They certainly were small in real life, like a big toy. Right on the ground. She didn't think she'd like that.

There was a fold of red silk waving from the passenger door like a flag.

'I think it was Pearl,' she said.

'Another new man!' said Jolly. 'Where is your husband this evening?' he asked, after a moment or two.

'Indisposed,' said Sylvia.

'Of course! You said.'

Their footsteps echoed metallically on the pavement.

'End of another year!' said Sylvia.

'Yes, it is!' said Jolly.

'I'll be glad when this one's over,' said Sylvia.

'Not long to go!'

'Been a bit of a funny one for me, nineteen fifty-nine,' Sylvia reflected. 'What with the strawberry fool, and the accident . . .'

'Accident?'

'The brake cable on my bike snapped. Luckily I've always been a bit timid on bikes, and I wasn't on the steep part of the hill, so just some cuts and bruises. And a touch of wounded pride!' she said.

'Poor you!' said Jolly.

'You would have thought you'd be safe with a meat pie! Still, they say bad things come in threes,' said Sylvia. 'So let's hope that's an end to it.'

'Roll on nineteen sixty!' said Jolly.

Liliana King's preference would have been Charades. The fewer elements of unpredictability involved in a party game, the more successful the outcome.

With Charades, there was always a player whose slowness or lack of ingenuity amused, as there was one whose quick wits or talent surprised (her son-in-law Eddie was particularly adept at mime and always had everyone in stitches. She put it down to long spells on boats with nothing better to do). Sardines, Murder in the Dark, even Hide and Seek often had more dangerous overtones, especially in a building with floors up and windows out for redecoration.

Or perhaps she was just getting more anxious as she grew older, Liliana thought. How tiresome it was of Jennifer to have gone into labour this very evening and deprive her of her friend Ruby's company.

The hotel had gone very quiet indeed, but as Liliana lay in bed, she was sure she could hear a noise above her. As if there was someone in the tower.

A mile or so away, Kingshaven's church clock began to strike the hour.

Chapter Eight

1 January 1960

Bong!

In London, Tim asked, 'Will you marry me?'

Bong!

'Yes!' said Claudia.

Bong!

In the Windsor Suite of the Palace Hotel, Mr Carney asked, 'May I? May I? Lady Elizabeth?'

Bong!

'Yes! Yes! Yes! YES!' Libby panted.

Bong!

In the tower, Liliana King shone her torch, and asked, 'Is anybody there?'

Bong!

'No!' said Angela King.

Bong!

In the Summer House, Mrs Farmer urged, 'Just one more push, Jennifer!'

Bong!

'Is it a boy?' Jennifer asked.

Bong!

'Yes!' screamed the midwife.

Bong!

In Cherry Avenue, Sylvia Quinn waved at Jolly Allsop as he

hurried off home. 'Michael?' she said, opening the door to their house.

Bong!

'Yes?'

Bong!

'Happy New Year!' said Sylvia.

Michael took a deep breath and waited for the house of cards he had built of his life to come tumbling down around him.

'Aren't you going to say it, then?' Sylvia asked. She was very pink and her eyes were very bright, and she was smiling.

'What?' he asked.

'Happy New Year!'

'Happy New Year!' Michael replied.

Sylvia gave a last twirl of her dress, before kicking off her shoes.

'So, what was it like?' he asked, wondering if his voice sounded normal to her. To him, it was a hollow echo in his head.

'Lovely!' she said. 'Apart from the pie.'

'Are you sure you're all right?' Michael asked, putting his palm against her forehead to test her temperature after she'd explained.

'All it needed was a bit of fresh air. I didn't actually eat any of it.'

'I'll make you a cup of tea,' he volunteered.

'That would be nice,' she said, sitting down at the dining table.

He wondered whether Sylvia had been drinking, or whether it was still the after-effects of the taste of oyster. There was something a little feverish about her.

'Dr Payne brought you home, did he?' Michael placed a cup of tea in front of her.

'No, Mr Allsop accompanied me. He's a gentleman!'

Should he infer a hint of criticism? Was this the beginning of the onslaught? Sylvia was behaving so differently from how he'd been dreading as he sat waiting for her, watching the last seconds of the old year tick away.

'What are your New Year's resolutions, then?' Sylvia asked.

Was her question as innocent as it appeared or was she trying to trick him into a confession? He had been so convinced that Pearl would throw a histrionic scene. Perhaps, after all,

Mrs King did know her daughter better, and he had been granted a reprieve?

A new kind of horror immediately began to seep into his mind. If his secret was to remain hidden, would it bind him to the Kings? It was tempting to confess and take his punishment now.

'So, are you going to tell me, or not?' Sylvia asked, looking at him over the rim of her teacup.

'What?' he asked, alarmed.

'New Year's resolutions! No, wait a minute, New *Decade*'s resolutions,' she corrected herself.

'No nuclear weapons, the abolition of private education—?' he suggested.

'It's not a party manifesto. It's about things you promise yourself you'll try to do,' Sylvia interrupted crossly.

His heart was racing. If he didn't answer soon, she'd suspect something even if she didn't know already. 'I will try to be a better person . . .' he faltered.

Sylvia rolled her eyes impatiently.

'What about you?' he asked.

'You won't laugh?' she said, sitting forward on the dining chair, putting her cup down on the tablecloth.

'No . . .'

'I'd like to get a shop of my own,' she confessed. 'You're thinking what shallow, materialistic ambitions she has . . .' she added, looking at him.

'I am not . . .' he protested, but he was alarmed at how she had seen through him.

'Not like you, of course, with all your world peace and being a better person,' she went on, 'which isn't, in fact, what you really want at all.'

'Isn't it? So what is it I really want?' he asked.

If he had it coming, better to get it over with.

'I've seen you watching the letterbox every morning. What you really want is to be published. You wouldn't give a fig about being a better person if you could see your book in a bookshop, would you?'

He felt diminished by the pathetic transparency of his hope.

'Have you been drinking a lot?' he asked.

'A bit,' she admitted, unbowed. 'And you know what they say?'

'What do they say?'

'*In vino veritas!* It means the truth comes out when you've had a drink. Mrs Farmer told me.'

'She should know.'

'That's typical of you, isn't it?' Sylvia went on. 'Always criticizing other people, and never looking at yourself. You should hear yourself. Sneer, sneer, sneer . . .'

'All right, all right!' he said, holding his hands up against the battering, which was so unlike Sylvia that he was beginning to find it almost amusing. 'How about I make it my New Year's resolution to be less critical. OK?'

Sylvia suddenly stopped her tirade. 'Do you think,' she said, reaching her hand tentatively across the table. 'Do you think you could have a New Year's resolution to try to like me a bit more?'

It was such a small request, so childlike in its innocence.

He knew that this was the moment to be honest. She would forgive him if he told her. But it would hurt her so much. It would be too cruel to hurt her now.

'Yes,' he said, taking her outstretched hand in his. 'I will do that. I'm sorry.'

'Oh, it's you, Angela!' said Liliana King. Her granddaughter was squashed into an alcove and in her long white nightgown she looked like a statue too big for its niche. 'You gave me quite a fright.'

'Who did you think it was then?' Angela wanted to know.

'Nobody,' said Liliana quickly. 'A rat, possibly.'

'Or a ghost,' said Angela, ducking out of her hiding place and picking her way down the steps.

'What makes you say that?' Liliana asked.

'Christopher says there's a ghost. A ghost of a little boy.'

'Does he say he's seen it?' Liliana asked evenly.

'Of course not. There's no such thing as ghosts!' said Angela triumphantly.

'Quite right!' said Liliana. 'Now come along. It's hours past your bedtime.'

'I wanted to see the New Year in,' Angela told her as they

walked back along the corridor in their nightdresses. 'But nothing happened.'

'What on earth do you mean?'

'I thought that nineteen sixty would *look* different,' said Angela.

For a moment, Liliana remembered exactly how it felt to be a child staying up until midnight for the first time: the heightened reality brought on by forcing yourself to keep awake; the mounting anticipation as a first adult rite of passage drew ever closer; then the chimes and . . . what? A few cheers, a chorus of 'Auld Lang Syne', and everything went back to being exactly the same as it was before, except that you were now so tired, you were completely unable to sleep.

In the hall downstairs, the Victorian clock began to chime the hour, a good fifteen minutes late.

'We're rather behind the times here,' Angela said.

Liliana laughed. 'Very good!' she said. Perhaps Angela did after all have potential?

'It's what Pearl always says,' said Angela.

Liliana looked at her granddaughter. Ten years old and her whole life ahead of her. At the end of this new decade, Angela would still not have reached her prime, and she would be an old lady. She was filled with a sudden impossible urge to stop the clock and hang on to the present for dear life.

'Yes!' said Claudia.

It was suddenly so wonderfully clear, like a neat solution to a crossword clue. She'd struggled with all sorts of convoluted layers of meaning, but when she finally saw what the simple answer was she couldn't think how she hadn't got it before.

'Are you sure?' Tim asked doubtfully. 'How much have you had to drink?'

'Yes, I'm sure, and not that much,' she told him.

He grabbed her hand and pulled her up the steps to the mezzanine.

'Ladies and gentlemen!' he shouted.

A few of the more drunken guests were still singing 'Auld Lang Syne'.

Tim nodded at the drummer, who did a loud roll on his snare drum, making everyone stop and look up.

'I have an announcement!'

He looked down at Claudia for a second, uncharacteristically uncertain, as if he doubted her sincerity. She nodded to reassure him.

'Claudia and I are getting married!'

A huge cheer went up. Another drum roll.

And then he bent his face towards hers.

Crazily, to kiss him seemed like a much bigger step than to marry him.

Tim saw the panic in her eyes, and dropped his mouth lightly on to hers, the briefest touch.

Amid the wolf-whistles, a loud, lascivious voice heckled, 'Come on, you can do better than that!'

'Later!' Tim shot back, gripping Claudia's hand hard. Protecting her.

And then everyone was surrounding them, congratulating them.

When it was finally Tim's father's turn, he held both her hands and looked levelly into her eyes, and said, 'I hope you will make each other very happy.'

'We already do,' she replied brightly, somehow knowing that this was not quite what he meant.

'I'm going to walk Claudia home,' Tim interrupted.

'Isn't it rather a long way?' Claudia asked as Tim helped her into her coat.

'Not if we go by the park.'

She still found distances in London confusing. Some tube stops were almost next door to each other, others were miles apart. The leafy avenues of Belsize Park were quite a different landscape from the grimy terraces around Mornington Crescent where she lived, three stops down the Northern Line.

'Are you tired?' Tim asked as they set off in the dark.

'Not at all!'

At the top of Primrose Hill they stopped, and he put his arm around her. The lights of London stretched as far as they could see.

'Where shall we live?' Tim said with an expansive gesture as if he were offering her the whole city.

'I don't know. Bloomsbury?' She was half joking, thinking it might be fun to have an address with all those literary connotations. 'Or Fitzrovia?' She walked each morning through Fitzroy Square. There were huge trees there and the sound of a breeze through the leaves blew the rumble of the city from her mind, and allowed her body a moment of peace before all the noise at work. She thought she would like to live somewhere where she could feel just a little connected to nature.

'How about Ladbroke Grove? You can get a lovely house quite cheaply if you're prepared to put some work into it,' Tim suggested. 'And it would be very convenient for the new Television Centre . . .'

He was already plotting his career through the BBC. This evening Claudia had understood where his extraordinary self-belief came from. If you grew up surrounded by creative people, you knew about literature because you knew writers, and film because you knew directors, and television because you knew producers. You assumed these jobs were open to you because they were what people around you did. It was the same as her always thinking she should be an academic, because that's what her father did. It wasn't exactly arrogance.

They would live in Ladbroke Grove then, Claudia thought, wondering why he had even bothered to ask her.

'Where is Ladbroke Grove, by the way?' she asked as the sky over the city grew lighter.

'Over there!' he said, throwing out his arm. He turned and smiled at her, and he took her face in his hands and kissed her a little longer than before, and then he unwound the tinsel from her neck and draped it around his like an opera scarf as they ambled down towards the Outer Circle of the park.

They were how a young couple should be, Claudia thought. They complemented each other. He was outgoing, quick, charming; she was more reticent, thoughtful, an observer. He gave her the wings of confidence, and she gave him a kind of grounding when his flights became too fanciful.

He kissed her again outside her door, for much longer this time. She allowed her mouth to relax against his.

'Mmmmm,' he said when he eventually drew away.

'Mmmm,' she replied with a little giggle.

'I've been waiting such a long time for that,' he said.

'I'm sorry.'

'No, it was worth it.'

She smiled at him, not knowing what came next.

'Shall we go away for a weekend?' he asked her. 'Some seedy hotel by the sea?'

'Oh no!' she said.

He was right that they needed to do it now. Soon. And she was glad he had not suggested that she spend the night at his house. His parents were certainly liberal enough not to mind, to encourage even, but she did not want to encounter his father's knowing eyes at breakfast.

But a hotel would be worse. The thought of the chambermaids' speculations as they made the beds . . .

'Not a hotel,' she said, wanting to show that her objection wasn't prudish.

'My mother has a cottage in Suffolk,' he said. 'But it's freezing at this time of year.'

'We wouldn't freeze,' she said.

'No?' He looked surprised at the implication.

What did he think? That being a virgin disqualified you from discussing sexual intercourse?

'I'll arrange it then,' he said.

Another kiss. A longing look. She turned and ran up the stairs.

'Sleep well!' he called, looking at the sky which was almost light.

From the top of the steps she waved at him all the way down the street. It was only when she put the key into the front door that it occurred to her neither of them had said anything about love.

Tom Snow's studio was above a Chinese restaurant in the red-light area of Lowhampton.

'Have you ever eaten Chinese?' he asked Pearl.

'Certainly not!'

'But you'd love it! Sweet and sour all in one mouthful. Rather like you!'

A little oriental woman wearing an emerald-green silk dress popped her head around a door at the bottom of the staircase when she heard the key in the lock. Her face popped back just as quickly as she registered that he had company.

'Who was that?' Pearl wanted to know.

'Miss Chu keeps an eye out for me!'

'Does she indeed?' said Pearl, picking her way up the dingy staircase in her ball gown. She'd never have imagined such an exotic side to the photographer, who had always appeared such a clean-cut example of middle-class Englishness.

There was a somewhat Chinese flavour to the narrow hallway he showed her into after more locks at the top of the stairs: a fringed lampshade in fuchsia pink; a hall mirror in a carved black frame with golden dragons roaming over it. Pearl wondered what the flat had been used for before he moved in.

'Welcome! I haven't had a chance to do it all up yet,' Tom explained. 'Bedroom, kitchen, darkroom.' He pointed at the doors off the narrow corridor. 'Studio!'

The flick of a switch flooded the sparse white room with light so bright it made her blink. There were screens, an open umbrella and a couple of chairs at one end. At the other, the space was taken up with lighting and tripods and photographic equipment. On the back wall four large frames displayed black and white prints of his work.

'I prefer to use the same model,' he said as Pearl stared at the pictures, startled to recognize herself.

One of the photographs had her looking surprised as her hat blew off one Sunday as she was coming out of church; another had her glancing at her watch as she waited underneath the clock tower; the third was the moment of a kiss on the disused pier at Quarry Point, a couple too far away to be recognized making a dark silhouette of passion against the white crash of a wave breaking behind them.

'This is my favourite,' he told her, pointing to a close-up of her face asleep against the striped cloth of a deckchair. She was gratified to see the evenness of her dark eyebrows and the matt quality of her skin.

'Imagine waking up next to such a perfect nose,' he said softly.

'Are there any more?' Pearl asked.

'Oh, hundreds!'

It was slightly unnerving to discover that her most ordinary moments had been observed, but the pictures were beautiful and sent a thrill right through her. In the process of recording her doing nothing, he had made it seem as if she was doing something, as if her life had a purpose. He was an artist, and she was his muse.

'Would you like to see my darkroom?' he asked.

'How many women have you said that to?' she flirted.

'Very few,' he said.

She felt a twist of irrational jealousy that there had been any others. She had not expected him to give her an honest reply.

It was not completely dark. There was a red glow in which she could see washing lines of prints pegged out to dry. As her eyes grew accustomed to the dim light, she saw that the walls were papered with scenes of Kingshaven daily life.

After some minutes of looking, she turned and said to him, gleefully, 'You are very naughty!'

'Makes two of us!'

And then, sensing the opportunity, he moved closer to her, took her face in his hands and kissed her fiercely on the mouth.

She had never been kissed by a man of similar height, and it felt different. Passion had always been the swoon of giving herself up to a man's dominance. With Tom, it felt equal, friendly, rather nice.

When he drew away, she decided she wanted some more, so she took his face between her hands and kissed him back, and they both sank to their knees, and he made love to her on the darkroom floor. And at the moment of climax, her arm stretched up in ecstasy and brought down a string of prints all over them, and they lay panting among Kingshaven's peccadilloes.

'You,' he told her, kissing her nose, 'are the best I've ever had.'

'Better than Miss Chu?' she fished.

'No comparison.'

'For me, too,' Pearl told him, suddenly feeling extremely happy.

He sat up and held her face to his chest, stroking her hair.

'Tell me what it felt like,' he said.

'What do you mean?'

'Describe it!'

'I can't!' she cried. It wasn't the sort of thing you talked about.

'Try. Try to describe what it felt like!'

Her body tingled at the very thought of breaking a taboo.

Pearl rolled on to the floor beside him and stared upwards. The light was so dim, she couldn't see a ceiling. It was like being in a cave.

'Well,' she said, trying to think of an appropriate analogy. 'Before, it's always been like being on a wave, rising and rising, but never quite breaking,' she said. 'But with you it felt more like being on a lovely raft on a great river . . .'

She glanced at the side of his face to see how she was doing. He was listening, nodding. To her astonishment, she was getting excited by describing what she had felt.

'Slow and lazy at first, drifting along, wonderfully relaxing, and then suddenly the current starts to get faster, and faster, and then, oh my God, it was going over the top of the Niagara Falls . . . terrifying, amazing . . .'

'Do you want to do it again?' he whispered.

'Oh, yes, yes, please!' she cried.

'Where is my boy?' Jennifer called from the bedroom. 'Is someone going to bring me my baby?'

Downstairs, Ruby Farmer looked at Dr Payne and then at Jolly Allsop.

Both men shook their heads.

Ruby took a deep breath and went back upstairs.

'Where's my baby? Where's my little boy?' Jennifer said, smiling.

She looked so beautifully wan. The midwife had helped her change into a nice clean nightie and brushed the long hair which fell around her shoulders like in a Pre-Raphaelite painting.

Ruby had been present at the birth of all the babies, but she'd never seen her daughter like this, sitting up eagerly, proud of herself.

'Jenny, my dear Jenny.' Ruby sat down on the bed.

Her daughter's smile immediately faded. 'What's wrong? Is

something wrong with him?' she asked, agitated. 'There's something wrong. I can see it in your face. What's wrong, Mummy?'

Ruby felt so sad. 'The truth is,' she began, 'the baby's dead.'

There was no way of disguising it, but she should have said something a little more poetic. Passed away. Gone to a better place. Something to soften the blow.

'What do you mean?' Jennifer stared, uncomprehending.

'He was a beautiful little thing. Perfect. Must have been his heart or something. We don't know yet.'

'My baby's dead?' Jennifer said, as if she had only just understood. 'My little boy?' She sat there, propped up in bed, very still.

Ruby bowed her head and shook with grief, not daring to let her tears make a sound in the awful silence.

'I'd like to see him,' Jennifer suddenly said, making Ruby stop crying.

'Dr Payne's taking the body away. For tests. They have to, apparently,' she told her.

'But I want to see him,' Jennifer said.

'I'm sorry, love.'

'I want to see my baby!' Jennifer was suddenly shrieking.

Jolly burst into the room.

'Will you for God's sake stop shouting!' he yelled at her. 'It's not your baby. It's dead. Dr Payne has taken the body away now, and as soon as you're feeling a bit better, he'll do some tests.'

'Tests?' Jennifer repeated.

'He'll do some tests to see why you don't seem to be capable of producing a healthy boy!'

'Jolly, I really don't think now's the time . . .' Mrs Farmer interrupted.

'The sooner we find out, the sooner we'll be able to put things right,' said Jolly, a little more considerately. He went over to the bed and put an awkward hand on his wife's shoulder.

It was as if Jennifer had died too, Ruby thought, right in front of her. Like an electric bulb which had gone out and all the shaking in the world was not going to make it fire up again. One second alive, the next dead. You couldn't see the life going, but when it had gone, you knew it wasn't there any more.

*

Michael awoke from a dreamless sleep. He could see from the seam of light between the curtain edges that it was growing light. Beside him, Sylvia was still sleeping peacefully.

He found his trousers and jumper downstairs on the sofa where he had thrown them off a few hours before. They had made love on the living-room floor, as fumbling and sweet as when they were teenagers. What an effort it must have been for Sylvia, he thought wryly as he picked up the clothes which were left strewn around, to have resisted the urge to tidy up afterwards.

They were both trying hard to be nice to one another.

Hugging his donkey jacket around him, he strolled towards the seafront. He passed no one as he walked along the promenade, through the narrow streets of the Harbour End and up the hill to the track above the landslip. Far in the distance, he could see the avenue of trees leading to the Castle and the little gatehouse. No smoke was coming from its chimney. Everyone was still asleep. He felt as if he was the first person in the world yet to have woken up to the new decade.

From the clifftop path the open sea looked quite different from the bay. There was a swell. At certain times of the year, dolphins could be spotted and Michael sometimes thought he glimpsed their smooth curves cresting the waves. When Iris was with him, she always insisted she'd seen them. But they both knew in their hearts that they had not yet been lucky, and it was only desire playing tricks with perception.

Up here, away from the shelter of the town, with the wind biting through to his skin, Michael always felt as if it were possible to change.

If he could just accept that it was enough to have a family, a secure job, a reasonable life . . .

He stared into the wild churn of water. He accepted that the dolphins were out there. It wasn't essential to experience seeing them to know that they were. If he could only stop himself thinking all the time that there was more for him out there somewhere beyond his reach, he would be a happier man, he thought. A better man.

The sun broke through the mist as he turned towards home, blinding him with unexpected glare.

Pushing open the front door, he stepped on a letter which had fallen, address up, almost exactly in the centre of the mat.

The letter was postmarked WC1. The 'e' of the typewriter was slightly misaligned. The same typewriter had acknowledged the receipt of his typescript, months ago.

As his finger levered under the flap, Michael tried to suppress the hope which made his heart beat faster and his fingers shake. Ridiculous, to be almost thirty and behaving no differently from when he received the results of his School Certificate.

Sylvia's face peeped round the kitchen door, much as his Auntie Jean's had then, eager, anxious, dying to rip the letter from his hands, but knowing she had to stay back.

Dear Mr Quinn,
    THE TEACHER
    Thank you so much for giving us the opportunity of reading this novel which I think shows considerable promise. Your characters are all too believable and I think you communicate splendidly the disillusion of your young hero.
    In principle, I feel that you are an author we would be most interested in publishing, and I hope you will not find it presumptuous of me to include some editorial notes about the structure, in particular the ending of the book, which I have jotted down.
    Perhaps when you have had a chance to mull over these suggestions, you will get in touch with me and we can take things further from there. I shall hold your manuscript here until I hear from you.
    With best wishes, and congratulations on an impressively powerful piece of writing.
    Yours sincerely,
    Roman Stone
    PORTICO BOOKS

'Is it good news?' Sylvia asked.

Michael looked up and was touched to see how much she wanted it for him. 'Yes.' He smiled at her. 'Yes, I think it is.'

Chapter Nine

July 1961

'Whose bright idea was it to invite in the Russkies?' Eddie asked, helping himself to scrambled eggs.

'Actually it was Pearl's,' said Libby. 'Do put the lid back on that dish!'

She hated the smell of eggs in the morning and couldn't imagine why anyone would want to start such a bright summer day with something so indigestible. She attributed Eddie's morning appetite to his impoverished childhood. If you didn't know where the next meal was coming from, then it was certainly sensible to fill up while you could.

'Bloody hell, she never lifted a finger while she was here, and when we finally get shot of her, she lands the bloody Kirov Ballet on us.'

'It's the Kiev Ballet,' Libby corrected. 'She and Tom mix with the arty set in Lowhampton. The director of the Festival Theatre's a neighbour. Apparently, there were a few worries about putting the company up in a place like Lowhampton so Pearl suggested us. Far easier to keep tabs on them in Kingshaven.'

'Well, they're a miserable lot,' said Eddie.

Libby couldn't help but agree with this.

On stage, the dancers were so beautiful, so ethereal in their white costumes. During the day they slouched round the hotel in drab rags, filling the corridors with gloom and the smell of their foul cigarettes. It was as if Monsieur, the company director, like the wicked wizard he played, really had cast a spell which turned them into swans for a few hours.

In real life, Odette and Prince Siegfried were married, but they were far from being the harmonious couple their pas de deux on stage suggested. The sound of them screeching at each other set the other guests on edge. It was always awkward to witness an argument, but somehow worse if you could not understand a word of what was being said. After a performance, the principals were allowed to sleep in, so at least breakfast time was relatively undisturbed.

'They certainly know how to drink,' said Eddie, who had come up from the bar both nights in a fug of brandy fumes.

'You're not obliged to match them glass for glass,' Libby told him.

'I hope they're paying in sterling!'

'Pearl's taken care of all that.'

'The translator is a friendly enough chap,' said Eddie. 'The only one you can have a bit of a laugh with.'

'He's probably the spy,' interjected Liliana, stirring a teaspoon of sugar into her cup of Earl Grey tea.

'Sergei? A spy?' Eddie repeated.

Libby noticed that her husband's face fixed mid-expression, the way it did when he'd been caught out and thought you wouldn't notice. Had he been indiscreet? He had in the past made the mistake of thinking that a conversation with a stranger was by its nature confidential.

'I'm sure they always bring a spy,' continued Liliana.

Since Pearl's marriage, Liliana had taken over the role of the one who sparred with Eddie at meal times.

'But they're ballet dancers!' protested Eddie.

'Spies don't generally give spying as their profession . . .'

'What interest could Kingshaven possibly be to them?' Eddie asked.

For once in their lives, Angela and Christopher were listening intently to the conversation. Christopher was so transfixed that his spoon had stopped midway between bowl and mouth, its load of porridge quivering.

'It's a good landing point,' Liliana suggested.

'I hardly think the Russians would bother with a launch party in Kingshaven Bay!' Eddie scoffed. 'Not when they can put a man into space!'

'I would like to be a-a-a . . .' Christopher suddenly interrupted.

All eyes looked at him, which probably made his recent tendency to stutter worse, Libby thought as she willed her son to get the word out, just as she used silently to urge her father on when he stammered.

'A spy?' Angela suggested.

Christopher shook his head. 'A-a-a-a . . .'

A wincing combination of embarrassment and sympathy gained momentum the longer Christopher struggled, until Libby's temptation to supply the word became irresistible.

'Astronaut?' she said.

Every little boy wanted to be Yuri Gagarin these days.

'A dancer,' Christopher finally managed.

The blob of porridge finally fell back into his cereal bowl splashing milk up on to the new short-sleeved summer shirt Libby had bought him in Mrs Farmer's Summer Sale. Not for the first time, Libby wondered how her son would manage at his new school, which was said to be even stricter than the prep school he had just left.

'Well, you can forget that,' said Eddie immediately.

'Why?'

'No son of mine's going to be a bloody ballet dancer.'

'Why?'

'Stop saying why all the time!'

'Is it because they wear women's clothes?' Angela asked disingenuously.

Eddie guffawed. 'You could say,' he chuckled into his cravat.

'They're not women's clothes, they're costumes,' said Libby, feeling sorry for Christopher with everyone laughing at him.

The reason he wouldn't be able to be a ballet dancer was that he was a terribly clumsy child. No co-ordination at all. An image of him prancing around the stage, knocking over the lines of the corps de ballet like dominoes, came to her mind, and she had to fight back the smile which was trying to break over her own face.

'There's nothing effeminate about some male ballet dancers, I can assure you,' Liliana suddenly announced with a kind of authority that put an end to the discussion.

The scrape of cutlery on china resumed.

Libby was thinking about Prince Siegfried on stage in the little gold and white brocade jacket which stopped at his waist and those tight white tights. Pearl and Tom had reserved a box at the Festival Theatre for the first night and invited all the family to join them.

'Those tights don't leave much to the imagination,' Pearl had whispered over the haunting oboe theme of the swans, and Libby had had to bite her tongue to stop herself giggling.

It was just like old times with Pearl these days. Now that they were both wives and mothers, their relationship seemed to have reverted to the sisterly one they had shared when they were both single. Marriage and motherhood suited Pearl astonishingly well and it was lovely that they'd produced little boys one after the other. Adrian and Damian. It would be good for the boys to grow up together. Libby often thought Christopher might have been more normal if he'd had a brother instead of Angela.

She scooped a spoonful of sieved porridge from the nursery bowl, and offered it to baby Adrian, who was sitting in his high chair next to her. His mouth made a very serious and deliberate O as he took the food and swilled it round his mouth. Then he smiled a lovely gummy, porridgy smile at her. He was such a robust, cheerful little baby, with his dancing blue eyes, she didn't seem to mind all the mess he made down his bib as she had with the others.

Claudia spooned sugar into two cups of tea on the breakfast trays she was preparing. The spoon made no sound at all in the liquid, and only the slightest chink on the saucer as she replaced it. Whenever someone made a cup of tea on radio, she was required to do much clattering with the studio teacup. People in radio dramas never exited a room without slamming the door. There was never a staircase without a creaky floorboard halfway up. Real life was much quieter, Claudia thought as she padded up two flights of threadbare carpet from the basement kitchen to the first floor.

She knocked softly on Mr Boyce's door and put the tray down on the floor outside. Mr Boyce sold Rolls Royces in a showroom in Berkeley Square. He was always very well turned out in a dapper suit and a clean white collar, but his room was so untidy, he forbade anyone to cross its threshold, or even to look in. Claudia never heard his door open, but somehow, when she returned on her second trip with Mrs Anton's tray, he had always managed to slide his breakfast tray in unobserved.

Claudia returned to the kitchen for the second tray and climbed the three flights of stairs to Mrs Anton's door.

'Come in, my dear!'

Mrs Anton was a lady of a certain age with white hair scraped back into a tight bun (even this early in the morning; Claudia had never seen her with her hair loose), who tutored a stream of reluctant boys for their Common Entrance exams.

'I could have been a don, you know,' she often told Claudia. 'But in my day, women had to choose between academia and love. I chose love.'

One of the first women to go up to Oxford, she had been swept off her feet by a flamboyant Polish count. They had lived a giddy life, until he had died quite suddenly in the South of France, leaving her with nothing but gambling debts. She had drifted back to London, like so much of the flotsam and jetsam on the tides of European instability which washed up in the many bedsits of the once-elegant terraces of the capital.

Mrs A. and Mr B. had come with the house Claudia and Tim had bought in Kensington. The terms of their sitting tenancies included breakfast. Claudia did not find it a particularly onerous duty, but it irked her that Tim had never once offered to perform it himself, even in the first few months of their marriage before he left the realms of Broadcasting House for his new job in the gleaming citadel at White City. They used to walk down Ladbroke Grove to the tube station together, and once, when he'd teased her for yawning, she pointed out that she had been up long before him to make sure that the tenants' breakfasts were done. He had simply kissed her on the nose and said, 'I'm sure they'd rather see you than me in the morning!'

Her husband was terribly good at compliments, which she

never saw coming and which always disarmed her. And when she jokingly raised the subject another day, he simply said, 'Oh, not that again!' as if she was being dreadfully boring.

It wasn't as if she really minded. She liked Mrs A. and enjoyed the tales of her exotic past, but it niggled that they had gone into the marriage promising to share everything. Claudia enjoyed some of the chores – like shopping: in this area of London, you could walk a hundred yards and breathe spices and aromas from all over the world – but she objected to the assumption that her time was less valuable than his. She was always the one who had to wait for the electricians and plumbers and builders to arrive.

'If I'm late again, I think I'll lose my job,' she had protested recently, only half joking.

'Would that be such a bad thing? You're always complaining about how boring it is,' Tim had replied.

The unspoken assumption was that she would soon fall pregnant and then her job wouldn't matter. In the meantime, Claudia felt as if she were existing in a kind of limbo. She was considered fortunate to have kept her job at all. Tim had some-how managed to make the story of his own move from radio into the cutting-edge world of television a kind of wedding present to her, for husband and wives were not generally allowed to work in the same department at the BBC.

Claudia swished back the old velvet curtains, letting light flood into Mrs A.'s sitting room.

'A little sad today?' said Mrs A.

She was sitting in her straight-backed armchair, fully clothed and neat, just like Claudia's tutors at Cambridge, and just as perceptive. Claudia smiled at the old woman. She found her observations friendly rather than intrusive. On the wall behind Mrs A.'s chair was a small oil portrait of her dashing husband, looking as if he came from another century, which, of course, he did. When Mrs A. had married, she had had to choose between a career and a husband. Things had changed beyond recognition in the forty years since then, and yet, to Claudia, the options for a young woman didn't seem so very different today.

If she were to lose her job, it would allow her to concentrate all her efforts on Tim's other project of turning the empty two floors

they occupied into the kind of contemporary modern apartment a dynamic young television producer and his family should live in. The trouble was that Tim was so much better at all the issues of decoration. Stone or ceramic for the kitchen floor? Matting or stripped boards in the hall? Curtains from Liberty or the Design Centre? The truth was that Claudia didn't really care all that much. Somewhere in her core, after so many years of frugal living, there was a part of her which felt it was immoral to expend so much mental energy and money on things which did not ultimately matter at all.

Claudia stared out of the long window at the flickering patterns of blue sky above the red leaves of the Japanese cherry tree whose boughs in spring were laden with abundant bundles of impossibly pink blossom. A woodpigeon cooed soothingly. At work, she had to be very careful about playing the right birdsong for the right geographical area and season. If you got it wrong, people wrote in.

'Far too nice a day to be gloomy,' said Mrs A. briskly.

When most couples were in bed with each other, there was not a lot of talking, but the Russian Prince and Princess never shut up. It sounded as if they had so much to say they had to talk very quickly and urgently. And this morning, when the Prince finally started kissing the Princess, she was crying so hard he had to stop and let her blow her nose on the sheets before he could continue. Then they were interrupted by a knock at the door. The Prince got up and put a towel around his waist and spoke to the man at the door, and when the man at the door had gone away, and the Prince got back into bed with the Princess, the two of them started giggling so much they had to hold the pillow over their mouths. When they started doing it, it looked much more beautiful than when anyone else did it, with the woman climbing all over the man and him lifting her off his chest as if she weighed nothing, like the dance they did on stage, and her legs stretched so wide apart they made a straight line with a pointed foot at each end.

The Prince fell asleep afterwards, and the Princess kissed him ever so softly on the forehead, and slipped out for morning class in the ballroom where Monsieur had set up a barre.

Angela had been crouching for so long, there were pins and needles in her legs, and when she stood up, she lost her balance accidentally knocking over the stepladder which was used when a lightbulb needed changing. It made an awful noise. Angela froze and waited for the sound of footsteps, or a knock on the door, terrified that she was about to be discovered. But no one came.

The chambermaids must have started on the other wing. Far away in the ballroom, she could hear the sound of the piano thumping out the same tune again and again as the dancers repeated their exercises, and the sharp impatient clap of Monsieur's hands as he stopped and corrected them.

Angela decided the coast was clear.

She pushed open the door a crack.

Nothing.

As she slipped out of the darkness into the corridor, a heavily accented voice said, 'What are you doing, little girl?'

He removed his grease paint each evening with cotton wool, but there were still dark rings accentuating the Prince's eyes, and the stain of red lipstick had not been entirely kissed off by the Princess. In daylight, his skin was pocked and pitted like pictures Angela had seen of the surface of the moon, not smooth and white like it was on stage, but he was still the most handsome man she had ever seen. His cheekbones were high and defined, and he held his head differently from normal men, chin in the air, nostrils flaring, as if he was permanently holding his breath.

'Are you spying on me?' he asked. His eyes were so bright, they almost seemed to flash.

'I didn't know you spoke English,' Angela stuttered.

'I have been learning,' he said with a short laugh.

'Why?' asked Angela, playing for time.

'Perhaps so I can tell your mother what you do.'

'Please don't,' said Angela. 'Or she won't buy me a horse.'

'But I think she would like to know that her child spies on her guests.'

'I promise I won't do it again.'

'What good are your promises to me?' He stooped and

brought his princely face very close to hers. 'Why should I keep your secret?'

'I . . . I don't know,' stuttered Angela.

'Unless I had a secret too . . .' he whispered menacingly. 'Then perhaps we could, how do you say it . . . ?'

'Swap?' Angela suggested timidly.

His sudden smile lit up the dim corridor just as it lit up the stage.

The Rhododendron Mile wasn't actually a mile of rhododendrons, but the reduced size of the Summer House at the end of the avenue made it look further away than it was. The rhododendrons were past their best: a great dense mass of shiny green foliage in the bright summer sunshine. The remains of purple flowers were withered and brownish like paper scorched by the summer heat. Lying in his pram, Adrian looked up at the dancing patterns of shadow and light and smiled.

'Rhododendrons,' Libby said to him.

She let the spaniels, Earl and Countess, off their leads and they dashed about, sniffing among the roots of the shrubs for rabbits.

It was lovely to be out in the air away from the pounding of the piano and the foul smell of those black cigarettes.

Jolly Allsop had erected a fence around the pretty cottage garden he had made at the front of the Summer House. Libby couldn't remember him asking permission to do so, but she didn't think she would take exception to it. Jolly didn't really qualify as the usual sort of sitting tenant, and the improvements and extensions he had made to the house would certainly add value to the property when the time came for him to move up to the Castle.

The little Allsop girls, Joanna and Jackie, were playing unsupervised on the front lawn.

'Where's your mother?' asked Libby.

Joanna pointed towards the open front door.

The motion of the pram had made Adrian fall asleep. Libby parked him outside the front door of the chalet and tied the dogs' leads to the gate.

Inside, Jennifer was staring into the unlit fire, sucking on a cigarette as if her life depended on it. Upstairs, the new baby was crying in the gasping, panicky way that babies had when you didn't attend to them.

The sound transported Libby back to the guilt of those awful nights when Nanny had banned her from going to pick Christopher up, insisting, wrongly as it turned out, that he would soon cry himself out. And then, almost as soon as he'd grown out of the screaming, there'd been the bed-wetting, but at least they didn't have to worry about waking the hotel guests with that. She had forgotten about all that with Adrian, who was altogether a much easier baby.

Jennifer's dress did not look very clean and there was white baby dribble all over the shoulder and sleeve of one arm.

'You look well,' said Libby automatically.

Jennifer stared at her with hollow eyes.

'The baby's crying!' said Libby, pointing.

Jennifer looked at Libby's finger, but did not move.

'I'll fetch her, shall I?' said Libby.

The nursery was decorated with blue and white wallpaper with a design of yachts. The baby was hot with tears, but calmed almost instantly as Libby cradled her and stroked the damp fronds of hair very gently back over her forehead. An impossibly tiny fist clasped Libby's little finger. Soft little raspberry lips whimpered. Her eyes were almost closed, only the deep blue irises visible. Through the thin damp covering of nightdress, Libby could feel the baby's fragile little bones. It was like holding a kitten.

'She's hungry,' said Libby, presenting the baby to Jennifer, who looked at the child impassively, then started unbuttoning her shirtwaister dress.

Libby averted her eyes.

'Perhaps you'd like a cup of tea?' she suggested.

The kitchen was much as it had always been, with a long oak refectory table and the cast-iron range which conjured happy childhood memories of their father's younger brother, Alex, who had sometimes pitched up late at night, before the war, in a convoy of cars with a crowd of his London friends. She and Pearl would hear them from their bedroom, and in the morning, they would sneak down the Rhododendron Mile with milk and sausages begged from the kitchen staff, and Uncle Alex would give them a silver threepenny piece each.

'Nothing beats camping!' he would say, turning the sausages in the large black pan on the range. And all his friends would cheer. They were a very amusing crowd.

Uncle Alex used to tell them ghost stories, Libby suddenly remembered, about a boy who had been banished to the Summer House to live away from polite society. When Pearl had repeated the tales to her mother, Liliana had called him a bad influence and tried to stop them seeing him. But Alex had promised that when the war was over he would take them to London, to cocktails in the Café Royal and shows and nightclubs.

How different things would have been if Alex had survived!

But if he had survived, Libby thought, then of course the hotel would have passed on to him after her father died, and all their lives would have followed different courses. In a way, she had his death to thank for her present situation. Which was ironic, she thought, tipping boiling water from the huge kettle on the range into the teapot, because she had always liked him enormously.

The milk in the jug on the table was on the turn. Libby splashed a little into the teacup and took it back into the reception room.

'She's a dear little thing,' said Libby, putting down the tea. 'Have you decided what to call her?'

Libby was slightly expecting to be asked to be godmother. Liliana was to Joanna, and Pearl, of all people, to Jackie. But no invitation had so far been forthcoming.

'Julia,' said Jennifer.

'Julia,' Libby repeated. 'That's a lovely name!'

Jennifer's face brightened momentarily. 'Do you think so? I chose it.'

'May I?'

Jennifer deposited the fragile bundle into her waiting arms.

'She's a very pretty baby,' Libby said. 'Although it's never a good guide to how they'll grow up. Angela was a beautiful baby. Everyone said so.'

Jennifer lit another cigarette and blew a few mesmerizing loops of smoke from her lips.

'Hard to believe,' said Libby – it was a struggle to pass the time of day with no response – 'so tiny now, but all too soon, she'll be a grown woman like you.'

How old was Jennifer now? Libby did a quick calculation. Was she only twenty-five? She looked much older.

'I don't feel like a woman,' said Jennifer suddenly. 'I feel like a cow.'

'A cow?' Libby repeated.

'A cow who is inseminated and milked each year . . .' Jennifer went on.

Libby cradled her hand around little Julia's head. Inseminated wasn't a word to use in front of children.

'. . . until I produce a boy, and then I might be put out to grass.'

An extraordinary outburst!

'Not really like a cow, then,' Libby corrected. 'Because generally the boy calves are the ones sent off for slaughter. Little girl cows are the ones who are prized.'

Jennifer threw her cigarette butt into the grate.

'If I were you, I'd get Julia on to the bottle straightaway,' Libby advised. 'Much healthier for everyone concerned, and she does look as if she could do with the nourishment. Have you thought about a nanny?'

'Where would we put one?' Jennifer snapped. 'This place is so small, I can hardly stand up straight.'

Rather an ungrateful comment in the circumstances.

'You're obviously exhausted, poor thing. Nobody can be expected to look after three children on their own,' said Libby, trying to be helpful. 'I'll have a word with Jolly about it, shall I?'

Sylvia was unwrapping a brown paper package from the uniform suppliers when the gaggle of ballerinas entered the shop, chattering away and pawing the merchandise. She didn't understand what they were saying, but she suspected that they weren't used to this kind of quality and variety where they came from.

'Here, let me show you,' Sylvia said, reaching up to the high rail with the hook on a pole and getting several garments down so that the girls could have a closer look.

There were still several of the summer skirts Mrs Farmer referred to as tropical skirts because of the bright sunset scenes printed on the fabric. The ballet dancers pointed and giggled at the black silhouettes of palm trees against the blazing slashes of orange and blue.

'We try?' one of the girls asked Sylvia.

'I think you'll find them a bit too big,' Sylvia said.

Even a size eight, which was the smallest size Ruby Farmer stocked, would hang off this lot, Sylvia thought. And the size eight had gone long ago. She thought that there were only twelves and fourteens left. She flipped through the waistbands looking at the size labels. 'No, nothing,' she said.

'We try?' the girl repeated.

'Up to you,' said Sylvia, swishing back the curtain of the fitting room.

Were they born like that, or did all the training they did keep them as petite and flat-chested as little girls?

Sylvia remembered the competitiveness amongst her peers at school about who would be the first to get a bra and whose breasts were largest. It must be completely different in the changing rooms of a ballet school. Going up a cup size would be a cause for sympathy, not envy as it had been amongst the developing Etherington girls.

Iris had all that to look forward to, Sylvia thought as she went back to her parcel and pulled out her daughter's brand-new school blazer. It was very dark navy blue, almost black, with an embroidered gold crest. LGGS. Lowhampton Girls' Grammar School.

Sylvia sighed. She'd always thought that having a daughter would be like having a friend when she was old enough. They would do women's things together, like she and her mother used to, like shopping and having their hair done in adjacent seats in the salon, perhaps even going to the cinema together. But she couldn't see that ever happening with Iris. When Iris didn't have her head in a book, she wanted to do boys' things. She had the brains to pass the eleven plus (the highest mark in the county, Michael had discovered) but Sylvia wasn't sure how much her headstrong daughter was going to like the jolly-hockey-sticks atmosphere of the strictly all-girls Grammar School.

Sylvia put the blazer on a hanger. It looked a bit big, but Iris was growing so fast it wouldn't be big for long. She didn't want people thinking that Iris had a big blazer because they couldn't afford to buy her two in a year. There was enough money for that now, with Michael's book sold to a publisher, even though it wasn't yet printed, and more money promised from America, too. They called it an advance in the publishing trade. Sylvia was never quite sure if that meant they'd have to pay it back, even though Michael explained it wasn't them that would have to pay it back, but the book. Truth be told, she thought they both worried about money arriving when they hadn't even asked for it. Neither of them could quite allow themselves to trust it.

'Why don't we open a bank account for the moment and see how we go,' Michael had suggested. 'If it continues like this, we'll put money down on that shop you wanted.'

She'd been so touched that he remembered, it had made her cry. All the money in the world couldn't buy that thought. Of course, you couldn't have the thought in the first place without the money. It felt so grown-up to open a bank account.

The bell above the door pinged as Audrey Potter came in after sorting the second post, ostensibly to look at handkerchiefs for her sister's birthday.

'We've some very pretty ones with a little bit of Swiss embroidery in the corner,' Sylvia said, extracting the appropriate tray from the chest of glass drawers and placing it on the counter between them. 'Or she might prefer a monogram?'

'A shame about poor Jennifer,' said Audrey, leafing through a set of four with a rose pattern and hand-rolled edges. 'Apparently the midwife had to tell Jolly it was a girl. No one else dared.'

'She's a lovely, healthy baby, at least,' said Sylvia. 'Julia. A little princess, Mrs Farmer says.'

'But what hope does she have when she's unwanted from the moment she comes into the world?' Audrey asked.

Sylvia was looking over her friend's shoulder towards the fitting room. 'I've got the Russians in,' she explained.

'You want to keep an eye on them,' said Audrey darkly.

'Iris's uniform has arrived,' Sylvia said, showing Audrey the blazer.

'A very clever girl, is Iris,' said Audrey.

A couple of holidaymakers came in to enquire whether Farmer's stocked souvenir headscarves of Kingshaven.

'No, but it's an idea,' Sylvia said, smiling. 'Souvenir headscarves! Have you ever heard of anything so common,' she added as soon as they were out of earshot.

Mrs Turlow popped in to enquire about her order for elastic stockings, and as Audrey was deciding that she would have a bit of a think about the handkerchiefs, the ballerinas trooped out of the fitting room.

'How did we get on?' Sylvia called over to them.

They stopped in their tracks and stared at her anxiously.

'Any good?' she tried again.

Then the only one with any English at all said, 'Very big!'

'I thought so,' said Sylvia slowly and loudly. 'You are very small!'

The girls burst into peals of giggles again, which stopped abruptly as a Russian man came in and said with an impeccable accent, 'Allow me to offer my assistance.'

The girls filed out soundlessly beneath his stern gaze.

Shops could be like that, Sylvia thought, when she found herself suddenly alone again. You could go for hours without a customer and then they all came at once and messed the place up. If she ever got her shop, she planned to keep it small with only the very latest fashions, and no extras like elastic stockings and sanitary towels under the counter.

She slightly wondered whether there would be enough customers for a shop of her own in Kingshaven, now that Pearl King had moved away. Pearl had promised that she'd be her first customer when Sylvia confided her dreams, but then she'd upped and left without even saying goodbye. And she'd got married without even asking Sylvia to make her wedding dress, which made her wonder whether she'd accidentally done something to offend.

Sylvia folded the handkerchiefs neatly back in their tray, then went to the fitting room to get the skirts. There were two size twelves and one size fourteen hanging on the hook when she was sure that she had taken four skirts in. Her first instinct was to run down the street and challenge the Russians, but she could hardly leave the shop unattended. She remembered the terror in the eyes of the girls as they walked silently past the man who was looking after them. Guarding them, more like. Sylvia thought it was a shame if pretty girls weren't allowed something pretty to wear if they wanted it enough to steal it. Anyway, the shop was so busy in the summer, any of the 'foreigners' might have filched a skirt. She decided she wouldn't bother Mrs Farmer with it. She had enough to worry about at the moment.

From the steps of the hotel, Eddie watched the dancers returning from their morning excursion into town. They were walking in pairs, like schoolchildren, with their toes pointed out and their steps perfectly synchronized.

You had to hand it to the Reds, they knew a thing or two about discipline.

'And now,' said Sergei after he had counted them back into the Palace, 'I am available for the spot of lunch.'

'Good,' said Eddie. 'Would you rather walk or shall I drive?'

'Shall we not partake of the local fare within?' asked Sergei.

'Thought you might like to see my yacht. It's got a couple of features I think you might be interested in,' Eddie said with a wink. 'Being a naval man!'

Sergei hesitated.

'I can't imagine there'll be any translation needed at lunch. It's a choice of cod or beef, I believe,' said Eddie with a backwards nod at the hotel.

Sergei smiled uncertainly. 'Just an hour,' he said, looking at his watch.

'The workers have to have a lunch hour,' said Eddie, opening the passenger door.

So much for Liliana's theories. If Sergei was a spy he'd have jumped at the opportunity of seeing a bit of the town, he thought.

They parked on the quay and Eddie rowed them out in the tender to the *Brittany Anna*. There were far too many boats in the harbour at this time of year. The place was like a boating lake with all the brightly coloured dinghies. In contrast, the polished wooden deck of the *Brittany Anna* gleamed like the walnut dashboard of an expensive car.

Nobby Wolfe, a boatbuilder and captain of the lifeboat, had agreed to crew.

'Very shipshape!' said Sergei.

'How long were you in the Navy?' Eddie asked.

'Ten years.'

'We've abolished National Service here,' said Eddie. 'Bloody shame if you ask me, which nobody ever does, of course!'

'Of course!' agreed the translator.

The sea was an inky blue, and there were only a few high wispy clouds in the sky. The *Brittany Anna* was moored far enough from the golden beach for the sound of children shrieking at the Punch and Judy Show to be virtually inaudible. The South Cliffs shone white in the sunshine and the fields were lush and green on top.

This was picture-postcard England at its best, Eddie thought, surveying his territory with pride. He couldn't imagine they had anything like this in the Soviet Union, which he always imagined as a bitter, grey place, permanently cold and unforgiving.

'Over there, I think.' Sergei waved his right hand. 'The quarry caves where smugglers concealed their botty.'

'Booty,' Eddie corrected. How on earth did the Russky know that?

'Also the skeleton of your extinct predecessor . . .'

'Beg pardon?' said Eddie.

'A giant lizard from the Jurassic period?'

'Oh, you mean the dinosaur!'

Sergei had clearly swallowed the guide book whole and was simply regurgitating it.

'That's in the Natural History Museum, I'm afraid. It's only a pile of bones. Can't understand why people get so excited about it myself.'

'Shall I start up, Mr King?' asked Nobby.

'That's right, a short trip around the bay. We won't bother with sails.'

'Aye aye, Captain!' Nobby said, starting the motor.

'I hope I'm right in thinking...' Eddie ushered his guest towards the steps down into the cabin. '... there's something prepared for us below.'

On the table was a bottle of champagne chilling in a bucket of ice, and a platter of smoked salmon and cucumber sandwiches. Lounging on the benches on either side were Norma from the Yacht Club, and her friend Tina, the brunette, whose cat-like green eyes were, in their sultry way, just as enticing. They both sat up and smiled very attractively.

Norma was wearing a red bathing costume which showed off her hourglass figure to perfection. The brunette was slimmer and more flat-chested in black, but an aura of dirtiness crackled around her.

'I thought you might like to sample some traditional English delicacies,' said Eddie, offering Sergei the platter of sandwiches.

He could see that his companion was finding it difficult to choose, but he knew he would be happy with whatever was left over.

'Business or pleasure?' said Stanley Ironside through the ticket office window.

'A bit of both, I hope,' said Michael, making an effort to be sociable.

'That book of yours in the shops yet?' asked Stanley.

'It should be soon,' Michael replied.

It had never been his intention to tell people about his upcoming publication until it actually happened, but after the American publisher bought the rights for a sum which was apparently a record for a first novel, there was a mention in the *Times* Diary. The author's name had registered with the beady-eyed Mrs Turlow over her toast and marmalade. She had pointed it out to her husband, who called Michael in to confirm the facts, and then informed the editor of the *Kingshaven Chronicle*. In the piece which subsequently ran, Mr Turlow was quoted saying that he had always suspected that the teacher of his middle class was something of a dark horse, a phrase which Ivor never let Michael forget, making clippety-clop noises whenever he entered a room, and whinnying softly behind him when it was his turn to take assembly.

Miss Phelps had ordered a copy for the library, and there was already a waiting list, but Michael could tell that people were beginning to doubt it would ever happen. He didn't really believe it himself. He hadn't known about publishing schedules and how long it took to go through all the stages of editing, and copy editing, and designing, and proof reading, and subscribing, and printing a book, before it ever got into the shops.

As the day of publication drew nearer, he thought that he would start to feel more like an author somehow. But even when the publisher sent him a copy of the dustcover with his name in big letters, it still felt as if it had little to do with him. He put this down to the change of title. The novel was now called *The Right Thing* (*What do you think?* his publisher had written. *I think it's got a Kingsley Amis-ish ring to it, which should help it sell in droves!*), and the image on the jacket was bold and daring – a photo of a glass with a lipstick stain: not at all what Michael had expected. In fact, he had hidden it rather than show it to anyone, which he knew was absurd, since sooner or later the whole town would be able to see it in the library. He sometimes wished that the publisher had suggested changing his name as well as the title.

'I'm going up for the publication party,' Michael told Stanley Ironside.

'What's that then?'

'I'm not really sure,' Michael confessed.

The two-fifteen was already in the station. Michael got in and sat down. The locomotive decoupled and ran round beside the carriages, returning to the front with an impatient hiss of steam.

The platform clock ticked away the minutes until departure.

Just as the guard blew his whistle, a woman wearing a headscarf ran out of the Ladies' toilets and made a dash for the door next to which Michael was sitting. He could see the panic on her face as the train started to move. He pushed down the window, put his hand on the door handle and opened it. The train was gathering momentum.

'Come on!' Michael grabbed her outstretched hand.

The platform was fast running out. He didn't know how long he could hold her. Would it be more dangerous to try to haul her in, or to let go?

'Come on!' he urged.

Suddenly she took off, an enormous leap which knocked him back as she dived half on top of him into the compartment. For a moment, her face was right next to his. Her breath stank of cigarettes. Her complexion was terrible despite her heavy make-up. He averted his eyes. She got up hastily, brushed her skirt down and, without saying anything, let herself out of the compartment into the corridor.

'Claudia, your husband's on the phone.'

The senior studio manager spoke to her through the studio microphone. Claudia looked up at the gallery. Her boss looked cross and exasperated, but indicated that she should go to take the call.

It had been an endlessly trying afternoon. The leading actor in the drama they were recording had been particularly temperamental, complaining about everything and making them run way over schedule.

'Not the weather to be stuck inside the windowless bowels of Broadcasting House,' the actor remarked, mopping the sweat from his brow with a large white handkerchief, making it sound as if bowels generally had windows, which Claudia found quite funny.

'Darling! Did I catch you in the middle of something? Sorry!' said Tim.

'No, it's quite nice to get out of the studio.'

Claudia wondered why she always made it easy for him. Tim was quite aware that her producer didn't appreciate being interrupted. Sometimes she suspected he made a point of ringing at inconvenient moments just to remind his erstwhile colleagues in radio that he was now an important person in television, with his own extension number.

'Is anything wrong?' she asked.

'No, but something's come up. That trip to New York. We're

having a meeting to discuss it this evening, so I'm going to be late for Dad's party.'

'How late?' she asked.

'Just depends, darling. I can't tell at the moment.'

'I'll wait.'

'Why don't you go on your own?' Tim suggested.

'Because I don't really want to,' said Claudia.

'But Dad will be so disappointed if neither of us shows.'

'So you're not going at all?'

There was a sharp intake of breath at the other end of the phone. 'Obviously, if things get interesting here, I can't just say I've got to go to a party with my wife!'

'No, I don't suppose you can,' said Claudia.

'So you'll go?' Tim pressed her.

'I'd rather not.'

'Just this once?'

This was why Tim would always rise up the ranks of whatever organization he was in, whether it was the university cricket team or the BBC, Claudia thought. He simply would not take no for an answer.

'I really don't want to.' She made one last effort, knowing as she spoke that she was already defeated. She could hardly explain over the phone why it was that she didn't want to go to the party when she hadn't been able to explain in person.

The producer was on his way out of the studio as she came back in.

'I'm calling it a day,' he said crossly. 'If no one else wants to make the effort, I might as well not bother.' He looked at her as if the failure of the production was entirely her fault.

'I'm terribly sorry,' said Claudia, employing all the soothing skill she had amassed over the years dealing with another irascible old man, her father. 'Come on. We can't give up now. I'll stay as late as you want . . .'

'Oh, very well, Claudia,' he said, as if he were the one granting her the favour.

As the train was pulling in beside the long platform at Waterloo station, the woman slid open the door from the corridor into

Michael's compartment again. He held the door for her to step down on to the platform in front of him, wondering why she had no luggage, not even a handbag. She did not say thank you, but seemed to hesitate, and wait for him, then walked along uncomfortably close beside him in the low-heeled white shoes which didn't seem to fit her properly, and seemed at odds with the full, brightly coloured skirt. There was something familiar about the shoes. He wondered if Sylvia had a similar pair. At the end of the platform, the woman suddenly grabbed his arm and asked, in a heavy foreign accent, 'Excuse me, please, Bow Street?'

Michael shrugged and peeled away down the steps to the Underground and then, remembering the map he had spent so much time studying before his first visit to London, he placed Bow Street just north of Waterloo Bridge. He pushed up against the stream of people coming down the stairs, and scanned the station forecourt for the woman, but she had disappeared into the crowd.

Michael's brother Frank had once taken him potholing, and he felt the same paralysing terror now as the escalator plunged him into the depths of the tube. The tunnels were smaller than he had imagined them and his brain was unwilling to trust that the weight of earth and brick above was adequately supported. The train was packed. As it lurched off, he grabbed one of the smooth round handles which felt warm from the touch of so many other hands and stared at the line map pasted above the window. They must now be travelling under the Thames. He could almost feel it pressing down, ready to collapse at any moment, crushing tunnel and train and sweeping all the passengers along in a chaotic flood, like a vision of hell in a medieval painting.

Michael's knee accidentally touched that of a pretty woman in nurse's uniform who was sitting in the seat below his armpit. She smiled at him sympathetically as if she had read the fear on his face. His eyes returned to the map. The train jolted to a halt. He was thrown forward, and then back again.

Charing Cross. Underground, the stations were as featureless as they were on a Monopoly board.

The nurse was still looking at him. He held her eyes, and then it was her turn to blush and look away. When she stood up to get off, he caught a whiff of the scent of her in the warm Underground air. A complex tang of carbolic and femininity. It was the end of her shift, he thought, and she was on her way home. He pictured her in a dingy room with a view of rooftops, sponging her arms with water from a basin. As the train pulled out of the station, he craned his neck for a last glimpse.

A sound of distant chatter and music, like that produced by a summer fête, drifted through the open front door of the house. Michael checked the address on the invitation again. It was the right street, the right number.

It would be his first meeting with Mr Stone. He had telephoned to accept the offer the publisher had made from the kiosk on the promenade, taking a bag of coins with him and letting others in the queue go before him so that he could talk undisturbed.

Mr Stone sounded posh. 'Dear boy, that's the most marvellous news. I shall drink a glass of champagne to you,' he'd told him.

Which was not at all what Michael had expected and he'd been glad of the written evidence to convince him that it wasn't all some elaborate practical joke.

Since then, they had exchanged a number of letters, including the most recent communication, an invitation to celebrate the publication of *The Right Thing* by Michael Quinn, on the back of which Mr Stone had scrawled in black ink, 'Plenty of room for you to stay if you need to.'

Michael stepped uncertainly into the vast hall. The staircase wall was entirely shelved with books, and the other was covered with pictures. A tall, rather beautiful middle-aged woman with long dark hair appeared at the end of the hall accompanied by a blast of loud laughter which was dampened as the door behind her closed. She was wearing a very simple sleeveless black dress and smoking a French cigarette,

'Hello?' She peered at him enquiringly.

'I'm Michael Quinn,' he said.

Her languid, slightly haughty expression instantly lifted into a welcoming smile. 'So you are! Pippa Stone.'

She approached him holding out a hand, which sported several large rings, as if she expected him to kiss it. There was a slightly awkward moment as he swapped the briefcase he was holding in his right hand into his left, then took her hand and shook it.

'Can I relieve you of that?' she asked.

Sylvia had bought him the briefcase as a congratulation present, emptying her Post Office savings to purchase the best leather one with his initials tooled in gold.

'Thanks,' said Michael, handing it over, glad that it wasn't a rucksack, and yet, from the slightly disdainful look that flitted across Pippa's face, guessing that it wasn't quite the appropriate luggage for an overnight guest to be carrying.

Pippa smiled at him. 'You ought to get a better author photo,' she said, giving him a direct look.

When Roman Stone had written to ask him to send a black and white photograph for the jacket of his book, Sylvia had been all for him getting a professional job done by the photographer who used to work for the *Chronicle*, who was now married to Pearl King. Fortunately Ivor had come to the rescue with his Box Brownie, which had recorded every performer whose name had appeared on the bill at the Pier Theatre since he was twelve years old. Although his subjects included such legends of the entertainment world as Jimmy Edwards, Freddie Frinton and two of the Beverley Sisters, nobody could pretend Ivor was much of a photographer. The shots in which Michael was smiling were blurred, and the close-ups, Sylvia had remarked, looked like the mug shots you saw in the paper when the police were looking for a man to help with their enquiries.

'Well, you're supposed to be an Angry Young Man, after all!' Ivor had defended himself.

Following his hostess towards the door at the end of the corridor, Michael felt a tremendous pressure to make small talk.

'Are those real?' he asked, pointing at the signature of Picasso on several of the framed drawings on the wall.

'I certainly hope so,' she replied, with an almost inaudible breath of laughter.

The door at the end of the hall opened on to a kind of balcony overlooking a room like an enormous greenhouse filled with people instead of plants. Through the open doors, steps led into a garden where a jazz band was playing.

'Red or white?' Pippa asked, pointing at a table covered in bottles of wine and glasses. There was a scattering of freckles over the slightly papery skin of her thin bare arms.

'Red,' Michael said. 'Please.'

Her eyes focused on his mouth as if she knew that he was not used to drinking wine. It was slightly warm and tasted of blackberries and licorice, with the roughness of sandpaper in his throat as he swallowed. 'Very nice,' he said.

'Come and meet some people,' she said.

An eruption of laughter from a loud group of men. Michael couldn't help feeling that they were laughing at him.

The style of dress was informal. The women were in summer dresses; the men were mostly in shirtsleeves. Michael was overdressed in his three button suit and narrow tie.

'Pippa, darling!' A youngish man with prematurely grey curly hair grabbed the hostess and kissed her with fervour on both cheeks. The top button of his shirt was undone and he was wearing a yellow silk cravat with a small paisley pattern in red and black. 'Amazing news about our mutual friend!' said the man, drawing Pippa into a coded conversation about some unnamed person. As Michael stood by his hostess's side, trying to laugh at the appropriate moments, Cravat frowned at him as if he were an unwelcome intruder.

In the packed room, it felt as if as if everyone was watching him and ignoring him at the same time. Michael drained his glass of wine. It was replenished by a young woman with a bottle in each hand.

'Warm work for you,' Michael said, trying to initiate communication with someone.

She giggled and moved on.

On a side table, he was startled to see a tower of copies of his book. He picked up the top copy. It had a new, chemical smell and the spine cracked as he opened it. He put the book back on the pile again.

The little groups of people who were standing talking in the garden appeared even more impenetrable than the mass inside. Michael positioned himself a short distance away from the jazz band, tapping his foot with the music as if he hoped to blend in with them, a player without an instrument.

The waitress reappeared to fill his glass.

'Do you know which one Roman Stone is?' Michael asked her.

'Over there,' she said, then, looking at him again, she said, 'Oh my God, I'm so sorry. You're Michael Quinn, aren't you?'

'Yes,' he said.

'Hattie,' she said, transferring one of the wine bottles to her armpit so that she could shake his hand. 'I work in publicity. Not a very good start, I'm afraid! I'll take you to Roman.'

She inclined her head in the direction of a man who looked far too short to be Pippa's husband, who suddenly glanced in Michael's direction and made a beeline towards him, leaving the gaggle of people he was with mid-conversation.

'My dear boy! How long have you been here?' he said with a hearty handshake.

Michael had no idea whether it was five minutes or an hour.

'Welcome!' said his host. 'Now, who do you know?' He put a hand on the small of Michael's back, pushing him gently but firmly back into the party.

'Have you heard about the Russian?' The receptionist in the circular lobby area at the front of the building was on the edge of her seat.

'No, what?' Claudia asked, instantly alarmed.

East–West relations were so volatile these days that she continually feared the world was about to erupt into nuclear war.

'It was just on the news. Another ballet dancer's defected. In London, this time!'

Claudia's first thought was that she should ring Tim. If he could get an in-depth interview, it would be exactly the sort of scoop he'd been looking for to put his topical arts programme on the map. But he was bound to know already. Television Centre would be buzzing with it. And he would ask whether she was already at his father's house.

Regent's Park was full of people enjoying the fine weather. Rounders and cricket matches overlapped. Claudia fielded a ball that fell at her feet, throwing it so accurately that she got out the batsman, a boy in school uniform with his tie askew who scowled at her and protested because she wasn't officially part of the team.

'Sorry!' she called as wolf-whistles followed her all the way up to the Rose Garden.

A group of small children were playing Hide and Seek, crouching behind the floribunda roses, tiptoeing from post to post in the pergola, then making a dash for the central bed of standard roses which they had designated home. There were couples rowing on the lake. A medley of hits from musicals drifted across the flowerbeds from the bandstand. The air felt soft and balmy. It was the sort of perfect summer evening which made strangers smile at each other as if to acknowledge the shared good fortune of being alive in such a place at such a time.

Claudia walked as slowly as she could across the open fields towards the perimeter of the Zoo. It was getting towards eight o'clock. With any luck the party would be over by the time she arrived.

The final performance of *Swan Lake* was cancelled and the entire company had been corralled into the ballroom of the Palace Hotel along with the staff and guests of the hotel.

Accusations were flying.

Sergei was blaming Monsieur for letting Prince Siegfried enjoy a lie-in. Monsieur blamed the translator for abandoning his charges at lunchtime. Nobody could work out how the Prince had managed to get all the way to London without being spotted.

Everyone had a different theory: he had hidden on the farm truck which had delivered this morning's consignment of strawberries; he had concealed himself in the coach which was taking the North Herts Association of Rose Growers on a day excursion to the Tropical Gardens twenty miles along the coast. There was even a rumour, started by a family with two boys who had been down on the beach, that he had made his escape in a pedalo.

'There's no way you could pedal to London in that time,' Eddie informed them authoritatively.

Nevertheless, a constable was dispatched to check with Nobby Wolfe and returned with the news that the number fourteen pedalo was missing. Later on, the honeymooning couple who had taken it round the headland in search of a secluded cove were escorted back by the lifeboat, pink with sunburn and embarrassment.

'If the last sighting was this morning and he's in Bow Street by six o'clock, he must have driven, or taken the train,' Eddie informed the police sergeant.

'If I may say so, you seem very sure of your facts,' Sergei commented suspiciously.

A call went to Stanley Ironside who was certain that no one except Mr Quinn had bought a ticket that afternoon.

'Mr Quinn, eh!' said Eddie.

'Who is this Mr Quinn?' asked Sergei.

'His wife works in the dress shop!' said Libby.

Several of the dancers shifted uneasily on their tiny bottoms.

'He's a bit of a Red himself,' said Eddie.

'I do wish you'd keep your ideas to yourself,' Libby hissed at her husband. 'Can't you see that they already think you're involved?'

The idea that her husband had been party to a plan to snatch a defector for the West seemed utterly laughable, but she didn't like the looks he was getting.

The local sergeant really didn't have a clue what to do but thought it was best to keep everyone in one place until he had instructions from London, but then Liliana had the ingenious idea of telephoning her husband's old friend and fellow Rotarian, the Chief Constable of the county.

Was it really appropriate for the hotel to be swarming with officers, Liliana wanted to know, when as far as she knew no crime had been committed or warrant issued? In a free country, a man had every right to go to London if he pleased. The hotel was not a prison.

In the wake of the police retreat, the dancers were bundled into a coach and taken back to Heathrow Airport, but another wave of invasion was already on its way as the men of Fleet Street got out their road atlases and searched the index for Kingshaven.

It hadn't crossed Michael's mind that people would have read his book already, and he didn't know whether to accept the praise or shrug it off. It was like receiving an unexpected and over-extravagant gift.

It was gratifying to hear people sharing his vision, arguing about it, even, but the more they did, the less he felt it had anything to do with him.

What were you supposed to say when somebody you had never met told you she had fallen in love with your central character?

'But you couldn't have!' a male reviewer chipped in. 'He's an absolute bastard!'

'But he's so attractive!' said the woman, who had rippling dark hair and an Australian accent, and had introduced herself as Shelley, publicity director of Portico Books.

'I hear paperback rights have gone to Pan,' said Cravat, who turned out to be an influential literary editor, and appeared to have forgotten that he had snubbed Michael earlier.

'So intriguing to be given an insight into what really goes on in men's minds,' said Shelley with a flirtatious smile at Michael.

'Are you writing a sequel?' demanded Cravat.

'Oh, you simply can't,' said Hattie. 'It was wonderful the way you just left them there. That final image, of the family when they arrive at the seaside . . . everything's picture perfect, but you just know it isn't . . .'

'I cried!' Shelley claimed.

Michael was sure she hadn't. She didn't look like the sort of woman who cried easily.

People kept asking him questions, and as he struggled to think of answers, someone far more articulate and confident than he was would step in and the conversation rolled on without him ever having to contribute to it. And if there was a hiatus, all he had to do was ask, 'And how do you come to know Roman Stone?'

And that would set them off again.

It was so hot in the greenhouse he swigged back each glass of wine as soon as it was poured. He seemed to be getting used to the wine, feeling more sober as the evening wore on than he had after his first glass, until it hit him quite suddenly that he was among the last guests and he had not noticed anyone leaving.

And then somewhere at the back of his brain, he heard Roman Stone saying, 'Come and meet our guest of honour!'

And then Claudia was walking towards him and it didn't even cross Michael's mind to wonder how it was that of all the houses in all the streets of London, someone he knew had walked into this one.

She was wearing a simple sleeveless dress in emerald green cotton which fitted her slim body exactly. The colour made her long hair blacker and her skin paler than ever.

'The party's almost over!' Roman chided her as she walked towards him and allowed him to kiss her on both cheeks.

'I'm so sorry. I had to stay late at work,' Claudia explained.

'Allow me to introduce Michael Quinn.'

Wine slopped alarmingly near the top of Michael's glass as he transferred it from his right hand to his left.

He heard himself saying, 'And how do you come to know Roman?'

Claudia had assumed someone would have told him she was married. If not Papa, then surely one of the Paynes. Edith had flown back from Texas with her own new husband especially for the wedding and pronounced Tim 'real cute' in her new American drawl.

Perhaps it was a sign that Claudia had truly escaped from Kingshaven that nobody there cared enough about her to pass on the gossip.

She turned over and buried her face in the pillow.

Perhaps Michael was so drunk he had forgotten.

After they had all sat down for the inevitable post-mortem of the party, Michael had almost immediately fallen asleep and started snoring.

'I don't think they're used to drinking red wine in Kingshaven,' Roman said, regarding his star guest slumped on the sofa.

It was a particularly patronizing remark, but Claudia had fled like a coward rather than stay to defend her friend, offering the idiotic excuse that she had to get supper for Tim.

Claudia lay in bed, listening to the sounds of their house.

Above their bedroom, Mr B. was listening to Mozart's fortieth symphony. At the end of the slow movement, Claudia waited expectantly for the fast final movement, but Mr B. walked across the room and turned it off, and the silence that ensued seemed somehow more profound because she had been expecting more music.

Gradually, her ears adjusted to the familiar noises outside: the random shouts of men coming out of the pub at the crossroads; a police siren wailing in the distance.

When Tim's key turned in the lock, he called out as he walked across the hall to their bedroom with no thought that he might be waking anyone up: 'Claudia?'

Her eyes blinked as her husband flicked on the harsh electric light.

'Must get a shade for that,' Tim said, leaping on to the bed next to her. 'They've got some unusual ones in Heal's.'

'How did it go?' Claudia asked.

'The short answer is they loved the idea and I'm going!' he said, bouncing up and down like a child. 'Had to twist their arm a bit. A little bird told me that the duty desk had a number of calls praising my piece on the Establishment Club . . .' He was high on his triumph and his energy was infectious.

She sat up. 'Twist their arm?' she asked, laughing.

'I just dropped in that I might be thinking of leaving for a lucrative job in advertising . . .' said Tim.

'Wasn't that rather risky?'

'Oh no! They're paranoid about losing good people with ITV in the ascendant, and the new channel on the way,' Tim said.

'But has someone offered you a lucrative job in advertising?' Claudia asked.

'As a matter of fact, several people have,' Tim said.

She didn't know why she should feel a little hurt that he hadn't mentioned this to her before. She told herself it was probably because he knew she thoroughly disapproved of an industry which wasted creative talent on trying to make people buy things they did not want or need.

'So when do we go?' she asked.

She had assumed that they would go to New York together. It had been her idea, after all. Just as the piece on the Establishment Club had been. She read all the time. Tim did not. He wouldn't have known much about the Beat generation if she hadn't briefed him. But when she saw his face, she suddenly realized she wasn't included in the plan.

'I'd love you to, darling, but it's really work,' he said, placing his hand on her arm, which she found so infuriating she felt as if rage would burn a hole in her skin where his fingers touched. 'Anyway, who would look after Mr B. and Mrs A.?' he added.

Claudia was so cross she could not look at him.

'God, you're pretty!' he said, putting a finger under her chin and turning her face towards his.

He could clearly sense the turbulence going on inside her, she thought, but he imagined that a compliment would cheer her up when in fact it only added to her distress.

She didn't know whether she was supposed to say, 'God, you're handsome!' back, or, 'Thank you!' or just smile.

She felt a similar kind of panic when he began to make love to her.

She never could bring herself to ask whether she was doing it right. Did he want her to actively respond, or was it preferable to lie quiescent as he pumped up and down on top of her?

Like everyone else, she had rushed to buy *Lady Chatterley's Lover* as soon as it became available the previous November, devouring its pages in the hope of enlightenment, but finding little to help her. Did all other women achieve the kind of peaceful fulfilment that Connie did, she wondered, or were there some like her who remained awake for hours feeling strangely dissatisfied after their husbands had made love to them?

Michael opened one eye and discovered that he was lying fully clothed in an unfamiliar bed. His tongue felt like a doormat. He sat up quickly. The room swam in front of his eyes. A stiletto of pain pierced the frontal lobe of his brain.

There was a knock at the door.

'I've made you a prairie oyster,' said Pippa Stone.

'A what?' The pain intensified on speaking.

She walked towards the bed with a glass in her hand. She was wearing a man's silk dressing gown. 'Drink it,' she said. 'You'll feel a lot better.'

Like a sick child swallowing his medicine, Michael did as he was told.

She perched on the bed, close enough that he could smell the sweet mustiness of recent sex emanating from her body. Some of her hair was muzzed into a nest at the back of her head. For a split second, before memory started to filter back, he wondered: Had they?

An embrace in the hall, her head pressed against a few simple pencil strokes which somehow conjured a rounded naked woman from a plain sheet of paper. Matisse's signature right in front of his eyes.

And then Roman had been there. 'Behave yourself, darling!' A friendly warning, but a warning nevertheless. And the sting: 'We don't want to damage the merchandise, do we?'

Michael looked at his watch. 'My train,' he said.

'Stay for breakfast,' said Pippa. The edges of the dressing gown gaped slightly, revealing the sprinkling of freckles on her chest.

'No thanks.' Michael leaned forward to put on his shoes. The cocktail she'd given him lurched biliously to his mouth, but he swallowed it back. 'I'm expected home. My wife's working . . . someone has to keep an eye on the kids . . .'

Her face betrayed a total lack of interest in his domestic arrangements.

'Thanks for having me,' he said, offering his hand awkwardly at the door, like a child remembering his manners after a birthday party.

There was one thing he had to do before leaving London.

At Tottenham Court Road, he asked directions to Foyle's.

As Roman Stone had promised, one window was full of copies of his book. A notice read:

DO

'THE RIGHT THING'

READ

MICHAEL QUINN'S SENSATIONAL FIRST NOVEL!

Michael wished he had Ivor's Box Brownie camera to record the moment when he felt at last like a real author.

The man sitting opposite him in the compartment was reading *The Times*. The lead story was another defection. Michael squinted at the small type, trying to make out the details, but the motion of the train made him slightly queasy.

He opened his eyes just as the train was pulling into Kingshaven. There was a patch of damp on the scratchy upholstery of the headrest where his mouth had fallen open in sleep. His throat was parched and his breath tasted mouldy. Michael stood up and pulled the window back to breathe in gulps of fresh salty air, and did a double take.

Unlike the previous afternoon, when there had been no one about, the platform was crowded with people rushing at the door as he opened it. Flashbulbs exploded in his face. Men in pork pie hats called, 'Over here, Mr Quinn!'

'How did you do it, Mr Quinn?'

'The *Mirror*, Mr Quinn. How about an exclusive? We'll make it worth your while.'

As he tried to step down from the train, camera lenses were thrust in his face.

For a moment, the only event his befuddled brain could relate to this surreal scene was newsreel he had seen of Arthur Miller and Marilyn Monroe arriving in England as newlyweds. The sheer volume of press had prevented them from moving and there'd been a glimmer of fear just behind Marilyn's eyes as she smiled and blew kisses, clinging on to her tall, serious husband.

Michael spotted Iris, pushing through the crowd towards him. 'Please!' he shouted.

A sudden hush fell as the journalists waited for his words.

'Let her through!' he said.

Bodies parted to make a way for Iris, who leaped into his arms through another explosion of flashbulbs and shouted, 'How did you do it, Daddy? How did you help the Prince escape?'

Chapter Ten

December 1962

The death of the barmaid sent shockwaves through the town. Norma Barker had been a familiar figure behind the bar of the Yacht Club (a little too familiar, some of the wives had thought on Ladies' Nights when they observed the ease with which she bantered with their husbands), and she was young, although, at thirty-six, not quite as young as she had led people to believe, and beautiful, even though her platinum-blond hair was clearly out of a bottle.

The body was discovered some hours after she had dialled 999. (The duty sergeant who answered the phone had consumed a measure or two from the bottle of Johnnie Walker which Percy Bland of the Ship always sent up at Christmas, and had formed the definite impression that the call was a prank.) The constable found her on the floor behind the bar of the Yacht Club in a halo of her own vomit, clasping a bottle of sleeping pills in one hand and the telephone receiver in the other.

Accident or suicide appeared to be the only question for the Coroner to adjudicate, but he was new to the county and un-familiar with the ways of the place, and wanted things to be done by the book. An inquest was opened and formally adjourned, and the police instructed to provide a full report surrounding the circumstances of the death.

And that was when everyone started asking questions.

Why would a lovely girl like that want to take her own life? And, if that's what she had done, why had she changed her mind – if this was the explanation for her emergency call? Could it have been a lonely cry for help, which everyone was too busy enjoying themselves to hear?

A collective guilt descended on the town, taking the shine off the traditional build-up to Christmas. The coloured lights strung across the High Street remained unilluminated; there was a heated argument amongst the members of the Kingshaven Amateur Dramatic Society committee as to whether this year's pantomime should proceed.

The editor of the *Chronicle*, Mr Otterway, took the view that while an investigation was in progress, any facts that emerged should be given sub judice status, but the paper's reporting of the church bazaar and the Women's Institute Children's Party, when there was only one subject in the minds of the readers, only served to escalate the growing feeling that the full facts surrounding the barmaid's death were not being divulged, and the ordinary people of Kingshaven were left to come up with their own theories.

'They say that she was having it off with just about everyone, from the Mayor down,' Ivor told Michael after the schoolchildren had gone home on the last day of term.

They were standing on chairs at either end of the classroom, taking down the Christmas decorations.

'Who are *they*, exactly?' Michael asked, wondering where Ivor got his information from.

There seemed to be no genuine sympathy for the girl, who was not a local. Her mother, a blousy woman who looked exactly as one would have imagined the barmaid looking if she had lived another twenty years, had come from Swansea to make arrangements for the transportation of the body. Michael had been behind her in the queue in the bank, and witnessed the cashier pretending not to understand her accent.

'They say she slept with the KGB man . . .' Ivor continued.

'Well, they would, wouldn't they?' said Michael.

The town had made a mountain out of the molehill of celebrity afforded by the defection the summer before last. From the way people talked, one might have thought that the Berlin Wall, which had gone up a short while after, had been erected solely for the purpose of stopping further dissidents from behind the Iron Curtain making their own escape to Kingshaven.

'I don't see what her sex life's got to do with it,' Michael said.

He noticed Ivor's instinctive look over his shoulder, checking whether the headmaster was lurking. 'They say there's a connection with the Palace,' Ivor whispered.

'What sort of connection?'

'She was a regular on the *Brittany Anna*. A touch of droit de seigneur, if you get my drift,' said Ivor.

Michael put down the claw hammer he was holding. 'How do you always know so much about the Palace?' he asked.

Ivor concentrated on levering a drawing pin out of the top of the blackboard.

'Have you got a girlfriend up there or something?' Michael asked, trying to see Ivor's face, which seemed to have gone a bit red. 'Well, congratulations! It's about time!'

Ivor usually maintained a bit sheepishly that the right girl hadn't come along yet. 'What's her name, then?' Michael asked.

'None of your business,' said Ivor, winding the final crêpe-paper streamer round his hand and putting it back in the Christmas-decoration box. 'Feels funny taking stuff down before Christmas,' he said. 'They say it's unlucky.'

'Be more unlucky to have to come in during the holidays,' said Michael, switching off the lights. 'Do you fancy a quick drink?' They usually did at the end of term.

'I can't tonight,' said Ivor.

'Oh. I see,' said Michael knowingly. 'Don't let me get in the way of love's young dream!'

Even though it was dark, he could tell Ivor was blushing again. It was fun to give him a taste of his own teasing.

Iris had grown so tall she was often mistaken for much older than her twelve years. Towering over her peers and uninterested in their chatter ('Nothing but ponies,' she said dismissively when Sylvia had pressed for details), Iris had quickly gravitated towards the back of the bus where the older girls sat openly flouting the school rule which forbade Lowhampton Girls from talking to Lowhampton Boys (or indeed any other members of the opposite sex) while wearing school uniform.

Iris had become particularly friendly with Winston Allsop, who was also very tall, and the two of them often lingered at the bus stop talking before making their way home in opposite directions.

Sylvia worried about this development.

'You're very young to be talking to boys,' she said, when reports started to come back. 'Why don't you make friends with someone your own age?'

Winston was seventeen now, very clever, and hoping to read Law at Oxford University.

'Are you sure you don't mean my own colour?' Iris responded coolly.

'It's got nothing to do with that. He's only half-coloured anyway,' Sylvia had replied, flustered.

'I shall speak to whom I please,' Iris told her imperiously. 'It's a free country.'

Iris was passionate about politics. While other girls her age slept with pictures of Elvis Presley under their pillows, Iris had a newspaper photograph of Martin Luther King on her bedside table. She and Winston were the founder members (only members, as far as Michael could tell) of the Kingshaven Civil Rights Movement.

'It's a meeting of minds,' he had assured Sylvia.

'Well, I certainly wasn't allowed to meet any minds at that age,' Sylvia said.

'You met me instead,' he teased her.

'But that was different,' his wife said. 'You weren't . . . so much older.'

Now, as Michael approached his daughter and Winston deep in conversation at the bus stop, there was something about the angle of her head as she looked at Winston that made Michael see his wife's suspicions were well founded. Iris's interest in the boy, whether she was conscious of it or not, was not purely intellectual.

A combination of emotions curdled inside Michael. His daughter was becoming an adult, and he was proud to think that she was going to be the sort of adult he would like to know. He admired her bravery in daring to be different when most children of her age did their best to be the same as one another. At the same time, he knew how lonely it could be to go against convention, and he was afraid for her. And part of him was simply jealous, when he saw his clever girl with eyes for another man, and it dawned on him that he would very soon no longer be the most important person in her life. He was shocked by how the warm feelings he'd always had towards Winston suddenly cooled, as he viewed him as a suitor, someone Iris might need protecting from. She was only twelve, after all.

'Good afternoon, sir,' Winston said politely as he approached.

Michael observed that the boy took a step away from Iris. 'Good afternoon, Winston.'

'Dad?' Iris asked. Her blue eyes were alive with excitement.

'Yes?'

'Some of Winston's friends are playing a gig at the church hall. Can I go?' Iris asked.

'A gig?' Michael repeated.

'They're in a rock-and-roll band,' Iris explained with a heavy sigh, as if Michael were impossibly old-fashioned for needing it spelled out.

'I don't think so, Iris.'

'Why not?' She was immediately on the offensive.

'Because you're too young to go out at night,' he said.

'But it's not at night,' Iris trounced him. 'It's in the afternoon. Saturday afternoon. What's wrong with that?' She stared at him defiantly.

'We've got our party on Saturday evening,' said Michael, searching for a reason.

'So what?'

'Are you coming home, Iris?' he said, hoping that they could discuss it and find some sort of compromise.

'No,' she said, glaring at him.

'Well, don't be too long,' he told her.

Was it like this for all parents? By the time he was Iris's age, both his parents were dead, and he was living with Auntie Jean and Rita, who let him do more or less what he liked. But he had been a boy and it had been the war. Things had been different.

If he'd ever thought about what sort of parent he would be as his children grew up, he'd imagined himself liberal-minded and tolerant. He still thought of himself as young, as someone who rebelled against people in authority. He was an Angry Young Man. It said so in the newspaper. And yet he was behaving like a clichéd father, trying to prevent his daughter spreading her wings. Surely it wasn't possible for him to have become middle-aged at thirty-two years old? He realized he had put Iris in an impossible situation, refusing her perfectly reasonable request for no good reason, and now either she or he would have to lose face by backing down. Michael wished they could just go back and start the conversation again.

The new hors d'oeuvres trolley was a source of enormous pleasure to Libby King. There was something completely satisfying about the design, which reminded her of those metal toolboxes carpenters carried, which concertinaed out into an unbelievable number of trays for essential bits and bobs, and all slid back together again neatly for convenient transportation. The trolley was a similar masterpiece of engineering (sadly Swedish rather than English, but they had after all invented the idea of a buffet with their smorgasbord). The four spinners were like miniature Ferris wheels, each holding six dishes which were cleverly weighted to rise and stop exactly where the previous dish had been. Twenty-four separate dishes offered a kaleidoscope of mouthwatering choice to the discerning diner, whilst only requiring one waitress to push it and serve.

By happy coincidence, the trolley had arrived at the same time as the new chef, Jean-Claude, who paid attention to the appearance of things. An artiste with a piping bag, Mr Pocock called him. Jean-Claude could turn half a hard-boiled egg into a delicate swan, and make a cheerful clown's face from a simple stuffed tomato. And his talent was not limited to the hors d'oeuvres. No ham was allowed to go unglazed or unbejewelled with glacé cherries. No salmon was permitted to leave the kitchen without an intricate coating of cucumber and lemon scales in a frame of mayonnaise swirls. The restaurant had become so renowned that they had decided to open it to non-residents and they had taken bookings right up until Christmas Day, when Jean-Claude was promising to do something spectacular with a turkey.

It was just as well, because takings were down. It hadn't been so noticeable the previous year, when the unexpected arrival of journalists from all over the world boosted profits in that time just before the school holidays when things were often a bit slow, and had more than made up for the bar bill the Russians had left without paying. But after Kingshaven's brief appearance on the world's stage, things had rapidly returned to normal.

There was a marked decline in bookings all over the country.

The commonly held view was that people were choosing to fly to warmer climes by aeroplane. (Libby couldn't see that lasting very long. Two weeks of dreadful foreign food and primitive plumbing was enough to make people yearn for a place they knew and trusted, Libby had told a recent meeting of the Southern Hoteliers' Association.)

In the current climate, the last thing Kingshaven needed was a death.

Death clung like a limpet to the reputation of a place. Which visitor to Bournemouth nowadays could amble down the peaceful pine valleys to the sea without their thoughts turning to the grisly murder in the Chine, even though it had happened a good fifteen years ago? Statistics showed that victims were usually murdered by someone they knew, but holidaymakers simply weren't logical about these things.

Not that there was any evidence to suggest that Norma Barker's death was murder, Libby reminded herself. According to the pathologist who conducted the post-mortem, asphyxiation by vomit was the cause of death, which had been brought about by the ingestion of an enormous quantity of alcohol and sleeping tablets. Why she had taken them was anyone's guess. She was Welsh, after all. It was a mystery why the Coroner was wasting everyone's time and taxpayers' money on further investigation. All members of the Yacht Club were being quizzed on their knowledge of the girl, and were being asked to provide an account of their movements on the night in question. It really was a bit much. Bad enough to have a suicide on the seafront, without everyone being branded as suspects. At this rate it would drag on and make next year's season even worse.

It was the unpredictability of the hotel business that Libby found frustrating. However meticulously you planned and budgeted, there were always things which had nothing to do with you at all, which could change everything.

Libby gave the hors d'oeuvres trolley an impatient little tap. The magical mechanism made the little tray of Hawaiian Melon Cocktails disappear and a tray of Prawn and Cucumber Boats instantly appear in its place. It calmed her nerves.

Claudia pulled apart a thick loaf of rye bread she had purchased in a delicatessen at the end of Portobello Road, sniffing the soft flesh of the bread inside the hard crust, its strong sour flavour sweetened by caraway seeds, a taste so complex and delicious she could happily eat nothing else for the rest of her life.

She and Tim were eating supper in their newly refurbished kitchen.

'This is delicious soup!' said Tim, taking a spoonful.

'Heinz tomato,' said Claudia.

'From a tin?'

'Yes!'

'I'll have to send you on a cookery course,' Tim said, only half joking.

'I can cook,' Claudia defended herself.

'My mother makes wonderful soup,' said Tim.

'It's not difficult if you have the time,' Claudia said pointedly.

Pippa Stone dressed in bohemian clothes and struck left-wing attitudes, but she came from an upper-class family and had been educated at a Swiss finishing school. She knew how to do things like Beef Wellington with a perfect crust decorated with pastry leaves, which people at Roman's dinner parties went into ecstasies about. But Pippa didn't work, and she had a cleaner to do all the clearing up afterwards.

'Just a minute ago, you were saying how delicious this was,' Claudia reminded her husband.

She found it slightly surreal to be having this conversation beneath a large screen print of a Campbell's soup can, which Tim had brought back from Andy Warhol's Factory in New York and installed as the main feature of the open-plan kitchen and dining room. If a soup can was art (and Claudia had no doubt it was), what could be aesthetically displeasing about eating its contents, as Tim's expression of distaste seemed to imply?

'If Christmas dinner came in a can, you'd eat it,' said Tim.

'And what would be so wrong with that?' Claudia asked levelly.

'Don't let's have a fight,' said Tim, which was what he always said when she responded to his undermining comments, making it sound as if she was the one who had been provocative in the first place.

Claudia stood up and rinsed her plate under the tap.

Tim pushed away his bowl, the soup half eaten.

If she had claimed to have made the soup herself from real tomatoes and cream, would he have eaten it up? Claudia wondered.

'I've decided to go down to see my father,' she announced, knowing that it wasn't a good time, but wanting to get the resentment over with in one.

'When?' Tim asked.

'I thought this weekend.'

'But we were going to go Christmas shopping.'

'You're far better at choosing.'

The ritual exchange of expensive gifts she had experienced on her first Christmas in the Stone household had made her uncomfortable. The conspicuously extravagant generosity felt to her like a substitute for genuine affection.

'I didn't go home last Christmas or the one before,' she said.

'Christmas doesn't matter to him, you said so yourself.'

'I don't think he's very well.'

'Why now, though, when there's so much to do?'

'I hardly ever see him!'

'Yes, well . . .' said Tim. 'Whose fault is that?'

Papa had not bothered to hide his feelings at the wedding breakfast Roman had thrown for them at the Ritz. It had been embarrassing, and she had only seen him once since. With work and the house, it was difficult to find enough time to travel down to Kingshaven for the weekend, and it was impossible to do in a day with cuts in the train timetable, unless you only wanted five minutes in the place while the engine turned round. Inside she knew this wasn't the real reason she had avoided him. Papa had not taken to Tim despite her new husband's determined charge of charm. Worse than that, she found the contempt that her father was too old to conceal had resonated with feelings of her own, and had made her shiver with disloyalty.

The giant poinsettia confirmed Libby's worst suspicions. Eddie never bought her flowers, unless he was feeling guilty.

'What have I done to deserve this generosity?' she asked him, staring at the flowers, which were so bright and red and papery, it was hard to believe they were real.

'A little bit of Christmas cheer!' he said. 'A token of how much I appreciate all your hard work at this time of year. Any time of year, as a matter of—'

'That's very thoughtful of you,' she cut him short.

She could tell that he was worried from the way his eyes anxiously tracked her round the room as she tried out various placements for the plant. It didn't look quite right anywhere: too big for the mantelpiece, not big enough to stand alone in the corner. If it went on the dining table, people on opposite sides would have to lean to see round it. The more Libby carried it around unable to find a place for it, the heavier the pot seemed, and the more eager she was to put it down, before it started to become a symbol of some greater failure in their lives.

Eventually, she stood it next to an arrangement of white chrysanthemums on the little pie-crust table in the bay window.

'You'll need a mat under that,' Eddie advised.

'Yes, I do know that!' she said impatiently.

Eddie gulped.

People always took Eddie at face value. They saw the jokes, the twinkling smile; thought him a bit of a wag, a good cove. He performed the role well – so well that even Libby could sometimes be lulled into believing that nothing bothered him. It was only on occasions like this, crisis points, that she caught a glimpse of the vulnerability which had drawn her to him the very first time they met, at the quayside in Lowhampton when Uncle Cyril returned from India.

In his white Navy uniform, Eddie had been handsome and full of youthful vitality, but his darting eyes had betrayed such eagerness to be liked that she had found the confidence to talk to him, even though she was only thirteen and he five years her senior.

Now, they both stood staring at the bright red flowers of the poinsettia. All of a sudden there seemed to be rather a lot at stake and neither of them wanted to be the one to break the silence.

Were they in fact flowers, or leaves? Libby wondered.

It had been love at first sight on the quayside. For her at least. Not for him. Love was rarer amongst men. Years of observing other people's relationships had made her aware that her father's devotion to her mother was not the norm, and had probably given her false expectations. But if Eddie hadn't loved her as she had loved him, he had needed her in different ways, and on the whole they'd managed to achieve a balance in their marriage. Over the years, a certain amount of flexibility had been required, but neither of them had taken their wedding vows lightly, and even if they'd been stretched on occasion, the shared assumption had always been that the two of them were in it together, for the duration, for the good of the family and the hotel.

In the fifteen years since she had solemnly sworn to love, honour and obey until death relieved her of the duty, now was the first time Libby had seriously wondered whether things had gone too far for those promises to be kept.

How wrong people were who thought that wealth and privilege could protect you from the grubbiness of life.

'Were you sleeping with the barmaid?' she asked quietly.

'No,' he replied instantly.

'I need the truth, Eddie, because I will probably be called to give evidence to the Coroner's officer.'

'Of course I wasn't!' he said, more confidently. 'A little tart like that!'

'If you think I'm concerned about your morals, you're mistaken. It's the reputation of the hotel that interests me.'

'Yes, well, I might have known that!' Eddie said, leaping to the offensive. 'You care more about this bloody place than you do about me!'

'Oh, don't be so childish!' Libby scolded, but inside she did wonder whether it was all her fault. Was ownership of the hotel, which had after all been her greatest attraction, also the source of his perpetual need to seek comfort elsewhere, or would it have happened anyway? It was something she could never know for certain.

She gazed beyond the poinsettia through the window, over the lawns and out across the murky-looking bay. There was no sun at all and the sky looked almost yellow, as it sometimes did before snow. Bad weather was forecast over England, but she was praying for it to stay away for just another few days. White Christmases were rare in Kingshaven. The probability of snow was so small that she and Mr Pocock had dreamed up the Christmas Bonus (Mr Pocock had heard of a similar scheme in a hotel in St Mawes, Cornwall), which offered to reimburse the cost of the holiday if there was more than half an inch of snow on the ground.

A small advertisement in the *Telegraph* had proclaimed:

> Dreaming of a White Christmas?
> And a Free Holiday?
> Whatever the Weather
> You're Sure of a
> Warm Welcome at the Palace!

It had seemed like a good idea in a very empty October and resulted in more bookings than they had anticipated from all sorts of people who had never previously visited.

Libby had been surprised how readily people from different ends of the spectrum were prepared to gamble on a free holiday. There was an income tax inspector with his mother in tow and, in the next-door room, a bookmaker with a much younger woman he said was his wife. The income tax inspector had let slip that he had a friend in the Met Office who had predicted a seventy-five per cent chance of snow; the bookmaker was prepared to give odds even at this late stage.

'Oh, all right then!' Eddie suddenly blurted out.

'What?' Libby's mind was still on the logistics of the Christmas bonus. The small print on the booking form had made it clear that it was only the standard room rate that would be reimbursed, not meals or other extras. Nevertheless, there was bound to be feeling. How long would snow have to settle to trigger the repayment? Could they insist on twenty-four hours, in which case, if it didn't arrive until late on Christmas Day, might they just get away with it?

'Do I have to spell it out?' Eddie asked.

'What?' Libby asked again.

Her husband sighed long and hard. 'I was, having . . . you know . . . with Norma!' he finally admitted.

Libby had known, of course, but she hadn't realized how peculiar it would feel to hear him admit it. She saw her life as being like one of those huge chests of drawers behind the counter at the dispensing chemist, with different compartments for each bit, all carefully labelled and closed when they weren't needed. Now, it felt as if a bomb had just dropped, blasting all the drawers open. Rules were flying about, secrets spilling out and emotions dripping into each other. In the disarray, she couldn't seem to keep hold of any thought except the one that kept reiterating in her head that this must go no further.

'Anything can be dealt with,' Libby clearly remembered overhearing her mother saying, long ago, 'so long as it remains utterly oyster.'

Eddie's face was twisted in a most peculiar manner. It took her several seconds to understand that he was crying. For a moment, she felt tremendous affection for him as he sobbed pitiably in front of her, his face in his palms. Her hand hovered just above his heaving shoulder for a moment before patting it. Her touch made him stop, sniff a loud, watery sniff, and look up at her with red eyes. She couldn't tell whether he was expecting forgiveness, or punishment.

'Did you love her?'

Libby didn't know why she had asked. It made no difference now.

'Of course not,' said Eddie resolutely. 'I'm not the only one who's strayed . . .' he added meaningfully.

'Hmm, yes, well.' Libby was flustered. 'But this is . . .' Her brain searched for the right expression. '. . . so very public!' she finally said, unable to disguise the squeal of desperation in her voice. 'Were you there the evening she died?' she demanded.

'No,' said Eddie, looking away and sighing, as if exhausted by the interview. 'Well, all right, if you must know, I was, but she was right as rain when I left her.'

'Oh, how could you make such a bloody mess of things?' Libby suddenly shouted at him.

The heater in the train wasn't working and Claudia was squashed against the window. It was bitterly cold, but with four people and their assorted parcels on her side of the compartment, the air was stuffy too. A little girl bundled up in hand-knitted scarf was sitting on her mother's knee opposite, staring at her. Claudia smiled at the child. In the condensation on the window, she drew a round face with a smile on it. The child copied her.

'Don't do that,' the mother scolded. 'You'll make your mittens all wet.'

The child frowned at Claudia.

Claudia got a paperback book out of her handbag, the Penguin edition of a novel that had caused a bit of a stir when first published. It was about an unmarried, pregnant young woman, turned out of her home by her father, who goes to live in a squalid bedsit. Curiously, Claudia found herself slightly envying the girl's life with her eccentric neighbours and bug-filled bed. After a few pages, she closed the book, and stared at the barren fields racing past.

Pregnancy was the worst thing that could have happened to the character in the book, but if Claudia had fallen pregnant, she thought, it would have changed everything for the better.

It had all looked so straightforward. She and Tim were a bright, healthy young married couple, with enough money to start a family. The private communal garden their house backed on to was a safe place for children to play, with big shady trees, swings and lots of lawn to run about on. The only blight on the otherwise rosy future that lay in front of them was that each month Claudia's period arrived.

Claudia wasn't sure whether it was her inability to conceive which had made Tim lose respect for her or whether it had happened before that, as far back as the moment she agreed to marry him. The more time she spent with him, the more she realized that Tim measured his life in goals. It was as if, having achieved her, his mind had gone on to other ambitions.

But there was no point in blaming him because it was as much her fault. In her heart, Claudia knew she was paying the price of marrying for logic rather than love. She had wanted a new beginning to her story, and she had got one, but she hadn't imagined a story in which she would be defined solely as a wife and potential mother, which were roles she didn't seem to be particularly well equipped to play.

Her father was asleep when she arrived home. She bent to kiss the side of his face, which was bristly with several days' growth of beard. His white hair had taken on a slightly yellow hue, like the fingers of people who smoked.

He opened his eyes and smiled with such pure, unguarded delight she was moved to see how much he loved her.

'You've come!' he said happily, and drifted off to sleep again.

It occurred to her that perhaps he had always been frightened of showing love, afraid that anything he loved would be snatched from him, as it had been before. She was cross with herself for being so wrapped up in her own life that she had not stopped to think about what her leaving home might have felt like for him.

Her father began to cough. It was a horrible, wet, chesty cough that convulsed him and turned his ashen face pink. Claudia stood helplessly beside him, her hand on his bony shoulder as it heaved up and down.

'Good journey?' he said, awakened by the paroxysm.

'Sssh!'

She waited for his breathing to calm, but there was still a distinct wheeze on his chest.

'The heater wasn't working in the compartment, so I was rather cold,' Claudia told him.

'Silly girl, why didn't you move?' Even though he was in feeble health, his capacity to find fault was not diminished.

'Train was packed. People coming home for Christmas,' she explained.

'Are you home for Christmas?' he asked immediately.

His eye sockets seemed to have drooped, she noticed, leaving the eyeball more exposed in its watery surround, and his hope less easy to disguise. She didn't have the heart to say that she was planning to go back to London.

'If I'm welcome,' she said.

'Well, you'll have to get some food for yourself,' he said shortly. 'I've nothing in.'

But she could tell that he was pleased.

Michael watched the expression on Sylvia's face as she ladled punch for their guests, realizing that this was a moment his wife had waited for. Sylvia looked completely at home in the role of hostess, with her long blond hair done up in a sophisticated top-knot, a constant patter of pleasantries falling from her pale lipsticked lips and 'Moon River' playing softly in the background on the Dansette he had bought her for her birthday.

In his opinion, the cut-glass punch bowl, which had been their wedding gift from Sylvia's parents, was a quintessential reflection of Doreen's pretensions. He'd forgotten they even owned it, but Sylvia had clearly stored the memory as safely as she had the gift, wrapped in its original box and tissue paper, transported quietly from one house to another, and secreted in the attic until the day came when they would be the sort of couple who would invite their neighbours in for a glass of punch at Christmas.

An image of Sylvia when she was a little girl flew across his mind: that game she had always wanted to play when it was her turn to choose. He could see her now with all her dolls arrayed under the big oak tree at the bottom of her parents' garden, serving them acorn cups of egg nog. She made the drink with a teaspoon of lemon curd mixed with water. He could almost taste the thin sugary liquid and the little globules of curd which would never entirely dissolve.

Polite conversation had not come easily to him even then.

'We can't have you standing in the corner like a wallflower,' Sylvia would say to him, prising him away from the tree. 'Come and meet Heidi.'

And he would obediently shake the doll's hand, but find himself lost for words.

'Talk about the weather,' Sylvia would suggest through clenched smiling teeth, before greeting the next doll with her miniature jug of refreshment. 'So pleased you could come!'

The little black velvet dress and single string of cultured pearls she wore now were more sophisticated than the summer frock and plaits, but essentially she was just the same, Michael thought. She had been rehearsing for this moment all her life.

He felt an ache of fondness for her. She was so vacuous his brain always told him not to like her, but so well-meaning and pretty his heart said otherwise. And her greatest quality was that she didn't bear grudges. It was the important respect in which she differed from her poisonous mother, who'd always choose to dwell in the past rather than try to make a go of it. Sylvia understood almost nothing about him, he thought, but she was prepared to love him, nevertheless. And he in turn had tried very hard over the last couple of years to love her. And they had been surprisingly happy, he realized, if he didn't allow himself to think too much.

'Mr Allsop,' Sylvia said, guiding the new arrival across the room to where he was standing.

'Oh, call me Jolly, everyone else does!'

'I don't think you know my husband, Michael?'

'Only by reputation,' Jolly said.

Michael flinched.

'Our local author,' said Jolly Allsop, extending his hand amiably.

Michael didn't think Sylvia would appreciate it if he responded, 'Our local toff!' so he just said, 'Hello!'

'We're all so busy these days, aren't we?' Sylvia said. 'We hardly know who's living at the end of our street!'

A shadow of displeasure passed across Jolly's face at the implication that he was living in the vicinity of council houses, but his eyes followed Sylvia's backside appreciatively as she sashayed back across the room to greet another guest.

'Very cold weather,' Michael said.

'They say it's going to snow,' said Jolly.

'Do they?'

'The berries were very plentiful this year,' said Jolly.

'That's a sign, is it?'

'So they say.'

Michael struggled to think of some other weather-related issue. Had the sea ever frozen in Jolly Allsop's experience? Did sheep shiver if the temperature dropped beyond a certain point?

'Are you writing another novel?' Jolly suddenly asked.

'Trying to,' said Michael, immediately wishing he had simply said yes.

One of the unforeseen aspects of being a published writer was that people expected you to talk about it.

'I expect it's hard to find the time,' said Jolly. 'I find it difficult enough writing a letter!'

For Michael, the problem was not time, but staring at a blank exercise book for hours on end. Roman Stone was pressing for another novel, even offering to pay him some money up front, but Michael felt he would be in trouble if he took money for something that might never come into existence. The problem was not money. Even if there was enough money to give up his job, which he didn't think he would ever feel comfortable doing, he wasn't sure that he would ever write again. He wondered if he was suffering from writer's block, a condition he'd never seriously believed in because he'd always written, since the day he'd been able to hold a pen, until, ironically, the reality of being published had entered his life.

'Second novels are always a problem,' Roman Stone had told him. 'Don't be afraid of writing a sequel.'

Michael suspected this advice had more to do with capitalizing on his investment than any question of artistic integrity.

'Not much of a reader myself,' Jolly Allsop was saying. 'But my wife found it interesting, didn't you, Jenny?'

'I always wonder where writers get their ideas,' said Jennifer Allsop.

Was there a flicker of mischief on her face?

'Jennifer, have you met Ivor?' Sylvia ushered over the latest arrival. 'He's a colleague of Michael's.'

'Another novelist?' Jennifer enquired, although Michael was sure she knew that Ivor was not.

'Teacher, I'm afraid,' said Ivor good-humouredly. 'Those who can't and all that.'

'Are you on your own, Ivor?' Sylvia said, handing him a glass of punch. 'We were hoping we were going to meet your girlfriend.'

The sheer mortification on Ivor's face made Michael ashamed that he had said anything to Sylvia. How crass and disloyal of him when Ivor had been so resolutely discreet on his behalf.

'Who's that then?' Jennifer immediately picked up on Ivor's discomfort.

'I think you've got the wrong end of the stick,' said Ivor, recovering quickly. 'I'm still available,' he said with a wink at Sylvia, who giggled.

From elbow height, Anthony offered a plate of Ritz crackers in one hand and a plate of Twiglets in the other.

'Where's Iris then?' asked Patsy, the next-door neighbour.

'She's not feeling too well,' said Sylvia.

'It's that age,' said Audrey knowledgeably.

'She's sulking,' said Anthony.

Jennifer turned to Sylvia. 'Love your dress. Didn't you make one like that for Pearl King?'

'Yes,' Sylvia said.

'You must make some for Mummy to sell!'

'It's hardly worth it with the percentage your mother takes,' Michael found himself saying, even though he could feel Sylvia beside him silently willing him not to. Sylvia liked to keep everyone friendly, but Michael thought that people exploited her. Mrs Farmer always expected her to step in to run the shop during the summer months when it was busy, then dropped her during the winter, and she took such a big commission on Sylvia's dresses, there was barely any profit in it.

'Would you like a nibble?'

Anthony was holding a plate with a half-grapefruit which was stuck with cocktail sticks threaded with cubes of Cheddar and tinned pineapple, which he and Sylvia had spent the afternoon preparing.

'Thank you, young fellow!' said Jolly, helping himself.

'How are Joanna, Jackie and Julia?' Sylvia asked Jennifer, refilling her cup of punch.

'Fine,' she said, distractedly. 'Libby King had tickets for the pantomime this evening, but, of course, it's been cancelled.'

'Such a shame,' said Sylvia.

'Of all the years to choose *Sleeping Beauty*! Bloody bad luck, I call it,' said Jolly.

Everyone nodded in agreement.

The one subject certain to cut across all social boundaries and make the party go with a swing was the death of the barmaid, Michael thought.

'There's a rumour going round,' Ivor said, checking that Anthony had moved out of earshot with his cheese and pineapple hedgehog. 'She was pregnant.'

'Surely a type like that would be on the Pill nowadays,' Audrey Potter suggested, demonstrating how up to date she was, even though she was the oldest at the gathering, and a spinster.

'But Dr Payne won't prescribe it even to married women,' Jennifer exclaimed. 'I'm told,' she added as her husband gave her a sharp glance.

'What if she had no intention of killing herself?'

'You mean it was an accident?'

'Or someone laced her drink . . .'

'Why would anyone do that?'

'If she were blackmailing someone?'

'She was Welsh, of course.'

'You mean, if she was going to say whose baby it was?'

'If she knew . . .'

General sniggering.

'The consensus is pointing towards murder then, is it?' Michael asked.

There was an intake of breath at the boldness of this statement. It wasn't done to go beyond innuendo.

'Well, there's a thought for your next novel,' said Jennifer. 'You could write a murder mystery!'

'*Murder at the Harbour End*,' Audrey mused.

'How about *The Last Resort*?' Ivor offered.

'I say, that's rather good!' said Jolly.

'Wasn't there a famous detective novelist who used to stay at the Palace?' Jennifer asked.

'Daphne W. Smythe, of course!' said Miss Potter.

'That's the one!'

They were all looking at Michael.

'I don't write murder mysteries,' he said.

'Maybe you should have a go,' said Ivor encouragingly.

'Oh, do have a go!'

Michael felt there was a hint of impatience creeping in. Why not? Call yourself a writer? He wished he could go upstairs and shut himself in his room like Iris. The small talk was worse than the sickly punch. The first sip was tolerable enough but if you had too much it left a nasty taste in your mouth.

When everyone had finally gone home, Michael carried Anthony, who had fallen asleep under the stairs with a small sausage in one hand and an empty cocktail stick in the other, upstairs and tucked him under his blankets still fully clothed.

Sylvia was emptying the ashtray which Jennifer had filled when he came back down.

'Do you think it was a success?' she asked him anxiously.

'A great success.'

'Did you enjoy yourself?'

'Up to a point,' he said.

'Oh good!' She smiled at him. There was a slight pink flush on her face from the punch and the excitement of it all.

'Jolly Allsop couldn't take his eyes off you,' he said.

'Don't be silly,' Sylvia protested.

'I don't blame him,' said Michael. 'Come here.'

'What?' she asked, looking at him warily, as if he were about to ravish her on the carpet.

'I've got something for you,' he said. 'Christmas present.'

'Keep it 'til Christmas Day,' she said, like a child.

'No, I want you to have it now.'

He wanted it to be a moment when it was just the two of them. He wanted to have the innocent pleasure on her face just to himself.

He dangled a key in front of her eyes.

'What's that?' she asked.

'A key.'

'I can see it's a key. What's it for?'

'I've taken a twelve-month lease for you on the little shop next to Offard and Lye.'

'A key to my own shop?'

'I would have had a sign painted, but I didn't know what you'd want to call it,' he said.

Sylvia took the key from his finger and twirled it in front of her eyes, as if she couldn't quite believe it was real.

'I wish you had given it to me when everyone was here,' she said, finally.

During the Christmas Day service, the stained-glass East window, the Kings' window as it had become known, glowed with the candles in front of it. Libby was finally convinced that it had been the right decision to be bold and go for a modern design by one of Pearl's upcoming artist friends, rather than try to recreate the previous window, which had only been Victorian and not original after all. If they could get away with modern in Coventry Cathedral why not St Mary's, Kingshaven?

The depiction of Christ was traditional enough, but the slabs of colour were bold and bright (and a good deal less expensive, of course, than all those tiny pieces) and the words 'KING OF' spelled out vertically in the six panels down one side and 'HEAVEN' down the other, really did say it all, very simply and directly.

As the congregation rose in unison to sing the first carol, Libby felt buoyed up by the presence of all her family around her. Traditionally, Pearl turned out for the morning service very reluctantly, and for the last two Christmases she hadn't come at all. Tom was great fun and good for Pearl in many ways, but Libby suspected there wasn't much religion in his life. This year, Pearl had telephoned to invite herself and Tom and little Damian over for three days, almost as if she sensed that Libby needed the moral support.

Libby watched proudly as her own son Christopher ascended the pulpit steps to read the first lesson. It was a momentous occasion for him, the first Christmas since he was six years old that he hadn't sung the first verse of 'Once in Royal David's City' solo. Finally, at the age of fourteen, Christopher's voice had broken, and although it didn't feel quite the same in the church without his wobbly soprano trilling up to the eaves, at least she no longer had to squash a spare pair of trousers into her handbag in case of an accident under his surplice.

His stutter over the Angel Gabriel's tidings had the curious effect of giving the words a certain awe, and as he raced through to the end in one breath, and sighed loudly with relief, several people actually clapped, which gave the service a very festive feeling.

When the Reverend asked the congregation to kneel, Libby closed her eyes tight and prayed very hard.

'Our Father, which art in Heaven, Hallowed be thy name . . .'

There was nothing in the Lord's Prayer specifically about telling the truth, she thought as she spoke the words by rote. Might it be possible that there had been times when even Jesus had told a little lie, for the greater good of his family?

If called upon by the Coroner to swear on the Bible, would she physically be able to stand there and lie about Eddie's whereabouts on the night in question?

'Forgive us our trespasses . . .'

The implication was, surely, that it was possible to trespass and be forgiven? But Libby didn't know whether that included knowingly trespassing, and it wasn't the sort of thing you could ask the vicar.

Libby prayed fervently for guidance.

Please God, could you just point me in the right direction? And, also, if you could hold off the snow for another day or two . . .

In the five years since the hotel had started staying open for Christmas, a tradition had been established that the King family and their guests would eat their lunch at a long table in the public dining room with the guests.

Pearl and Tom had brought with them a job lot of crackers, which Pearl doled out like rations, insisting that everyone put on the paper hats and read the jokes out loud. It got things off to a flying start and helped fill the time while the hors d'oeuvres trolley went round with the starter (no choice on this occasion) of a smoked salmon rosette perched on a piped swirl of pink mayonnaise.

A few of the crackers contained defective snaps which didn't go off at all. One (fortunately at the bottom of the box, and therefore allocated to the King table) appeared to have an excessive quantity of explosive. Glowing fragments spattered out burning little black holes in the tablecloth and briefly igniting Liliana's yellow tissue paper crown. Eddie was very quick with the water jug, but the slight taint of singed hair remained in the room throughout the meal until the lighting of the pudding with brandy provided more mellow fumes.

Chef's turkey, which was boned and stuffed with a chestnut forcemeat, was certainly a memorable centrepiece to the feast.

'Well, it beats cooking Christmas dinner yourself!' Pearl was the first to come up with a positive comment.

'Certainly beats your cooking,' said Tom, which made Pearl swipe him playfully with her napkin.

Libby wished she wouldn't because it made it so much more difficult to tell the young ones off.

'Pearl left the giblets in the bird last year,' Tom told the table.

'I'd never heard of giblets!' Pearl admitted, cheerfully.

'You can barely imagine the taste!' said Tom.

'Was it worse than this?' asked Angela, pushing a bit of dark meat around her plate.

'Angela, I am quite capable of selling that horse before you've ever ridden it,' Libby warned under her breath.

The decision to buy Angela a horse for Christmas meant that Libby had had to give up a valuable negotiating tool.

Angela was meant to receive the horse the previous Christmas, but when the truth about the ballet dancer's disguise had emerged (and in a national newspaper, of all places), Libby had had second thoughts. It was bad enough that Angela had for a short time become something of a heroine in the town without rewarding her theft. Libby wouldn't have minded quite so much if it hadn't been her favourite headscarf Angela had chosen to give the defector, along with the shoes she had worn on Coronation Day, which had sentimental value even though they were several sizes too big.

'I'm afraid I can't eat it because I'm a vegetarian,' Christopher said, pushing his plate away. It was another of his worrying fads, but he seemed quite serious about it, to the point of declining bacon at breakfast.

'I'm a vegetarian too!' Joanna Allsop piped up, after tasting the meat.

Ruby Farmer's seven-year old granddaughter had developed a rather amusing crush on Christopher, trailing around after him and copying everything he said.

'So am I!' said Jacqueline, her younger sister.

'Don't be ridiculous,' said Jennifer Allsop. 'You don't even know what a vegetarian is.'

'Do!'

'What is it, then?'

'Someone who doesn't eat animals!' said Joanna triumphantly.

'How could anyone eat an animal?' Jackie wanted to know. 'They've got fur and everything?'

'They skin the fur off,' Joanna explained.

'That's enough!' said Jolly desperately.

'Try pouring gravy over it,' Eddie urged Jolly as the older girls clamped their mouths shut when their father tried to make them eat. 'Drowns the taste.'

The three little Allsops had inherited their mother's looks in reverse proportion, Libby thought as she watched them sitting at the children's end of the table wearing identical tartan dresses with white collars and black velvet bows. Joanna, the oldest, had the rich chestnut hair; Jackie had the hair and a hint of the delicacy of feature; but little Julia, at just eighteen months, was already a beauty, with Jennifer's large, soulful eyes. Julia and Adrian, who was sitting next to her, made a very handsome couple, Libby thought, and she was an even-tempered little thing in spite of the fact that her birth had been such a disappointment to everyone.

After lunch, there were mince pies and Charades with the guests in the ballroom.

There was much hilarity as the Squadron Leader and his oriental wife picked *Bridge on the River Kwai* out of the hat; Mrs Farmer, Jennifer and Jolly's team got *Spartacus*, which took a little longer to guess, partly, Libby suspected, because everyone was enjoying the spectacle of Ruby and Jolly pretending they were in a boxing ring for the syllable Spar.

When it was Eddie and the boys' turn, he put three fingers up. 'Three words?'

Eddie nodded, then he got down on all fours and started roaring.

'Lion!' called Angela.

Eddie nodded vigorously.

The little children shrieked with laughter.

Eddie grabbed Adrian from Libby's lap and put him on the floor beside him.

'Come on, son, be a lion!'

The two-year-old started roaring.

Christopher was laughing at the spectacle of his father and brother prowling round the floor. Eddie beckoned to him.

'M-M-Me?'

'Yes, come and be lions with us.'

Unbelievably, their oldest son, normally so reticent and shy, went down on the floor too. Libby looked at her three lions prowling around the floor and felt suddenly very proud. What a good father Eddie was when he was like this. How nice it was to be a family, laughing all together, and making guests welcome in their home.

Was this, she wondered, the sign she had asked the Lord for?

'Three lions?' she guessed.

Eddie nodded.

'Is that the answer, *Three Lions?*'

'What's another name for three lions?' Eddie asked.

'Is it *The Lion Family?*' Ruby Farmer guessed.

'I've got it! England!' suggested Jolly. 'There are three lions on the flag. Aren't there? On those paper sandcastle thingummies?'

'It's England, then, is it?' Libby asked.

'It has to be three words!' Pearl told her.

'A pride!' said the income tax inspector. '*A Pride of Lions.*'

'Exactly,' said Eddie, pointing at him. 'Three words, first word "pride".'

'*Pride of England?*' suggested Liliana.

'It's not anything of bloody England,' said Eddie, exasperated.

'*Pride and Prejudice*?' said the tax inspector's mother suddenly, surprising everyone who had assumed she was gaga.

'Well done!'

'That's it?'

'Of course that's bloody it!'

'But why didn't you simply stick your nose in the air?' Libby asked. 'Everyone would have got it straightaway.'

'Wouldn't have been half the fun, though, eh?' said Eddie, getting up, brushing his trousers and looking at her with shining, eager-to-please eyes.

More spaniel than lion now, she thought.

It must definitely be a sign.

The first snow fell on Boxing Day, and by the afternoon virtually all roads in and out of Kingshaven were impassable. On the coast road, twelve bus passengers who were returning from Lowhampton after visiting relatives had to be rescued by helicopter.

By the time Claudia reached the railway station, all services on the branch line had been cancelled.

'Until when?' Claudia asked Stanley Ironside, her breath turning to clouds in the freezing ticket hall.

'They're saying on the radio there's no prospect of it lifting until the New Year. You're not dressed for it,' he observed as she stood, unable to stop her teeth chattering. All she'd had to put on was her old school coat because she had not brought anything suitable with her; she'd only been intending to stay a couple of days.

'Here, borrow this!' The station master let himself out of the ticket office and handed her his black uniform winter coat. The leather-clad sleeves swamped her arms and the coat hung like a heavy suit of armour on her shoulders. The wool fabric was as stiff as a wall, and inside it was chilly, like when you came home to a cold house before you lit a fire. The coat stank of years of soot.

'But what will you do?' Claudia asked the station master.

'I've only fifty yards to my house,' he said.

'You're very kind. Could I leave a deposit or something?'

Mr Ironside laughed. 'I know where you live,' he said.

It occurred to Claudia that the insularity of the town had a value she had not previously discerned. In Kingshaven, they had always been the odd ones out. During the self-conscious years of adolescence at the Grammar School, Claudia had found it extremely difficult. She had always felt as if the town had awarded her an identity – the poor little refugee girl with the mad Commie father – which had little to do with what she was like, but was as inescapable as an unflattering passport photograph.

Claudia had dreamed of living in a crowded, cosmopolitan city, the sort of place where a saxophonist might blow a plaintive jazz riff from his room above a street market, and a trumpeter would join in at another window, and people would spontaneously start to dance; a place where people would have conversations across the streets, and share their food, and help each other. But in London people did not hold conversations across the street. If a station master in London had told her he knew where she lived, she probably would have inferred some kind of threat. Nobody in London would lend their coat.

In London, you could go for whole days in close proximity to thousands of people without speaking to anyone. Different races lived side by side, but they kept within their own communities. Even though she and Tim were liberal-minded and lived only streets away from hundreds of West Indians, they did not have a single friend of Caribbean origin. She could see now that her utopian vision had a lot to do with newsreels of spontaneous street parties at the end of the war, all mixed up with a short film about New Orleans she had once seen before the main attraction at the Regal.

The snow was falling as thickly as feathers from a burst pillow-case. Flurries which looked as pretty and harmless as glitter in a snow dome were beginning to settle and drift. It would be too dangerous to go the direct way up the lane back to the gatehouse.

Kinghaven's main street was silent apart from the muffled thud of her footsteps. Streetlights were blurred little suns in the dense white air. The town itself seemed much smaller than it did in her memory. In Kingshaven, streets stopped for a road or for the gardens on either side of the little river, or because they reached the sea, or the edge of the cliff. In London, she had become used to streets which joined other streets and went on seemingly without end. One weekend when Tim was away working, Claudia had, out of curiosity, taken the Central Line right out to Ealing and all the way back to Ongar at the far eastern end. Even when the tube train emerged from its tunnel and trundled across open landscapes (she had not been able to work out whether it was actually going slower in the open air, or whether this was an illusion), there were still endless rows of semi-detached houses, stretching further than the eye could see.

Now, walking down the main street which was Christmas-card pretty under its blanket of snow, protected by the huge house of a coat, she discovered to her surprise that she felt quite happy to be trapped in Kingshaven a while longer, her free will denied by the blizzard.

'It's stopped for a bit,' Sylvia said, looking out of the window. 'Why don't you all go out for a walk and blow away the cobwebs?'

Iris knew her mother wanted them out of the house so that she could get on with her sewing undisturbed. The black and gold Singer had come out on to the dining table first thing after breakfast on Boxing Day. The living-room floor was covered with paper patterns. Iris had been ordered to help, then shooed away when she got the nap going the wrong way on a bodice. Fortunately, her mother had spotted the error just before slicing into it with the satisfying crump of her dressmaking scissors.

'Anthony and I are going sledging,' her father announced, stamping his feet on the doormat. They had been clearing a path to the front door. His nose was very red. Anthony's face was hardly visible, with his knitted bobble hat pulled down and his matching scarf wound right over his mouth. Their grandma had sent each child a hat and scarf set for Christmas. Anthony's was blue with a knitted design of large white snowflakes; Iris's was red with a row of brown robins with square sides and black French knots for their eyes. Iris thought she'd rather die than be seen wearing it.

'Are you coming?' her father asked.

It was ages since they'd last had snow. Iris remembered climbing up and whizzing down the ramparts of the Iron Age fort countless times until it was almost dark, and Daddy tugging her on the sledge all the way home (Anthony had been far too little to come with them), and mugs of Cadbury's drinking chocolate too hot to hold in frozen hands, and the anguish of waking up the next morning to rain and all the whiteness sliding into puddles of black water.

'Oh, all right then.' Iris feigned reluctance.

'Make sure you wear your hat!' Sylvia called from behind her sewing machine.

To save another argument, Iris put it on, but as soon as she got outside, took it off again and shoved it into the pocket of her duffel coat. The air outside was as cold as when your hand went in to get a choc ice from Mr Green's yellow chest freezer. It was so cold it seemed to get right inside Iris's head, almost as if her mother had told it to in order to make her wear the hat, which she definitely was not going to do.

'Where's the best place, do you think, Iris?' her father asked her.

'The fort?' she suggested.

'Good idea!'

He smiled at her across the top of Anthony's head. She knew he was trying to make friends with her again, and sometimes, when he caught her unawares, she'd smile back. But then she'd remember the way he'd spoken to her in front of Winston, and be just as furious with him as she had been at the bus stop.

'I wish you'd hurry up writing your new book,' Iris said.

'Why?' he asked.

'Because we could move to a bigger house.'

'When I was your age, Iris, I didn't even have a house,' he told her calmly.

'Here we go,' she sighed.

'What?'

'The lecture about how lucky I am compared to poor old you. When I was your age,' she whined mockingly, 'I didn't have a house, or a family, or anything!'

'That's right,' he said in a cold voice.

'Well, lucky you!' she shouted at him, stamping off.

He grabbed the hood of her duffel coat. 'Iris!'

'Don't do that! I'm not a child!'

'You're behaving like one!'

'At least you didn't have anyone telling you what to do all the time,' she said, somehow unable to stop herself from pushing it further.

She could almost feel the heat of his rage in the frozen air.

'You're right, I didn't,' he said finally. 'But your life isn't that bad, you know. And you don't know as much as you think you do. Wait . . .' He held up his hand to stop her interrupting. 'I promise I will try to trust you a bit more. How does that sound?'

Her instinct was to talk back, but she could think of nothing to say that wouldn't make her sound childish. 'All right,' she agreed.

They started walking again, side by side.

'Iris is impossible, isn't she, Dad?' Anthony chirped up.

Her brother looked like a gingerbread man with his big jumper wedged under his coat and making his arms stick out straight. If she pushed him over into the snow, he would make a print like one of those chains of paper men they did in Infants, Iris thought.

'Iris is not impossible, she's just growing up,' their father corrected him.

Behind his back, Iris stuck her tongue out at Anthony.

The last time, the whole hillside had been bobbing with people with toboggans and tea trays. Now, the three of them were completely alone, and the snow was beginning to fall again. With all hope of seeing Winston gone, Iris pulled the dreadful hat out of her pocket and yanked it right down over her ears.

The air was thick with snow, the sea barely visible except where great waves met the rocks in a crash of white spray, as if the elements were competing with each other for whiteness.

The sledge stuck instead of sliding. Anthony caught his finger underneath and started crying, but stopped as soon as Dad said they'd have to go home. Dad took Anthony down the rampart and they both fell off laughing.

It was all right for boys, Iris thought, because they could wear trousers. She had on a tartan kilt and woollen tights which the snow came right through, and were too short in the leg and chafed the insides of her thighs.

The wind was blowing so hard against them on the long walk home Anthony had to get off the sledge and walk with them. They were all so bent against the wind, none of them noticed the enormous coat which appeared out of the snow like a phantom, and said, 'Hello!'

Iris was surprised to see a lady peeping out from beneath the collar. There were no hands visible at the end of the sleeves.

The face was so extraordinarily pretty, Iris was sure it must be famous.

Her father said hello back. His voice sounded so peculiar that Iris turned her head sharply and saw him smile as if he had just tasted something delicious.

'What brings you back?' he asked the woman.

'Christmas!' she said.

Anthony was staring at the bottom of the coat, looking for evidence of feet. He trudged around the woman and was relieved to find a trail of footprints behind her which were fast being erased by the snow.

'Is your husband with you?' Dad asked the lady.

'No. He's in London.' The lady looked down. Not smiling any more.

'How is your father?'

'Not so good, I'm afraid,' she said.

'I offered to take up some Christmas dinner, but he didn't seem to want me to.'

'He's very obstinate.' She gave a little laugh. Then she said, 'Thank you,' and looked at Dad again.

'How long are you here?' he asked.

The woman tilted her face to the sky, as if to say it was in God's hands. Snowflakes stuck to her long black eyelashes.

Iris suddenly remembered the poster for the film that had been on at the Regal during the summer, which her mother had been to see three nights in a row. The lady in the poster had a long cigarette holder in her mouth and diamond earrings on, but it was definitely the same face.

'Will you be all right getting home?' her father asked the woman, hugging his donkey jacket around him.

The woman nodded.

They stared at each other with a silent, shining look, then Dad said, 'Better get going, then,' stepping out of the woman's way at exactly the same time as she stepped to the same side so that they were blocking each other again.

'Come along, Iris,' Dad said crossly, as if she had done something wrong.

The woman was barely out of earshot when Anthony piped up, 'Was that a ghost?'

Their father laughed as if it were a much funnier thing to say than it really was.

'Why?' he asked Anthony.

'I don't think she had a body,' he replied, very seriously.

'Was it Holly Golightly, the craziest heroine who ever crept between the pages of a best-selling novel?' Iris guessed.

'Of course it wasn't,' said her father crisply.

'Well, who is she, then?' Iris wanted to know.

'A friend.'

'Mummy says men can't have friends who are ladies,' said Anthony.

Dad hesitated. 'She's the daughter of the professor I sometimes go to see.'

The public rooms of the Palace Hotel were deserted, and the few staff who remained padded around quietly and spoke in whispers. The corridors of the bedroom floors were eerily quiet, apart from the occasional groan, and the regular flushing of toilets.

Initially, it was assumed that the turkey was responsible for the outbreak of food poisoning. When pushed, even Libby had to admit that it had tasted off, but when none of the children except Christopher succumbed to the agonizing explosions of diarrhoea and vomiting, suspicion fell on the hors d'oeuvres which had been considered too sophisticated to waste on immature palates.

When the number of victims rose to over a dozen, Dr Payne advised Eddie that he was obliged to notify the Inspectorate.

The news sent Libby rushing to the bathroom again.

In the brief moment of cold, sweaty relief after heaving, she wondered where all the sick was coming from. Any food in her stomach must be long gone. It felt as if the poisoning was breaking down the very tissue of her gut and expelling it.

'What's it like out there?' Libby asked as she climbed weakly back into bed.

'It's a plague ship, according to Angela. Everyone's sick and nobody can get off.'

'I think she's doing the Middle Ages in History.'

'We're going to have to reimburse the guests,' Eddie said.

'So annoying when the snow held off until they were supposed to go home,' Libby sighed, looking at the opaque greyness outside. For days, the hotel had been engulfed in thick cloud. It was hard to remember there had ever been a view.

'Can't be helped. But how long we're going to have to put them up is anyone's guess,' said Eddie.

Eddie had taken over the running of the place with admirable efficiency, which had given Libby a glimpse of why he had been decorated in the war. His seafaring constitution had shaken off the sickness as if it were a common cold. Instead of water, as the doctor advised, his remedy had been as much brandy as he could drink. On the basis that he'd actually managed to pickle the hostile organism in his stomach, Libby had tried a sip of brandy herself, but even the fumes had sent her straight to the loo.

'I've squared it with Otterway at the *Chronicle*,' Eddie continued.

'The *Chronicle*?' Libby swooned back against her pillows. The illness was so completely overwhelming, she hadn't even considered the effect on the hotel's reputation.

'He'll have to report an outbreak of food poisoning, obviously, but he's agreed to do it in the context of us sacking Jean-Claude. Chef out. Problem solved. Can't trust the French.'

'I don't think Jean-Claude really was French,' said Libby.

'Well, serves him right for pretending,' said Eddie.

Poor Chef! She would miss the joy of inspecting the hors d'oeuvres trolley each day in its pristine state, an experience she found almost as thrilling as viewing rings in a jeweller's shop, each tray covered with rows of regularly spaced morsels glistening . . .

Libby made another dash for the bathroom. Surges of acid shot through her throat into her mouth.

'Are you all right in there, old girl?' Eddie put his head round the door.

She was too nauseous to speak, and still the vomiting came.

Eddie knelt on the floor next to her and began to rub her back gently. It was such a tender act, she felt as if she would cry, but she didn't have a handkerchief. Eddie pulled a large clean cotton square from his trouser pocket and handed it to her. 'There, there,' he said as she gave in to tears. 'There, there.'

In the thin grey light of a snowstorm, on the cold, unforgiving tiles of the bathroom floor, with the smell of sick all around her, it occurred to Libby that *this* was the sign.

Other women came and went, but Eddie was loyal only to her, and he was the only person in the world she could bear to see her like this.

It was a curiously intimate moment.

'You're a cheat!' said Iris.

'You're the cheat,' said Anthony. 'You're not allowed to have a hotel until you've got four houses.'

'Stupid game, anyway!' said Iris, kicking over the Monopoly board as she stood up.

'You did that on purpose!'

'Didn't!

'Did!'

'Didn't!'

'Oh, for God's sake,' said Michael.

'It was her fault!' said Anthony.

'No, it wasn't!'

'Be quiet! Both of you!' Sylvia said. 'And go to your rooms.'

Anthony was the first to make a dash for the door. Iris quickly followed. There were thumps and squeals as Iris caught his leg and made him trip and he kicked her in the ear.

'Why don't you go to the library?' Sylvia suggested to Michael.

'Why?'

'You can't expect the children to keep quiet all day when

they're stuck inside. And you're getting on my nerves pacing around the whole time.' She smiled at him, hoping that the dark cloud, which had descended on him just like it had over the weather maps of England, might lift. The 'Big Freeze', they were calling it.

'Do you think the library will be open?' Michael asked.

'Worth a try,' she encouraged.

With her husband in this mood and the children all cooped up, Sylvia couldn't wait for the beginning of term. It was always the same with the school holidays. You longed for them to arrive, but once you were a few days in, you couldn't help wishing they would end.

'There!' Sylvia tucked the ends of her husband's scarf into the neck of his coat automatically, as if he were one of the children she was seeing off. He hesitated on the doorstep, as if he were about to say something, and his eyes were so troubled, she shuddered with a kind of presentiment that it was the last time she was ever going to see him. 'Off you go!' she urged. 'You're letting all the heat out of the house!'

You never knew what it was with Michael because he could worry about things that no one else even thought about. In the autumn, a travelling salesman had come to the door, trying to sell them a portable fire extinguisher, when Michael was glued to the television news about the Cuba crisis. It said 'Domestic Use Only' clearly on the container. If it had been up to Sylvia, she would have taken advantage of the trial offer. Safety was never a question of price, as the salesman had pointed out. Instead Michael had shouted, 'We'll need a lot more than that!' and slammed the door in the salesman's face, although he'd never said the extinguisher would be any use in a nuclear war.

'I think I'll go and see if any of the shops are open,' Claudia told her father.

'They won't have anything,' he told her. 'They're going to have to airlift supplies in.'

This information had come from the man Sir John Allsop had sent down to the gatehouse to check that he was all right. The farmhand was usually a reticent man, but the crisis had made him eloquent. Apparently, the stream had frozen and people were skating on it. Sir John had ordered a pig to be slaughtered and roasted on a spit over a fire in the Victoria Gardens. Claudia imagined a bustling snowy scene like the Bruegel painting on several of the Christmas cards she and Tim had received. She was quite keen to see it for herself.

'I won't be long,' she told her father.

'Be as long as you like,' he said brusquely. 'Makes no difference to me.'

The smell of illness seemed to have seeped into the fabric of the gatehouse even though she had swept and cleaned and dusted every surface with a damp cloth. Initially, she had been cross with her father for letting dirty crockery pile up in the sink and a coating of ingrained grime to be trodden into the carpet, but, over the course of a week, she had been forced to acknowledge that it wasn't a matter of him not having the will for cleaning, it was that he had ceased to see the environment around him as unhygienic.

In the years since she had left home, the balance between them had tilted, and now she found herself in the role of parent with him as recalcitrant child. She resolved that in the spring she would come down and get the windows open, give the walls a coat of fresh paint, and bash the rugs on the washing line with a carpet beater.

The snow lay thickly on the conifers and iced the skeletons of deciduous trees. The only sound was the muted crunch of her shoes marking a trail. The chill, alpine air was refreshingly pure and felt as if it was cleansing her body from the inside out. Claudia turned a full circle to embrace every angle of the frozen landscape, relishing the sparkling moment of perfect aloneness, until the numbness of her nose and the chill of the ground seeping up through the soles of her shoes urged her on.

Making her way into town was an exhausting business. On occasion she sank right down into drifts and lay in the snow, listening to herself panting with the effort of getting up. When she finally reached the promenade, a well-trodden path of compacted ice had been carved out by other people's boots.

Claudia walked quickly past the red telephone box, thinking guiltily that she should phone Tim, but not really wanting to. The last time they had spoken, he had made it sound as if her inability to return to London was wilful.

'You will be back for my parents' New Year party?' he had insisted.

'If I possibly can,' she had told him.

'I'm missing you,' he had said at the end of the conversation.

Her pause must have only been a second or two, but the distance between them had echoed down the line.

'Me too,' she had finally whispered, as if it would not be so much of a lie if spoken quietly.

Michael knew it would be Claudia without looking up from his library desk, but when he saw her standing there in her old school coat, he wondered if his imagination was playing tricks on him. All the times he had sat in this place and felt the draught as the door opened, and had not been able to stop himself checking . . . Now she was here, and he didn't want to believe it. When she smiled at him and walked across the parquet floor, and sat down in her old seat opposite, all the feelings he had ever had for her opened like a great sponge inside his chest, filling the emptiness which he had created by squashing them down.

There was no one else in the library except Miss Phelps. Michael had a blank notebook in front of him and a pencil in his hand, but he did not want to stop looking at Claudia for even the moment it would take to scrawl *Hello!* across the page. He mouthed the word silently at her, and she mouthed her reply. And then he inclined his head towards the door and she nodded.

When they were outside, his voice sounded much too loud in the empty street. 'Still here, then?'

'I hoped I might find you,' she said with disarming frankness. 'I wanted to give you my telephone number. And I have a favour to ask . . .'

'Yes?'

'I wondered if you could let me know if my father gets any worse? I think he's on the mend now, but he still seems very frail . . . It's just that I know he won't tell me. He's very proud and . . .'

'No problem.'

There was a thump of disappointment inside him. What had he been expecting her to say? he asked himself. What had he hoped?

'I'll give you my telephone number.'

He took out his blank notebook and a pencil.

Claudia began to tug the fingers of her gloves with her teeth.

'Look, do you want to have a coffee, or something?' he asked as nonchalantly as he was able to.

The Expresso had opened the previous summer in the vacant lot between the Happy Plaice Fish and Chip Shop and the new amusement arcade. With its Gaggia machine, and Italian proprietors, who were hoping to replicate the success of their other coffee and ice-cream parlours in Torquay and Weymouth, it had put several other establishments out of business, including the Coffee Bean. Ironically, the same traditionalists who had protested against the original purveyor of coffee-bar culture in Kingshaven had bemoaned its decline as yet another indicator of how standards were dropping. Privately, everyone admitted that the brothers Mario and Rocco Rossi served a better cup of coffee (if you liked a continental strength and flavour) and worked very hard (for Italians), open all hours and very eager to please.

'Good afternoon!' the younger brother, Rocco, greeted Michael and Claudia as they sat down at one of the red Formica tables.

The plate-glass window was a solid wall of mist between the bitter cold outside and the friendly steam within.

Rocco put down two tiny white cups in front of them. 'I sorry. The farmer he can't deliver no milk.'

The coffee was so rich there was a creamy foam on top.

Michael looked at Claudia's tiny hands as she took off her gloves, noticing for the first time the gold wedding band on her left hand.

'*Bellissima!*' Rocco nodded at Claudia, then at Michael. An exchange of friendly masculine appreciation which made Claudia's complexion redden.

The mellow sound of Acker Bilk's 'Stranger on the Shore' wafted out of the jukebox, evoking an awkwardly romantic mood.

'The last time I saw you—' Michael began.

'On the promenade?' she jumped in.

'No, I meant in London . . . I didn't know you were married,' he said. 'And I felt such a fool.'

'I'm sorry . . . I should have let you know.'

'Did you tell your father-in-law to publish my book?' Michael blurted. 'Was it your doing, me getting published?'

Claudia looked amazed, then burst out laughing. 'Roman doesn't take any notice of anyone else. You must know that! Actually, he didn't even know that I knew you before the party. You were the one who revealed it . . .'

Michael felt doubly embarrassed. 'Why didn't you tell him you knew me, by the way?' he asked quietly.

She sighed. 'I've asked myself that,' she said. ' At first, when he was going on to everyone about this wonderful discovery he'd made, I suspected he might not appreciate me saying that I had discovered you first!' She looked up and smiled at him. 'And then suddenly it got too late to say anything. However casually I dropped it in, it would seem a little peculiar that I hadn't mentioned it before. I'm sorry I left the party without saying goodbye. But you were a little bit . . .'

'Unconscious?' he suggested.

She laughed.

Rocco Rossi came over to the table with two large slices of light fruited cake on small white plates with red and green borders.

'Christmas cake from Italy,' he said. 'On the 'ouse!'

'It's *panettone!*' exclaimed Claudia.

'*Si, panettone!*' said Rocco, delighted with her. 'You speak Italian?'

'*Mia madre era italiana!*' she said.

She and the waiter had a rapid conversation in Italian, and then both suddenly stopped, as if they had realized that they were excluding Michael.

'Your 'usband no speak Italian?' said Rocco.

'*Non è mio marito,*' she replied.

'*Ahhh, capisco,*' said Rocco knowingly.

'What's he saying?'

'He says he understands!' said Claudia. 'But I don't think he does!'

'I didn't know that you spoke Italian,' Michael said.

'I won a travelling scholarship at Cambridge, and spent three months in Italy.'

'With your husband?'

The irrational stab of jealousy at the idea of her on holiday with someone else was as searing as it had ever been. Someone else taking a photograph of her standing by the golden Baptistery doors in Florence; someone else sitting under a vine-canopied restaurant with her, or kicking up the dust of an ancient ruin, or gazing up at the ceiling of the Sistine Chapel. It obliterated all other thoughts.

'Long before I married Tim,' she said.

There was a wistfulness to her tone that made him look up sharply.

'Eat some *panettone*,' she instructed. 'It's meant to bring good fortune.'

It tasted like a light and very superior hot cross bun, much nicer than the strong, burnt flavour of English Christmas cakes and puddings.

'It's getting dark,' Michael said, making a porthole in the steamed-up window.

'How long since I last walked you home?' he asked as they trudged along beside one another.

'Must be seven or eight years.'

Such a lot of time, and yet he couldn't think of a single thing that had happened in between. In the silence of the snow, he could convince himself that time with Claudia was in a different dimension. It wasn't eight years, it was just a moment ago.

'How's your second novel coming along?' Claudia asked.

'You sound like Roman!' he told her.

'God forbid!'

'You don't get on?'

'You haven't answered my question,' Claudia said, shooting a sly smile at him.

'Promise you won't tell him?'

'Cross my heart!'

'The answer is that I haven't written a word.' It was a relief to admit it to someone.

'Why do you think that is?' Claudia asked with genuine concern in her voice.

'I don't know.'

'But you had such wonderful reviews!'

'Except for the one in *The Times* that said my characters were embodiments of a particular kind of social thinking rather than living, breathing people . . .'

'And that's the only one you remember!' Claudia chided. 'What about all the others?'

'I was amazed,' he admitted. 'I have a kind of novelty value – they keep calling me a "working-class novelist". Where I come from, being a teacher's middle class. Nobody calls anyone a middle-class novelist, do they?' He paused for breath, surprised at the flood of irritation. 'I don't like the way they assume they know me,' he went on.

'I think writers always get that,' Claudia said, 'even those of a middle-class persuasion.' She smiled at him.

'I used to write because I thought that if I didn't, my life would just pass by and there'd be nothing to show for it,' Michael tried to explain. 'And it was a kind of private place, somewhere I could be on my own . . .'

Claudia had always enabled him to explore thoughts that were only half formed in his head.

'A bit like a diary?' she suggested.

'Maybe,' he said. 'Maybe that's why I don't want to do it any more. It's like knowing someone is reading your diary, so you end up trying to write for them, but you don't really know what they want.'

'You have to go with your instincts,' she told him.

'But I don't seem to know any more what my instincts are . . .'

'You will find out,' she said calmly. 'I know you will.'

It was quite dark now, but the whiteness of the snow cast a kind of light. He paused for a moment beside the wall of the church-yard and faced her. 'Thank you,' he said.

'What for?'

'For believing in me,' he said, acknowledging the corniness of the words with an embarrassed shrug.

She smiled, but her eyes were still sad.

'What about you?' he said.

'Me?' she repeated.

'What's your life like?' he asked.

'You don't really want to know,' she said.

It was a disturbingly accurate answer. He wanted to know about her, but he didn't think he could bear to hear her say she was blissfully happy. And yet he somehow knew he would not have asked if he'd thought that would be her answer.

'Explain,' he said.

Claudia sighed. 'Unlike you, I haven't found anything I'm particularly good at yet,' she said. 'No, it's the truth. I'm not particularly suited to the BBC; I'm not particularly good at being a wife . . .' She held her hand up as he tried to interrupt again. 'I'm not interested in cooking or home improvements. The only book I cannot bear is a book of wallpaper samples!'

He loved the categoric way she stated her position. He found himself on the point of laughter when he saw that she was crying.

Why was she telling him this? Claudia asked herself. Why were tears as hot as boiling water running down her chilled cheeks? Why was she letting the disappointment of her marriage ripple into every other aspect of her life and turn her into a weak person, because she was not weak, she was sure of that. Yet how corrosive failure could be!

Michael stood with his arms half outstretched, mid-gesture, as if the snow-capped gravestones that peeped over the top of the churchyard wall might be watching them and report any affectionate display.

She had hoped that he would understand. She knew that his marriage could not be ideal. She had sometimes overheard his wife chatting in the street, or gossiping in Farmer's. There was one summer day Claudia remembered long ago, when she'd contrived three separate reasons to visit the shop: needle, thread, thimble.

'This one would forget her head if it weren't attached to her body!' Sylvia Quinn had remarked to Mrs Farmer, pleasantly enough, but it was impossible to imagine what she and Michael must talk about at home.

They started walking again suddenly, as if their bodies had

both reached the point where they knew they would freeze to the spot unless they moved, and then Michael said, 'He can't have married you to choose his wallpaper!'

The outrage in his voice gave her heart.

'I think he was fascinated by me because I was unattainable,' she said. 'But then I wasn't any more, was I?'

'Unattainable?' Michael queried.

'I loved someone else.' The cold was making her reckless. 'Who was already married,' she said.

It was crazy, but she couldn't help it now. She didn't have anything to lose any more.

They stopped outside the school at the entrance to the boys' half of the playground.

'Why did you stop writing to me?' she asked.

'I promised your father,' he said.

It seemed such an odd thing for a grown man to say, especially when his head was framed by an arch with the word 'BOYS' carved into it. So absurd to think of the two men making decisions about her, in her absence, without either of them asking her opinion.

'Could I ask you another favour?' she said as they stared at each other.

Her teeth were chattering. She wondered fleetingly whether too much snow went to your head, like too much sun did. Did incipient hypothermia turn you mad? But if she didn't ask now, she might spend another eight years wondering, hoping . . .

'What?' he asked.

'Could you please kiss me?' she asked him.

He looked surprised, then bent and kissed her cheek quickly.

'No,' she said. 'I meant properly.'

The bike shed was open one side, with a thick layer of snow on the roof, like the stable in a Nativity scene. Inside it was dry and smelled of creosote. It was impossible for anyone to see them here, behind the school, but Michael pulled her by the hand into the deepest, darkest corner. He took off his gloves, made a quick, futile attempt to warm his fingers, before taking her solemn, trusting, beautiful face in trembling hands and placing his lips on hers.

It was like an act of reverence, profound and true, and her face was cold, like a statue. And then her body seemed to sigh against his, and a transfusion of warmth and energy passed between them, as if some magical chemistry had made her part of him, as if there had always been a Claudia-sized space inside him, and now she was in it and he was complete.

In that moment, he understood what it was to be happy.

Their mouths finally separating, they drew back their heads a fraction to look at each other as if neither of them could believe what had happened.

'Was that proper enough?' Michael asked.

The happiest, wickedest smile lit up Claudia's face.

He kissed her again and when he drew away to look at her again, her face was flushed, and her eyes shining, and they went straight back to kissing urgently, with the back of her head pressed against the shed wall. And it was as if a long-dormant passion had woken up, ravenously hungry, and they were trying to consume each other.

The loud click of a lock and the whispered muttering of low voices close by brought them up short. They both held their breath, realizing that there were people inside the darkened school, who were about to come out of the back door.

The spotlight of a torch stopped on Michael's face just long enough for the person who was holding it to recognize him, and for Michael to recognize them. Then the beam dropped, and he watched it jiggling across the snow as muffled footsteps ran away towards the open ground.

Claudia exhaled. 'Who was that?' she whispered.

'A colleague of mine. Ivor.'

'A friend?' she asked hopefully.

'I thought so . . . Did you see who he was with?' Michael asked.

'A man?'

'I'm sure it was the man from the hotel. What's his name? The one who slinks around the place?'

'Mr Pocock?'

'That's it!'

'Goodness,' said Claudia.

'What do you think they were doing in the school?' Michael asked.

She gave him a knowing look. 'What do you think?'

'In the school?'

'Not really the weather for the public conveniences in the Gardens,' she said.

'Is that where that sort go? How do you know all this?'

'I was a chambermaid at the Palace, remember? It's a hotbed of sin among the live-ins.'

An unwanted image of Pearl King kneeling before him in all her lascivious glory floated through Michael's mind.

The bike shed now felt like a tawdry and shameful place.

They followed Ivor's fast-vanishing footprints across the playground.

'Do you disapprove?' Claudia asked when they were safely outside the school grounds again.

It disturbed him that he'd never guessed Ivor was that way inclined, although it seemed so obvious now. He was camp and theatrical and he never had a girlfriend.

'Don't you?' he asked.

'Not really. Quite a few people I knew at Cambridge were.'

'Pansies?'

She nodded.

'Good God!'

They walked the rest of the way to the gatehouse in silence.

Eventually he said, 'Do you think I should tell anyone?'

'And get him arrested?'

'No, you're right,' he said.

As liberal-minded as she felt about another person's illicit romance, she wished that it had not blighted theirs.

It seemed like a sign that it was never meant to be.

The two of them stood awkwardly outside the little wrought-iron gate which was almost buried under the snow.

'Won't you come in to see Papa?' Claudia asked.

Claudia's father was asleep in his armchair, with his mouth hanging open.

'He needs a lot of sleep at the moment,' Claudia said kindly, putting her hand on her father's forehead to test his temperature, then pulling a blanket made of knitted squares up over his knees. 'Would you like a cup of tea?'

Michael followed her into the tiny kitchen.

Claudia tidied up the sink, filled the kettle, put it on the stove to boil, smiled at him.

The electric lightbulb that hung from the ceiling seemed particularly bright. It made him think of that painting he admired in the book about modern American art in the library – a stark study of a brightly lit bar on the corner of a street by an artist called Edward Hopper. The more Michael looked at it, the more his mind wanted to create stories about the man and woman in the picture. What had happened to them before? What would happen after?

And now he thought that if someone were to look in through the curtainless window from outside, they might want to create a story to fill the space between him and Claudia.

It was Claudia who broke the silence. Claudia was the brave one.

'Did something happen to us back there, before we saw Ivor and—'

'No,' he interrupted.

She looked alarmed; hurt.

'Not back there,' he qualified. 'Eight, no, nine years ago.'

'What happened nine years ago?' she asked, her voice abrupt with swallowed emotion.

'I fell in love with you,' he said.

For a moment, her eyebrows went up. 'Really?'

He nodded.

'Oh, God!' she said, and then she was in his arms, and the space between them was gone for ever.

The Food Hygiene Inspectors found the Palace Hotel kitchen reached satisfactory levels of cleanliness, but they took exception to the position of one of the preparation tables, which lay directly under the hook from which the Christmas turkey had hung.

'The mayonnaise may have been contaminated with turkey blood,' Eddie reported when the Inspectors had left.

Bile lurched up her oesophagus but, this time, Libby managed to keep control of it. A good sign. Like most vices, vomiting could become a habit if you weren't extremely firm with it.

'Just the Coroner's officer now,' she said, ticking off a mental list of problems.

'What are you going to say?' her husband asked.

She could see Eddie was nervous, and there was no harm in letting him suffer a bit.

Eventually she said, 'I shall tell them that on the night in question you were in the hotel. I have a very clear recollection of it, and so does my mother.'

To her surprise, Eddie marched across the room and kissed her firmly on the lips, which was something he had not done for a very long time.

'Attagirl!' he said, squeezing her waist and slapping her bottom.

'As a matter of fact, Mother and I have been talking about a number of things,' Libby went on, slightly flustered by her husband's unanticipated physicality. She could feel herself blushing furiously. 'We both feel that you've handled this crisis magnificently. We were wondering if, in the circumstances, you'd be prepared to become Chairman of the company?'

'With shares?'

Libby frowned. 'I suppose something could be arranged.'

The idea had been to come up with a clear signal of solidarity to the outside world, and if it gave Eddie a bit of a boost, so much the better. But you couldn't blame him for trying for more.

'A fresh start,' she said brightly.

'I like the sound of that!' said Eddie with a wink.

Her husband's face was particularly attractive in triumph, Libby observed with a frisson of excitement.

Part spaniel, part wolf.

The drip, drip, drip of melting icicles outside Claudia's tiny bedroom window was calling time on their miraculous imprisonment.

Michael came to the house each afternoon when her father slept and, whispering and kissing, they stumbled up the little staircase into her room in the roof of the tiny house, and made love on her child's bed, under her single blankets, and it was so fantastically, totally wonderful, she craved more when he dozed next to her, and more on the stairs when he left, and in every waking moment between his visits, and in her feverish dreams when she finally managed to sleep.

Sex with him was all her body seemed to want or need.

She had no appetite for food, found it impossible to read, could hardly talk to her father without the thought of it making a silly smile creep involuntarily on to her face, as if she were a fool.

She had been a fool to think that they could deceive her father.

This morning he had looked up from his book and asked, nonchalantly, 'Are we expecting your lover today?'

'You don't object?' she asked, shocked.

'If you are determined to make your life difficult, I don't see that there's much I can do about it,' he had replied.

'You tried to stop us,' she said.

'It is frightening to see your child in the grip of someone who loves her so much he would ruin them both. But it is far worse to see her with someone who loves only himself,' he replied.

He made it sound like a Confucian proverb because he was so unused to expressing his feelings, she thought.

She went and knelt beside his armchair, and held his hand. He squeezed hers very hard for several seconds, and then released it. And when she looked up into his rheumy eyes, there were twinkling tears she knew he did not want her to see.

Drip, drip, drip.

In the outside world, trains were running again; people were going back to work; the boiler in the school had been lit, the playground swept. Kingshaven was waking up, casting off its eiderdown of snow.

Sounds that had been frozen were now buzzing in the air: the clip-clop of horses' hooves; the stuttering growl of a dustbin lorry; the random shrieks of children on toboggans desperate to make the most of every last minute of the fast-melting snow.

Claudia and Michael had been suspended in an icy cocoon, but the thaw was about to release them back into reality, and she didn't know how they would survive.

Her body was curved around his back, shaped to him like warm candle wax. She loved the hard bumps of his vertebrae, the softness of his warm skin against hers, his smooth strong arms, his pianist's fingers . . .

She prodded his shoulder. 'What are we going to do?'

'Ehh?'

How was it that the male constitution was so different from the female that it allowed a man to sin and then sleep so peacefully?

'What are we doing to do?' she whispered into the warm shell of his ear.

He turned over. The bed and bedclothes were so small, it was difficult to manoeuvre into a new position without the cold air rushing to bite their hot skin.

'Just another minute,' he mumbled without opening his eyes, and kissed her.

His breath tasted warm and muzzy. His face was so close, she could see every tiny dot of stubble in every pore on his chin. She was filled with an irrational desire to count each one, to memorize his dimensions, so that her imagination would be able to recreate them when she was away from him, and count them back when he came back to her again. If he ever did.

'Wake up!' she urged him softly.

'Just another minute!'

'No! You have to go!' she said, laughing at the absurdity of trying to make him do what she least wanted.

He rolled over suddenly on top of her, pinning her to the bed. 'Just a little longer?' he pleaded, his pale blue eyes looking down into hers, seeing into her soul.

It made her think of the scene in *Romeo and Juliet* when they wake the morning after making love and, as time runs out, try to convince themselves that the dawn chorus of the lark is the evening song of the nightingale.

She shivered with a sudden dread that she and Michael were doomed lovers too.

'What are we going to do?' she asked him.

Chapter Eleven

November 1963

Sylvia had moved her sewing machine down so that Sylvia's Boutique could become her workshop too, and she could make use of the hours that passed between customers. It was hardly worth keeping the shop open in the late afternoon now the clocks had gone back, but she liked the idea of people looking in from outside and seeing her there, working steadily and silently, like a busy elf in the pumpkin-lantern glow of the interior.

Sylvia had asked Mr Coral, a local builder, to knock down the dividing wall between the shop and the little kitchen at the back and she'd run up a couple of long curtains out of the last few yards of purple velvet left over after making costumes for the KADS and St Mary's Choir joint summer production of *The Gondoliers*. One of the drapes hid the sink, draining board and electric kettle, which she used to make friends a cup of tea if they stopped in for a chat; the other was fixed on a rail and swished across to create a changing cubicle. Mr Coral had cadged a huge mirror from an associate of his in demolition who had a warehouse outside Lowhampton full of interior fittings from a cruise liner that was being broken up. The art deco etchings looked incongruously glamorous fixed along the side wall of Sylvia's narrow little shop. To return the favour, Sylvia had made a wedding dress for Mr Coral's daughter Carole free of charge.

Sylvia was putting the finishing touches to her first evening wear range just at the time the landladies of Kingshaven were starting to think about what they might wear to social events at Christmas. She had decided to continue with separates. Her hunch that people were more inclined to part with money for items they could wear in a variety of ways was confirmed by the success of the summer season, for which she had designed a range of navy and cream sleeveless blouse tops, with flap pockets and matching skirts in both colours. On a slim figure, the navy on cream had proved smart enough for semi-formal occasions. Jennifer Allsop had been pictured in the *Chronicle* wearing hers at the Yacht Club Regatta, along with her three little girls all dressed in navy sailor dresses from Farmer's. That had given Sylvia another idea: children's clothes as chic as their mothers', and, after that, a range of affordable fashions for that difficult age between girl and womanhood Iris was at, where little girls' clothes looked silly, and women's sizes were still a bit big. Sylvia had even thought of a name for it. Quinn-Teen.

But that was all for the future. She had to force herself to take it step by step, otherwise all her ideas started to run away with her. First, the evening separates must be finished off and displayed.

With the increasing popularity of trousers for casual and formal wear, and the flattering line of a dropped waist, Sylvia was gambling on tunics with skirts or trousers in black or gold with a band of contrasting beaded embroidery at the neck and hem. The rayon fabric was slithery, and was proving tiresome to sew, and Sylvia was concentrating so hard that, when the bell over the door pinged and she looked up, she was surprised to see that it was already quite dark outside.

Michael was standing in the doorframe with his rucksack slung over one arm. She'd tried to persuade him of the benefits of a small suitcase, but he always went back to the scruffy old thing he'd bought from the Army Surplus before they were married.

'Hello. What have you done with Anthony?' she asked.

Usually, when Michael was going up to London at the week-end, he dropped their son off at the shop on his way to the station.

'Iris was home early and she's looking after him,' he replied.

'I thought it was Iris's drama club tonight?' Sylvia was

suspicious that Iris had invented her school drama club as an excuse to get home late on Friday afternoons.

'Apparently the Beatles may be appearing on *Ready Steady Go!*' Michael explained.

'In that case, I think I might hurry home myself,' Sylvia said as she came to the end of the line of black bugle beads and bit off the thread.

Everyone had their favourite Beatle. Iris's was John Lennon. Sylvia's was the baby-faced Paul McCartney. She sometimes felt a bit sorry for the other two lads because nobody seemed to like them best.

Michael stayed in the doorway as if he was uncertain whether he wanted to enter or not.

'Close the door if you're coming in!' she said as the draught blew a wintry chill through the cosy somnolence of the shop. 'You're getting the six o'clock, are you?' she asked.

'Yes,' he replied.

'Well, hadn't you better get going?'

He sighed. The air in the shop suddenly felt heavy and oppressive.

'Can't you face it?' she asked.

'What?' he asked.

'Another journey to London. It's a long way just for one night, isn't it? Couldn't you do the work here? I'll try to keep the children out of your way.'

'It's a collaborative effort,' Michael said.

'How long does a film take to write, then?' Sylvia asked him, starting off a new row of embroidery and concentrating hard so that the fabric didn't bunch up.

He was spending virtually every weekend in London working with the director of *The Right Thing*.

'Depends . . .' he said.

'Will you be staying at Roman Stone's again?' she asked.

Later, she wondered whether, if she hadn't looked up from her sewing at that moment, she might not have seen him looking shifty, and everything might have turned out differently. Some instinct – honesty or self-destruction, she never could decide – made her remark, 'You don't seem very sure.'

'What are you getting at?' he challenged, aggressive and yet unable to look at her.

Michael was more difficult to read than most people, but she'd heard that tone before.

It all rushed into place: the mood swings from excessive kindness to black, impenetrable depression; the way he'd sometimes stare when she or one of the children were talking to him, not listening to a word they said; him not asking for sex, which had been so welcome when she was working hard she hadn't wanted to question it; the scent of his skin when he returned home on Sundays. Cussons Imperial Leather. Not a soap she'd ever liked the smell of. Why would he have a bath on Saturday night unless he had something he wanted to wash off?

'Are you having an affair?' Sylvia heard herself asking, recklessly.

If she hadn't asked, she often reproached herself afterwards, she wouldn't have been any the wiser, and he'd probably never have had the courage to tell her, and it might have fizzled out with time.

Each second that elapsed without a denial thumped inside her chest.

'There is someone I've been seeing,' he said finally.

'To do with the film?' Sylvia asked. Inside she felt as if she was wailing, but her voice sounded peculiarly calm.

'Not really.'

Michael let out another long sigh and stared at the floor.

'Is it over?' she asked.

'I've tried, Sylvia, believe me, I really have!'

'Look at me!' she ordered, just as she did to Iris when she was being insolent.

Michael's face was all crumpled with guilt, just like it was after the first time, when he'd stood on her parents' doorstep the morning after he'd been found out, and refused to leave, even when her mother slammed the door in his face.

Sylvia had pitied him then and forgiven him.

Now, she felt as if he'd conned her.

'Is it over?' she repeated, matter-of-factly.

'I'm so sorry.' He looked at her with hollow-eyed despair.

Did he want her to feel sorry for him?

'So you should be!' she said, allowing herself to feel slightly superior.

'I've never wanted to hurt you,' he said.

'Well, you have.'

She wished she was the sort of person who could think of vicious or witty things to say when the occasion demanded it.

The silence seemed to last an age, then he said, 'We'll have to discuss what to do.'

'Well, I don't know about that,' she said. He wasn't going to get away with it that easily.

'It's not the right time to make arrangements now . . .' Michael said. 'We both need to think about it.'

'Yes.'

'I will always look after you and the children.'

'Pardon?' Sylvia didn't understand.

'When I move to London.'

Suddenly, it was like being in a nightmare. The surroundings were familiar but what was happening was completely illogical. It finally dawned on Sylvia that he meant it was over between *them*. She wasn't even going to be given the chance to decide whether she would forgive him or not.

'You're leaving me?' she whispered.

'I'm sorry,' he said.

She wished he would just answer the question: yes; not keep saying sorry.

In sudden fury, she picked up the nearest heavy object, her pinking shears, and hurled them across the room at him, but he stepped back and they bounced off the floor in front of him.

He bent to pick them up.

'DON'T YOU DARE TOUCH THOSE!' Sylvia screamed at him.

'I'm sorry,' he said again, backing away towards the door, bewildered by the sudden change in her.

'What about the children?' she shouted.

'We can't go on living a lie. It's not fair to any of us . . . It's no good for them either.'

What he was saying sounded perfectly reasonable, but it wasn't right, it was all topsy-turvy.

'It wasn't a lie,' Sylvia said, trying to hold on to the facts. 'Not for me!'

He didn't love her. He hadn't ever loved her. Two thoughts going round and round in her head obliterated any others. She felt as if she should be crying, but she just felt numb.

'Syl . . .'

She looked up, imagining for one split second that he was going to say it was all a misunderstanding, but instead she caught him glancing at his watch.

He'd just broken her heart, but he didn't want to miss his train!

'You're not going to London now?' she asked in disbelief.

'Wouldn't it be better? Give us both a chance to think about it rationally?'

Rationally. The word hung in the air between them like criticism of her. As if she were the one to blame for not understanding that it had all been a sham.

'I'll tell you one thing that's rational,' she told him in a chilly voice that didn't sound very much like hers. 'If you leave now, you're not coming back.'

He looked a little surprised. 'But we'll have to talk – what to do about the children . . .' he stuttered, understanding that she meant it.

'You've obviously made your decision,' she said coldly.

'But I still have to see them . . .' he protested.

'But not me?'

Sylvia wished she hadn't let herself ask. It was so crucifyingly humiliating when he didn't reply. She felt as if she was reduced to nothing at all. Every tenderness, every touch, every happy moment they'd ever shared was meaningless.

A single tear rolled down her cheek.

'OK,' Michael conceded. 'You're right. Of course I can't go to London. We'll discuss it.'

It was an empty victory, but it gave Sylvia a glimmer of confidence back.

'No, we won't.' She heard her voice echoing in her head. 'Because you can bloody well get out! Go to your fancy woman in

London and make her life a bloody misery, just like you make everyone else's.'

She never swore. Swearing was common.

Michael was looking at her as if he didn't recognize her.

She finally found the courage to stare straight back at him.

After what seemed like an age, he meekly picked up his rucksack and let himself out of the shop.

The urge to chase after him and plead with him not to go was so strong Sylvia had to hold on to the arms of her chair.

Finally she gave herself permission to cry, folding her arms across the top of the sewing machine and sobbing against them for a long time, until, amid all the mingling of pain and memory, it crossed her mind that someone might look in and see her, and then she would have to start explaining before she'd worked out what she was going to say.

There was no one else in the street. Mrs Farmer had done her window up for Christmas already. The mannequin was wearing the same pink chiffon party dress she had been wearing for the last three years. Sylvia caught her own reflection.

Alone.

Her mother had always said Michael would never make anyone happy. And she'd thought, with all the arrogance of youth, what did mothers know? But mothers were always right.

Sylvia stared at the silent televisions in the window of the Rediffusion shop. She must have missed *Ready Steady Go!* by now. It looked as if the news was on. There were pictures of a crowd cheering a cavalcade of long American open-topped cars.

What was she going to tell the children?

Sylvia tried to envisage herself on the sofa afterwards, with an arm around each of them, having a little cry, and then something nice for tea. She always kept a tin of fruit cocktail and a tin of Carnation milk in the kitchen cupboard for badly grazed knees and other emergencies, but she knew that wouldn't be enough. Anthony would ask question after question and Iris would try to put the blame on her.

Sylvia stood outside her front door for a moment, taking deep breaths. She didn't know whether she had the strength to tell them tonight.

When she opened the door, she could hear that Iris was already upset because Anthony was saying to her, 'Why won't you tell me what's the matter? What's wrong?'

For a moment, Sylvia thought Michael had not gone to the station after all, but instead come home the back way and told them himself, twisting all the words and making it sound like it was all her fault.

She slammed the door furiously to announce her presence.

Iris came hurtling out of the living room shouting at her, 'Mum! Have you heard?' Her daughter's eyes were puffy and her face was red from crying.

'It's all right, Iris,' Sylvia said, trying to sound calm. 'We'll be all right.'

'But it's so horrible! I can't believe it!'

Tentatively, Sylvia opened her arms and her daughter, who was almost as tall as she was, flung her face against her shoulder and allowed herself to be folded in her arms. It was so long since Sylvia had had any physical contact with her great big, angry daughter, it was lovely just to hold her, and smooth her unruly hair away from her hot wet face, and absorb her sobs in her chest.

'We'll manage, I promise. We'll be fine.'

The soothing words were for her own benefit as much as Iris's.

'But why would anyone want to kill him?' Iris asked, sniffing and drawing her face back. 'He's a good man. He was going to change the world . . .'

'Beg pardon?' said Sylvia.

'Why?' Iris insisted.

'Why what?' Sylvia asked.

'What do you mean?' Iris said, dropping her arms as if the embrace with her mother was suddenly embarrassing.

'I don't know what you're talking about,' Sylvia said, bewildered.

'President Kennedy's been shot, you idiot!' Iris shouted in her face. 'Why else would I be crying?'

There was no one on duty in the entrance hall when Libby arrived back at the hotel from her appointment with Dr Payne. In normal circumstances, she would have summoned the under-manager for an explanation, but this evening, she was privately quite pleased that Mr Pocock wasn't around. He had an uncanny knack of spotting when she was particularly happy or sad, and he was good at winkling the reasons out of her, which was odd, because she knew almost nothing about him. She was not unaware of the rumours, but her own view was that Mr Pocock was married to his job, and had neither the time nor inclination for other pursuits.

Libby took off her headscarf and shook her head so that her hair wouldn't look flat.

The bar was deserted, which was odd at this time of evening, even when the hotel was less than half full.

In the dining room, a solitary waitress was laying tables.

'Where is everyone?' Libby asked.

'Watching television,' the girl replied.

Libby tutted. The billiard room was so little used these days, it smelled mouldy. It seemed that people would rather gawp at the dreary customers of a fictitious Northern working-class pub than have a real conversation in the well-appointed lounge bar of a select hotel.

Still, the good thing about television was that it relieved her of having to talk to the guests. Libby had never understood why they seemed to think that she, who lived there, would be interested in learning what they, who didn't, had discovered about Kingshaven.

The Canadians were the worst. A pair of recently retired brothers with a fortune from a fish-freezing plant in Newfoundland were spending the 'fall' tracing their family tree, and kept her constantly updated with facts they unearthed in the church records. Their great-grandfather owned a boat. Amazing! His first two children had died at birth. How sad! After a couple of evenings, Libby had found it difficult to feign interest, but still they lay in wait for her, beetling over as soon as she appeared to regale her with further details about their astonishingly un-remarkable family.

Libby preferred the guests who kept themselves to themselves, although sometimes they presented other problems. In August, three men had pitched up in a sports car with a large suitcase, which, she couldn't help noticing during a surreptitious room inspection while they were at breakfast, was stuffed with used bank notes. No hotel wanted that kind of notoriety, especially in the high season. But no responsible citizen wanted to see the Great Train Robbers on the loose either. She'd been relieved to read that they had been arrested a couple of hours after their departure *following an anonymous tip-off*, the newspapers said.

Libby found Eddie upstairs giving Adrian his bath. She stood in the doorframe watching them sploshing each other. They were so involved in their noisy game that neither of them noticed her there.

Both she and Eddie spent a lot more time with Adrian than they had with the other children when they were little. She wondered if it was because Adrian was so much more winning than the first two, or simply because they were that bit older and more experienced as parents. Poor Christopher had come along before Libby and Eddie had really had a chance to get to know each other. She did wonder whether leaving him at the hotel for such long periods with her mother and father might account for her older son's peculiar disconnection from them. But as an officer's wife her duty had been to be with Eddie, and her father and mother had doted on their first grandson.

'Where's the duck gone?' Eddie asked Adrian, squelching the yellow rubber duck in his great big hand and hiding it behind his back.

'It's in your hand!' squealed Adrian.

'Which hand?' Eddie said, putting both behind his back.

'That one!'

Eddie held out an empty hand.

'That one!'

A swift duck transfer. Another empty hand.

Adrian was mystified.

'Look, he's behind you!' said Eddie, pointing at the end of the bath.

The little boy twisted round. 'No, he's not!' he said a little warily.

'Oh, no, how silly of me, he's been in front of you all the time,' said Eddie, putting the duck back on the water in front of Adrian just before the child turned round again.

Eddie was very good at timing, Libby thought. Whenever she tried to play a similar game, she always let the mystery go on just a little bit too long, and it would end in tears of frustration, rather than the delighted laughter which now pealed through the bathroom.

'Are you staying?' Eddie asked, finally catching sight of her standing there, still in her winter coat.

'I've got a surprise for you!' Libby said.

'For me?' asked Adrian.

'Well, for both of you, really,' said Libby.

Eddie and the boy exchanged excited glances.

'I wonder what Mummy's bought us,' said Eddie.

'A surprise! A surprise!' Adrian shouted eagerly.

'Well, actually, it's not something I've bought,' Libby cautioned.

Adrian's face fell.

'But it's much better than something you could buy,' she said encouragingly.

'What is it?' asked the three-year-old, a little suspiciously.

'A baby,' Libby said.

Eddie did a double take.

Libby remembered a rather different expression on his face when she had told him she was pregnant with Adrian. Then, they'd stared at each other, unsmiling, unblinking.

'Well, that's a bit of a surprise!' he'd finally remarked.

And that was all that had been said on the matter.

Libby thought it was sometimes the unspoken words that bound families together more than the spoken. Utterly oyster, as her mother would say.

Now, her husband's eyes were positively sparkling with pleasure and pride. He stretched up his soapy, wet hand to take hers. Still in her coat, she knelt down by the bath beside him and he kissed her resoundingly on the cheek.

'When's it due?' he asked quietly.

'Next April. Apparently on the same day as Jennifer's!' she whispered back.

'Where is it?' Adrian asked, craning his neck to peer round the back of her as he had with the rubber duck.

'Where's what?' Libby asked, distracted by her husband's fingers squeezing her waist.

'The baby!' said the little boy.

'You'll have to be patient,' said Libby, wondering whether it had been such a good idea to introduce the subject in this way after all.

'Why?' Adrian wanted to know.

'It will take a few months to grow . . .' She searched for a way of explaining that he could understand. 'You see, it's rather like a bulb in the garden,' she said. 'You know how we bury them in the earth and in spring they shoot up and become a lovely flower?'

Adrian nodded.

'Well, babies are the same – sort of, I mean . . .'

'The Allsop girls are getting a baby too,' Eddie came to the rescue. 'And they all want a brother. Do you think you'd like a little brother or a little sister?'

'I want my duck. Where's he gone?' Adrian asked, which made them laugh so much, he joined in too.

Libby took a big white towel from the airing cupboard. It was fluffy from drying in the hotel's new industrial-sized tumble-dryer. She knelt down again and draped it over her knees. Eddie lifted the chubby three-year-old from the bath and placed him on the towel, and she wrapped the child up like a parcel and cuddled him. Spontaneously, Eddie put his arms around both of them and they sat there on the floor for a few wonderful, warm seconds like a family of Russian dolls, all fitting together nicely.

'Oh, there you are!' said Liliana at the door. 'I've been looking for you everywhere.'

Libby wished that sometimes her mother would knock.

'What is it?' Eddie asked Liliana brusquely.

'President Kennedy's been shot,' Liliana announced.

'Dead?'

'So it seems.'

'Good Lord!' said Eddie.

'It's what comes of trying to change things,' said Liliana.

The warm intimacy of bathtime disappeared instantly, and it

suddenly felt rather chilly. Libby remembered the same sensation of numbness when Mr Chamberlain had announced the country was at war with Germany, the same sense that she was living a moment of history and that nothing was going to be the same again. It seemed a bit disrespectful, somehow, to be sitting on the bathroom floor in the circumstances.

'Granny Lily?' Adrian piped up, oblivious to the significance of the news.

'Yes?' said Liliana.

'Mummy's buried a baby in the garden.'

Sylvia would get over it. Ultimately she'd be happier without him, Michael thought. She'd find another man. Sylvia was most men's idea of the perfect wife. And she was resourceful. He'd been surprised at her tenacity and determination to make the shop work.

Had he really made her life a misery? he wondered. Or was that just a cheap shot?

He realized now that there would never have been a right time or place to tell her. Claudia had been right about that. She had not said it to put pressure on him, but with a look of defeat on her face, as if she thought he would never be able to bring himself to do it, and he had felt that he was letting her down too.

He had been planning to wait until after Christmas, for no other reason than that when he rehearsed in his head, he could almost hear Sylvia saying, 'You could have waited until after Christmas . . .'

It probably would have been better to tell her at home, he thought, although the shop had the advantage that there was no chance of the children overhearing.

He hadn't meant it to come out as it did, but he'd found he simply couldn't lie to her any more. Not when she asked a direct question.

Anyway, it was done now, and nothing could change it.

The whistle blew and the train began to pull out of Kingshaven.

Michael stared out of the window as the train raced across the South of England, carrying him further and further away from his wife and children. The relief of owning up gradually began to replace the guilt of confession and from time to time excitement at the prospect of telling Claudia shivered through his body even though he knew he ought to be feeling sad.

After all the years of waiting, they would start their life together sooner than they'd ever dreamed! He hoped he would be sacked from his job, rather than having to work notice. They'd get a bigger flat, and the children could come up and stay. Sylvia would soon see the sense of that. Iris would love London. He'd take her to the Houses of Parliament and to the theatre, and it would be good for Anthony to see a bit of real life instead of thinking the world revolved around Kingshaven.

Stepping onto the platform at Waterloo, he couldn't stop himself running. In minutes, Claudia would open the door of her little rented flat in Bloomsbury, and he would tell her his news, and her face would light up. He would kiss her, and they would fall down on to the floor, barely remembering to close the door in their haste to clamber all over each other.

Afterwards, they'd go to the little Greek restaurant on Charlotte Street and drink wine that tasted of pine resin and eat salad with cubes of sharp white cheese, and meat with a charcoal crust. They'd eat and talk, as hungry to hear what the other had been doing all week as they were for food. They'd walk home – home! – past the tall, monumental university library, where she'd worked since leaving her husband; across Russell Square, where the bushes rustled with clandestine couplings in the dark; through the narrow Dickensian streets, talking all the way, the flow of conversation interrupted only by the frequent urge to kiss. And then they would go to bed.

And tomorrow they would be able to spend the whole day with each other, from waking to sleeping, and then, every day, a blissful unhurried series of days without end. In the mornings, he would no longer wake from his unconscious world and check to see whom he was sleeping next to, but instead lie propped up on his elbow beside Claudia, watching her face, so peaceful, so beautiful he had to touch her soft cheek to check that she was real.

He rang the bell, an unsuppressible grin spreading from ear to ear across his face as he heard her footsteps approaching. But when she opened the door, her face did not light up, and she did not leap into his open arms when he told her his news. Instead she pulled him inside, her eyes full of tears.

'What?' He was suddenly filled with foreboding.

'Haven't you heard?' she asked, impatient with his ignorance. 'President Kennedy's been assassinated!'

Years later, when it had become a cliché that everyone remembered exactly what they were doing when they heard the news, Michael would always recall his optimism, running down the fog-bound London street to Claudia's flat, and how quickly it had become grief as he learned of faraway events on a sunny boulevard in Dallas.

Chapter Twelve

May 1964

For the older residents of Kingshaven, the deafening roar of motorbikes recalled the sound of fighter planes taking off from the nearby Coombe Hill airfield during the war, and the prospect of an invasion of British teenage gangs was almost as terrifying as occupation by divisions of German soldiers.

Following the events at Margate and Brighton, any seaside town with a beach big enough to stage a fight had become a possible destination for the Mods and Rockers. Most people in Kingshaven were of the opinion that television was to blame for giving young people ideas, and agreed that the obvious solution was the reintroduction of National Service. In the meantime, shopkeepers had taken to boarding up their premises on Sundays and Bank Holidays just in case Kingshaven was next on the list.

For Iris, who ran to the end of Cherry Avenue to watch the bikes streaming down Hill Road, the sheer numbers were exhilarating. They *were* like armies in uniform: first the Rockers, all black leather, oily quiffs and silver studs glinting in the sunlight, and shortly afterwards, a pack of Mods in their parkas.

Iris considered herself a Mod, although she could never get her hair straight or tidy enough to truly look the part. Her mother, who encouraged any interest her daughter showed in fashion, had bought her a white PVC mac for her birthday, which was the envy of her peers, but Iris was growing so quickly that it was already shorter than the grey skirt she was wearing with her black polo-neck jumper. This morning, her mother had gone out visiting, and Anthony was away for the weekend at scout camp, so Iris had experimented at her mother's dressing table with a thick coating of mascara to her eyelashes and a smear of pale lipstick.

As she watched the Mods swoop past, Iris was confident she looked as old as any of the girls they had with them. Bringing up the rear was a guy without a pillion, on a Lambretta GT 200 with a shining array of rear-view mirrors which stuck out like antlers. He wolf-whistled. Iris glanced behind her, expecting to see Milly Bland, or one of the older girls who always wore make-up and skinny-rib jumpers, but she was the only person on the street. She'd never been whistled at before. Usually boys shouted something about her red hair. Normally she shouted back. But now, she couldn't stop a blush spreading all the way up from her brown shoes to the hair she had flattened using most of a can of Sylvia's hairspray.

Iris set off walking into town. With Dad gone, and Winston up at Oxford University, Kingshaven had become a lonely place at weekends. During the winter months, she'd virtually gone into hibernation, sometimes spending the whole day in bed reading or sleeping. Her mother was so busy keeping up appearances, she didn't seem to care how long Iris stayed in her room as long she didn't let the untidiness spill out into the rest of the house.

When the spring sunshine beckoned to her round the edges of her bedroom curtains, Iris occasionally dragged herself to the Expresso, where a group of the older girls from school sat awarding scores to the 'talent' hanging out in the amusement arcade. They tolerated Iris because her reputation at school was unimpeachably bad. Cheekier in her confrontations with the teachers than anyone else dared to be, Iris was approaching the school record of detentions, even though she was only in the third form. There was a sort of cachet attached to having a father who'd abandoned his family, especially if you gave the impression of not caring.

'I can't really blame him for leaving my mother,' Iris would declare, which made even the ones who smoked reel with shock.

She wasn't just saying it for effect. She did find it difficult to understand why her parents had ever got together. They'd had to marry because of her own imminent arrival, of course, her mother had told her this enough times, but how come they'd been 'doing it' in the first place?

Her father was working-class, left-wing, deep. Her mother was so irredeemably bourgeois, right-wing and shallow that when her father had left them, she'd taken comfort from the fact that 'You'll Never Walk Alone' by Gerry and the Pacemakers was at the top of the charts, and played the single so many times on the Dansette that the neighbours complained.

The girls at school thought her mother was groovy for liking pop music and envied her collection of Beatles' singles, but they didn't have to listen to her singing along to 'Anyone Who Had a Heart' with even more strangulated emotion than Cilla Black.

Iris thought her mother's sole attraction was her pretty face. Were looks alone enough for men to take leave of their senses? Or was everything about sex? Sylvia, for all her prudishness, had clearly been prepared to lose her virginity before she was married, as Iris had pointed out to her in the midst of a particularly heated row.

Her mother had been momentarily silenced by the nerve of it and then she had screamed, 'Yes, and look where it got me!' and burst into self-pitying tears, which used to work with Dad, but made Iris hate her even more.

If she couldn't blame Dad for leaving Mum, Iris knew she'd never forgive him for leaving her to deal with Sylvia alone.

Iris kicked a small stone hard at the tailfin of a passing black Ford Zodiac, then shrugged her shoulders as the driver braked and stuck his head out to look behind, feeling her cheeks colour for the second time that day as she recognized the handsome face of Mr Spivey, a new arrival in town who'd taken over the premises next to her mother's shop.

The tide was up, leaving no immediately obvious place for the rival gangs to mass.

By the time Iris reached the seafront, the Rockers had taken the direct route to the Harbour End, driving their motorbikes in formation along the pedestrian promenade, tearing the notices stating 'No Leather' off Saloon Bar doors and occupying all the pubs.

At the New End, the Mods, who were London boys from their accents, and unused to the ways of the sea, were gathered around the clock tower blaming each other for the impasse.

Iris stood at a distance under the striped awning of the Beach Stores, trying not to look like she was watching them.

'You said there was a beach!' one Mod whined.

'There was when I came here with me nan!'

'That's a load of bloody use!'

A couple of the Mod girls had purchased cornets, and were sitting astride scooters, taking long suggestive licks from swirls of Mr Whippy.

The extra policemen, who'd been drafted in from Lowhampton in expectation of trouble, wandered round inspecting the scooters, trying to look as if they were in command of the situation, and eventually decided to confiscate two cricket bats.

'But, officer, we've only come for a game of cricket on the beach,' said the lippy one, who appeared to be leader.

Iris, who was pretending to be interested in a spinner of colour postcards, caught the eye of the boy who'd whistled at her. He had straight black hair which flopped over his eyes, and a smile which crinkled up his pale face horizontally, exposing his nice white teeth, a bit like a chimpanzee. He winked at her. Iris quickly looked back at the spinner.

'No beach at present,' a policeman pointed out.

'You on holiday?' Monkey Face was right behind Iris now. He was much taller than he looked on the bike. Taller even than she was.

'Unfortunately, I live here,' she replied, keeping her eyes fixed on an aerial view of the town which was so out of date, it didn't even show the council estate, let alone all the new bungalows that were being built further up the hill. The photograph had obviously been taken on black and white film and the colour printed on afterwards, but the alignment wasn't quite right. The brown of the town had strayed into the green of the fields and the beach was half yellow and half blue.

'Nice,' said the Mod, looking over her shoulder. He was standing uncomfortably close to her.

'Actually, it's a dump,' Iris told him, turning round.

The youth stepped back. He had dark eyes which sparkled with mischief (or was it drugs? Iris wondered. It said in the newspapers that Mods took a lot of pills). His skin was unhealthily white and his hair was so black it looked like he had dyed it.

'You can come to the station and claim the bat when it's low tide, can't you?' the sergeant told the leader of the gang.

He and the officers got into the police car and drove off to monitor events at the Harbour End.

The leader put two fingers up at the back of the police car.

The Mods applauded.

Monkey Face looked sideways at Iris and winked again, as if she was one of them.

'There goes our game of cricket,' said the leader with exaggerated disappointment.

The Mods booed.

'We'll have to find something else to do.'

Another mass sigh.

'There's always the Gardens,' Iris heard herself suggesting.

'The Gardens?' said the leader, focusing on her.

'There's putting, table tennis . . .' Iris faltered, wishing she hadn't said anything now. They weren't the sort to play ping-pong. There was a restlessness around them, like a pack of hounds waiting to go hunting.

'What we like doing in gardens . . .' the leader said, his eyes fixing on a stack of tin buckets just to her left, '. . . is digging.'

As Mr Ball of the Beach Stores later told the reporter from the *Chronicle*, there was very little he could do. A sand spade was not an offensive weapon, and the boys paid cash in full, not even requesting a discount for quantity. It was lucky really that he'd only had nine in stock. A week later, he'd have taken delivery of a gross for the season. The Mods had been very polite, but there'd been at least twenty of them in the shop, and he didn't want to think about what might have happened if he'd refused to serve them.

From the subsequent flurry of letters to the *Chronicle*, it was clear that the majority of the residents of Kingshaven considered that the destruction of the interior of the Beach Stores would have been a price worth paying.

'Blue for a boy,' said Sylvia, peering into the cradle of the new Allsop baby, which was decked out in blue and white gingham.

Jennifer Allsop put her coffee cup down and lit a cigarette. She wondered whether it was a shopkeeper's habit to speak in clichés or whether it was something Sylvia had picked up from her own mother. At times, Sylvia seemed so very like Ruby, one might almost have thought that *she* was her daughter. Sylvia was everything Ruby would have liked her daughter to be: industrious, clever at sewing, capable of taking over the business when the time came . . . except she wasn't her daughter, Jennifer thought smugly, and therefore would never be given the opportunity. Although, with the success of Sylvia's Boutique, Jennifer was increasingly uncertain there would be anything left of Farmer's for her to inherit when her mother eventually passed on. She thought Sylvia had a bit of a nerve, frankly, insinuating herself into her mother's shop and then setting herself up as a rival.

Biting the hand that fed her, as her mother put it.

'Boys are so much more affectionate,' said Sylvia with a smile.

'Until they grow up,' Jennifer remarked.

There was something about Sylvia's aura of serenity which gave Jennifer an almost irresistible urge to prick it. Since her husband had abandoned her, Sylvia had somehow managed to acquire the status of a blessed martyr.

'I've brought you a lickle present.' Sylvia spoke into the cradle with a silly, lispy baby voice.

Jennifer unwrapped the pale blue tissue paper to find a most exquisite white matinée jacket with a blue silk ribbon tie. How on earth did Sylvia have the time for such intricate knitting these days? It crossed Jennifer's mind that perhaps Sylvia had knitted the jacket for the birth of Julia three years before with the idea that she could attach pink or blue ribbons at the last minute, and then thought better of it when Julia turned out to be a girl. She had not come with a gift then, Jennifer remembered with bitterness. Few people had. They'd all been too embarrassed to show their faces.

'Sweet of you,' Jennifer said, holding the jacket up for a moment, then putting it down on the arm of a chair.

'Have you decided on a name?' Sylvia asked.

'James,' Jennifer replied with a sigh. 'But I want him to be known as Jamie. Libby King is godmother.'

'Very fitting,' said Sylvia. 'She's had a little boy too, I hear?'

'Yes. Edwin. And Pearl's had a girl, Susannah.'

'What a lot of babies!' Sylvia's lip quivered slightly.

Was the idea that everyone ought to feel sorry for her because she was no longer in a position to have a baby herself? Jennifer wondered. Fat chance!

Sylvia certainly knew how to play it. Eyes brimming with tears, a resigned little shrug of her shoulders.

'Would you like another cup of coffee?' Jennifer asked, hoping to accelerate her departure.

'Oh, that would be lovely!' Sylvia said. 'It's a real treat for me, this. I don't get many chances to go out socially these days.'

In the kitchen, Jennifer clattered the kettle against the tap, and poured water on to the spoonful of instant coffee long before it was boiling.

A police siren wailed in the distance.

'Sounds like trouble down there,' Sylvia called through.

The baby started to cry.

Sylvia had him out of the cradle before Jennifer could get to him.

Undissolved coffee powder floated on the surface of the pale beige liquid Jennifer offered her.

'Ooh, do be careful,' Sylvia admonished. 'We don't put hot drinks next to babies, do we?' She indicated with a nod of her head that Jennifer should put the drink down on the coffee table.

'I'm trying not to pick him up every time he cries,' Jennifer informed her curtly as she stood redundant, waiting for Sylvia to hand her son over. 'Don't want to get him into bad habits.'

'Poor ickle boy,' Sylvia cooed over the baby. 'What a horrible mummy you've got!'

'Hardly,' Jennifer said. 'He's bound to be tremendously spoilt.' She flicked ash carelessly over the white matinée jacket. A burning ember sizzled a black pinhole in one of the blue ribbons.

'Seeing that he is the heir to the Castle,' Jennifer added, just to re-establish the hierarchy.

'Any news on that front?' Sylvia asked, looking up from her Virgin Mary pose.

'Sir John's as healthy as ever,' said Jennifer with a heavy sigh.

'Jolly must be very proud,' said Sylvia.

'I should bloody well hope so.' Jennifer pulled hard on her cigarette.

'He's ever so nice, your husband,' said Sylvia. 'Did you see the lovely planting he did for me?'

'Yes, I did,' Jennifer replied.

Jolly had done a window box for outside Sylvia's shop before he'd even attended to the ones on his own house. Sylvia Quinn didn't have a husband any more but she certainly knew how to flutter her eyelashes and get men rushing to her aid.

'You don't always get what you see, though, do you, with husbands?' Jennifer said in a low, confidential tone.

'Be thankful you've got one,' Sylvia replied evenly.

'You seem to be managing very well without,' said Jennifer.

'I'm doing my best.' Another drawn-out sigh. A brave little smile.

'Of course, it can't have been much of a surprise,' Jennifer went on, the temptation to wound finally irresistible.

'Beg pardon?' said Sylvia. Serenity gone in an instant, like a cloud passing over the sun.

'Well, your husband wasn't exactly a saint, was he?' said Jennifer. 'It wasn't the first time, I mean . . .'

'How did you know that?' Sylvia asked.

'Everyone knew, didn't they? Shall I take Jamie now?'

Jennifer smiled her nicest, most sympathetic smile at her guest as she handed over the baby.

'Knew what?' Sylvia asked in a barely audible little voice.

'Well, they weren't terribly discreet, were they?' said Jennifer. 'But then Pearl rarely is.'

'It's the perfect metaphor,' Iris whispered to Monkey Face.

They were crouching behind the kiosk where the balls and putters were kept, watching the digging-up of the flowerbeds, an act so subversive and thrilling she scarcely dared to look.

'A group of Modernists destroying Britain-in-Bloom's Runner-Up . . .'

'What are you on about?' he asked.

The leaders of the Mods were standing in the main display bed, which featured the words Kingshaven 1964 written in orange double marigolds, tossing spadefuls of newly planted bedding plants over their shoulders, creating an almost perfect circle of mess on the surrounding lawn.

Monkey Face took out a packet of ten Embassy and offered Iris one.

She shook her head and shivered as he put his arm around her and drew the stiff top half of her body towards him.

'What's your name?' she asked him as their lips grew uncomfortably near.

'Vic.'

Iris didn't know whether she was supposed to put her own arm around his back too. Despite her mother's suspicions, she had never even held hands with a boy, let alone kissed one. She wriggled a bit.

'You're pretty,' he said.

'I'm not pretty!' she protested.

'Your legs go on for ever.'

She'd never thought of her legs as an asset – more a nuisance because she couldn't get a pair of trousers that were long enough.

The Mods leaned on their shovels and viewed their work with satisfaction, and then a scraggy little one, who had not been allowed a spade, picked up a clod of earth and threw it at the War Memorial. There was a suppressed gasp, a moment of silence as the others considered whether this was a taboo too far, and then, suddenly, the destruction escalated into something darker and more frenzied.

Iris could suddenly see that the consequences of this prank were going to stretch long into the future. Had anyone noticed her with the Mods? Hers was the only white PVC mac in Kingshaven.

Vic's face moved towards hers.

Was it understood that a girlfriend was a good enough excuse not to join in? Iris wondered.

'Don't you like vandalism?' she asked uneasily.

'Not really,' he said.

'Why are you a Mod, then?'

'It's a day by the sea after being cooped up all week.'

'Do your parents know?'

'My mum's dead. It's just me and my brother.'

It sounded so grown up.

'Where do you work?' Iris asked.

'In a theatre. Box office. Come here!'

He moved towards her again.

Were you supposed to stay still or move too? When your lips touched, should you have your mouth open or closed? Iris wished she'd paid more attention to the conversations of her peers when they were changing for Games. She was always so intent on shrinking invisibly into the coats to hide her flat chest, she didn't really listen to what they were saying, although she'd gathered there was a kind of points system for what you should allow and when. A French kiss was worth more than an ordinary one, but Iris didn't know what the difference was.

She could taste the acridity of the cigarette on his breath, and she suddenly realized that she didn't want to kiss him at all, and broke away.

'What's the problem?' he asked, blowing out a smoke ring.

'I don't know you,' she told him. 'There's a kind of intimacy created by the shared thrill of voyeurism, that's all.'

'Bloody hell!' he said. 'You're weird!'

'Do most girls immediately succumb to your charms?' Iris asked.

He took another long drag on his cigarette and smiled his smile, which was oddly attractive now that she was used to it. She wondered if she had been wrong to put him off. Perhaps it would be useful to try kissing out with someone she didn't love, so that if the time ever came for someone she did love, she would know what to do.

The Mods were now tearing up the turf from the putting green and dumping it in the little river that ran though the Gardens.

One of the leaders rammed the metal flag for the eighteenth hole into the top of the pile, like a flag on a sandcastle.

And then the leader held his hand up for silence. From the Harbour End came the distant rumble of motorbikes.

'Let's get out of here!' Vic took Iris's hand.

'No! This way!' Iris yanked her arm away and ran as fast as she could for the woods, not stopping to look round to see if he was following her. She collapsed panting amid the roots of an old pine tree and watched the sunlit events outside, as if they were happening somewhere else, or on television. She couldn't see where Vic had gone.

The Rockers arrived in a great roar of exhaust, driving down the wrought-iron gate, which had escaped melting down for armaments during the war owing to the particularly fine dedication to Queen Victoria's Diamond Jubilee. Furious at having been pre-empted by their rivals, they surged into the Gardens, hell bent on destroying anything that was left, smashing both the all-weather ping-pong tables and urinating en masse in the wishing well.

They began to rock the wooden kiosk where Iris and Vic had been hiding just moments before. When they had brought it down, they fell upon the metal putters inside like revolutionaries lighting on a government arms cache. Brandishing their weapons, they charged towards the Mods who stood in a tight battalion holding up sections of picket fence as shields.

Iris put her hands over her eyes as the fight began, but she could hear the ugly clang of metal on metal, and the smack of fist on flesh, and then suddenly, as if at some secret signal, the noise stopped and the armies scattered as a police car screeched into the Gardens over the fallen Jubilee gate and attempted to corral the fighting youths like wild horses.

On Sundays, Michael always got up early and went to buy all the papers. Then he brought Claudia tea and toast in bed. It was the smell of burning which usually woke her up, or the swearing from the kitchen as he looked up from the colour supplement to see that he had yet again neglected to watch the grill. She would pretend to be sleeping still as he tiptoed in, just so that she could have the pleasure of being woken with a kiss. Hot sweet tea, toast with specks of charcoal in melting wedges of yellow butter, the sandpaper scrape of her lover's unshaven cheek, and lazy Sunday morning sex . . . it was the best way in the world to wake up.

Later, she would read the papers while Michael played the piano, which was the principal reason they'd decided to rent the little mews house in Hampstead. When they'd come to view the property, he'd paid scant attention to any of the other features, like the impractical arrangement of living room on the first floor with kitchen and bedroom below, or the ramshackle bookshelves made of bricks and planks which looked as if they might collapse at any moment. The owner was an academic. Claudia could tell as soon as he opened the door into a living room which shared many features with her father's study. He was explaining that he was letting the house because a university in America had offered him a visiting lectureship, when Michael had pointed at the upright piano, which had piles of scores stacked on top.

'Is it in tune?'

'Of course,' the owner had said.

'We'll take it, won't we, Claudia?'

And she had simply nodded, enjoying the opportunity to make him happy.

Since her old boss from BBC days had introduced them to Ronnie Scott's club in Soho, Michael had become fascinated by jazz. He played with his eyes closed, almost in the same way as he made love, his fingers instinctively feeling for the notes. Occasionally he would open his eyes and smile at her, and she would smile back, and it felt so perfectly harmonious, it almost hurt.

When he closed the lid of the piano this morning, he said to her. 'You know Gabriel Oak?'

She laughed.

'Not personally.'

'But you know what he says in *Far From the Madding Crowd* about marriage?'

'Remind me.'

' "Whenever you look up, there I shall be – and whenever I look up, there will be you." '

'Yes,' she said hesitantly.

'I used not to understand how anyone could want that. But now, I do.' He looked at her. 'I shall do one thing in this life – one thing certain – that is love you, and long for you, and keep wanting you until I die,' he said.

She smiled at him across the dusty beam of sunlight coming through the window, and then she said, 'Let's go for a walk. It's such a lovely day.'

They lived in the centre of Hampstead, but the house was tucked away in the warren of steep little streets between the High Street and the Heath. Friends, even those who had been there several times, had difficulty finding it. Often they would receive a phone call from the telephone box outside the pub, not fifty yards away, asking for directions. Hampstead was a village, but it was not the kind of place where any stranger you stopped in the street would automatically be able to point you in the direction of somebody's house. Londoners liked to preserve their boundaries.

'Do you find it oppressive?' Michael asked her as they walked down the road towards the Heath.

The air was beautiful, still fresh but warm. Summer air.

'What?' she asked.

'Me saying things like that.'

'Not oppressive, exactly,' she said. 'But one person can never be enough for someone else. It wouldn't be right.'

A day didn't go by without Claudia thinking of the bright little face of his son, inquisitive and innocent as he traipsed round her in the snow looking for feet, and his daughter, tall enough and suspicious enough to be a woman, but still only a girl.

Anthony had rung recently from the telephone kiosk on the promenade and Michael had assaulted him with such a barrage of questions that there had been no time for the child to reply before the pips went.

Iris had not been in touch since the Sunday evening Michael had returned to Kingshaven to find the locks had been changed on his house. He had spent the night at the Riviera Guesthouse, been sacked from his job the next morning, and left Kingshaven for good on the afternoon train.

He wrote to Iris almost daily, but she returned all his letters unopened.

When Claudia had suggested sending postcards, thinking that even the most determined girl could not stop herself reading those, these had been returned too, in an envelope which had made Michael's hands wobble in anticipation when he recognized his daughter's handwriting on the front, and then stare in disbelief as a blizzard of torn-up pieces of postcard settled all over the floor.

It was then that Claudia had realized that the damage they had done might never be healed.

She watched the side of Michael's face as they walked towards the Heath together, wishing he would talk about how he felt about it all. He had that stubborn, male reluctance to talk about his feelings. Not just about his immediate family he had left in Kingshaven, but the others, the parents who had been killed in the first air raids, his brother Frank, the lively aunts he had lived with, who had gone to America after the war. Very rarely, he let slip a tantalizing glimpse of one of these ghostly figures but if Claudia pushed for more, he clammed up. That's all in the past, he'd say with quiet insistence.

At the first sign of spring, there were those in Hampstead who would race to swim in the ponds, even though the sun was not yet strong enough to dry their skin when they got out. Today the Heath was like a beach, swarming with people walking dogs, kicking balls, spreading picnics out on the ground, flying kites or simply lying in the grass, eyes closed and faces tilted to the sun.

At the top of Parliament Hill Fields, Claudia and Michael stood looking over the city. In front, buildings as far as the eye could see; to the left, Alexandra Palace watching over North London. If you knew where you were looking, you could just make out Big Ben in the distance, and each year, new landmarks like the tower blocks of council flats and the slim tube of the Post Office Tower sprang up out of the urban sprawl. The stretch of the city, the fact that you could not see where it ended, nor begin to imagine all the lives that went on in it, always filled Claudia with a sense of her own inconsequence which she found oddly liberating. As if he shared that feeling, Michael suddenly picked her up and twirled her round with her feet flying out in a circle, like a child, until giddiness got the better of them and they fell over, laughing.

'Coffee and cake?' Michael asked, looking down at her. She couldn't focus on his face because the sunlight was so bright behind him, shining through his light brown hair, making it a bright white halo.

Sometimes she felt this time was like a holiday, except that she went out to work. He was meant to write, but he seemed to spend most of his mornings playing the piano and his afternoons at the cinema, or theatre matinées. So many aspects of London living were still treats for him which he gobbled up with the appetite of a child. He loved to spend Sunday afternoons in the Austrian café, which smelled of freshly ground coffee and had a refrigerated window full of gleaming strawberry tarts and perfectly smooth chocolate discs of Sacher Torte, and where the clientele was mostly rich widows of a certain age with middle-European accents and lots of rings on their veiny hands who looked disapprovingly at Michael and Claudia's casual attire.

'Or how about an ice cream?' Michael suggested.

A smart ice-cream parlour had recently opened at the bottom of Haverstock Hill with a mosaic of pure fruit water ices in gleaming stainless-steel trays, just like the ice-cream parlours they'd visited on their real holiday when she'd introduced him to Italy.

It had been the most dreamy time, even though Michael was an exhausting companion with such an appetite for knowledge that he wanted to see every fresco and mosaic, and even had her teaching him Latin so that he could read the inscriptions on the stones in the Forum. He was a good pupil.

'*Semper Claudiam amabo*,' he told her, using the correct conjugation of the verb and declension of the noun. I will always love Claudia.

He was so taciturn by nature, she found herself equally thrilled and embarrassed by such open declarations of love, which made him seem somehow vulnerable, almost childlike for a grown man.

Sometimes she felt as if they were floating over the surface of life, and needed to be grounded. The money from sales of his first book continued to roll in, but sooner or later it must surely stop, and then the holidays would be over, and there would be no escape from the reality of earning the privileges they now enjoyed, and from facing the consequences of what they had done.

The sunshine had drawn the rhododendrons out of their buds. Violet flowers were peeping through the shiny green foliage, colours so beautifully matched that, if you looked away and back again, they shaded into one another, like shot silk.

Sylvia was walking down the Rhododendron Mile tormented by unanswerable questions. Tears came involuntarily to her eyes. It felt as if she'd gone right back to November when she'd cried every night until there wasn't enough liquid in her body for her to cry any more and her pillowcase was too wet to sleep on.

Patsy, her next-door neighbour, who was training to be a Samaritan, said that there were these phases to bereavement, and even though Sylvia was not technically bereaved, it was much the same thing. Sylvia thought it was worse. If Michael were dead, she could feel sorry for him, not be tortured by thoughts of him up in London enjoying himself.

Now, Sylvia felt she might as well not have gone through that whole journey of emotions. Just as she was getting used to him snatching her future away, he'd taken her past as well.

Was it really true about Michael and Pearl?

Jennifer Farmer had a very cruel streak.

But Sylvia knew inside that it was. She'd known immediately, and the more she thought about it, the more little odd moments, like stray pieces of a jigsaw, seemed to slot into the picture.

All those times she'd told herself not to be silly, she hadn't been silly at all.

Where had it happened, for goodness' sake? In the Palace itself? How could he do that – after the way he used to go on about the Kings?

And when had it finished? Had that been when he started up

with Claudia, or had there been a bit of a gap? Had everyone in Kingshaven known?

What a fool she must have looked!

Sylvia stood and stared at the Palace Hotel, fighting the urge to scrape up handfuls of the gravel drive and throw it at the windows, silently vowing a better revenge. One day, they would hurt as she was hurting now.

In the meantime, there was no point in getting herself arrested.

Turning her back on the Palace, Sylvia walked down Hill Road.

There were a few wisps of cloud in the azure sky. Baskets of bright begonias hung in the guesthouse porches, and newly painted 'Vacancies' signs creaked in the breeze. Over on the South Cliffs, the grass was green and lush and spotted with ewes and their lambs.

It didn't seem right for your life to be ruined on such a lovely day.

Wiping her face with the sleeve of her cardigan, Sylvia walked wearily up to her front door. She felt drained by it all, defeated. She took a deep breath as she put her key in the Yale. She felt like curling up in a ball and going to sleep so she didn't have to think about any of it, but there was tea to do. Anthony was bound to be starving after a weekend of baked beans in a billy can.

'Oh, God, you're not crying again!' said Iris, who was in the hallway, wearing her white mac. 'What's the matter with you?' Her daughter had that sing-song voice on which drove Sylvia mad.

'Just go to your room,' Sylvia said. 'I'm not in the mood for it. Not after what I've just found out.'

'What's that, then?' Iris asked with such exaggerated lack of interest, it made Sylvia look at her closely.

Iris was staring at her, unblinkingly defiant as she always was when she had something to hide.

'Did you know?' Sylvia asked quietly.

'Know what?' Iris shrugged her shoulders with infuriating insolence.

Daddy sometimes sleeps at the Palace . . . A statement filed away all those years ago now chimed like a bell in Sylvia's head. What a funny thing to say, she'd thought at the time.

'You knew, didn't you, you little cow!' Sylvia erupted like a volcano suddenly blowing its top.

Iris took a step back. 'I didn't mean to!' she protested.

'You egged them on, didn't you?'

'I didn't know all that would happen!' said Iris.

'You, you bloody little cow . . . if it hadn't been for you I wouldn't have been with him in the first place!' Sylvia hit her hard across the face.

Iris just stood holding her cheek, eyes brimming with tears. She looked young suddenly. Not like an adversary, but like someone who needed protecting. A little girl. Of course she hadn't known!

'You're wearing make-up,' Sylvia said quietly as a pink weal bloomed where her hand had made contact with Iris's cheek, below an eye plastered with far too much mascara. She went to touch her daughter's face more softly.

'Don't touch me!' Iris screamed at her.

'Sssh. The neighbours will hear!'

'I don't give a damn about the fucking neighbours!'

'Iris!'

Sylvia stepped in the way as Iris tried to get to the door, noticing for the first time consciously that Iris was taller than her now, and stronger, and there was no way she could physically stop her going out.

Sylvia sank impotently to the floor, buried her head in her hands, and wept.

'You're pathetic!' Iris said, stepping over her and walking out. 'No wonder Dad left.'

Michael loved the sensation of emerging into a light afternoon from the cinema; the stale smell of cigarettes clinging to his clothes made him feel as if he was playing truant. It didn't really matter whether the film was Bergman or Bond, whether it was the Everyman Hampstead or the Empire Leicester Square.

Watching *Cleopatra* should have been the perfect way to spend Sunday afternoon, but he thought that the huge audiences who had been drawn to see whether the real-life passion between Elizabeth Taylor and Richard Burton would spill into their roles were probably disappointed. The performances were curiously lacklustre given the lavishness of the setting and the great expectation after all the news reports.

It was getting dark outside, and the air had a freshness that reminded him that it was not yet summer.

'What did you think?' Claudia asked him.

'Oddly dull,' he said.

She said nothing for a moment, and then she looked at him and said, 'Elizabeth Taylor looks very like Pearl King, doesn't she?'

He'd always wondered whether Claudia knew, and now, just in case he was left in any doubt, she added, 'And you actually look quite a lot like Richard Burton.'

'Thank you,' he said, 'but I'd never wear a skirt like that.'

Claudia let out a yelp of laughter.

He went to take her hand. She gave him one of her disapproving looks, but did not break away. Then he put his arm around her. She fitted so well against him, it was like the two of them were made of the same stuff.

He looked up at the tall trees in the middle of the square. There was a huge swirl of starlings above, sweeping round in the semi-darkness. He wondered whether they ever slept, or whether they stayed all night on the wing, never realizing that the sun had gone in, that it was only neon creating a perpetual twilight.

'Did you love Pearl?' Claudia asked.

'No,' he said. 'No, I think perhaps I hated her.'

He couldn't explain it himself. It all seemed so long ago now, it was like a different life. The only reasons he could offer were so selfish and unworthy, and any psychological explanation made the liaison look like an insane attempt at self-destruction. There was really nothing to justify or redeem his behaviour, and he had always harboured a sense of dread that he and Claudia would come to this conversation, and he would lose her because of it.

The second-hand bookshops on Charing Cross Road where they often browsed were closed. A faint smell of roasting meat and sticky sweet sauce drifted over from the Chinese restaurants in Gerrard Street, making him feel ravenously hungry, but he didn't want the intensity of sitting in a restaurant together right now.

'I didn't know how to end it,' he offered.

'Your marriage?' she asked.

He had meant the relationship with Pearl, but perhaps he had subconsciously been looking for a way out of his marriage too. Claudia was perceptive about these things.

'Maybe,' he said.

'Very cowardly,' she said.

'Yes. I was. Unforgivably,' he said, quietly.

As they walked, he kept shooting surreptitious glances at the side of her face, trying to anticipate what she would say next, but she did not speak. And gradually, the tension in his body began to dissipate as he realized that she was not going to. It was enough for her to bring it out into the open, for him to acknowledge his responsibility, and to leave it there. There was a kind of stillness about her sometimes that he had only come to know through spending time with her. She did not needle, as other women did, intent on whittling out every last little detail. Maybe it was because he had never lied to her, as he had to the others.

A group of Mods were sitting in the Expresso with Coke floats in front of them. One of them had a cut on his face, another was drumming fingers rusty with blood on the Formica table top, making the other customers nervous. Iris breathed the odourless smell of fear as soon as she stepped in.

Vic beckoned her over. His dark eyes were feverishly bright, his mouth deep red and swollen. He smiled lopsidedly. One of his perfect teeth had been knocked out.

'What happened to you?' he asked, pointing at her cheek.

Iris glanced at her reflection in the mirror behind the bar and saw that a purple bruise was blooming from where her mother had hit her, and her eye had puffed up. The scraggy Mod stared, then pulled a chair up to the table for her, as if she had earned her place with them because she had the scars to prove it. Iris could feel the astonished eyes of Milly Bland and her friends on her back as she sauntered over to the jukebox and made a selection.

'A World Without Love', by Peter and Gordon. She thought it was suitably Mod.

'All right?' she asked Vic, trying out their language. She'd noticed they never said hello.

'All right,' he said.

The scraggy one pushed the scoop of vanilla ice cream round the top of his Coke float, creating a creamy beige foam like that you sometimes saw on the tideline when the breakers had been whipped up in a storm.

'I don't like this,' he said.

He picked up the glass and looked around the room as if he was looking for someone to throw it at.

Iris felt the intake of breath. Rocco Rossi had been polishing the same tiny white cup with the same tea towel ever since she came in. All the other customers prepared to take cover.

'I'll have it,' Iris said, taking it from the Mod.

There was a collective exhalation as she took the glass and put the straw to her lips, hoping he hadn't spat in it.

Several people took the opportunity to leave.

Vic took a clip of notes out of his back pocket, peeled off ten shillings and put it on the table.

'Better be getting off ourselves,' he said.

The promenade was virtually deserted, the Gardens quiet, apart from the tranquil trickle and plop of water in the little river.

Vic climbed on to his Lambretta, and checked his cut lip in one of the many mirrors.

His two friends climbed on to a Vespa and drove off, with the scraggy one leaning right back, making rude gestures at anyone who dared turn their heads in their direction.

Iris shifted her weight from one foot to the other.

'D'you wanna lift?' Vic asked her.

'All right,' Iris said.

'Hop on, then!'

Iris had never been on a scooter before. Gingerly she hitched up her skirt and climbed on. Her long, bare legs felt very exposed. By the clock tower, she noticed Mr Makepeace leaning on his walking stick. He'd become a bit of a sad figure, wandering round town in his dressing gown. They said he couldn't even remember who his wife was, but from the way he was staring at Iris she had the feeling that he was taking it all in.

'Where to?' said Vic.

'Just up the hill,' Iris mumbled, wanting to get out of town as quickly as possible. If nobody had seen her before, someone was bound to have by now. They were probably already on the phone to her mother.

'Put your arms round my waist, then,' Vic instructed patiently, as if he realized that this was her first time.

Tentatively, she placed her hands on his parka and then grabbed him tighter as they suddenly lurched off.

It felt much faster than it looked.

The wind blasted her hair back from her face, making her eyes sting, blowing every thought out of her head except fear, but once she realized she wasn't going to fall off, it was so exhilarating she wanted to scream.

As they puttered up the hill out of town, the mirrors attached to the front of the bike became lights bathing her face in the bright orange reflection of the western sky.

'Where do you want to get off?' Vic shouted over his shoulder.

They were approaching her council estate. Four lines of identical houses on the left side of the road. In one of them her mother was sitting waiting sourly for her.

'I don't want to get off,' Iris shouted.

'All right!' Vic called, pulling back the throttle.

The bike shot past the end of her road.

She'd meant it as a joke really, but now she didn't know how to take it back.

With every second, the distance to her house was getting longer to walk.

What was the point of going home?

'I give up on you, Iris,' her mother would say, and this time she'd really mean it.

When she was expelled from school, which was bound to happen when word got round, she'd throw her out anyway.

As the bike passed the last house in Kingshaven and pulled round the long bend to the brow of the hill, Iris thought, Why not? If it's inevitable, why put it off?

'Sure?' Vic shouted back at her.

Another second and it would be too late to change her mind.

'Sure!' she shouted.

'What's your name?' he called back.

Iris braved a glance back at the great expanse of sunset, and the town, now in shadow, dropping away from them.

'My name is Sarah Bird,' she shouted.

Sylvia was sitting on the bottom step of the staircase in the hall watching the door whilst talking to Audrey Potter on the phone. When Iris got home, she was going to kill her, she thought, as Audrey Potter told her that her daughter had been spotted with the Mods.

As if she didn't have enough to worry about.

Sylvia was desperate for an opportunity to ask Audrey: Did you know about my husband and Pearl King? Did everyone know?

But Audrey was full of the day's events.

'Did they cause any trouble?' Sylvia asked.

'Trouble?' Audrey laughed in an ominous way down the telephone line. 'Devastation, more like. There's to be an emergency council meeting tomorrow. The whole Gardens are under water, including the tennis courts. The lifeboat crew have had to wade through in their waterproofs to unblock the dam those hooligans built. And d'you know what?'

'What?' Sylvia asked, beginning to feel sick.

'Two of those disgusting yobs were taken to Lowhampton Hospital in an ambulance! At the taxpayer's expense. Can you believe that?'

'No,' said Sylvia.

'Disgraceful!'

'Were they badly injured?' Sylvia enquired.

'A couple of broken toes.' Audrey snorted with contempt. 'Serves them right for trying to kick down the model village.'

'No!'

'It'd take more than a couple of yobs to bring Little Kingshaven down!' Audrey said with satisfaction. 'That was built to last!'

'Was anyone else arrested?' Sylvia asked nervously.

Not Iris, please, not that.

'What can half a dozen coppers do against a mob like that?' said Audrey.

'Iris wasn't involved, though, was she?'

'Somebody said they saw her with a black eye.'

Sylvia caught her breath. 'I'll kill her when she gets in,' she muttered. 'Hang on, that's the door!'

'I'll say goodbye then,' said Audrey.

Sylvia set her face into an angry frown as the front door opened.

'Hello, Mum!' said Anthony.

'Oh, it's you,' she said, looking at her son's smiling, grubby face. 'Have you seen Iris?'

'No.'

'Where is she?' Sylvia stuck her head out of the door and looked down the empty street. The cherry trees were growing so fast, it was beginning to look like a proper avenue, but there was no sign of her daughter.

'Did you come back through the town or the Gardens?' she asked her son. The scout camp was on the fairground field up the valley.

'The Gardens are flooded. It's a right old mess down there. We Scouts have volunteered to help with the replanting instead of doing Bob-a-Job week!'

'Are the Mods and Rockers still down there?'

'No, they've all gone. A plague of locusts, Mr Bland said. They just swarmed in, stripped everything, then left.'

Michael heard the ringing as they passed the pub, but it was only when they were close to the house that he realized it was their phone. He felt a sense of urgency to answer it, and quickened his step towards the house. Nobody who knew them would keep ringing so long, because anyone who had been to their house would know that it would only take a few rings to get to the phone. Which meant it must be bad news, or a wrong number. He tried to calm himself as Claudia seemed to take an age fumbling with the keys and finally pushing open the door.

She picked up the receiver. 'Hampstead 5102.'

She listened for a moment then put her hand over the mouthpiece and mouthed 'Sylvia' to him.

He braced himself. One of the children.

'Hello, Sylvia?'

Silence.

'Where are you? Do you want me to call you back?' Surely she wasn't in the kiosk on the promenade at this time of night?

'Sitting on the stairs in the hall,' Sylvia said.

'You've had a phone installed?'

'Why shouldn't I?'

'No reason.'

'I don't need your permission, you know,' she told him.

'It's a good idea,' he said.

There was another long silence.

'Are you all right?' he asked.

'As well as can be expected,' she said curtly.

'And the children?' he asked.

'As if you care!' she shouted. 'After what you did with Pearl King!'

He held the receiver away from his head as if the blast of anger down the line would harm him physically. So this was the reason. It was almost as if the film they had just seen was a warning, the first tremor as the tectonic plate of his past bumped against the present.

'I'm sorry,' he said. It was utterly inadequate, and yet he didn't know what else to say. There was another long pause. He couldn't work out if she was still there.

'Hello?'

'Look, Iris isn't with you, is she?' Sylvia finally asked.

'With me? No, why?'

His heart leaped from despair to joy. Had Iris decided to forgive him?

'She's probably just trying to frighten me,' said Sylvia with a hollow little laugh.

'She's not there?'

'She'll probably be back any moment.'

'How long's she been gone?' Michael tried to keep his voice level.

'She was here this afternoon, and then she went out and she hasn't come back.'

Michael looked at his watch. It was almost midnight.

'When this afternoon?'

'I don't know. I had other things on my mind!' Sylvia spat the words down the phone, then collected herself. 'Mr Makepeace says he saw her going off on a motorbike, but he's a bit doolally . . .'

'Motorbike?' Michael repeated. Iris was far too young to be on a motorbike.

'There were those Mods and Rockers in town. He probably got mixed up.'

'Have you told the police?' Michael asked.

'No!'

'For God's sake, Sylvia, it's midnight and she's only fourteen!' Iris! Iris! he was screaming inside.

'We had a bit of an argument—' Sylvia explained.

'What sort of argument?' he interrupted.

'Don't you dare try to make it my fault she's gone, you bastard!'

'Sylvia!'

'Don't Sylvia me! Not after what you did!'

'Look, this is about Iris,' he said, trying to keep calm.

Sylvia started crying. 'Yes, and she wouldn't do this if you were here!'

'Do you want me to come down?' he asked.

'Don't you think you've done enough damage?' she screamed.

'You must call the police.'

'And as soon as I do, she'll turn up and how will I look?'

'Well, if you don't, I'm going to,' he said. 'And they'll come and get details from you.'

'All right, all right, I'll do it,' she said. 'If she comes to you, you'll ring?'

'Of course I will,' he said, taking down the number.

'Well.' She didn't seem to know how to end the conversation. 'Ring the police.'

'All right. Bye.'

Her voice sounded so lost, he wanted to go to her straightaway. What a mess he'd made of things. She was right. If he'd been there, Iris wouldn't have gone. If she had gone. What if she'd been abducted? Murdered?

Iris!

He sat up all night, listening to every gust of wind in the tall trees outside and rushing to the window at every hollow footstep on the pavement outside. When dawn began to break, it suddenly occurred to him that Iris might be within yards of the house but having difficulty finding it, so he stood outside in the street, hugging his jumper around him in the misty dawn air, watching for any movement. Gradually, the street began to wake up. The milk van clanked along. Curtains were drawn back; the sun came out; men in suits, with folded newspapers under their arms, hurried up the hill towards the tube, checking their wristwatches. The postman delivered letters just as if it were any normal day.

Iris did not come.

Then it occurred to Michael that there was no logical reason to think she would. It was only Sylvia saying it which had given him the idea, and he had wasted the whole night waiting when he could have been out looking for her.

Chapter Thirteen

February 1965

The death of Mr Makepeace seemed to symbolize the passing of an era. He had been a towering figure on the council for as long as anyone could remember and Captain of Kingshaven's Home Guard during the war. Tales of his bravery at Dunkirk and during the debacle with the E-boat, which got among the landing craft practising for D-Day, eclipsed any embarrassment he had caused in more recent speeches he had made as Mayor before people became fully aware of his failing health.

The *Chronicle* included a special illustrated spread entitled 'Memories of Makepeace', with a blurred picture of him as a young man presenting to Queen Victoria a small globe carved of stone from the quarry he later managed. There was also a more recent photograph of him at the ceremony held to recognize his lifetime's achievement, when the new Mayor had awarded him a silver replica of Kingshaven's clock tower, and Miss Kingshaven had presented him with a posy of forget-me-nots, which, people remembered with a sad chuckle, Mr Makepeace had tried his best to eat.

Liliana King, who had been friends with Mr Makepeace since her marriage, felt his loss profoundly. Mr Makepeace had been one of the last remaining bastions of the traditions her generation held to be important. He was the sort of man who downed a pint of ale with his workers once a year, and occupied any spare time with cricket and charitable acts. He wouldn't have dreamed of venturing further than Torquay for his annual holiday. His deeds exemplified all that was good about England: bravery, chivalry and pride in one's country; and his views, though they had become rather extreme in recent years, still chimed with many of the older residents, even after the full extent of his dementia had been recognised.

Mr Otterway, the editor of the *Chronicle*, also a long-time friend of Mr Makepeace, penned an editorial which summed up the man's influence. Kingshaven had been safe in his hands. Mr Makepeace's decline had coincided precisely with the decline in the town's fortunes. It was fitting that he should die so soon after his hero, and the man he in some ways resembled, Sir Winston Churchill. He and his like had galvanized the public to fight for their freedom, and it was scarcely believable that, after all their sacrifice, people had simply squandered the rewards on socialism, short skirts and holidays in sunny Spain. If it was unrealistic to think that Kingshaven could resist the white heat of revolution ushered in by the nasal Northern socialist who now led the country, with Mr Makepeace's death, a sense of decency, which had been stretched thinner and thinner like an elastic band around society, finally snapped into flaccid, useless fragments.

Liliana King considered the new generation of councillors a feeble, untrustworthy lot by comparison. They were property developers and estate agents, intent on making as much money for themselves as quickly as possible, unlike the quarriers and engineers of old who had built things to last.

The new Mayor, Mr Moor, was Captain of the Yacht Club and liked to sail to France for his holidays, whence he brought back wine and stinking cheeses, which filled his hobnobbing parties with a filthy aroma he clearly considered the height of sophistication.

Mr Makepeace had expressed the desire to be buried at sea (to lie, Liliana suspected, alongside the men he had been responsible for all those years ago), but even that simple request seemed to be beyond the council's powers of organization. The Labour government's regulations on things which had previously always taken care of themselves, from fishing to hygiene, got in the way of the most straightforward arrangements these days. After some debate, a compromise was agreed. The coffin would be towed for its final journey round the bay on the barge which had been used for decoy lights during the war. A funeral service at St Mary's would be followed by tea at the Palace. There would be a private cremation at Lowhampton. The precise resting place of Mr Makepeace's ashes would be a matter for his family alone, but it was understood that the authorities would turn a blind eye to any unauthorized disposal. Sir John Allsop, however, let it be known that permission to scatter on or from his land would be considered trespass, on which sour note, a number of councillors had been heard to remark that it was high time the rest of the older generation popped their clogs.

'Of course, they don't mean you, Mummy!' Libby interjected hurriedly after Eddie reported this titbit from the chamber, which irritated Liliana because she hadn't until then entertained the possibility that they might.

'I haven't quite outlived my usefulness, then?' she responded with heavy sarcasm.

'Far from it,' said Libby with a kindly smile.

Her daughter's generation seemed to have forgotten about the important things, Liliana thought. Libby was adamantly refusing to allow the hearse to come up the drive on its way from the Chapel of Rest. These days, the staff had better things to do, apparently, than line up and bow their heads as the coffin passed. There was no respect. Pearl had to be bribed even to turn up at the funeral. It was increasingly costly seeing Pearl these days. Her husband was so tolerant, so gullible, or perhaps such a rascal himself, that Liliana's usual trump card of disclosure no longer had the slightest effect.

Liliana was determined the Palace would give Mr Makepeace a proper send-off, even if she had to cut the sandwiches and make the sponge cake herself. The ladies would drink tea and the men would drink whisky, even if it stuck in Mr Moor's Francophile throat. There were some customs which were set in stone, Liliana had told Mr Pocock, who had remarked that it was rather an apt metaphor, given Mr Makepeace's former profession as a quarrier.

*

It was almost possible to believe you could find silence on a dull winter day in the park, when there was no one much around, no leaves on the trees for the wind to rustle, no sunshine to make the birds sing, and the temperature was so raw that small children walked stiffly in coats buttoned up to the hood, red faces too frozen to chatter.

Michael sat eating his sandwich in the deserted bandstand, looking over the still, black surface of the lake. Even with the air a blur of drizzle, the constant drone of London's noise went on: the background hum of traffic and construction and trains; the ever-present noise of a million lives being lived.

Sometimes Michael felt that if the sound would just stop for a moment, and if in that moment he was concentrating hard enough, he would be able to sense where Iris was, just as when they had played Hide and Seek together up on the South Cliffs. He had always closed his eyes tightly and counted loudly while she ran away to find her hiding place, but even though she was very good at keeping still, and able to wait much longer than most young children, he had known where she was immediately, and had to pretend to look in lots of other places before stumbling upon her.

There had been one exception. One long-ago summer afternoon, he had been lying in a sheltered dip in the ramparts of the Iron Age fort while Iris collected wild flowers, bringing each bruised little blossom back to show him and asking again and again, 'What's this one called, Daddy!'

Speedwell, Dandelion, Eggs and Bacon . . .

He must have dozed off in the soft sea sunshine.

When he opened his eyes she had disappeared.

'Iris!'

He jumped to his feet.

'Iris!'

He walked, then ran, up and down the ramparts to the centre of the fort for a better view.

'Iris!'

No reply. No sound except his breath panting and the distant crash of waves breaking.

'Iris! Where are you?'

The effort to keep his voice calm, not wanting to frighten her, suddenly breaking into panicky anger.

'Iris! It's not a game! Come out, now!'

Silence. And in the silence, his mind had gone into an over-drive of imaginings: perhaps a hole had opened up above the quarries and swallowed her, or she had fallen over the cliffs to her death, or a stranger had come and stolen her?

And after what seemed like a lifetime, but may have only been a fraction of a second, her tiny voice had called, 'Daddy!'

He had raced to it and found her with one spindly leg lodged in a rabbit burrow, and he had dropped to his knees and hugged her, shouting, 'Iris, don't EVER do that to me again!' as a bitter-sweet confusion of terror and gratitude coursed through his body.

And he had held her so tightly as he carried her home, so aware of her preciousness, so grateful for his luck, promising himself that he would never ever let such a lapse happen again.

Michael knew it was a kind of madness to search for her now without knowing where to look. However hard he tried to apply a logic to his mission, taking a London postcode each day, walk-ing each street, making enquiries at all the coffee bars and cheap places to eat, at the Labour Exchange and the library, logic told him that even if he found the right area, he could be within a few yards of her and she might walk down a parallel street, or even the very same street just seconds after him, and he would miss her.

He didn't even know if she was in London.

He didn't even know if she was alive.

And like that moment long ago on the South Cliffs, his mind created myriad stories to explain her absence.

The plots followed whatever direction his mood took him. On optimistic days, when he woke up, so rested that it was a moment before he remembered what had happened, he would find himself imagining that Iris had stowed away in Lowhampton on a liner to New York, or she had joined a circus . . . With few facts to include, the direction of the story relied heavily on the character of the protagonist. Iris would be excellent at pretending to be a poor orphan for the authorities on Ellis Island, or at charming a rich benefactor on board ship, but he couldn't see her as a high-wire artiste, or performing stunts bareback on a prancing horse.

More often, as he fidgeted in bed, unable to find the oblivion of sleep, his imaginings would be closer to the adult themes of thrillers than the adventure stories he had loved as a child. Iris was being held captive; Iris was on the streets; Iris had been brutally murdered.

Wandering the grimy treeless streets and faceless modern estates made him acutely aware of another London which co-existed alongside the comfortable circles he now moved in. There was a whole world of homeless people sleeping rough in the Embankment Gardens, whose bundled-up shapes he approached with trepidation, desperately wanting one of them to turn over on their bench and be Iris, and not wanting it almost as much.

The only certainty was the starting point of the story, when she had left Kingshaven on the back of a scooter, although even the witness to that was unreliable.

Michael had spent every weekend the previous summer in seaside resorts along the South Coast fraternizing with the gangs, showing them the most recent school photo of Iris, adding that she was wearing a white PVC mac. Some of them promised to look out for her, but nobody, even the ones who were proud to claim responsibility for the havoc wrought on Kingshaven, could remember her. He described Iris as tall and very thin with a mass of curly red hair (which was not obvious in the school photograph because it was in black and white and Iris's hair was tied back). Sometimes, if he judged his listener sympathetic, he added that she was quite a character. Very argumentative. You'd know her if you met her, he would say. And then he stopped saying that, because it felt disloyal. And he stopped mentioning the PVC mac, in case it became an integral part of the way people looked for her, and they would fail to report someone in a different colour coat.

Her identity was slipping away from him. It was difficult to hold on to all the facets of a person's character without their physical presence. When he tried to remember what it was like to be with her, he increasingly thought of the face in the black and white photo. In dreams, when his subconscious played the cruel trick of making him think he'd found her, it was the photograph's face staring at him in monochrome from the opposite seat in the tube, or walking towards him across Waterloo Bridge, or floating lifelessly past in a canal. And even in the landscape of the dream, the great flood of relief was tempered by doubt that it was really her.

Some days, his anger with her for doing this to him was so powerful it asphyxiated every other feeling inside him. Other days, he felt so guilty the only solution he could contemplate was suicide, but then his tortured mind would compose another story – that perhaps Iris had fallen off the motorbike and suffered a blow to the head, and was at this moment languishing in a hospital bed with amnesia. He imagined her sadness when she eventually remembered who she was, and when she discovered that she had inadvertently brought about his death. Because she did love him, he told himself over and over, even though she was justifiably angry with him. And he desperately hoped that she knew he loved her too, even though he had been stupid and selfish enough to think that she would understand him leaving her mother, and that it would not affect their relationship.

At Claudia's suggestion, Michael began to write down his stories about Iris, trying to imagine what she might be thinking in the situations he gave her to confront, but he became increasingly uncertain that it was possible to understand another person's consciousness, and he sometimes thought his attempts to write about her had nothing to do with her at all, and simply disguised his efforts to maintain his own sanity.

He'd never understood before that the expression 'put to rest' was as much about the survivors of a loss as the victim. Some days he felt so exhausted by the weight of not knowing what had happened that he simply wished they would find her body.

On one occasion the police contacted him to identify a corpse that fitted Iris's description. Michael braced himself, but nothing could prepare him for the deadness of the dead body and the shudder of sheer elation that it was not Iris. The woman, who had red hair, but little else in common with his daughter, had been murdered. There were ugly bruises on her neck. Michael had passed out, and the officer hadn't been able to conceal his disappointment when he came round and told him it was not Iris.

'You're quite sure, sir?' he'd asked, several times.

Did grief make people make mistakes?

As he walked away from the hospital where the body was, Michael had been tortured by uncertainty again, and almost inclined to go back and check.

Michael scrunched up the greaseproof paper Claudia had wrapped his sandwich in, unable to remember eating it, or what the filling had been. He had no appetite and ate only so that he could say he had when she asked. He opened his *A–Z*. He decided to try all the West End theatres again. If Iris was in London, it was the obvious place for her to head. He envisaged her hanging round stage doors, pestering the stage manager until it was less trouble to give her a job than keep turning her away. That was how she'd got round Archie Mills at the Pier Theatre, where she'd been an usherette for the last two Summer Extravaganzas even though she wasn't legally old enough to work.

There was a crowd gathered at the edge of the park under some large oak trees. They were staring up into the branches, looking for the eagle who had escaped a week before from London Zoo. Each day when Michael crossed the park, he could tell where Goldie was perched by the people underneath with binoculars, whose numbers grew each day, and were now accompanied by a BBC outside-broadcast unit and several press photographers.

Michael had developed a grudging admiration for the eagle who evaded the authorities and looked down on his followers with an imperious disdain. Why should he be trapped in an aviary? Why should he not fly free? He wondered why it was that a single bird had captured the public imagination. Was it possible that people trapped in their material world identified with the eagle and his determination to return to nature?

It crossed Michael's mind that Iris might have seen Goldie on the television news. He imagined her shouting at the zookeepers with their nets, 'Why can't you leave him alone!'

He could hear the exact timbre of her voice as she used to shout at her mother, 'Leave me alone!'

The thuds as she stamped upstairs.

Sylvia shouting after her, 'Don't you dare speak to me like that!'

And he remembered standing outside Iris's locked bedroom door, speaking through the keyhole. 'We just don't want you to come to any harm, that's all.'

And her saying, 'Why can't you just trust me? I'm not a child any more.'

And Michael wondered suddenly if this was what Iris was trying to tell him now and he hadn't heard because there was so much other noise.

In a sudden moment of clarity, the anxiety ebbed away from his head.

And then an image of her grey body lying in some unmarked moorland grave barged into his thoughts, and the cacophony of fear returned.

Jennifer Allsop had always looked good in black and her figure was back to its pre-pregnancy size. Standing in front of her dressing-table mirror, she held a pair of earrings to her ears, wondering if she dared. They were large cultured pearls, surrounded by a circle of tiny sparklers – not real diamonds, of course, though you would never have known, and they gave her face a real lift under the black hat. To hell with it! Jennifer clipped them to her lobes. It wasn't as if Mr Makepeace's death was exactly a tragedy. In his heyday, she was sure he would have appreciated a woman making an effort to look her best for him. She had to keep reminding herself that it was a funeral she was going to. It still felt like such a treat to go out without even having to think about the children.

With hindsight, Jennifer kicked herself that she hadn't asked Libby King to be godmother much earlier (Jolly had insisted on waiting for a boy), because Libby took her responsibilities towards James very seriously (unlike Pearl, who even had to be reminded of Jackie's birthday), including granting free access to Moira, the Scottish au pair she'd employed to look after her own sons, Adrian and Edwin (whom the Kings insisted on calling Winny, poor thing, instead of Little Eddie, which was surely the obvious diminutive). Moira was so capable she didn't seem to mind if Julia tagged along with Jamie too, and Julia and Adrian had grown inseparable.

The odd thing was that with Moira taking charge of all the things Jennifer was not very good at, like baking biscuits with faces on and sewing dresses for dolls, Jennifer found she could be the mother she wanted to be. She enjoyed the satisfying sense of peace as she smoothed the older girls' hair on their pillows as they slept. She no longer resented time spent listening to Julia's rambling make-believe, or playing 'This Little Piggy' on Jamie's chubby toes. She had even come to enjoy the look of amazement when she told people she had four children (though, occasionally, she choked on the number, feeling it was disloyal not to say five, but not wanting to have to explain and embarrass everyone).

Jolly was less demanding than he had been since their wedding day. He had even remarked recently that it was lucky the first three were girls because it didn't matter so much that they couldn't at present afford to send them to boarding school. Best of all, he had agreed to her mother's proposal to lend them the money for a proper house now that she was selling up the shop, since it didn't look as if Sir John was ever going to die.

The worst was over, Jennifer thought, smiling at herself in the mirror, and she had just about managed to hang on to her looks and her sanity. She was about to apply a slick of Scarlet Passion to her lips when she remembered the reason for her day out, and chose the more muted beige of Champagne instead.

If she walked quickly, there would just be time to call in at the estate agent on her way to church to see if anything new had come on to the market.

Sylvia looked up as Jennifer Farmer walked past her door and ran to catch her, but Jennifer had already gone into Spivey and Co., and Sylvia could see her flirting with the estate agent through the gaps between advertisements for houses in his window. Then Mr Spivey came outside and opened the door to his Zodiac, and they drove off together, so absorbed in their mission they didn't even notice Sylvia standing there. She hoped that this time they were going to view a house that would take Jennifer's fancy, because she seemed to be spending an awful lot of time seeing ones she didn't like. If it wasn't resolved soon, Sylvia would have to pull out of buying Mrs Farmer's shop and look for alternative premises, which she didn't want to do because Farmer's would suit her down to the ground.

Sylvia's plan was to move the retail side of the business down to Farmer's and keep the mail-order side in the little premises she now occupied. The mail-order business had been an inspired idea of Audrey Potter's, but neither of them had predicted the deluge of orders one little advert in the *Lowhampton Echo* would bring in. It was a simple sketch of a shift dress with a contrasting border at the hem and a matching kerchief, but the price was carefully calculated (enough to make a profit, Sylvia had decided, but not enough for the customer to think it worth the bother of making it themselves) and the orders had kept on rolling in throughout the summer. She'd had to buy in bales of the two fabrics, and it was quite handy to have Iris's old room to store them in, since it didn't look like her daughter was ever coming back. The rest of her house had become a sweatshop. She'd had to buy three new machines and train some local girls up to use them. Audrey Potter's front room had become a packaging depot. Even though Sylvia had given her a good share, there was more than enough money left after expenses to impress the bank manager with the future business plan she'd drawn up with a bit of help from Mr Spivey.

The idea was that Sylvia would move into Mrs Farmer's flat with Anthony and refurbish the shop from top to bottom, changing the layout and décor. The storerooms would be converted to sewing rooms and the basement to packing and storage. If things went well, she saw herself eventually taking over the café next door, which had never found the right proprietor since the early days of the Coffee Bean, and her customers would be able to combine the pleasures of shopping and chatting over coffee, a kind of up-to-date version of those long-ago afternoons Sylvia and her mother had spent together in Etherington's Stapely and Penney.

'Sad news, I'm afraid.' Anthony's voice brought her back to the present.

'I thought you were down at the harbour?' Sylvia said. The schoolchildren were supposed to be making a guard of honour down the slipway for Mr Makepeace's coffin.

'It sank,' said Anthony. 'What's for dinner?'

Sylvia had forgotten that the school dinner ladies had been given the day off for the funeral. The whole of Kingshaven had stopped for the day. Most of the shop windows had black ribbons. Sylvia had gone one better and dressed her mannequin entirely in black from the bar shoes to the necklace made of imitation jet.

'The coffin sank?' she clarified. At least Mr Makepeace got his final wish!

'Not the coffin, the barge,' Anthony said, exasperated, as if she must be the only person in the world who hadn't heard.

'What's happened to the coffin?' Sylvia asked.

'Mr King's trying to lasso it from the *Brittany Anna*, but the tide's against him and it's a bit choppy out there.'

'It floats? Well, for heaven's sake! I'd have thought with the size of him, he'd sink like a stone,' said Sylvia.

'Do you want to come and see? Everyone else is!' Anthony grabbed her hand.

'Not everyone else has a business to look after,' Sylvia reminded him, retreating back into the shop.

'But nobody's shopping,' said Anthony, looking at the deserted street.

'I've got to stay here,' Sylvia told him, smoothing his lovely blond hair which had been ruffled by the wind. 'Tell you what, why don't you report back? And get yourself some sweets,' she added, ringing up a No Sale on the till and handing him a sixpence.

'I've got something a bit special for you today.' The estate agent turned his head to give Jennifer one of those smiles that made her feel as if her insides had turned to liquid and she was going to wet herself.

She loved the times they spent together. It felt almost illicit going into other people's houses when they weren't there, sitting on their furniture, touching their ornaments.

'Intriguing,' she said.

'I'm not showing this to any of my other clients,' said Mr Spivey, turning off the road on to a lane she must have passed many times but had never been down before.

The car bumped along for a couple of hundred yards and then drew to a halt.

'What do you think of that?' he asked.

'The field?' Jennifer asked, craning her neck to see over the hedge.

'The view!' he said.

The sky was piled high with bulging clouds, but there was thin sunshine which made the sea look like rippled pewter.

'Looks like a storm's coming,' she ventured, not knowing quite what he wanted her to say.

'You seaside folk!' he said, turning back to her with a wide grin. 'Don't know when you're born, you lot! Londoners would pay a mint for that view!'

Jennifer nodded.

'When you're buying a house,' the estate agent explained, 'you're looking for a place to live, right?'

Another nod.

'And what else?'

Jennifer was completely unable to think of an answer.

It was the structure of his face, those cheekbones, that chiselled chin, lines as clean as a square-jawed hero in a strip cartoon . . .

'An investment,' he prompted her.

'Oh, yes, of course,' she said.

'Those earrings suit you,' he said, putting his forefinger under her chin and tilting her face to the light for a better look. 'Have you got time for a quick one?'

Their place – Jennifer felt she could think of it as 'theirs' now that they had come here a second time – was a dingy 1930s pub called the Stop Inn, out on the main road north, a convenient roadside resting place for lorry drivers on their way up from Cornwall. In the large, unmade car park, Jennifer could imagine criminals having clandestine rendezvous, and dodgy deals being transacted below dashboards.

The musty bar, with its dartboard and fruit machine, was the kind of place that Jennifer would not normally have been seen dead in, but it was the very seediness which excited her.

'So what do you want your investment to do?' Mr Spivey asked, putting her sherry down on the table in front of her.

'Grow bigger?' she guessed, glancing involuntarily at his besuited crotch, right at the level of her face.

He drew up a stool and sat down opposite her with a glass of beer.

'Correct,' he said. 'You want an investment that's going to appreciate, don't you? And what's the only kind of house that will appreciate in this economic climate?'

'I've really no idea,' she confessed.

'Lucky you've got me to offer you this exclusive opportunity, isn't it?' He drank his half-pint down in two gulps, then looked at his watch. 'But you've got to go to a funeral, and I've got to get back to the office. Phone never stops ringing at the moment.'

Jennifer's spirits plummeted.

'Opportunity?' she asked.

'Next time, I'll show you the plans, if you're genuinely interested . . .'

Her heart leaped at the suggestion of another meeting. Normally she was the one who initiated the viewings, but she had turned down so many properties, she had been beginning to wonder whether he was losing patience. And her mother said she couldn't hang on much longer.

'I'm definitely interested, Mr Spivey,' she said.

'Alan, please. The advantage of a new build is that you have a hand in the specification,' he explained as they got back into the car and he put his key in the ignition.

'But I don't really know anything about specifications,' Jennifer said anxiously.

'Which is why I'm here to hold your hand,' he said, smiling at her.

All her attention zoomed to her right hand, which was lying on her lap pulsing with the desire to be taken by his hand and placed on his trousers just to the right of the fly buttons. He'd done it once before, and she'd felt his hardness straining against the fabric, and then she'd taken her hand away, and he'd changed gears so nonchalantly she wondered whether she'd just imagined what he'd done.

'. . . and you don't have to put all the money up front,' he was saying. 'A ten per cent deposit is all it takes nowadays to secure your dream home. How does that sound?'

Jennifer was struggling to choose a suitably enthusiastic word when there was a sudden loud explosion in the sky.

'What the hell was that?' he said, slamming on the brakes.

'You Londoners,' Jennifer echoed his earlier taunt. 'Don't know anything, do you?'

Sylvia Quinn was out of her shop as soon as they drew up, almost as if she'd been waiting for them.

'Sylvia!' said Mr Spivey.

When had she become Sylvia rather than Mrs Quinn? Jennifer wanted to know.

'Hello, Alan,' said Sylvia.

The boyishness of Sylvia's geometric haircut made her face more sweet and feminine than ever, and the long mascaraed lashes accentuated the blue of her eyes.

Not for the first time, Jennifer wondered whether she should have her own hair cut like that.

Jolly couldn't abide short hair – 'How could she?' he'd cried when her mother had reported the news that Mrs Quinn had taken herself off to Vidal Sassoon in London – but Alan Spivey clearly didn't mind.

'Are you going to the church?' Sylvia asked Jennifer.

'Of course,' Jennifer responded curtly.

'Well, there's been a delay.'

'A delay?' Jennifer repeated imperiously. She didn't quite like the fact that Sylvia was more au fait with arrangements than she was.

'They've had to send the lifeboat out—'

'We heard the flare go up,' said Jennifer.

'For the coffin,' Sylvia explained. 'Why don't you come in and wait with me?'

'I'll leave you two ladies to it, shall I?' said Mr Spivey, slipping back into his office.

'He's ever such a nice chap, isn't he?' said Sylvia, holding the door open for Jennifer.

Jennifer bristled. Had Alan taken Sylvia to the Stop Inn? Had he put her hand on his you-know-what? Had he given her ear-rings? She fingered her right earlobe.

'Nice,' said Sylvia, her attention drawn. 'It's amazing how realistic they can make paste these days, isn't it?'

'And now,' said the presenter on the radio, which was always on in Sylvia's shop, 'The Kinks are "Tired of Waiting".'

'It's funny, isn't it,' said Sylvia, 'how some songs just sum up just what you're feeling?'

'I don't really follow pop music,' Jennifer informed her loftily.

Sylvia was wearing black, but the shortness of her straight shift with its boat neckline made Jennifer's outfit suddenly feel dowdy.

'Did you see anything you liked?' Sylvia enquired.

Was it the boy's haircut, or was it simply a bit of money which had given Sylvia confidence? Jennifer wondered. She used to be so eager to please, so easy to put down. Most people would have folded after what had happened to her, but Sylvia had risen phoenix-like from the ashes of her ruined life and taken everyone by surprise. The girl who would have been glad to sweep the floor Jennifer walked on – and, in fact, often had, when she was looking after the shop for her mother – was now a businesswoman in her own right whom she had to keep sweet, and Jennifer couldn't quite work out how it had happened.

Jennifer was half inclined to tell Sylvia to mind her own business, but she was in the ghastly position of being dependent on her, since Sylvia was also the only person who had shown the slightest interest in buying her mother's shop.

'There is something I'm interested in,' Jennifer said carefully.

'I don't want to hurry you,' Sylvia said.

In Jennifer's limited experience, business negotiations often demanded that people say exactly the opposite of what they meant.

'But I'd hate to have to let anyone down by pulling out—' Sylvia went on.

Jennifer's mind was still a little bit muzzy from the hastily gulped sherry. She tried to pay attention and look uninterested at the same time, and then, belatedly, realized what Sylvia was getting at.

'No!' she interrupted. 'No, you mustn't! Alan has the solution. I haven't had a chance to speak to Mummy yet, but she'll agree, I'm sure . . .'

'I'll speak to Mr Lye, then, shall I? Set a timetable for exchange and completion?' said Sylvia.

'Certainly,' said Jennifer, regaining her composure and trying to look as if the whole subject was beneath her.

Both women looked towards the door as the bell pinged.

'They've caught it in a trawler net,' Anthony announced. 'And they're reeling it in now.'

Pearl found it slightly strange being back in St Mary's Church, seeing everyone again, and everyone seeing her and her hand-some husband, who did look nice in a proper suit. She regretted not bringing her children down so that everyone could have a good gawp at them too. One of each and both very attractive, especially in comparison to Libby's offspring, which was probably why her sister had insisted that funerals were not suitable places for children.

There were more white heads than grey now amongst her mother's generation, Pearl observed. Among her own con-temporaries, the demands of current fashion were unforgiving for tummies and bottoms which had never completely recovered from the disfigurement of pregnancy. Pearl was gratified to see that she was not the only one smoothing down the creases across the thigh area when she stood up.

The same people still occupied the same pews, but in just five years, children had become adults and babies had become school-children who were sitting together in the choir. She recognized the two oldest Allsop girls only because they'd both inherited their mother's hair. Mr Turlow, who had always looked exactly the same age, sat at the end of one of the rows, and behind him the young teacher who used to have a quiff and play in a skiffle band. He now sported a Beatles mop and winked at Pearl as her gaze fell on him. Cheeky!

As the congregation rose to sing Mr Makepeace's favourite hymn, Pearl glanced back to see who was behind. Mrs Farmer sobbed ostentatiously as the coffin entered the church. Next to her sat Jolly and Jennifer, and behind them, ranks of shopkeepers and landladies.

A couple of the lifeboat crew, still in their oilskins, lent a hand as the undertaker's men staggered under the weight of the coffin.

A slim woman with pale blond hair cut in a sleek modern style slipped into the church behind the pallbearers, nipped down the aisle to the vacant space beside Audrey Potter and fumbled about with the hymn book looking for the correct page. When she looked up, she did not return Pearl's smile, and when Pearl turned to the front of the church again, she had the oddest feeling that Sylvia Quinn's eyes were still fixed on the back of her head.

' "O hear us when we cry to thee, For those in peril on the sea." '

The final, resounding chord reverberated long into the silence.

'Please be seated,' said the Reverend lugubriously from the pulpit.

His over-long address was punctuated by the irregular dripping of water from the catafalque on to the stone floor.

The waterfront spectacle had actually been quite fun, in a ghastly sort of way, Pearl thought, a bit like Regatta Week, with everyone willing on the boats and a cheer going up when the coffin was finally landed. Pearl tried to suppress the urge to giggle which often overcame her in church, mindful of her mother's presence beside her. She concentrated on the coffin, forcing herself to think of the huge dead body inside. Would the sodden casket present a problem for the crematorium? Presumably it could not extinguish the furnace flame, but would it smoke like an open fire when the coal was damp?

Liliana issued a look capable of stopping an arrow in flight as the irresistible spurt of laughter escaped Pearl's lips.

Pearl had never seen her mother more affected by a death. Normally, Liliana specialized in dignified composure. Even when her father died, Pearl couldn't remember tears. Perhaps there had been more to her mother's relationship with Mr Makepeace? It was always difficult to imagine the older generation at it – although Pearl had a distinct memory of investigating a noise in the shuttered-up Windsor Suite during the war, and stopping long enough to see a man's bare bottom, a bottom considerably more pert and youthful than her father's, or, for that matter, Mr Makepeace's, rising and falling over her mother's elegant, bestockinged legs.

The address finally over, it was Libby's turn to address the congregation. Mr Makepeace, she said, had been like a father to her after her own father had died. That was a bit rich, Pearl thought, when the truth was that Libby had invited Mr Makepeace to the Palace once a year for a meal she called the Duty Dinner. He would sit for hours like a great cigar-smoking toad at the end of the table.

The schoolchildren were beginning to fidget. One of the older boys caught Pearl's eye and stared at her. He had pale blond hair and blue eyes which sent a shiver of recognition through her, which her mother, still alarmingly good at reading Pearl's thoughts, seemed to sense.

In answer to Pearl's unspoken question, Liliana mouthed the word, 'Gone.'

Gone?

Where?

Deep inside Pearl, an ember of desire caught in an unexpected draught of hope and flamed again.

' "Dear Lord and Father of Mankind, Forgive our foolish ways . . ." '

Michael's son had the voice of a choirboy which soared above the other children's bored, flat notes. Pearl thought his piety must have come from his mother.

Gone?

Where could Michael have gone?

Pearl had assumed he would never leave Sylvia. For all his revolutionary ideas, essentially he was a typical man. A coward.

If she'd known he was capable of leaving, things might have been very different.

Where was he? Lowhampton? The idea that they had shared the same city, walked the same streets, shopped in the same shops was simply too much to bear.

Finally the Reverend gave the blessing and, to a brisk rendition of 'Fight the Good Fight', the coffin was carried out of the church.

Everyone began to gather up their handbags and gloves.

'Where is he?' Pearl whispered to her sister as soon as they got to the porch of the church.

'Who?' Libby asked.

'You know,' Pearl hissed in exasperation. 'The teacher . . .'

'Mr Turlow?' Libby asked distractedly.

'Mr Quinn!'

'Oh, him. I think he's gone to London.'

It was too windy to put up an umbrella. They ran towards the car, the wind making their faces wet.

'Because of me?' Pearl asked as they stood waiting for Eddie to bring the car round.

Her sister stared at her, perplexed.

Did Libby really not know? Pearl wondered. For a hotelier, a good proportion of whose business came from providing a discreet location for extra-marital sex, and for someone married to Eddie – for heaven's sake! – Libby was either naïve to the point of blindness, or simply chose not to see. Pearl was never sure which.

'He took up with some local girl, I believe,' Libby informed her.

Pearl's flame guttered and died.

They stepped back from the kerb to avoid getting spashed as Eddie's car pulled up. Tom was already sitting in the back, Liliana in the front. Her mother wound down the window.

'If you two don't get a move on, we'll be the last people to arrive at the tea,' she said.

Libby got in and held the door for Pearl against the wind.

'Actually,' said Pearl, holding on to her hat. 'I think I'll walk. I could do with a bit of air.'

Claudia's best friend, Josie, one of the few university friends who had stayed loyal to Claudia rather than Tim, often popped in on her way home from work.

'Where's Michael this evening?' she asked, taking a mug of coffee from the tray Claudia was offering her and lying back in the dilapidated sofa.

'Out,' said Claudia, sitting down on the floor and cupping the other mug of coffee in her hands.

It was cold in the little house. She plugged in the electric-bar fire. It filled the room with a smell of scorched dust, but barely made any difference to the temperature unless you were sitting right next to it.

'Out where?' Josie asked.

Josie had always had an ear for the unspoken, which was why she was a good journalist. She was now working for the *Sunday Times*.

Claudia sighed. 'He spends a lot of time looking for Iris,' she admitted, knowing almost before she had said it that Josie would have a theory about this. Josie was a great believer in analysis. Claudia half wished she had just told her that he was at the cinema. 'I don't think he knows what else to do.'

'He won't find her,' said Josie decisively. 'She obviously doesn't want to be found.'

'Assuming that she has any choice in the matter,' said Claudia.

'Is there any reason to think she might have been abducted?' Josie asked.

'Well, she was last seen on the back of a motorbike with a gang of boys . . .'

'What pubescent girl wouldn't want to be on the back of a motorbike with a boy!'

'She might be dead,' Claudia stated.

'Wouldn't they have found a body by now?' Josie argued.

'Well, what should he do, then?' Claudia asked, suddenly irritated by Josie's pronouncements, when she knew so very little of the situation.

'He's clearly searching for something, but I very much doubt it's his daughter,' Josie suggested. 'I could recommend someone.' She'd recently done a big feature for the paper about London's fashionable psychiatrists.

'But that's absurd,' Claudia argued. 'Whatever difficulties Michael may have, it is a fact that Iris is missing and he wouldn't be searching for her if she weren't . . .'

'Why are you so resistant to the idea of analysis?' Josie asked her.

'I'm not!' Claudia protested. 'I just don't think it's the answer to everything.'

'From where I'm sitting, it looks like Iris is doing exactly what she wanted to do,' said Josie.

'Which is?' Claudia felt exhausted by the relentlessness of Josie's diagnosis. If she ever ventured to contradict anything Josie said, her friend accused her of being in denial. When Claudia had once joked that she couldn't win, Josie had replied, 'Why do you think winning is so important to you?'

'What Iris wants to do is drive a wedge between you and Michael,' Josie said.

There was always an element of truth in Josie's observations, which gave them a kind of persuasiveness that was difficult to resist unless you were feeling very confident. It wasn't exactly true that Iris had driven a wedge between them, Claudia thought, more that she seemed to be there the whole time. Her absence felt much more like a presence. It dwarfed everything else. She and Michael no longer talked about issues or what was going on in the world. If they were to go on the Aldermaston March this year, she knew that Michael's principal interest would be in searching the crowds for Iris, just as he examined the blurred background of every photograph of every demonstration that appeared in the paper.

The previous October, when Harold Wilson had stood victorious on the doorstep of 10 Downing Street, a huge moment for any socialist, Michael had been so absorbed in scanning the mass of people the television cameras showed cheering the new Prime Minister in, he had not even listened to Wilson's words.

'I saw your divorce in the *Telegraph*,' Josie said.

'A bit cheap, I thought,' said Claudia.

The diary column had reported the news that Michael had been cited as co-respondent, under the headline 'Author of The Right Thing does The Wrong Thing'. Apparently, Tim was already engaged to his researcher.

'Is Michael divorced yet?' Josie wanted to know.

'Not yet,' said Claudia guardedly, knowing her friend was not above passing on information to her own colleagues.

Sylvia had declined to divorce Michael, and since Iris had disappeared, Michael hadn't felt able to press her. Claudia told herself it didn't matter. Neither of them believed in marriage, as they had both shown.

'Why don't you come round for supper soon?' said Josie, finishing her coffee. Since her return to England, she had bought a big house in Highgate where she rented out rooms. 'Just turn up with a bottle of plonk. We eat at eight. You're always welcome,' she told her.

'We'll try,' said Claudia, returning her friend's warm hug.

Claudia was curious to see what Josie's experiment in communal living was like, but she knew she would not persuade Michael to go. The only time the two of them had met, they had all gone for a meal together in a vegetarian restaurant. Claudia was inclined to vegetarianism herself and anyway more interested in talking than in the food, but Josie's loud American certainty had inspired contrariness and carnivorism in Michael. He had spent the evening pushing butter beans round his plate in a sulk, despite the fact that he'd eaten in the same restaurant quite happily on many occasions.

'He's extremely good-looking, but how do you put up with him?' Josie had asked when he went to the toilet.

Amusingly, when Claudia and Michael were walking home afterwards, he had said more or less the same thing about Josie.

The room was dark when Claudia went back inside, apart from the red glow of the bar fire, but she did not turn on the light, preferring to sit in the darkness alone and try to regroup her thoughts.

Was Michael's constant search for his daughter a form of denial, as Josie had implied? Was Iris really so manipulative and cruel that she had deliberately brought this despair on her father, or was she just an unhappy teenager who had run away? Would there ever be a resolution, or would they stay for ever in this limbo if Iris did not turn up?

And at what point would it become unbearable?

Claudia almost wished Josie would come back and they could talk it all through again, because at least if you were talking about things they did not magnify and loom like terrible shadows.

It occurred to her that she might be feeling gloomy because of the arrival of her period this morning, which often seemed to make her mood dip. She had allowed herself to hope after not having a period for three months that she might be pregnant, but it appeared she was not.

The disappointment was of a completely different quality from that she had experienced in the first months of her marriage to Tim. Then, whenever she had felt the familiar sensation of blood leaking, there had been a certain frustration. As time went on, the frustration had become a sense of failure. The day she had greeted the blood with relief instead of disappointment was the day she had realized that her marriage was over.

It was only when she and Michael had made love for the first time that she had really understood what it was to love someone so much you wanted to conceive another person with them, and she had been almost surprised that the perfect fusion of their bodies had not produced a baby instantly.

Claudia wondered if it was because of Iris's disappearance that she felt ever more desperate to have a child. Was she sub-consciously trying to give Michael another child, perhaps, or even just get his attention back? Josie would be sure to have a theory about that, but she didn't think she'd discuss it with her. Or was it a purely physical yearning, as she grew ever closer to thirty: the demands of biology overwhelming her sense of perspective?

'And your solicitor?' Mr Lye was saying to Sylvia. 'You'll be using Mr Humble, I assume.'

'Surely there'd be a conflict of interest, what with him being Mrs Farmer's solicitor?'

The estate agent looked over the top of his half-rim spectacles. 'I can assure you, my dear, that in my not inconsiderable experience, Mr Humble has never proved himself anything less than professional.'

Sylvia took a moment to sort out all the negatives.

'I'm sure I've no reason to doubt it,' she replied. 'Nevertheless, I've decided to instruct Mrs Tyler.'

The Tylers were new to Kingshaven. The husband was some-thing to do with oil tankers in Lowhampton; the wife, a solicitor, had taken an office above the greengrocer's. The general consensus among the landladies and shopkeepers of Kingshaven was that it would be foolish to trust a woman with their business, but Sylvia thought it was about time the men got a bit of a shake-up. She'd been surprised at how little mystery there was to business if you had a good idea and were prepared to work hard. She'd begun to suspect that the private members' clubs and guilds were just an excuse for men to have a drink together and look as if they were doing something.

'She's fully qualified,' she informed Mr Lye.

'As you wish,' the old estate agent sighed.

So that was settled. Sylvia walked out of Mr Lye's office. In less than a month, Sylvia's Boutique would become Sylvia's of Kingshaven. Perhaps one day there might even be a Sylvia's of Lowhampton, or even – in her wildest dreams she dared to envisage the label in her clothes with a little woven Union Jack beside the words – Sylvia Quinn, London. She'd have a very plain script, black on white. The Secret of Sixties style is Simplicity, Sylvia had read in the paper. The words had such a nice look about them, she immediately imagined a future advert for her own line, swapping the word 'Sixties' for 'Sylvia's'.

If she felt a little twinge of sympathy for Mrs Farmer, as she walked back up the hill past her drab, old-fashioned window, it soon disappeared when Sylvia reminded herself about her betrayal. People she'd respected and trusted had known and looked on and done nothing. Perhaps they'd even enjoyed her humiliation.

But they didn't know everything, did they? Sylvia thought with a little skip inside, because if you'd have told her at the beginning of the decade that she'd have her own clothes label and her own retail outlet (soon to be two), she wouldn't have believed it herself.

Mrs Farmer and all that generation had had their day.

Times were definitely a-changing, just like that whiny American kept singing.

A dumpy figure dressed in black was peering into the window of Sylvia's Boutique. The huffy rise and fall of the woman's shoulders was enough to identify her even at this distance. Perched on her head at a jaunty angle was a cap with a crown almost as tall as a chef's hat, made of shiny black plastic. Pearl King had always been sensitive about her height.

Sylvia took a deep breath, drew herself up from the waist and thanked God that she had decided to wear her black patent heels even though it wasn't the weather for them.

'Pearl! I hardly recognized you!' she said.

Pearl spun round. 'Sylvia!' she said, as if Sylvia were the last person she had expected to see. 'Looking very à la mode!'

Sylvia took out her keys and summoned up all her reserves to prevent her hands shaking as she opened up.

'Love the hair,' said Pearl, touching her hat as if she expected a comment in return.

'I fancied something new,' said Sylvia.

Pearl followed her in without invitation and watched as Sylvia removed her gloves.

'I've just heard about your husband,' Pearl said, adding with false-sounding sincerity, 'I'm so sorry.'

'Are you?' said Sylvia, too quickly.

It was a moment she'd been practising for, but she'd never imagined it quite like this, she and Pearl alone together, on her territory. There was nothing Pearl could do to hurt her now, but Sylvia still felt as nervous as if she were sitting an exam. Take your time! Her heart was palpitating and when she spoke she couldn't seem to hear her own voice.

'It's really for the best,' she began, looking directly at Pearl, wondering whether she dared. She had never managed to say the perfect sentence convincingly even when she was speaking to her own reflection in the mirror.

Pearl raised her eyebrows.

'I was getting a bit sick of him hopping into bed with every little tart who threw herself at him,' Sylvia said.

The words came out a little too quickly, but Pearl visibly recoiled.

'Were you looking for something in particular?' Sylvia asked, after a suitably uncomfortable pause, as Pearl flipped through the hangers of clothes. 'We don't really cater for the fuller figure, but you might just about get into one of the large sizes.'

'Actually, I don't really see anything I like,' Pearl countered quickly.

'No,' Sylvia concurred. 'I'm designing more for the younger generation these days.'

Revenge is a dish best eaten cold, so the saying went, but as Sylvia watched Pearl strutting off down the street, she didn't know if that was quite right. She thought revenge was more like a cup of strong coffee. It picked you up for a minute or two, made you feel on top of the world, but quite soon afterwards, you felt just the same as before, maybe even slightly let down, and with a bit of an acid tummy. Sometimes she wondered whether the desire for retribution was turning her into a horrible person, but, as her mother had always told her, nobody ever got anywhere by being nice.

Chapter Fourteen

September 1966

The qualities of Sir John Allsop which made the citizens of Kingshaven view him with suspicion – the liberal-mindedness which had driven him to adopt Winston and vouch for a German-speaking refugee during the war; his philanthropy in allowing prime building land to become a scout camp; his recent support for a naturist colony (before Liliana King got wind of it and orchestrated such a fierce opposition in the pages of the *Chronicle* that the naturists took flight before it got past the planning stage); and his general lack of interest in money and possessions – were exactly the things which endeared him to Claudia.

During her childhood, he had been like a benign distant relation, who occasionally gave her enthusiasms the benefit of his particular focus. Sometimes he would be visiting her father when she arrived home from school, and once, when she had shown him a painting she had brought home, he had appeared the next day at the gatehouse all covered in cobwebs, carrying a walnut box thick with dust. Inside, there was a set of watercolours, dry and crevassed with age, and fine brushes with brown wooden handles as smooth and glossy as just-opened conkers.

On another occasion, she had mentioned how much she liked reading Greek myths, and he had rifled through his cabinets for a little shard of red-on-black Attic pottery showing a boy's face and the top of a lyre, one of the souvenirs brought back from his

Grand Tour by his ancestor Benjamin Allsop. The sensation of holding something in her hands which had been moulded and painted by the hands of an artist over two and a half thousand years before had been one of the most memorable of Claudia's childhood.

But now, when she picked up the phone to hear his distinctive voice barking her name, she was subsumed by foreboding. Sir John came from the generation who believed that the telephone was for use only in emergencies.

'Your father . . . not well at all. Won't see a doctor. Thought you might talk some sense into him.'

'I'll come down,' Claudia said, and then realized that she was speaking to a dead line. Sir John, having delivered his message, had hung up.

Michael was in the bathroom swearing at himself in the mirror, trying to tie a black bow tie.

'Here, let me help you,' Claudia offered, placing her hands on the shoulders of his dinner jacket and turning him gently round to face her. The smooth black jacket and the gleaming white shirt of the hired dress suit, and the sharp points of the collar jutting towards his chin, threw a harsh light on to his face, accentuating the lines which anxiety had etched, but making him look even more handsome than he did in the heathery Harris tweed jacket with leather patches at the elbow that he usually wore. She felt a moment of pure molten desire for him all spruced up and smart.

'Who was that?' Michael asked her as she patiently tied the black tie.

'Sir John Allsop. My father's quite ill.'

'Do you want to go down now?' Michael asked, concerned.

'No. I'll go tomorrow.'

She knew that she couldn't let Michael down at this moment, and the relief on his face made him look suddenly vulnerable in his finery.

'I'll come with you, if you like,' he offered.

She knew how difficult that would be for him, and she was on the point of declining. And then she thought that perhaps it would be a good thing to allow him to support her when she needed help, as she had supported him.

'I'd like that,' she said.

On the way to the tube, people looked at them, all dressed up to the nines in the middle of the morning. Claudia was wearing a bright yellow crêpe shift with a high round neckline and cut-away shoulders, which Josie had insisted suited her, but made her feel very exposed.

'I feel like bloody James Bond,' Michael said as the lift at Hampstead station dropped slowly down into the underground cavern of the tube. He looked at her as if noticing her outfit for the first time, and said, 'You look lovely.'

'I've never been to the Savoy before, have you?' Claudia said in the rush of warm air that preceded the train as it shot out of the tunnel into the station.

'No,' he replied as they got in and sat down.

The double fear of the tube and the impending awards ceremony had rendered him practically catatonic.

Publishing events were always a bit of a trial. Michael tended to get very nervous and drink too quickly. Either he made no attempt to mingle at all, or he said the wrong thing loudly. It wasn't that he was deliberately rude, just that he didn't know the rules of the literary establishment. Literary London was a peculiar kind of village with a consensus of values just like any other village had. You were marked if you didn't fall in with the latest thing the clique of opinion-formers agreed upon. Most of them had been to Oxford or Cambridge, and whilst they might be inclined to admire the writing of a working-class man, his inability to perform sherry-party small talk made them snigger about him behind his back, and left Claudia dying inside.

Most of the invitations Michael ignored, but he was virtually obliged to attend the Annual Awards Lunch at the Savoy, since his second novel, *Hide and Seek*, published earlier in the year, had been shortlisted for the British Booksellers' Award. Even though Michael refused to entertain the possibility that he would win the prize, Claudia had made him write an acceptance speech just in case, and practise the faces he would make on hearing the news that he had won, or that he had lost. The knowledge that the Award was going to be filmed for her former husband's late-night review programme had magnified her pre-lunch nerves.

'Well, well, well, Michael and Claudia!'

They jumped apart guiltily at the instantly recognizable voice of Roman Stone. He and a woman who was not Pippa were approaching, and Claudia's former mother-in-law, wearing a mint-green floaty dress, was deep in conversation with a man just behind. It was inevitable, since they were sitting at the same table, they would have to talk at some point during the ceremony, but Claudia did not feel ready for the encounter.

'Claudia!' Pippa rushed forward and kissed her on both cheeks.

Her mother-in-law was too civilized to be publically rude, but the over-enthusiasm of the greeting was almost worse.

Roman turned to his companion. 'Martha, this is Michael Quinn.'

'Oh my God! I'm so pleased to meet you! *Hide and Seek* is absolutely my favourite on the shortlist.' The woman was American. She laughed at her own enthusiasm, and held out her hand to Michael who shook it, but said nothing.

'Martha Lacock,' said Roman. 'She's said the same thing to everyone,' he added with a wink.

'What a very striking outfit!' Pippa drew Claudia to one side. 'Have you said hello to Tim? He's around somewhere.'

'Not yet,' said Claudia.

Pippa stared at the dress. 'He certainly won't be able to miss you.'

'How is he?' Claudia felt obliged to ask.

'On top of the world. Did you know I'm a grandmother now?' Pippa's expression said she was used to having people exclaim in disbelief at this news.

'No,' Claudia stuttered. 'No. I didn't. How lovely!' she added belatedly.

She knew she should ask whether it was a girl or a boy, whether the baby had a name, when the happy event had taken place, but she didn't trust herself to speak.

'Terry just loves the book,' the American was bubbling on to Michael. 'He wants Richard Burton for the lead—'

'I'm not sure I want it to be made into a film,' said Michael bluntly.

The woman's face seem to freeze: the bright smile was still there, but the promise drained from it.

'Shall we see you at the table?' said Pippa.

As she walked away, Claudia heard her saying to the American woman, 'You have to understand he's an autodidact, and you know what they're like: egotistical and ultimately nauseating, as Virginia Woolf herself said.'

'You're kidding me? Who did she say that about?'

'James Joyce, I think it was.'

The American shrieked with cruel laughter.

It was impossible to tell from Michael's face whether he had heard or not.

'Who is Terry?' he asked Claudia.

'Terry Lacock, the director.'

'Oh, I see.' Michael replaced his empty champagne glass on a tray being carried by a waiter and took another one. 'I admire his stuff. Do you think he's here?'

Each time a floorboard creaked or a tractor drove past, Jennifer froze and Alan Spivey would look up from his task until the frisson of danger ebbed away again. The sheets were crumpled but clean, although there was no getting away from the faint note of manure which seemed to impregnate the fabric of the farmhouse. On the window sill, a very large sleeping tabby cat occasionally opened one eye and looked at them, as if to say that he had seen it all before.

In time, the patient, continuous lapping of the estate agent's tongue pushed such an unstoppable rush of pleasure up through Jennifer's body, she wouldn't have allowed him to stop even if her husband had walked into the room with a gun.

'I love you,' she said, not knowing how else to express her gratitude for the pure joy he gave her.

The cat got up, stretched, yawned dramatically, then jumped down from the window sill and slid out through the half-open door.

'Do you think he's gone to tell on us?' Jennifer asked, as both their eyes followed their witness's departure.

'They're at it like rabbits in the bedroom!' said Alan in a miaowy voice.

Jennifer laughed and lay back, basking in the warm pool of sunlight. It had been such a wonderful hot summer.

Alan reached into his jacket pocket for a packet of cigarettes, lit two and handed her one. There was a brimming ashtray on the chest of drawers next to the bed, but even so, it was taking a big risk to leave fresh cigarette smoke in someone else's bedroom. Jennifer drew in a thrilling lungful. She loved the way Alan kept upping the ante: a kiss stolen in the cold bathroom of a mock-Tudor semi; a furtive touch of her breast as they inspected the view from the luxury flat in the block that had just gone up near the Victoria Gardens; his hand slipping up into her knickers as she ascended the spiral staircase in the ultra-modern upside-down house on the cliffs in Havenbourne; their first, ravenous grappling in a four-poster bed said to have been slept in by the Duke of Monmouth the night after his ill-fated landing down the coast; and now, languorous afternoon sex in a farmhouse so picturesque it might have featured on the lid of a biscuit tin.

'Why is this house on the market?' Jennifer asked, staring up at the cracked plaster ceiling.

'The farmer's children don't want to take it over. Sadly, it's the same story all over the country. It's what comes of giving every-one a free education,' Alan said with a knowing wink. 'It'd make a very attractive property for someone prepared to put some work into it,' he went on. 'And it's priced very attractively too. In need of some modernization, obviously . . .'

She'd noticed that when it came to talking about houses, he always used estate-agent patter.

'Translation, please,' Jennifer asked.

'Riddled with dry rot,' Alan informed her.

She flung herself back among the old feather pillows with their complex sweet scent of starch and human and animal. She loved it when he allowed her into the secrets of his trade. It felt terribly intimate, as if he trusted her completely.

'How is my brand-new rot-free house coming along?' she asked, throwing a languid arm across his chest, playing with the little tufts of hair around his nipple.

Sometimes she found herself wishing that the new house would never be finished because there would be no further excuse to pop into Alan's office, or drive off with him in his car on the pretext of seeing how the building was going. She didn't know what would become of them after. Would he still come to her? Would they make love in the bed she shared with Jolly? It wouldn't be quite the same in her own home.

'That's something I want to talk to you about,' said Alan, suddenly getting up and pulling on his trousers.

They put their cigarettes out and arranged the bed as they had found it, then went down the creaking stairs and out through the hall, past a row of mud-caked wellington boots.

In Alan's car, she turned in her seat for a last glimpse of the thatched farmhouse with its late pink roses round the porch, where she had been so briefly happy.

At the building site, they got out of the car. No visible progress had been made since the last time they had come. The shell of new grey breeze blocks looked curiously like one of the old abandoned stone farmhouses you sometimes saw with air where the roof had once been. The sun had lost its warmth for the day, and there was a nip in the air which made her shiver.

Alan turned to face her and took her hands in his. 'You're going to hate me for this, Jen . . .'

He looked so serious, she knew it was something very bad. Was he married?

'The builders have gone bust. Scarpered,' he said.

'Oh . . .'

Not as awful as she'd feared. Or was there more to come?

'I feel rotten, I really do . . . with you of all people . . .' He hung his head.

'It's not your fault.' Her automatic instinct was to console him.

'If I could get my hands on them . . .' he said with a little growl a bit like the sound he always made when he caught his first glimpse of her underwear.

'I'm sure there are plenty of other builders,' she said.

'Trouble is,' he confessed, 'the money's gone too. Not just yours, mine as well. Cash-flow crisis. I'm going to have to do a runner.'

'Leave Kingshaven?' she cried.

'No choice, darling. No two ways about it.'

She half expected his face suddenly to light up as it did when he was teasing her, but his eyes remained unfathomably dark.

Jennifer burst into tears. 'You can't!' she said through her sobs. 'You just can't! I can't live without you.' She clasped his broad shoulders and looked into his face, pleading.

'Do you mean that, Jen? Do you really mean that?' he asked.

She sniffed and pulled away. 'Of course I do,' she said.

'Then come with me!' he said.

'With you?' she repeated tentatively.

'I've done it before,' he said. 'There's no shortage of people willing to lend you money if you look the part. And with you by my side . . .' He stood back as if appraising her like a fine work of art. 'Class!' Another growl.

She blushed and giggled.

'We'd make a good team, you and me,' he said. 'And we wouldn't always be looking over our shoulders, listening for keys in the door.'

There was a part of her that quite liked that bit.

'Where would we go?' she said, trying to pin it down, this dream. It was a dream, wasn't it? An adventure, full of risk: being on the run, pitching up somewhere where no one knew them, making love whenever they wanted?

'World's our oyster!' he said.

It was such a beautiful evening when Claudia and Michael arrived that they decided to walk from Coombe Minster Junction, the branch line to Kingshaven having finally succumbed to the recommendations of the Beeching Report some months before. There was no bus for an hour, and the idea of ringing for a taxi and all the questions such a journey would involve was more arduous than the prospect of a five-mile hike with light luggage.

The air had that distinct edge of crispness Michael remembered from the beginning of every school year, which confirmed that however clement the summer had been, it was now over. A brisk stroll was exactly the remedy for the blurry remnants of the hangover he was suffering as a result of the previous day's excess of champagne and Chianti. Even though *Hide and Seek* had not won the prize, he had spent the lunch, and many long hours after, toasting its success.

When the Savoy bash was over, their party had adjourned to a pub on the Strand, and then to a cheap Italian restaurant Terry Lacock suggested in Soho, where Michael had consumed an enormous bowl of spaghetti in a belated attempt to mop up some of the alcohol in his stomach, but there was still a sour taste in his mouth which no amount of hot sweet tea out of the flask Claudia had prepared seemed to swill away. Occasionally, on the long journey down, cooped up in a compartment which conspired to be both draughty and airless at the same time, flashes of the previous evening's conversation had returned to him.

'Did I agree to him filming it?' he had suddenly asked near Salisbury.

'I'm sure no one would hold you to what you said last night,' Claudia told him, barely glancing up from the novel by Iris Murdoch she was reading.

Michael had got on well with Terry, whose grittily realistic documentaries he admired. But it would be Terry's first drama. Could he really trust him?

'What do you think?' he asked Claudia.

She shrugged. He could see that however much he pushed, he was not going to get her to add her weight to whatever decision he made. He liked the fact that she made him take responsibility for his actions, but sometimes he found her rigour quite stern.

Now, as they approached the milestone to Kingshaven where the road forked, another snippet of conversation flashed through his brain.

'Was something said about Julie Christie?' he asked.

'Do you really not remember?' Claudia asked him with a disbelieving smile. 'Terry wants her to play the daughter. You said no, in no uncertain terms. In fact, you gave a full critique of why she had been so unsuitable for the role of Lara in *Dr Zhivago* . . .'

'Did I? How embarrassing!'

Claudia smiled at him. 'I ended up feeling quite sorry for her.

And it's difficult for any woman to feel sorry for Julie Christie, I can tell you.'

'But we parted on amicable terms?' Michael asked. 'Terry and I?'

' "Best mates! We're best mates, mate. That's what we are! Mates," ' Claudia did a loud, slurred imitation of their drunken bonhomie, flapping her arms about and zigzagging into the road.

Michael grabbed her by the hand as a black car swept round the corner and roared past them, pulling her into his arms and kissing her ferociously. Then he looked at her beautiful face, which was laughing with mischief, and kissed her again, tenderly.

'Thank you for bringing me home,' he said finally.

'Here?' she said, surprised.

'No, home. Our home. Last night,' he said, unsettled by the moment of uncharacteristic misunderstanding. 'That little house we share in Hampstead, remember?'

All the senses which had been numbed by the hangover now jangled discordantly in his head.

Even at a distance, the gatehouse looked empty. The panes in the diamond lattice of the leaded windows were dark and unfriendly; the shrubs in the garden were overgrown.

'You don't think they've taken him to hospital?' Claudia asked as they approached, her voice trembling a little.

'I don't think anyone's lived here for a while,' said Michael, seeing that grass was growing up through the gap between the doorstep and the front door.

And then, in the distance, they saw Sir John walking towards them waving a walking stick. 'Ah, there you are!' he said, as if they had just gone out for a five-minute stroll. 'Your father's been living at the house for the last little while. Suits both of us. Can't think why he didn't come up years ago!' He peered at Michael. 'I don't think we've met.'

'As a matter of fact we have. A long time ago,' Michael reminded him. 'I taught Winston.'

'Of course!' said Sir John.

'How is he?' Claudia asked.

'Winston?' the old man asked.

'My father!'

'Bearing up, bearing up,' said Sir John.

Professor Liebeskind was in the conservatory at the back of the house, sitting in an old planter's chair made of teak and fraying basketwork. He was asleep, and his breathing was shallow and rapid, like a child with a temperature. The white paint and putty of the fretwork of the conservatory was cracked and shedding, a couple of the panes were broken, but the room was warm from the sun, and there was a wonderfully evocative smell of geraniums.

He looked shockingly older than when Michael had last seen him.

As if he had sensed his daughter's presence, the professor opened an eye, and, bringing her into focus, smiled with such incandescent pleasure that Michael had to gulp back emotion as he witnessed their reunion. The sight of Claudia's lovely face on waking from a troubled sleep was like an anointing of happiness. He did not want to intrude on this moment between them.

Wandering back through the house, Michael found Sir John reading a copy of *The Times* a couple of months old, in a large room with several armchairs and a concert-sized piano with a blanket thrown over it. A couple of chickens strutted around the Persian rugs on the floor, pecking randomly at balls of dust.

'I don't think we've met!' Sir John stood up with difficulty, his manners impeccable, even though his short-term memory appeared rather flawed.

'Michael Quinn.' He held out his hand. 'I used to teach Winston.'

'So you did. He's up at Oxford now, you know. Thinking about becoming a barrister.'

Sir John went back to his paper.

Michael wondered how many times he had read it, and whether England's win against Germany in the World Cup came as a surprise each time he did.

'Does anyone play?' Michael asked.

'Winston is more of a cricketer.'

'I meant the piano.'

Sir John looked at the piano as if it were unfamiliar to him. 'I can't remember anyone playing,' he said, frowning at it.

'May I see if it's in tune?'

'By all means!'

Michael put a pile of folios on the floor beside the piano and rolled back the blanket. Underneath, the polished wood of the lid shone like a mirror.

He played the A then whizzed through a simple Mozart minuet. The instrument was hopelessly flat.

'Claudia!' said Sir John, rising from his seat. 'This good fellow has come to play for us.'

'This is Michael. We came down from London together,' she told him gently.

'Play as long as you like.' Sir John waved at Michael. 'I usually go for a stroll at this hour anyway.'

They could scarcely contain their laughter until he had left the room.

'Is it just the two of them here?' Michael asked Claudia as she slid on to the piano stool next to him.

'I found Mrs Burns in the kitchen. Apparently she comes up twice a week, and some of Sir John's men keep an eye,' Claudia said.

'Mrs Burns?'

'She used to be the cook at the Palace, under the old regime.'

He raised an eyebrow. 'How is your father?'

'Physically very tired, but mentally alert.'

'Unlike Sir John.'

'He's always been a bit forgetful,' Claudia told him. 'But his instincts are good.'

Michael could see that Claudia was enjoying being back, revisiting things she'd forgotten, or at least had never talked about to him. He found it disconcerting to think that the house, and the little network of lives surrounding it, had been going on all the time he had lived not three miles away, and he had not been aware of it. He felt very much the outsider, like John Ridd, who had stumbled upon the secret world of the Doones and their beautiful daughter Lorna.

While he and Claudia had shared the same ambition to escape from Kingshaven, they had known two different Kingshavens. For him, the town was an intellectual desert with only the meagre oasis of the library for succour; for her, the town library must have been, in a sense, a banal respite. At the Castle, there were books everywhere: on shelves, in bookcases, in cardboard boxes and apple panniers. Many of them had been left open, as if the reader had been distracted mid-way and never returned.

The four of them sat down to a supper of Mrs Burns's meat pie, with pastry which was golden and shiny on the outside and deliciously puddingy where the gravy had soaked in underneath.

Sir John suddenly turned to Michael. 'Is there any money in piano-tuning?'

Michael hesitated.

'He can't tune the piano!' said Claudia's father impatiently.

'My dear Rudy, the fault may well lie in the instrument,' said Sir John with a conciliatory smile at Michael.

'Michael is a writer,' Claudia explained. 'A writer who plays the piano.'

'Well, he can't play it in that state,' said Sir John. 'How does one find a piano-tuner, I wonder? In the past, I believe one used to find us. I never knew how. He was blind.'

'But they're only here for a day or two!' protested Claudia's father. 'It would be a complete waste of money. Neither you nor I play, and the only instrument Winston is interested in is his infernal guitar.'

'Nevertheless, Rudy, I shall have it tuned,' said Sir John, asserting his authority.

'They're like an old married couple,' Michael whispered to Claudia in bed later that evening. 'They bicker and quarrel and get on each other's nerves.'

'And look after each other,' added Claudia.

'Did you persuade your father to see the doctor?'

'Apparently he did come to see him and prescribed penicillin, which my father insists made him much more ill when he took it before, so he refused it. He says he's just got bronchitis again.'

'And what do you think?'

'I think he's worse than last time, but he's very strong-willed and I get the impression he's determined to stay alive just to prove the doctor wrong.'

'He's enjoying having you here,' Michael said.

'I think so. It's always so difficult to tell,' she said with a little bubble of laughter.

Michael hugged her close to him. The sheets seemed finally to be warming up although the room was still chilly. Sir John had told them to choose any room they wanted. He seemed to assume that they were married, or perhaps he didn't care one way or the other. He was such a strange mixture of out-of-date manners – 'No need to dress for dinner!' – and free-thinking, it was impossible to predict which issues he would feel strongly about.

He was fervently in favour of the abolition of capital punishment, arguing vehemently against the professor who had argued for it in the case of crimes against humanity.

'My dear Rudy, I fear you are letting understandable emotion interfere with your logic,' he had said, which had sent Claudia's father into a furious paroxysm of coughing.

However, he was against nuclear disarmament because he thought the Japanese would never have given up without Hiroshima.

'If you're so keen on the sanctity of life,' the professor had snorted, 'why do you discount two hundred thousand Japanese?'

Sir John thought for a while. 'I suppose my argument is utilitarian.'

'But you're not prepared to allow me mine . . .'

Michael watched the two old men quarrel over dinner and wondered if they did this every evening. Did they ever agree? And if they did, would one of them play devil's advocate just for the fun of it?

Sir John was kind to his workers, Michael saw, as the old man sympathized with Mrs Burns's lumbago and asked after her grandchildren, appearing to know all their names and occupations, but his concern was essentially patrician, and left no one in doubt that he was still lord of the manor.

The room they had chosen to sleep in was in the East Wing, an unused part of the house. The two old men occupied the downstairs rooms of the West Wing, only venturing infrequently up the grand staircases that curved up each side of the vast oval entrance hall for a bath. A bed for the professor had been brought down into the dining room. It stood beneath the ornate stucco ceiling rose where the table would have been, looked upon by glass-fronted cabinets displaying a complete dinner service with a gilded border and a painted pheasant motif. Sir John had his own bed in the scullery next to the kitchen – not, he informed them, from any inherent asceticism, but simply because it was the warmest place in the house.

Michael and Claudia's room, with its high ceiling and panels of hand-painted Chinese paper, was stunningly beautiful, but the windows which Michael estimated must be at least twelve feet high on both the front and side elevation made it freezing cold, even at this time of the year.

'Listen,' Michael whispered to Claudia as they huddled together under an eiderdown which reeked of years inside a cedar cupboard.

'What?' she said.

They both held their breath to listen better.

'Nothing,' said Michael finally. 'Silence.'

'Are you OK?' Claudia asked anxiously in the darkness.

'Yes,' he said, suddenly realizing that the headache which had troubled him all day had disappeared. 'It's good to get away from London.'

'Mummy?'

Julia Allsop was afraid of the dark, and always clamoured to have her mother sit on her bed and hold her hand until she fell asleep. Usually Jennifer told her not to be so silly, that there was nothing to be afraid of, but just this once she granted her wish. Her daughter's eyes were huge with tiredness after her first week at school, so she was bound to go off in no time. It was hardly going to become a habit, Jennifer thought. It was quite nice, sitting in the dark, thinking, planning, with her daughter's little warm hand gradually slipping out of her own. Julia's breathing was so peaceful, Jennifer could almost have fallen asleep right next to her.

'Mummy?' Just as Jennifer was tiptoeing out of the room, Julia chirruped and sat up as if she wasn't tired at all.

Jennifer sighed. 'Yes, darling?'

'Does it need to be a real pea?'

'I'm sorry?'

'We didn't have a pea, so I put one of Adrian's marbles under my bed. But I can't feel a thing.'

'What are you talking about, darling?' She was a curious little thing at times, Jennifer thought. In a world of her own.

'"The Princess and the Pea"!' said Julia. 'We're reading it at school.'

'Can you read already? Clever you!' said Jennifer distractedly.

'No, Mrs Evans reads and we sit very still and listen very quietly,' Julia told her.

'Is it the one about the princess who doesn't laugh?' Jennifer asked.

'No, silly,' said Julia, 'that's "The Golden Goose". "The Princess and the Pea" is about this princess but nobody believes she's a princess so they put a pea in her bed . . .'

'Oh, yes, I remember. And they put twenty mattresses on top—'

'And twenty quilts,' Julia went on excitedly, 'but in the morning she's all black and blue with bruises from the pea, so they know she is a real princess.'

'That's it,' said Jennifer. 'Go to sleep now.'

She made for the door again.

'I love you, Mummy,' said the little voice in the darkness.

Julia was such a sweet-natured child. It was almost as if being unwanted had made her want everyone else to feel needed. It would never have occurred to the older girls that Mummy might deserve a little affection from time to time, Jennifer thought. She doubted they would even notice if she wasn't there, and Jamie was too young to know the difference.

Jennifer sat down on the bed again. 'Julia?'

'Yes, Mummy.'

'Can you keep a secret?'

'Yes, Mummy.'

'I'm going to go away for a little while.'

'Where?'

'It's a secret.'

'That's two secrets!' The child was as excited as if she had managed to wheedle a double portion of dessert. 'Is it a holiday?'

'I suppose you could call it that. In a little while, I'll come back and fetch you too.'

Jennifer was glad the room was dark because she didn't want Julia to see the tears which had sprung to her eyes.

The room was quieter than ever. Then Julia murmured, 'Mummy?'

'Yes?'

'Do you think the princess was staying at the Palace?'

'What?'

'Why else would there be so many mattresses?'

Julia was still thinking about princesses and peas, Jennifer realized. Which was probably just as well.

'It's just a fairy story, darling. Goodnight.'

'Mummy?'

'Yes, darling?'

'Do you think the princess might have fallen off all those mattresses and in fact that was why she was all black and blue?'

Jennifer laughed. 'It could be,' she said.

Julia was sitting up again, excited. 'When I grow up I'm going to marry Adrian and be a real princess in the Palace,' she told her mother.

'You'll probably have to marry Christopher if you want to do that,' replied Jennifer mischievously.

'Don't be silly, he's far too old!'

'Lie down, and go to sleep!'

'Mummy?'

'What now?' Jennifer asked.

'Is your secret place lovely?'

'I hope so, darling,' Jennifer replied.

It was still dark when Michael woke from a dreamless sleep. He crept down the corridor to the bathroom and when he switched on the light, he was greeted by a very loud and startling chorus of 'Cockadoodledoo!'

Three roosters were perched on the wooden drying rack suspended above the deep claw-footed bath.

The ancient plumbing rumbled as he pulled the chain of the lavatory.

He tiptoed guiltily back to the Chinese room.

'What's that?' Claudia mumbled, still half asleep. She was all soft and warm and sweet-smelling under the eiderdown now, and he cuddled up close to her, putting his feet, cold from the tiled floor of the bathroom, against her warm legs.

'Dawn arrived early for the cockerels,' Michael whispered. 'Wouldn't you have thought they'd know the difference between electric light and sunlight?'

'Mmm,' Claudia murmured and turned over, pulling the eiderdown right over her head. Clearly, she was not yet ready to begin a new day, but Michael could not fall asleep again. As quietly as he could, he crept out of bed and pulled on his corduroy trousers and jumper, and then he tiptoed downstairs and out into the garden.

There was an old orchard with apples almost ripe enough to be picked. In the long wet grass he picked his way carefully between mushy brown windfalls, which tainted the chill air with a faint whiff of yeast. Beneath ancient raspberry nets beaded with dew, brambles had taken over. Michael stooped to pick a blackberry, the taste transporting him to the scrubby edges of the cricket field where Frank used to play on Sunday afternoons. Michael would pretend to be looking for lost balls, all the while popping fruit into his mouth, squashing each little soft capsule of juice individually with his tongue. And when he got home his mother would take one look at the purple stains at the corners of his mouth and warn him he'd have stomach ache.

The heavy wooden door of a walled garden looked as if it was locked, but creaked open as Michael pushed it. It was still possible to make out a grid of vegetable beds all gone to seed. In one corner there was a dilapidated greenhouse housing a couple of withered palms in terracotta pots, with dry brown fronds which looked as if they would turn to dust if he were to touch them. A sudden rainbow of bright morning sunshine split by a prism of broken glass bounced across the slatted wooden shelf inside. In the slightly steamy interior, Michael felt a kind of well-being seeping through his body. He wondered if human beings experienced something like the physical process of photosynthesis he could recall illustrating in his biology book with a diagram of a plant and lots of arrows.

The thought blossomed that he would be able to write here.

In the rose garden, some of the ramblers had gone wild, and there were shiny hips among the fragile pink flowers. Michael snapped off the dead heads he could reach, occasionally pausing to put his nose inside one of the full-blown blooms and inhale that delicate, elusive scent of rose, so immediately recognizable and yet so impossible to imagine just an inch or two away.

'Are you a gardener?'

He had not heard Sir John's approach, and he jumped.

'No, I'm Claudia's friend. We came down from London together,' Michael explained, holding out his hand.

'Good God, man, have you forgotten I ate dinner with you last night?'

There was a glint of mischief along with the impatience, which made Michael wonder if Sir John's absent-mindedness might be a tactic to gauge how people reacted.

'I used to help my aunts with their garden when I was a boy. It was nowhere near the size of this,' Michael told him.

'Your aunts?'

'In Etherington. They went to America after the war.'

Sir John looked perplexed, as if considering why he should be the least interested in this information.

'My son Jolly calls himself a landscape gardener now, you know. He considered farming to be beneath him. I told him he'd have to fend for himself in that case. He'll get all this lot when I go, of course.' Sir John shook his stick at the neglected garden.

'Is there no alternative to the system of primogeniture?' Michael asked.

Sir John scowled at him, and he couldn't tell whether he was appalled by his ignorance, or his familiarity.

'Does he still live in the grounds of the hotel?' Michael asked, searching for a more neutral subject.

'Oh, yes, indeed, he's very keen to hobnob with the Königs!'

'The Kings?' Michael corrected.

Sir John stared at him. 'You can change your name, but you can't change who you are,' he said.

'König. Is that a German name?' Michael was fascinated.

'The heir apparent used to wear a brown shirt in the thirties. Had to send him away when he became too much of an embarrassment.'

Was this intriguing titbit true, or just another tease?

'I always assumed their name had something to do with the town,' Michael said.

'That's what they'd like everyone to think, but they're neither landed nor gentry. They had a successful butcher's shop in the East End,' Sir John elaborated.

Now, Michael couldn't tell whether Sir John's principal objection to the Kings was to the fact that they were originally German, or originally trade.

'Jolly married a shop girl, you know,' Sir John went on. 'I gave them an Attic lecythos as a wedding present. Priceless, of course. Apparently, they threw it away because it was cracked!'

Michael wasn't exactly sure what an Attic lecythos was, but didn't dare to display ignorance again.

'Her mother invited herself to tea and informed me that my house could be very nice with a bit of updating,' said Sir John, giving a surprisingly good impression of Mrs Farmer.

Michael laughed.

'Ghastly woman!' said Sir John.

When it became apparent that Mrs Farmer's stay at the Palace was going to be longer than initially expected, Libby King had negotiated a reasonable long-term rate, but she never quite managed to rid herself of the notion that she was doing her mother's friend a favour. Indeed, now that Mrs Farmer had sold her shop and was no longer in a position to offer benefits in kind, Libby rather felt that Mrs Farmer had become something of an imposition. And the same could be said about her daughter, Jennifer.

'Kiss for Mummy,' said Jennifer, bending down to toddler height and offering her cheek to her small son.

Jennifer's skin was as smooth as porcelain, Libby noticed, as James grimaced on tasting his mother's face powder. Wasn't it a little early in the day for make-up?

'You will be picking the girls up?' It was a statement rather than a question.

Libby was quite happy to help with James's early education – he was, after all, her godson, and would eventually become an important neighbour, and Moira cost the same whether she was looking after one toddler or two – but Jennifer had got into the habit of telephoning the hotel in the middle of the day and telling Moira to pop down and collect her girls from school. Anyone would think that Jennifer was building her new house with her own bare hands, the time it was taking.

Mr Maurice, whose salon window was directly opposite the bow-fronted premises Mr Spivey occupied, had apparently mentioned at her mother's last hair appointment that not a day went by these days when Jennifer didn't hop into the estate agent's car of an afternoon. There was nothing wrong, in his opinion, with a woman taking an interest in property matters, Liliana had quoted the hairdresser at dinner, adding, just in case Eddie failed to spot the irony, 'I told him that was just as well, or my family would be living on a boat!'

She and Mrs Farmer had snorted for an almost indecently long time over the joke, until Eddie stood up and went for his brandy and cigar in the bar.

Sometimes Libby wished that Mrs Farmer would take her meals in the restaurant like the real guests did. At first, she found it quite sweet the way Liliana and Ruby went everywhere together, chatting and giggling like schoolgirls. Libby had been glad she was there to cheer Liliana up after the recent spate of deaths. But she was beginning to tire of walking into a room and having the two old girls stare at her as if she was interrupting some secret parley. And they were always ganging up on Eddie.

Libby wasn't sure about Eddie's idea of sailing solo round the world in the *Brittany Anna*, but she very much doubted it would get to that, and in the meantime, she didn't mind him spending so much time, tinkering around with all those halyards and booms and other bits and pieces if it made him happy. If she had learned anything from nearly twenty years of marriage, it was that there was no point in trying to force Eddie to be the quiet, modest and dutiful man her father had been.

Her mother, however, liked to make people be as she wanted, and suffer if they resisted. Libby sometimes wondered whether her father had ever made a risqué joke, or pinched a maid's bottom, or dreamed up a madcap scheme before Liliana's iron will squashed any enjoyment out of him.

After depositing little James in the nursery with Winny, Libby was quite relieved to see that it was just her daughter at breakfast.

Her mother and Mrs Farmer generally rose late – partly, Libby suspected, as a result of the number of gin and Dubonnets they consumed in the evenings. Liliana had never drunk in public before Mrs Farmer came to stay, although Libby knew she kept a bottle of Dubonnet in her room for guests, and had once found her siphoning gin into it from the optic in the bar.

'Morning, Mummy,' Angela said through a mouthful of toast, without looking up from the current issue of *Horse & Hound*.

'Lovely day,' said Libby.

'Bye, Mummy!' Angela said, swallowing the last of her tea and wiping her mouth on her sleeve.

'Would you mind putting your napkin back in its ring?'

Angela sighed loudly, but did as she was told.

'Where are you off to today?' Libby asked, suddenly desperate not to sit and eat alone.

'The stables, of course!' said Angela.

Libby had an impetuous thought. 'Why don't we go for a ride together?' she asked brightly.

Angela's face fell. 'Do we have to?'

'It'll mean a lift to the stables,' said Libby.

On horseback, she would be able to get a good look at how Jennifer and Jolly's new house was coming along. She'd no idea how the builder had ever got planning permission to build on such a site right in the middle of a beauty spot. It had made Eddie wonder whether the Planning Committee might look favourably on granting permission for some luxury houses on their land, if things at the hotel didn't pick up fairly soon.

Libby couldn't remember a time when she and her daughter had gone out specifically with the intention of doing something enjoyable. They used to go to Lowhampton for Angela's school uniform, and sometimes take tea together in the restaurant on the top floor of Gillie's. She'd try to ask relevant questions about what went on at school, while Angela shovelled ice-cream sundae into her mouth with a long-handled spoon, but she never did find out whether Angela enjoyed any particular subject. Her daughter's reports indicated mediocre performance all round, although she had once been awarded school colours for high jump. Libby, who had always considered Angela rather advanced for her age, wondered about the standards of teaching. But it was difficult to look as if you were criticizing when Angela's disciplinary record meant that the school would expel her if offered the slightest excuse. Nevertheless, it did seem a huge amount of money to have spent over the years for only two poor 'O' levels to come out at the end.

'This is fun, isn't it?' Libby said, giving her daughter's jodphured thigh a little pat.

'Awfully good fun!' Angela sneered.

At least she spoke with the right sort of accent, Libby thought, and that was one thing in life you could not do without. She'd noticed the older Allsop girls, who attended the local school, had begun to pick up the local vowels.

'Can't you go a bit faster?' Angela asked.

'Why are you in such a hurry?'

'Well, if you must know, the selectors for the Eventing Team are coming, and I do want Spit to be looking his best.'

'How exciting!' said Libby. 'What do you think your chances are?'

'It's between me and Stella Sherbourne. Spitfire's a better jumper, but we're hopeless at dressage. Oh, I do so hate dressage! What's the point of it?' Angela stamped her foot on the floor of the car.

'I used to feel just the same way,' Libby told her.

'Really, Mummy?'

Angela was a different character when it came to horses. Animated and eager to learn. Her dedication and enthusiasm, which had endured far longer than most adolescent girls' crush on all things equine, reminded Libby of something Mr Carney had once said: 'We've got horse in our blood, you and me, Lady Elizabeth.'

The memory of him made Libby sigh. She rarely found the time to go out on rides now that he and his large family had moved back to Ireland to run a stud in Tipperary.

'When I was a reserve for the County Juniors,' Libby reminisced, 'it was always Patricia Sherbourne, Stella's aunt, who got picked in front of me. Damn dressage!'

She took her eyes off the road to smile at Angela. Angela smiled back.

'I never knew that,' she said.

'Between you and me,' Libby went on, emboldened by her daughter's interest, 'I used to wish that Patricia Sherbourne would fall and break her neck!'

Angela clapped her crop with delight. 'So what happened?'

'The war came, and we all had other things to worry about,' said Libby, a little wistfully.

People had said then she had the potential to go beyond county level, perhaps even to represent the country, but then Mr Hitler had intervened, and she met Eddie, and suddenly there were other things to do. If you were going to compete at an international level, it had to be your life.

Perhaps, Libby thought with sudden optimism, all this time Angela was spending at the stables would actually lead to something rather than just being a way of keeping her daughter out of trouble until they decided what to do with her.

The school had made it clear that they would not have Angela back even to sit retakes, which did mean that she was at a bit of a loose end. The idea of a Swiss finishing school was a non-starter. Nobody could honestly see Angela lasting long at cordon bleu cookery or needlepoint.

'I say, good luck today,' said Libby as she drove the car into the courtyard of the stables. 'And don't worry, I'll keep out of the way. I know how off-putting it can be to have a proud parent watching!'

'Oh, thanks, Mummy!' Angela said, leaning over and giving Libby an entirely unexpected kiss on the cheek.

From the bridleway along the top of the ridge, Michael looked down on the Castle and its land, able now to discern the pattern of features Sir John had shown him on the scroll of the original plan of the garden, which his host had unearthed in an ancient cardboard tube tied with a watered silk ribbon.

Although Michael had walked this route dozens of times before, he had never seen the clumps of trees and the ribbon of small lakes as anything other than naturally occurring features of the landscape. The new perspective threw him slightly off kilter, and made him question why he had accepted the view of people whose opinions he otherwise despised that Sir John was a barmy old aristocrat clinging to his crumbling pile. In person, Sir John was much more like the sort of man Michael had imagined when he first read Dickens and dreamed of having a secret, rich benefactor, in a great ramshackle mansion, who would one day reveal himself.

Michael stopped to get his breath, and to enjoy the panorama. The closer you were to the sky, the bigger it appeared to be, and it crossed his mind that the ambition which impelled men to climb mountains, and countries to conquer space, might be as much a desire to acknowledge man's insignificance as to claim superiority. The view of Kingshaven from this distance was like a map of man's interaction with nature, but as Michael's steps took him nearer, he began to distinguish features which were textured with individual memories: the stone obelisk on the edge of the cliff where a new wreath of artificial poppies appeared each Remembrance Day; the conifer bent over by the wind which Iris had always called her tree. The pang in his chest as he pictured her bouncing on its single branch became sharper as he realized he had not thought about her since he had woken up. Sometimes, hours went by now without the sharp ache of loss catching him mid-activity and stopping his heart for a moment. Human beings were designed with an extraordinary capacity to cope with pain, but he hated himself for letting her slip from his consciousness even for a second, let alone a minute, an hour, a day.

As he approached the Harbour End, Michael could hear the metallic tapping of a fossil hammer, and his eyes picked out a lone lad down on the beach below the South Cliffs methodically tapping at a rock.

'You'd have more luck with the one next to it,' he called

as he clambered towards the boy with a view to helping him.

There was something uniquely thrilling about cracking open a smooth stone and discovering the rings of an ammonite hiding inside. And there were plenty to be found, but only if you knew what you were looking for.

It was only when the boy looked up, startled by Michael's voice, that he realized he was addressing his own son, a child he knew little better now, he thought, than when he had first looked at the lines of newborns sleeping in the nursery of Lowhampton Hospital and wondered which was his. A bristling impatience with Anthony for not knowing the first thing about fossils was overwhelmed by the flood of guilt that he was not there to teach him about such things.

Michael stared at the hammer the boy was holding. It was the hammer he had bought for Iris. Iris had been able to list all the dinosaurs by period. Iris had tired of ammonites when she was about seven, and set herself the task of discovering an ichthyosaurus at least as big as the one another little girl, Mary Anning, had found over a hundred years before, further down the coast at Lyme Regis.

'What are you doing here?' Michael asked Anthony, and then realized that it was the question his son was probably wanting to ask him. 'I mean,' he said a little more gently, 'why aren't you at school?'

'It hasn't started yet.'

'Hasn't it?' Michael was surprised. It was already two weeks into September.

'Does Mummy know you're here?' Anthony asked, regarding Michael warily.

'No, she doesn't. You see, I'm visiting a friend who's not very well,' Michael stammered.

'I see,' said Anthony.

Both of them looked out to sea.

The sound of water gently pulling at the gravel seemed extraordinarily loud inside Michael's head. He could not think of any way of starting a conversation.

Finally, he said, 'How about England winning the World Cup, then?'

Anthony turned and half smiled at him. 'Great!'

'Do you play football at school?' Michael asked.

'Rugby, I think,' Anthony replied.

'Do you like rugby?'

'I'm not sure.'

Michael had never known whether Anthony was simply unintelligent, or whether he intimidated him, making him appear slightly imbecilic.

'Did you get the postal order I sent you on your birthday?' Michael asked.

'I wrote to say thank you.'

'So you did.'

Another lengthy silence.

'Did you find anything interesting to spend it on?'

'I bought a new satchel.'

'Good. How is school?'

He realized he hadn't spoken to Anthony since he'd gone up to Lowhampton Boys'.

The boy looked a little apprehensive. 'It might feel a bit different at first, but I'm sure I'll get used to it in no time,' he said.

Michael could hear the echo of Sylvia in this peculiarly stiff response.

'What are you going into? Third form, is it?'

'I don't know if it's called that at Harrow,' he said.

'Harrow?' Michael repeated.

'Harrow School.'

'What are you talking about?' Michael demanded.

Anthony flinched as if he'd been hit. 'I'm going to Harrow School, sir.'

'Don't call me sir!' Michael struggled to keep the explosion of anger under control. 'Don't you have to sit an exam to get into Harrow?' he asked quietly, still not prepared to believe what he thought he was being told, although he knew that Anthony wasn't devious enough to have invented such an apt lie.

'Common Entrance,' Anthony said. 'Mr Brown helped me with that.'

'Ivor?'

Ivor had helped his son apply for public school? How could he?

Ivor knew his views about public schools. There had been a time when he had shared them.

So, this was Sylvia's revenge! After driving his daughter away, she was sending his son to a public school. His wife had become a modern-day Medea.

'Who's paying for you to go to Harrow School?' Michael asked. Had Sylvia found herself some terrible Tory? The sort of man her mother always wanted for her?

'Mummy has a lot of money now,' said Anthony loyally. 'People say she's an overnight success, but they forget about all the years of hard work that went into it.'

His mother's cadences again.

'You don't want to go to Harrow School, do you?' Michael appealed to the boy.

'I don't see how I could be lonely with all those other boys, do you?' His son was clearly nervous, but determined to toe the party line. 'Harrow's quite near London, I think. Perhaps you could come to see me sometimes?' Anthony ventured.

'I wouldn't be seen dead in Harrow School,' Michael told him.

Whenever Sylvia Quinn heard 'These Boots are Made for Walkin'' by Nancy Sinatra, she always wondered what sort of boots they were. Sometimes she imagined sturdy leather walking boots, like the ones worn by the really serious walkers who stayed at the cheaper guesthouses and went off at the crack of dawn in breeches and thick wool socks after eating the landladies out of Shredded Wheat. Other times she thought Miss Sinatra, who was, after all, a sophisticated New Yorker, was more likely to be talking about a stylish pair of calf-length white vinyl chisel toes, or even black, knee-high, kinky boots, laced all the way up the front, like the ones she'd seen in a photograph of models on the Kings Road, Chelsea.

'And now,' said the presenter on the Light Programme, 'how's the weather where you are?'

The orchestral intro to 'The Sun Ain't Gonna Shine Anymore' filled the shop, but in the pause just before Scott Walker was about to sing the word 'Loneliness . . .' the shop door jangled and Michael walked in.

It wasn't a complete surprise. The previous afternoon, Jennifer Allsop had marched in with feverish spots of colour on her cheeks and made Sylvia guess whom she had passed walking towards town with his girlfriend. The barb of betrayal Sylvia thought she had expelled had been suddenly just as sharp and toxic as it was the day he left her.

Michael stood looking at the ceiling for a moment, as if trying to identify the song. She turned the volume knob right down, and then the shop was so silent, she wished she hadn't.

'Can I help you?' Sylvia asked, hating the petulant sound of her own voice.

He hadn't shaved that morning, and – maybe it was just the light – the stubble on his chin looked grey. She could feel the intensity of his pale blue eyes upon her, but she couldn't meet his gaze.

'What are you playing at, Syl?' he launched straight in, no pleasantries, no small talk. 'It's not fair on him.'

'What?' she asked, disingenuously.

'Sending Anthony to public school. I saw him on the beach. He's obviously terrified.'

'And what do you propose to do about it?' she asked.

His anger was boiling so near the surface she could almost hear the moment the crust popped. 'I'm still his father!' he shouted.

'You don't contribute to his upkeep.' She kept her voice as level as she could.

'Only because you send my cheques back!'

'We manage quite well without you, thank you very much!'

'Looks like you've done well for yourself,' he said, looking round the shop. Changing his tune, trying to take the heat out of the conversation, she thought.

'No thanks to you,' she was unable to resist saying.

'I'll take you to court if I have to,' Michael threatened, suddenly nasty again.

'I doubt very much whether the courts would want to interfere with my wish to give my child the best education,' she responded coolly.

He didn't expect that, she could tell. Didn't realize that she moved in better circles these days. It wouldn't have occurred to him that she counted a solicitor amongst her friends. He hadn't quite worked out that she'd had all the time in the world to think of a defence because she'd anticipated just this reaction if he ever bothered to ring and find out how they were getting along.

'But it's not the best education!' Michael said.

Sylvia took a deep breath. 'Well, there's your opinion on one side, and on the other there's just about every successful person in the country,' she said.

'I think you'll find the Prime Minister's on my side,' Michael retaliated.

She wanted to say, Yes, and look what a mess he's making of things, but she stopped herself. There was no point in getting into politics with Michael.

'I doubt whether your average judge would be on your side, though, don't you?' said Sylvia.

He recoiled.

He wasn't the only one who could make threats, Sylvia thought with satisfaction.

'Won't you be lonely if he's away?' Michael asked.

'Fat lot you care,' she snapped at him.

He tried another tactic. 'Surely you can't believe it's right, Syl . . . Education shouldn't be about who's got the most money. It's unfair.'

'What's more important to you, your principles or your son's education?'

'That's not the point.'

'Isn't it? I think you're just jealous of people who have what you didn't,' she told him.

'You mean like institutionalized bullying and buggery?' he asked, suddenly furious again.

'Don't you dare use language like that in my shop!'

'No doubt Ivor Brown's prepared him for that too! Private lessons, one to one! I bet he enjoyed that!'

'What do you mean?' She'd forgotten how vicious he could be when crossed. Lashing out at everyone.

'You silly cow. You've got no idea, have you?' he shouted.

The words hit her like blows.

Nobody was going to speak to her like that in her own shop.

'Get out!' she ordered him.

'Don't worry, I'm going. You're good at getting people out, aren't you? You got Iris out, now you're getting Anthony out too!'

'I'm doing what's best for him!' Sylvia screamed. 'But you wouldn't know anything about that, would you? You only ever think about what's best for you. And I wasn't the one who drove your darling daughter away, either. You're the one she hated. You! You!'

She stabbed the air and looked him right in the eye, amazed to realize that she didn't feel the slightest love for him standing there in his old jumper looking like some pathetic tramp. The fight seemed visibly to drop from his shoulders.

'Just go,' she told him, unnecessarily, as he turned away.

The fillip of triumph as the door closed behind him lasted only a couple of seconds before the hollow emptiness inside her opened up again.

Sylvia turned the volume back up on the radio.

Dusty Springfield was belting out, 'You don't have to say you love me . . .'

Sylvia watched him marching off up the street, not looking back. However much she tried to make it into a victory for herself, the truth was that he had left her, and that was something she could never change.

It was only when he disappeared from view that it occurred to her she still hadn't told him about Iris.

'Sarah!' a voice called up from the kitchen in the basement of the Luna Caprese café in Soho, London.

'Hang on a mo!' Iris smiled at the two men who'd just come in to the café.

'Sarah!'

'How about the booth at the back?' She pointed.

'Sarah,' came the disembodied voice. 'How long you want people to wait for spaghetti?'

'Not such a dumb waiter, is it?' Iris remarked as she showed the two men past the food lift down to the kitchen.

The shorter, wiry one, who was good-looking but kind of rough around the edges – a bit like David Bailey, who'd been in the previous week – smiled at the joke she made almost every day.

He looked familiar, but Iris wasn't sure whether that was because he was famous, or she'd just served him before.

The customers at the Luna Caprese – the Cap, as it was known locally – were a disparate bunch. There were market traders from Brewer Street like Louis and Sid, who always brought in a damp smell of bananas with them and gave Iris over-ripe tomatoes for nothing when she shopped at their stall, or asked her to try some new exotic fruit that had come into Covent Garden market, like avocado or prickly pear, or, once, a yellow fruit in the shape of a star which looked gorgeous, but tasted like cat's piss, in her opinion. There was Jilly G., a boutique owner from Carnaby Street, who smoked cigarettes through the long triangle of hair which hung over one half of her face, and wore short dresses with bits cut out. When Iris got her hair cropped very short, like Jean Seberg, Jilly had told her she could be a model, and Iris, thinking of Sylvia, had informed her curtly that she wanted to be an actress, not a clothes horse. A couple of months later, when everyone was talking about how much Twiggy was earning – ten guineas an hour, it said in the papers – she'd regretted having been so categoric.

There was Agatha Brown, a literary agent with an office in Golden Square, who brought in under-nourished writers and talked in a loud voice while they crammed food she was paying for down their throats, and Inigo, a poet, who was a bit of a dedicated follower of fashion, with his velvet trousers and flamboyant jacket which was made of the sort of chintz Mrs Farmer used to cover her armchairs.

Occasionally, a pair of weary female shoppers would wander off the beaten track of the department stores in Oxford Street and slump at one of the corner tables, surrounded by stiff paper carrier bags, but most of the customers Iris knew by name.

The two men who'd just arrived shifted their bottoms along the leatherette seat of the booth.

'I'll get you a menu,' Iris said, taking the one with the suit's raincoat to hang up on the hooks behind the counter where the till was.

'We'll both have the spaghetti with clams, love, ' said the wiry one, barely glancing up. He had a London accent like Vic and his brother Clive.

'Two spaghetti alle vongole,' Iris said, putting on her best Italian trill, and writing the order with a flourish on an imaginary notebook. They must be regulars to order the special without looking at the menu, she thought. Probably evening customers.

At the end of the day, her final duty was to remove the red-and-white-checked oilskin cloths from the tables and bring out squares of crisp white linen which smelled deliciously of starch when she shook out the folds. She would put a Chianti bottle with a candle in it on each table, and, suddenly, even though it was serving exactly the same food, the café would magically turn into a restaurant, which was favoured by musicians in evening suits with worn, shiny collars, and tiny ballet dancers who smoked so hard their pretty fingers were yellow from nicotine, and, later, when the theatres turned out, critics and famous actors and actresses wearing furs and dark glasses, talking in loud, bored voices about how hellish it was having to sign autographs.

Iris was rarely required to do the evening shift, which was the preserve of the owner's niece, Anna Maria, who was not inclined to swap because tips were much more generous when people were drinking large quantities of red wine. On the rare occasions Anna Maria was indisposed, Iris would leap at the chance of working back-to-back shifts for the thrill of encountering her idols, and boasting about it to Vic afterwards, when he came to meet her out of work. As they sped through the dark streets of Soho together on his Lambretta, catching snatches of stripper music as they passed the brightly lit doorways of clubs, or a jazz riff floating up from some seedy basement on a curl of cigarette smoke, and out into the daylight neon glow of Piccadilly Circus, the sheer luck of being here would rush through her, and she wouldn't be able to resist hugging Vic's waist hard to reassure herself that she was right in the middle of Swinging London where just about anything was possible.

Vic's secret ambition was to be a dancer and he was saving enough money to enrol in a school. Iris was determined to be an actress. On her walk to work from the Tottenham Court Road, where Vic dropped her off, she passed the stage doors of several

West End theatres and could hear them rehearsing inside. She kicked herself for refusing to learn ballet and tap dancing, as her mother had wanted her to, at Cynthia Clark's Dance Academy in Lowhampton where Dr Payne's girls had all gone. If she'd known how to dance, Iris was sure that she could have wangled her way in as a chorus girl, but even she could see that the world was not yet ready for her Nora or Ophelia.

In the meantime, she and Vic saw every film and show and play in the West End, taking full advantage of Vic's job in the box office at the Dominion and the unwritten code between box offices all over London that fellow workers were comped into any performance they wanted. Sometimes, if a film was good, they'd sit through it twice, and afterwards, on the journey home, they would compete with dreams of being invited to premieres, and accompanying each other to glittering parties, and calling each other 'Darling'.

'Sarah!' Another call came up from the kitchen.

'Sorry!' Iris picked up the two large shallow bowls of pasta from the dumb waiter and ferried them to the booth. 'Spaghetti alle vongole,' she said, putting one down in front of each man.

'Thanks, love.' The London one smiled at her.

There was a kind of edgy energy about him she liked. The way his eyes held hers made her think that if she could just think of the right thing to say to him, they would end up having a conversation. Nothing funny, like the blokes who bantered and then pinched her bottom when she turned round. More like the art critic who'd told her about the Courtauld Gallery and the Wallace Collection, as if he could tell she was more intelligent than the average waitress.

'Parmesan?' Iris asked.

'Why not?'

She went to the shelf for a little glass pot of granulated cheese which she thought smelled of sick. When she returned to the table, the man was talking earnestly to his companion and didn't even look up, so Iris retreated to her position by the kitchen lift.

It wasn't that she didn't like the Cap, it was just that she'd got the hang of being a waitress now, and was itching to try out a new role.

When she first arrived in London, she had been acting all the time and it had felt as unreal as marching around in her mother's stilettos when she was little, or being the Nurse in the school production of *Romeo and Juliet*.

Iris played the role of Sarah Bird as a bit like the capable sister in a children's book: responsible, good at household chores. It was amazing how tasks like tidying up and cleaning, which she hated doing at home, became positively enjoyable when you were on an adventure. She was Susan in *Swallows and Amazons*, except that the two brothers she lived with weren't related to her.

When Vic had first told her in his cockney accent that he lived with his brother, she had created an image of urchins surviving in a warren of narrow Dickensian city streets, and she had cast Vic, with his monkey face, as a kind of Artful Dodger, taking care of a younger, frailer sibling.

The reality, she'd discovered the morning after she left Kingshaven, was very different. Vic's brother Clive was not a boy at all. He was several years older and much bigger than Vic, trained in a boxing gym, worked in a nightclub until the small hours and played Frank Sinatra LPs on his record player. When she first saw him, Iris had already spent the night in his flat on the twenty-first floor of a gleaming concrete block in an area called Hackney, and was cooking a fried breakfast in the kitchen.

Clive stood in the doorframe, naked except for a towel tied round his hips.

'Can my friend stay here for a few days 'til she gets herself sorted out?' Vic had asked, straight out, as if he wanted to take advantage of Clive's state of undress.

Clive looked her coolly up and down as she stood by the cooker, fish slice in hand, and asked, 'How old are you?'

'Sixteen,' Iris replied, possibly too quickly, because he stared at her quite hard then, but she didn't blink.

'Do your folks know where you are?'

'Yes.'

She handed him a plate of bacon and fried bread and eggs, whose yolks she had managed not to break, hardly daring to look at his bare chest, or speak again in case she blew her chances.

'What's your name then?' he asked her, pointing at her with a forkful of fried bread.

'Sarah Bird,' she replied.

'Sarah Bird!' he'd mimicked her middle-class accent, with the faint trace of a smile on his face.

That morning, after she'd done the washing up, she had gone straight down in the lift to find a phone box to ring her mother, because she was sure that she wouldn't get away with lying to Clive again. She had informed Sylvia that she was staying with a friend and their family (a phrase she was quite proud of coming up with because it sounded so innocuous, but was also true) and assured her that she would ring occasionally and let her know how she was getting on.

'And you're safe?' Sylvia had asked.

'Yes,' Iris had replied without hesitation.

'And I don't suppose you're coming back?'

'No.'

Playing a grown-up could have disadvantages. The first café Iris had got a job in after seeing a postcard in the window had scratched tables, plastic ketchup bottles shaped like giant tomatoes, and an owner who touched her up every time he passed the sink where she was washing up. She warned him enough, but when he persisted, she tipped an entire bowl of hot dirty water all over him, and got the sack.

When he heard about the antics of her boss, Clive had gone straight up there and brought back a week's wages for her in lieu of notice, along with the jar of tips from the counter.

'I had a word,' he said laconically when she'd asked how he'd managed it.

After that, Clive had got her the job at the Cap, a couple of streets away from the club where he worked.

'A nice family-run establishment,' he'd told her. 'I've had a word.'

'Sarah!' the proprietor called up from below. 'You clearing tables?'

The men in the far booth had made inroads into their pasta. The portions were so big, it was rare for anyone to finish them.

'Have you finished?' Iris asked.

Without looking up, they pushed the large plates in her direction.

'Burton's interested,' the wiry one was saying. 'They're setting up their own production company, you know.'

The suit's eyebrows went up.

Iris began to wipe crumbs of parmesan off the oilskin with the tea towel she kept tucked into the belt of her apron.

'And the girl?' he asked.

'I suggested Julie Christie, but he won't have her. Says she's too well known . . .'

Iris's ears pricked up. She thought the wiry one must be a film director, or producer, she didn't quite understand the difference. Maybe she had seen him on *Late Night Line-Up*.

'God save us from writers and their artistic bloody integrity!' the one with the suit said, pushing the slim hardback book across the table.

The title was written in bold white letters over a grainy black and white photograph of a darkened alley with the distant silhouette of a woman disappearing into the night.

Hide and Seek by Michael Quinn.

As casually as she could, Iris picked up the book in one hand as if she were just moving it out of the way of her wiping.

The blurb on the back read: *When Martin Quest's daughter goes missing, his search for her takes him almost to the limits of his sanity. But is he trying to find out where she is, or who she is? Can we ever really know another person?* A powerful exploration of identity, love and loss.

Iris's eyes scanned the reviews:

'The author of *The Right Thing* gives us a chilling thriller where nothing is ever as it seems.' *The Times*

'A heart-wrenching tale of a father's love for his daughter.' *Daily Mail*

'You all right, love?' The London man was looking at Iris.

'Yeah.' Iris could feel her voice wobbling. 'Is it any good, this?' she asked, recovering herself.

'Fabulous!' he said.

'Hey, could I borrow it?' She tried to make the request sound as casual as she could.

'Help yourself!'

'Do you like reading?' asked the suit.

Patronizing sod! Sounded like he was surprised she *could* read. She hated it when people treated her as an inferior being just because she was wearing an apron. Sometimes Sarah Bird would have to fight back the impulse to be Iris Quinn with a smart response, as her mother would have called it.

'Thanks, I'll give it back,' she said sweetly.

Then she turned away from the booth a little too quickly and tripped over the handbag lying on the floor beside the next booth, sending herself falling 'arse over tit', as Vic would say.

Chapter Fifteen

May 1967

A flutter of white sails on an ink-blue sea presaged the beginning of the season as the shops on the High Street prepared for the influx of Whitsun visitors. Inflated lilos flapped on lines like brightly coloured washing in the breeze. A strong gust knocked over a tower of plastic buckets, sending the top one clattering down the street as if it could not wait to get to the beach. But Kingshaven remained empty of holidaymakers.

The wreck of the *Torrey Canyon* earlier in the year had dealt a blow to the struggling economy of the resort, at the very time when the attractions of package tours to Majorca were being advertised on the television. With pictures of the stricken super-tanker on the news every evening, and reports of oil washing up on the beaches of Cornwall, bookings, which had been diminishing year on year as people chose the sunny costas of Spain in preference to the sand-in-sandwiches seaside of the South Coast, now dried up completely. Several of the smaller guesthouses had already gone out of business. The Summer Show at the Pier Theatre had been cancelled.

In her office behind the reception desk, Libby looked at the reservation book. What had seemed a clever idea of Eddie's the previous year, to capitalize on the increase in ownership of small craft by throwing in a temporary mooring at the Yacht Club with the price of a double room at the Palace, had never been given a

421

chance to succeed. Nobody wanted to sail on an oil slick, and water-skiing was out of the question. Fast cars and motorways had done for the weekend trade. If people could get to the seaside and back in a day, why would they go to the expense of spending a night away?

However often her mother reassured Libby that these things went in cycles, and the trick was to hold one's nerve, Libby sometimes wondered, as she gazed at the full board of room keys, or listened to the china clock ticking away time in the empty hall, whether in an increasingly fast-moving world there was still a place for the traditional holiday the Palace had to offer.

'The Show Must Go On!' was Liliana's rousing call to arms, but increasingly Libby found a subversive thought creeping into her mind.

Why? Why must the show go on? Why did they have to struggle against the odds to keep up appearances? Why couldn't they just cut their losses, sell up and live normal lives like any other family?

'Mrs King?' Julia Allsop interrupted her daydream.

'Come in, Julia, dear.'

With their grandmother in apparently permanent residence, the younger Allsop children treated the Palace as their home, tricycling up and down the deserted corridors and playing rounders in the ballroom when it was raining. Libby had developed a soft spot for Julia whose forlorn little face seemed perfectly in tune with her own mood. She thought perhaps the child sensed her disapproval of the acrimonious custody battle her father Jolly was waging against Jennifer.

Nobody could dispute that what Jennifer had done was unforgivable, but Jolly's relentless drive to deny her access to the children seemed unnecessarily cruel, and Mrs Farmer's decision to testify against her own daughter in court was an unspeakable lapse of judgement. Ruby Farmer had always been socially ambitious, but she had allowed the desire to see her descendants occupy the Castle outweigh any consideration of loyalty or good taste. To cap it all, without so much as a by your leave, Jolly had called Moira, the nanny whose wages Libby paid, to stand in the witness box and give evidence against Jennifer.

The older Allsop girls had been sent away to school, which was probably for the best, and little James was still too young to understand, but at six, Julia was old enough to know what was going on. Julia had been closest to her mother and looked so much like her. It was Julia who missed her most. You could see the suffering in those huge blue eyes.

Libby put a tentative arm around the little girl, who immediately snuggled in close against her bosom. Julia was a real little girl whose favourite colour was pink and who liked fairies and princesses and things that little girls were supposed to like. So unlike Angela had been.

'Mrs King?' she asked.

'Why don't you call me Auntie Libby?'

'Could you read this letter to me, Auntie Libby?'

'Of course!'

The light was rather dim, but she immediately recognized Jennifer Farmer's handwriting.

'Where did you get this, Julia?' she asked, knowing that Jolly had forbidden communication between Jennifer and the children.

'I found it in Daddy's pocket.'

'Julia, dear, you mustn't go through Daddy's pockets.'

'It was an accident.'

'Even accidentally. Men's trouser pockets are not things for little girls to put their hands in,' said Libby, inadvertently making it sound rather more sordid than she had intended.

'You won't tell?' Julia's large eyes welled with tears.

Libby could feel her trembling, all shivery skin and bone, as helpless as when she had first held her as a tiny baby.

'We'll keep it between ourselves, just this once, shall we?'

Julia nodded solemnly. 'What does it say, Auntie Libby?'

Libby was rather touched by the child's trust. She unfolded the single piece of paper and held it at arm's length. 'Let me see. *My dearest Julia,*' she read. '*Do you remember the story of Cinderella?*'

'Yes, I do,' Julia interrupted.

'Do you want me to read it or not?' Libby asked.

'Yes, please,' said the child, meekly.

'Well, don't interrupt, then! Here we go . . . *In life, as in fairy stories, terrible things sometimes happen and little girls get separated*

from their mothers, but in the end, if you hope and pray long enough,
everyone will live happily ever after. I think of you every day, my
darling, and I send you a big hug and a kiss. Be a brave princess. All my
love from Mummy.

'There!' said Libby. 'Isn't that nice?'

'No, it's silly!' said Julia, suddenly cross.

Libby was inclined to agree. Why couldn't Jennifer just say something straightforward, instead of wrapping it up in flowery make-believe when she knew the child had a tendency to be over-imaginative?

'Cinderella's Mummy is dead!' Julia sobbed.

'I don't suppose your mother meant it quite like that,' Libby said, starting to regret allowing herself to be drawn in. 'She probably means that if you're patient, and good, sometimes nice things do happen when you least expect them.'

'But I don't have a fairy godmother!' said Julia. 'I don't even have an ordinary godmother because nobody wanted to be mine.'

'Oh, I'm sure that's not true.'

'It *is* true,' the child insisted. 'Mummy told me. It's because I'm a girl.'

'Well, if you really don't have an ordinary godmother,' said Libby, clutching at straws, 'I'm sure that must mean you have a fairy godmother.'

'Really?' Julia's eyes shone.

Libby was surprised that Julia was prepared to swallow this without challenge. Angela had always taken issue with any white lie she tried to fob her off with, unless it involved cash, like the tooth fairy.

'Will I get glass shoes?'

'Possibly,' said Libby, trying to rack her brains to think of a more practical equivalent the child might accept as a substitute. Some beach sandals were made of transparent plastic, she thought, although they tended to take on a nasty yellowish tinge with wear.

'Will I go to Mummy in a golden carriage?' Julia asked.

Somebody said Jennifer and the estate agent had gone to Scotland. Libby couldn't imagine him lasting long there. The Scots wouldn't be so keen to part with their money on a promise.

'That's really for your fairy godmother to decide . . .' said Libby, standing up and brushing invisible lint off her skirt.

On the whole, it was always a mistake to get too embroiled in other people's problems. It wasn't as if she didn't have enough of her own to cope with.

When she was a little girl, Claudia had been forbidden to go into the walled garden. Being an obedient child, she had never dared to push open the heavy wooden door and look inside, but she had often stood at a safe distance, looking at the high red-brick walls and wondering what secrets lay beyond. She had imagined dangerous convicts lurking there, or dragons, or ghosts. Even now she still retained a slight echo of foreboding, left over from childhood, as she approached the walls, although she had recently discovered that the reason she had not been allowed to go in on her own was Sir John's fear she would sever an artery on the broken panes of the glasshouse.

The lemon trees in terracotta urns on either side of the entrance gave off a sweet citrus fragrance. Claudia lifted the heavy iron latch. The door creaked as she pushed it open. The bright sunshine inside was a surprise after being in the shadow of the wall, almost as if she had stepped outside again. The garden was a patchwork of rectangular beds with neat rows of vegetables at different stages of growth.

In the far corner, Michael was digging. The walls gave shelter from the fresh sea breeze, and he was working in his shirtsleeves. When he saw her walking towards him, he stopped, leaned on his spade and gave her a smile which sparkled so much it caught her unawares and made her fall in love with him all over again.

Claudia had a secret so precious she could hardly contain the desire to skip with joy along the brick path towards him.

Michael lifted a spadeful of new potatoes. She was always amazed at how many there were under each plant. They thudded into the zinc bucket beside him, releasing an aroma of freshly dug earth.

Together they walked hand in hand back to the East Wing of the house, removed their wellington boots and went straight up to bed to enjoy the delicious luxury of making love in the afternoon. Afterwards they sat up side by side in bed, watching the sky turn gold and then, fleetingly, pale pink before an unequivocal darkness descended as rapidly as the moment after an electric light is switched off.

'Do you fancy going to the flicks tonight?' Michael asked.

Claudia leaned her head on his shoulder, listening to his heart-beat, and the slow, reassuring fall and rise of his chest.

On Friday evenings, they often walked to the Regal. Out of season, the cinema struggled to attract an audience which now received moving pictures in their living rooms. The last time they had gone, Claudia was sure she had heard mice nibbling at discarded Kia Ora cartons and scuttling behind the double 'love' seats in the back row.

'I'd rather stay right here,' she said, slipping her leg over his.

'God, woman, you're insatiable!' Michael said, kissing her quickly, and then softly and persistently until she stopped knowing where she ended and he began.

Later, in the darkness of the room, she wasn't sure whether he had fallen asleep.

'Michael?'

'Hmm?'

'I went to the doctor today . . .'

'Hmm?'

Claudia could tell that he was drifting.

'I'm pregnant,' she whispered softly as she kissed the secret goodbye, silently wishing it luck on its way out into the world.

The sky was so clear, there would be a hard frost in the morning, but the longer Michael stared up, picking out constellations, the milkier with stars it became.

On a night such as this, long ago, he remembered telling Iris that there were more stars in the sky than all the grains of sand on all the beaches of all the world.

And she, always sceptical, had asked, 'How do you know that?'

He had attempted to explain the concept of infinity to her and she had listened, her face frowning with the effort to understand. And a little later on she'd said, 'But, Daddy, if there are an infinite number of planets like Earth which all have sandy beaches, the infinite number of grains of sand must be bigger than the infinite number of planets.'

She must have been about nine at the time because she was in his class at school. He had always found it difficult to be fair to Iris in class. She was so clearly the most intelligent child, but he was scrupulous about not showing favouritism. There were some children whose hands went up whenever he asked a question even if they had no idea of the answer, and he had to plough through their suggestions, or their 'don't knows', trying to make it look as if his failure to pick Iris was entirely random.

'Why do you always choose me last?' she once asked him. 'And why don't you ever say, "Well done, Iris," like you do to the others?'

When he tried to explain to her that he didn't want her to become unpopular because she was the teacher's daughter, she said, 'I don't particularly mind about being unpopular.'

That had horrified Sylvia when he told her, but Michael had found it rather admirable.

'We have to respect her as a person,' he told Sylvia when she went on about Iris not being like other little girls.

'But she's a child!' his wife had replied, regarding him as if he were mad.

'In infinity, are there infinite Irises?' his daughter had asked him.

The logic of the proposition seemed to deny the reality of her uniqueness, and Michael hadn't known how to respond.

Michael's memory of Iris was so clear tonight, he couldn't believe it was possible that she was not still alive, still thinking her complicated thoughts, still questioning everything around her. Perhaps even looking up at the same stars.

Iris.

When Claudia had told him earlier in the evening that he was going to be a father again, his first thought had been of her.

How could he have another child when he had lost his first?

Michael knew how much Claudia wanted a baby. He affected an interest in all her reading about nutrition and naturopathy. He had indulged her wish to take up Sir John's invitation to stay at the Castle when the lease came up on the house in Hampstead, wanting her to have the satisfaction of knowing that they had tried everything. Claudia had convinced herself that nature would take its course if only she was close to nature, but Michael had never believed or really wanted that to be true.

When she had whispered this evening that they were going to have a baby, he had been glad it was dark and she would not see the fear in his eyes.

It was a similar apprehension to that he'd felt when Sylvia had fallen pregnant with Anthony, almost immediately after they'd arrived in Kingshaven. People said that a parent's love was infinite, but even though Michael had tried to feel as much love for Anthony as he did for Iris, he hadn't. The simple fact was that he did not love his son as he did his daughter. Even when he tried to concentrate on Anthony's babbling, if Iris butted in he would find he had turned to her without even realizing that he had stopped listening to Anthony.

Curiously, Anthony had never appeared to mind. He was a good little lad, and didn't bear grudges, as Iris did. He was still like that now. When Anthony had come up to the Castle to visit him at Christmas – a pretty brave thing to do in the circumstances – he had chatted on confidently, impervious to Michael's total lack of interest in fives or rowing or whatever it was they did at Harrow School. Claudia said it was a useful quality, and Anthony would go far because of it.

There was a part of Michael which was excited at the prospect of seeing Claudia's particular sympathetic intelligence directed at the project of nurturing another life. But that was balanced against the knowledge that their own relationship would be different. The very moment she told him, and he realized that she had kept the secret from him for several hours, he had known that the child would change the way they were together.

And, selfishly, he longed for it to stay just the way it was.

He wondered if the new baby would put Claudia off sex as motherhood had Sylvia. Was this ultimately the reason he had not warmed to his son? Michael wondered. If Claudia's recent amorousness was anything to go by, pregnancy seemed to be having exactly the opposite effect on her, but Michael knew he would never handle her slim, girlish body in quite the same way, and that they would never again enjoy the pure exclusivity of loving one another.

'Whenever you look up, there I shall be – and whenever I look up, there will be you.'

There were so many stars this evening.

If you believed in an infinite universe, then there existed the possibility of a world in which a Michael and a Claudia remained exactly as they were this afternoon before she told him, and Michael envied them a little.

The bus from Lowhampton was on time. At the stop next to the clock tower, Claudia stepped back as the doors opened with a hiss to let the passengers come down the steps: a couple of visitors dragging heavy suitcases behind them; and then Josie, their first weekend guest, with a fringed suede handbag over her shoulder, an open book in one hand and an unwieldy raffia bag in the other.

Claudia went to hug her friend.

'Just a minute,' said Josie, finishing the page she was on.

'*The Magus*.' Claudia ducked under the book to see the title. 'John Fowles wrote *The Collector*, didn't he?'

'I've never read anything like this,' said Josie. 'It's utterly compelling.'

'I think he lives down the coast,' Claudia said.

'Oh my God! Do you think we could drop by?'

'No,' said Claudia, laughing. 'I expect he's come down here to get away from metropolitan journalists like you. What on earth have you got in here?' she asked, trying to grasp both of the little scratchy handles of the raffia basket in her small hand. There was an assortment of clothes, several newspapers and a biscuit tin all thrown on top of one another.

'Later,' said Josie, putting a finger of secrecy to her lips.

They began to walk up the High Street.

'So, this is what you've come back to,' said Josie, with a decidedly unimpressed glance at the shops.

'It doesn't really feel like coming back,' Claudia told her. 'More like a progression. We found we were coming to the Castle most weekends, and then our landlord came back suddenly from the

States, and my father needs a bit of looking after, so it just seemed like the solution for us to move down here for a while,'

'You're taking this back-to-nature thing a bit seriously, aren't you?' Josie said, looking pointedly at Claudia's mud-caked wellington boots and the big jumper of Michael's she was wearing.

Claudia imagined the expressions on the faces of the customers of the Ship Inn should Josie walk in with her purple-and-orange-striped Biba suit with trousers that flared out from the knee.

'Are the locals hostile to you and Michael?' Josie pressed on, as keen as ever to have all the facts.

'I get a few looks. I don't know whether because we're living in sin, or simply because we're living at the Castle. Sir John's always attracted controversy. The popular view is that if he had handed the estate over to his son, the wife wouldn't have run off with the estate agent . . .'

'Instead he welcomes an adulterous novelist and a glamorous divorcee to keep chickens in his garden . . . your very own *Forsyte Saga*,' said Josie.

'I expect similar things happen in every small town,' said Claudia. 'And the chickens were there already,' she added dryly.

'What about Michael's wife?'

'Actually, that's her shop.' Claudia pointed at the double-fronted store which had been Farmer's Outfitters, where she purchased her school uniform when she was growing up. The jointed mannequins with their unlikely hourglass figures had gone, and instead Sylvia's bright summer shifts were displayed like festive bunting against a painted backdrop of white beach huts. She doubted whether Sylvia sold uniforms now. 'It's what she always wanted, according to Michael,' she said.

'Oh, lucky her, then!' said Josie with heavy sarcasm.

Claudia was beginning to feel a little embattled.

'Have you made friends down here?' Josie enquired.

'A few,' Claudia lied.

There were really only Barbara and Peter who had bought the Riviera Guesthouse after Ivor Brown and his mother moved away. The sign outside now declared it was a vegetarian guesthouse, which had given Claudia the excuse to strike up a conversation with Peter who was often in the front garden. They discovered they had things in common. Peter and Barbara had both been teachers and Barbara was now studying homoeopathy. They'd talked about buying free-range eggs from Claudia, and Claudia was always saying that they must come over for supper, but she hadn't got round to fixing a date because she slightly dreaded introducing people to Michael. He could be so charming on certain days, and so difficult on others. At Christmas, when Edith Payne had come over from America with her four sturdy children, she had invited them to Dr Payne's Christmas soirée. It was a tricky enough social occasion, but Michael had made things much worse by holding Edith's American husband personally responsible for the Vietnam War.

'How much further?' Josie asked wearily as they walked past the abandoned railway station. Old green paint was peeling on the awning and there were wild hollyhocks growing out of the tracks.

'Not too far now,' said Claudia.

'Half of Hampstead seems to be escaping the rat race these days,' said Josie. 'Everyone's buying up old rectories and raising goats and lettuces; that sort of thing.'

She made it sound like a fashion decision rather than a choice about how you wanted to live your life.

'Don't you miss going to the theatre and parties and all that civilized stuff?' Josie demanded.

Claudia felt slightly as if she were being interviewed for one of Josie's articles. She wondered if she would open the colour supplement in a couple of weeks' time and find her answers quoted under a title such as 'The New Landed Gentry'.

'You were always more gregarious than me,' she said neutrally.

'Are you working?' Josie wanted to know.

Living at the Castle was much harder work than they had imagined. Michael got up early and usually managed to do some writing in the mornings, but most of Claudia's day was taken up with attending to the garden, cooking lunch for her father and Sir John, doing everyone's washing, or walking into town to buy provisions they could not grow themselves.

It left her with little time or energy for the painting she had planned to do. In the evenings, she was so physically tired, she would immediately succumb to dreamless sleep.

When they were more accustomed to their chores, she thought there would be more time. There would always be weeds to pull up, but not the wilderness Michael had had to hack through, like the Prince on his way to Sleeping Beauty, in order to get the vegetable beds going. The time would come for her to paint, but she was in no hurry. The pace of life was different here.

'Michael's writing a screenplay,' she offered, unwilling to start justifying herself to Josie.

He found the work difficult and frustrating, especially when Terry Lacock sent back his drafts with suggestions for changes, but the money had bought them a year, and Michael would never have let anyone else adapt *Hide and Seek*.

'And your role is to support him?' Josie said, aghast. 'Haven't you read Betty Friedan?'

'Of course I have!' Claudia defended herself. 'I don't see myself as seeking fulfilment *through* Michael, but alongside him . . .'

Josie looked dubious. 'But what do you do all day?' she asked, exasperated.

'I'm pregnant,' Claudia suddenly admitted.

It wasn't how she had wanted to tell Josie, but it felt somehow dishonest to go any further in the conversation without saying it.

Josie raised her eyebrows, but said nothing for a few moments as she puffed along beside Claudia, finding it difficult to keep pace on the steep incline in her impractical city shoes.

'Do you remember how it was at Cambridge – all those times you prayed to God that if he could only make it so you weren't pregnant, then you'd start believing in him?' she finally said.

Claudia did remember Josie's frequent pregnancy crises, but she had herself remained a virgin until her engagement to Tim. By Josie's standards, she was lamentably inexperienced.

'Is Michael happy about it?' Josie asked.

'Of course,' said Claudia with more certainty than she felt.

He had said all the right things, but she sensed that an

ambivalence remained. There was no way she was going to admit that to Josie.

'I suppose I ought to say congratulations,' said Josie finally.

'Thank you,' said Claudia, flattened by her friend's reaction. 'So, what are you working on at the moment?' she asked, trying to divert the conversation.

'I'm doing a big piece about psychedelia. Obviously I've had to do a lot of research in the field of mind expansion . . .' Josie winked.

'Drugs?' Claudia asked, a little shocked.

'I've dropped acid a couple of times,' said Josie casually. 'It's an experience, but on the whole I prefer hash. I'm taking a class in TM. We're thinking of going to India for a whole summer of peace and love, man.'

'Is "we" anyone special?' Claudia was aware how out of date she sounded.

'Baby, I'm not really into the limitations of a relationship with one person,' Josie told her. 'Thank God for the Pill!'

They stopped for breath, and looked at the view over Kingshaven. The sea was blue and mirror-shimmery like the wing of a tropical butterfly. Surely even a trendy metropolitan cynic like Josie could not fail to wonder at the breathtaking beauty of the bay.

'Wow!' said Josie eventually. 'That is truly mind-expanding!'

Claudia felt a leap of triumph in her heart.

'What's that monstrosity?' Josie asked, pointing.

'It's the Palace Hotel. The Kings are the town's first family,' Claudia told her.

'The Kings? In the Palace? You are kidding me, aren't you?' Josie asked.

'Do you know, I'd never thought of that,' said Claudia. 'It used to be quite glamorous in its day, by all accounts. Noël Coward stayed there, and Daphne W. Smythe, you know, the detective novelist, even Edward and Mrs Simpson, I believe . . .'

'It kind of spoils it, though, doesn't it?' said Josie, not really listening.

'Michael would agree with you on that,' said Claudia.

'That would be a first!' said Josie, laughing.

*

The question of what would become of Christopher when he left school in the summer constantly simmered in the King family's thoughts. He was such an introspective young man, it was difficult to know what career he could successfully pursue.

'The Navy's the obvious thing,' Uncle Cyril said, trumping Liliana's queen of hearts from his hand, palming his fourth trick across the blue baize surface of the card table.

Cyril had always claimed a special friendship with his great-nephew, producing pennies from behind Christopher's ear when the boy was at an impressionable age, and awarding him the skin of a mangy tiger he said he'd shot during his days in the Raj. (It had given Christopher nightmares and had to be removed from his bedroom wall and stowed in the attic.)

The reason behind Cyril's uninvited visit to the Palace this evening Liliana hadn't as yet gleaned, but it was typically bumptious of him to think his opinion about his great-nephew should carry as much weight as everyone else's.

'Snap!' cried Eddie from the other card table where he was playing the children's game with Libby.

'Christopher detests the cadet corps. He always has,' Liliana said, demonstrating the fact that she was her grandson's chief confidante.

'You're not supposed to *like* it,' Eddie scoffed.

'The Navy'll make a man of him,' Cyril offered, trumping Ruby's ace of spades.

'Do try to count, Ruby,' Liliana hissed at her bridge partner.

'That is exactly what you said about his school,' she reminded Cyril.

If anything would make a man of Christopher, Liliana knew it was not a crowd of bullies but a determined woman. Privately, she put her hopes in the idea that a capable girl would take the boy under her wing, just as she herself had done with Basil, whom Christopher so closely resembled. There was a definite propensity to feebleness on her husband's side of the family, what with Rex and Alex and, to be honest, Basil himself, until she (quite literally) got her hands on him.

'Snap!' cried Eddie again.

Liliana tutted. What an example to set! She and Basil would never have dreamed of playing anything less demanding than bezique. You could hardly blame Christopher for his failings.

Her truculent granddaughter Angela was less of a worry these days. There would always be a well-bred young man in need of a presentable horsewoman for a wife. Angela was not pretty enough to be a prize for a first-born son, but she would certainly be up to scratch for a second, and, sometimes, with a bit of luck, the first son met with an untimely end, as Liliana knew only too well.

Technically, of course, her brother-in-law Rex had not yet met his end, Liliana had been reminded recently when one of his irritatingly cheery postcards had arrived with a picture of the Pagoda at Kew. The scrawl informed her that he was recuperating in a major London hospital from an operation. *All visitors welcome!* he had written.

Liliana had been sorely tempted to write back, *Something serious, I hope?*, but she had kept her dignity and her silence. Nevertheless, the postcard had disquieted her. London was rather close for comfort, and, to his credit, Rex had never suggested a reunion before. Liliana tried to reassure herself that it was probably just the sentimental wish of a dying man, but the bat squeak of foreboding in her head was as difficult to budge as the real-life bats who had recently taken up residence in the roof of the tower and swooped around her windows at twilight, unsettling her with their unpredictable trajectories.

Liliana watched Cyril's devious face deliberating between two cards.

'Anyway, what's the point of Christopher going into the Navy if he's destined to run a hotel?' she asked as she scooped up the trick Cyril should have made, tapping the four cards neatly on the table and placing them in a horizontal pile on top of her growing stack. Now she had control, Cyril didn't have a hope of making three clubs, let alone four. Not that it was entirely his fault. The dummy hand Christopher had put down bore no relation to his bid. When they next had a quiet moment together, she would have to try to explain the basic principles of bidding to her grandson again.

'I sometimes wonder whether he's really cut out for running the hotel,' Libby ventured.

'He needs to learn on the job,' Liliana told her daughter.

'But there's so little for him to do here these days,' said Libby dismally.

'I was thinking perhaps of another hotel,' Liliana continued.

'Who'd have him?' Ruby Farmer interjected.

Not for the first time, Liliana wished her friend wouldn't put her oar in during discussions that were none of her business.

'To be honest, Ruby's got a point. I don't think any of the hotels round here need more staff in the present climate,' Libby said.

'I was thinking of somewhere further afield,' snapped Liliana.

'Didn't you used to have a friend at the Savoy, Lil?' Ruby Farmer remembered.

Liliana glared at her. 'There may be a string or two I could pull,' she said.

'Really, Mummy? That would be marvellous!' said Libby.

'What would be marvellous?' asked Christopher, returning to the room to see Uncle Cyril losing the rubber.

'How would you like to work in London?' Libby asked him.

'As an architect?' Christopher asked optimistically.

'Darling, you have to go to university to be an architect,' Libby explained patiently.

'You never know, I might pass some of my retakes,' Christopher said, looking round the room for support.

Ruby picked up the *Radio Times*.

Uncle Cyril concentrated exceptionally hard on shuffling the deck.

'Doesn't anyone here have any faith in me?' Christopher cried.

There was a resounding silence.

Liliana watched as he turned and ran out of the room. The most worrying aspect was that the poor thing had no idea of his own limitations.

Cyril was the first to break the embarrassed silence. 'Talking of hotels,' he said, although nobody now was, 'my sister-in-law Adela has written to ask me to put her case.'

So this was it, the wily old fox, Liliana thought. Cyril always had an instinctive knack of capitalizing on awkward situations.

'What case is that?' she asked with feigned disinterest.

'She would like to come and stay here.'

'For how long?' Libby asked politely.

Cyril gave one of his infuriating, knowing grins, and Liliana observed her daughter's face fall as she realized that he wasn't talking about a holiday.

'Why didn't Mother ask us herself?' enquired Eddie, belatedly cottoning on.

'I don't think she wanted you to feel under any obligation,' said Cyril, giving his nephew a ghastly pious smile.

'But why now?' Eddie asked.

'It appears she has run out of money,' Cyril explained. 'What little she had, she has, unfortunately, lost.'

'Lost?'

'They've no idea how she managed to get to the casino, and everyone's surprised she was let in wearing her habit . . .'

Cyril paused as the assembled company tried to picture the scenario.

'Eddie's mother affects to dress as a nun,' Liliana explained to Ruby, whose mouth was hanging open.

'Poor Mother,' said Eddie eventually.

'She fervently believes it was God's will,' Cyril elaborated. 'Says she heard him telling her to put it all on black. As chance would have it, red came up.'

'Can't you sue the sanatorium for negligence?' Liliana suggested, desperate to come up with an alternative plan. She'd only met Adela on one occasion, at Libby and Eddie's wedding, and it certainly wasn't an encounter she wanted to repeat on a daily basis.

'I've gone into all that,' Cyril explained wearily. 'They claim there's nothing in the terms of engagement that obliges them to confine an inmate to the premises . . . and Swiss lawyers probably cost a bob or two . . .'

'What about the casino?' Libby suggested.

'Again, difficult to ascertain whether we'd have a case. By all accounts, Adela appeared to be sober and compos mentis. Apparently, she wasn't the first person of a religious persuasion they'd had through their doors . . .'

'Sounds to me like she's barking mad!' Ruby declared.

Liliana wished again she would keep her opinions to herself. Couldn't she see where this one was heading?

'But surely she needs specialist care?' asked Libby with uncharacteristic panic in her eyes.

'I'd be lying if I said she wasn't eccentric,' said Cyril. 'But she's still quite spritely. No problems with her movements, if you get my drift. Harmless really. I'd have her myself, but with the size of my bungalow . . .'

His eyes travelled round the huge, empty lounge.

Liliana stared at Eddie, willing him to come up with some excuse. It had to come from him. Adela was his mother, although a fat lot of use she'd been to him. Given the emptiness of the hotel, and the presence of Ruby Farmer, who was not even a relative, it was going to be difficult to argue logically that Adela shouldn't be allowed to take up residence.

'I don't see how another old girl would make much difference, do you?' Eddie said to Libby with the casual tactlessness he always seemed to find when tensions were running so high people were practically spitting at each other.

Libby glared at Liliana. 'I told you so,' her daughter seemed to be saying. She had made it clear that Ruby had outstayed her welcome on a number of occasions, and now – too late though! – Liliana was of a mind to concur.

'Well, that's settled then,' said Ruby Farmer, folding her arms. 'Now, does anyone mind if I switch on *The Forsyte Saga*?'

When Michael had rented the television, Claudia had explained to Sir John and her father with some trepidation that he needed it to watch the *Wednesday Play* and learn about writing scripts himself. She had expected an outcry against this modern intrusion into their bookish world, but, to her great surprise, both elderly men had become almost instantly addicted to the object they referred to as the 'goggle box', turning it on each evening 'for the News' (although she couldn't help noticing they always managed to catch *The Magic Roundabout* too), and watching continuously until close down.

Television opened up a whole new world of arguments for

them: BBC1 or BBC2? Malcolm Muggeridge or Kenneth Clark? Abortion – a fit subject for television drama? Dougal or Zebedee?

Tonight, as Claudia brought their supper to them on trays in the old music room, she couldn't help overhearing a schoolboyish discussion about whether Nyree Dawn Porter was more attractive than Joan Bakewell.

'How can you compare when one's in Edwardian costume and the other's wearing a skirt up to her backside?' said Sir John, who preferred blondes.

'It's not Joan Bakewell's legs I'm interested in, it's her brains,' responded the professor.

'Really, Papa,' said Claudia, placing the tray on his lap.

'Can't you tell your friends to keep the noise down?' her father replied irritably, without taking his eyes off the screen.

The sound of laughter was echoing through the whole house from the vast oval entrance hall, where, at Josie's suggestion, Michael had set up the long refectory table, and placed a candle on each step of the curving staircase, transforming it into a glittering film set.

When Claudia returned from the West Wing with the request that they be a bit quieter, Josie and Michael laughed even more.

'I was just asking your man here how it felt to be lord of the manor,' said Josie.

'And I was informing her that we are mere tenant farmers,' said Michael.

'You're the only socialist I know who could reject consumerist values in order to take up residence in a stately home,' Josie declared.

'And you're the only socialist I know who tries to deny the fact she's a landlord by calling her house a commune.'

'I thought you were supposed to be into communes,' Josie challenged.

'Not when Joe Stalin's in charge,' he said.

There was a long pause, and then, much to Claudia's relief, Josie said, 'You bastard!' almost affectionately.

'I do wish you two would stop arguing,' said Claudia, sitting down in her chair halfway down the long table.

'We like arguing,' Josie told her. 'Have a brownie!'

Josie sent a silver platter of cake squares hurtling down the table.

Claudia had cooked a cheese soufflé for supper, and afterwards an apple crumble made from the last of the Bramley apples they had picked and wrapped in newspaper in the autumn. The idea of eating fruit they had watched grow from blossom was wonderful, but if truth be told they were both getting rather tired of apples, and the gooey chocolate brownie made a delicious change.

'Where did these come from?' Claudia asked.

'I made them myself!' said Josie. 'With a special recipe.'

'Oh, they're not hash brownies, are they?' Claudia asked, detecting a slightly herby aftertaste at the back of her first bite.

'From my very own yard,' said Josie. 'Tastes so much better when you've grown it yourself,' she said, mockingly echoing one of Claudia's comments at dinner and collapsing into another fit of giggles.

Claudia felt slightly left out, but hesitated to eat any more of the brownie in case it might harm the baby inside her.

The ring of the telephone made Michael suddenly stop laughing and look up.

Claudia went to answer it.

'Terry Lacock,' Claudia told Michael, holding her hand over the mouthpiece. 'He thinks they may have found a girl . . .'

Michael rose immediately from his carver chair, his eyes shining with hope as his intoxicated brain misinterpreted the information.

He thought she meant Iris!

'He wants you to go up tomorrow and see her audition,' Claudia explained, as he walked towards her to take the call. His shoulders suddenly slackened as reason reasserted itself, and Claudia had to look away as she handed him the receiver, unable to bear the defeat in his eyes.

The dingy green room was full of proper actresses greeting each other with kissy-kissy affection and chattering dramatically about other auditions they had attended. They were ostentatiously friendly with one another, but none of them appeared to notice Iris. When she happened to focus on one who was pretending to

check her lipstick, whilst in fact looking over the top of her compact mirror calculating the odds against her rivals, the actress
stared at her with open hostility, and then nudged her neighbour,
who also stared.

'How tall is she?' Iris could lipread the whispered words.

'At least six feet.'

More tittering.

Iris was half inclined to supply the correct figure. Five feet ten
and a half, in fact. But she knew it wouldn't win her any friends.
It was a bit like being back at school. She never had been any
good at all-female gatherings.

Each time one of them was called, the other girls fussed
around, making sure she had the script, and telling her how good
she looked, and then they'd all chorus, 'Break a leg!'

There'd be a short phase of silence, and then the chatter would
resume again as soon as the candidate was out of earshot, with an
artificially sympathetic anecdote about how sorry one had felt for
her, when some embarrassment or mishap had befallen her at a
previous audition.

One by one, as the afternoon dragged into evening, they left
the room, until Iris was alone.

Was being last a good or bad sign? she wondered.

'Sarah Bird!'

The woman with the clipboard put a tick against her name as
Iris automatically stood up. All her confidence seemed to drain
down through her legs into the floor, making her wobble. She felt
as if she had temporarily forgotten how to walk, and she had to
talk herself through the motions. One foot; now the other. Her
heart was pounding so loudly inside her head she couldn't understand what the woman with the clipboard was telling her, and
when she followed her into the studio, the lights were so bright it
was like looking at the sun, which you weren't supposed to do. Iris
shielded her face with her hand.

This was her moment, Iris told herself, trying to calm her
breathing down. She had put so much effort into preparing for it,
waiting every night at the Cap in case Terry Lacock came, and,
when he finally did, returning Dad's book to him and remarking,
casually, as she had practised a thousand times in the mirror above

the bathroom sink, that she was born to play the part. He'd smiled at the cliché, but she thought she'd have the last laugh, insisting as he regarded her curiously, 'It's true!'

'Are you an actress?' he'd asked her.

'I am,' she'd asserted. 'Resting at the moment.'

She'd heard real actors talking, and that was what they said.

She didn't know whether he believed her, but he'd been intrigued enough to offer an audition the very next day. The project had been taken up by the BBC, he told her, and they were keen on new faces.

'OK, Sarah?' Terry Lacock's familiar London voice came from behind the camera. He sounded friendly, but she couldn't see him.

She wasn't an actress at all, Iris suddenly realized.

She was nothing like an actress.

'OK. Rolling.'

Somebody stepped out of the darkness beside her and snapped a clapperboard in front of her face. Iris jumped, and stood, staring into the blinding white lights, waiting for someone to tell her what to do.

After several seconds, Terry's voice spoke again.

'Cut! Is there a problem?'

It took Iris a moment to realize he was talking to her.

'I was waiting for you,' she explained, feeling a total idiot.

'Don't wait for me, just go ahead and say your line,' Terry instructed.

She could hear impatience creeping into his voice.

'Rolling . . .'

The clapperboard snapped in front of Iris's face again.

'Action,' offered Terry's voice helpfully.

She couldn't do it – despite all she'd read about Method acting, where you lived the person you were acting, so you weren't really acting at all. Just be yourself, Vic had told her this morning, unaware of the irony of his advice.

Come on!

Iris stared straight ahead and tried very hard to imagine that the camera was her father.

The day he left had been just like any ordinary Friday up until teatime, when everything changed. He was packing his rucksack to go up to London, like he did most weekends, and she'd agreed to look after Anthony on condition that her brother didn't speak for the whole of *Ready Steady Go!* She was concentrating so hard on the television screen that she didn't even look up when her father left the house.

Afterwards Iris had been tortured by the thought that if only she had said goodbye properly he might not have gone.

When her mother had come back in a state, Iris had thought she was upset because President Kennedy had just been assassinated.

She'd always wondered whether, if she'd listened properly to what her mother was saying, she could have run after Dad and stopped him at the station, or gone with him, or even just said goodbye . . .

The tears in Iris's eyes made the lens swim as she remembered she was supposed to be speaking her line.

'Hello, Dad,' she said.

There was a long, empty silence, and then Terry Lacock shouted, 'Cut!'

Iris could hear some whispering behind the camera, but she couldn't hear what they were saying.

'I don't want you to look at the actress, look at the monitor,' Terry instructed Michael. 'People look different on television.'

'Right,' said Michael, staring at the tiny screen.

'This is Sarah Bird,' said the studio manager.

Michael wished he'd never touched Josie's brownies. They'd put him in a permanent state of hallucination. On the train on the way up to London, he'd been sure that people were looking at him, aware that he'd recently taken drugs. In the studio, a stream of posh girls with RADA voices had paraded surreally in front of him, pretending to be his daughter, and now, suddenly, Iris's face sharpened into focus on the black-and-white monitor, just like the school-photo face which he always kept in his wallet, which loomed out of his dreams.

But it wasn't the same face. The hair was cropped. Older, thinner, frightened.

Then the face was gone again, replaced by white numbers flashing on the screen.

'Oh, dear,' Terry whispered to him.

Michael didn't trust himself to speak.

'Cut! Is there a problem?' Terry said to the actress.

'I was waiting for you.' Iris's disembodied voice calling out of the darkness.

Not Iris. Sarah, Michael told himself. Sarah.

Michael tried to test his senses. The studio, which was in a part of London he'd never visited before, smelled of damp, like school the first day after the holidays. The floorboards were pocked with cigarette burns.

Was the damage to his brain permanent, or would the effect of the brownies wear off?

'Rolling. Action.'

A long silence filled with doubts he could almost taste.

Michael found himself silently urging her on.

Come on! Come on! You can do it.

Not Iris, his brain kept saying. Sarah.

She stared at him with exactly the same bewilderment as the last time he'd seen her, when instinct had made him turn and look up as he walked away from the house in Cherry Avenue that he'd been locked out of.

He'd raised his hand to wave at her standing at the upstairs window and she had dropped the net curtain in front of her face.

Now, a tear welled in her right eye and spilled a ribbon trail of wetness over her freckles which she brushed away with an impatient fist.

It was not the face, not the voice, but that one little gesture, her face screwed up with self-criticism, that made him sure, finally, that he wasn't hallucinating.

Iris would look different now. Iris was three years older.

'What's her name again?' Michael stuttered.

'Sarah Bird,' said Terry.

Sarah Bird. Sarah Bird.

The name was like someone calling inside Michael's head. The girl was Sarah Bird and she was auditioning for the role of the daughter in the film of his book.

'She's not formally trained, but the camera loves her,' Terry was murmuring.

Michael stared past the camera.

'Hello, Dad.'

'Cut!'

'It *is* her,' Michael whispered.

'I thought you'd agree.' Terry seemed pleased. 'Lights!' he called.

The studio lights were suddenly switched off. It took a moment for his eyes to adjust.

Terry walked round to the front of the camera.

'Well, Sarah,' he said.

Sarah Bird! Of course! Iris's imaginary friend, who'd been responsible for all the paint Iris had spilled and all the dresses she had torn when she was little.

'Shall we tell her now, or shall we let her suffer a bit?' Terry called back to Michael.

'Tell her now!' he said, and saw her blink with surprise at his voice.

'Congratulations!' said Terry.

Iris stared at the director.

'Lost for words? That makes a change,' he said.

Michael watched his daughter. She had been a girl when he left, and now she was a woman, but suddenly her smile was innocently wide, and she leaped into the air, all unsophisticated arms and legs.

Trying to get a hold of himself – he was trembling all over – Michael emerged from his hiding place behind the camera.

'Sarah, this is Michael Quinn, the author!' said Terry Lacock.

'Were you watching me?' she asked, astonished.

'Yes,' Michael replied.

'Was I any good, then?' she asked, proud and defensive at the same time, just like she used to be when she wrote poems and made him read them there and then in front of her, peering over his elbow, scanning the lines quicker than he could, demanding to know his opinion before he could get to the end.

'Perfect!' he said, stepping towards her. 'Well done . . .'

He was about to say her name, but her eyes sent a message which said, 'Please don't tell on me!'

'. . . Sarah,' he finished, offering her his hand, thinking how bizarre this meeting was, and how much more complex than any of the scenarios he had ever dared to imagine.

The sensation of holding her hand in his was so precious, he never wanted to let it go. That familiar warm bundle of bones he had grabbed to cross roads and jump over puddles, and held on to so tightly as he swung her round and round in great looping circles over the rippled wet sand when the tide had gone out.

'You might have let me know you were alive,' he whispered as Terry went to take a phone call.

'I hadn't a clue you didn't know until I read your book,' Iris replied, with no trace of apology.

He didn't think about the implications of this enigmatic statement until later.

'When was that?' he asked.

'A few months ago . . . I rang your Hampstead number, but nobody ever answered. Anyway, you invented an interesting way of finding me, so now I've found you back,' she told him.

Each word of the impossibly idiosyncratic explanation confirmed the reality of her presence. Michael knew that his brain, even under the influence of drugs, was incapable of inventing such uniquely Iris-like thoughts. There was a brittleness about her he hadn't seen before, and he wondered whether she had acquired it fending for herself, or whether it was a result of the damage he had inflicted by abandoning her.

But there was no room now for guilt or self-recrimination, only love so elemental he couldn't stop smiling at her, even when she frowned at him, and he half expected to hear her say, 'Stop looking at me with that stupid face,' as she had done on reaching the age of self-consciousness, when, almost overnight, she had stopped clamouring for praise and started being embarrassed by it.

Iris could tell her father was struggling to keep up the pretence that he had never met her before. He would surely blow her cover if she wasn't careful. He kept calling her Sarah, far more than anyone would in normal conversation, and she was sure that

Terry was finding it a bit weird, but she couldn't think how they could go back now they'd started. Terry was the type of working-class-made-good bloke with a big chip on his shoulder, and he might easily take it the wrong way, and think they were taking the mickey.

Iris sipped the half-pint of lager and lime she'd asked for. She much preferred the sips of wine she'd swigged from the bottom of Chianti bottles at the Cap, but she didn't think they served wine in pubs.

Dad was already on his third pint.

'So, Sarah,' he said. 'What did you like about the book?'

She could see Terry was surprised at the way this usually laconic man kept pressing her with personal questions. Did she have a job? Where did she live?

'I liked the fact that the father eventually grew to respect the daughter,' she replied pointedly.

'That's very interesting, Sarah.'

The urge to say, 'Oh, just shut up!' was as strong as when she had gone up to the Grammar School and they still treated her like a little girl at home. It troubled Iris that, in the presence of a parent, she was feeling about twelve years old again. She'd become Sarah because she'd wanted to leave Iris behind in Kingshaven. But now Iris seemed to be back, as cross as ever, and the Sarah disguise was as unconvincing as a joke false nose, to anyone who knew her.

Terry stood up. 'I've got to be off,' he said. 'Martha's got tickets for Covent Garden.'

He looked from Iris to Michael, as if he expected them to drink up and follow his lead.

'Are you working at the Cap tonight, Sarah?' he asked.

'No,' she told him. 'I'm off home after I've finished this.'

'Are you staying in London?' Terry asked Michael.

'I hadn't planned to,' he said.

'Where do you live now?' Iris heard herself asking, letting her guard slip for a moment.

Her father's face reddened.

'Kingshaven. It's on the South Coast,' Terry answered for him. 'Sounds idyllic.'

'Kingshaven?' said Iris, aghast. 'Never heard of it,' she added quickly.

'Good day's work,' Terry said to Michael, and nodded at Iris, who smiled at him.

And then he left the pub, glancing back from the door, as if he were slightly anxious about leaving them together.

'We're going to have to tell him, or he'll think we're lovers,' her father said.

'Yuck!' said Iris.

When she'd first seen her father's face, she had been shocked by how much he had aged. She didn't think anyone could mistake them for a couple.

With Terry gone, they were momentarily stuck for words.

Iris's finger played with a ring of spilt beer on the table top. When she looked down, she saw that it had written Iris. She crossed it out.

'You're back in Kingshaven?' she asked, her voice thick with the effort not to care.

Her father started on a long explanation about Claudia's father needing to be looked after and, with all the space in the Castle, the solution being for them to move in. He talked about how interesting it was to be there, excavating documents and artefacts from the attics, and how he'd come to enjoy the physical labour of growing food and living from the land. He was so full of it, Iris felt he was trying to excuse himself to her, as if it hadn't really been his decision to go back there, but he had simply been overtaken by the obviousness of it.

As if she cared!

She could see now that he was more contented than he'd ever been. Weatherbeaten but happy.

Part of her – the Sarah part – was glad for him, but the Iris part felt as confused and angry as if he'd left all over again.

'So, do you think that this affair with Claudia will last?' she asked.

He was startled by the question, as if the thought that it could end had never crossed his mind.

'Yes,' he replied. 'Yes, I do.' He hesitated. 'As a matter of fact, we've just discovered we're going to have a baby.'

'That's not always a guarantee of happily ever after,' Iris replied tartly.

He looked so crestfallen, she felt rotten for being so churlish. In the ensuing silence, she wished she could take it back.

'I'm sorry, Iris,' he finally said. 'So sorry. I know it must be hard for you to believe this, but I never thought that things would change between *us*. I was stupid. I thought we'd be the same, only I would be in a different place . . . It was very selfish of me . . .'

She knew that if she were a good person, she would tell him it was all right.

'Yeah, well,' she said. 'Doesn't matter now.'

She couldn't find it in herself to forgive him, and yet she hated the distance that now sprawled between them again.

'I can't believe that Mum didn't tell you I was OK,' she said, wanting to be conspirators again, the two of them, bound by their shared dislike of her mother.

'I behaved appallingly to Sylvia,' he replied guiltily.

Why did parents, however badly they got on, put up an automatic defence of the other parent to the child? Her mother used to do it too. It drove Iris mad because it was so dishonest and unfair.

'Yes, well,' Iris said, gathering all her resources together. 'I'd better be getting home now.'

She could see that he was longing for a detailed description, an invitation, even, but it was too soon for that. There was a truce, but it was still fragile, and she needed time to steady herself, otherwise she would slide straight back to being his antagonistic daughter again.

'Can I take you?' he offered. 'In a cab?'

'No, thanks. I'll get the bus, like I always do,' she said.

'Of course,' he said, but he looked so lost, she felt she had to give him something to hold on to.

'I expect we'll see a bit more of each other now,' she offered as they walked the short distance to the bus stop on Shaftesbury Avenue.

'Yes! I'll be coming to London for the shoot . . . and you're always welcome at the Castle—'

'No,' she interrupted. 'I'll never go back to Kingshaven.'

'No,' he said.

And then the bus was there.

'Bye, then, Dad,' she said, kissing him quickly on the cheek.

'Bye!' He went to hug her but she slipped out of his reach on to the platform. 'Iris?'

'What?' she said as the conductor pulled the bell twice and the bus lurched off.

'You . . .' He was running alongside.

'Yes?'

'You've grown up . . .' he said.

'Have I?' Iris could feel the stretch of the grin spreading right across her face.

And then he stopped running, and stood waving the bus all the way down the street, as if he was letting her go.

Iris climbed the stairs to the upper deck and found a seat at the front. She stared out of the window as the bus trundled through the streets of London. The route was familiar to her now, but there was always something new going on, new advertisements pasted on hoardings, new restaurants opening up with exotic names – Taj Mahal, Sam Pan, Kalamata – and hot, spicy cooking smells drifting from their doors.

I'd better be getting home now.

She wasn't sure that she'd thought of the flat as home until then. The arrangement worked well enough. She stayed in the spare room and paid the brothers rent, but she'd always thought of it as their home, not hers. How could the flat be her home when Vic and Clive didn't even know her real name? And she could never tell them the truth after all this time, because Clive wouldn't like that at all. Clive set great store in trust.

Home, in her mind, had been somewhere she'd run away from. And now it felt strange that both her parents were back in Kingshaven, but there was no home with either of them.

She would never speak to her mother again, she had decided that already.

Her father had a new family with Claudia and a baby on the way, a family that made him happy and successful instead of sad and thwarted.

Iris used to be the one who could cheer him up, but he didn't need her now.

For the first time since she had arrived in the capital, staring out of the window of a red double-decker bus, glimpsing strangers' lives in the first floor offices and bedrooms of Holborn, Islington, Newington Green, Iris felt lonely.

Vic was out. Too late, Iris remembered she was supposed to be meeting him after the audition. She wondered guiltily how long he had waited outside the Odeon.

Clive was about to go into town to work, wearing his usual sharp suit and pressed white shirt. Most men wore their hair a little longer these days, but Clive's was short and slicked back with Brylcreem, and his eyebrows were so dark and straight, Iris sometimes wondered if he plucked them. Clive's face was as perfect as the man in the cigarette advert on the hoarding next to the Angel, Islington.

Iris had practised grown-up and sophisticated in the mirror a million times, but when Clive looked at her, she always felt young and silly.

He made a little twirling motion with his forefinger. She obediently turned 360 degrees.

'You should wear make-up more often,' he said finally. 'How did it go?'

She was surprised he remembered what she was doing today. Clive never took much notice of her, although sometimes she had felt him looking at her, and once he had said, 'I've never met a woman like you, Sarah,' which she'd decided to take as a compliment – he'd said 'woman', after all – although she wasn't sure he'd meant it that way.

'Oh, I got the part,' she said.

'"Oh, I got the part"!' Clive mimicked her flat voice. 'You got the part?'

She nodded.

'She got the part!' Clive did a little shimmy on the spot. 'You know what, girl? You're a natural!' he said. 'Come on, you deserve a glass of bubbly,' he declared.

'At your club?' she asked disbelievingly.

She and Vic were always hankering to be invited, but Clive just laughed dismissively when they pleaded with him.

'At my club,' he confirmed.

*

Iris sank as elegantly as her mini-skirt would allow into the low leather seat of Clive's red MG. On the rare occasions he gave her a lift, she always felt like she was in *Alfie* with Michael Caine. Clive even sounded a bit like Michael Caine, if you closed your eyes.

The car had a distinctly masculine aroma of cigarettes and leather and astringent aftershave. Sometimes when they came up in the lift together, or when Clive was sitting at the kitchen table and Iris was washing up, she would catch a waft of him, and it would put her into a kind of trance for a second.

She wondered how many girls he had leaned over and kissed as they lay in this seat beside him.

As they whizzed back into town with the top down, Iris hoped that the people who looked enviously at the car mistook her for his girlfriend. Did she look old enough? Everyone always assumed she was Vic's girlfriend.

When she'd left Kingshaven on the back of his bike, she'd decided that it was a deal she'd be prepared to make for her freedom, but Vic had never even tried to kiss her again after the first time.

After a while, it had made her wonder if there was something the matter with her, but when she'd finally plucked up the courage to ask, Vic had confessed that he didn't really like girls like that.

'So why did you try to kiss me in the Gardens?' she'd asked him.

'It's what they expect,' he said, referring to the gang he sometimes tagged along with at weekends.

It had made her feel a bit funny at first, having 'one of them' as her best friend, but she liked having a secret of his to keep in exchange for his knowing where she came from. She understood without Vic spelling it out that her presence in the flat helped limit the chances of Clive asking difficult questions, just as her presence on the back of his Lambretta at weekends allayed any suspicions the gang might have.

From the outside, the Zebra Crossing Club looked like any of the other buildings in Soho, except that the windows at street level were filled in. Inside the shiny black front door, Iris and Clive walked down steps, carpeted alternately black and white, past a hat-check counter, and into a vast subterranean lounge which appeared to go on for ever. The effect, Iris later realized, was created by mirrored walls at the back of the dimly lit booths around the edges of the club. There were two semi-circular tiers of tables surrounding the dance floor. The carpet was zebra print and the entire room furnished in chrome and black vinyl. On either side of the stage was a Belisha beacon.

'Champagne cocktail,' Clive told the bartender. 'She's going to be on television.'

'You an actress?' asked the bartender as he eased the cork out of a bottle of champagne with a controlled pop.

Iris nodded, perching uneasily on a chrome bar stool.

A useful discovery she had made since coming to London was that people took you at face value. If you donned an apron and said you were a waitress, then you were a waitress. If you wore make-up and said you were an actress, you were an actress. If you added three years to your age, nobody questioned it.

There was a sugar cube in the bottom of her glass. She watched the trails of pinhead bubbles snaking up through the golden liquid before putting her lips to the rim of the shallow glass. Almost instantly, the effervescence seemed to enter her blood-stream, shooting to her head, obliterating the pockets of doubt inside her brain.

She noticed that there were multi-coloured lights under the dance floor.

'Better?' Clive asked.

'Very,' Iris declared, and then remembered that you couldn't be very better.

A hint of the smell of extinguished candles still hung on the cool air in the oval hall when Claudia went to answer the phone. When it rang late at night, there was always the slight fear that it would be the police with bad news. Claudia usually practised her greeting out loud to steady herself before picking up the receiver.

'Hello?'

'Claudia?'

It was Michael. The relief made her relax her cheek against the cold, heavy Bakelite receiver.

'I've found Iris!'

Claudia said nothing, remembering his mistake the previous evening.

'Claudia, are you there?'

'What do you mean?' she asked carefully.

'I've found her! I'm getting the last train.'

He sounded as if he might have been drinking.

'You've really found Iris?'

'I've really found Iris,' he repeated impatiently, as if it was slightly unreasonable of her to demand clarification. 'Or she found me, I'm not sure.'

'And she's well?' Claudia asked, holding on to her caution, in case he was wrong. Someone had to be strong to pick up the pieces.

'Very well. Very grown-up. Look, I'll tell you all about it . . . I'm going to miss my train.'

'I'll wait up. Michael, are you OK?' Claudia asked.

'I'm insanely happy!' he shouted.

It didn't sound like him at all.

'See you later, then,' she said.

'See you later!'

She was about to replace the receiver when she heard him still on the line.

'Claudia?'

'Michael, you'll miss your train—'

'Claudia, I'm really pleased about our baby, you know,' he said.

'Go and get your train!' she told him strictly.

But inside she began to let herself feel mad with happiness too.

When Iris woke up, the sunlight through the windows made it feel like she had those sparklers you waved around on bonfire night behind her eyelids. She pulled the blanket up over her head, trying to go back to sleep, but her heart was pumping champagne instead of blood, and her brain felt like it was floating somewhere just out of her reach. She wasn't in pain, but she wasn't convinced her legs would support her if she tried to stand up, so she lay, trying to slow down the stream of images racing across her vision.

She could remember the sequence of events up to when Clive had brought his bosses over to meet her. They were brothers, big men who bore a strong family resemblance to each other. Their faces were coarse and pitted like the market traders she served at the Cap, but their bodies were encased in immaculate dinner suits, with shiny lapels and braiding down the leg. Their hands were huge and soft, with big gold rings which crushed her fingers when they shook hands. One of them asked if she was a model, and when she said no, Clive had stepped in and said she was an actress and was very good at impressions. She'd offered Marilyn Monroe followed by Barbara Castle, and they'd laughed and wished her luck, and Clive had nodded at her, as if she had done well, before disappearing with them somewhere backstage.

After that, the club seemed to fill up and she talked to all sorts of people at the bar. Her glass was constantly refilled. She had a sense that the champagne had made her dazzlingly witty, but she couldn't remember anything she'd said. The only other thing she did remember was sitting for so long in a stall in the Ladies that the outline of the lavatory seat was imprinted in red on the back of her thighs. She got up when a fat black woman started banging on the door, saying, 'De boss is lookin' for ya, darlin'.'

Clive let her have the top down on the way home even though it was chilly in the early hours (now, as her head swam, she wondered whether she'd threatened to be sick). She seemed to remember singing 'Strangers in the Night' at the top of her voice as they sped along the Essex Road.

God! Now she recalled trying to go to sleep on the floor of the lift, and Clive carrying her into the flat like a newlywed and dumping her unceremoniously on her bed, where she now lay, still fully clothed, wondering how she would ever live it down.

Clive was in the kitchen reading the *Mirror*. 'All right?' he asked, pouring a cup of tea.

'Fine,' Iris replied brightly. When he didn't look up, she added, tentatively, still not sure of the extent of her misdemeanours: 'I'm sorry about last night.'

He looked up and smiled at her. 'You were on fine form,' he said.

She wanted him to explain exactly what he meant by that, but she didn't dare. 'Where's Vic?' she asked.

'Gone to work.'

'I was meant to go with him!'

'I explained you were a bit the worse for wear,' said Clive. 'You've never had champagne before . . .'

'How do you know?' Iris asked, pouring herself a cup of tea.

'You told me enough times.'

'Oh . . .'

Had she told him other things she could not remember?

'What you need is fresh air. Do you fancy a drive?' he asked.

The shade of Epping Forest was so complete and the carpet of bluebells so dense it made the air seem blue too. There was profound silence only interrupted by the soft low burble of an unseen woodpigeon.

'I come here to get a bit of peace of mind,' Clive said.

She almost made the mistake of laughing, because she didn't really associate Clive with troubled thoughts. His philosophy of life was based on a rigid moral code. If you worked hard, respected your family and took care of your appearance, you got what you deserved: a bit of money and a nice car. The idea that he might come to this quiet place and try to puzzle out the meaning of life made Iris look at him differently.

She remembered the first time she had seen him, standing in the doorframe of the kitchen rubbing the sleep from his eyes. It was the only time she had ever seen him looking vulnerable. The contours of his chest were so hard and smooth, it had made her want to touch his skin to see if it was soft and warm like anyone else's.

There was nothing but trees and bluebells as far as she could see. Iris could not now remember which way they had come in, and for a moment she was frightened that they were lost.

When they came to a peaty ditch, Clive offered his hand to jump her over it, and then he didn't let go. It felt odd holding his hand, almost as if her hand wasn't part of her any more; Iris didn't know whether she should point out that he could let go now, or just relish the sensation while it lasted.

She promised herself that she wouldn't speak unless Clive spoke first. He didn't do a lot of talking, and whenever she asked him questions about his work or his interests, he gave so little back that she became nervous, and spoke more and more quickly, making it worse.

Suddenly he stopped walking and faced her.

'I've never met anyone like you, Sarah . . .'

He looked so strange, so darkly, diabolically good-looking, it crossed her mind that he had discovered that she had lied about who she was, and he was going to kill her. There was no point in running because he would catch her up; no point in screaming because no one would hear. Her body would be found one day by a dog who had bounded off the lead. The cool, eerie stillness of the place gave it the solemn atmosphere of a graveyard.

And then he kissed her – out of the blue, she would later think, picturing how they must have looked, the two of them knee-deep in bluebells. The sensation was strangely familiar, and only then did she remember that he had kissed her the night before in the car, when she drunkenly told him she wouldn't get out until he did. But now he was the one who was demanding and she succumbing in astonishment.

He stopped suddenly and pushed her away.

'What?' she asked, frightened by his unpredictability.

'Vic,' he said, looking away from her.

'It's not like that, me and Vic. We're just friends,' she stammered, promising herself she wouldn't say anything more. She wouldn't betray her best friend. Couldn't. Mustn't.

Clive was looking up and down her body, making her feel naked.

Iris shivered, almost expecting to hear a cockerel crowing at her silence.

And then he was kissing her again, clasping her body to his so hard it squeezed the breath out of her, and when he finally stopped and looked at her, his eyes bright with surprise, she couldn't think of anything except the words of the song going round and round in her head, telling her not to spoil it all by saying something stupid like she loved him.

Chapter Sixteen

March 1968

It was the first day it had been warm enough to sit outside. The sunshine felt kind, and the scent of mimosa filled the air. Great clusters of yellow pompoms dusty with pollen cascaded from dark green fronds, the colour no more improbable than the trumpets of daffodils scattered round the orchard, and yet, to Claudia, the mimosa trees had always looked and smelled as if they would be more at home in some Southern clime, framing a view of the Bay of Naples perhaps, or among the white cubes of a Greek island.

Her father was sitting in the planter's chair with a baby in the crook of one arm, and a book held as far away from the half-moon glasses on his nose as his other arm would allow. At his feet, on the grass, the other baby made comically determined efforts to raise himself up to a crawling position, as if he were doing press ups.

Claudia sat on the edge of the hammock Michael had put up the previous summer between two apple trees, swinging gently backwards and forwards, and watched her father and her twins with pleasure so acute it was almost agonizing.

They had called the little boy Bruno Francis. Bruno because of the head of dark brown curls he had been born with, and Francis after Michael's brother. The girl was Fiammetta Monica. Fiammetta because when she was delivered there had been a twist of red hair at the top of her head like a little flame, and Monica because it had been Claudia's mother's name. They were as individual in character as they were in looks: Fiammetta always preferring to be close to the warmth of another person; Bruno always striking out on his own. He could roll from one end of a Persian runner to the other in no time at all. Now, leaving attempts to support his weight on his arms for another day, he set off across the orchard like a barrel, reaching the roots of the hawthorn hedge in the time it took Claudia to jump up off the hammock and chase after him.

'Where do you think you're going?' she asked, scooping him up and holding him in outstretched arms high above her head.

Bruno gurgled with pleasure. A string of drool dropped from his little wet mouth on to her face.

The delicate pink blossom of the almond trees above his head reminded Claudia of confetti caught in the branches.

'Bruno, do you want to come and listen to this story about a bear called Paddington?' Claudia's father called.

Claudia carried the baby boy over and deposited him on her father's lap with his sister. The book engaged Bruno's interest. He stretched out his hands towards it.

Claudia wished she could take a picture of the three of them, her two babies staring at the book, and her father squinting with concentration at the distant type, looking as self-satisfied a grandfather as there ever was.

From the moment she had announced her pregnancy to him, with some trepidation because she had never been able to predict how he would react, he had revealed a soft, almost sentimental quality that had taken her by surprise.

'My dear, I am so happy for you,' he had told her tearily, grasping her hand for a long time. 'I know how very difficult it has been.'

Until then he had given no indication that he had even noticed her childlessness, let alone sympathized with her distress. She would never have dreamed of talking to him about it. Whilst her father appeared to accept Michael's presence as inevitable, she had always been under the impression that her choice of life was a disappointment to him. She had assumed that this stemmed from her failure to pursue an academic career. But now she wondered if all along he had simply wanted her to do the thing that any daughter could do, regardless of education, but which she had found so difficult, which was to produce grandchildren.

The advent of a new generation of her family caused Claudia to reflect on her own history. Her father was an old parent who had been in his late forties when she was born. When Claudia went back to the large trunk of her mother's possessions which had come with them when they escaped through Hungary, and searched out the sepia photo taken on her parents' wedding day, she saw that her mother had been a much younger bride than she had previously realized. Her parents must have been married over ten years before she was born, she calculated. Perhaps her mother had experienced the same excited acceleration of hope each month and the same sudden brake of failure?

When Claudia eventually became pregnant, she had felt close to her mother in ways she had not before, and when it was confirmed that she was carrying twins, the first thought that had popped into her mind was how glad her mother would have been. It was such a comforting feeling of presence that, had she been a religious person, Claudia might have been inclined to describe it as her mother watching over her from another dimension – heaven perhaps – and smiling.

'Now, where were we?' her father was saying as he found his place in the story about a refugee bear who'd found a home in England.

He took the duty of reading to the twins very seriously even though, at just six months, they must be far too young to make any sense of the stories, and could only listen to the rhythms of the sentences and the cadences of his voice.

His battered panama hat was bleached white by the sunshine, and the children both had white sun bonnets on. For a moment Claudia saw them as a Renaissance painting in a shaft of sunlight on an Italian church wall: a bearded saint and two cherubs resplendent in their haloes.

Months of sleepless nights had put her brain into a heightened state where images often seemed brighter and more redolent with meaning than usual and she felt as if she was existing just a little out of step with reality. Sometimes her body was so tired she would find her eyes had closed briefly, even if she was hanging out washing or changing a nappy, and she would jolt awake, alarmed to have lost control even for a split second of time passing. The experience of motherhood was so different from the calm satisfaction she had imagined. It was like being gripped in an alternating vice of pleasure and fear, which made her acutely aware of her strength and her frailty.

Content that the twins were safe for the time being, Claudia lay back and allowed her eyes to close. She could feel the dappled sun patterns on her face moving as the hammock creaked gently, hear the faraway barking of a dog, and the murmur of her father's reading voice growing gradually more distant, like a musical box winding down, gently soothing her to sleep.

Liliana couldn't get the phrase she'd heard at the hairdresser's out of her head.

'It's a shame to see the Palace going to the dogs, isn't it?' Sylvia Quinn had said with exaggerated concern to Verity Dyer as they chatted away, cataloguing their neighbours' misfortunes.

The opinion had not been intended for Liliana's ears. Mrs Quinn hadn't known that she was behind the screen having her hair washed. Or perhaps she had. Liliana wouldn't put it past Verity Dyer, who was very keen to ingratiate herself into Mrs Quinn's favour, as so many others seemed to be. It was astonishing what a bit of money could do, and nobody had any respect for age any more.

Verity had never been very deferential, even when she was employed to sweep up the hair from the floor – although rumour had it that she'd always been ready to go down on her knees for Mr Maurice. Why else, Liliana asked herself, would he have bequeathed her the salon? Now Verity was in charge, and had renamed the place Get Set, she clearly considered herself above even the simple courtesies.

'Of course, there is a growing need for old people's homes,' Sylvia had continued, eliciting a coarse snort from Verity.

With the hose running over her head to rinse off the shampoo, Liliana lost the next few exchanges, although, from the tone of the laughter, they were in a similar vein.

'Do you really think so?' Sylvia was saying when the girl finally turned off the water and wrapped her head in a large towel.

Louder laughter, which stopped abruptly as the girl brought Liliana round and sat her on the opposite side of the salon from Sylvia, so that they were sitting back to back, but could see each other's faces in the mirrors.

To cap it all, Sylvia had smiled at her reflection sweetly, and asked, 'How's business?'

'Ticking over nicely,' had been Liliana's automatic response.

The recent outbreak of foot-and-mouth had put off the walkers. The 'I'm Backing Britain' campaign the government had dreamed up to mask the devaluation of the pound was a charade. People might put Union-Jack stickers in the rear windows of their cars, but they still chose to go to Europe for their holidays.

In a world where the holiday business was battling for new, young customers, there were certain advantages in concentrating on a more mature clientele. Libby had had to offer cheaper rates to old people's clubs, but they were normally returning block bookings with relatively low expectations. It was enough for most of them to purchase a postcard of the luxury hotel they were staying in which showed its beautiful blue swimming pool. Very rarely did one of them ask if the pool was ever going to be filled with water, and if they did, they were usually satisfied by the response that it was closed for repainting. Most of the old women (and they were mostly old women) were pleased enough, after a lifetime's cooking, to be served with a roast dinner in the evening, without thinking too much about the quality of the joint. As long as the meat was easily cut, the Yorkshire pudding light enough not to cause problems for dentures, and served with ample gravy, they ate up gratefully.

There was no longer a need to go to the expense of hiring a chef with a reputation. Since Mr Pocock's departure, the hotel had reverted to finding most of its staff locally.

Going to the dogs, indeed! So ungrateful, after all they'd always done for the town.

In the past, Liliana would have had a word with Mr Otterway and the next time Sylvia Quinn or Verity Dyer appeared in the paper it would have been the most unflattering picture he could find in the archives. But since the editor's retirement, and the impending closure of the *Chronicle*, which seemed inevitable unless a buyer could be found, there was no longer a way of striking back.

Liliana couldn't help noticing that Eddie's mother, Adela, was dropping titbits of her evening meal on the carpet, which were eagerly snapped up by Lord and Lady, Libby's latest generation of spaniels.

It had been agreed that Liliana, Mrs Farmer and Adela would eat with the guests, in order to give her daughter and Eddie some semblance of a normal family life, and, after a recent incident with a chicken bone, it did seem advisable for somebody responsible to be in the dining room to keep an eye on things. The arrangement was not without its drawbacks. It was a constant struggle to keep Adela from upsetting the guests.

It wasn't usually a problem having a nun on hand to say grace, although the Jewish Ladies' Bridge Club from Bournemouth had complained about her making the sign of the cross above their table. (Astonishingly, Adela redeemed herself by recounting some elaborate fantasy that she had hidden a family called Cohen during the war. When the ladies returned to Bournemouth, they had sent her a commemorative set of playing cards as a token of their appreciation for her bravery, and because they knew how much she enjoyed a game of canasta.)

Less easy to explain was a woman of the cloth smoking cheroots during, as well as after, the meal.

And there were her outbursts.

Much to Liliana's amusement, little Winny had unintentionally nicknamed his other grandmother Granny Addled.

Ruby Farmer's word for it was barking. Perhaps that's what they meant by going to the dogs! Liliana allowed herself a private snigger.

This evening, Adela seemed intent on throwing her entire meal piece by piece on to the carpet for the spaniels.

'Please stop doing that,' Liliana requested quietly. 'Gravy stains are the worst to get out and you'll only make them fat.'

'I'll give it to her to taste then, shall I?' Adela asked, pointing her fork aggressively at Ruby Farmer.

'I don't want it, thank you,' said Ruby, jerking her head away from the proffered meat.

'As I thought,' Adela growled.

'What did you think?' Liliana asked, trying to humour her.

'Don't think I don't know what you're up to,' Adela suddenly shouted, pushing her chair back and standing up.

'Adela, dear, do sit down. You've hardly touched a morsel,' said Liliana through gritted teeth.

'I know all about you, Liliana King! I've been warned! You won't get rid of me so easily!'

It wasn't so much the loudness of her voice as the German accent which always attracted attention.

The room collectively held its breath.

'My dear Adela, why on earth would I want to get rid of you?' Liliana asked, with deliberate irony, flashing a little glance around the room. She was pleased that her quicksilver wit, as Basil used to call it, had not rusted with disuse. A number of faces offered sympathetic smiles.

'You won't poison me!' said Adela.

'Oh, do calm down, Adela dear, you'll be giving me ideas,' Liliana said with a tinkling laugh, inviting her supporters to proclaim their own lack of senility by joining in the joke. Obligingly, Ruby started off the giggling, then everyone began laughing so much the dogs started barking too.

Liliana relaxed against the back of her chair.

Adela, still standing isolated, looked rather lost. She relit the end of her cheroot. 'I shall pray for your soul,' she announced before striding out of the room with rosaries rattling.

'Well, that's a kind thought, anyway,' said Ruby Farmer.

If Adela went on repeating her mad accusations over and over, would people continue to assume that her demented brain was making things up, Liliana wondered, or would they begin to believe that the layers of social convention that protected sensitive information were simply rotting with age, leaving facts exposed?

And what exactly did she mean when she said she had been warned?

The days were drawing out, and the sunshine had brought people on to the promenade for an evening stroll. Even the most disapproving of Kingshaven's citizens found it impossible not to smile at the twins sitting up facing each other in the big, old-fashioned pram, looking, Michael thought, a bit like members of the royal party at Ascot peering over the sides of their carriage as if they owned the place.

Little bastards they might be, but such beautiful little bastards! Bruno was facing out to the world, his dark brown eyes fringed with long lashes which were the envy of every woman who stopped to look. Fiammetta's eyes were as blue as periwinkles. Michael noticed that most people, wary of mispronouncing the babies' Christian names, referred to them, with grudging affection, as the Dearchildren.

Claudia had looked so peaceful sleeping in the hammock, Michael had thrown a blanket over her when the sun started to lose its warmth, wanting to let her rest for as long as possible.

After giving the twins their evening bottles, he'd decided to take them out in the pram in the hope that they would fall asleep and be ready to be transferred into their cots when they got home.

The pram was the one place where the babies synchronized their behaviour, and he wondered if this was because they felt more relaxed when occupying the same enclosed space (as they had for the best part of nine months), or whether they were already competitive, and couldn't bear the idea of missing something the other might see. Awake, they were alert and curious about everything, but when they decided it was time to sleep, they would go down within seconds of one another.

He had suggested to Claudia that they should let them sleep in the pram at home, but she worried that they'd never get used to a cot, suggesting, only half jokingly, that they would have to build bigger and bigger prams.

He'd wanted to tell her that they would sleep in time. When you had your first child you thought that every stage would go on for ever and you couldn't envisage a time when suddenly, for no apparent reason, your baby decided to do things differently. He found it strange being the experienced parent, knowing these things without even realizing he did, and he had to be careful not to sound patronizing.

Two perfectly untroubled little faces were nodding into their chins. He shifted each baby down in the pram and tucked the little yellow and white pram blanket around them.

The smell of frying fish and chips wafting along from the Harbour End had given him an appetite.

Michael sat on the harbour wall with the pram parked up beside him.

The sun went quickly down and, for a few moments, the sky was pink with little grey clouds like smudges of ash.

The appetizing steam as he opened the hot wrapped package, the lacy crunch of the batter, the delicious soggy bit underneath the fish, the uneven distribution of salt and sharpness on the fat chips brought a powerful memory of the time Michael had gone over to see Frank when he had been stationed in Scarborough.

They'd climbed up the promontory between the North and South Bay with their parcels of fish and chips. Michael's was the biggest piece of fish he'd ever seen, but when he'd finished it, he'd wished there'd been more, or that he'd eaten it more slowly, because it felt so good just sitting there with his brother, looking out to sea, sharing his company.

He remembered thinking that he would come again. It wasn't that far from Etherington to Scarborough by train, and Frank didn't seem to mind that he'd turned up.

He'd asked him, 'Do you always get leave at weekends?'

And Frank had laughed shortly. 'No, Mike. I was only allowed to see you because they're sending us all down South tomorrow. The lads think we're going back in . . .'

And Michael's perception of the encounter had taken on a

different meaning as he realized that Frank was not staring at the pale beauty of the silver sea, and the dark, almost purple, sky before the rain came down, but at the perilous journey he was about to face. What Michael had enjoyed as a comfortable, reassuring silence was, for Frank, charged with uncertainty, and when his brother had put a companionable arm around his shoulder, he had not been saying, 'It's good to spend some time with you, Mike!' but, 'Goodbye and wish me luck!'

It was the last time Michael had seen him.

As darkness began to fall, the lamps along the promenade came on, their globes of light so bright in the fading grey that for a moment they were the only visible things. As Michael's eyes adjusted, the familiar silhouette of the pier emerged, and the clock tower in the distance, and the terraces of the houses of the New End, and, high up on the North Cliffs, the shadowy shape of the Palace Hotel, as monochrome in the fast-falling darkness as the postcard Frank had sent of it.

Another grand hotel! Frank had written. *Only the best for the RAF, mate. Still waiting to learn what happens next.*

Memories of his brother had faded as other uncertainties had preoccupied Michael's life. And then Fiammetta had come along with his same red curls, as if to remind him again. Almost as if a message Frank was trying to send him hadn't got through the first time.

When you had a baby, the lack of sleep could make you think all sorts of weird things.

'I woke up and everyone had disappeared,' Claudia said, a little out of breath.

'I'm sorry,' said Michael, seeing that he had inadvertently worried her by bringing the twins out without telling her. 'How did you know where we were?' he asked.

'There aren't many routes flat enough to push that pram!' she said.

He offered his hand to help her up on to the wall beside him. 'Chip?'

'You were far away,' she said. 'I was waving and waving from the promenade and you didn't even see me.'

'I was thinking about Frank,' he admitted. 'The last time I saw him we had fish and chips.'

'Do you think of him every time you have fish and chips?' she asked.

Michael looked at her intense, serious face. She still sometimes asked questions with all the innocence of a child, and he loved that about her.

'I think it's because I'm eating them out of newspaper' – he imitated her seriousness – 'Sylvia always insisted on a plate.'

It was quite dark now, and the lamps along the promenade glowed orange.

'You've never really told me what Frank was like,' Claudia said tentatively.

Michael was aware that he did not talk as much as she would like him to about his family. Claudia believed that you couldn't properly live in the present unless you understood the past, but he could never see the point of raking it all over, making yourself miserable when there was nothing you could do to change it.

'Well, he was full of charm,' he offered, trying to think how to describe Frank's quintessential Frankness. 'Women were all over him. He wasn't what you would call conventionally good-looking, but he had this smile that kind of changed everything . . .'

'Like you,' she said.

'Do I?'

He had no idea what he looked like when he smiled spontaneously.

'Would I have liked him?' Claudia asked.

Michael considered this for a moment. 'I think you might have disapproved of him,' he said. 'He was a bit of a chancer.'

'Would he have liked me?' she asked.

'I wouldn't have let him anywhere near you!' said Michael.

He jumped down from the wall, then put his hands around her waist and jumped her down too.

'Do you miss him?' she asked.

Michael pushed the pram at a brisk pace. 'There are some questions I'd like to ask him.'

'Such as?'

'Such as why . . .'

'Why he died?'

'Yes.'

'It was the war,' she said.

Michael sighed heavily. 'No, it wasn't the war,' he revealed.

People always assumed that because, if they asked, you gave the year, not the month. And they thought they understood. And you let them. Because it was easier not to have to explain.

'He had an accident,' Michael said. 'Just after the war. Between VE and VJ day . . .'

That's what they had said and Michael had told himself it must have been an accident because that's what his aunt Jean had told him. And he couldn't believe that Frank meant to die like that.

'That's what you had to say if you wanted him buried on consecrated ground,' he admitted now.

'He committed suicide?' Claudia whispered, and he could see the thoughts flying across her anxious face. Curiosity, sympathy and, with a fleeting glance at the sleeping twins, fear. Could a disturbed personality be inherited along with looks? 'Why?' she asked.

'I don't know why,' Michael said impatiently. 'Because he didn't bother to leave a bloody note.'

'People see terrible things in war.'

'But he was one of the lucky ones. He wrote to me on VE night, and that's what he said. *I'm one of the lucky ones . . .*'

Golden boy, their mother had always called him.

'Why would he do that and not tell me?' he blurted.

This was why he hated talking about it. Because it changed him into a fifteen-year-old boy again who felt so alone in the world he'd thought he would never stop crying.

Michael stopped walking, held on to the promenade railings, trying to get a grip of himself. Beside him, Claudia's hand hovered near his arm, unable to decide whether it would be better or worse to touch him. Eventually, without looking at her, he stretched out his hand and she took it and squeezed it hard, as if she was trying to hold him together.

Eventually, she said, 'Have you ever thought about trying to find out why?'

'Wouldn't bring him back, would it?' Michael said curtly, his words blurred with the tears he was trying to keep back.

'No,' she said. 'It wouldn't do that.'

He began walking again so fast that she had to run with the pram to keep up with him.

'You've always thought something happened here, haven't you?' Claudia asked.

'Have I?' he asked.

'Why come here?'

'It was the first place I got offered a job . . .' he told her.

'Was it?' Claudia asked.

He wondered how she knew these things without ever having been told.

Iris had never been on a demo before. It had started peacefully with a rally in Trafalgar Square. Vanessa Redgrave addressed the crowd, and although Iris couldn't really hear what the actress was saying through the PA system, she cheered as enthusiastically as everyone else. Miss Redgrave was her role model, an artist and an activist at the same time, and a woman who was both tall and sexy.

It was when the crowd started to march towards Grosvenor Square that Iris sensed an escalating feverishness. After the depressing impotence of watching pictures of the Vietnam War on the news, it felt like doing something, being here, as if together they could change things. The adrenalin of excitement surged through Iris's body; the volume of her shouting rose to stoke up her courage. Word spread that they were going to storm the American Embassy.

Iris fell in with a group of students from the LSE who told her about the strikes and sit-ins they had been involved in, and she felt they would know what to do, but when she entered the square and saw the cordon of uniformed police protecting the Embassy, some primitive survival instinct made her want to get out fast. There was no way the Americans were going to let them take the Embassy, she suddenly realized. The protestors were going into a battle they could only lose. But it was too late. The crowd had a momentum; the only way was forward.

There was a peculiar hush as the crowd spread out. She spotted several of her comrades stooping to pick up stones. And then, at some silent, invisible signal, the group she was with turned their banners like jousting sticks and charged towards the line of policemen. And Iris knew she had to go with them, because if she didn't, she would be swamped.

Long ago, before she had learned to swim, she had ventured out to waist height in the sea. The water had been calm, but the tide was on the turn, and sticking close to one of the breakwaters had not been the safe thing to do. As she waved to her father, the sand had suddenly dropped away from under her feet and she had found herself flailing in a bottomless pool. She had gone under several times. What she remembered most was the noise: the slurp of her bubbling lungs as she went down; that strangely peaceful hum of silence underwater; the shrieking of children on the beach each time she surfaced.

Now, there was the squelch of boot on flesh, the scream of obscenities, the clash of violence, but it was the same terrifying feeling of having lost control of her destiny.

Pearl King, who had been on the promenade at the time, and had a life-saving badge from Girl Guides, had rescued Iris. Their photograph was taken for the report in the *Chronicle*, and Miss King had extended a public offer to teach her to swim in the Palace's new swimming pool.

That bright turquoise rectangle; the blinding sunlight; Iris's hair dripping with water as she emerged from the water.

Regaining consciousness, Iris put her hand to her face and was bewildered by the warm stickiness of blood. She appeared to be lying in a forest of red tulips. It was quite soft and comfortable and she felt that if she closed her eyes, she would sleep, and maybe when she woke up, the demonstration would all have gone away. But then the volume of the screaming suddenly magnified, and another sound reverberated through her skull: the metallic clatter of horses' hooves on tarmac; and Iris realized that if she did not get herself up and start running, the pillowy earth of the flowerbed might soon become her grave.

Disorientated, tottering, Iris stumbled and ran, and kept running until the noise was far, far in the distance, then she slumped down on the steps of an official-looking building. The street had the odd quietness that falls over a city's busy thoroughfares on a Sunday. She could hear a bird singing a spring song. She leaned against the railing and allowed her eyes to close.

And then – was it hours or seconds later? – she became aware of a voice saying, 'Iris?'

There was a tall man with a huge Afro hairstyle and a placard which read 'ALL YOU NEED IS LOVE' stooping over her. As her focus swam, he smiled.

'Winston?' Iris said, struggling to sit up.

'Long time, no see. Are you OK?' he asked, looking at her face.

'I think so,' she said.

'I'll see you guys later,' he said to the group of demonstrators he was with, and sat down on the steps next to her. Iris shifted along, suddenly feeling awkward.

'Getting scary back there,' he said. 'They say there are snipers on the roof with orders to shoot if they get over the gates.'

She shivered.

'Why don't you come back to my place and get yourself cleaned up,' he said, pulling her to her feet. 'It's just round the corner.'

He lent her his arm, but when it was clear she could manage on her own, Iris dropped it.

'Dad said you ran away,' said Winston.

She'd forgotten how odd it sounded when he called Sir John Allsop 'Dad'.

'I was half expecting you to pitch up at the porter's lodge,' said Winston.

Had he laughed at the crush she had on him, and all the letters she had written to him when he went up to Oxford, full of adolescent philosophical thoughts and poetry quotations, trying to show how intelligent she was?

'What would you have done if I had turned up at your college?' Iris asked.

Winston looked her slowly up and down. 'The Master might not have taken too well to us shacking up together,' he said with a grin which gave her a little kick of satisfaction.

'Do you see anyone from Kingshaven?' Iris asked as they walked.

'Not if I can help it,' Winston said.

She laughed.

'Wait a minute,' he remembered. 'I did run into Christopher King the other day . . .'

Iris raised an eyebrow.

'I was in the American Bar at the Savoy with some clients, and there he was . . . the waiter!' Winston had always been a good raconteur. 'I liked hearing him call me "sir" so much, I kept asking for more peanuts. I think he must have thought I really was a monkey!'

Iris threw back her head and laughed, suddenly feeling much better.

'Your father's living at the Castle now,' Winston said.

'Yeah, kind of weird, isn't it?' she said.

'And they've had twins!'

'Yes.'

'Have you seen them yet?'

'No,' said Iris. 'No, I'll never go back to Kingshaven.'

'They'll have to come and see you, then,' said Winston.

'Maybe when they're a bit older,' Iris agreed.

She sometimes saw her father when he came to London, but she didn't really want to hear about the details of his present arrangements any more than she wanted him to know about hers.

Winston's place was a four-storey Georgian townhouse in an elegant square on the north side of Oxford Street.

'Very grand,' said Iris.

'It's only a temporary address,' said Winston, winking at her.

Instead of going in the front door, he led her round to the mews at the back. The basement windows were boarded up but when Winston tapped four times, a couple of the boards were levered out by someone inside.

'Ladies first,' Winston said.

'We're breaking in?' Iris asked.

'Not exactly.'

With a quick look over her shoulder, Iris climbed in. Winston followed. It was quite dark inside. Winston took her hand and led her further in, opening another door. They were at the bottom of the stairwell of the building. There were dust motes dancing in the bright natural light filtering down from above. The air smelled a bit like the incense which wafted out of some of the shops on the Kings Road.

Winston led Iris up the wide stone steps to a hall. The crumbling paint was powder blue and there were cracked white stucco decorations which reminded Iris of Wedgwood china. Above the huge front door was a glass fanlight through which sunshine poured in.

'Lovely building, isn't it?' said Winston. 'Shame to leave it empty when there are people with nowhere to live.'

He pushed open the door to a vast reception room whose walls were the same blue with white stucco cornicing and an ornate ceiling rose. On the opposite wall, above the biggest marble fireplace Iris had ever seen, a more recent decorator had painted a rainbow, and huge flowers growing up from the floor. The word 'PEACE' was written in letters the size of people.

There was no furniture apart from several battered, dirty old armchairs which looked as if they might have come from the back of a rag-and-bone cart. The wooden floor was stained dark brown around the edges, but there was a large square of untreated boards in the centre, where Iris imagined a Persian carpet would originally have been.

A student-looking type with a beard, who had been among the gang of demonstrators with Winston, was sitting beside the fireplace licking roll-up cigarette papers and sticking them together. Two others watched intently.

'Guys, this is Iris,' Winston announced.

'Hey, man,' the beard murmured, barely glancing up from his task.

'I'll give you the guided tour,' said Winston. 'We're claiming squatters' rights,' he told her as he showed her round gracious high-ceilinged rooms with old mattresses, sleeping bags and blankets in untidy heaps on the floor, one of which grumbled about being disturbed.

Iris noticed that there were two pairs of feet sticking out.

'Sorry, guys!' said Winston.

'If we can occupy the building long enough, we can claim legal possession,' he explained. 'That'll never happen, of course. We've already had a couple of visits from the local constabulary suggesting we go quietly. But since what we're about is largely symbolic, we're determined to be evicted.'

Winston had always had a talent for putting ideas into action. When a group of his friends at school were trying to form a band, Winston was the one who'd taken himself into Lowhampton and blagged a spot at the Tavern nightclub. At Oxford, he'd got his name in *The Times* for organizing a demonstration outside the Oxford Union where Enoch Powell had been invited to speak. Winston had been quoted as saying that the Union was a right-wing anachronism, which would be first in line to extend hospitality to Adolf Hitler were he to be found alive.

'Where would you go?' Iris asked.

'Belgravia would be groovy,' Winston said, looking out of a long sash window on to the square. 'There are lots of empty buildings in London.'

'But isn't it illegal?' Iris said.

'That's something we intend to test. Squatters' rights are centuries old,' said Winston.

'But are lawyers supposed to be involved in this sort of thing?' Iris asked.

'I've given up the law. I'm in the music business now.'

'You've given up, after all that studying?'

'All that studying makes me sound like I know what I'm talking about.' Winston smiled at her. 'Now, let's get you cleaned up.'

He showed her into a bathroom with a marble basin and huge deep bath. Beside the taps was a row of milk bottles filled with water.

'The utilities are switched off, obviously,' Winston told her, pouring water down the side of her face. 'But we fill bottles from the drinking fountain in the square. I think it's only superficial. There's always an alarming amount of blood with a head wound.'

He sounded as if he had some experience.

Iris looked at herself in the mirror. She had taken a hit on her cheekbone.

'It was you, wasn't it?' Winston said, looking at her reflection. 'In that film on telly.'

'Yes,' she admitted.

'You call yourself something different now.'

'Sarah Bird. It's a bit of a long story,' she said.

'You were great! It was your father's book, wasn't it?'

'Yes. It was made for me, that role,' she said.

It was nice to be with someone who just understood because he'd known her for ever, instead of having to edit her life as she usually did.

'So what are you up to now?' he asked.

Iris had a second call for a television series they were making called *Please, Sir!* It was a pretty neat idea – an innocent teacher comes to a tough school and learns lessons in life from the pupils – but she could see the way the casting was going. Among the girls, they were looking for a sexy voluptuous one, and a swot, and she wasn't particularly keen on being typecast as the gawky one with glasses.

'Believe it or not, there aren't a lot of parts around for a lanky, red-headed teenager,' Iris said. 'And I don't have any training.'

'Why don't you go to acting school?' Winston asked.

'I'm thinking about it. I'm not so sure I want to act,' Iris said.

She'd not admitted this to anyone else yet.

Winston raised an eyebrow.

'Things are a bit different when you actually do them . . .' she tried to explain.

'Oh, I agree,' said Winston. 'I had this vision of myself as the noble attorney. A black Atticus Finch, battling for people's rights. Mostly I found I was pleading on behalf of some petty crook who didn't want a coon defending him.'

'Really?' said Iris, shocked. 'Well, it's not as bad as that, obviously, but most acting jobs are in advertising and they only want my legs. You've probably seen them on the tube, advertising pantyhose. Not exactly what I wanted to do . . .'

'Great legs, though,' said Winston, holding her eyes so long she had to look away.

They went back downstairs again where the three men were now passing round a long, loosely rolled cigarette with a cardboard filter, which Iris assumed was a spliff. The bearded man passed it to her. She realized that this was the smell she'd been unable to identify when she came in. She'd taught herself to smoke Consulate cigarettes when she came to London, but it had never become a habit because she didn't like the taste. She took a tiny puff and held the smoke in her mouth. It wasn't as acrid as plain tobacco. Winston was watching her. She took another longer drag, and passed the spliff on.

Iris felt much more relaxed about having a second toke when the joint came round again, and a third, and then she lost count how many tokes she had, so involved was she in the conversation, which seemed interesting and profound at the time, although later she would struggle to remember a word of it.

At some point the man and woman who had been making love upstairs joined them, and then Winston disappeared and returned with handfuls of Mars Bars and Iris exclaimed how totally far out it was that he'd known she had a craving for chocolate, and every-one started giggling.

Sitting under the word Peace, Iris had a sudden epiphany.

She heard herself saying to Winston, 'I am where I should be.' And she thought it sounded really deep, like something a philosopher might say.

She felt his arm go round her, drawing her towards those lips she had imagined kissing so often when she was younger . . .

In her head, she heard herself saying to her mother, 'His mouth is pink inside like anyone else's.'

And her mother's retort. 'Don't be so disgusting!'

Iris lay back on the hard wooden floor, feeling the skin stretch-ing over her ribcage and her stomach becoming concave, and Winston's big, gentle hands touching her in the gap between her jeans and her skinny-rib top, making her squirm with pleasure. As she gazed at the tall windows, she saw that it was getting dark out-side, and she suddenly remembered she wasn't where she was supposed to be at all.

'What's the time?' she asked, struggling to sit up.

The bearded man looked at his watch.

'Nearly seven o'clock, man.'

'Seven o'clock in the afternoon?' she asked.

Everyone fell about laughing again like they would never stop.

First she tried the front door, twisting the handle in greater and greater desperation, until she realized there were boards nailed across it. Then she remembered how they'd come in, and felt her way across the darkened room, rattling the boards in frustration until Winston came up behind her.

'Why are you so keen to leave?' he asked.

He caught her hand as she went to climb out through the window.

His eyes were shining. She wondered if her eyes were shining too. Whether it was obvious that she had been smoking dope.

'You all right?' he asked, concerned.

'I have to go,' she said.

There was usually another agenda when Pearl telephoned to ask how everyone was, but this evening, Libby was struggling to work out what it could be.

'Susannah and Damian?' Libby asked.

'Thriving! Adrian and Winny?'

'Winny's great friends with James Allsop. Adrian and Julia are inseparable. I don't know what she'll do when Adrian goes off to school . . .'

'You talk about Julia Allsop as if she's one of yours,' said Pearl.

'Well, I have grown fond of her, it's true,' said Libby.

'And Granny Addled?' Pearl asked.

'Actually, you know, I've grown quite fond of her as well,' said Libby. 'She's got some fascinating stories to tell. I don't know how many of them are true!'

'Has Eddie got used to having his mother around?' asked Pearl.

'Eddie's in the doghouse, I'm afraid,' said Libby crisply. 'He was breathalysed on his way back from the Yacht Club the other evening, and apparently it's an automatic ban.'

'Can't Mummy have a word with the Superintendent?'

'Retired, I'm afraid. Poor Mummy. All her generation seem to be retiring or dying these days.'

'Poor Mummy!' Pearl echoed. 'It must be horrible to lose one's grip on things.'

'Still, The Show Must Go On!' they both said, in unison, and then there was a long silence.

'And Tom?' Libby suddenly remembered she had forgotten to ask after Pearl's husband. She had a sense that things were not as happy as they might be between the two of them.

'Well, that's partly what I was ringing about,' said Pearl excitedly.

Libby wondered whether she had just led herself into a trap.

'Something terribly exciting's come up. Tom's got a big commission.'

The number of times she'd heard this . . . Libby knew what was coming next. Pearl was about to request a loan to tide them over until Tom's payment arrived.

'He and this journalist friend of his are going to do a series of articles for the *Sunday Times* colour supplement!'

'Congratulations!' said Libby evenly.

'It's called "The State We're In". The idea's that they do a family from every level of society, interviewing them, photographing them, seeing what affect the Swinging Sixties has had . . .'

'Sounds fascinating,' said Libby dutifully.

'And the best bit is—' said Pearl.

'The trouble is, I really don't think our cash flow can—' Libby jumped in.

'He wants to start with you!'

'With me?' Libby repeated.

'You plural, silly. Us, really. The Kings. The Palace. In a national newspaper!'

That was the carrot.

Libby waited.

'So, what do you say?' Pearl asked.

'Will there be any money involved?' Libby asked cautiously.

'Well, obviously he's not going to pay you when he's giving you a giant advert. In colour, for God's sake!'

'You know that's not what I meant,' said Libby.

'What did you mean?'

'Never mind.'

It all seemed rather too good to be true. Libby was sure there must be a catch.

'Our prayers have been answered!' said Liliana with a glance towards the ceiling when Libby went to tell her about it in her private suite. 'Haven't I always said that if only people knew the best England had to offer, they'd never think of flying off abroad!'

'It's really about the family, I think,' said Libby cautiously.

'You must insist on editorial control,' said Liliana. 'We can't allow anything to give the wrong impression.' She pointed up again.

Libby realized she was referring to Adela, who slept in the room above.

'I doubt they'd give us that,' said Libby. 'It's the *Sunday Times* we're talking about, not the *Chronicle!*'

Liliana frowned. 'Nevertheless, don't you think it might be as well if Adela were off the premises?' she asked.

It wasn't the first time her mother had tried to manipulate Libby into agreeing to put Adela into an institution.

'It'll be for the best. She won't even notice,' said Liliana. 'My sister never did. After a very short time, she couldn't recognize any of us! And nobody had to be embarrassed.'

'I never knew you had a sister, Mummy,' said Libby.

'My point exactly,' Liliana replied with equanimity. 'So that's settled, then.'

'No, Mummy. I'm sorry, but I just can't. We can trust Tom, can't we? I mean it would hardly be in his interest to make it look like a lunatic asylum!'

Her mother sucked in her breath.

'My worry is the hotel is looking a little shabby.' Libby tried to move the conversation on.

'Oh, they can do all sorts of things with proper lighting,' said her mother impatiently. 'I gather Tom's a dab hand with the air-brush,' she added with an impish smile, showing she was quite aware of the sort of magazines Tom generally worked for.

With the lights on, and two women in overalls hoovering, the interior of the Zebra Crossing Club looked shabby, and Iris noticed for the first time that the carpet was strafed with cigarette burns. As she watched the staff arriving in their street clothes and disappearing behind the stage to emerge transformed, the waiters in spotless white jackets, the dancers in tight red Latin dresses and feathered headdresses, she wondered if it was the marijuana which had made her suddenly see through the illusion of glamour.

The bartender busied himself emptying trays of ice into a big refrigerated bin under the bar and preparing little glass dishes of cocktail cherries, olives and finely sliced lemon on the counter at the back, under the long row of spirit bottles. Iris could see his reflection in the mirror as he concentrated on his work. Occasionally, when he thought she wasn't looking, he glanced at her, then looked away again, as if he knew she was in trouble. Once or twice she tried to smile at him when their eyes met, but he didn't wink at her like he usually did.

Finally, Clive decided to acknowledge her presence. He flicked his thumb towards the back room, as he did to the hostess girls when they spent too long with a customer who wasn't buying enough champagne.

Reluctantly, Iris followed him.

'What happened to you?'

'I fell over.'

'Where the hell have you been?' he asked coldly.

She'd told him that her father was in town and wanted to have lunch with her.

'We went to the Cap and we were at the back, and you know how it's dark back there, and I lost track of the time.'

She was breaking her own rule that when telling a lie, you should always stick as close to the truth as possible. She told herself to keep quiet. You do not have to say anything, but anything you do say may be used in evidence against you.

'The Cap's closed on Sundays,' said Clive.

He came up close to her and sniffed her hair, which she could see in the mirrored wall opposite was so unruly after her run to the club, it was almost as Afro as Winston's. The side of her face was swollen.

'You been smoking pot?' Clive asked.

Iris said nothing.

'You know what I think about drugs.'

'You sell enough!' she said.

Clive's almost undetectable glance at the mirrored wall indicated he thought they might be being watched from behind the glass.

'I've got to work late,' he said coldly.

Iris sat at the front of the bus thinking how much she missed Vic and his Lambretta, and the sensation of wind blowing through her head, clearing out all the confused thoughts. Vic had moved out soon after it became obvious that Clive and Iris couldn't keep their hands off each other. Iris hadn't wanted him to go. She'd asked him why it made any difference, and he said it felt like his best mate had suddenly become his stepmother, which had made her laugh.

'Don't you approve?' she'd asked him.

'You and Clive are different types,' he'd warned.

'Opposites attract,' she'd said.

In the first flush of their romance, she'd been convinced that love was an unstoppable force which had no regard for boring rationality. She'd loved it that they were different, that Clive was a grown-up, that he drove a car, that he introduced her to a whole world she'd only seen on the movies. Clive's girl. Even the words sounded like something someone in a movie would say. Each week, he bought her a little present. A bunch of flowers; a half-pound of Milk Tray; sometimes a bit of jewellery; once a watch with a diamanté face, which she showed off to the other girls at the auditions she went to, who told her how lucky she was. At last, other girls admired her, because she had the kind of boyfriend every girl wanted. A good-looking bloke with a bit of money to splash around, who looked after her.

Iris imagined Clive's face if he found out what she had done today. She'd broken just about every rule. Clive despised drugs, coloured people, long hair and demonstrations, even though he worked in a place where drugs changed hands, where they employed immigrants to do the jobs nobody else wanted to do, and where the owners wore short back and sides, but had recently been arrested for conspiracy to murder. Not that she was supposed to know any of this. She was only a woman, after all.

The lift was broken again. Iris started the long haul of stairs up to the top floor of the block of flats.

When she had first arrived, the view that stretched for miles and miles, and the feeling of being in the sky, had given her such a sense of freedom, she used to stand for hours just looking out of the window over the never-ending city.

Now, the curtains were open and it was dark outside, and the wall of pure blackness that greeted her made her feel as if she was entering a prison.

The sweet scent of fudge wafted from the door of the confectioner's. In the window, Mrs Green was arranging a pyramid of sample boxes which she removed during the winter to prevent the colour photo of Kingshaven's seafront fading. As the pram with the twins sitting up passed in front of her eyes, her face broke into a spontaneous smile, but when she caught Michael's eye, she looked away.

The Beatles' latest hit, 'Lady Madonna', wafted through the open doors of Sylvia's dress shop.

'See you three later, then,' Michael said to Claudia.

He leaned over and kissed her on the nose, then watched her as she pushed the pram down the street.

The floor of Sylvia's shop was made up of large black and white squares, and the dresses were displayed on bentwood hatstands dotted about like giant chess pieces. Large mirrors with ornate gilded frames cast Michael's reflection back at him. Standing on a white square, he felt like a vulnerable pawn who had ventured into enemy territory.

'Oh, it's you,' said Sylvia with determined nonchalance, emerging from behind one of the hatstands wearing a similar dress to the one which was hanging on the display.

'Can I have a word?' Michael asked.

'About what?' Her tone was hostile.

'In private,' he said.

'Milly, can you hold the fort for five minutes?' Sylvia called. 'I'll be upstairs if you need me.'

Michael followed her up to the flat and she showed him into the long living room. The room was painted white, and curtains with a jazzy pattern of pink and burnt-orange circles flapped beside the open French windows. A huge sofa made of tubular steel and soft padded leather was a matching orange. The only untidiness was a grey box file on the floor beside the sofa which had a big label with 'Properties' written on it in Sylvia's girlish looping handwriting. Seeing him looking, she picked it up and put it on the sofa beside her.

'Habitat,' Sylvia told him, kicking off her shoes and curling her legs up under her.

Michael felt at a disadvantage, standing up, but the moment had passed to sit down, and he sensed that she was enjoying holding court, and it wouldn't help his case if he attempted to make himself at home.

'You match the furniture,' Michael finally said.

The dress she was wearing was short with long sleeves in a pink and orange striped stretchy fabric. She'd always had an unerring instinct for the latest colours.

Her face puckered into a frown, as if she couldn't work out whether he intended this as a compliment or a criticism.

'Very attractive,' he said.

A very brief smile broke through the frown for a moment, and he was relieved to see that she wasn't always as hard as she appeared. On the last few occasions they had spoken, he had seen only a vicious, unforgiving replica of Doreen.

'I'm sure you haven't come to tell me how nice I look,' she said with a flirtatious toss of her hair, which she was wearing long again, fair and straight, with a parting down the middle.

'I've come to ask you to give me a divorce,' Michael said as evenly as he could.

He saw her wince and open her mouth, then close it again, suppressing the urge to say something.

The silence yawned between them. He knew that the one who broke it first would look the weaker, but he was determined to get it over with. It had gone on long enough now.

'It must be better for both of us, mustn't it?' he said. 'You'd be free—'

'And you'd be able to be the perfect little family,' she interrupted. It had probably been a mistake to part from Claudia and the twins right outside the shop, he thought. Not the most sensitive approach.

'I'd prefer the children to be legitimate, yes, I admit it,' he said.

'I'm surprised at you, Michael, for being so conventional,' Sylvia taunted him. 'I was under the impression you were keen on free love ... and what about all those starving people in the world, if you keep producing more mouths to feed?'

Michael winced as she repeated his own specious argument back to him. He hadn't wanted more children with Sylvia and he should have had the guts to say so.

'I know I behaved badly to you,' he said, trying to keep his temper. 'But can't we just get on with our lives now? Not keep going back over the past?'

'And how am I supposed to get on with my life with you swanning around the whole time with your mistress and your babies?' she said, looking away from him.

'I didn't intend to come back,' he began to explain, but she cut him short.

'Oh, that's so typical! You never intend, do you? Things just happen and you're never responsible. So, it was *her* idea to come back, was it? It wasn't enough that she took you away, she has to bring you back to rub my nose in it too!'

Michael realized that he had only considered how difficult it would be for him. He hadn't really thought about how it would be for Sylvia, and that had been wrong and selfish of him.

'It's not Claudia's fault,' he said.

'I can see she's really got you under her thumb. Bet it was her idea that you come here today, too, wasn't it?'

He hated the fact that Sylvia was right about that too. He would probably have let things continue as they were, but Claudia wanted to get married. Not for herself, for the children.

'Look, I could probably sue you for divorce on grounds of mental cruelty after you not telling me about Iris all that time . . .' Michael went on the attack.

Sylvia looked the other way.

'I'm giving you the chance to sue me for adultery instead.'

'And what if I decide not to take up your tempting offer?'

Sarcasm had never suited Sylvia. It made her pretty face ugly.

'This government's pledged to make divorce easier ... In a couple of years, I'll be able to divorce you whether you like it or not!'

'Well, that's typical, isn't it!' Sylvia exclaimed. 'Divorce, abortion, queers. All easier with your lot ...'

'My lot?' he repeated.

'I'm a Conservative now,' Sylvia said proudly.

Michael had suddenly had enough.

'Are you going to give me a divorce or not?' he asked.

'I've got a lot of important decisions to make at the moment ...' Her hand patted the box file on the sofa next to her.

He could tell that she was dying for him to ask what. But he wouldn't.

'I'll have to think about it,' Sylvia told him, twisting a lock of her long hair round her finger.

It was the power she relished, and he knew that she'd never give that up voluntarily.

'Bloody hell, Sylvia!' he said despairingly. 'Haven't you had your pound of flesh? I wanted to kill myself when Iris was missing. Are you determined to torture me for ever?'

'Torture you? What about me?' she shouted.

They'd been through this all before. The same old arguments. Round and round in a never-ending circle of blame.

'I've said sorry to you, but you're so—'

She put her hands over her ears like a child not wanting to hear more. 'Sorry doesn't make it better!' she screamed at him.

'Now, we're going to have your six-month check,' Claudia told the twins.

She knew people thought she was a little crazy holding one-sided conversations with her babies, pointing out colours, shapes and sounds. Sometimes she suspected it *was* a kind of madness, brought on by six months' lack of sleep, which made her so enjoy the undemanding occupation of pushing a heavy pram containing two infants – her instant family, as people called them, not knowing about all the years of trying.

Claudia was relieved to find that it was Mrs Jarvis at the surgery. She was the health visitor who had supported her during the first few weeks after the twins' birth. Claudia had never felt comfortable with Dr Payne's avuncular manner when she was a child, and he seemed to treat her with exactly the same patronizing attitude as an adult. He was also getting rather old and unreliable. Although he had listened to her belly with an ear trumpet on several occasions, it was only when she and Michael had attended National Childbirth Trust classes in Lowhampton that they discovered she was expecting twins.

The babies behaved perfectly as Mrs Jarvis put each of them on the scales, and reported that they were thriving.

'And how are you?' the health visitor asked, as Claudia put the twins down on the floor where Bruno did roly-polys and Fiammetta lay staring at the ceiling with a look of concentration as if she was trying to work out a complicated mathematical theorem, but probably meant that she was about to do a poo.

'Fine,' Claudia said, gazing proudly at them. 'A bit exhausted . . .'

'I'm not surprised! Any problems at all?'

'Apart from lack of sleep?' Claudia asked. 'Not that I can think of.'

'And you're all healed up nicely,' said the health visitor, pointing at Claudia's belly.

To Claudia's intense disappointment, after months of breathing exercises and visualization, the twins had been born by emergency caesarian section in Lowhampton General Hospital.

'I'm fine,' said Claudia, touching where the scar was.

'You look as if you've lost weight,' the health visitor said. 'Are you sure you're eating properly?'

Claudia's eating had become as erratic as her sleep patterns, and she often found herself stuffing a handful of breakfast cereal into her mouth at four o'clock in the morning whilst walking round with one or other of the babies who refused to go to sleep.

'Your health is important, you know,' the health visitor admonished her gently. 'Make sure you're getting enough iron.'

'Yes,' said Claudia obediently.

She knew that the health visitor didn't think a vegetarian diet gave all the necessary nutrients, and she didn't want to go into all that again.

'Oh, one of my breasts is a bit hard . . .' she suddenly remembered. 'My friend Barbara says it's mastitis. She told me to put hot flannels on. I've tried, but it doesn't seem to work.'

'Do you want me to have a look?'

Claudia went behind the screen and pulled up the black V-necked sweater she was wearing.

'Any pain?' said the health visitor, locating the bump and pressing it gently as Claudia kept an eye on the children, slightly embarrassed to look at the health visitor at such a close distance.

'No, not painful at all,' said Claudia, feeling guilty for even mentioning it as she fastened her bra again and pulled her sweater back down.

'Your body's had some big changes,' said Mrs Jarvis. 'It'll probably go away on its own.'

'I always had difficulty feeding with that breast.'

'Yes, I remember.'

Mrs Jarvis had come to the house every day to support her efforts to breastfeed the twins. Claudia had done her best, but eventually she'd had to give in to bottles.

'Could be a cyst, I suppose,' said the health visitor. 'I'll ask Dr Payne to get you an appointment to have it drained.'

Claudia winced.

'Doesn't take a moment. Once they've drawn the fluid out, it normally settles down nicely.'

'And that's it?' said Claudia.

'That's it,' said the health visitor.

'And if it's not a cyst?' Claudia asked, sensing that the health visitor had left something unsaid.

And then Fiammetta started to cry and it went right out of her mind.

Claudia knew from the stoop of Michael's shoulders that his mission had not been a success.

'She refused,' he said when she caught him up.

'Doesn't matter,' she told him with such haste that she gave away her disappointment.

'What did the health visitor say?' he asked, gently adjusting the pram blanket over Bruno's chubby legs in a gesture so tender it made Claudia gulp.

'That they're thriving,' she said.

She gazed at the children, reminding herself how lucky she was.

Clive was still asleep when it was time to leave the flat.

Iris looked at his face, peaceful like a great big child.

The night before, she had lain awake in fear of his return, but when he had come in the small hours, he had been all contrition instead of anger, even when she told him she had been on the demonstration.

He was worried about her, that was all, he'd said, and he'd apologized for being cross with her at the club and making her get the bus home. He didn't like being lied to, that was all, and what with the proprietors in custody, he had a lot on his mind at the moment.

When he was apologetic, Iris found it almost harder to deal with than when he was in a temper, because his assumptions about what was important to her were all so wrong. He'd even suggested that on his next day off they go up to Mappin & Webb and look at engagement rings.

Clive thought that a solitaire diamond was every woman's ultimate desire.

Once, when they'd been watching *The Lucy Show* on Saturday night, Clive had remarked that Iris was a bit like Lucille Ball: a tall, funny redhead. Iris had told him that he was a bit like Desi Arnaz with his dark Latin good looks and his old-fashioned manners (pity, she'd said, that he couldn't sing). It had occurred to her, as they sat on the sofa together and she glanced from time to time at the side of his face as he laughed on cue at the simple set-ups which he, like Desi, never saw coming, that maybe he thought that Lucy and Desi really lived in that three-sided room, and that Lucy was really silly and scatty, and not a major player in Hollywood, just as he thought that Iris was a nice girl with a few funny ideas, who really wanted to marry him.

It was not his fault, Iris reminded herself. She was the one who was dishonest, not him.

Dear Clive, I'm leaving. I'm sorry. I do love you, but I've got lots I want to do before settling down. Thanks for all you've given me. Love, Sarah.

Iris reread the note. It seemed so inadequate and she knew she ought to be brave enough to say it to his face, but she didn't think she'd ever make him understand. She imagined him puzzling over the note, mystified.

She thought he'd take the last sentence to mean his presents. And she didn't know if he'd be more offended if she left them, or took them with her. After a moment's deliberation, she took her jewellery out of her bag, and left it beside the note. It was nearly nine o'clock, she saw on the face of the diamanté watch.

She closed the door of the flat with a click, and tiptoed down the first flight of steps, and then ran the rest.

The clinic was as new as the estate. It was nice and clean inside, with bright posters on the noticeboard and an alphabet frieze around the wall for children to look at while they waited for the doctor.

'You can go in now.' The receptionist looked at her face, and Iris remembered she had a cut on her cheek.

Usually there was a long wait with everyone pretending to read dog-eared *Reader's Digest*s, surreptitiously inching away from the one with the cough, and Iris wished she'd had a breathing space after her run from the tower block.

The doctor was a youngish man. He was opening a brown envelope with her name on it from which he extracted a piece of paper.

'Congratulations! You're pregnant.'

Iris had imagined hearing this news a hundred times, trying to face down fate with her certainty. But fate wasn't going to be tricked so easily.

The doctor was smiling with his mouth, but his eyes were looking at her swollen face.

She couldn't seem to stop her lip from wobbling.

How could she have been so stupid?

How could she have been as stupid as her own mother?

'Are you sure that's my result?' she asked.

He checked, and nodded.

She tried to brush away the tears with her fist, but her knuckles caught the cut, and then she was sobbing. She could hear the gasping sound she was making, yet it was as if it wasn't her. Iris couldn't stand women who cried.

The doctor looked like he would have been top of the class at medical school, but nothing had prepared him for this.

'No chance of marrying the father?' he asked.

Why did people always think that marriage would solve anything?

Truth be told, when Clive had suggested they get engaged, it was really because he didn't approve of girls who slept with men before marriage. Iris had thought she'd better agree, because the look in his eyes after they'd had sex always made her feel dirty for encouraging him. Nice girls didn't do that. So she'd said yes, but she'd never had any intention of marrying him, or anyone else, ever.

Iris registered the way the doctor was looking at her cheek. She could tell he was thinking she'd been hit, and she felt doubly disloyal to Clive for lying about his willingness to marry her, and for letting the impression go unchallenged that she'd been the victim of domestic violence. Clive had never hit her. Sometimes she'd thought he was going to. But he never had.

'I can't have it,' Iris whispered.

'I'm sure you'll want to have a think about it,' said the doctor.

'No, I don't,' Iris blurted.

She knew she had to pull herself together right now or that would be the end of the appointment, and the next time she'd get the woman doctor with the ribbed beige stockings and stout brown lace-up shoes who'd told her she was certainly not prepared to prescribe the Pill to an unmarried teenager.

'I've thought about it already,' Iris said clearly. 'I've got enough money.'

'I see.' The doctor stared at her face again. 'Terminations can only be performed on medical or psychiatric grounds,' he said, writing something down on a piece of paper.

'What does that mean?' Iris asked.

'You'll have to see a psychiatrist,' he said, unable to look her in the eye.

'And pretend I'm barmy?' Iris asked.

'It's a legal formality,' he said, handing her a piece of paper with a name and address on it.

There were still notices in the window of Gillie's of Lowhampton advertising the clearance sale.

'Ah, Mrs Quinn! Delightful to see you again,' said the solicitor as he met Sylvia outside with the keys. 'I thought we might bring Mr Quinn with us today.'

'Why?' Sylvia asked sweetly, watching his already ruddy complexion turn almost puce.

'Without further ado, then!' said the solicitor, shaking the keys. 'The administrators have asked me to let any prospective purchaser know that the fittings are not included in the price, although I'm sure they'd be quite flexible in negotiating a separate fee,' he said as he pushed the door open.

'Oh, I wouldn't be interested in keeping any of this,' said Sylvia, waving her arm around. 'I'd be looking to refurbish throughout.'

'Indeed?' said the solicitor.

Three floors of retail space to fill, and a restaurant. It was a bigger step than she had planned, and it would be a stretch, Sylvia thought. But if she didn't take it now, the chance might never come up again. Gillie's of Lowhampton would be taken over by one of the big chains, House of Fraser perhaps, or maybe even something common like C&A, and the opportunity would have gone. She couldn't think of another store along the South Coast which suited her wish list as well as Gillie's did.

But it was a dream, wasn't it?

When she'd seen the article about the department store closing, she'd made enquiries and the administrators had forwarded details. She'd had a good look round once already, trying to envisage what she'd do with it, but she'd only been able to imagine two floors.

The ground floor would host the range of make-up, handbags, pantyhose and other accessories she was developing, and, at the back, men's clothes in a small boutique-style space at first, with its own entrance from the street behind, but also accessible through

493

the main shop. First floor was always ladies' fashions, but Sylvia's would have fashion with a difference – up-to-the-minute clothes in a lush, luxurious art deco setting. She had already secured the warehouse of fittings from the cruise liner which Mr Coral's friend in demolition had never found a buyer for. There was everything from mirrors to chandeliers to the curving banisters of a grand staircase which Sylvia could see the models walking down on opening night.

Sylvia Quinn's department store would host a unique fusion of modernity and glamour. Instead of being a duty, shopping would be an event in itself, as exciting as going to a ball. The changing rooms would be roomy, with upholstered banquettes to sit on. There would be waiters with trays of drinks, and music from the store's very own radio station. She'd even thought of a name for the shop which would perfectly reflect the combination of fairy tale and fashion: Cinderella Rockafella.

But even dreams had limits, and Sylvia hadn't been able to get beyond that fabulous first floor, until the most unlikely person had given her a clue.

'You match the furniture,' Michael had said.

Soft furnishings. Once the idea was planted, she couldn't get it out of her head. Why not curtains made of the paisley fabrics her customers couldn't get enough of? Why not bright silk cushions like those she'd made for the chaise longue in her shop, which people always remarked on (and, occasionally, shoplifted). Why not sheets and towels in purple and crimson and gold, and embroidered bedspreads imported from India? Why settle for a department store when you could have an emporium?

Sylvia thought she could probably rent out the restaurant for the time being. And later, if the store was a success, she'd open up a roof garden . . .

'Has there been much interest?' Sylvia asked as she walked through the ghostly skeleton of Gillie's: empty racks, worn carpet, silent tills.

'Plenty of enquiries,' said the solicitor. 'But it's a difficult time in retail, as in everything else, with the price of imports.'

In her mind, Sylvia cancelled the order for Indian bedspreads until the pound recovered its strength. Most of her suppliers were in the North of England, and so the devaluation hadn't made such an impact on her business as it had on others. There appeared to be an ever-growing market for her designs. Two boutiques in London were now selling her clothes, and a journalist from Fleet Street had recently telephoned to ask if she'd like to feature in a series of articles she was writing about how the Swinging Sixties had affected the lives of ordinary people.

Sylvia Quinn was riding the crest of the wave. She didn't seem able to put a foot wrong.

'When's the auction?' she asked.

'Next week,' said the solicitor. 'But if you were thinking of a pre-emptive offer . . .'

'I'll have to do my sums,' said Sylvia with her sweetest smile.

'Talk it over with Mr Quinn,' said the solicitor.

'My husband's not actually involved in the business,' Sylvia told him firmly, making him go puce again. He clearly wasn't used to dealing with a woman, which Sylvia found often worked to her advantage.

There was just time for a quick cup of tea in the café at the bus station before the next service back to Kingshaven.

The song blaring from the radio behind the counter was 'Congratulations' by Cliff Richard, which seemed like a good omen.

Sylvia sat on a high stool by the window stirring her tea.

The green bus from Kingshaven was parking up in its bay a little early. She watched as several people she did not know came down the steps, and then Claudia. Sylvia held her breath, expecting Michael to appear behind her with a baby in each arm, but he did not. His girlfriend was alone, and she didn't look very happy, Sylvia thought, blowing across the top of the teacup.

They'd never spoken. Sylvia didn't even know what Claudia's voice sounded like. She knew what she looked like, of course, because she had always been a very pretty girl, a bit like Audrey Hepburn, with the same effortless, slight figure, and the same kind of surprise in those wide almond eyes, as if everything was new to her. But she'd lost that innocent look, Sylvia thought as she tracked Claudia walking across the bus station. Now she looked anxious, as if she wasn't quite sure where she was going. That was what years of being with Michael Quinn did to you.

'I almost killed myself when Iris was missing,' he'd told her.

And Sylvia had found herself feeling a bit sorry for his girl-friend, because she knew what he was like when he was depressed, as if he wanted to punish everyone around him.

Sylvia remembered her mother remarking, after the news about Frank's accident, 'Anyone would think he was the only person who'd lost anyone in the war!'

But Sylvia had thought that Michael felt things more deeply than anyone else. His endless staring silences had made him even more elusive and romantic. Her one desire in life had been to make him happy.

When Iris went missing, he must have thought that everyone he loved had abandoned him, Sylvia realized now, feeling rather ashamed of herself.

It wasn't as if she'd planned not to tell him. She'd just wanted him to know what it was like, being kept in the dark.

And then, after a couple of months had elapsed, she'd been frightened. It had become a bigger thing to tell him than not to.

But she'd never lied exactly, because he'd never asked. If he'd rung up occasionally to see how she and Anthony were getting along, well, things might have been different. He had only him-self to blame, really.

Anyway, Sylvia had always told herself, Iris knew where he was. She could get in touch with him herself if she wanted to. Why should Sylvia be her messenger?

If she gave him his divorce, Sylvia thought, would that make up for it?

Claudia's face passed within inches of hers, separated only by glass, so intent on wherever she was going, she wasn't noticing anything around her.

Sylvia decided she'd have a think about it when she had less on her mind.

It was an anonymous suburban street, with detached mock-Tudor houses set back from the road, which could have been almost anywhere on the outskirts of London. As Iris walked along looking anxiously for the right number, she was shaking with fear. There had been a sign to Epping Forest just before the bus stop, and she was terrified that Clive was going to drive past at any moment in his red sports car and ask her what the hell she was doing. If she told him, he would probably kill her.

At last, the Gables Nursing Home.

A girl of about her age was walking down the gravel drive towards her, hugging the edges of a raincoat around her even though it was a warm day. She didn't appear to see Iris as she walked past.

Iris took a deep breath, and walked towards the door.

The nurse was ample-bosomed and smiling, and she had a large syringe in her hand.

'It'll be a little prick and then we'll draw out the fluid,' she said as Claudia sat up on the hospital bed wearing a surgical gown, with one breast exposed and her arm in the air. 'Shouldn't hurt too much.'

Claudia looked away, not wanting to see the needle going in. For a moment, she wished that she had let Michael come. It would have been comforting to have his hand to hold, but she knew she would never relax if the babies were left in the care of the two old men, and it seemed such a palaver bringing them all on the bus.

'Brave girl,' said the nurse. 'There, that's the worst bit over.'

Claudia looked down. The needle was in her breast. It was painful, but it was bearable.

'Now,' said the nurse, trying to pull the plunger back. 'It is sometimes a bit stiff.'

Finally she managed to move it, and the pain was suddenly searing, as if Claudia had been stabbed. She took a deep breath, looked at the nurse, expecting some comforting phrase, but instead the motherly face was frozen with alarm.

Claudia saw that there was no fluid in the tube.

'Is something wrong?' she whispered.

But she didn't need to ask, because the drumbeat of

apprehension, which had started as a barely audible murmur at her visit to the health visitor, was so strong now, it was pulsing through her veins.

'I think I'd better find a doctor,' the nurse replied.

Chapter Seventeen

19 July 1969

It had all been a dream!

For one sweet second, a wave of relief washed over Claudia as she opened her eyes.

But with the next tick of the clock on her bedside table, the pain gnawed into her awakening senses, insistent and relentless, and though she tried to breathe through it calmly, her brain was racing with panic.

She was running out of time.

When there had been hope, she had felt it would be defeatist and morbid to make plans for what might happen. Then she had believed that if hope ran out, there would be a period of acceptance during which everything could be organized, but now she knew that there would never be enough time. Nothing was going to make it all right.

When the doctors were telling you that people did recover from cancer, you didn't want to ask how long in case it sounded as if you didn't trust them, or you weren't willing to try.

At first they'd said that if it hadn't spread from the breast the chances were good. When they told her there were secondaries, she'd actually thought for a moment it was positive news. 'Secondary' didn't sound very bad, somehow. The doctors clearly thought her reaction was so brave, she hadn't wanted to spoil it by howling with fear when she belatedly realized what they meant.

After that, there had been no more talk about people recovering.

Claudia could tell from the whiteness of the light coming round the edge of the curtains that it was going to be a hot summer day. She could hear the distant clank of scaffolding poles as the stage went up for Winston's festival. The smell of bacon wafted up from the kitchen. In the brief periods before the pain took over, her body was greedy for sensation. Had bacon ever smelled so bacony before?

'How is it all going?' she asked as Michael came in with a cup of tea for her.

He sat down on his side of the bed, and though he wasn't touching her, the change in pressure was such agony she couldn't stop herself crying out, and she had to point to the chair. He leaped up, his face stricken with anxiety that he had inadvertently caused her pain, and she was irritated with him for not disguising it better.

How was he ever going to cope?

Michael went over to the window and drew the curtains back. 'When Winston said Folk Festival, I thought we were talking about a couple of bearded blokes with guitars and a girl playing the tambourine,' he said, looking out. 'But a pantechnicon of speakers has just arrived, and a generator and a back-up generator. Winston's saying that Bob Dylan might come. I think that translates as he's invited him, but he's heard nothing, and until he gets a definite no, then there's still the possibility . . . It's a free concert, but he's charging people two quid to camp. Winston's pretty good at seeing money-making opportunities in the midst of peace and love—'

'Oh, for heaven's sake!' Claudia interrupted sharply.

'Can't you stand it? Shall I ask Winston to cancel the Festival?' he asked.

'No! It's not that!' she said.

She knew he was only chatting away to fill the awful sombre silence that sometimes fell between them, but she didn't want all this information. There were more important things they needed to discuss, like what he would tell the children. His usual way of dealing with difficult issues was not to talk. But that wouldn't do now. Would he be brave enough to explain what had happened? Did he realize that the way he behaved was absolutely crucial to their ability to cope?

'What are you going to tell the children?' she demanded to know.

'I haven't decided,' he said.

'You must not tell them that I've gone to sleep,' Claudia said. 'Because that will make them frightened of sleeping.'

'I know that,' he said patiently.

'So what will you say?'

'I don't know!' he said. 'I don't want to think about it right now, OK?'

He looked out of the window, as if to say: on a lovely day like this. But she knew that there weren't going to be many more days, and she could see that he didn't realize how soon it would be. In movies, there was always a Cathy and Heathcliff moment in which issues were resolved, undying love declared, the possibility of an afterlife introduced, but she didn't think that real death was so picturesque or so patient.

'Have you thought about what it's going to be like for them growing up in a household full of men?' Claudia demanded, and then the terrifying thought crossed her mind that he would find another woman, and the twins would call someone else Mummy.

'We'll manage.' He looked at her. 'There's no way of making it right. It won't be as you want it to be . . . as I want it to be. But I promise we'll survive.'

'But I don't want them just to survive,' she insisted. 'I want them to have wonderful lives! And you mustn't go to pieces. You mustn't think about yourself all the time . . .'

She hated herself for being so cross with him. It made her wonder if some primitive instinct made a dying person cruel to the ones they loved, to lessen the sting of parting.

'I'm sorry,' he said.

'And don't keep apologizing!'

Michael shrugged his shoulders.

Even that gesture irritated her so much she wanted to scream at him. But the pain liquefied the scream to tears.

'Claudia!' Michael went to put his arms round her, stopping just before he touched as he saw her brace herself.

'I need some paper and a pen,' she said, sniffing back the tears with a loud, unladylike snort, which made them both finally smile.

My dearest Fiammetta, Claudia wrote. *My darling daughter* . . .

She tried to imagine at what age this letter would be given to her child. Should she write a date for it to be opened, or should she leave it to the judgement of others? All these decisions about how to present oneself in the future were so fraught, she wondered if it was safer not to try. Her daughter could come to her own conclusions about her.

It hurt so much that they would be too young to remember her. But possibly it was better that way, Claudia thought, because they would not consciously miss her so much.

She remembered how she had traced her finger over her mother's name in the front of her books, the handwriting bringing her closer than a photograph ever could. She wondered if her mother had experienced the same dilemma as she was in. Had she made a conscious decision not to write a letter to Claudia? Had she simply believed that they would be reunited? Had she even known she was going to die? Had she known how unbearable it was to think of what your child would do without you?

Would answers to these questions have made it easier or more difficult for Claudia when she was growing up?

Claudia looked at the writing paper in front of her, her tears mingling with Fiammetta's name, streaking in watery blue rivulets down the page.

It was impossible to convey her identity, to demonstrate her love, to support her daughter as a mother should. No words she could ever write would impart the simple warm presence of a hug.

My darling Fiammetta,

I don't know how to start this letter because you are so little now, and I am so sad that I am going to miss finding out what sort of person you will become. I already know that you are clever, because you can recite nursery rhymes. Your favourite is

'Mary, Mary' – I think because you like the soothing rhythm of
the words, not because you are contrary. You are a very
co-operative little girl. Everyone remarks on it. They say you
look like a china doll because of your pale skin and your
beautiful red curly hair and bright blue eyes, and because you sit
still. Dearest Fiammetta, it is good to be well-behaved, but
always remember that you are just as important as anyone else,
and don't let anyone boss you around. My hope is that you stay
as sweet-natured as you are, but grow up strong too.

There are so many things I wanted to show you, like
mountains with snow on top, and Alpine flowers so tiny and
perfect you think that fairies have made them, and the
Mediterranean sea as blue as ink, with porpoises playing in the
wash of an island ferry, and Venice, and all the places I wanted to
go with you for the first time, Athens, India, Egypt, Mexico . . .

Michael had always wanted to travel, and when the twins had
arrived, they'd talked about buying a dormobile van, as soon as
they were out of nappies, and taking off round Europe like
gypsies. There was the small matter of learning to drive, but
everything had seemed possible then. It had felt like the beginning of their future.

Claudia shifted position to try to get a little more comfortable,
but the pain was becoming savage now, attacking her whichever
way she moved. She started writing faster.

Fiammetta, when I was a little girl, I sometimes felt very sad
and lonely that I didn't have a mother, and sometimes I forgot
about it completely. I want you to know that if you forget about
me, I will understand and I won't mind at all. And one day you
will understand that we have experienced the same thing, and
that I am close to you, even though I'm not there . . .

Claudia read back the paragraph. She didn't want to create
problems which might never have occurred to the child. She was
inclined to scrunch the paper up and start another draft, but the
pain was now ravenous inside her. Soon the nurse would come to
give it morphine, and then it would subside for a while, and

nothing would matter. But the periods of clarity between shots were getting shorter. Each day, the pain got greedier, and needed a bigger dose to keep it satisfied. The time was fast approaching when there wouldn't be any gaps between the spells of oblivion. Curiously the pain had begun to feel almost like a friend. As long as it was around, Claudia knew she was alive.

She started on a new sheet of paper, her writing so frantic it was almost illegible.

My darling Bruno,

You are such a bundle of energy, and you love to laugh. Listening to your laughter is the best sound in the whole world. You give me the tightest hug, and then you fall asleep so peacefully I have to put my hand on your cheek several times a night, just to check you are warm, and also because I can't quite believe my luck in having you. You love music and jumping and the dustbin lorry. Your first words were ''Ello, mate!', which is what the dustmen said to you. And that is how you greet people and it makes me laugh every time. You give me such joy because I thought I wouldn't know what to do with a boy baby, but you make it so easy. You are so affectionate, standing up in your cot to kiss me goodnight so that I don't have to bend over when my back hurts . . .

Claudia threw down the pen, scrunched up the letters and threw them across the room in a wild gesture that hurt so much she felt as if she would be sick.

It was futile!

There was no way of addressing them individually without invidious comparisons being made. Would Fiammetta think she loved Bruno more? Would Bruno think she valued him less? Better to let them each build their own picture of her, to make up the mother they would have wanted. It was difficult enough to know another person when they were alive.

Claudia suddenly remembered how, in the beginning, she and Michael had talked only about books, finding out about each other that way, creating a language to speak of things they could not talk directly about.

She began to scribble furiously on a new sheet of paper.

Children, these are the books I most loved because they made
me think, or dream, or sometimes just laugh: *Persuasion,
Middlemarch, Ulysses, Great Expectations, Far From the Madding
Crowd, Anna Karenina, Women in Love, Howard's End, Brideshead
Revisited, Our Man in Havana, Love in a Cold Climate, The Girls of
Slender Means, Lucky Jim, The Country Girls, The Golden
Notebook* . . .

Was there anything distinctive about this list that made it
different from any list of classic books any other person would
choose? Should she put the children's books in too?

Then it occurred to her that she was going to miss them dis-
covering Mrs Tiggy-Winkle, or the Flower Fairies, or
Milly-Molly-Mandy, or The Family from One End Street, or
Emil and the Detectives, or *The Tale of Troy* by Roger Lancelyn
Green, and all those stories about girls who had been Claudia's
friends in her lonely childhood: *What Katy Did, The Secret Garden,
A Traveller in Time, The Far-Distant Oxus, Little Women, Anne of
Green Gables* (how she had longed for a friend across the valley to
flash messages by torchlight!) . . .

'Mummy! Mummy! Mummy!' A joyous high voice and little
footsteps running down the hall; squeals of laughter followed by
the heavier tread of their father running after them.

'Ssshush,' Michael said. 'Mummy's not feeling very well.'

'Want to see Mummy!' Bruno said impatiently.

Claudia could almost hear Michael's hesitation.

'Can I hear visitors outside my door?' she said as loudly and
brightly as the pain would allow.

'Mummy!' Bruno ran in and threw himself head first on to the
bed.

Claudia tried to shift herself up on her pillows.

'Come over here with Fiammetta, and tell Mummy what you
can see out of the window!' Michael suggested. He was holding
their daughter's hand. She was sucking her thumb, looking at
Claudia warily.

'No!' said Bruno, snuggling up next to Claudia.

The pain was so excruciating, Claudia felt herself reeling in and out of consciousness. She tried to grip it, to use the pain as a handle to support her as she attempted to lift her arm and draw the little child against her chest.

People always said of Bruno, as he insisted on walking instead of going in the pushchair, or ran away when it was time to leave the beach, 'He's full of life!' Claudia felt as if she was drawing strength from the vital little body against hers.

She must have closed her eyes for a moment, perhaps longer, and when she opened them, Bruno was staring up into her face curiously, giving her that look he had given her as a baby at the breast when she had run out of milk.

'Where does it hurt, Mummy?'

'Everywhere,' she said, unable to dissemble or stop the tears running down her cheeks.

He clambered up the pillow and gently kissed her wet face.

'There,' he said, as if attending to a grazed knee or a nettle sting. 'All better now!' he said, and dashed out of the room unperturbed.

Claudia and Michael watched him go.

'Is there anything you need?' Michael asked.

'I need a kiss from Fiammetta too,' said Claudia, making a huge effort to stretch out her arms.

Michael lowered their daughter over her so that she could kiss her mother's cheek without touching her, a kiss as soft and delicate as a petal falling from a blossom tree.

'Oh, that was the best kiss in the world!' Claudia said, and the solemn little face broke into the most wondrous smile, and she went tottering off to tell her brother.

'Don't always tell them to be quiet around me,' Claudia told Michael. 'I don't want them to remember me as someone they couldn't talk to.'

'I'm sorry.'

'Will you promise to read her *Milly-Molly-Mandy*?'

'Of course I will.'

'I want her to know the books I liked, not just the books you liked . . .' she insisted.

'I was a teacher,' he tried to reassure her.

'When you tell them what I was like, please tell them the bad things too,' Claudia said.

'What bad things?'

He was being so sweet, and she still couldn't make herself kind to him.

'I hate it when nobody dares to say anything bad about people who have died,' she told him brusquely, unable to look at him.

'OK,' he agreed.

'So what are my bad points, then?' she wanted to know suddenly.

'Sometimes you can be a bit demanding,' he said, as light-heartedly as he could.

'What's wrong with that? Women should be more demanding.'

'Now you're beginning to sound like Josie!'

'Oh, God! I'm surely not that bad, am I?' she said.

Finally, she looked at him, and he smiled at her, and she saw that he understood her ill humour and forgave her, and it made her feel even more wretched that she was so ill that now she had to be indulged.

'Do you think the nurse is on her way yet?' Claudia asked.

The last time the hotel had thrown such a party was for the Coronation. Libby gazed out of her bedroom window in her dressing gown, enjoying a moment's reflection before going downstairs. Then it had poured with rain, but today looked as if it was going to be gloriously sunny. Then she had been hopelessly inexperienced, but now she'd got the hang of it.

Just as the party in 1953 had been organized with the dual purpose of celebrating the Coronation and the safe stewardship of the hotel's affairs through a turbulent period in its history, so today's would mark another new beginning.

For the moment at least, the fortunes of the hotel were on the up, and she hoped that throwing a party would draw a line under the difficult times. Robin Knox-Johnston's very English victory in the Round the World Yacht Race had put sailing back on the map and breathed new life into the marina development at the Harbour End. Several of the flats had already sold, and the company was investing the money in a secure fund which would see Adrian and Winny through their education.

Thanks to the article in the colour supplement, which had cheekily portrayed them as a kind of Royal Family of the South Coast in the same week as the film about the real Royal Family went out on television, bookings at the Palace had increased significantly. It was too early to say whether it would last, but after a decade in which everyone else seemed to be having fun, Libby had decided it was time the Kings let their hair down too.

Libby had purchased a dress with a hemline a good two inches above the knee in cream-coloured crimplene. On her brother-in-law's advice, she had bought a pink shirt with ruffles for Christopher, but she didn't know whether it was really appropriate. When Eddie had seen it, he'd asked if she was trying to make their son look even more like a flaming queer than he already did. Tom Snow could get away with such flamboyance in the artistic circles he moved in.

Libby had come to appreciate her brother-in-law's élan. He'd been such a help in organizing the party, printing the invitations, designing the platform on which Libby would hand over the keys of the Palace to Christopher. If you wanted a good photo in the paper, Tom advised, you had to create it yourself, which was something Libby would never have thought of.

Libby held the dress up in front of her and was looking at her reflection in the cheval mirror, enjoying the sheer practicality of the fabric (it never creased or bagged and you could wash it in an automatic washing machine!) when Christopher himself wandered into her bedroom, still in his pyjamas.

'I don't understand why the whole town has to come to my birthday party,' he said.

'It's your twenty-first,' said Libby, slightly flustered to have her son see her before she'd even pulled a brush through her hair. 'And you're going to be deputy manager. That's an event in somewhere the size of Kingshaven.'

'I never asked to be deputy manager,' he said sulkily.

A year ago, with the hotel teetering on the brink of bankruptcy, giving him such a title would have been meaningless, but Libby had decided to capitalize on the moment. It would be better as far as his authority with the rest of the staff were concerned to bring him back from London rather than having him sent back, which looked increasingly likely with the number of pranks reported, although he had assured her that the incident when he'd ended up in the Savoy wastebins was just a bit of harmless fun.

'There'll be your friends too,' she tried to reassure him.

'I'm not sure how many of them will turn up,' he said sheepishly.

'There's the pop group. Dancing. It's going to be great fun,' said Libby determinedly.

'It just seems such a palaver,' said Christopher, staring up at the ceiling.

Libby had suddenly had enough. Fury boiled up inside her like a volcano. 'Well, if that's really the way you feel about it, why don't you go and find yourself a job somewhere else?' she exploded. 'I'm certainly not going to stop you! In fact, it would make my life a great deal easier if I didn't have to defend you to your father all the time!'

Christopher cowered, glassy-eyed, like one of the spaniels when she told them off. She realized that she had never shouted at him before. Perhaps she had been too soft, as Eddie had always said.

'And don't you dare cry!' she added as she saw her son's lip wobbling. 'You're twenty-one!'

There was a long silence, in which she could only hear her own breathing, and she tried to imagine how she would feel if her son did walk out. Relieved, she decided. Of course, she'd have to make up some excuse for the *Chronicle*. But she'd be relieved, and completely astonished, of course, because in her heart she knew there was no way Christopher would take the opportunity to go off on his own.

'I'm sorry, Mummy,' he said, quietly. 'Of course I'm grateful, so grateful for everything you do for me.'

She had an almost irresistible urge to say to him, 'Oh, for God's sake, go! Go on! Don't get stuck here, when there's so much else to do in the world. It's not much of a life, this, having to humour difficult guests, and placate envious neighbours who think that just because you've got a big hotel and a bit of land that everything in the garden's rosy; always worrying whether you're going to survive the next downturn in the economy; always being dependent on the fickleness of public opinion, which can be bought for the price of an airfare and a couple of jugs of sangria . . .'

Instead she simply said, 'Yes, well . . .'

Christopher walked across the room towards her with arms outstretched, but she turned away and fiddled with the brushes on the dressing table, feeling it wouldn't be appropriate for her grown son to embrace her when she was still in her dressing gown.

Sylvia had toyed with calling the men's section the Mighty Quinn, as a bit of fun. There were so many names which seemed perfect the moment she thought about them, like Wonderful World or Xanadu, even if, as her mother had remarked, it sounded a bit foreign. Sylvia's market was primarily the younger generation, but she was aware that it was the postal orders grannies gave on birthdays which often paid for the cheaper items, such as the purple and black horizontally striped over-the-knee socks which had been such a success during the winter season.

In the end, she'd decided to keep it simple and name the shop Sylvia Quinn. Now, as she stood on the pavement outside, looking up at the sign on the top of the building – her name with a conch shell beside it in pink neon, which was visible for miles when it was switched on at night – she knew she'd made the right decision, because she didn't think it would be quite the same thrill if it wasn't her own name up there for all the world to see.

'Happy, Mum?' Anthony asked.

Her son towered over her now. Sylvia looked up at him. His lovely head of thick fair hair – a bit longer than the school would allow because it was the holidays – was right in line with the sign. Her two proudest achievements, Sylvia thought, smiling up at him and linking his arm as they turned to have their photo taken.

The man from the *Lowhampton Echo* now took photographs for the newspaper group which had bought up the *Echo*, the *Chronicle*, and a list of other struggling local papers along the South Coast. With any luck, a picture would appear in all of them. Sylvia had considered asking Miss Lowhampton 1969, who was on duty later in the day as Carnival Queen, to cut the wide pink ribbon across the main door, but when she'd realized that that would be the photograph the paper would use, she'd decided to cut it herself instead, wearing one of her own dresses made of stretchy black jersey with pink dots, which was smart, but short enough to show off her legs.

'Very happy,' she said.

A satisfying rasp of sharp scissors on silk, a smattering of applause from the crowd who'd gathered outside, then two liveried doormen opened the doors for her. Even though she'd been through a thousand times over the past frantic year, Sylvia took a deep breath, imagined that she was her own first customer and savoured the beauty of the interior.

It was like going into a palace of mirrors and flowers, all black and silver and shell pink.

'A bit claustrophobic,' her mother had remarked the day before when Sylvia had given her a preview. But Sylvia wanted people to be wrapped up in the experience of her shop, to forget there was a world outside, to feel glamorous simply by being there, just like her products, which were wrapped in beautiful black and pink packaging, which lent even the most ordinary blue eye shadow a special desirability, and meant you could charge twice as much as Rimmel.

There was no smell Sylvia liked more than the ground floor of a department store. It conjured memories of happy moments: her first test of a lipstick; her first squirt of perfume; her first American Tan stockings stretched over leg-shaped bits of card in flat, elegant packages; and all the times she'd held little white velvet squares with earrings she couldn't afford next to her ear, dreaming of having an occasion to wear them.

The scent of her own store had been the most difficult thing to get right. As yet, there was only one Sylvia Quinn perfume. It was heady with lots of sandalwood; not exactly what she'd have worn herself, but it suited the exotic quality of the shop, and it would suffice until she had time to learn a bit more about perfumery. But when she'd squirted it around, she'd realized, even before her mother had said it, that she needed to lighten the fragrance if she didn't want the place smelling like a tart's boudoir. The solution had arrived quite naturally with the florist who was dressing the shop for the opening with silver ice buckets of Stargazer lilies on every available surface, which gave off such a wonderfully fresh and light scent, it crossed Sylvia's mind that they should always have a small florist's barrow in the entrance, so that there would be the constant fragrance of fresh flowers, and, importantly, the opportunity to purchase bunches – wrapped gratis in shell-pink tissue paper, perhaps – since she dreaded to think what the florist was going to charge for this lot.

The shop assistants were all wearing black bell-bottom trousers and short-sleeved shell-pink blouses Sylvia had made up specially. Sylvia never thought it was a good idea to have your sales staff wearing the patterns you were selling. People didn't want to buy something that a shop girl wore.

Sylvia took it all in with a quick glance, then nodded at the doormen who dropped the shell-pink rope they were holding and allowed the crowd in.

Amid gasps of delight at the look of the place, came the final innovation: a disc jockey's voice welcoming customers to the store through concealed speakers, and playing the first song she had chosen to launch Radio Sylvia.

'If Paradise is Half as Nice', by Amen Corner.

By the time the song faded away in la la las, there was another sound, just as wonderful, of cash registers pinging, as excited customers fell upon the merchandise.

When Winston Allsop had telephoned to ask – extremely politely, you'd never have known he was coloured from his voice – whether there were any rooms available for some friends of his who were in a band, for some reason (possibly thinking of the Black and White Minstrels) Libby had pictured men in white suits with brass instruments – a trombone, a trumpet, perhaps even a saxophone. She'd half had it in mind to invite them to play a fanfare when she handed over the symbolic keys to the Palace to Christopher. She was extremely surprised when Winston drew up in a Volkswagen van with a garish psychedelic pattern all over it, and four young white men with long hair, wild eyes and cigarettes dangling from their mouths fell out of the back along with bits of a drum kit.

Libby put them as far away as possible in the suite at the top of the tower, which was free because she'd over-estimated acceptance of the party invitations by Christopher's friends. Still, the noise they were making was audible throughout the hotel and gardens, even though she'd sent Christopher up twice already to ask them if they'd mind doing their drumming with a little more thought for others.

When she'd telephoned the Castle to complain, Winston had assured her that they would not be there during the party since they were playing at the Castle that evening. He would personally pick them up, and he doubted whether they'd be back before the small hours. He'd been so charming about it all, Libby had felt it would be churlish to go back on her promise, and, as she and the family took lunch on the terrace, she couldn't help a sly smile crossing her face when she thought of Sir John's reaction to such a racket.

'Goodness, Libby, the music sounds a little avant-garde for you!' Pearl exclaimed.

Her sister could never just arrive, Libby thought. She always had to make an entrance, normally accompanied by a drift of heavy perfume, always wearing something eye-catching, and usually late, although today, capriciously, she was several hours early. Pearl was wearing a clinging mini-dress printed with a bright pattern of dots, and a floor-length sleeveless cardigan thing, which did not conceal the roll of flesh above the line of her girdle as well as Pearl probably imagined it did. Around Pearl's neck there seemed to be at least a dozen strings of beads, and she was wearing a hat in the same fabric as the dress with a wide brim that flopped over half her face.

'I simply adore your outfit, Auntie Pearl,' said Joanna, the oldest of the Allsop girls. 'Is it from Sylvia Quinn?'

'As a matter of fact, it is,' said Pearl, as if she hadn't really put any thought into what she was wearing. 'I don't usually care for her stuff,' she said with a glance at Mrs Farmer.

'What? You were practically first in the queue this morning!' said Tom.

'Is the new shop totally fab?' asked Joanna excitedly.

'It is quite fun, I suppose,' said Pearl coolly.

'Jack and I are desperate to go, but Granny won't let us,' said Joanna with a scowl at Mrs Farmer.

'When you're old enough to pay for your own clothes, you can choose them too,' Mrs Farmer said, folding her arms.

'I'm fourteen!' said Joanna huffily. 'All my friends have Sylvia Quinn clothes.'

'Sylvia Quinn?' said Jolly Allsop, as if he'd just woken up.

'She's taken over Gillie's in Lowhampton now,' Mrs Farmer informed him.

'Has she, by George! Good for her!' he said with a beaming smile, which faded as it met the thunderous look on Mrs Farmer's face.

'Please will you take us there, Father?' Joanna tried to press home the advantage.

'Well, you know, shopping's not really my bag,' he said.

'Mummy would have taken us,' muttered Jacqueline, wincing as her older sister kicked her hard under the table.

Libby felt a certain sympathy for the Allsop girls, who were sitting in a row wearing identical pink dresses with patch pockets and a deep frill at the hem. The style suited Julia well enough because she was still a little girl, but it did not flatter the other two, who were approaching puberty. She remembered how Liliana had insisted on dressing her and Pearl in identical winter hats and coats when they were young (just like the Little Princesses, people always said), and how she had always felt big and ungainly beside her pretty little sister. It crossed her mind that she might, as a treat, take the Allsop girls into Lowhampton herself since it was the school holidays, and see what all the fuss was about.

A sudden torrent of swear words rained down from the tower, and everyone looked up to see a drumstick somersaulting through the air and landing in the bright blue water of the swimming pool where it floated for a moment, before the youngest of the spaniels tore away from the terrace, and plunged into the pool to retrieve it.

A head of long hair appeared over the top balcony and shouted, 'Shit!'

'Oh, my goodness! I think that was Dexter Strange!' said Pearl. 'Who did you say the band was upstairs?'

'They're friends of Winston's,' said Libby. 'But they've not got his manners, I'm afraid. When I asked their names, they all looked at me as if I was mad and said, "What?"'

'All that drumming has probably damaged their hearing,' Liliana observed.

'You are kidding?' said Pearl. 'You've got the What staying at the hotel and you've no idea who they are?'

'What?' repeated Libby. 'Whoever they are, I hope Winston comes to collect them before the guests start arriving. I'm a little surprised no one's here yet.' She looked at her watch.

'They're probably stuck in traffic,' said Pearl. 'We took an age, didn't we, Tom?'

'The weekend queues have normally disappeared by now,' said Libby.

'My God, are you the only person in the country who hasn't heard?' asked Pearl.

'*Heard?*' echoed Liliana.

'The Kingshaven Folk Festival. Everyone who's anyone is coming!' said Pearl, exasperated. 'Thousands. From all over the country!'

'Thousands?' said Libby.

'It's been on every radio station!'

'I've been far too busy to listen to the radio.'

'Oh, do make him drop it, Libby, and let me take it back up,' said Pearl, trying to pull the drumstick from the dog's mouth.

'Good boy, Baron!'

The dog obediently dropped the drumstick at Libby's feet.

'They can come down themselves if they want it back,' she said firmly, confiscating it and putting it beneath her chair.

Pearl looked as if she was going to stamp her foot and make a fuss, but then she changed her mind and sat down as everyone else finished their lunch.

For a few minutes, the peace of the afternoon was interrupted only by the chink of silver on china as the family ate their individual summer puddings, and pretended to ignore Granny Adela as she took a hairpin from under her wimple and used it to dig blackberry pips out of the gaps between her teeth.

Then suddenly the pleasant atmosphere was rent by a noise far louder and more penetrating than anything the What could manage upstairs, as banks of speakers inside the Castle grounds blasted into operation.

'Help!' Adela cried, covering her head with her hands, as if the booming was coming from an overhead aircraft about to drop its payload of bombs.

'It's started!' Pearl said, exchanging a look with her husband. 'So exciting! Bob Dylan's coming, but I didn't know the What were on the bill too! Shall we go across and see what's happening, Tom? Libby, we can leave the children with you for the afternoon, can't we?'

'As long as you're back for the photo,' said Libby, relieved not to have Pearl teasing her during those awful moments before the party, when you worried that nobody was going to turn up.

It was such a hot afternoon that swirls of invisible heat distorted the view of the stage from a distance. The air stank of cannabis and patchouli oil, and people smiled with glazed, unfocused eyes when Michael walked past with Bruno holding his right hand and Fiammetta his left.

Most of the men had taken their shirts off and their bare chests looked very white in the bright sunlight; a couple of women had stripped down to their knickers and bras. One large-breasted girl had dispensed with the bra too, and was dancing euphorically.

Bruno stared at her with a look of utter astonishment on his face.

'Is that a lady?' he asked, as if the girl might belong to a different species. Even when Claudia was breastfeeding, her breasts had never been larger than half an orange, and these were melons.

Michael laughed out loud. 'Yes, it's a lady,' he replied. 'But she's not really behaving like one.'

It made him feel rather middle-aged, observing what the young people were up to, knowing that he would never have dared strip off, or openly defy the law by smoking pot, or even kissing in public, certainly not with the girl lying on top of him as one couple were doing, her long hair tenting their faces as they made love with their mouths.

Michael had assumed Winston was exaggerating when he'd estimated thousands rather than hundreds of people would turn up, but as the corrugated iron fence had to be moved down a field to allow more campers in, and traders appeared with bundles of coloured T-shirts in their car boots, emblazoned with the words 'Kingshaven '69', it was increasingly clear that something big was happening.

How on earth had Winston persuaded all these bands to perform for no money? How did he know all these people when he was only twenty-four? Where had he got the confidence to think he could stage such an event in a sleepy backwater which hadn't seen such an influx of outsiders since half a million American troops had gathered in the surrounding area during the weeks running up to D-Day?

Michael was slightly anxious that the sunny atmosphere of peace and love might suddenly grow darker as the light faded, and people began to feel the effects of sunstroke and overcrowding. Winston had assured him that nobody without a pass issued by him personally would get inside the house itself, but all day there had been people coming to the Castle: first the disenchanted drivers of lorries containing the equipment, until Winston put up directions from the road; and then the better-prepared campers who'd caught early trains down from London, or hitch-hiked, with tents and sleeping bags rolled up on the top of their rucksacks, and who stood on the doorstep with expectant smiles on their faces, making Michael feel like the grumpy warden of a youth hostel as he turned them away.

At their recent free concert in Hyde Park, the Rolling Stones had hired a gang of Hell's Angels to keep order, but Michael couldn't see that Winston's long-haired friends, who had spent the night on the floor in the oval hall and eaten them out of bacon, would provide similar protection.

It was going to be a very long weekend, he thought as he carried the tired twins back up the avenue to the Castle.

The nurse's bike was leaning against the wall outside.

Inside, the Castle was very dark after the bright sunlight.

Michael put the children down without giving them their bath.

They no longer clamoured for a kiss from their mother at night, and it made him sad that they had adapted so quickly, but gave him hope too. Children were naturally heartless, and it was probably better that way.

Claudia seemed peaceful when he checked on her. He leaned over and kissed her very gently on the forehead.

The nurse was waiting for him downstairs, and his heart missed a beat because he knew she wouldn't have stayed to tell him good news.

'I don't think it'll be long now,' she said. 'There's fluid building in her lungs.'

'No!'

However much he had braced himself for this, he didn't seem to be able to control his body shaking, and then his nostrils were streaming, and he didn't have a handkerchief in his pocket.

'How long?' he asked, wiping the back of his hand under his wet nose.

'I think probably days,' said the nurse.

'Days?'

What had happened to weeks?

At first it had been years. 'Some people live for years after a mastectomy.'

Then it had been months. 'I'm afraid it's spread. We're probably talking about months.'

Now it had jumped straight to days. They'd been cheated. It had all gone too quickly.

Sometimes Michael found it difficult to believe her illness was real and not some terrible nightmare like the one where you tried to run and your legs wouldn't let you. Sometimes he wondered, perversely, if her decline would not have been so rapid if she'd not gone to the doctor. She'd been perfectly healthy, but as soon as she'd had the test, then the mastectomy, then the further tests, she was irrevocably dying.

Claudia thought that he didn't confront things, but he sometimes wondered whether if she'd said nothing, done nothing, she would still be walking around now.

Or should he have done more? Forced her to go to London for

a second opinion? Insisted she have more radiotherapy, or try new experimental drugs? She'd wanted to combat the disease naturally, but now he wondered whether she had secretly wanted him to intervene, to take charge? He didn't know and he didn't dare ask, and now it was too late.

'We've had so little time,' he told the nurse with a pathetic watery sniff.

Even though she was younger than he was, he could see she'd seen it all before.

'It's just . . .' He tried to make this death the special one, different from the others. 'It's just that I love her so much,' he tried to explain.

'I know you do,' said the nurse. 'And so does she.'

The sunset was very like the one Sylvia remembered on the day she and Michael had first arrived in Kingshaven, the forget-me-not-blue sky and cherry-blossom-pink clouds so bright that if she were to design a fabric with exactly the same pattern, she knew people would say it was artificial and garish.

As she drove over the North Hill, the town was already in shadow, but the sky above was as light and iridescent as the inside of the abalone shell Anthony had bought from the Shell Shop for her birthday, which she kept on her desk in her office at the shop.

After the frantic scramble to get it all ready in time for the summer holidays when visitors poured into Lowhampton with cash in their pockets, Opening Day itself had been more serenely successful than Sylvia could ever have wished. Now it was over, and she had counted the cash (three times her most optimistic budget!), it had only just dawned on her that Opening Day wasn't the end, to which all her thoughts and energy in the past year had been directed, but in fact the beginning of uncountable days ahead.

Already, she learned some lessons. In future, there would be no carrier bags for purchases under a pound (she'd telephoned this afternoon to ask the supplier to run up quotes for a cheaper quality bag, with paper handles instead of cord) and she might have to employ an undercover assistant to keep an eye on the make-up counter. They had run out of Flower Power lipstick by three o'clock in the afternoon, but Sylvia was sure that stock-taking would prove not all of it had been purchased. The maxi-length lacy cardigans had sold out and she was slightly worried that her crochet ladies would not be able to keep up with demand. Sales in the second floor SQ Home Department had been slow, but the men's shirts and velvet jackets had been flying out of the shop, and if it continued like that, she decided she would swap the two departments around.

Sylvia had predicted that when the day was over, she would simply collapse in an exhausted heap, but as she drove home with the windows wound down, she was still buzzing with energy, and she couldn't imagine ever being able to fall asleep. It was only when the car drew to a standstill in stationary traffic on Hill Road, and the air seemed to be pulsing with a loud bass beat, that she remembered today was also the day of the Festival, about which there'd been so much controversy in Kingshaven.

'What on earth's that racket?' asked her mother, who was sitting next to her in the front passenger seat.

Sylvia listened intently, trying to decipher a tune from the blur of sound.

In the battered open-top 2CV in front of them, a girl was standing waving her arms around to the music. She had a woven band tied round her long hair, Red-Indian style, and a loose peasant blouse with floaty sleeves. She looked so happy swaying in time with the music, Sylvia felt like getting out of the car and joining in.

'Drug addict, I expect,' said Doreen, pursing her lips with distaste and folding her arms.

Her mother had been quite a pretty woman, but as she had grown older, her mouth had begun to curve downwards at the corners. Even on a triumphant day like today, she had been waiting for something to go wrong, and when Sylvia had proudly announced the day's takings, all her mother had said was, 'Don't let it go to your head.'

Was it simply that she was from the generation who had the best years of their lives blighted by the fear of not knowing what was going to happen that made her suspicious and thrifty, unwilling to trust in good fortune? Sylvia wondered. Or had

Michael been right in thinking that Doreen was a particularly joyless person?

Sylvia pictured the best room at home in Etherington with its salmon-pink curtains and hard armchairs with perfectly white starched antimacassars, the carriage clock her father had been given to mark twenty-five years in the tax office ticking loudly on the mantelpiece. She thought of her father sitting beside a fire which was rarely lit, and she couldn't remember ever having heard him laugh.

Ominously, her mother had been making hints since he died that the house was too big for her to rattle around in all on her own; that the climate when she came to Kingshaven seemed to suit her arthritis. So far, Sylvia had managed to ignore the opportunity to invite her mother to stay permanently, but she knew the time was coming when she'd have to decide whether to take pity, or blatantly resist.

Anthony leaned forward. 'Could I go up to the Festival, Mum?'

With his long legs, he looked as if he had been folded in two on the back seat.

'On your own?' said Doreen.

'Dad'll be around, I expect,' said Anthony, as if this news would make a positive difference to his grandmother's opinion. 'I'll probably bump into some people I know.'

Sylvia found herself on the point of saying no, but then she looked across at her mother, all tense and sour, and said, 'I don't see why not.'

'But it'll be full of hippies!' Doreen interjected, echoing the concerns of the older residents of Kingshaven. 'And cults!'

'As long as you're sensible,' Sylvia said as the traffic moved down the hill through the traffic lights and they came to a standstill beside the clock tower.

The sunset had almost disappeared now but the sky was patched with pale gold, and the sea was milkily silver.

Sylvia remembered standing on the promenade the night they'd arrived in Kingshaven, all those years ago, watching the sky until it was quite dark, with Iris dancing round her legs, demanding again and again, 'When are we going to our new home?'

Sylvia had been so certain then that everything was going to be all right. How could it not be in a place where the breeze was balmy and the scenery so beautiful it didn't look like England at all, more like she'd imagined the Isle of Capri in that song her father sometimes played on the wind-up gramophone.

If someone had offered Sylvia three wishes that day, her first would have been to stay just as they were, at that moment on the promenade. Her next would have been to have a house of their own. Her third, the silly one, would have been to own a shop with her name above the door.

And now that the unattainable had come true, Sylvia wondered whether she would swap it for the first wish, if she had the chance.

Or had that moment of pure contentment on the promenade been an illusion, as ephemeral as the mother-of-pearl sky? Had she and Michael ever really been happy together?

They'd tried to be. Pretended to be. She'd spent her whole life trying to be what she thought he wanted her to be, and failing, because she didn't know what that was, and, in fairness, he probably didn't either.

Even that day they travelled down from Etherington, they'd bickered on the train, Iris had prattled on giving her a headache, and the bottle of lemonade had leaked and turned their sandwiches to slime. And Sylvia hadn't been very happy when she'd seen the filthy hovel they were to live in, nor when she was beating the dust out of the carpet the following afternoon.

It was easy to blame other people for making your life wrong, Sylvia thought, with a glance at the side of her mother's face. Misery could become a bit of a habit, and then your life was over and you had forgotten to live it.

The traffic began to move forward again.

Perhaps it was time to give Michael his divorce. A new beginning for both of them.

Apparently his girlfriend was ill. Cancer, Sylvia assumed, because nobody ever said. Doreen said it served her right, but Sylvia wouldn't wish that on her worst enemy.

'You'll be wanting to get yourself a bigger place to live now, I suppose,' Doreen said as they went upstairs to the flat.

'This suits us fine for the time being,' Sylvia told her mother firmly.

It was too warm an evening to have the French windows of the ballroom closed, but the racket from the Festival made it impossible to hear the tunes which the five fresh-faced young men who called themselves the Chimps were playing.

'Are we going to get this photo done now?' asked the photographer from the *Chronicle*.

Libby looked at her watch. It was already half past eight and the light was all but gone.

'The editor wants me up at the Castle when Bob Dylan arrives,' the photographer explained.

A sudden crescendo of distant cheering made him even more fidgety and Libby could see that if they didn't do the photo soon, there wouldn't be one.

'Everyone out on the terrace! It won't take a minute,' she called to the few guests who were dotted round the perimeter of the ballroom.

When it had been developed and printed, the photograph would show the entire family except for Angela, who practically lived at the stables, and Pearl who did not return from the Festival until much later on. The photographer managed to capture everyone looking at the camera but there was something slightly peculiar about the picture. The faces in the back row were all old: Liliana, Adela, Uncle Cyril, Mrs Farmer, Mr Otterway, Dr Payne, the Reverend Church and other distinguished elders of the town; and the faces at the front were all children: the three Allsop girls, Adrian, Winny and their cousins Susannah and Damian. Libby and Eddie stood at the centre with Christopher, who was holding the ornate replica key looking embarrassed, like an uninvited guest at his own party. There was no other member of his generation.

What the picture did not record was the moment of silence after the photographer called 'Ready!' when the quantity of decibels the What were putting out over the other side of Kingshaven blew the Festival speakers, finally allowing the guests at the Palace to listen to the Chimps playing 'For He's a Jolly Good Fellow', and other appropriate tunes.

'Is Mr Murphy coming, do you know?' Libby ventured to ask the photographer as he packed up his kit.

'Couldn't say, love.'

'Really,' Libby remarked. 'It's one thing to decline an invitation, but when you've actually accepted, it's so rude!'

'He's Australian,' Eddie said, as if that would account for it.

The news that the *Chronicle* had been gobbled up by a newspaper group with a successful track record for making ailing local newspapers profitable had caused consternation. Most people in Kingshaven were of the opinion that the *Chronicle* would fast turn into a scandal sheet which relied on the wishes of advertisers instead of sticking to the rigorous editorial standards Mr Otterway had always insisted on. The announcement that the new editor was to be a young Australian journalist presently living in London was doubly perplexing.

'Apparently, he's a surfer,' said Eddie, with the grimace locals reserved for the vanloads of unwashed youths with boards who set up camp most weekends these days among the sand dunes of Havenbourne just down the coast.

'We know all about Australians, Liliana, don't we?' Adela suddenly remarked, downing her champagne in one and throwing the glass over her shoulder as the party went back inside. Luckily, Eddie caught it before it shattered on the terrace and caused a hazard.

'Do we?' Liliana asked through thin lips.

Adela tapped the side of her nose.

'We used to get letters from Australia,' Christopher said. 'I remember Grandpa Basil showing me how to steam off the stamps for his collection.'

'Probably some of his naval friends,' Liliana said. 'He used to get stamps from all over the world.'

'Australia is full of convicts, refugees and other unwanted people, isn't it, Liliana?' Adela persisted.

'Oh, really, I'm sure it's not that bad. I know some awfully nice Australian chaps who live in Earls Court,' said Christopher.

'Well, why didn't you invite them?' Libby said, looking around the virtually empty ballroom.

'I did. They probably went to the Festival instead.'

Mrs Farmer had persuaded the Reverend Church to partner her in a military two-step. Ruby was rather common, Libby thought, but she did know how to get a party going.

In the far corner of the room, Adela whirled round and round, her habit fanning out to reveal surprisingly shapely legs and a pair of metallic pink dancing shoes she had borrowed (without asking) from Liliana.

At the other end of the room, all the children were gathered around Joanna Allsop, shrieking with glee as she spilled Ribena all down her party dress. Except little Julia, who was doing shy little ballet poses beside the Chimps.

'Why don't you ask Granny Lily to dance?' Libby urged Christopher desperately.

'Do I have to?'

'Eddie, will you please dance with Mummy?' Libby pleaded.

'Oh, very well,' said Eddie.

Libby mustered her best smile and launched herself in the direction of Mr Turlow, who had two left feet, but kept his hands on a lady's waist, unlike Uncle Cyril, whose fingers were inclined to slip to the buttock.

'Lovely party!' said Mr Turlow, as they bowed and curtsied and promenaded in rather ridiculous fashion to the nonsensical words of 'Lily the Pink'.

'Thank you,' said Libby with a weak smile.

She'd rarely felt more disappointed in her life.

It had been such a thrill to turn prospective guests away with the excuse, 'I'm so sorry, but the hotel is fully booked for a family function that weekend.' For once in her life, Libby had put the family's needs before those of the general public, throwing caution, and income, to the wind. She should have known better. Fifty did seem rather a large number of party guests for a boy who'd always had difficulty making friends. Perhaps Christopher had simply been trying to please her, Libby thought to herself as Mr Turlow attempted to twirl her.

When they'd righted themselves, Libby was pleased to see that Christopher had finally plucked up courage to ask someone to dance. Or possibly his partner had asked him. Julia Allsop was standing on his feet gazing up at him as if he were a prince, and Christopher's face broke into a smile as he gently twirled the little girl.

Christopher wasn't tall or dashing or witty or intelligent, Libby thought, and he had no charm like his father, but, unlike most young people these days, he wasn't interested in drugs or loud music, and he was kind to old people, animals and children, which would always stand him in good stead.

'They make a lovely couple, don't they?' Mrs Farmer nudged Libby crudely in the ribs as the dance came to an end.

Michael wandered around the Festival grounds, not really knowing why.

He kept seeing glimpses of people he had known. A mouth with a cigarette would bend into the flame of a lighter and he would recognize the briefly lit face as one of the children he had taught, now grown-up, but still defensive when he caught them doing something naughty.

His son, Anthony, lumbered up to greet him and introduced him to a crowd of friends from Harrow wearing leather thongs round their foreheads. They shook his hand and said, 'How do you do?' in incongruously posh voices.

'How is Claudia?' Anthony asked.

'She's very ill,' Michael said.

Nobody should know she was about to die if Claudia did not. Michael didn't know whether he was going to be able to tell her. Or even whether he should. Everyone else he had known who had died had done it without him there. His parents; Frank. He didn't know what you were supposed to do.

'Send her my love!' said Anthony.

'Yes,' Michael agreed, adding, as if obliged to affect some kind of paternal authority, 'Take care!'

'Don't worry, Dad,' said Anthony confidently. 'I don't much like pot.'

'I see,' said Michael.

He drifted on, unable to remember whether or not he had said goodbye to Anthony.

The mood of the Festival was calmer since the speakers had blown. A single male folk singer was on stage accompanying himself with a guitar, a drum on his back which he played with a lever to his foot. Projected behind him was a light show of moving blobs, which Winston had demonstrated on a bare wall of the oval hall to the wonder of the twins. It was simply a matter of putting oil on a slide in front of the lens, he'd explained, but to Fiammetta and Bruno, Winston was a magician.

The crowds began to thin out as those who had enjoyed too much sun, or cider, or pot, retreated to their tents. There was a pervasive smell of frying onions from a hot-dog van which had appeared, like so many other vehicles, having heard about the Festival on the radio.

'Hello? It's Michael, isn't it?' A young woman was standing in front of him. She had long brown hair and glasses, and was wearing a loose dress in some dark colour he could not make out in the dusk. 'I thought we might see you here,' she said.

Michael recognized the short vowel sounds of Etherington, but couldn't place her. She was in her twenties and serious-looking. Was she old enough to have been a pupil in his year of teaching practice?

And then she smiled.

'You're Rachel's daughter!' he cried.

'Clare,' she said.

'Yes, of course, Clare! What are you doing here?'

'Same as everyone else, I suppose,' she said with a shrug.

He missed the dourness of the North, sometimes. People down South made a meal of things.

'Same as everyone else,' he repeated. 'Is your mother here?'

Although he hadn't thought about her much for many years, he was suddenly brightened by the prospect of seeing someone he could talk to, perhaps cry in front of, someone who knew him and would understand.

'Didn't you get the letter?' Clare asked.

'Letter?'

'Mum died last year. The last address we had for you was the school.'

Rachel was dead!

Michael slumped to his knees, his face in his hands. The girl knelt in front of him, her hands hovering beside his shaking shoulders, and when she patted his arm, tentatively, all the emotion inside him seemed to rush up as he grasped her, held her, feeling the warmth of her skin as his tears soaked through her cheesecloth dress.

'Are you all right, Clare?'

A man's voice above them.

Michael tried to pull himself together. What would an observer make of this needy embrace? He didn't want to make trouble for the girl. But when he looked up, he saw that the boy was far too young to be her boyfriend. The voice had sounded gruff because it must only recently have broken. He had a soft, almost effeminate beauty, with long waves of fair hair. He had not yet begun to shave.

Michael stood up. The boy was about his size. His eyes were pale and full of hurt.

'You must be . . .' He struggled to remember the name. Was it Keir? Or Karl? Something socialist, he knew that.

'Clem,' said the boy suspiciously.

'I was a friend of your mother's,' Michael said.

The boy looked down.

'What did she die of?' Michael asked Clare, calmer now.

'Lung cancer,' she replied.

'I'm very sorry,' Michael said to the two of them, thinking how young they suddenly looked. 'I liked your mother very much. She was a good woman.'

It sounded so inadequate.

'She shouldn't have smoked,' said the boy in his abrupt, gruff voice.

Michael wanted to tell him that it wasn't Rachel's fault. People could live blameless lives and still get cancer.

He couldn't imagine Rachel without a cigarette in her hand, conducting Mozart opera with it, or, straight after sex, sucking in the smoke as if it were cold mountain air.

'Is your dad still teaching?' he asked.

'Yes,' said Clare.

'So's Clare!' said the boy, proudly.

'Are you? Where?' Michael asked.

'I'm down in London now,' she said. 'Clem came down last night and we hitched here this morning.'

'What about you?' Michael asked the boy.

'He's just starting his 'A' levels,' said Clare, in a firm voice that sounded a bit like a teacher, a bit like a mother, as if it had been quite a job to persuade him.

'My son's just gone into the sixth form too,' Michael said, looking around in case Anthony was nearby. He realized he had no idea which 'A' levels Anthony was going to take.

'I want to go to Art College,' said Clem.

'Good luck!'

Michael thought they were probably out of things to say now. He did not want to burden them with Claudia's illness, and any further talk of Rachel might reveal things they did not know, although he suspected Clare had always known. Even as a child, she had made him feel uncomfortable, as if she could see through his lies.

'Enjoy yourselves!' he said, thinking how middle-aged he sounded.

As he turned to leave them, he became aware of someone shouting his name.

'Michael!'

Pearl Snow rushed up to him, kissing him loudly on both cheeks. In the half-light, she looked like a gypsy with her long curly hair around her shoulders. He couldn't help noticing that she had put on a lot of weight, and the skin of her cleavage was looser than it had been, and then he couldn't believe that he had looked.

'I was just about to come looking for you,' she said.

He hadn't seen her for almost ten years, and yet she was speaking as if they were out for the evening together.

'Rob's desperate to go backstage . . .' she wheedled.

'Rob?'

'Robert Murphy, the editor of the *Chronicle*. The editor of the whole *Echo* group, actually!' she said, as if that would impress him. 'We're just over there!'

She pointed at two men talking at the side of the stage, one short, the other tall and wearing a cowboy hat.

She slipped her hand through Michael's arm, as if she wasn't going to let him get away again.

Clare and Clem were staring at her as if she were a creature from another planet. Michael felt obliged to introduce them.

'Er, Pearl, this is—'

'Let me guess, you're Anthony?' Pearl interrupted. 'My goodness, you've grown up,' she added, as Clem shifted awkwardly, but said nothing.

'Not Anthony, although he's around somewhere. This is Clem, and Clare,' Michael told her. 'They're friends of mine from the North.'

'Of course!' said Pearl, as if she had known that all along.

Clare was giving her the same wary look she had given Michael as a child.

'Come along, now!' Pearl tugged at Michael's arm. 'You must speak to this horrid security guard who won't let us go backstage without a pass.'

The new editor of the *Chronicle* was standing with his back to the stage and the spotlight was very bright behind him. When he removed his hat an explosion of curly, almost woolly, hair framed his face.

'Rob Murphy?' the man said, in a distinctive Australian accent. 'Michael Quinn.'

'Good to meet you, Michael.' The man gave a very firm handshake. 'I'm told you're one of our local notables?'

He nodded at Pearl, who squeezed Michael's arm possessively.

'Love to do an interview sometime?'

'I'm a bit busy at—'

'No hurry . . . Give me a call anytime?' He presented Michael with a business card. 'Don't suppose you could point me in the direction of Mr Winston Allsop?'

'Sure,' said Michael. 'I think he's probably backstage.'

He unpeeled Pearl's fingers from his arm.

'When's Bob Dylan arriving?' asked the editor.

'You'll have to ask Winston,' Michael said, showing a backstage pass to the burly bouncer.

'Good to meet you?' Rob repeated.

Every time the editor used the unfamiliar inflexion, which made his sentences sound like questions, Michael felt as if he was being made fun of. He kept hesitating before replying, expecting the man to say, 'Gotcha, Mike!' because he looked so like his brother Frank, Michael had to keep reminding himself that Frank would have been in his forties now, and this man was no more than twenty-five.

Or perhaps he had just hallucinated the similarity, after inhaling too much of other people's pot, or perhaps he'd been sent into a trance by Winston's twirling lights.

But didn't they say that when you died, your whole life passed before you? Were these strange presentiments happening because Claudia had already died? Had she slipped away, like everyone else he had ever loved, without him?

On the stage, the folk singer was singing 'Where do you go to, my lovely?'

Michael pushed his way back through the crowd, sprinted up the avenue, took the stairs two by two, ran down the corridor, stopped outside the bedroom door, listened, but could hear only his own breathing, and a ripple of distant applause, and then . . . snores.

Claudia's father had fallen asleep in the armchair.

Claudia was lying perfectly still on the bed, but as Michael rushed to her, he could see that she was still breathing, little shallow breaths, which became quicker when lines appeared across her smooth forehead, as if she was having a bad dream.

'It's OK, my love,' Michael whispered to her. ' I'm here.'

His chest heaved with relief. He dropped a kiss on her hair, and dabbed with the corner of the sheet a tear which had fallen on to her cheek.

'Well, at least everyone who came seemed to have a good time,' Libby embarked on a post-mortem of the previous evening as she and her husband enjoyed the luxury of morning tea in bed.

'Uh-huh,' Eddie said, from behind the *Sunday Telegraph*.

The headline was all about Apollo 11 orbiting the moon.

Libby found it completely impossible to imagine three men in a tin can all that way away.

'At least the weather was nice,' she remarked.

'At least we got in a bit of sleep before the party started,' said Eddie dryly.

They had been woken up at three in the morning by the noisy return of Winston's friends accompanied by Pearl, Tom and a brassy girl Libby couldn't place, but thought was local. Libby had found them in the bar, drinking the champagne which was left over from the toast because the children hadn't been allowed more than a thimble each, and the bubbles didn't agree with most of the older generation. Libby had ordered them all up to bed, wondering whether or not she should allow the local girl to stay, and deciding she simply couldn't be bothered to start an argument.

'We've learned some useful lessons, anyway,' said Libby, trying to ignore the fact that under the covers, her husband's hand was stroking soft little circles on her inner thigh.

'Such as?' he murmured.

'Young people obviously want to do their own thing. These days, families only come together for funerals.'

'Hmm,' said Eddie.

'Eddie, I really don't think . . .' Libby started to say as his finger popped inside her. 'I really don't, Eddie . . .'

'No guests to worry about,' he whispered close to her ear.

'Yes, but the dogs are in the room . . . Goodness me, Eddie, in the morning? We're in our forties, for heaven's sake!'

Her husband kissed her. His mouth still tasted of brandy.

Despite her best intentions, she found herself sinking down into the dark warmth under the sheets.

They were disturbed by a loud knocking on the bedroom door.

'Go away!' Eddie shouted.

'It's rather important,' said Christopher nervously, outside the door.

Had he heard anything? Libby sat up quickly, adjusting her nightie and tucking her hair behind her ears.

'It's his first day in charge, remember?' she whispered to Eddie. 'He's probably trying to impress. What is it, dear?' she called.

'Dexter Strange is in bed with Millicent Bland and they're refusing to come down to breakfast. They say they're protesting for peace and they want room service.'

'Just tell them not to be so silly,' Libby instructed. 'We never offer room service.'

'I'll give them bloody peace,' Eddie declared, throwing back the bedclothes.

'Oh, and I think you should have a look out of the window,' said Christopher.

Libby got out of bed and went over to the bay window. Sunlight poured in as she drew back the curtains. It was another beautiful day. The sea was a bright, deep turquoise; the sky had a misty haze which the sun was fast burning off. The lawns going down to the cliffs were as green and smooth as a billiard table, and the herbaceous border was red, white and blue with delphiniums and red-hot pokers.

'Yes, it's a lovely day!' she called.

'Look in the pool,' called Christopher from the other side of the bedroom door.

Libby craned her neck. 'Oh my God!'

Libby's first thought was that it must be a member of the band. Pearl said the What were almost as famous as the Rolling Stones, and everyone had heard about Brian Jones in his swimming pool.

How odd, Libby thought, that she hadn't heard the splash when whoever it was now floating face down in the pool had hit the water.

Visions of police and journalists swarming over the hotel flew through her mind. It would be the end of them!

'I think you'd better come and look,' Libby said quietly to Eddie. It was for emergencies like this that she did wish Eddie would wear pyjamas.

'Oh my God! cried her husband as he looked out of the window. 'Mother! She probably thought she could walk on water!'

The curtains were drawn, but occasional wafts of breeze from the open windows made them balloon into Claudia's room.

When Winston's amplified voice announced the next band, she

stirred, but the two infants taking their afternoon nap on the bed beside her slept on, blissfully unaware.

Michael put his book down and got up from the chair to close the window.

'Don't!' Claudia whispered. 'I love this song.'

He hadn't realized that she was awake.

Listening intently, Michael recognized the Kinks' song 'Days' played with a folk beat and too much tinny tambourine.

'Most love songs are about the nights, not the days,' Claudia said. Her eyes were closed. 'But it is the days you remember, isn't it?'

He thought of the summer day they'd gone up to Cambridge on the train, and walked in the gardens of her old college where there were girls on lawns talking earnestly, and the institutional smell of cabbage wafted from the canteens. Claudia had shown him the bench where she had written him letters, and afterwards they'd sat outside the Anchor, watching students in cricket flannels drift past on punts, and he'd told her how much he wished he had been with her there, and she'd said, 'Well, you are today,' as if that was enough.

He remembered the day she'd insisted they go to Kew Gardens. Scrunching ankle deep in leaves, breathing the smoky autumnal air, he'd thought how lucky he was to be with a person who would journey more than an hour across London just to look at the crimson leaves of a rare maple.

Those endless, ochre days in Rome, the sun scorching the ancient paving stones beneath their sandals, seeking refuge in the cool, sacred air of Santa Maria in Trastevere. And drinking tiny cups of bittersweet espresso and tall glasses of ice-cold water in a peaceful square, relaxing against the slatted backs of aluminium chairs, gazing up into the yellow canopy of a Cynar umbrella, wondering if life ever got better than this.

Those first days making love in her child's bed at the gatehouse under a blanket of knitted squares, listening to the icicles melt as the grey light of a winter afternoon turned to darkness . . .

On the big double bed next to her slumbering children, Claudia was so tiny and weak, yet her presence was still so vibrant, so physical, he could not imagine how all their lives would go on without her.

'I've loved every day,' Michael whispered, kneeling beside the bed. 'Thank you.'

He felt her hand reaching out to touch his hair.

'What about the nights?' she whispered.

'And the nights.'

The night they'd gone up to the top of Parliament Hill and watched fireworks going off all over London, and she'd pulled a packet of sparklers from her coat pocket, and they'd written their names with fizzing silver wands in the chill night air.

The night in Florence when they'd wandered over the Ponte Vecchio, stopping to listen to a busker playing the mandolin, and perused the windows of the souvenir shops. He'd bought her a triangle-shaped purse with golden fleurs-de-lis stamped on it and a popper that said 'Firenze', which had given her such girlish pleasure he had wanted to buy her many other trinkets, but she wouldn't let him, saying that he had paid far too much for this already, yet she had nursed the soft leather in her small hands like precious treasure.

The night they'd gone to the Opera House in Covent Garden, with its lush red and gold tiers, and, as the pretty candlelights went down, Claudia had taken his hand and he could feel her excitement. He had not expected to enjoy the ballet, but he had wanted to see his old travelling companion, the Russian defector, in his debut with the Royal Ballet. But his lasting memory was not of the Prince, but instead the moment the prima ballerina came on to the stage, so fragile and yet so vital, and her eyes looked out and up into the audience, sparkling with an expression of enchanted delight he had witnessed once before, on the day that Claudia had stood in the entrance to the ballroom at the Palace Hotel.

'I never taught you to play the piano,' he said now.

'We didn't have time,' she whispered.

He lay his hand on the bed next to her hand, close enough for her to feel its warmth, but not touching because he knew it hurt her.

'Michael?'

'Yes?'

'If you want to marry someone else . . . If you think it's the best thing for them . . .' Her other hand fluttered over their sleeping children.

'There could never be anyone—' he began.

'But if there is,' she interrupted. 'I don't believe in an afterlife.'

'But if there is?' he teased.

'I suppose I might be a bit cross when you get there.' She smiled, seemed to drift again, and then opened her eyes suddenly as she heard the sound of the tyres of the VW van on the gravel drive.

As if she'd been waiting for it, Michael thought.

'Do you think it really is Bob Dylan?' she asked.

Winston had received a mysterious phone call in the late morning and had immediately rushed off to Lowhampton station.

'Meeting a special guest,' was what he'd told Michael as he'd hurled back the sliding door of the VW and jumped in.

Michael went over to the window.

The psychedelic van stopped in a spray of gravel.

'You don't suppose he would come and sing "Lay Lady Lay" to me?' Claudia asked.

Michael laughed, not really knowing whether she was joking. There was so much he still had to find out about her. They didn't have time.

He leaned out of the window to see who it was getting out of Winston's van.

Not Bob Dylan.

The new arrival spotted him hanging out of the window and waved vigorously.

He turned to give the news to Claudia.

'Iris has come!'

Iris had expected the children to be smaller. She was still thinking of them as babies, but although they possessed the rounded features of cherubim, they were little people who could walk and talk, and had ideas about what they wanted to do and what they did not. They both immediately accepted that she was their sister when their father introduced them, and happily took one of her hands each, as he told them to, when they walked upstairs.

When Winston had phoned to tell her that he thought Claudia was dying, Iris had imagined her perfect face lying serenely on a white pillow. Instead she was on a bed in the middle of an extraordinary painted room, like an exhibit in a museum, half propped up against an old brown velvet cushion, as if she had struggled to raise herself up, but fallen asleep when she hadn't the strength to get any further. Her breathing was shallow, and Iris felt as if she was intruding on her privacy as she sat there with a twin on each knee, whispering nursery rhymes which seemed to come straight from her unconscious memory to her lips.

'Round and round the garden, like a teddy bear . . .'

Fiammetta reached a small round hand up to touch Iris's hair, which was now longer than it had ever been in her life and fell around her shoulders. Blue eyes stared at Iris, as if she somehow recognized her.

'Again!' demanded Bruno.

As Iris tickled him, unable to stop herself joining in with the laughter that gurgled out of him, she suddenly found herself trying to work out how old her own baby would have been. Then she put the thought away, as she became conscious that Claudia's eyes were watching her.

'Again!' shouted Bruno.

'Hello,' Iris said.

'Hello,' Claudia replied.

Iris didn't know whether she was more nervous about whether Claudia would like her, or not like her.

'Fiammetta likes my hair!' she said. 'She looks like me, doesn't she?'

To prove the point, she stood Fiammetta up on her thigh, so that her face was next to hers for comparison.

Claudia smiled. 'Yes, she does!' she agreed, attempting to push herself up the cushion, her face stricken with pain.

Iris instinctively looked at her father to help her.

'Michael, will you take the children, please?' Claudia said. 'So Iris and I can get to know each other?'

Each word was a huge effort, and she looked awful, but her smile was still as luminous as it had been that snowy day on the promenade when Iris had thought she was Holly Golightly.

'Shall we go and see what's happening at the Festival?' Michael asked the twins as he scooped them up.

'No!' said Bruno.

Which made Iris laugh.

'I don't like them to see me in pain,' Claudia explained as she allowed Iris to make her more comfortable when they were gone, though each movement was clearly agony.

Her body felt as light and bony as a bird Iris had once found under a tree when she was little. She had tried to pick it up with such care, but the bird had quivered in her clumsy hands, and she hadn't known whether to clasp it tighter, or to drop it.

'So,' Claudia said as Iris drew up a chair. 'You've come back to Kingshaven.'

'Winston rang me . . .' Iris started to explain, then stopped, not knowing quite what to say. He'd told her he thought Claudia was dying. And Iris had found herself saying, 'I'll come down.' And she hadn't been aware that she was doing what she said she'd never do until she was on the train.

'I know how difficult—' Claudia began.

'It's fine,' Iris interrupted, embarrassed, not wanting her to waste her breath.

'So, what are you up to?' Claudia asked.

Iris hadn't been expecting to talk about herself. She hadn't really known what to expect. She'd come because she thought she might be some practical use. Because she wasn't involved, she would be able to hold the fort if everyone else went to pieces. But when she set eyes on the children, happily enacting their little routines with no idea what was about to happen, and her father, pole-axed by fear, she'd felt so shaky herself, she realized that she was involved after all.

'At the moment, I'm waitressing again, and going to night school,' Iris said. 'Because I've decided I want to go to university.'

'Bravo!' said Claudia.

'I haven't told Dad yet.'

'He'll be so pleased.'

He won't, Iris thought to herself, because nothing will ever cheer him up again.

'You were at Cambridge, weren't you?' she asked, trying to keep a normal conversation going.

'Yes.'

'I'm thinking of going somewhere up North. Explore my roots. I don't know yet.'

Claudia sighed. 'I'd love to talk more,' she said, 'but, as you can see, I can't.'

Claudia was trying her best to make it easy for everyone else. She was a lovely person, Iris decided, just as Dad had said. Iris was sure she wouldn't be so selfless if she was the one who was dying.

Iris stood up.

'No! Don't go!' Claudia almost shouted.

Iris sat down again.

The effort of conversation seemed to have drained Claudia. Her eyes lolled in and out of consciousness.

'Look, I don't really know what to say, or what to do,' Iris told her, seeing that the time to be polite was over. 'Just tell me what you want.'

'Could you try to love my children?' Claudia whispered.

Iris had been thinking more along the lines of a glass of water, or adjusting Claudia's pillows.

They weren't going to be able to build a friendship gradually and tentatively. Time was so short, it had to be more like an ultimatum. Do you like me or not? Yes. Well, this is what you have to do, then.

'I do love them,' Iris said, surprising herself with the simple truth of the statement. 'I'm their big sister, aren't I?'

Claudia tried to smile. 'I don't want them always to be surrounded by gloomy old men . . .' she rasped.

Iris blurted with laughter at the implied inclusion of her father in this description.

'I want them to have an intelligent woman who cares about them,' Claudia said. 'Just sometimes.'

'I'm not sure I know what to do . . .' Iris stammered, at once flattered and terrified by the responsibility Claudia was prepared to give her.

'The children will show you,' Claudia said.

Iris could see she was fading. She wasn't making sense.

'I'll try,' she said, putting her hand over Claudia's; taking it away again as she saw the involuntary wince.

Iris remembered carrying the baby bird into the kitchen to make a bird hospital for it, and her mother telling her she should never have touched it. Iris had put it in a shoe box, on a scrap of velvet stolen from Sylvia's sewing basket, and tried to feed it water with a baby doll's bottle. But it had still died.

The last band played out the Festival with 'Those Were the Days' and the sound of thousands of voices singing a poignant farewell rolled across the fields and down to the sea.

Michael and Iris were sitting silently in the kitchen when Winston finally returned to the house in the small hours after sending the last lorryload of equipment on its way.

The Castle grounds were strangely still and silent as the kitchen door opened and closed behind him.

Winston threw a pair of lilac ladies' panties on the oak refectory table.

'Amazing what people forget to take with them,' he said.

'Any sign yet of Bob Dylan?' Michael teased.

'He called and said he's definitely coming to the Isle of Wight next month,' Winston informed him.

'The Isle of Wight?' echoed Michael in disbelief. 'Who on earth's going to go to the Isle of Wight?'

'People came to Kingshaven,' said Iris.

'Yes, they did.'

Michael noticed Winston's hand linger on Iris's shoulder for a moment.

Were they together? he wondered. Iris told him very little about her life, and he had to be satisfied with that. It was enough to have her back, he always told himself. He gathered that she'd stayed at Winston's squat after she'd left the council flat, where, he presumed, she'd lived with a boyfriend. Now she seemed to live with several other friends in a big house Winston had bought in Clapham. Did they share a room? Michael wondered. He thought he'd probably be glad if they were together. Winston was a man of principle, and he had a natural gift for making money. A rich man of principle. Isn't that what every father wanted for his daughter?

'Isn't anyone going to watch the moon landing?' Winston asked.

'God, I'd completely forgotten,' said Iris. 'Are you coming, Dad?'

'No, it's my shift,' said Michael, taking a cup of coffee upstairs with him. 'Call me if they land.'

Claudia's father insisted on taking a turn at his daughter's bedside every evening even though he was very tired and frail and usually went to sleep as soon as he sat down in the old armchair beside the bed. But tonight when Michael returned to the Chinese room, the old man was alert and watching her and, as he looked up at Michael, his eyeballs were watery like oysters in their sunken sockets, and dull with dread.

With difficulty, the old man bent over the bed and kissed Claudia's hair.

'Good night, my dear child,' he said.

In her morphine-induced sleep, she did not stir.

'Wrong way round,' the professor muttered as Michael helped him back to his own bed, sensing he was more impatient than ever with himself for clinging on to life when his daughter could not.

The bedroom was a little stuffy.

Michael pushed up the bottom half of one of the sash windows. Outside, it was still warm and a little hazy, but the moon was high in the sky. He stared at it, unable to believe that there were three men all that way away, orbiting, and that through the miracle of man's invention, pictures of them landing on the moon's cratered surface would fly invisibly back to a television set in this ancient place where, ever since human beings had made tools from flint, they had gazed at the moon in awe, possibly even worshipped it.

'Dad! Dad! They've landed!' Iris called from downstairs.

Michael knelt beside Claudia. 'I'm going to see the men on the moon, my darling!' he whispered. 'I'll be back in a minute.'

Claudia stood looking at the heavy wooden door of the walled garden, wondering what secrets lay beyond. She still retained a slight echo of foreboding left over from childhood.

In the distance, she heard Michael saying, 'I'm going to see the men on the moon, my darling!'

For one sweet second, a wave of relief washed over her. It had all been a dream!

Claudia lifted the heavy iron latch. The door made no noise as she pushed it open. The bright sunshine inside was a surprise after being in the shadow of the high walls. The vegetable beds were a tapestry of colour and, beyond, there was an orchard of blossom trees.

Claudia began to walk soundlessly along the red-brick path, petals dancing around her like snow.

In the chill grey moments just before the dawn, Michael found himself standing outside the gatehouse, startled to have walked the length of the Castle drive and unable to remember a single step.

The garden was overgrown now, and the windows boarded up. The silence was so profound, he could almost hear a whisper from another moment in time, long ago.

What are we going to do?

Michael gazed back up the long avenue of beech trees, but knew he could not return to the house just now. Claudia was not there any more. He would have to look for her in other places.

There was no one standing at the bus stop by the clock tower. The school yard was deserted for the holidays. It would be several hours before Miss Phelps unlocked the door of the library. It was too early even for the Expresso bar.

Michael stood on the empty promenade, staring at the gently undulating pewter surface of the water melting to silver as the reflected sun gathered strength for a new day.

As he turned towards the Harbour End, he glanced back up at the Palace Hotel, its windows shining like mirrors, and his vision blurred with the memory of a girl in a red dress standing in a golden frame, with an expression on her face which had made him think that his life had only just begun.

Iris and Winston, the professor and Sir John were all sitting round the kitchen table in silence.

Iris shivered and pulled on a cardigan. 'Right, I'm going to go after Dad,' she said decisively, but the professor put his bony, liver-spotted hand upon her arm.

'No. You must leave him to himself,' he said in his heavy middle-European accent. 'One kind touch, and he will disintegrate. I know about this!'

His rheumy old eyes looked so certain, Iris sat down again.

And then all of them, the old man included, jumped as a high, clear voice rang out from the twins' bedroom: 'Mummy, Mummy, Mummy!'

Iris took a deep breath, and stood up again. 'I'll go,' she said.

Bruno was standing up in his cot. ''Allo, mate!' he said.

Iris couldn't help laughing.

She swished back the curtains. 'Good morning, Fiammetta!' she said gently as the little girl opened her eyes and smiled up at her.

'Sit-ter?' she said.

'That's right, I'm your sister,' Iris translated. 'I'm going to be looking after you today, so what are we going to do?'

'Beach!' shouted Bruno gleefully.

The children will show you.

Acknowledgements

In the course of researching this first of a trilogy of novels, I have enjoyed scouring many websites, reading and rereading novels, biographies, autobiographies and works of local history. I am particularly indebted to the following books for the inspiration and pleasure they have given me: *Royal: Her Majesty Queen Elizabeth II* by Robert Lacey; *The Queen* by Ben Pimlott; *The Windsors: A Dynasty Revealed 1917–2000* by Piers Brendon and Phillip Whitehead; *Philip and Elizabeth: Portrait of a Marriage* by Gyles Brandreth; *Princess Margaret: A Life of Contrasts* by Christopher Warwick; *The Little Princesses* by Marion Crawford; *A Royal Duty* by Paul Burrell; *The Coronation Cookbook* by Marguerite Patten; *This Sceptred Isle* by Christopher Lee; *Guinness World Records: British Hit Singles* (16th edition); *Chronicle of the Twentieth Century*; *Fashion Sourcebooks: The 1940s–The 1980s* by John Peacock; *50s Popular Fashions* by Roseann Ettinger; *A Century of Fashion* by François Baudot; *Thames and Hudson 20th Century Fashion*; *The 50s and 60s, The Best of Times* by Alison Pressley; *Dorset 1900–1999: The Twentieth Century in Photographs* by David Burnett; *The Hulton Getty Picture Collection: 1940s; 1950s; 1960s; 1970s; 1980s* ed. by Nick Yapp; *Poole: A History and Celebration* by Roger Guttridge; *The Memories Series: Golden Years of Poole and Memories of Bournemouth*; *Swanage and Purbeck Photographic Memories*; *The Book of Swanage*; *Bridport and Lyme*

Regis by Rodney Legg; *A Short History of Lyme Regis* by John Fowles; *The Centre of the Bed: An Autobiography* by Joan Bakewell; *Toast: The Story of a Boy's Hunger* by Nigel Slater; *Baggage: My Childhood* by Janet Street-Porter; *The L-Shaped Room* by Lynne Reid Banks; *Saturday Night and Sunday Morning* by Alan Sillitoe; *A Kind of Loving* by Stan Barstow; *Room at the Top* by John Braine.

I am very lucky to be published by Transworld, and am enormously grateful to the fantastic team for taking the project and running with it. I am indebted to my agent, Mark Lucas, for his humour and general brilliance, and to Alice Saunders and everyone else at LAW for their support and efficiency, and also to Nicki Kennedy at ILA for her skill and friendship.

Huge thank yous to Wilfrid Duggan and Kathleen Parker for their recollections; to Becky Parker for her unique brand of energizing enthusiasm; and to Caitlin Atkin for her inspiring imagination.

Without my wonderful son, Connor, and my unbelievably patient husband, Nick, I could not have written this book. They know, I hope, how much I love them.